The East Asian
Story Finder

ALSO BY SHARON BARCAN ELSWIT

The Jewish Story Finder: A Guide to
668 Tales Listing Subjects and Sources, 2d ed.
(McFarland, 2012)

The East Asian Story Finder

A Guide to 468 Tales from China, Japan and Korea, Listing Subjects and Sources

SHARON BARCAN ELSWIT

McFarland & Company, Inc., Publishers
Jefferson, North Carolina

The present work is a reprint of the illustrated casebound edition of The East Asian Story Finder: A Guide to 468 Tales from China, Japan and Korea, Listing Subjects and Sources, first published in 2009 by McFarland.

LIBRARY OF CONGRESS CATALOGUING-IN-PUBLICATION DATA

Elswit, Sharon.
The East Asian story finder : a guide to 468 tales from China, Japan and Korea, listing subjects and sources / Sharon Barcan Elswit.
p.   cm.
Includes bibliographical references and index.

ISBN 978-0-7864-9548-1 (softcover : acid free paper) ∞
ISBN 978-0-7864-5355-9 (ebook)

1. Tales — East Asia — Bibliography.
2. East Asia — Folklore — Bibliography.   I. Title
Z5984.E18E47 2014   [GR330]   016.3982095 — dc22   2009006464

BRITISH LIBRARY CATALOGUING DATA ARE AVAILABLE

Cover art © 2014 Shutterstock

Printed in the United States of America

McFarland & Company, Inc., Publishers
Box 611, Jefferson, North Carolina 28640
www.mcfarlandpub.com

For Michael

Acknowledgments

I wish to thank all of the librarians in the Asian and Middle Eastern Division of the New York Public Library, especially John M. Lundquist, Chief Librarian, and librarians Sumie Ota and Qi Xie for their invaluable help and enthusiasm for this project.

I am indebted to Myra Barcan and Mark D. Szuchman for technical indexing assistance and to Junmei Zhang for her political insights.

Thank you to the grownups, Susan Skolnick, Kate Elswit, Benjamin Gimpert, and Dan and Betsy Elswit, who ask me to tell these stories, and to the children at Claremont Preparatory School who sit up a little straighter when I do.

Thank you, Kathleen Ragan, Ed Young, and Laurence Yep for bringing folklore in new, compelling ways to our world. And to Reina Barcan and Jane Eisenstadt for knowing that collecting these stories is my passion.

I also wish to thank my fellow librarians in the Hudson Valley Library Association for their advice and support when *The East Asian Story Finder* was still a glimmer.

And, finally, I am grateful to M, the prince of backups, who took this long journey with me.

Table of Contents

Preface

If the people of the world could be gathered around the common hearth fire and listen to each other's folk tales there would come a deeper understanding of each other, as interpreted by the past. — Y.T. Pyun, TALES FROM KOREA

A good story has the power not only to entertain us for the moment, but to penetrate walls and come to reside within us — to explain why things are the way they are in the world, to warn of dangers, teach lessons, to create fantastic characters and adventures that grab the imagination, and to open minds and hearts to change. Adventuring, laughing, and empathizing with a protagonist who may look different or come from a different place may be a first step toward understanding the ties that bind us as a human family, a step toward tolerance. But, how do you find the right folktale from so many, one that makes just the connection you are looking for?

The East Asian Story Finder follows the format of my other Story Finder work, in this case giving you a subject guide to folktales from regions in China, Japan, and Korea and letting you know sources for those stories. I've gathered what I feel are the most meaningful folktales of each culture, grouped them by their main significance, and indexed them by all the different connections I think they make to the listener's heart. I'm not going to tell you each story word by word, beginning to end. I'll summarize to give you the feel of the story, and then I'll tell you where to go to find the full text. I will also link that particular story to variations by pointing the way to similarly told tales among all of the East Asian cultures.

What makes this Asian guide especially exciting is that the folklore in it has only been available in English for, at most, one hundred and twenty-two years. People had been spinning wonder tales and telling humorous stories to each other for thousands of years, but the East Asian provinces were closed to Westerners until the nineteenth century.

In 1887, *Japanese Fairy Tales* by Theodora Ozaki appeared; it was the first collection of Japanese folklore published in English. The American Lafcadio Hearn, who went to Japan to teach English, is responsible for bringing a variety of folk and ghost stories west in the beginning of the 1900s. And from Korea, one of the earliest collections was *Korean Tales*, published by Horace Newton Allen in 1889. *Korean Folk Tales: Imps, Ghosts and Fairies*, translated from the Korean of Im Bang and Yi Ryuk by James S. Gales, followed in 1913.

With the rise of nationalism around 1917–1918, China began taking an interest in collecting first its own folksongs in Chinese and later, stories. Between 1957 and 1960, the five translated volumes of *Folk Tales from China* were published by Foreign Languages Press, featuring common people from many regions as the heroes, women and men. Wolfram Eberhard, a teacher at Peiping and Peking Universities, edited and translated Chinese tales from a variety of Chinese print sources into English in 1937. Eberhard's book was more widely available outside of China and is still used as a touchstone for story adapters. In the introduction to his 1965 edition, Eberhard discusses the difficulties in identifying true Chinese folklore. Coming across some stories presented as historical fact and others possibly created by the Communists for propaganda, he originally selected tales from older sources. His revised edition does include some additional tales, including one where a greedy landlord is called the "Living King of Hell."

Bit by bit, with the popularity of post-modern interest in cross-cultural curricula that began in the 1970s and continues now with, for example, multicultural Cinderella units, more stories from Asia are circulating in English. The array is breathtaking. I will lead you to tales where dragon kings live in sparkling palaces at the bottom of the sea; where a wife may be a crane, a shell, a fish, a snake, a frog, or a pine tree and a husband a toad, a monkey, or a frog; where a baby boy pops out of a peach and goes on to successfully fight demons; where foxes and badgers change form to play tricks on people or beguile them into falling in love. I will show you where to find heart-stopping drama when a young woman plunges off the side of a cliff with a dagger in her teeth to challenge a cruel sea serpent or when fierce tigers leap over walls and pace outside of huts, looking for humans or animals to eat. And I will show you the many places where the charmingly outrageous magical Monkey King resides, managing — almost always — to get his own way.

For thirty years as a librarian and a mother, I have shared my favorite stories. We read aloud *Tikki Tikki Tembo*, where a Chinese boy gets into big trouble because of his very long name, and *The Funny Little Woman*, where a Japanese woman follows her runaway dumpling down a hole to the house where the wicked *oni* live. Children internalized these stories and gave them back in their own words as stick puppet plays. Years later, they still remember which characters they played. When it has been useful to illustrate the need for cleverness and patience in solving problems, I have called upon the Korean story of the woman who must acquire a tiger's whisker to help heal her husband's psychological wounds.

With all their differences, China, Japan, and Korea share some universal folktale characters. The hardworking peasants and wicked landlords, noodleheads, tricksters, mean stepmothers, clever wives, jealous brothers, wise judges, and brave heroes common to stories all around the world are here. Like their counterparts in Europe, the folktale characters of East Asia show strengths of courage, self-sacrifice, and compassion. They also show frailty, greed, jealousy, and cruelty. There are ghostly encounters and battles with demons. Cleverness is valued as a way out of a bad situation, and kindness is rewarded.

However, there are also some characteristic themes and motifs that are specific to East Asia. Many of the stories share a reverence for nature, filial piety, and respect for weaving and the production and decoration of cloth. In plots from all four countries, animals help people who are worthy, and extraordinary children born propitiously with help from deities or spirits go on to accomplish amazing deeds. Water, both too much and too little of it, often forms the setting for a tale and plays a central role. There are supernatural loves; men and women fall in love with spirits from the natural world — pheasants, shells, foxes, trees, snails, and toads who have taken human form. Across the East Asian stories, magistrates and emperors frequently seize workingmen's wives to be their own, and individuals sacrifice for the good of the community. These larger themes grew into organic chapter divisions for this book.

There is a colorful cast of supernatural creatures in Asian folklore. Japanese dragons may have three claws where Chinese dragons have five and may also fly, but dragons that live in the waters are common to all three cultures. Others, like the witchy yamaubas; winged, trouble-making tengu with long noses; and a flesh-eater who consumes the bodies of the dead, shroud and all, are specific to Japan. In both countries, talking badgers are never up to any good. Maidens who appear suddenly are often not as innocent as they seem.

These similarities and disparities demonstrate that, although I chose to focus on folklore from one geographical area, there isn't one kind of East Asian story here. East Asia encompasses four political divisions with almost sixty ethnic groups. Each group has its own rich stories and legends and its own way of telling them. They encompass scholars, princesses, khans, emperors, monks, priests, rice farmers, lords, poets, thieves, soldiers, hermits, and beggars. They reflect their lives as individuals and as members of communities as diverse as Tibetan farmers, Mongolian herdsmen, Zhuang woodcutters, Miao lacemakers, Ainu hunters, Chinese scholars, and woodcutters in a village outside of Seoul.

Fantastic creatures and magical events often grow from moral and social traditions. With the help of a snake-hunting dog, a sharp sword, and some rice balls, brave Li Chi fights the dragon that has been terrorizing people in the Yung mountain range. A miserly landlord gets his comeuppance when a cherry tree grows out of his head, and he is too stingy to see a doctor. Sea water becomes salty when a greedy man steals his brother's magic mortar without knowing how to make it stop producing salt. A white hare that has tricked and then mocked some crocodiles loses all of his fur. Cats, drawn by a boy who is in trouble because he cannot keep from drawing them, come alive to battle the goblin rat that has brought terrible drought to his village. A young man who is heading to pray at a shrine detours to the dreaded Black Swamp to deliver a letter to the parents of a young woman held captive in other waters. Another young man unselfishly asks the Dragon King for a Golden Dipper to help flooded farmers bail out their fields, instead of choosing the luminous pearl that could win him the hand of the princess. A young woman is ready to sacrifice her life to the god of the mountain rather than keep secret a source of water that can help her community.

It is fascinating to lay these stories side by side and compare how the same basic tales, characters, or intent changes when the story moves from one culture to another. A villainous wolf in a tale told by the Han Chinese majority might be a tiger when told by Koreans or Tibetan People. Cross-cultural analysis uncovers deeper threads, too.

Take the different reflections from one popular mirror tale. This is a story told in China, Japan, and Korea. A husband brings a mirror back to his remote village. When she gazes into the mirror, his wife is sure he has replaced her with a pretty young woman. She seeks out others to back up her indignation. Each person who looks into the mirror, though, sees someone else and offers a new interpretation. In one Japanese variation, an abbess reassures the family that everything is all right now, pointing out that the young woman in the mirror feels penitent for the trouble she caused them and has shaved her head. Simple Wang and his family are whipped by the village magistrate at the end of one Chinese variation. The magistrate believes that they are mocking him by bringing in an impersonator. In a Korean telling, comical misunderstanding results in destruction of the mirror itself by a man who punches the bully he sees.

The East Asian Story Finder has a subject index that points the way to stories with universal themes, such as kindness, tricksters, greed, foxes, and friendship, and to culturally specific characters, like the bewitching kitsune, a Japanese fox woman; Nasreddin, the Muslim Chinese trickster; and O-sung and Han-um, two young Korean friends.

Here are access points to the popular stories that most children within a culture hear and most adults know that may also be meaningful to others outside of that culture. The purpose of this guide is to reach out with stories from East Asia, to celebrate the tales and, through the subject guide, to suggest connections for educators, folklorists, and storytellers, which may be of use in sharing them with general audiences. Story summaries flow by related topics within each chapter.

The East Asian Story Finder includes widely retold tales, such as "Urashima Taro," about the young Japanese fisherman who rides off on the back of a turtle with a mysterious princess of the sea; "The Wonderful Pear Tree," from China and Japan, where a magic tree "bears" instant fruit that seems to have mysteriously come from the cart of a stingy pear peddler; and the tale from Korea, China, and Japan, where a young stonecutter wants to be transformed into something greater — becoming first a prince, then the sun, a cloud, a windy storm, and a mountain — only to discover in the end, a humble stonecutter chipping away at his base. The book also includes *Football on a Lake*, which haunted me though I found it only once.

How do you ensure that the translated, published story you want to promote captures the spirit and heritage of its original teller? I have made it a point to reference stories that read well to contemporary listeners, as well as to include early touchstones upon which others based their retellings. Some of the earliest translations may only be present in rare book rooms, but the Internet is continually making so much more available. You don't have to travel far to see B. H. Chamberlain's marvelous little crepe-paper books from 1888. His stories from the Ainu have been scanned and now appear whole on the web. *Stolen Charm* inspired Ed Young's powerful *Silver Charm*, where a brave puppy and fox kit outwit an ogre in the woods to save the young boy they love. Still, it is something to hold the little hundred year-old crepe-paper books with colorful woodblock illustrations from the *Japanese Fairy Tales Series* in your hands.

For each tale in this volume, I have chosen one story to summarize and listed variants and where they may be found. Some of the stories, like the tale of the dancing badger who takes up residence in a priest's teakettle, are tales especially told to children, but many others were intended to be shared with older audiences.

Reading stories in a language other than the one in which they were created does raise some challenges. A world of nuance in the picture symbols of China and Japan is flattened by literal translation. Many of the first collectors in English were missionaries, and they presented the stories in terms that an American or European reader would understand. They may call the spirits of Japanese tales *fairies*, for example, or the king demon *Satan* and the underworld *Hades*. The introductions to some of the turn-of-the-century volumes are sometimes objectionably condescending. However, the collections I have included represent a sincere desire to bring home unfamiliar stories that the listener found prominent and exciting. The tales themselves do not contain language that demeans the people who told them.

In oral performance, there are culturally expected forms and structures to tales that often do not appear on the page. In Japan, it is customary for a storyteller to begin "Mukashi mukashi, aru tokoro ni," the English equivalent of "Long, long ago in a certain place." In Korea, the folkloric "Once upon a time" is often referred to as "When tigers smoked pipes."

Japanese stories include frequent use of onomatopoeia, with the sounds of words repeating and often replacing description for an action: "doki doki" represents a frightened heartbeat; "soro soro" tells listeners that someone is walking slowly across the floor. Korean listeners expect to hear lists of, for example, the many types of food that are consumed at a dinner.

Chinese tellings may be musical, with the last part or word in a line repeated at the beginning of the next.

The traditional Korean p'ansori teller holds a fan in one hand that emphasizes the action. Many Miao and Mongolian stories are accompanied by a fiddle. Traditional Chinese Han tellers often use clappers and p'i-p'a. Painted silk scrolls often illustrated Tibetan stories, and in Japan, the kamishibai man carried a twelve to sixteen card set of pictures to go with his story. Some modern writers have taken care to try to capture the particular time and place and be true to the culture of the tale they are telling through language and illustration. One of my favorites, for example, is Tony Johnston's version of *Badger and the Magic Fan* with comic-book style panels by Tomie dePaola. It is one totally modern telling that captures the playfulness of the Japanese story.

The East Asian Story Finder contains summaries for 468 basic story plots and points the way to a total of over 1,645 stories that tell them. Look up a specific topic in the subject index or peruse chapters where stories have been gathered into broader, cross-cultural themes. Check the comprehensive title index if you are trying to track down one particular story that you know by name. Turn to the appendix in the back, where stories are listed by country. Find the stories to read in one or more of the almost 450 books and websites listed in the bibliography. Check the glossary for definitions of unfamiliar terms.

Which Stories Are Here

Chosen for this volume are timeless short tales written in English from China, Japan, Korea, and Taiwan that may resonate with modern listeners, both children and adults, from all different cultures. I know that they can work when you make the beginning connection to engage an audience's attention.

I have selected stories that make the leap beyond a country's borders. This means that I have not included some historical legends of local or national interest only, such as the battles between the Taiga and the Heike clans of Japan or stories to explain the presence of local rock formations in China. But I have included the haunting story of Hoichi, a blind biwa player who is summoned years later by the dead Heike to retell their tragic story, because we come to care about him as a character.

It is sometimes difficult for humor to jump from reception in one culture to another. Sometimes the punny ending to a Chinese or Japanese story depends on someone knowing the homonyms in those native languages. I have also not included stories which might offend, with humor that belittles any group, ethnic or sexual. That still leaves room for many earthy stories, however. There are two stories with breaking wind at the core; in one, it actually turns out to be a woman's talent and the reason why houses now have separate rooms.

Obviously, not every appearance of a tale in English can be documented here, nor should it be. Along with stories retold by non–Asians, I have included summaries of tales that many Japanese, Korean, and Chinese writers heard in their own tongues and have published in English. I selected my favorites among many story variants of all kinds: print collections and picture books, electronic texts, audio, and video. Some variants were bare outlines for tales, rather than satisfyingly fulsome stories. I have included only stories which I have read myself.

To be here, a story had to have a compelling plot, memorable characters, or thrilling mysteries and wonders. It also needed to be well-told in its sources. I provide summaries, such as a book reviewer might, outlining basic plots and hinting at the personality of the tales. Retellers are skilled experts at their craft. Characters spring to life for an audience with the intriguing details and gracefully wrought phrases of the actual stories from the actual collections. To share them, readers will want to turn to the books where these stories may be found.

My summaries are the bare bones, but I tried to capture each reteller's unique style by preserving his tone and spelling. The tales themselves come from an oral tradition where English was not the original language. Renderings of names and spellings are all over the place. The user of this subject guide will meet a fearsome yamanba or a yamauba in the Japanese mountains, depending on a particular storyteller. The diversity will help you choose the character of a tale you desire, but rest assured that only one of these terms has been selected for the subject index.

Featured Stories and Variations

Such is the way of the oral tradition that a story changes according to the teller. Not only have some folktales popular within in a particular country been told in different ways, but they also vary from one country to another within the region. For each of the 468 stories in this book, I picked one to summarize and gathered other versions of that story to suggest as alternatives. It was often hard to choose which story to highlight. All of the retellings are worthy narratives, or they would not have been included here. I could only annotate one, but have briefly indicated major differences in characters or plot for the others, along with their cultural identity. There is no ethnic bias or intent that places a particular story on top. Often, the lead story is one which appears in a collection or as a picture book readily available to a contemporary reader. The way it is told called to me personally.

Variations are divided into two categories:

"Where Else This Story Appears" refers to an exact retelling of the feature story in another collection or in another source.

"How Else This Story Is Told" points the way to different versions of a story, as it has been retold by others, and sometimes the same author, within a particular culture and across others in East Asia.

Characters may have different names or appear as different creatures, but if the narrative thrust of the story is close, if why a person would choose this story is the same, it has been included as a variant. Story spellings (and misspellings) in the variations and *Title Index* appear as I found them in print.

For main story and variation entries, author and editor names are given as they appear on the title page. However, they appear in standard English form with last name first in the bibliography. Since many Chinese and Japanese family names often appear first in English translations, you may have to try both names to locate the book a particular story has been drawn from in the bibliography. A rule of thumb is that the surname will usually be a single syllable. A first name often appears as two syllables, written as one word.

After a year of soul-searching, I divided the variant tales along current political lines: Chinese, Japanese, Korean, and Taiwanese. This was a difficult decision. Stories from the minority Tibetan people differ more from the majority of Chinese stories than tales from Taiwan, which are basically Han Chinese. With 55 cultural minorities and one majority people represented by China, parsing every story with every cultural variation would have made this volume cumbersome. Chinese minorities, as well as the Han majority, are all listed under "Chinese variations." Cultural distinctions have not been lost, however. As identified by the retellers, specific cultures are named beside each story title. You may also find stories told by the Mongolian People as a group, for example, referenced in the Subject Index.

Because you will also not want to miss a particular supernatural creature, I catch the special characteristics of variant tales in the Subject Index. In the Han Chinese story *The Outsize Candy Figure* goblins beat a magic food-producing drum. A variation of that story from the Tibetan People features fairies in the cave and a wishing cup. Magic hammers, mallets, sticks, and clubs wielded by tokkaebi, ogres, ghosts, and goblins appear in different Korean variations. Variant story terms are also included in the Subject Index and will lead you to the main story number where you can find a story that contains them.

Using the Subject Index

The Subject Index catches all. When teachers ask me to recommend stories, they are looking for nuances. I have included many useful handles in the "Connections" section which accompanies each main story, looking for every possible reason why this tale might answer someone's need. As I worked with the stories, certain themes specific to the East Asian stories arose. Some formed main chapter divisions, such as "Devotion," of children to parents and husbands and wives to each other. The subject *Kindness to animals* is part of the reverence for nature in the chapter "Cherishing the Earth."

Identifying *Water* as an essential element happened early on. Those who seek to relieve the suffering of their villages from flood or drought are valued characters and fill the "Heroes" chapter. You will find them under *Water; Drought; Floods; Heroes, men* and *Heroes, women*. By story number, the Subject Index will lead you to other heroic men and women wherever they are throughout the guide, perhaps also in the chapter with "Problem Solvers" and under "Devotion."

The subject list grew from an analysis of the stories and the reasons why someone would want to turn to them. *Eyeballs, Stone horses, Wife-stealing*, the *Dragon Princess*, and *Imperial examination* (on which the future of so many people rested), all became subjects, as well as *Compassion* and *Outsmarting supernatural opponents*.

Because these stories are translations of tales written or told in other languages, defining subjects in English posed particular difficulties. Dragons, when they are not gods of lakes and rivers, may be considered fairies in Chinese lore, as are some ogres and Japanese tengu and foxes. Fairies, though, may conjure up a totally different magical being to an English speaker than to a Chinese native. Perhaps tellers reinterpreted what they found, but how they present a story in English is how the reader will find it. The Subject Index here reflects this. If an editor identifies a character as a *demon*, it is listed as such.

Each main story has been given a number, and references are to that story number. In story # 253, *The Old Man with a Wen*, the characters he meets are referred to as *dwarves, goblins*, and *elves*, depending on which version of the story you read. Some white-haired old men who help protagonists along the way may be *mountain gods* and some are *spirits*. I chose to include all of these terms in the Subject Index exactly as the reader will find them. So, if the Subject Index indicates that a goblin is to be found in story # 253, it may not be in the featured story, but will be identified in one of the variants listed below.

Distinction is made between the place where a story originated, which is listed as, for example, *Niigata, Japan, stories from*, and *Niigata*, the place mentioned within a story. Countries are not specified for geographical locations inside stories because many, like the Eastern Sea, are sites that exist only in the imagination.

Place names often reflect what the countries were called at the time that the stories were told and capture the flavor of a particular tale. Cross-references will carry the user from Peking to Beijing and vice versa. For all of the tales, geographical locations and people appear as reported by the authors and retellers in their collections and anthologies. You will want to check their scholarly notes for further information. Every attempt was made to unify variously found spellings within the Subject Index.

Which Collections Are Included

I have drawn upon both individual picture books and story collections for the 448 titles listed in the bibliography. The purpose of *The East Asian Story Finder* is to make it easy for people to use and to share Asian stories. If I am going to point the way, then readers need to find the books that these stories are in. With the growth of the Internet, I widened my definition of qualifying material from my earlier work *The Jewish Story Finder*. Trade books listed in *The East Asian Story Finder* include those in print at the time of preparing this manuscript, plus those out-of-print collections, anthologies, and picture books which were widely distributed and may be easily found in libraries or with used-book dealers or have now been scanned online. The book also includes story presentations in video and alternate print formats, such as the Japanese kamishibai storycards. I did follow the lines of sources given by retellers, but a few led to dead-ends and did not seem to exist. For the integrity of this guide, I have only included references to texts I could read for myself.

The stories included in this guide also needed to be readable. I wanted readers to be able to turn to the recommended tale and feel confident in sharing the proffered story from there just as it is. Through the given variations, a reader may choose the version of a tale to her liking. Many of those books in turn, through their notes on the origins, history, significance, and folkloric archetypes of a particular story will lead readers who desire to know more to primary source and scholarly material in reference books.

The breadth of what is available in English has come a long way since *The Five Chinese Brothers*, who looked identical, but used unique individual talents to help each other escape punishment. Other memorable characters now fill my story bag—the brave young wife who goes to seek her husband taken by a cruel emperor to build the Great Wall of China, the hunter who saves a snake from a crane and receives a stone from the Dragon King's mouth that enables him to understand the language of animals, the young boy who accidentally injures his father's prize cricket just before a match with the emperor's champion, the woodcutter who buys another man's dream of treasure when he sees a bee fly out of his sleeping friend's nose, the poor man who finagles his way inside a miserly rich man's house by purchasing the shade of his mulberry tree, and the sensual fox woman who will trade her life to save the priest she has come to love.

It gives me great pleasure to point the way to the sources for their stories, where you will find laughter, delight, and wonder. Preparing this guide to 468 Asian tales has been an incredible journey. Like Marco Polo, I traveled east from the Eastern European stories I knew so well. Indeed, I found some of the stories highlighted in The Jewish Story Finder among stories told by the Uygur People of western China and by the Koreans. Perhaps these tales traveled with the trade routes long ago.

The Japanese culture identifies eight types of storytellers. From a region rich in oral storytelling tradition, after centuries of our not having had access to Asian stories, we can now all become new Katarites, professional educators who share stories learned from books and call forth insights into the views and imagination of people from other times and places. We can observe how the characters handle disaster and life's hardships, how they make moral choices, and what they do when there is not always justice in the world. Seeing how they help each other and how sometimes they are helped by spirits and other fantastic beings, seeing how cleverness often extricates people from unhappy situations, we, too, grow stronger and better able to survive.

~ I ~

Kindess Rewarded and Lessons Learned

1. Bamboo Hats and a Rice Cake

Ann Tompert. Japan

The New Year is approaching, and a poor old couple will have no rice cakes for the first three days, no way to invite good fortune in for the year. The old man reluctantly agrees to sell the old woman's kimono. Along the way, he stops by six statues of Jizo, the protector of children. He bows and brushes off the snow that covers them. When he meets a woman who has had no luck selling her fans, he kindly trades his fans for the kimono she admires. He trades the fans for a little gold bell. It is getting late. No one wants to buy the little bell. But then the old man feels sorry for a young man who still has five bamboo hats left. They make a trade. On his way home, the old man stops and ties one hat onto each bare stone Jizo's head to keep them warm. He ties his own hat onto the sixth statue. He comes home covered in snow, but his wife is pleased with his kindness to the Jizos. They hear a thunk. Opening the door, they see one enormous rice cake. Six statues are walking away, down the path, leaving their thanks and good fortune for all the years ahead.

CONNECTIONS. Animation. Changes in fortune. Compassion. Deities. Fukushima, Japan, stories from. Golden bell. Hats. Jizo. Kindness. Magical objects. New Year's. Poverty. Rewards. Rice cakes. Snow. Statues. Traditions.

HOW ELSE THIS STORY IS TOLD. The Grateful Statues— Florence Sakade, *Japanese Children's Favorite Stories* and *Little One-Inch*. *Hats for the Jizos/Kasa Jizo*— Miyoko Matsutani on kamishibai story cards. Kasa Jizo— Yei Theodora Ozaki, *Japanese Fairy Book*. Kasa Jizo— Cathy Spagnoli, *Asian Tales and Tellers*. Kasajizo/Hats for Jizos— *Kids Web Japan*, Online. New Year's Hats for the Statues— Yoshiko Uchida, *The Sea of Gold*. The Sandal-Seller— Florence Sakade, *Urashima Taro* and *Japanese Children's Favorite Stories*, Book Two. Sedge Hats for Jizo— Fanny Hagin Mayer, *Ancient Tales in Modern Japan* and online at *Learning to Give* (from Fukushima).

2. Two Brothers

Suzanne Crowder Han, *Korean Folk and Fairy Tales*. Korea

Two brothers divide their rice field evenly, but at harvest time, the older brother brings an extra sack to his younger brother's storehouse at night, thinking his younger brother will need more rice as he has recently married. And yet, in the morning, the older brother cannot understand why the sacks in his own storehouse number the same as before. So, the next night, he places another sack in his brother's storehouse. But he himself still has the same number of sacks. On the third night, as he is carrying a sack over for his brother, he meets his younger brother heading towards him, also bearing a sack. The younger brother has been thinking that his older brother will need additional rice as his family is larger.

11

CONNECTIONS. Brothers. Compassion. Farmers. Generosity. Helpfulness. Kindness. Rice.

HOW ELSE THIS STORY IS TOLD. The Two Brothers—*Long Long Time Ago*.

3. One Word for Happiness

Margaret Read MacDonald, *Three-Minute Tales*. China

The emperor hears how the many people in Chang Kung's household all get along, and he wants to learn the secret. Chang Kung writes *kindness* on a sheet of paper. In a proclamation he desires Chang Kung to post outside his gate, the emperor expresses his happiness at discovering Chang Kung's family. In the future, Chang Kung becomes known as the Kitchen God, and his image graces many kitchens.

CONNECTIONS. Chang Kung, Kitchen god. Community. Curiosity. Emperors. Family life. Gods and goddesses. Happiness. Harmony. Kindness. Kitchen God. Kao-tsung, Emperor.

HOW ELSE THIS STORY IS TOLD. God of the Kitchen — Isabelle C. Chang, *Tales from Old China*. The God That Lived in the Kitchen — Frances Carpenter, *Tales of a Chinese Grandmother*. The House of Harmony — Lim Sian-tek, *Folk Tales from China* (here the magic word told to Emperor Kao-tsung is "forbear." This story does not include the Kitchen God).

4. Drinking Companions

P'u Sunling in Moss Roberts, *Chinese Fairy Tales and Fantasies*. China

The young man Hsü often brings a bottle of wine when he goes fishing. Before he drinks, Hsü always pours some on the ground to honor those who have drowned. One day, Hsü isn't catching any fish, but he invites the young man who appears to share his bottle. They sit companionably, and then the young man offers to send fish upstream. He disappears, and Hsü soon finds the river full of fish. He thanks the young man, whose name is Liu-lang, Sixth Born. For half a year they meet by the riverbank, but then, one night, Liu-lang tells Hsü that this will be their last night to share a drink together. He is really the ghost of a man who has drowned in the river and is now going to be reborn somewhere else. A woman will replace him. The next day, Hsu sees a young woman with a baby in her arms fall into the river. She throws the child to safety, but begins to sink. The woman struggles and then manages to pull herself out of the river. Hsü is puzzled. That night, Liu-lang returns. He tells Hsü that when he saw the baby, he could not let the woman drown and pushed her out of the water. A few days later, Liu-lang says that the gods are rewarding him for his kindness to the woman. They are making him a local god in the town of Wu in the province of Chuyuan, which is far away. He invites Hsü to come visit him, and one day Hsü does make the journey. He stops at an inn in Wu and is surprised that the host knows his name. Indeed, everyone in Wu knows who Hsü is. They say the local god told them his friend would be coming and to help him. That night Liu-lang appears to Hsü in a dream and tells him that he is a good friend. When Hsü leaves, a small whirlwind accompanies him on the road for a bit and then vanishes. Back at home Hsü becomes comfortably rich; Liu-lang did not forget him, even when he became a god.

CONNECTIONS. Acceptance of life's changes. Chuyuan Province. Fishermen. Friendship. Generosity. Ghosts. Gods and goddesses. Kindness. Rebirth. Shape-shifting. Taiwan, stories from. Transformation. Underworld. Wind. Wine. Wu, town.

WHERE ELSE THIS STORY APPEARS. Drinking Companions— P'u Sunling in Joanna Cole,

Best-Loved Folktales of the World. Drinking Companions—P'u Sunling in Jane Yolen, *Favorite Folktales from Around the World*.

HOW ELSE THIS STORY IS TOLD. ***Chinese variations:*** The Drinking Companions—John Matthews, *The Barefoot Book of Giants, Ghosts and Goblins*. The Fisherman—Young Lee in Brian Brown, *Chinese Nights Entertainments: Stories of Old China*. The Fisherman and His Friend—P'u Sung-ling, adapted in *Strange Stories from a Chinese Studio*, Online. ***Taiwanese variation:*** A Wealthy Landowner, a River Spirit, a City God—Gary Marvin Davison, *Tales from the Taiwanese* (the King of the Underworld raises the river spirit, who was once a landowner who was killed by robbers, to the status of City God after the fisherman cries out to warn the woman whose spirit is going to be traded for the landowner to be reincarnated as a human again).

5. Koichi and the Mountain God

Yoshiko Uchida, *The Sea of Gold and Other Tales*. Japan

One day, while up in a tree cutting branches, Koichi sees an old man eat the lunch his mother has packed for him without asking. Koichi is sure the man must be hungry. The next day, Koichi brings two lunches, and the old man finishes them both. Still, Koichi feels sorry for the old man. On the third day, the old man reveals that he is God of the Mountain and tells Koichi to go to the temple at Tenjiku. If Koichi is as kind to people along the way as he has been to him, the old man says he will have good fortune. Koichi's mother borrows money and food for his journey from the richest man in the village, who asks only that when Koichi reaches the temple he pray for his daughter to recover from a long illness. Although he may only ask three questions, Koichi gives up his own, promising to ask for help for a man whose cherry trees will not bloom and for a woman who has been stuck in the river mist for one thousand years. When he reaches the temple, the God of the Mountain appears and asks if anyone requested help. Koichi asks what answers he should tell them. The God of the Mountain gives him specific instructions for each of them and turns into an old oak tree. Koichi gives thanks for a safe journey and prays for the sick girl. On his return, he delivers all the messages. Grateful, the man and the woman each reward him with a special treasure, and the girl offers her healing cup of wine to Koichi for him to become her husband.

CONNECTIONS. Compassion. Deities. Dragons. God of the Mountain. Gods and goddesses. Guanyin, Goddess of Mercy. Healing. Helpfulness. Han People, stories from. Hui People, stories from. Hunger. Illness. Kindness. Kun Lun Mountain. Magical objects. Mysteries. Ningxia, China, stories from. Oak trees. Old man, supernatural helper. Poverty. Quests. Questions. Tenjiku, temple. Transformation. Unselfishness. Woodcutters. Xinjiang, China, stories from.

HOW ELSE THIS STORY IS TOLD. ***Chinese variations:*** *The Fourth Question: A Chinese Tale*—Rosalind C. Wang (a young man journeys to Kun Lun Mountain to discover why he is so poor). Kuan-yin, Gentle Mother of Mercy—Lim Sian-tek, *Folk Tales from China*. The Living Kuan-yin—Carol Kendall and Yao-wen Li, *Sweet and Sour* (a man, who has been good to others, but is now so poor, journeys to ask questions of Guanyin). Musa—Li Guifang in Shuijiang Li and Karl W. Luckert, *Mythology and Folklore of the Hui* (from Xinjiang). Olive Lake—*Folk Tales from China*, First Series (from the Han People. This one includes a dragon that wishes to rise to heaven). Yinbolaxi—Ma Shenbao in Shuijiang Li and Karl W. Luckert, *Mythology and Folklore of the Hui* (from Ningxia). ***Korean variation:*** The Distant Journey—James Riordan, *Korean Folk-tales* (with a dragon, apple trees that bear no fruit, and a young woman who wants to know whom she is to wed).

6. A Compassionate Scholar and an Ungrateful Wolf

Haiwang Yuan, *The Magic Lotus Lantern and Other Tales from the Han Chinese*. Han People

Mr. Dongguo is on his way to Zhongshan take the imperial examination when a grey wolf flings itself before him. An arrow is sticking out of its buttocks. The wolf begs the terrified scholar to hide him from hunters. Mr. Dongguo is unsure, but the wolf promises to repay his kindness. Mr. Dongguo empties bamboo books out of the sack tied to his donkey and helps to stuff the wolf inside. When the hunters arrive, Mr. Dongguo lies for the first time in his life. The hunters ride off. Once out of the sack, the wolf announces that he will now eat Mr. Dongguo for he is hungry. The scholar says that tradition demands that a dispute must be settled by the judgment of three elders. The old maple tree and the cow do not decide in Mr. Dongguo's favor, but an old man who comes along listens to both stories. He calls for a reenactment in order to assess the situation better. He tells Mr. Dongguo to put the wolf back into the sack, which he then whacks with his hoe until the wolf is dead.

CONNECTIONS. Compassion. Consequences. Deceit. Deer. Foxes. Han People, stories from. Helpfulness. Henan People, stories from. Imperial examination. Justice. Kindness to animals. Monks. Problem solvers. Rabbits and hares. Scholars. Snakes. Tails. Tibetan People, stories from. Tigers. Traditions. Wolves. Zongshan, place.

HOW ELSE THIS STORY IS TOLD. *Chinese variations:* (In most of the stories from the Han People, a wolf is the ungrateful animal, and an old man saves the scholar. Tales from the Tibetan People more resemble those from Korea; a rabbit is the wise one, and a tiger is often the ungrateful party.) Bagged Wolf — Carol Kendall and Yao-wen Li, *Sweet and Sour*. Gratitude — Cheo-Kang Sié, *A Butterfly's Dream and Other Chinese Tales* (here, the trickster is an ungrateful fox). The North Country Wolf — Ma Chung-hsi in Moss Roberts, *Chinese Fairy Tales and Fantasies*. The Rabbit Judge — Carolyn Han, *Why Snails Have Shells* (from the Tibetan People). The Story of Good Faith — W. F. O'Connor, *Folk Tales from Tibet* (the tiger that is freed by a musk deer is shut up again in a house by a hare). The Story of the Snake — Zhang Yan in Howard Giskin, *Chinese Folktales* (in this variation from the Henan People, it is the snake that is ungrateful and a dog who convinces the rabbit to put him back where he was). The Three Aged Worthies and the Wolf — Lim Sian-tek, *Folk Tales from China*. The Ungrateful Ones — Louise and Yuan-Hsi Kuo, *Chinese Folk Tales*. The Wolf and the Scholar — Mingmei Yip, *Chinese Children's Favorite Stories*. The Wolf of Zhongshan Mountain — Ma Zhongxi in *Ancient Chinese Fables*. *Korean variations:* (In some versions, the tiger and the monk who will not kill him run round and round in circles.) Clever Rabbit — Gillian McClure, *The Land of the Dragon King and Other Korean Stories*. The Hare's Judgement — James Huntley Grayson, *Myths and Legends from Korea*. The Rabbit's Judgment — Suzanne Crowder Han (rabbit is the wise one who saves the man from the tiger). The Rabbit's Judgment — Suzanne Crowder Han, *Korean Folk and Fairy Tales*. Another Tiger by the Tail — Lindy Soon Curry, *A Tiger by the Tail*. A Tiger by the Tail — Lindy Soon Curry, *A Tiger by the Tail*. A Tiger by the Tail — Suzanne Crowder Han, *Korean Folk and Fairy Tales*. The Tiger's Tail — Yu Chai-Shin, Shiu L. Kong, and Ruth W. Yu, *Korean Folk Tales*. The Traveller and the Tiger — Y. T. Pyun, *Tales from Korea*. The Ungrateful Tiger — Gim Gwang-Sob in Zong In-Sob, *Folk Tales from Korea* and at D.L. Ashliman, *Folktexts*, Online. The Unmannerly Tiger — William Elliot Griffis, *The Unmannerly Tiger and Other Korean Tales* and at D.L. Ashliman, *Folktexts*, Online.

7. The Tiger's Grave

James Riordan, *Korean Folk-tales*. Korea

A boy from Zangsu Province travels over the mountain to get healing herbs for his sick mother. On the way back from Unbong, he drops the herb bag to help a merchant who has been holding a tiger's tail so the tiger will not bite him. The merchant asks the boy to hold the tiger's tail so he can get his knife, but then leaves him there, running off with the medicine bag. The boy holds on until he can hold the tail no longer and faints. But the tiger vanishes. Down the mountain, though, the boy finds his medicine bag, along with pieces of the merchant. Back at home, he prepares the herbs for his mother, and her health improves. Months later, he hears shots, and a tiger suddenly appears. The boy recognizes his tiger and protects him from the hunters. The tiger leaves when the danger has past. Soon after he reappears carrying a young girl, who fainted when she saw the tiger. They let her parents know that she is safe. The boy and girl fall in love and marry. When the tiger shows up dead in their yard one day, they bury him. Good fortune smiles on them ever after, and a persimmon tree grows from the tiger's grave.

CONNECTIONS. Deceit. Filial devotion. Healing. Illness. Journeys. Kindness. Matches, marriage. Merchants. Mothers and sons. Persimmon trees. Punishment. Rewards. Tails. Tigers.

HOW ELSE THIS STORY IS TOLD. The Tiger's Grave — Lindy Soon Curry, *A Tiger by the Tail.* The Tiger's Grave — Gim Du-Hon in Zong In-Sob, *Folk Tales from Korea.*

8. The Man Who Saved Four Lives

Chai-Shin Yu, Shiu L. Kong, and Ruth W. Yu, *Korean Folk Tales.* Korea

A young man's mother tells him that they haven't always been so poor. Long ago their family freed many slaves, and now she wants him to try to sell the document for money. He does, and the freed slaves gratefully give him nine hundred coppers. On the way home, he finds a weeping family. First the old man, then the old woman, and then the young girl try to throw themselves into the freezing river, and the others stop them. They tell him that their son is to be executed because he spent public funds he cannot repay. The young man offers to use his coppers to pay the son's debt. When he returns home, his mother is proud of him for saving their lives. When she dies, years later, he is still poor, but seeks a poong soo to find the best grave site for her burial. The poong soo indicates a nearby mountain, and the son climbs to see the man who lives in the mansion on top. Mr. Kim invites him in without question. Then, a young woman suddenly embraces him. She tells her husband that he was the one who had saved their lives many years ago. Mr. Kim said they had searched for him and now open their house to all travelers, hoping one will be the man who helped them. They give the man a grave site for his mother and a place where he may live on their mountain.

CONNECTIONS. Family life. Geomancers. Gratitude. Helpfulness. Heroes, men. Kindness. Life bringing/saving. Poverty. Reunions. Suicide.

9. Pao Hsüan and the Horse

Karl S.Y. Kuo, *Classical Chinese Tales of the Supernatural and the Fantastic.* China

On his travels as Official Who Presents Accounts, Pao Hsüan of Shang-tang meets a student who suddenly becomes ill. Pao-Hsüan massages his chest, but the student dies. Searching to see who the student might be, Pao discovers a scroll of writings and ten ingots of silver. He sells one of the ingots to pay for the burial and hides the scroll and the other ingots inside the coffin. Still, he does not know the identity of the student and prays that the student's soul let his family know where he is. When Pao Hsüan arrives in the city a magnificent horse follows him everywhere. It will only let Pao Hsüan come near. A while later, west of Han-ku Pass, he loses his way and seeks shelter at the house of the marquis who lives there. The servant tells the marquis that the man outside has stolen his horse. The marquis recognizes Pao Hsüan's name as that of a respected scholar and brings him in to talk. As Pao Hsüan tells about the student who died on the road, the marquis realizes that the young man was his son. He visits the burial site and opens the coffin. For his kindness, Pao is made Director of Retainees, a position passed on to his son and grandson.

CONNECTIONS. Death. Fathers and sons. Gratitude. Han-ku Pass. Helpfulness. Horses. Kindness. Mysteries. Officials. Scholars. Spirits. Transformation.

10. The Mourner Who Sang and the Nun Who Danced

Frances Carpenter, Tales of a Korean Grandmother. Korea

A king who goes about checking on the welfare of his people disguised as a farmer is surprised to hear merry singing coming from a poor hut. Inside, he sees a strange sight. While an old man weeps, a mourner is singing, and a nun dances. The king asks what has happened. It turns out that the sister has been selling strands of her hair to buy the family food, but now, she has no hair left. Their father is crying because he thinks she really has become a nun. The brother and sister are dancing and singing to cheer him up. The king wants to help them. When he sees an excellent poem on the wall that the young man has written, he leaves him money for supplies and tells him to show up for the King's Examination. The theme is An Old Man Weeps! A Mourner Sings! A Nun Dances! The young man easily wins the competition. When he is brought to court, he recognizes the king. The king now makes him a paksa, rewarding both his good writings and his regard for his father. This insures that the family will now have enough to eat.

CONNECTIONS. Changes in fortune. Compassion. Family life. Filial devotion. Hunger. Identity. Imperial examination. Kindness. Kings. Misunderstandings. Officials. Poetry. Poverty.

11. The Orphan Yen Jan

Folk Tales of China, Fifth Series. Kawa People

The orphan Yen Jan goes off to the forest to escape from bad treatment in the village. One day, he rubs a leaf over his mosquito bites and they vanish, but when he rubs it over his lips, they grow too long. He rubs his lips again, and his face returns to normal. He rubs a dead crow and then other animals back to life with the leaf. He heals village people. One day, when he stops and asks for water, a pretty maiden invites him to stay, but when she goes to cook, a fierce-looking man, wearing a hoe and a sword, comes in and throws Yen Jan out. Yen Jan stops with a blind, old woman, who is kind to him. He rubs his wonderful leaf over her eyes and they get better. When Yen Jan hears that the Princess has died, he tells his adoptive mother that he will offer to bring the Princess back to life if he can marry her. He does revive her and recognizes her as the kind maiden who gave him water, but her father does not want his second daughter to marry a commoner. The headman gets the village toughs to provoke a fight. Yen Jan suggests that the Princess might want to marry someone else, but she does not. Yen Jan goes to the roof where the crow, peacock, tiger, and leopard fight fiercely on his side. The village toughs flee. The bride's eldest sister, though, tricks the Princess in giving her the healing leaf. Just as the Princess is about to hand it over, the moon intervenes and takes it away. The villagers are angry with the sister for losing them the wonder leaf. They build a ladder to the sky. A dog climbs up, but as it reaches the sky ants chew through the bottom wood, and the dog is stuck up there arguing with the moon. Yen Jan and the Princess disappear, but people continue to call for Yen Jan in hopes that he will come to help them.

CONNECTIONS. Ants. Blindness. Chieftains. Deceit. Dogs. Fathers and daughters. Healing. Kawa People, stories from. Kindness. Leaves. Life-giving. Magical objects. Matches, marriage. Moon. Orphans. Poverty. Princesses. Rebirth. Rising to the sky world. Sisters. Social class. Transformation.

12. The Green Leaf

Kim So-un, *Korean Children's Favorite Stories*. Korea

A hard rain floods the land, and an old man in a boat rescues a child, a deer, and a snake. He brings the deer and the snake to safety, but cares for the child, who is alone. Much later, the deer brings the man to a cave full of treasure. The adoptive son, though, has become selfish and idle and tells people that the old man's money came from looting during the flood. Officials arrest the old man. He is awaiting sentencing, when the snake he saved slithers across the dungeon floor and bites him. Then, puzzlingly, the snake brings him a green leaf, that immediately soothes the swelling and pain. Now the jailers are shouting that the lord's wife has been bitten by a snake. The old man knows just what to do. He heals her with the green leaf and tells the overlord his story. The overlord brings the boy to the dungeon. The kind old man requests his son's release, and this time, the boy really has learned compassion from the old man.

CONNECTIONS. Adoption. Boats. Captivity. Deceit. Deer. Fathers and sons. Floods. Forgiveness. Gratitude. Healing. Ingratitude. Kindness. Leaves. Rain. Rescues. Snakes. Treasure.

13. Sweet and Sour Berries

Linda Fang in David Holt and Bill Mooney, *More Ready-To-Tell Tales*. China

Tsai Shun's mother becomes ill in a time of hard drought, One day the eight year old comes home without any wild cabbage for them to eat and finds his mother on the floor. Robbers have taken all of their rice and chickens. Tsai Shun goes out to the woods and fills a basket with sweet, dark blackberries. The next day, he brings two baskets along. He can only find a few sweet berries and puts them in one basket for his mother. The sour red berries he puts into the second basket for himself. He is singing aloud as his picks them. On the way home, a highwayman stops Tsai Shun and demands money. Tsai Shun has only berries. The highwayman begins to eat all of the sweet berries, and Tsai Shun cries. He tells the highwayman that those were for his sick mother. Since he was singing so happily, the highwayman doesn't believe him. Tsai Shun answers that the song helped remind him to put sweet berries in his mother's basket. He sings his little sorting tune for the highwayman, who remembers his own mother and lets Tsai Shun go. The next day, Tsai Shun and his mother find a note with a big bag of rice by their door.

CONNECTIONS. Berries. Changes in attitude. Drought. Filial devotion. Hunger. Illness. Mothers and sons. Music. Thieves.

HOW ELSE THIS STORY IS TOLD. Two Dutiful Sons— Frances Carpenter, *Tales of a Chinese Grandmother* (here, the robber leaves everything, when a young man shames him for taking the copper pan he was going to cook breakfast in for his mother).

14. The Alchemist

Geraldine McCaughrean, *The Crystal Pool*. China

The laundryman, Mr. Chia, wishes he had money like the new neighbor, Mr. Chen. One day he offers Mr. Chen a bottle of wine and is invited in to share it. There Mr. Chia sees wonders. When Mr. Chen pours the last drop of wine, the jug fills itself again; when Mr. Chen rubs a stone against a vase, it becomes silver. When Mr. Chia asks about the stone, Mr. Chen replies that Mr. Chia's greed is well-known in Heaven. He also says that immortals are forbidden to teach mortals alchemy. Mr. Chia keeps pouring more wine until Mr. Chen collapses. The laundryman takes off with the stone. Without knowing the magic words, however, he cannot use it, so when Mr. Chen comes looking for his stone, Mr. Chia tells him he found it in the street. Again, he pleads to learn how to use it, just once. Mr. Chen does not want to appear ungrateful, but he suggests Mr. Chia transform something small. Mr. Chia holds up a bar of soap. After saying the magic words, however, Mr. Chia rubs the stone against his large wash-block, which becomes a hunk of solid silver. Mr. Chen is angry at the deception, but, one year later, the laundryman shows Mr. Chen all the good he has done for others, all the miseries he has washed away with the silver. Mr. Chen is now sure that Mr. Chia will now be welcome in Heaven.

CONNECTIONS. Alchemy. Changes in attitude. Changes in fortune. Charity. Deceit. Discontent. Forgiveness. Greed. Immortals. Jealousy. Laundrymen. Magical objects. Silver. Transformation.

HOW ELSE THIS STORY IS TOLD. The Alchemist — P'u Sung-ling, *Strange Stories from a Chinese Studio*, Online.

15. The Greedy Minister

Wolfram Eberhard, *Folktales of China*. Hupei, China

A boy finds an egg that he cares for without knowing what will hatch out of it. It turns out to be a little snake that grows bigger each day. He plays with it and the snake listens to him and sits in during his school lessons. But when the boy goes to the capital to take his examinations, he cannot bring the snake along. He asks the snake for a gift, in thanks for having taken care of it all these years. The snake spits out a large pearl. Having excelled in his examinations, the young man decides to present the pearl to the emperor, hoping to receive a good appointment. He becomes chancellor, but misses having the pearl. The young man returns home and asks the snake for another pearl. He steps forward to receive the pearl, and the snake swallows him.

CONNECTIONS. Chancellors. Changes in fortune. Eggs. Emperors. Gifts. Hupei, China, stories from. Imperial examination. Ingratitude. Magical objects. Mysteries. Pearls. Rewards. Snakes.

16. Once Under the Cherry Blossom Tree: An Old Japanese Tale

Allen Say. Japan

A grumbling, miserly landlord in a poor village swallows a cherry pit the wrong way and wakes to find some leaves sprouting from the top of his head. The tree continues to grow. One year later, just at festival time, the cherry tree on top of his head blooms. When villagers gawk, the landlord grows angry with them and rips the tree right out of his head, threatening to raise their rents. Now there is a large hole on top of the landlord's head, which summer rains fill with water. Even though he has to sleep sitting up, the landlord doesn't mind at all when carp begin to swim in the hole. After all, it saves him money on food. One brave boy and his friends decide to fish in the hole while the landlord is napping. But when a carp splashes water, the landlord wakes with a roar. He chases after the boys, but trips and falls, somehow disappearing into the hole in his head, until all that is left is a peaceful pond.

CONNECTIONS. Carp. Cherry trees. Children. Humorous stories. Kagoshima, Japan, stories from. Landlords. Misers. Physical difference. Transformation. Trees. Villagers.

HOW ELSE THIS STORY IS TOLD. An Exaggeration — Fanny Hagin Mayer, *Ancient Tales in Modern Japan* (from Kagoshima).

17. The Skeleton's Dance

Keigo Seki, *Folktales of Japan*. Japan

Two friends have gone to another country to find work. Shimo works hard, but Kami wastes his time. After three years, Shimo lends Kami money so that they can travel back home, but Kami kills Shimo in a mountain pass and steals all of his money. Back at home, Kami lies, saying that it was Shimo who was the wastrel. However, Kami ends up losing all of the money, gambling, and decides to travel again. In the same mountain pass, a voice calls his name. Then a skeleton appears that says it is Shimo and urges Kami to take him along to dance so Kami can make money. Kami does, but when he opens the box, the skeleton stays still. Kami beats it, and the skeleton gets up and tells the truth. Kami is punished, and the skeleton falls apart.

CONNECTIONS. Deceit. Friendship. Journeys. Justice. Murder. Revenge. Skeletons. Skulls. Thieves.

HOW ELSE THIS STORY IS TOLD. The Skeleton's Dance — Anita Stern, *World Folktales*. The Skeleton's Song — Keigo Seki, *Folktales of Japan* (in this variation, it is a skull that sings the truth).

18. The Two Travellers

Indries Shah, *World Tales*. China

An evil man plucks out the eyes of the generous man with whom he has been traveling and then abandons him. The blind man works his way to the top of a tree where birds are singing. He realizes that he can understand their chatter. The birds sing that if a blind man bathes his eyes in dew, he will be able to see again. They sing that if someone were to bring the King's daughter a certain flower, she would recover from her illness. The flower would also find water for the King's parched gardens. The blind man follows their advice and bathes his eyes in dew. Sight restored, he finds the special flower and brings it to cure the King's daughter and repair the King's garden. The good man and the princess marry. When the evil man hears this he climbs the same tree, hoping to acquire good fortune, too. The birds are complaining that someone must have eavesdropped on them before, for the king's daughter is well, and his garden is flourishing. They look around the tree and find the bad man up there and pluck out his eyes.

CONNECTIONS. Birds. Blindness. Cruelty. Eavesdropping. Eyes. Flowers. Greed. Healing. Journeys. Language of animals. Princesses. Punishment. Rewards. Talking birds. Tibetan People, stories from.

HOW ELSE THIS STORY IS TOLD. ***Chinese variations:*** In the *Kanjur* (from the Tibetan

People). The Gossiping Animals—Wolfram Eberhard, *Folktales of China* (there is no blindness in this story of two brothers from Central China). The Umbrella Tree — Frederick and Audrey Hyde-Chambers, *Tibetan Folk Tales.*

19. The Beggar Scholar

Louise and Yuan-Hsi Kuo, *Chinese Folk Tales.* Han People

Near Nanking, a beggar's daughter pulls a frozen man lying in the snow into the poor hut she shares with her father. When he revives, he tells them that he is an orphan, and old Chang invites him to stay on with them. Mo Kwei helps out, and he and the daughter become fond of one another and wed. The daughter encourages Mo Kwei to study for the public examinations. He passes and old Chang gives him money to travel to the capital to take the imperial examinations, where he also excels. Mo Kwei hires a large boat to take them all to the capital, but en route begins thinking that he needs a better wife than a beggar's daughter to fit his new appointment. He pushes his wife and then her father off the boat and into the river. One month later, a matchmaker says that the Minister of Justice would like to arrange a marriage between Mo Kwei and his daughter. He agrees, but on the day of the wedding, when he lifts the red veil covering his bride's face, it is his wife. The Minister of Justice accuses the scholar of being heartless; he had seen everything, since his boat was right behind Mo Kwei's. The daughter begins to hit her husband, and old Chang tells Mo Kwei that he owes his new position to Chang's begging money. Now, Mo Kwei truly regrets what he had done, and seeing that, his wife decides that she will not destroy a life she once saved.

CONNECTIONS. Beggars. Changes in fortune. Consequences. Deceit. Forgiveness. Han People, stories from. Husbands and wives. Ingratitude. Justice. Kindness. Love. Ministers. Nanking. Poverty. Rescues. Scholars. Selfishness. Social class. Unfaithfulness.

HOW ELSE THIS STORY IS TOLD. The Heartless Husband — Richard Wilhelm, *The Chinese Fairy Book.*

20. A Small Favor

P'u Sung-ling in Moss Roberts, *Chinese Fairy Tales and Fantasies.* China

Although he is wealthy and just, Ting Ch'ien-hsi nevertheless flees Chuch'eng in Shantung Province when he is accused of certain charges. In Arch'ie province, he runs into a rainstorms. He stops by a house where he is a stranger. Although Mr. Yang is away at his gambling den, Ting Ch'ien-hsi is shown gracious hospitality by Mr. Yang's wife. Mr. Yang's nephew even pulls thatch from the roof to feed his horse. Although Ting offers silver to pay for his meal, they refuse to take it. Many years later, there is a famine, and Yang comes to see Ting Ch'ien-hsi for help. Ting Ch'ien-hsi hosts him with warmth and respect for several days. Finally, worried about how his family is faring, Yang mentions something to Ting Ch'ien-hsi. It turns out that Ting Ch'ien-hsi already sent gifts of cloth and food to them on the very first day of Mr. Yang's arrival.

CONNECTIONS. Arch'ie Province. Changes in fortune. Gamblers. Gratitude. Hospitality. Husbands and wives. Journeys. Shantung Province.

21. Gentle Gwan Yin

Frances Carpenter, *Tales of a Chinese Grandmother.* China

The Emperor Po Chia loves his youngest daughter, Miao Shan, best, but she refuses to marry anyone to become Empress. Instead, she wants to help less fortunate people. To punish her, the Emperor orders the nunnery where she lives to give Miao Shan the hardest tasks. The Emperor of Heaven sends dragons, a tiger, birds, and spirits to help her with the chores. Still angry, the Emperor sends troops to burn the nunnery, but clouds quench the flames with rain. When the Emperor tries to behead Miao Shan, the axe falls to pieces, and a tiger rescues her and brings her to the dark underworld. There, a young man asks Miao Shan to pray for those being punished. She does, and light fills the underworld. Back on earth, she continues to pray for people. An old man gives her a peach that will not only feed her, but make her immortal. Transformed into a tiger, the God of the Neighborhood brings Miao Shan to the island of Pu To in the Southern Sea, where she prays for nine years. She is granted a place in Heaven as Guanyin, *She-Who-Hears-Prayers*. And it is to Guanyin that people pray when things seem hopeless.

CONNECTIONS. Anger. Buddha. Compassion. Despair. Dragon Princess. Emperors. Gods and goddesses. Guanyin, Goddess of Mercy. Han People, stories from. Helpfulness. Immortality. Jade Emperor. Kindness. Long Nü. Magical objects. Marriage. Miao Shan. Nunneries. Old man, supernatural helper. Peaches. Po Chia, Emperor. Prayer. Princesses. Punishment. Pu To, island. Tigers. Transformation. Underworld.

HOW ELSE THIS STORY IS TOLD. Guanyin, Goddess of Mercy—Haiwang Yuan, *The Magic Lotus Lantern and Other Tales from the Han Chinese* (in this more complex variation of a story from the Han People, Buddha takes Miao Shan as his disciple, and the Dragon King's daughter, Long Nü, becomes hers). The Little Goddess—Catherine Edwards Sandler, *Heaven's Reward*.

22. Lord of the Cranes

Kerstin Chen. China

Tian flies down from his mountain to the city on a crane one day to see if people are being good to each other. He trades his robes for a beggar's rags. No one notices him or drops any coins into his cup. He enters an inn, where the innkeeper invites him in to eat, even after he tells Wang that he cannot pay. For months, Wang feeds the old man. Then one day Tian says that he would like to repay Wang and paints a wonderful mural of three cranes on his wall. He sings and claps, and the cranes come to life. Tian disappears then, but the cranes remain. Although Wang becomes rich, as people stop in to see his cranes, he continues to feed those who need soup and cannot pay. Tian returns and tells Wang to teach others to be kind and generous. When Wang asks who he is, Tian plays a melody from heaven and the three cranes kneel before him. Then Tian flies off on the back of one.

CONNECTIONS. Animation. Changes in fortune. Cranes. Disguises. Generosity. Han People, stories from. Immortals. Innkeepers. Kindness. Old man, supernatural helper. Paintings and pictures. Tests. Transformation.

WHERE ELSE THIS STORY APPEARS. Lord of the Cranes—Kirsten Chen at *Learning to Give*, Online.

HOW ELSE THIS STORY IS TOLD. A Dancing Crane—Haiwang Yuan, *The Magic Lotus Lantern and Other Tales from the Han Chinese*. The Dancing Yellow Crane—Lim Sian-tek, *More Folk Tales from China*. The Paper Crane—Molly Bang.

23. The Pointing Finger

Carol Kendall and Yao-wen Li, *Sweet and Sour*. China

One of the Eight Immortals decides to test people to see if they have become less selfish. In disguise, he brings the first man to P'eng-lai, the Immortals' mountain island in the Eastern sea. The Immortal points to a pebble and turns it to gold. The first man does not think one pebble-sized gold is enough; he wants the Immortal to transform a pile of small stones. The second man thinks his family will need a boulder-sized amount of gold. The third man is not interested in taking the golden pebble. He wants to know about the magic and asks the Immortal to point at many different rocks. The Immortal thinks that perhaps he has found his unselfish man, but it turns out that what the man wants to own is the Immortal's finger itself.

CONNECTIONS. Disguises. Eastern Sea. Eight Immortals. Fingers. Gold. Greed. Humorous stories. Immortals. P'eng-lai, island. Tests. Transformation.

HOW ELSE THIS STORY IS TOLD. I Want Your Finger — Xiao Fu in *Ancient Chinese Tales*.

24. The Dissatisfied Benefactor

Wolfram Eberhard, *Folktales of China*. Chêkiang, China

Two Immortals come to test a respected rich man, known for his charitable deeds. Disguised as shoeless beggars, they get into a fight outside his house. The rich man separates them and brings them clothes and food, which they eat so slowly, they ask to spend the night. They spit all over the bed and leave the next morning without thanking him, but the rich man does not speak against them One day, when he jokes that he wishes the water in his well was wine, it becomes wine. He sells the wine. A customer criticizes, requesting spirits. The rich man asks for the wine to become brandy and makes more money. When someone else questions why he doesn't sell grape skins, he wishes for that. The two Immortals return and tell him that he has been too demanding, unsatisfied with what he has. They turn the wine back into well water again.

CONNECTIONS. Beggars. Changes in fortune. Chêkiang, China, stories from. Discontent. Disguises. Hospitality. Immortals. Magical objects. Priests. Rewards. Rich man. Tests. Transformation. Wine.

HOW ELSE THIS STORY IS TOLD. The Dissatisfied Good Man — Leslie Bonnet, *Chinese Folk and Fairy Tales*. The Wine Well — Chiang Ying-K'e in Moss Roberts, *Chinese Fairy Tales and Fantasies* (here it is a Taoist priest who comes to stay).

25. The Magic Pear Tree

P'u Sung-ling in Moss Roberts, *Chinese Fairy Tales and Fantasies*. China

A Taoist priest comes over to a farmer with a wagon load of pears, and the farmer shoos him away. The priest yells. Finally, a soldier gives the priest a few coins, so he can buy fruit. The priest eats a pear and plants the seed. Immediately the seed sprouts and becomes a tree, covered with delicious pears. The priest begins to give all the pears away. Then he cuts down the tree. The farmer has been watching, but now he finds that his wagon is empty of pears, and one handle is gone.

CONNECTIONS. Animation. Beggars. Consequences. Farmers. Magical objects. Misers. Pear trees. Pears. Priests. Punishment. Taoism. Transformation.

WHERE ELSE THIS STORY APPEARS. The Magic Pear Tree — P'u Sung-ling in Jane Yolen, *Favorite Folktales from Around the World*. Planting a Pear Tree — P'u Sung-ling in Michael Bedard, *The Painted Wall and Other Strange Tales*. Planting a Pear Tree — P'u Sung-ling, *Strange Stories from a Chinese Studio*, Online.

HOW ELSE THIS STORY IS TOLD. *Chinese variations: The Beggar's Magic: A Chinese Tale*— Margaret S. Chang and Raymond Chang. The Magic Pear Tree — Catherine Edwards Sandler, *Heaven's Reward. The Magic Pear Tree*— Wango Weng, director, Film. The Miserly Farmer — Richard Wilhelm, *The Chinese Fairy Book*. The Monk and the Pear Tree — Lim Sian-tek, *More Folk Tales from China*. The Pear Tree — Michael David Kwan, *The Chinese Storyteller's Book*. Planting a Pear Tree — Joanna Cole, *Best-Loved Folktales of the World*. The Wonderful Pear Tree — Frances Carpenter, *Tales of a Chinese Grandmother*. The Wonderful Pear Tree — Herbert A. Giles, *Chinese Fairy Tales*. *Japanese variation:* The Uneatable Pears— Yoshimatsu Suzuki, *Japanese Legends and Folk-Tales*.

26. The Lost Star Princess

Frances Carpenter, *Tales of a Chinese Grandmother*. China

The Jade Emperor wants to reward the old beggar Sing Wu for always sharing whatever rice he obtains. He sends his young daughter, one of the seven Star Princesses to earth for one year. She marries Sing Wu, and his life changes for the better. However, the wicked mandarin next door covets the Star Princess and offers Sin Wu his own wife in exchange. The Star Princess tells Sing Wu to accept, for she will only be able to stay on earth for a few more days. Sing Wu is sad. The Star Princess appears before the mandarin and chastises him for forsaking his own wife. She claps once, and he vanishes. She claps again, and his house becomes a lake, his servants fish, and his guests frogs.

CONNECTIONS. Beggars. Changes in fortune. Fathers and daughters. Generosity. Gods and goddesses. Husbands and wives. Jade Emperor. Kindness. Love. Mandarins. Punishment. Rewards. Star Princess. Stars. Supernatural wives. Trades. Transformation. Unfaithfulness. Wife-stealing.

27. Why Is Sea Water Salty?

Florence Sakade, *Japanese Children's Favorite Stories*. Japan

In a Taoi village Elder Brother turns his younger brother away when Younger Brother comes to borrow rice for New Year's celebrations. Elder Brother says Younger Brother shouldn't have gotten married if he couldn't afford it. Younger Brother helps an old man gather wood in the mountains. The old man hands him a wheat cake and tells him to take it to a cave behind the shrine, but not to give it to the Little People there, unless they will trade it for their Stone Hand Mill. Younger Brother finds the Little People and comes out with their treasured mill. The old man tells Younger Brother that when he turns the handle to the right, whatever he wishes for will appear. Turning the handle to the left will stop the mill. Younger Brother and his wife wish for rice and, then, salmon, a new house, and two horses. They get whatever they wish for and share their good fortune with the poor. But, peeking through the window, the elder brother only sees Younger Brother turning the handle of the mill one direction to start the mill;

he does not see him turn the handle the other way to stop it. Elder Brother steals the mill and sails away. After eating so much sweet, he now craves something salty. He turns the handle on the mill. Salt pours out and then more salt. Elder Brother cannot stop the mill. Salt sinks the boat and continues to pour into the ocean.

CONNECTIONS. Brothers. Deities. Greed. Kindness. Magical objects. Mills. Misers. Monsters. Mortars. New Year's. Old man, supernatural helper. Origins. Punishment. Rewards. Salt. Sea. Taiwan, stories from. Taoi, village. Thieves. Tokushima, Japan, stories from.

WHERE ELSE THIS STORY APPEARS. The Magic Mortar — Florence Sakade, *Urashima Taro and Other Japanese Children's Stories.*

HOW ELSE THIS STORY IS TOLD. **Chinese variation:** How the Sea Became Salty — Louise and Yuan-Hsi Kuo, *Chinese Folk Tales.* **Japanese variations:** The Handmill That Ground Out Salt — Fanny Hagin Mayer, *Ancient Tales in Modern Japan* (from Tokushima). The Magic Mortar — Yoshiko Uchida, *The Magic Listening Cap.* The Salt-Grinding Millstones— Keigo Seki, *Folktales of Japan.* Why Is Seawater Salty? — Yoko Kawashima Watkins, *Tales from the Bamboo Grove.* **Korean variation:** Why the Sea Is Salty — Suzanne Crowder Han, *Korean Folk and Fairy Tales.* Why the Sea Is Salty — Gillian McClure, *The Land of the Dragon King and Other Korean Stories.* **Taiwanese variation:** How Saltwater Came to Fill the Seas— Gary Marvin Davison, *Tales from the Taiwanese.*

28. When Rocks Rolled Crackling Wisdom

M.A. Jagendorf and Virginia Weng, *The Magic Boat and Other Chinese Folk Stories.* Yi People

In magical times when creatures and stones of the earth can speak, two brothers live in the same house after their parents die. However, Elder Brother is so miserly that Younger Brother leaves to live alone in the woods. One day he lays down his bundle of wood, and a rock tells him that the wood is too heavy for its head. The woodcutter apologizes and tells the rock how mean his brother is. The Talking Stone instructs him to reach down into a crevice and pull out a handful of gold dust, which he does. He thanks the stone and leaves. Elder Brother notices the change in Younger Brother's fortune and hears about the gold dust. Now, disguised in rags, he visits the Talking Stone and lies, saying that his brother is mean to him. The Talking Stone does not believe him, and when greedy Elder Brother thrusts both of his fists into the crevice to get gold dust, the stone closes its lips over his hands and will not let him go until he learns to be generous. His wife has to come and feed him for many days. Finally she says they have run out of food, and she will have to nurse him like a baby. Elder Brother stretches his neck towards her. The Talking Stone laughs. Its mouth opens, and Elder Brother pulls free. He runs off without gold dust, but is never mean and stingy again.

CONNECTIONS. Animation. Brothers. Changes in fortune. Disguises. Gold dust. Greed. Hui People, stories from. Humorous stories. Husbands and wives. Jealousy. Magical objects. Misers. Punishment. Qinghai, China, stories from. Stone. Stone monkey. Yi People, stories from.

HOW ELSE THIS STORY IS TOLD. The Stone Monkey — Ma Mingyi in Shujiang Li and Karl W. Luckert, *Mythology and Folklore of the Hui* (from Qinghai).

29. A Crane and Two Brothers

Li Ximing in Neil Philip, *The Spring of Butterflies and Other Folktales of China's Minority Peoples.* Tulong People

A poor younger brother is tricked by his elder brother, whose wife cooks the millet seeds before giving them to him to sow. One seed does sprout, but just as he goes to harvest it, a crane swoops down and takes it. When the younger brother yells, the bird brings him to the Sun Mountain. The younger brother is allowed to take one nugget of gold, and he gladly does. The older brother pretends to be poor, but when he is taken to Sun Mountain, he won't stop gathering nuggets, despite the crane's warning that it is time to go. The hot sun rises and burns the greedy brother.

CONNECTIONS. Birds. Brothers. Cranes. Deceit. Gold. Millet. Poverty. Punishment. Seeds. Sun Mountain. Trees. Tulong People, stories from. Warnings.

HOW ELSE THIS STORY IS TOLD. The Greedy Brother — Catherine Edwards Sadler, *Heaven's Reward*. Picking Up Gold — Charles J. Wivell, translator, in *The Lady in the Picture*. Sun Valley — Emily Ching and Ko-Shee Ching, *Sun Valley; a Stone Carver's Dream* (in this variation, the kindly younger brother is rewarded for not chopping down a tree at the tree's request). Women's Words Part Flesh and Blood — Richard Wilhelm, *The Chinese Fairy Book*.

30. The Farmer and the Badger

Yei Theodora Ozaki, *Japanese Fairy Book*. Japan

Angry that a badger ruins their crops every night, an old farmer finally catches the badger in a trap hole. He strings him up in the storehouse, telling his wife not to let the badger escape, for he plans to cook him. The wiley badger, though, is determined not to stay caught. He offers to help the farmer's wife pound barley and lets her know how sad and uncomfortable he feels, hanging upside down. After a while, farmer's wife feels sorry for him. When she unties him, though, the badger hits her with the heavy wooden pestle and makes soup out of her. He then disguises himself as the old woman until the minute he sets the soup in front of the farmer, when he transforms back into a badger, mocks the farmer, and runs off. The farmer weeps. A rabbit tells the farmer that he will avenge his wife's death. The rabbit calls out, suggesting that he and the badger cut grass together to store for food. They are carrying bundles of grass, when the rabbit sets his on fire and pretends not to know. Fire burns the badger's fur. The rabbit pretends to be sympathetic and makes a red pepper ointment that stings the badger even more. When the badger finally heals, the rabbit invites him to go fishing. He offers the badger a clay boat, which starts to fall apart in the water. When the frightened badger says he cannot swim, the rabbit says that this is for murdering the old woman and hits the badger with an oar. The farmer and the rabbit become fast friends.

CONNECTIONS. Badgers. Compassion. Consequences. Cruelty. Deceit. Escapes. Farmers. Husbands and wives. Ingratitude. Kindness to animals. Murder. Rabbits and hares. Revenge. Shape-shifting. Soup. Tanuki. Yamagata, Japan, stories from.

HOW ELSE THIS STORY IS TOLD. The Burning Mountain — Juliet Piggott, *Japanese Fairy Tales*. The Crackling Mountain — Pearl S. Buck, *Fairy Tales of the Orient*. The Crackling Mountain — F. Hadland Davis, *Myths and Legends of Japan*. The Crackling Mountain — Baron Algernon Bertram Freeman-Mitford Redesdale, *Tales of Old Japan*. The Hare and the Badger — Takeshi Nakajima, *Japanese Traditional Tales*. Kachi Kachi Mountain — Keigo Seki, *Folktales of Japan*. Kachi-Kachi Yama — Fanny Hagin Mayer, *Ancient Tales in Modern Japan* (from Yamagata). Kachi-Kachi Yama — Iwaya Sazanami, *Iwaya's Fairy Tales of Old Japan*. The Kachi-Kachi Yama, or the Crackling Mountain — Alan Leslie Whitehorn, *Wonder Tales of Old Japan*. *Kachi-Kachi Yama/Kachi-Kachi Mountain* — Kobunsha's Japanese Fairy Tale Series, No. 5. Kachikachiyama — *Kids Web Japan*, Online. The Slaying of the Tanuki — Andrew Lang, *The Pink Fairy Book*.

31. Ten Thousand Treasure Mountain

Louise and Yuan-Hsi Kuo, *Chinese Folk Tales*. Yao People

One day, as K'o-li and his mother urge each other to eat the little bit of pounded turtle foot plant that they have, a frail old man appears. He seems to need the food more, and they give it to him. Then K'o-li carries the man far from his farm in Kwangsi across gorges and up mountains to a big stone cave. Grateful, the old man instructs the maiden who has come out to meet him to turn her earrings into keys. She tells K'o-li that he will need the gold key to get into Ten Thousand Treasure Mountain and the silver key to get out. K'o-li visits Ten Thousand Treasure Mountain. The stone door opens with the gold key. He looks for a tool that will help him at home and chooses a white stone grinder. K'o-li lets himself out with the silver key. Back at home, the grinder produces so much corn that they have much to share with their neighbors, and the king sends an official to confiscate it. However, at the king's touch, the grinder becomes a heap of white lime. K'o-li next returns from Ten Thousand Treasure Mountain with a mortar that produces rice as it pounds. But, in the king's hands, the mortar turns to yellow clay. K'oli acquires a hoe that makes corn grow. This time, the king sends for K'o-li and demands to know where the magic tools come from. K'o-li tells him about the mountain and gives the king only the gold key. The greedy king becomes trapped inside. K'o-li is only sorry that he will not be able to return the gold key to the maiden, since it had been her earring. His mother suggests they go to visit. The old grandfather would like K'o-li to marry his granddaughter. The granddaughter happily goes home with K'o-li and his mother.

CONNECTIONS. Changes in fortune. Filial devotion. Generosity. Golden key. Grandfathers and granddaughters. Greed. Guangxi, province. Hunger. Kindness. Kings. Love. Magical objects. Mothers and sons. Mountains. Old man, supernatural helper. Poverty. Tools. Treasure. Yao People, stories from.

HOW ELSE THIS STORY IS TOLD. Treasure Mountain — Catherine Edwards Sadler, *Treasure Mountain*.

32. The White Hare and the Crocodiles

Eric Quayle, *The Shining Princess and Other Japanese Tales*. Japan

A little hare would like to get from the island of Oki to the mainland of Inaba, but he cannot swim and he fears the crocodile's teeth enough not to ask for a ride. Then, the hare thinks up a trick. He asks the crocodile whether he supposes more crocodiles exist than hares, and the crocodile is sure there are. Aloud, the hare doubts if there are enough crocodiles to reach all the way to Inaba. The crocodile takes the bait. Crocodiles all line up, each one holding the tail of the other in its mouth, and the hare hops safely across their backs to Inaba. Once on shore, however, he taunts the crocodiles, shouting that he deceived them all. The closest crocodile pulls out much of the hare's fur. Sons of the Emperor advise the hare to dip into the sea and then bake on the beach, but this is a mean trick, for the hare's bare skin tightens from the salt water and causes him much pain. The youngest son, who has been hauling all their baggage, feels sorry for the hare, but chastises him for tricking the crocodiles and then jeering at them. The little hare is now truly sorry, and the youngest son shows him how to soothe his skin and grow new white fur. The hare asks what he can do to thank the Emperor's son. The son says that he would like to marry Princess Yakami, but he is sure his brothers will arrive first. The hare reassures him that the princess would never marry anyone as cruel as his brothers. And, indeed, it comes to pass that the princess does choose the youngest son.

CONNECTIONS. Bodhisattvas. Changes in attitude. Crocodiles. Deceit. Gods and goddesses. Guanyin, Goddess of Mercy. Han People, stories from. Helpfulness. Inaba, place. Islands. Kindness. Oki Islands. Princes. Punishment. Rabbits and hares. Remorse. Sea. Skin. Tricksters. Turtles.

HOW ELSE THIS STORY IS TOLD. *Japanese variations:* The Counting of Crocodiles—Harold Courlander, *The Tiger's Whisker* (ends with the crocodile biting off the hare's tail). The Hare of Inaba—Lafcadio Hearn, *The Boy Who Drew Cats and Other Japanese Fairy Tales*. The Hare of Inaba—Lafcadio Hearn, *Japanese Fairy Tales*. *Inaba no Shiro-Usagi / The Hare of Inaba*—Japanese Fairy Tale Series, No. 11. The Rabbit and the Crocodile—Yoshiko Uchida, *The Dancing Kettle*. The Rabbit Who Crossed the Sea—Florence Sakade, *Japanese Children's Favorite Stories* and *Little One-Inch*. *Sh-Ko and His Eight Wicked Brothers*—Ashley Bryan. The White Hare—Takeshi Nakajima, *Japanese Traditional Tales*. The White Hare and the Crocodiles—Virginia Haviland, *Favorite Fairy Tales Told in Japan*. The White Hare and the Crocodiles—Yei Theodora Ozaki, *Japanese Fairy Book*. The White Hare of Inaba—F. Hadland Davis, *Myths and Legends of Japan*. The White Hare of Oki—Juliet Piggott, *Japanese Fairy Tales*. The White Rabbit and the Crocodiles—Alan Leslie Whitehorn, *Wonder Tales of Old Japan*. *Chinese variations:* Rabbit's Tail Tale—*Eleven Nature Tales: A Multicultural Journey* (from the Han People). The Sad Tale of the Rabbit's Tail—M.A. Jagendorf and Virginia Weng, *The Magic Boat and Other Chinese Folk Stories* (here, the rabbit counts turtles, instead of crocodiles).

33. Heaven and Hell

George Shannon, *Stories to Solve*. China

A man wishes to see the difference between heaven and hell before he dies. In hell he sees people frustrated because they cannot get food to their mouths with three-foot long chopsticks. Heaven seems to be the same. People also sit by food-laden tables with long chopsticks, but they have discovered that by feeding each other, all can eat.

CONNECTIONS. Cooperation. Food. Heaven. Hell. Helpfulness. Realization.

HOW ELSE THIS STORY IS TOLD. Heaven and Hell—Isabelle C. Cheng, *Tales from Old China*. Heaven and Hell—Margaret Read MacDonald, *Peace Tales*.

~ II ~

Cherishing the Earth
and All Living Things

34. Offering a Sacrifice to the Tiger

A Museum of Chinese Classic Stories, Volume 6. Hezhen People

Long ago, a Hezhan hunting family lives on the south bank of Three-River-Mouth where the Songhua and Heilongjiang Rivers meet. The husband goes off to the mountains to hunt for martens in the early spring. It is evening when the wife hears the door bang. She is frightened. A tiger's bleeding paw appears, with a thorn stuck inside. The woman works on the paw, and is finally able to pull the thorn out with her teeth. After that, the tiger brings them gifts of deer or wild pig. He becomes known as the Servant of the Mountain God.

CONNECTIONS. Compassion. Fear. Gratitude. Healing. Heilongjiang River. Helpfulness. Hezhen People, stories from. Hunters. Kindness from animals. Kindness to animals. Songhua River. Thorns. Three-River-Mouth. Tigers.

35. The Tiger General

Wolfram Eberhard, *Folktales of China*. China

One day a woodcutter hears whimpering and finds a tigress in labor. Her entrails have caught on thorns. She seems to be pleading for help. He runs to his mother, a midwife, who tells him they must dip the entrails in wine. They do this, and the tigress gives birth to four little cubs. Before they leave, the mother tells the tigress that she must bring a bride for her son, as they are so poor. One snowy night, a bridal party is surprised by five tigers. The attendants flee, and the tigers carry the bride to the woodcutter's house. He invites her in, and they marry. The rightful bridegroom complains to the magistrate that the woodcutter stole his bride. The mother goes to the tigress and asks her to appear as a witness. The judge asks the tigers if they had brought the bride to the woodcutter's, and when the tigers nod, the woodcutter is freed. Years later, the emperor orders the woodcutter and his five tigers to chase away a rebel who has wild beasts, and they do. The emperor names the woodcutter Five Tiger General, and he keeps peace along the border.

CONNECTIONS. Birth. Brides. Changes in fortune. Compassion. Fear. Generals. Gratitude. Healing. Helpfulness. Justice. Kindness to animals. Magistrates. Protection. Rewards. Thorns. Tigers. Woodcutters.

HOW ELSE THIS STORY IS TOLD. The Five Tiger General — Leslie Bonnet, *Chinese Folk and Fairy Tales.*

36. The Man in the Moon

Shelley Fu, *Treasury of Chinese Folk Tales*. China

In a time of famine in a poor village by the Yellow River, a boy finds a tiny sparrow with a broken wing. He brings it home and cares for it, until it can fly again. That day, the sparrow drops a tiny seed by the boy, which he throws away three times until his mother suggests that he plant it. He does, and the seed grows into a giant vine that bears one huge, golden gourd at the end of the summer. When the boy cuts into the gourd, precious gems spill out. Wu Gan, another boy from the village is jealous. He practices throwing rocks until he brings the sparrow down. Afterwards, he tends its broken wing. When it is well again, he orders the sparrow to bring him a reward. The bird drops a large seed, which grows into a golden gourd. One night Wu Gan dreams that an old man has offered him one sweet from a jar. In the dream, his hand gets stuck when he tries to grab too many. The old man scolds him and calls him cruel. When the boy awakes, he cuts open the gourd and is frightened when the old man from his dream emerges. He grabs his axe. The old man takes him by the hand, and they rise to the moon. The old man brings Wu Gan past silver boulders to a cassia wood tree with jade leaves and fruits of precious stones. The old man says that if Wu Gan can chop down the tree, he will be able to keep the gems and return to earth. Wu Gan tries over and over, but every cut with his axe heals over. Still, he keeps trying to cut down the tree and never hears the beautiful Tsang-O who wants to converse.

CONNECTIONS. Birds. Brothers. Cassia trees. Chang'e. Changes in fortune. Cruelty to animals. Dreams. Golden gourd. Gourds. Gratitude. Greed. Greedy neighbor. Healing. Helpfulness. Jewels. Kindness to animals. Magical objects. Melons. Moon. Old man, supernatural helper. Punishment. Rewards. Rising to the sky world. Seeds. Sparrows. Swallows. Tibetan People, stories from. Yellow River.

WHERE ELSE THIS STORY APPEARS. The Man in the Moon — Shelley Fu, *Ho Yi the Archer*.

HOW ELSE THIS STORY IS TOLD. *Chinese variations:* The Golden Squash — A.L. Shelton, *Tibetan Folk Tales*. The Hurt Sparrow — Pearl S. Buck, *Fairy Tales of the Orient*. The Man in the Moon — Wolfram Eberhard, *Folktales of China*. The Magic Melons — Tehyi Hsieh, *Chinese Village Folk Tales*. The Reward from the Sparrow — Louise and Yuan-Hsi Kuo, *Chinese Folk Tales*. The Story of the Two Neighbors — W. F. O'Connor, *Folk Tales from Tibet*. The Two Melons — Adele Marion Fielde, *Chinese Nights' Entertainment*. *Japanese variations:* The Five Sparrows — Patricia Montgomery Newton. The Sparrow with a Broken Back — Fanny Hagin Mayer, *Ancient Tales in Modern Japan*. The Sparrows' Gifts — Royall Tyler, *Japanese Tales*. *Korean variations:* (these usually involve two brothers, one kind and one greedy, but do not include the moon ending). The Good Brother's Reward — Frances Carpenter, *Tales of a Korean Grandmother*. The Gourd Seeds — Yu Chai-Shin, Shiu L. Kong, and Ruth W. Yu, *Korean Folk Tales*. Nolbo and Heungbo — Tae Hung Ha, *Folk Tales of Old Korea* (the wounded bird is a swallow). The Pumpkin Seeds — Kim So-un, *Korean Children's Favorite Stories*. The Pumpkin Sparrow — Claudia Fregos. The Queen Swallow's Gift — Suzanne Crowder Han, *Korean Folk and Fairy Tales*. The Swallow Queen's Gift — Lindy Soon Curry, *A Tiger by the Tail*. Two Kins' Pumpkins — John Holstein.

37. The Crane Maiden

Rafe Martin, *Mysterious Tales of Japan*. Japan

An old man frees a panicked crane from a snare. He is filled with wonder as the beautiful crane flies away. The next morning, the man and his wife find a young girl at the door who says she is lost and offers to weave for them. The old man and woman are delighted to have her with them. She asks that they not watch while she weaves. For a whole day, she shuts herself in with the loom and emerges pale, holding exquisite cloth. She tells them to sell the cloth, and they do. When that money is gone, she weaves another beautiful cloth. The next time the young woman weaves, they peek. At the loom is a crane, pulling feathers from its breast and wings and weaving with them. The crane sees them. This time, when she hands them the cloth, she says that she was the crane the old man had kindly saved. She has wanted to thank them, but now she must go. She transforms back into a crane and flies away.

CONNECTIONS. Changes in fortune. Cranes. Geese. Gratitude. Kindness to animals. Maidens. Nagano, Japan, stories from. Rescues. Sail makers. Shape-shifting. Shipbuilders. Spirits. Supernatural wives. Transformation. Weavers.

HOW ELSE THIS STORY IS TOLD. *The Crane Maiden*— Miyoko Matsutani. The Crane Who Said Thank You — Juliet Piggott, *Japanese Fairy Tales*. *The Crane Wife*— Odds Bodkin and on *The Blossom Tree* (the protagonist is a sail maker who marries the crane). The Crane Wife — Keigo Seki, *Folktales of Japan. The Crane Wife*— Sumiko Yagawa. *Dawn*— Molly Bang (here a shipbuilder rescues an injured goose, who becomes his weaver wife). The Fairy Crane — Florence Sakade, *Urashima Taro and Other Japanese Children's Stories*. The Grateful Crane — William Elliot Griffis, *The Fire-Fly's Lovers and Other Fairy Tales of Old Japan*. The Grateful Stork — Yoshiko Uchida, *The Magic Listening Cap*. The Stork Wife — Fanny Hagin Mayer, *Ancient Tales in Modern Japan* (from Nagano). *Tsuru no Ongaeshi*— Tomoji Noda at *Kids Web Japan*, Online.

38. The Great Flood

Kim So-un, *Korean Children's Favorite Stories*. Korea

When Talltree's celestial mother returns to the heavens, a flood covers the earth. Father-tree tells Talltree to climb into his branches. They float this way and that for days. Feeling sorry for the animals, Talltree asks his father if he may invite first some ants on board and then, mosquitoes. Father-tree agrees to ants and mosquitoes, but he is quiet about the boy Talltree also brings on board. They all disembark at an island high above the water; the ants and the mosquitoes thank Talltree and go their own way. Talltree and the boy find an old woman and two girls there. They work for the old woman, and when they grow up, she decides the most skillful young man should marry her real daughter and the other her adopted daughter. The other boy cheats, claiming that Talltree can separate millet from sand, and the old woman prepares a test. Just as Talltree is wondering how he will accomplish the task, grateful ants come to pick out the millet. Still, the other boy begs to marry her real daughter. The old woman puts one daughter in the east room and one in the west. A mosquito tells Talltree which is which, and he finds the real daughter in the east room. They have many children and grandchildren, and over time, the earth again fills with people.

CONNECTIONS. Ants. Deceit. Fathers and sons. Floods. Gratitude. Identity. Ingratitude. Kindness from animals. Kindness to animals. Matches, marriage. Mosquitoes. Mothers and daughters. Rescues. Taiwan, stories from. Tests. Trees.

HOW ELSE THIS STORY IS TOLD. **Chinese variations:** The Legend of Wang Xiao — Li Lianshan in Howard Giskin, *Chinese Folktales. The Magic Boat*— Demi (here, the male hero saves animals and one deceiving man with a toy boat). Tung Caho-chih and the King of the

Ants— Karl S. Y. Kao, *Classical Chinese Tales of the Supernatural and the Fantastic*. **Korean variation:** The Son of the Cinnamon Tree —*Long Long Time Ago*. **Taiwanese variation:** The Man Who Loved Tiny Creatures— Cora Cheney, *Tales from a Taiwan Kitchen*. *See also*, The Great Flood, story # 271.

39. The Grateful Ants

Yu Chai-Shin, Shiu L. Kong, and Ruth W. Yu, *Korean Folk Tales*. Korea

When torrential rain makes the river overflow into the rice paddies, a poor farmer fishes a round object out of the water. It is an anthill, which Han Baek Lee shelters under a rock, though others want to break it apart. He also gives the ants some food. When the rain stops, Han Baek Lee's wife shows him the neat piles of rice that have mysteriously appeared in their yard. Rice appears every day. They do not know who owns the rice, so eventually Han Baek Lee sells it, and he and his wife become rich. When famine comes and the governor opens the storehouse to distribute food, no rice is there. The governor hears about Han Baek Lee's rice and accuses him of stealing from the storehouse. A strange, tiny voice calls out that Han Baek Lee is not guilty. The governor sets him free, but Han Baek Lee has been troubled all along about where the rice had really come from. That night he hears the strange little voices in his dream. They tell him that they are the ants, repaying him for considering them important enough to save their lives. When he awakes, Han Baek Lee uses his wealth to build a dam for the community.

CONNECTIONS. Ants. Bowls. Captivity. Changes in fortune. Dreams. Drought. Farmers. Floods. Frogs. Golden ruler. Governors. Gratitude. Kindness to animals. Magical objects. Mysteries. Rain. Rebirth. Rescues. Rewards. Rice.

HOW ELSE THIS STORY IS TOLD. **Korean variation:** The Grave of the Golden Ruler — Richard M. Dorson, *Folktales Told Around the World* (this farmer puts tadpoles in a waterhole during a time of drought. The grown frogs reward him with an earthenware bowl that multiplies whatever he puts in it. The story goes on to describe another village where snakes keep reappearing until one snake gifts another man with a golden ruler that brings people back to life. Both men give their magic treasures to the king until the gods appear and tell him it is time to return the bowl and the ruler to heaven so people will not become lazy).

40. The Spider Weaver

Florence Sakade, *Japanese Children's Favorite Stories*. Japan

The young farmer Yosaku rescues a spider from being eaten by a snake. Soon after, a beautiful girl appears in his yard and says she will weave for him. In one day, she weaves enough cloth to make eight kimonos. She will not tell Yasaku how she does it, but orders him never to enter while she is weaving. One day, he peeks through the window and sees a spider at the loom. He recognizes her as the spider he'd saved. He crosses the mountain to buy more cotton for her thread and does not see a snake slip inside the bundle. At home, the snake surprises the spider as she begins to weave. The spider jumps outside in time, and Old Man Sun lifts her up on a beam of light to weave clouds in the sky. The story ends by saying that this is why the Japanese word *kumo* means both spider and cloud.

CONNECTIONS. Deceit. Farmers. Kindness to animals. Maidens. Origins. Rising to the sky world. Shape-shifting. Snakes. Spiders. Spirits. Transformation. Weavers.

WHERE ELSE THIS STORY APPEARS. The Spider Weaver — Florence Sakade, *Peach Boy*.

How Else This Story Is Told. The Cloud Spinner — Shirley Climo, *Someone Saw a Spider*.

41. The Maiden in Green

Margaret Read MacDonald, *Three-Minute Tales*. China

A student falls asleep while practicing his calligraphy late at night. He dreams that a beautiful maiden in a silk dress begs him to save her and disappears. He awakes to hear a little green bee buzzing. It is caught in a spiderweb, and the spider is drawing near. He quickly rescues the bee and gently lays it down on his inkstone. As the bee revives, it walks into the ink and then leaves tracks on his writing paper. On his paper is the character for "Thank you."

Connections. Bees. Calligraphy. Dreams. Gratitude. Kindness to animals. Rescues. Shape-shifting. Spirits. Students.

42. The Woodcutter and the Bird

Cathy Spagnoli, *Asian Tales and Tellers*. Korea

Hearing a bird cry out, a woodcutter runs to find a mother pheasant frantically trying to scare a large, white snake away from her nest. The man picks up a stick. Waving and yelling at the snake does not stop it from approaching the babies. When the snake rears back to strike him, the man hits the snake with the stick, and the snake dies. Several years later, the woodcutter is lost in those same woods. A very white woman invites him into her hut. He awakes in the night to find a white snake pinning his arms. The snake tells him that it is the spirit of the snake he killed. The man says that he tried to warn the snake first. The snake replies that she is warning the man now that he will die. The snake says she will let the man go only if the temple bell rings before dawn. The man does not hold out much hope, but just at dawn he hears a faint ringing. The snake slithers away. The man runs up the hill to the long-deserted temple. Who has rung the bell? Just then he sees the body of the mother pheasant he had helped before.

Connections. Bells. Birds. Captivity. Flies. Gratitude. Kindness to animals. Magpies. Mothers and children. Pheasants. Rescues. Shape-shifting. Snakes. Sparrows. Spirits. Transformation. Ultimatums. Woodcutters.

How Else This Story Is Told. The Grateful Magpies— Suzanne Crowder Han, *Korean Folk and Fairy Tales*. The Peasant and the Pheasants—Y.T. Pyun, *Tales from Korea*. The Pheasants and the Bell — Zong In-Sob, *Folk Tales from Korea*. The Revenge of the Serpent — Eleanore M. Jewett, *Which Was Witch?* The Sparrow and the Flies— Frances Carpenter, *Tales of a Korean Grandmother*. The Sparrow and the Snake — Yu Chai-Shin, Shiu L. Kong, and Ruth W. Yu, *Korean Folk Tales*.

43. The Grateful Monkey's Secret

Yoshiko Uchida, *The Sea of Gold*. Japan

One day when poor Kentsu hasn't sold any wine from his jars in a village far from his home, he hears high shrieking. The cries continue, and Kentsu brings his jars to the beach, where he sees a huge crab holding tightly to a monkey's paw. Kentsu hits the crab with a stick until it lets go of the monkey. Then he bandages the monkey's paw with his handkerchief and carries him up into the hills. A few days later, the monkey, still wearing his handkerchief, swings down from a tree, chattering, and pulls at Kentsu. Kentsu follows the monkey to a pool in the mountains. The pool is made of wine. Kentsu fills his jars at the pool and does brisk business selling his wine for less now. If he returns twice in one day to refill his jars, Kentsu finds the pool dry, but he is not greedy. One fill of the magic wine a day is enough for the rest of his life.

CONNECTIONS. Crabs. Gratitude. Kindness to animals. Magical objects. Monkeys and apes. Pools. Rescues. Rewards. Wine. Wine sellers.

44. The Singing Turtle

Elizabeth Scofield, *Hold Tight, Stick Tight.* Japan

A kindhearted man turns a turtle rightside up, and the little turtle suggests he make the man's fortune by singing songs in the village. He demonstrates the Turtle Song, the Pig Song, the Frog Song, and the Locust Song. The old man is delighted by the turtle. The next day, he holds the turtle in his hand, calling out for villagers to come and listen. They do and press coins upon him. The man's greedy neighbor grabs the turtle. For him, though, the turtle pulls into its shell and won't sing. People chase him away. The greedy man is so angry he kills the turtle. The kindhearted man buries the turtle in his garden, and the next day a tall tree grows there with hundreds of turtles crawling down the trunk. The kindhearted man is enchanted and holds out his hand for the turtles. To the old man's surprise, each one drops a gold piece into his hand and starts back up the tree. The greedy man breaks a branch off the tree and sticks it in his garden. Turtles start climbing down his tree too, but when they reach the mean man, they stick out their little tongues. He climbs up after them, but a branch breaks, and down he falls.

CONNECTIONS. Changes in fortune. Cruelty to animals. Cruelty to trees. Gold. Greed. Greedy neighbor. Helpfulness. Kindness to animals. Magical objects. Music. Punishment. Singing. Thieves. Trees. Turtles.

HOW ELSE THIS STORY IS TOLD. *Japanese variation:* The Singing Turtle—Florence Sakade, *Kintaro's Adventures* and *Japanese Children's Favorite Stories,* Book Two. **Korean variation:** The Talking Turtle—Y Chai-Shin, Shiu L. Kong, and Ruth W. Yu, *Korean Folk Tales.* **Chinese variations:** The Two Brothers—Neil Philip, *The Spring of Butterflies* (the greedy brother kills a little dog that helps the older one to plow, and then he chops down the money tree that has grown from the dog's grave. The good brother ends up owning precious dishes after he chases off monkeys from a winter melon that grows where he has planted branches from the money tree. This story is also told as How the Brothers Divided Their Property in *Folk Tales from China,* First Series. It overlaps with themes from The Man in the Moon, story # 36, and The Old Man of the Flowers, story # 47).

45. The Tongue-Cut Sparrow

Florence Sakade, *Japanese Children's Favorite Stories.* Japan

A childless old man keeps a sparrow for a pet, but his wife is impatient with all the attention he gives it. One day, when the sparrow is pecking at her laundry starch, she grabs a pair of scissors, cuts off its tongue, and orders the sparrow to fly away. Sad, her husband heads into the woods to look for the sparrow. It flies to him as a lovely woman dressed in a kimono. The sparrow invites him to her house. She brings a feast, and her daughters perform the Sparrow Dance. She offers him a choice of two baskets as a gift. He chooses the smaller, lighter one, so as not to be greedy. When he returns home, he finds that it is filled with coins and precious stones. His wife scolds him for not choosing the bigger basket, and the next day she heads out to find the sparrow. The sparrow also offers her tea. She chooses the biggest basket, but it becomes too heavy on her way home. She stops to see what is inside, and frightful things come out — a devil's head, stinging wasp, snakes. She runs home and never again is mean to birds.

CONNECTIONS. Changes in attitude. Choices. Cruelty to animals. Dancing. Fukui, Japan, stories from. Greed. Husbands and wives. Kindness to animals. Magical objects. Punishment. Rewards. Shape-shifting. Sparrows. Spirits. Tongues. Transformation.

WHERE ELSE THIS STORY APPEARS. The Tongue-Cut Sparrow — Florence Sakade, *Peach Boy*.

HOW ELSE THIS STORY IS TOLD. *Shitakiri Suzume: Tongue-Cut Sparrow*—Japanese Fairy Tale Series, No. 2. The Slit-Tongue Sparrow — Andrew Lang, *Pink Fairy Book*. The Sparrow with the Slit Tongue — Joanna Cole, *Best-Loved Folktales of the World*. The Story of Shitakiri Suzume, The Tongue-Cut Sparrow — Yuri Yasuda, *Old Tales of Japan*, Vol. I. The Tongue-cut Sparrow — F. Hadland Davis, *Myths and Legends of Japan*. The Tongue-Cut Sparrow — William Elliot Griffis, *The Fire-Fly's Lovers* and at D. L. Ashliman, *Folktexts*, Online. The Tongue-Cut Sparrow — Lafadio Hearn, *Japanese Fairy Tales* and at D. L. Ashliman, *Folktexts*, Online. The Tongue-Cut Sparrow — Virginia Haviland, *Favorite Fairy Tales Told in Japan*. *The Tongue-cut Sparrow*— Momoko Ishii. The Tongue-cut Sparrow — Fanny Hagin Mayer, *Ancient Tales in Modern Japan* (from Fukui). *The Tongue-Cut Sparrow/Shitakiri Suzume*— Miyoko Matsutani on kamishibai story cards. The Tongue-cut Sparrow — Helen and William McAlpine, *Oxford Tales from Japan*. The Tongue-Cut Sparrow — Baron Algernon Bertram Freeman-Mitford Redesdale, *Tales of Old Japan* and at D. L. Ashliman, *Folktexts*, Online. The Tongue-Cut Sparrow — Keshi Nakajima, *Japanese Traditional Tales*. The Tongue-Cut Sparrow — Yei Theodora Ozaki, *Japanese Fairy Book* and at D. L. Ashliman, *Folktexts*, Online. The Tongue-cut Sparrow — Eric Quayle, *The Shining Princess*. The Tongue-Cut Sparrow — Iwaya Sazanami, *Iwaya's Fairy Tales of Old Japan*. The Tongue-Cut Sparrow — Keigo Seki, *Folktales of Japan*. Tongue-Cut Sparrow: Shitakiri Suzume — Kazuo Tanaka at *Kids Web Japan*, Online. The Tongue-Cut Sparrow — Yoshiko Uchida, *The Dancing Kettle*. The Tongue-Cut Sparrow — Alan Lesie Whitehorn, *Wonder Tales of Old Japan*. The Tongue-Cut Sparrow — Teresa Pierce Williston, *Japanese Fairy Tales* and at D. L. Ashliman, *Folktexts*, Online.

46. Hold Tight and Stick Tight

Margaret Read MacDonald, *Earth Care*. Japan

A kind woodcutter finds a pine tree whose limb has been broken off. Sap is flowing out, He bandages the tree with a strip from his own clothes. The tree asks the man, "Hold tight or stick tight?" The man tells the tree to decide. Suddenly gold coins stick to him all over. At home, his wife helps to unstick the coins from his clothes. A mean neighbor wants to know where the coins come from. The kind woodcutter tells him, and the neighbor runs to the tree, breaks off three branches, and then bandages the tree. When the tree asks him "Hold tight or stick tight?," he expects even more coins for having broken three branches. However, sticky sap pours down on him, and it takes him a long while to pull free.

CONNECTIONS. Animation. Coins. Cruelty to trees. Ecology. Gold. Greedy neighbor. Healing. Helpfulness. Pine trees. Punishment. Respect for trees. Spirits. Rewards. Trees. Wakayama, Japan, stories from.

How Else This Story Is Told. Hold Fast or Stick Fast — Fanny Hagin Mayer, *Ancient Tales in Modern Japan* (from Wakayama). Hold Tight, Stick Tight — Elizabeth Scofield, *Hold Tight, Stick Tight*. The Sticky-Sticky Pine — Florence Sakade, *Japanese Children's Favorite Stories* and *Peach Boy*.

47. The Old Man of the Flowers

Yoshiko Uchida, *The Dancing Kettle*. Japan

A kind old couple love their dog Shiro. One day the old man digs where Shiro has been pawing and finds hundreds of gold coins. Their mean neighbor asks to borrow Shiro, for he, too, wants gold. He threatens to beat Shiro if he won't dig. The neighbor digs where Shiro barks, but only digs up rocks. He hits Shiro with his shovel and kills him. Filled with sadness, the kind old man and woman plant a pine tree over Shiro's grave. It grows quickly, and the old woman makes a bowl from the wood in which to make rice cakes in Shiro's memory. Rice multiplies in the bowl. When their mean neighbor borrows the bowl, it only produces rocks for him. and he burns it. As the old man carries the ashes home, wind scatters them over the winter cherry trees, which begin to bloom. His wife makes him new clothes, and he travels through the countryside sprinkling ashes and bringing out pink blossoms on the trees. The prince rewards him. When the cruel neighbor also tries to collect a reward, his ashes blow in the prince's face, and the prince has him taken away.

Connections. Ashes. Bowls. Changes in fortune. Cherry trees. Cruelty to animals. Dogs. Flowers. Gold. Graves. Greed. Greedy neighbor. Husbands and wives. Iwate, Japan, stories from. Kindness to animals. Loss. Magical objects. Multiplication. Murder. Punishment. Respect for trees. Rewards. Treasure. Tung People, stories from.

How Else This Story Is Told. **Chinese variations:** The Envious Neighbor — Pearl S. Buck, *Fairy Tales of the Orient*. How the Brothers Divided Their Property — *Folk Tales from China*, First Series (from the Tung People). **Japanese variations:** Dear Dog — Geraldine McCaughrean, *The Crystal Pool*. Hanasaka Jiisan — at *Kids Web Japan*, Online. *Hanasaki Jiji: The Old Man Who Made the Dead Trees Blossom* — Japanese Fairy Tale Series, No. 4. Jiu-Roku-Zakura — Lafcadio Hearn, *Kwaidan*. Old Man Flower-Blower — Iwaya Sazanami, *Iwaya's Fairy Tales of Old Japan*. The Old Man of the Cherry Blossom — Juliet Piggott, *Japanese Fairy Tales*. The Old Man Who Made Flowers Bloom — Fanny Hagin Mayer, *Ancient Tales in Modern Japan* (from Iwate). The Old Man Who Made Flowers Bloom — Keigo Seki, *Folktales of Japan*. The Old Man Who Made Dead Trees Bloom — Eric Quayle, *The Shining Princess*. The Old Man Who Made Trees Bloom — Helen and William McAlpine, *Oxford Tales from Japan*. The Old Man Who Made Trees Blossom — Florence Sakade, *Japanese Children's Favorite Stories* and *Little One Inch*. The Old Man Who Made Trees to Blossom — F. Hadland Davis, *Myths and Legends of Japan*. The Old Man Who Made Withered Trees to Blossom — Alan Lesie Whitehorn, *Wonder Tales of Old Japan*. The Story of Hanasaka Jijii, The Flower Blossomer — Yasuda, Yuri, *Old Tales of Japan*, Vol. I. The Story of the Old Man Who Made Withered Trees Blossom — Keshi Nakajima, *Japanese Traditional Tales*. The Story of the Old Man Who Made Withered Trees Blossom — Baron Algernon Bertram Freeman-Mitford Redesdale, *Tales of Old Japan*. The Story of the Old Man Who Made Withered Trees to Flower — Yei Theodora Ozaki, *Japanese Fairy Book*.

48. The Strange Apple Tree

Wang Qiu in Howard Giskin, *Chinese Folktales*. Heilongjiang People

On her way home from selling cloth one day, a poor mother gives her only penny to a beggar woman, who predicts that their fortunes will change if her son learns a skill and helps people. The mother tells her son. Nor-man tries different trades, but nothing sticks. His mothers tells him to herd cattle, and this, he enjoys. He is kind to the cattle. One of the herd tells Nor-man that he has been put with the cattle as a punishment, and that if Nor-man is ever in trouble, he should grab the cow's ears and say, "fly." When Nor-man sees heavy smoke one day, he tries it. He and the cow sail to the forest. Nor-man saves a small beetle trapped inside the fire. The beetle becomes an old woman who leads them to a cave in the mountain. She asks him to choose between taking red jewels to become rich and handsome or taking the apple tree to make his mother happy and help people. Nor-man chooses the apple tree and plants it in front of his house. His fruit cures people's illnesses, and he does not charge. However, the lord of the village steals the tree, and it withers. Nor-man goes looking for the old woman on the mountain. She gives him two types of apples. He takes the first kind to the lord's house, where everyone who eats one grows an enormously long nose. He trades them the second kind of apple to restore their noses for the apple tree itself. It revives, and Nor-man is able once again to do good for people.

CONNECTIONS. Advice. Apples. Apple trees. Beetles. Cattle. Choices. Fire. Generosity. Healing. Heilonjiang People, stories from. Herders. Kindness to animals. Long nose. Magical objects. Nobles and lords. Noses. Old woman, supernatural helper. Punishment. Shape-shifting. Thieves. Transformation. Trees. Work.

49. The Pine of Akoya

Rafe Martin, *Mysterious Tales of Japan*. Japan

More than one thousand years ago, as the governor's daughter is playing her koto outside at night, she hears a flute join in. The same thing happens the next night, too. Akoya asks the mysterious musician to appear, and a young man in a green robe holding a silver flute steps out. His name is Natori Taro. Together, they play music until dawn. He returns the following night and tells her that he must return to help his people at the base of Chitose Mountain, even though it will mean his death. Several days later, the governor tells Akoya that he had given orders to chop down a huge pine tree to repair a bridge across Natori River at the foot of Chitose Mountain, but all of his men together cannot move the log. Akoya asks to come see. She touches the great pine log and tells Natori she has come. Now, the log will lift. Underneath lies a silver flute inscribed with Akoya and Natori's names.

CONNECTIONS. Chitose Mountain. Ecology. Flutes. Love. Maidens. Music. Natori River. Pine trees. Respect for trees. Shape-shifting. Spirits. Supernatural beloveds. Transformation. Tree spirits. Trees.

HOW ELSE THIS STORY IS TOLD. The Woman Who Loved a Tree-Spirit — Richard Dorson, *Folk Legends of Japan*. Yayoi and the Spirit Tree — Yoko Kawashima Watkins, *Tales from the Bamboo Grove* (in this slightly different variation, the tree gives a girl who has befriended him the power to launch a ship made from his wood which will gain her the reward she needs to provide for her sick mother).

50. The Wild Goose Lake

Wolfram Eberhard, *Folktales of China*. China

In a time of drought when it is impossibe to farm, Chiao and his daughter Sea Girl go up Horse Ear Mountain above the village of P'o-lo to cut bamboo to make brooms to sell. Sea Girl finds a lake up there, where a wild goose carries off every leaf that falls on the water. She returns to the lake with an axe the next day to cut an outlet to let water flow down to the villagers below. The way is blocked by a stone gate that will not open. A wild goose tells Sea Girl that the gate requires a golden key, but does not tell her where to find it. She comes upon three parrots in the cypress forest who tell her that she must first find the third daughter of the dragon king. The girl follows a peacock in a pine grove south to a cinnamon tree in a canyon of the southern mountains. The peacock tells her to sing a folk song, for the third daughter loves songs. Sea Girl sings about snowflakes, about green grass, and about blossoming flowers. On the third day, the dragon king's third daughter emerges from the lake, despite her father's command not to have contact with humans. Sea Girl tells her about the drought. The compassionate third daughter tells Sea Girl that the key is guarded by an eagle in the dragon king's treasury. They have a chance to get it when the dragon king leaves the palace one day. Third daughter and Sea Girl take turns singing songs outside the treasury, and when the eagle comes to investigate, Sea Girl slips inside. She bypasses all the precious treasures and finally finds the key. She and third daughter return to Wild Goose Lake. Sea Girl takes the golden key and knocks at the gate three times. Water streams down to the canals of P'o-lo village. The stream is so strong, that Sea Girl brings straw to slow its flow. When the dragon king returns, he banishes his third daughter. She goes to live with Sea Girl and sing songs with the villagers.

CONNECTIONS. Birds. Dragon Princess. Drought. Eagles. Fathers and daughters. Geese. Helpfulness. Heroes, women. Horse Ear Mountain. Lakes. Music. Outsmarting supernatural opponents. P'o-lo, village. Parrots. Peacocks. Quests. Singing. Underwater kingdom. Unselfishness. Water.

WHERE ELSE THIS STORY APPEARS. Wild Goose Lake — Wolfram Eberhard in Ethel Johnston Phelps, *Tatterhood*.

HOW ELSE THIS STORY IS TOLD. Wild Goose Lake — Catherine Edwards Sandler, *Heaven's Reward*.

51. The Golden Carp

Louise and Yuan-Hsi Kuo, *Chinese Folk Tales*. Uygur People

When a merchant's stepson puts a beautiful golden carp back into the water, the merchant is furious and wants to kill the boy. His mother warns the young man to leave. She advises him to trust only companions who wait when he needs to go into the bushes. One day a young man becomes his friend and brother. They enter a city and eat, without knowing that the penalty is death for those who cannot pay. An advisor recommends that, instead of killing them, the chieftain send them to rescue his daughter who has been stolen by a demon. The chieftain gives them his saber and two horses. As they cross a high mountain, a terrifying woman demon appears. The older brother lets himself be sucked into her and cuts his way out with his saber, splitting her head in two. The lovely chieftain's daughter comes to fill a jug with water. She tells them the demon's sons will soon come home. When they arrive, the demon's sons smell humans, but the brothers fight and chop off both demon heads. They return with the chieftain's daughter. The elder brother says that he cannot have a wife, so the younger brother marries her. At the river, the elder brother reveals that he was the carp the boy had put back into the river. With a gleam of gold, he swims away.

CONNECTIONS. Carp. Chieftains. Demons. Fighting supernatural opponents. Friendship. Golden carp. Greed. Heroes, men. Kindness from animals. Mothers and sons. Rescues. Shapeshifting. Spirits. Stepfathers and stepsons. Transformation. Uygur People, stories from.

HOW ELSE THIS STORY IS TOLD. The Golden Carp — Yin-lien C.Chin, Yetta S. Center, and Mildred Ross, *Traditional Chinese Folktales.* A Golden Fish — Neil Philip, *The Spring of Butterflies.*

52. Yeh-Shen: A Cinderella Story from China

Ai-Ling Louie. China

After her mother dies, Yeh-Sen is treated cruelly by her jealous stepmother. The woman even kills the fish with golden eyes she has been feeding. An old man appears and tells Yeh-Shen to collect the fish bones and let them know when she is in need. Yeh-Shen speaks often with the bones, but she doesn't ask for anything until she is left home in rags during the spring festival. Magically, then, she finds herself dressed in a beautiful gown with tiny gold slippers on her feet. The spirit of the bones warns her not to lose the slippers. Yeh-Shen goes to the festival. As she flees, worried that her stepsister may recognize her, one slipper falls off. It is found by the king, who would like to discover to whom it belongs. Many women visit the pavilion where he has placed the slipper, but it fits none of them. When Yeh-Shen comes to take the slipper at night, the king, intrigued by her face, follows her. He requests that she put both slippers on, and when she does, her rags transform once again. The king marries Yeh-Shen. The wicked stepmother and stepsister are buried in their cave.

CONNECTIONS. Bones. Carp. Cinderella stories. Competition. Cruelty. Cruelty to animals. Fish. Gold slippers. Kindness to animals. Kings. Magical objects. Matches, marriage. Shoes. Spirits. Stepmothers and stepdaughters. Transformation.

HOW ELSE THIS STORY IS TOLD. A Chinese Cinderella — Lotta Carswell Hume, *Favorite Children's Stories from China and Tibet* (here the protagonist is called Shih Chieh). The Golden Carp — Tin-lien C. Chin, Yetta S. Center, and Mildred Ross, *Traditional Chinese Folktales.* Yeh-hsien — Judy Sierra, *Cinderella.*

53. The Third Son and the Magistrate

Folk Tales from China, First Series. Chung People

On his deathbed, a poor old man gives each of his sons a coin and tells them to each learn a trade. The third son buys two fishhooks and succeeds as a fisherman. One slow day, however, he catches only one big fish. Inside, there are many small fish, including a golden carp that is still alive. He cares for the carp, but one day, it just vanishes. The fisherman misses the fish. By the river, a young man appears and tells the fisherman that he is the carp, actually the son of the Dragon King. The son invites the fisherman underwater to the crystal palace, where the Dragon King thanks him. The young fisherman stays for a month. The Dragon King's son advises him to ask for a white chicken should the Dragon King offer him a gift. One day, the fisherman sees a girl cooking, who for a moment turns into a white chicken. She is the Dragon King's daughter, also grateful to him for saving her brother. They marry and return to land. However, the magistrate wants the fisherman's wife for his own. When the fisherman refuses, the magistrate demands one hundred twenty red carp. The Dragon King's daughter creates fish out of paper and makes them real. The magistrate then demands a blue cloth as long as the road and a flock of red sheep. With a magic gourd from underwater, the Dragon's King's daughter helps the young fisherman to fulfill these demands. But now the magistrate wants the magic gourd. He locks up the fisherman and asks for one hundred twenty monsters in three days. With charcoal and oil from the magic gourd, the Dragon King's daughter creates the monsters. The monsters scream and demand more and more food. When the magistrate gets up to feed them, they catch fire and everything burns.

CONNECTIONS. Animation. Captivity. Carp. Chickens. Chung People, stories from. Crystal Palace. Dragon King. Dragon Prince. Dragon Princess. Fathers and sons. Fire. Fishermen. Gourds. Husbands and wives. Kindness to animals. Magical objects. Magistrates. Monsters. Paper fish. Punishment. Rewards. Shape-shifting. Spirits. Transformation. Ultimatums. Underwater kingdom. Wife-stealing.

54. Three Treasures

Folk Tales from China, Second Series. Uygur People

Hoping to teach him how to earn a living, a widow sends her son off with three pancakes and an order not to come back empty-handed. He is sitting on the river bank when he sees a little snake that looks ill. He puts the snake in a little paper box and shares his pancakes with it. The snake grows bigger each day. The boy moves it to a pool. One day the snake requests to go into the river. The boy has been thinking he would be able to sell the snake and return home with money, but the snake assures the boy that he will be rewarded. When the boy tosses the snake into the river, it becomes a dragon with golden scales. A donkey appears by the boy. The dragon tells the boy to ask the donkey whenever he needs gold or silver, but not to reveal the secret to anyone. The boy asks an innkeeper to stable his donkey, but specifies not to ask it for gold. But the wiley innkeeper does and when gold appears, he switches his donkey for the boy's. Back at home, this donkey does not produce gold. The boy returns to the dragon, who gives him a tablecloth that will produce food. Unsuspecting, the boy returns to the inn and tells the keeper not to ask it for food, and the innkeeper again switches his cloth for the boy's. The boy tells the dragon that the magic things are not working. The dragon calls him ungrateful, but this time gives him a wooden stick. He instructs the innkeeper not to say "beat me" to the stick. The innkeeper does, however, and the stick whacks him until he gives the boy back the donkey and tablecloth he stole.

CONNECTIONS. Deceit. Donkeys. Dragons. Gifts. Innkeepers. Kindness to animals. Magical objects. Mothers and sons. Punishment. Rewards. Secrets. Snakes. Sticks. Tablecloth. Thieves. Transformation. Uygur People, stories from.

WHERE ELSE THIS STORY APPEARS. The Three Treasures—At D.L. Ashliman, *Folktexts*, Online.

HOW ELSE THIS STORY IS TOLD. Three Treasures—Emily Ching and Ko-Shee Ching, *Golden Needles; Three Treasures*.

55. The Wood-Cutter's Sake

Teresa Pierce Williston, *Japanese Fairy Tales*. Japan

A hard-working woodcutter, who struggles to support his aging parents, decides not to hunt the round badger he sees sleeping on the mountain. The badger awakes just then and says he will return the woodcutter's kindness. He directs the woodcutter to a certain smooth stone, where the woodcutter finds dumplings, rice, cakes and more waiting. The woodcutter cannot eat until the badger reassures him that he has already sent food down for the woodcutter's hungry parents. Then they feast. The woodcutter hears drumming followed by samisen music and realizes the badger is playing on his own stretched stomach. The badger vanishes. The woodcutter sees a waterfall that is also making sweet music and pouring sake. He fills his gourd and returns home to his parents. The next day villagers gather to visit the sake waterfall, but it only flows sake when the woodcutter comes alone.

CONNECTIONS. Badgers. Filial devotion. Harmony. Kindness to animals. Magical objects. Music. Rewards. Samisens. Transformation. Wine. Woodcutters.

56. The Deer of Five Colors

Yoshiko Uchida, *The Magic Listening Cap*. Japan

A beautiful, five-colored deer with white antlers rescues a farmer who has fallen in the river. When the farmer asks, the deer answers that the farmer can repay him by keeping his existence a secret, for the deer does not want to be hunted. One day a lord announces that he will reward anyone who can bring him to the five-colored deer he has dreamed about. Now the farmer renegs on his promise and brings the lord to the deer, for he would like to acquire those riches. The deer faces the lord, who keeps his men from shooting. The deer asks the lord how he knew where to find him and when the lord points, the deer chastises the farmer. When the lord discovers that the deer really did save the farmer's life, he lets the deer go. After that, the lord imprisons the farmer for betrayal and bans deer-hunting on his lands.

CONNECTIONS. Changes in attitude. Deceit. Deer. Farmers. Hunters. Killing. Nobles and lords. Promises. Rescues. Respect for life.

57. The Boy, His Sisters, and the Magic Horse

Gioia Timpanelli, *Tales from the Roof of the World*. Tibetan People

An old hunter grows angry that his son refuses to kill anything when the family needs food. He brings the boy to a large hole and shuts him up in there with a large stone on which he writes "Open or Not as You Please." The boy is scared, but he cannot move the stone alone. Three Buddhist monks help the boy out of the hole. They dress him in monk's robes so he can beg for dinner at his sisters' estates. One sister is sure he is their brother. They thank the monks for rescuing him and present the boy with a magic horse, a magic cow, and a magic sheep with a golden head. He climbs for a long time in the cold, and the magic horse says that the boy should kill him and spread his skin on the ground. When the boy will not kill him, the horse leaps off a cliff and dies. The young man places the horse skin the way the horse has told him with one foot in each direction. When he wakes, he is sleeping in a grand palace. The scattered horse hairs have become cattle, and the horse is alive in the stable. After a while, the boy puts on his monk's robes to visit his parents. His parents are forlorn and unmoving. He throws down two pancakes from the roof, and his parents become animated, joyful to see him. The young man brings his parents to the magnificent palace.

CONNECTIONS. Anger. Brothers and sisters. Changes in attitude. Cows. Cruelty. Fathers and sons. Golden-head sheep. Horses. Hunters. Killing. Kindness to animals. Magical objects. Monks. Pancakes. Rebirth. Reconciliation. Rescues. Respect for life. Sacrifice. Sheep. Skin. Tibetan People, stories from. Transformation.

HOW ELSE THIS STORY IS TOLD. The Young Man Who Refused to Kill — Frederick and Audrey Hyde-Chambers, *Tibetan Folk Tales* and online at *Learning to Give*.

58. The Tale of the Mandarin Ducks

Katherine Paterson. Japan

Shozo, a chief steward who has fallen out of favor, speaks up against the lord's capturing a wild drake, but the lord shuts the beautiful drake in a bamboo cage anyway. When the unhappy drake loses its shine, the lord has it sent to the back of the kitchen garden, but still will not let the drake go. The maid Yasuko feels sorry for the drake and releases it. The lord blames Shozo and strips him of his rank. Shozo and Yasuko fall in love, but the lord accuses them of conspiring to counter his command and orders that they be drowned. Two Imperial Messengers arrive saying the emperor has abolished capital punishment. The lord cannot object when they say they are to escort all prisoners to the Imperial Court. Marching for days, Yasuko and Shozo fall behind. The two Imperial Messengers appear and escort them to a hut. The messengers untie their ropes and feed them and prepare a bath to soothe them. In the morning, the messengers have gone, but a pair of mandarin ducks seem to bow to them before they fly off. Yasuko and Shozo happily live out their lives in that little hut.

CONNECTIONS. Captivity. Ducks. Gratitude. Husbands and wives. Justice. Kindness from animals. Kindness to animals. Love. Messengers. Nobles and lords. Punishment. Rescues. Servants. Shape-shifting. Spirits.

WHERE ELSE THIS STORY APPEARS. The Tale of the Mandarin Ducks— Katherine Paterson on *Asian Folk Tales*, DVD. Originally issued in 2003 by Weston Woods on *Stories from the Asian Tradition*, VHS. *See also* Oshidori (story # 162) in Chapter, V, Devotion.

59. Gombei and the Wild Ducks

Yoshiko Uchida, *The Sea of Gold*. Japan

Every day, just like his father, Gombei catches one wild duck in the marsh with a loop of rope. Now, however, he is feeling old and would like to trap one hundred at once, to make the next ninety-nine days easier. He lays one hundred loops in the icy marsh. One by one, ninety-nine ducks land in Gombei's loops, which he tightens. Suddenly, though, the sun's sparkle startles the ducks. As they all lift off together, Gombei is pulled with them up to the sky. He grips the ropes until he can hold on no longer, and then he falls. But as he falls, Gombei develops a bill, feathers, wings, and webbed feet. By the time he reaches the ground he looks and sounds like a duck. Hungry, he is heading to the marsh when he feels a loop tighten around his leg. He realizes what it must feel like for a duck to be caught. His tears break through the rope; his feathers disappear. He becomes a farmer and never traps another living creature.

CONNECTIONS. Captivity. Changes in attitude. Ducks. Flying. Greed. Hunters. Journeys. Transformation.

HOW ELSE THIS STORY IS TOLD. The Flying Farmer — Florence Sakade, *Urashima Taro* and *Japanese Children's Favorite Stories*, Book Two.

60. Kogi

Rafe Martin, *Mysterious Tales of Japan*. Japan

The priest Kogi is especially interested in painting fish. He studies them in a tub and then releases them in the lake. He gives up eating fish. One night, Kogi dreams that he is swimming in the lake, and a golden carp offers to transform him into a fish for three days. The carp warns him not to eat food from a baited hook. Kogi enjoys swimming effortlessly as a fish, but then he gets caught on the hook of someone he knows. He cries out, but no one can hear him, and the fisherman does not recognize him. Kogi feels the pain of the cook's knife and awakes. He has been in a coma for three days. During that time, the others found a fish that kept opening its mouth and gave it back to the lake. After that, Kogi's paintings look so real that the fish on one scroll actually swim away.

CONNECTIONS. Animation. Appreciation of nature. Buddhism. Changes in attitude. Fish. Fishermen. Golden carp. Harmony. Journeys. Killing. Kindness to animals. Knowledge. Kogi. Monks. Paintings and pictures. Respect for life. Transformation. Whales.

HOW ELSE THIS STORY IS TOLD. *Kogi's Mysterious Journey*— Elizabeth Partridge. Kogi the Priest — Rafe Martin, *The Hungry Tigress* and at *Learning to Give*, Online (in this story, a whaler experiences the beauty of swimming as a sperm whale and then the pain of being shot with a harpoon. He becomes a Buddhist monk, takes the name of the painter priest from folktales, and never kills whales again). The Story of Kogi the Priest — Lafcadio Hearn, *A Japanese Miscellany* and *The Writings of Lafcadio Hearn* (this is a longer and more complex telling of the adventures that befall Kogi with his art, outside of the water).

61. Screen of Frogs

Sheila Hamanaka. Japan

Lazy Koji scoffs at the peasants who have to work on his family's land. He himself never works to earn money, so that after his parents die, he has to sell off land piece by piece until all that is left are his house, one mountain and one lake. Koji is measuring his land when he falls asleep by the lake. He sees a woman in green walking lightly across the lily pads, but then a huge frog grabs his foot. The frog begs Koji not to sell the mountain, not to allow the land to be ruined by woodcutters which would leave animals without homes and wash dirt down into the waters. The frog disappears. Koji thinks perhaps he has been dreaming, but he decides to keep the land. He pays off debts by selling furniture and fixings from inside the house until all he has left is a futon and a black screen. That night, Koji wakes to a cacophony of frog sounds. He follows wet tracks on the floor to his screen, which is now filled with pictures of frogs that look almost alive. He begins to plant rice, barley, millet, and vegetables and to marry and raise a family on this land. When he dies, the frogs gradually fade from the screen.

CONNECTIONS. Appreciation of nature. Changes in attitude. Dreams. Ecology. Farmers. Frogs. Laziness. Magical objects. Paintings and pictures. Spirits. Transformation. Work.

62. The Story of Princess Hotoru

Alan Leslie Whitehorn, *Wonder Tales of Old Japan*. Japan

The daughter of a powerful old feudal lord is a friend to all the insects and birds in the garden, They call her Princess Hotoru, Princess Firefly. Then a fierce man, who says he is her uncle Hyō, arrives one night and kills her father, the Daimyo, and takes her to his castle over the mountains. She never had a chance to say goodbye, and the fireflies wonder where she has gone. A dove tells them what he has seen, and a stork tells them where she now lives. They fly to find her. At her uncle's house she is made to work as a servant. The fireflies hide until her work is done and then call for Princess Hotoru to open her shutters. They give her light to read by. Her bird friends bring her food in their beaks. She feels comforted to have their company, and they stay. A young Daimyo who has heard about her story arrives with men who kill Uncle Hyō and take his wife prisoner. Princess Hotoru marries the brave young Daimyo, and the fireflies and birds visit often.

CONNECTIONS. Birds. Captivity. Daimyos. Fireflies. Kindness from animals. Kindness to animals. Murder. Nobles and lords. Princesses. Rescues.

63. The Sea of Gold

Yoshiko Uchida, *The Sea of Gold*. Japan

Hikoichi seems slow, but at last, he is hired as a cook on a fishing boat. When the leftovers he stores takes up valuable space on the boat, they tell him to throw the food overboard. Fishermen laugh at Hikoichi for calling the fish to dinner before he tosses food into the water, but Hikoichi keeps doing it until he is old. One night, Hikoichi feels that the boat is not moving so he looks out, and the boat is sitting on sand. The sand seems to glitter, so he brings a bucket and gathers some of the sand to be able to remember this night. No one else awakens. In the morning, the boat is rocking in the water again. No one believes Hikoichi's story until he shows them his bucket now filled with gold. The oldest fisherman says the King of the Sea has rewarded Hikoichi for taking care of the fish all these many years. Hikoichi builds a little house by the sea. He continues to feed the fish, but no one ever laughs at him again.

CONNECTIONS. Boats. Changes in attitude. Changes in fortune. Fish. Golden sand. Kindness to animals. Magical objects. Rewards. Sand.

64. The Mother of Heaven

Wolfram Eberhard, *Folktales of China*. China

The ruler of heaven leaves his mother in charge for three days, saying that she must grant every human wish she hears. Traveling above on a cloud, the mother of heaven hears a man wish for a wind to sail with. She commands the wind to blow. Later, she hears another man ask for the wind to stop because it is blowing all the pears off his trees. The next day, she sends rain for an old man who wants to plant beans, but then a young girl asks for the rain to stop so she can dry her ginger. Confused, the mother of heaven stays home on the third day. When the ruler returns, he tells her that to help people, she must send different kinds of winds as well as rain at night and sun by day.

CONNECTIONS. Ecology. Heavenly Kingdom. Mother of Heaven. Mothers and sons. Rain. Weather. Work.

HOW ELSE THIS STORY IS TOLD. Li Jing—*Dragon Tales: A Collection of Chinese Stories* (a mortal man finds an old woman in a palace in the mountains where a Heavenly decree has come that her sons are to send down rain. Since the sons are not there, the mortal does the job and makes a mess of it).

65. The Butterfly Robe

Margaret Read MacDonald, *Three-Minute Tales*. China

Needing a respite from work, the prime minister is borne up into the hills. He alights from his chair and walks through a meadow. When a bee lands on his brightly-colored court robe, he cuts a piece of his robe off and tosses it into the air. The piece flutters from one flower to another. The prime minister keeps cutting pieces. His robe is shred, but brilliant butterflies flit all over the field. Refreshed, the prime minister returns to work.

CONNECTIONS. Appreciation of nature. Beauty. Bees. Butterflies. Fatigue. Harmony. Ministers. Peace. Perspective. Work.

~ III ~

Of Wonders, Magical Objects, and Enchantment

66. The Magic Teakettle

Florence Sakade, *Japanese Children's Favorite Stories*. Japan

A priest who enjoys drinking tea buys a rusty old teakettle and shines it up. When he goes to boil water in it, though, the teakettle comes alive. It grows a badger's furry head, four paws, and a bushy tail. The little badger teakettle jumps from the heat and runs around the room. Then it calms down, but the priest is sure the teakettle is bewitched and sells the kettle to a junkman. The teakettle tells the junkman that if he treats it well and doesn't put it on the fire, the teakettle will help make the junkman's fortune. The teakettle does tricks, so the junkman makes a little theater and sign for Bumbuku and sells many tickets to his show. People enjoy Bumbuku's acrobatics. After many years, the junkman suggests that the teakettle may want to retire and offers to take him back to the temple, where he is given a place of honor.

CONNECTIONS. Animation. Badgers. Changes in fortune. Cooperation. Enchantment. Junkmen. Kindness. Performance. Priests. Spirits. Talents. Teakettles. Temples. Transformation.

WHERE ELSE THIS STORY APPEARS. The Magic Teakettle — Florence Sakade, *Peach Boy and Other Japanese Children's Favorite Stories*.

HOW ELSE THIS STORY IS TOLD. **Chinese variation:** The Magic Kettle — Wenshi Hao in Howard Giskin, *Chinese Folktales* (Jiangxi Province). **Japanese variations:** The Accomplished and Lucky Tea-kettle — Baron Algernon Bertram Freeman-Mitford Redesdale, *Tales of Old Japan*. The Accomplished and Lucky Teakettle — Takeshi Nakajima, *Japanese Traditional Tales*. The Accomplished and Strange Teakettle — Pearl S. Buck, *Fairy Tales of the Orient*. Bumbuku Teakettle — Fanny Hagin Mayer, *Ancient Tales in Modern Japan*. Bunbuku Chagama — Shoichi Shiomi at *Kids Web Japan*, Online. The Dancing Kettle — Yoshiko Uchida, *The Dancing Kettle*. Fox Teakettle — Hiroko Fujita, *Folktales from the Japanese Countryside*. The Good Fortune Kettle — Virginia Haviland, *Favorite Fairy Tales Told in Japan*. The Good Fortune Kettle — Keigo Seki, *Folktales of Japan*. The Lucky Tea-kettle — Helen and William McAlpine, *Oxford Tales from Japan* and in Linda Jennings, *Stories from Around the World*. The Magic Kettle — Joanna Cole, *Best-Loved Folktales of the World*. The Magic Kettle — Andrew Lang, *The Crimson Fairy Book* and *The Rainbow Fairy Book*. The Miraculous Tea-Kettle — F. Hadland Davis, *Myths and Legends of Japan*. The Story of Bunbuku Chagama, the Lucky Cauldron — Yuri Yasuka, *Old Tales of Japan*, Volume II. The Tea-Kettle — Lafcadio Hearn and Others, *Japanese Fairy Tales* and *The Boy Who Drew Cats*. The Tea-Kettle — Grace James, *Green Willow*. The Tea-Kettle of Good-Luck — Iwaya Sazanami, *Iwaya's Fairy Tales of Old Japan*. A Wonderful Tea-Kettle — Alan Leslie Whitehorn, *Wonder Tales of Old Japan*. The Wonderful Tea-kettle — Japanese Fairy Tale Series.

The Wonderful Tea-Kettle — William Elliot Griffis, *The Fire-Fly's Lovers and Other Fairy Tales of Old Japan.* The Wonderful Teakettle — Teresa Pierce Williston, *Japanese Fairy Tales.*

67. Why the Dog and the Cat Are Not Friends

Frances Carpenter, *Tales of a Korean Grandmother.* Korea

Old Koo keeps a piece of amber in the jug in his small wineshop on the banks of a river, and the jug is always full. The magic amber was a gift from a stranger which whom he shared some last drops of wine. One day, however, the amber disappears. Old Koo thinks he may have accidentally poured it into someone's bottle. His dog and cat are also sad and decide to find it for him. They wait for winter to ice over the river so they can cross. Months later, on the other side, the cat smells the amber inside a closed box in a house. The dog and cat try to think how they will get into the box, without attracting the master's attention. The dog suggests they bargain to leave the rats alone for ten years if the rats will chew through the box now. The rats accept this deal. The hole is still too small for the cat's paw, so they send a mouse in to retrieve the amber. At last, the cat and dog are heading back to Old Koo, but the river ice has melted. Since the cat cannot swim, it is decided that he will ride on the dog's back and hold the amber in his mouth. As they near the other shore, some children laugh at the sight they make. The dog ignores them, but the cat laughs, too, and the amber falls into the river. The dog furiously chases the cat up a tree. One day, the faithful dog smells amber inside a fish and runs the fish to Old Koo's shop before the fishermen can stop him. Old Koo is delighted to have the amber back, but cats and dogs have been enemies ever since.

CONNECTIONS. Amber. Amount. Cats. Conflict. Cooperation. Dogs. Enmity. Kiangsu, China, stories from. Kindness from animals. Loss. Magical objects. Mice. Origins. Quests. Wine sellers.

HOW ELSE THIS STORY IS TOLD. ***Chinese variations:*** The Helpful Animals — Wolfram Eberhard, *Folktales of China* (in this tale from Kiangsu, a magic piece of iron pot disappears, and the animals compete to return it). Why the Cat and the Dog Are Enemies — Lim Siantek, *More Folk Tales from China.* Why Dog and Cat Are Enemies — Richard Wilhelm, *The Chinese Fairy Book.* ***Korean variations:*** In some of these tales, the dog is holding the amber and an indignant cat makes him answer her questions. The cat ends up as honored house pet. The Cat and the Dog — Zong In-Sob, *Folk Tales from Korea.* The Dog and the Cat —*Long Long Time Ago.* The Dog and the Cat — Suzanne Crowder Han, *Korean Folk and Fairy Tales.* The Enchanted Wine Jug — Ruth Manning-Sanders, *A Book of Charms and Changelings.* The Enchanted Wine-Jug; Or, Why the Cat and Dog Are Enemies — H. N. Allen, *Korean Tales.* How Cat Saved the Magic Amber — James Riordan, *Korean Folk-tales.* The Magic Amber — Eleanore M. Jewett, *Which Was Witch? The Magic Gem: A Korean Folktale About Why Cats and Dogs Don't Get Along*— Kim So-un.

68. The Magic Pot

Zhang Hong in Howard Giskin, *Chinese Folktales.* Liaoning Province, China

Xiaozhen and her mother work for a greedy farmer in a faraway mountain village. Xiaozhen offers her own food to an old beggar woman whom the farmer has turned away, and the old woman gives her an iron pot that she says is magic. It starts working with two magic words and stops with one other. Xiaozhen whispers these words at lunchtime, and the iron pot fills with porridge. She invites villagers in the field to share. The rich farmer hears the magic starting words and sees the food. In the night, he switches their magic pot for a plain one. However, the magic pot will not stop producing porridge and fills the farmer's house. Soon nothing is showing in the village but a few roofs above the porridge. Xiozhen stops the pot with the magic words. They rescue the farmer from the top of his house, and he is never greedy again.

CONNECTIONS. Amount. Beggars. Chants. Deceit. Farmers. Generosity. Greed. Humorous stories. Kindness. Liaoning Province, China, stories from. Magical objects. Porridge. Multiplication. Old woman, supernatural helper. Porridge. Pots. Rewards. Thieves. Words.

69. The Magic Moneybag

John Minford, *Favourite Folktales of China.* Korean Chinese People

After the fourth day that the bundle of firewood disappears from his house, a poor woodcutter hides himself inside a new bundle of wood. At midnight, a thick rope lifts that bundle up to the sky. The white-haired man who unties the bundle says that he has observed how hardworking the woodcutter and his wife are and would like to give them a treasure. Seven fairies escort the young man to a palace. They invite him to choose one sack from a room full of moneybags. The woodcutter is going to take the biggest moneybag, when the old man tells him that he will give him an empty bag from which he may remove one tael of silver a day. Back home, the woodcutter continues to cut wood, and his wife saves the daily silver taels. Finally, the husband decides that they should spend all the silver on a brick house. They do, but the husband forgets the old man's warning and opens the bag three times in one day for more silver taels. The fourth time he opens it, the brick house and the moneybag disappear.

CONNECTIONS. Babies. Bags. Changes in fortune. Coins. Consequences. Fairies. Generosity. Greed. Heaven. Husbands and wives. Korean Chinese People, stories from. Loss. Magical objects. Mysteries. Old man, supernatural helper. Parables. Rewards. Rising to the sky world. Silver. Warnings. Woodcutters.

HOW ELSE THIS STORY IS TOLD. **Korean variation:** Fate and the Faggot Gatherer — Eleanore M. Jewett, *Which Was Witch?* (the husband and wife here generously share their new wealth, but fear the arrival of the one "who will make great demands" — who turns out to be their new baby).

70. The Magic Vase

Suzanne Crowder Han, *Korean Folk and Fairy Tales.* Korea

When all, that a kind fisherman has caught one day is an old vase, his wife yells. There is a loud noise, smoke, and then a young man emerge from the vase. He grants them three wishes. The fisherman rubs the vase three times and wishes for rice. His wife wishes for them to be the richest couple in the village. Desiring more wishes, the wife sends the fisherman off to find another vase. While he is gone, she uses the last wish, wishing to be beautiful. She is thinking that now she will need to get rid of her husband, when everything disappears, including the wife and their house. A turtle brings the fisherman, who was not greedy, down to the palace of the Dragon King, where he lives happily with a loving new wife.

CONNECTIONS. Deceit. Dragon King. Fishermen. Greed. Husbands and wives. Magical objects. Punishment. Rice. Vanity. Vases. Wishes.

HOW ELSE THIS STORY IS TOLD. The Magic Vase — Linda Soon Curry, *A Tiger by the Tail.*

71. The Greedy Princess

Suzanne Crowder Han, *Korean Folk and Fairy Tales.* Korea

An elderly widow gives her three sons three magical treasures, which she tells them have been handed down through the family and must remain secret: a large marble, a bamboo flute, and an old vest. After her death, the two elder sons brag about the marble that rolls out a trail of coins and the flute that can call soldiers to their command. A greedy princess plots to obtain these objects for herself. Wanting to impress her, the brothers individually show her their treasures. She grabs the marble and the flute and has each brother thrown in prison. The youngest brother is worried when his brothers do not return. He approaches the palace wearing the magic vest, which renders him invisible. The princess calls her guards when she feels something brush against her, but they can find no one. The youngest brother runs out to a grove of apple trees and bites into one. The red apple turns his nose very long, but the yellow apple shrinks it down. This gives him an idea. He gathers red apples to sell, and the greedy princess buys the whole basket. When her nose shoots out long, he puts on his vest and reenters the palace to retrieve the magic objects. He blows the magic flute which brings soldiers to help him find his brothers. All together now, they leave.

CONNECTIONS. Apples. Boastfulness. Brothers. Captivity. Cleverness. Deceit. Enchantment. Flutes. Greed. Humorous stories. Inheritance. Invisibility. Long nose. Magical objects. Marbles. Noses. Princesses. Punishment. Rescues. Secrets. Transformation. Vests.

HOW ELSE THIS STORY IS TOLD. *Chinese variation:* Three Magic Charms—Tehyi Hsieh, *Chinese Village Folk Tales.* **Korean variation:** The Long-Nosed Princess—James Riordan, *Korean Folk-tales.*

72. The Golden Axe

Yoshiko Uchida, *The Magic Listening Cap.* Japan

When a poor old woodcutter's axe blade flies off into a pool of water, he prays to the goddess of the water to help him find it. He really does not know what he will do to earn a living. A mist rises, and a goddess in a golden robe holds a golden axe out to the woodcutter. She asks if it is his, and when he honestly replies that his was made of steel, she brings his old axe head up from the bottom. He thanks her. She gifts him with the golden axe, too. The woodcutter's fortunes change for the better after this, and his neighbor grows jealous. The woodcutter's greedy neighbor goes to the mountain and throw his axe blade into the pool. He, too, prays to the goddess of the water. When she rises with a golden axe, however, he says that it is his. She calls him a liar and descends back down into the water without ever returning his old axe head back either.

CONNECTIONS. Axes. Deceit. Gods and goddesses. Golden axe. Golden plate. Greed. Greedy neighbor. Honesty. Liaoning Province, China, stories from. Rewards. Truth. Water. Woodcutters.

HOW ELSE THIS STORY IS TOLD. *Chinese variations: Chen Ping and His Magic Axe*—Demi (when his axe falls in the river, a white-haired old man rises from the water and presents the honest boy with an axe that chops wood all by itself). An Honest Man—Li Honling in Howard Giskin, *Chinese Folktales* (in this story from Liaoning Province a golden plate stands in for the axe). *Japanese variation:* Golden Hatchet—Fanny Hagin Mayer, *Ancient Tales in Modern Japan.* **Korean variation:** The Flying Beauty—Tae Hung Ha, *Folk Tales of Old Korea.*

73. The Magic Pot

Pleasant DeSpain, *Thirty-Three Multicultural Tales to Tell.* China

A woodcutter places his axe inside a giant brass pot he has found and drags the pot home. His wife is surprised by the pot and by a second axe that shows up inside it. Excited, the woodcutter and his wife start placing other objects in the pot to see what happens. The pot doubles their dinner and their money. Coins fill the room. As the woodcutter dances with his wife, she accidentally falls into the pot. Now he has two identical wives who both claim him. They push the woodcutter into the pot. There are two husbands, and the two couples live in houses side by side.

CONNECTIONS. Amount. Axes. Changes in fortune. Coins. Humorous stories. Husbands and wives. Magical objects. Multiplication. Number. Pots. Woodcutters.

WHERE ELSE THIS STORY APPEARS. The Magic Pot — Pleasant DeSpain in David Holt and Bill Mooney, *Ready-to-Tell Tales.*

HOW ELSE THIS STORY IS TOLD. **Chinese variation:** *Two of Everything*— Lily Toy Hong. **Korean variation:** The Magic Pot — James Huntley Grayson, *Myths and Legends from Korea* (a greedy magistrate who takes the pot from a farmer ends up with many duplicate fathers).

74. Iron Crutch and Gold Finger Wang

Louise and Yan-Hsi Kuo, *Chinese Folk Tales.* Han People

North of the River Wei, lazy Wang has allowed his father's farmland to become overgrown. One day the Eight Immortals walk past to the river, ignoring him. Wang grabs the title to his ancestors' land and a few belongings and follows them. The river swells. The Immortals propose crossing on the foam to reach Chung-nan Shan. The last Immortal in line, Iron Crutch Li, asks about the young man following them. The Immortals decide he may come along if he can attain the Way. Iron Crutch Li tells Wang he must promise only to look straight ahead, to throw his possessions in the river without regret, and to cleanse his body by drinking enchanted soup. Wang would like to become an Immortal, but just in case, he throws his bundle close to the river bank. He cannot bring himself to drink the soup; it looks and smells disgusting. Iron Crutch Li tells Wang that he does not have what it takes to live in Paradise. He hands Wang the squash leaf the soup was in and tells him the leaf will bring good fortune if he is good to his neighbors. Wang regrets not having drunk the soup. He scrapes the one drop left on the leaf and licks his finger. It not only tastes wonderful, but the first two joints of his forefinger turn to gold. When diphtheria comes to the village that spring, Wang stays healthy. People who suck his finger also recover. But once Wang starts charging enormous rates to heal people, an old man with a long white beard, who sounds remarkably like Iron Crutch Li, bites off the golden finger.

CONNECTIONS. Cowardice. Eight Immortals. Fingers. Golden finger. Greed. Han People, stories from. Healing. Illness. Immortality. Iron Crutch Li. Laziness. Leaves. Loss. Magical objects. Punishment. Rivers. Selfishness. Soup. Tests. Transformation. Wei River.

HOW ELSE THIS STORY IS TOLD. The Eight Immortals— Richard Wilhelm, *The Chinese Fairy Book.*

75. Point to a Stone to Make It Gold

Zhang Zhiwei in Howard Giskin, *Chinese Folktales.* Liaoning Province, China

Across ninety-nine bridges and ninety-nine mountains, an already rich man travels to Lao Mountain to study with a magician he has heard can turn a stone gold by pointing at it. After one month, the magician tells the rich man that he may try. The rich man points to a tree, and it becomes gold. The magician warns him not to become greedy, but the man starts pointing at everything when he gets home. Even his wife turns to gold. He has gold, but he dies.

CONNECTIONS. Fingers. Gold. Greed. Lao Mountain. Liaoning Province, China, stories from. Magical objects. Magicians. Parables. Rich man. Stone. Transformation. Travelers.

76. The Magic Carrying Pole

Folk Tales from China, Second Series. Yi People

A poor cowherd acquires good fortune when he discovers a magic pole that will enable him to carry enormously heavy loads. Seeing it in action, a rich man pays a lot of money to acquire this magic pole. However, since it is old and cracked in places, the rich man has the pole sanded smooth. Now, however, the pole no longer lifts great weight. Its magic had come from cow hairs stuck in the old pole, not from the pole itself.

CONNECTIONS. Changes in fortune. Cow hairs. Herders. Magical objects. Poles. Rich man. Weight. Yi People, stories from.

HOW ELSE THIS STORY IS TOLD. The Magic Pole — Louise and Yuan-Hsi Kuo, *Chinese Folk Tales.*

77. The Rolling Rice Ball

Junichi Yoda. Japan

An old woodcutter tries to grab for one of his rice balls that is rolling away, but it drops down a hole. He hears a tiny voice singing about the rice ball, urging it to run. Curious, he drops his second lunch rice ball down a hole and then his last. A mouse pops out and thanks him and offers to take him down the hole. The woodcutter holds onto the mouse's tail. Underground, many mice await before a fine pavilion, and they ask him to stay for special rice cakes, which taste delicious. The mice give him a chest to take home, which he and his wife are delighted to find filled with gold coins. The greedy neighbor who has been eavesdropping forces rice balls down the hole. He doesn't wait for the mice to sing to him before barging down. The neighbor thinks he will scare the mice away and seize all the gold, but the mice leave him to try to find his own way out in total darkness.

CONNECTIONS. Changes in fortune. Chases. Coins. Gold. Gratitude. Greed. Greedy neighbor. Hospitality. Mice. Rats. Rice balls. Rice cakes. Songs. Treasure. Underground. Woodcutters.

HOW ELSE THIS STORY IS TOLD. *The Old Man and the Mice/Nezumi Choja*— Daiji Kawasaki on kamishibai story cards. Rat Jōdo— Fanny Hagin Mayer, *Ancient Tales in Modern Japan.* The Rolling Rice-Cakes— Florence Sakade, *Kintaro's Adventures* and *Japanese Children's Favorite Stories*, Book Two. The Roly-Poly Dumpling — Elizabeth Scofield, *Hold Tight, Stick Tight.* Roly Poly Rice Ball — Margaret Read MacDonald, *Twenty Tellable Tales.* See also *The Funny Little Woman* (story # 256).

78. The Monkeys and the Jizo

Elizabeth Scofield, *Hold Tight, Stick Tight*. Japan

An old farmer covers himself in flour to look like a scarecrow in order to chase monkeys from his grain field. No monkeys come, so he sits down and soon falls asleep. Monkeys come out of the woods. They think he looks like a kindly gray Jizo, a statue of the god who protects children, even though he is sitting down. They decide to carry this statue to the mountain shrine. The old man has awakened, but stays still to see what will happen. The monkeys pick him up, splash through a cold river, singing all the while about keeping him dry, climb to the shrine, and set him carefully down. It has been very hard for the old farmer not to laugh, but he does not. They leave offerings of food and go away. The old farmer gathers up the food and brings it all home to share with his wife. Hearing about this, their greedy neighbor covers himself with flour and goes to sit in the field. The monkeys think he looks cross, but lift this Jizo to bring him, too, to the mountain shrine. However, when they cross the river and sing their song, he begins to laugh, and the monkeys are so surprised to see a laughing Jizo they drop him in the river.

CONNECTIONS. Farmers. Food. Fools. Greed. Humorous stories. Jizo. Laughter. Misunderstandings. Monkeys and apes. Statues.

HOW ELSE THIS STORY IS TOLD. Monkey Jizo— Fanny Hagin Mayer, *Ancient Tales in Modern Japan*.

79. Ants

Lafcadio Hearn, *Kwaidan*. Chinese

In the province of Taishū, a pious man has been praying to a certain goddess for many years. One morning a beautiful woman in a yellow robe says she is that goddess and has come to reward him for his devotion. She anoints his ears with cream from a little box and tells him that he will now be able to understand what Ants are saying, but not to frighten them. She vanishes. He finds some Ants on a stone that supports a house pillar. One Ant is suggesting that they look for another place to live as the sun cannot warm the cold, damp ground because a treasure is buried underneath. When the Ants leave, the man digs up a number of jars, containing gold coins. He becomes wealthy, though he can never understand the language of Ants again.

CONNECTIONS. Ants. Changes in fortune. Coins. Devotion. Gods and goddesses. Language of animals. Prayer. Taishū Province. Treasure.

80. The Phoenix Fairy Flower

Folk Tales from China, Fifth Series. Han People

In a poor mountain village, talented Clever Girl decides to make a special wedding jacket decorated with images of the vegetables her betrothed has given her as gifts. When she pricks her finger, the drop of blood becomes a red flower; she turns her sweat into butterflies. The jacket is extraordinary. Her neighbor, Golden Flower, who is to wed a wealthy man, offers to exchange many clothes for it. When Clever Girl turns her down, Golden Flower runs off with the jacket and tosses it up where magpies catch it and fly away. Clever Girl refuses compensation. She fashions a big net for the roof and under it traps eighty to one hundred magpies, who fly her east to a wooded mountain. A fairy appears, wearing Clever Girl's beautifully embroidered jacket and offers her a trade. When Clever Girl will not trade, saying she made this jacket herself, the fairy hands it to her with good wishes. As she leaves, Clever Girl sees a phoenix fly off. Clever Girl meets her betrothed who has come to find her. They are happily married the next day. When Clever Girl wears the jacket to work in the fields, magpies circle her to guard the jacket. And when Golden Flower once again snatches the jacket, the magpies peck at her. Golden Flower's face and the jacket are in shreds. Colorful threads from the cloth drift off and become glorious flowers the next spring, with petals as red as flame and outstretched like phoenix wings.

CONNECTIONS. Betrothal. Birds. Cleverness. Determination. Embroidery. Fairies. Flowers. Han People, stories from. Jealousy. Magical objects. Magpies. Marriage. Origins. Problem solvers. Protection. Quests. Talents. Thieves. Trades. Wedding Jackets.

HOW ELSE THIS STORY IS TOLD. *Ling-Li and the Phoenix Fairy: A Chinese Folktale—*Ellin Greene.

81. Sister Lace

Katrin Tchana, *The Serpent Slayer and Other Stories of Strong Women*. China

Sister Lace's creations are so magnificent that the emperor sends soldiers to drag her from her village to make lace at his court. She cries that she will never marry him and scratches and kicks. He has Sister Lace thrown in prison, but says he will let her go if she makes him a live rooster from lace. Sister Lace works in her cell for seven days and makes a rooster that comes alive when she rubs a drop of her blood into the rooster's feathers and lets a tear drop into its mouth. When the emperor calls the rooster a trick and demands a wild partridge, the rooster breaks free from its lace and tears at the emperor with its claws, crowing that the emperor free Sister Lace or die. Courtiers kill the rooster. After Sister Lace makes a partridge, the emperor wants a dragon, and the partridge also scratches him. Sister Lace makes a little dragon. She is sure the emperor will demand something else, but he cries that she has made a snake, not a dragon. The dragon breathes out fire and burns the emperor to death. Sister Lace rides the dragon up into the sky. It is her lace that covers the night sky with stars.

CONNECTIONS. Animation. Captivity. Determination. Dragons. Emperors. Heroes, women. Lace. Magical objects. Origins. Partridges. Roosters. Stars. Talents.

HOW ELSE THIS STORY IS TOLD. Sister Lace — Hua Long, *The Moon Maiden*. Sister Lace — John Minford, *Favourite Folktales of China*.

82. The Magic Brocade

Joanna Cole, *Best-Loved Folktales of the World*. Zhuang People

A mother, so skilled at weaving that birds and other animals in her work appear to be alive, lives in a small village in southern China. One day, she finds a painting in the marketplace of a white house with fields and gardens. She would love to live in such a place, and her youngest son encourages her to weave the scene into a brocade. The mother devotes herself to that one piece for three years, day and night. Her eyes get sore. She weaves her tears into the picture as river and fishpond. When her tears turn to blood, she weaves them into the sun and red flowers. Just as she has finished and steps back to view the brocade, a wind carries it away. The mother is heartbroken. She asks her eldest son to go east to find it. A white-haired woman tells him that the brocade was carried away by fairies of Sun Mountain who desire to copy it. To get it back, he will have to knock out two of his front teeth and place them in the stone horse's mouth. The horse will eat red fruit and fly him through Flame Mountain and an icy sea, where he must not complain or he will die. When the eldest brother grows pale with alarm, the white-haired woman offers him a small box of gold instead. He takes the box and goes away. The second son also goes to the city with the old woman's gold, too ashamed to return home. The youngest son tells his mother that he will bring back the brocade. He passes through all the trials by fire and ice and finds one hundred fairies sitting at a loom on Sun Mountain, singing and copying his mother's brocade. They tell him they will return it the next morning. One fairy weaves herself into the original. He wakes to see the brocade there for him and gallops with it back to the old woman, who returns his teeth. She also gives him deerskin shoes which bring him swiftly home. The mother's sight returns, and as the son and she gaze at the picture, it grows larger until it all becomes real, her wish fulfilled. He marries the fairy standing by the fishpond, and they live happily.

CONNECTIONS. Animation. Brocade. Brothers. Courage. Determination. Devotion. Embroidery. Fairies. Filial devotion. Heroes, men. Loss. Love. Magical objects. Mothers and sons. Old woman, supernatural helper. Paintings and pictures. Quests. Stone horse. Sun Mountain. Supernatural wives. Talents. Teeth. Zhuang People, stories from.

WHERE ELSE THIS STORY APPEARS. The Magic Brocade — Eric and Nancy Protter, *Folk and Fairy Tales of Far-Off Lands.*

HOW ELSE THIS STORY IS TOLD. The Chuang Brocade — Catherine Edwards Sadler, *Treasure Mountain. The Enchanted Tapestry* — Robert D. San Souci. *The Magic Brocade: A Tale of China* — Aaron Shepard and at *Aaron Shepard's World of Stories*, Online. The Magic Brocade — Jane Yolen, *Mightier Than the Sword. The Magic Tapestry* — Demi. The Piece of Chuang Brocade — *Folk Tales from China*, Third Series and *The Peacock Maiden: Folk Tales of China*. The Silk Brocade — Tanya Robyn Batt, *The Fabrics of Fairytale.* The Silk Tapestry — Patrick Atangan, *Silk Tapestry. The Weaving of a Dream* — Marilee Heyer. The Wonderful Brocade — in *The Spring of Butterflies.* The Wonderful Chuang Brocade in M. A. Jagendorf and Virginia Weng, *The Magic Boat and Other Chinese Folk Stories.* Zhuang Brocade — Cathy Spagnoli, *Asian Tales and Tellers.*

83. The Wooden Horse

John Minford, *Favourite Folktales of China.* Uygur People

A carpenter brings a wooden horse to show the king his craftsmanship. He tells the king that if he loosens one screw the horse will fly, and if he loosens all twenty-six, the horse will take him around the world. The young prince begs to try the horse, but once aloft, loosens all the screws and takes off. He lands in a new town where the king has put his beautiful daughter in the sky to keep her safe. That night the prince secretly visits the princess, and they fall in love. The next day, however, the king can tell that the princess has touched a man. One courtier advises that the king paint her bed and chairs and arrest the person with paint on his clothes. The prince tosses his paint-covered clothes down from the sky, but then feels conscience-stricken and confesses when a poor old man is arrested for having them. The prince is about to be hanged, but he loosens the screws on his wooden horse and flies off with the princess. When she rides the wooden horse back alone to retrieve a gift from her mother, the king locks her in a room and arranges for her marriage to another prince. Meanwhile, walking through the desert, the prince eats peaches from a mysterious orchard. The fruit gives him a white beard and horns. He dreams that an old man tells him to eat dried fruit from under the trees to reverse the changes. When he wakes, he does eat the dried fruit and is no longer aged. The prince fills a basket with samples of the different fruits and walks west to the princess's kingdom. A procession also heading that direction stops. When the prince learns that the man in the carriage is the princess's intended bridegroom, he sells him two peaches and two pears in exchange for gold. Up ahead, the procession stops and waits for the fruit-selling prince. Because the bridegroom now has horns and a long white beard, he wants the prince to stand in for him and then lure the princess back to his kingdom. The prince bargains for more gold and then agrees. At first, the princess will not even look at him, but when she recognizes the prince she pretends that he is the bridegroom her father arranged for. Her father agrees to let her take the wooden horse back to her new home. At last the prince and the princess have a chance to escape. They fly the horse back to the prince's kingdom, where the prince thanks the carpenter for a fine adventure.

CONNECTIONS. Age, suddenly old. Captivity. Carpenters. Cleverness. Enchantment. Escapes. Fathers and daughters. Flying horses. Fruit, dried. Horses. Impulsiveness. Kings. Love. Magical objects. Matches, marriage. Peaches. Pears. Princes. Princesses. Problem solvers. Statues. Thieves. Transformation. Wooden horses. Uygur People, stories from.

HOW ELSE THIS STORY IS TOLD. The Wooden Horse—*Folk Tales from China*, First Series and *The Frog Rider*.

84. The Stone Horse

Xue Mei in Howard Giskin, *Chinese Folktales.* Hubei Province, China

Long ago near Baiyun Mountain, a cruel officer threatens an old sculptor that he must carve a statue of the officer riding a horse in a month or die. The sculptor carves the horse with his daughter Azhen's help, but he cannot make a statue of the officer that satisfies him. When the month is up and the statue is still not finished, many villagers intercede to save the sculptor's life. The officer sends him off to do hard labor. Azhen weeps by the horse, missing her father. The horse tells her that he will become fully real if she feeds him the golden flower that opens at dawn by Baiyun Mountain for seven days. She does this. The stone horse, now snow-white, takes Azhen on his back and flies into the sky. He lands beside Treasure Mountain to drink from the Gold and Silver River. Treasure does not interest Azhen. She wants only to see her father, and the horse does bring her to him. On their way home, the horse tells the sculptor and his daughter to take jewels from Treasure Mountain, so they do bring some home for poor villagers. Upon their return, the cruel officer sends men to take the horse. The horse tells the sculptor not to be afraid and flies the officer into the sky, where he disappears forever.

CONNECTIONS. Animation. Baiyun Mountain. Captivity. Cruelty. Devotion. Fathers and daughters. Flowers. Golden flower. Heroes, women. Horses. Hubei Province, China, stories from. Jewels. Magical objects. Officers. Punishment. Rescues. Rewards. Sculptors. Statues. Stone. Stone horse. Talents. Transformation. Treasure Mountain.

85. How Six Friends Sought Adventure

Eleanor Myers Jewett, *Wonder Tales from Tibet.* Tibet

Six friends—a future Magician, a Blacksmith, a Doctor, a Woodcarver, a Painter, and a Prince—decide to adventure before they take up their fathers' professions. Each plants a small tree at the beginning of one of six streams that lead off from a pond. They agree to follow these different streams and meet in a year. The health of the trees will indicate if any one of them is in trouble. The Prince's son falls in love with a beautiful girl who lives in a hut in the woods, but his happiness ends when the Khan's men find her ring in the stream. They take her away, and thrust him down a well. Gathering at one year and one day, his friends find the Prince's tree drooping. Working together with their various talents, they find him and heal him and make a great wooden bird that flies him to the Khan's palace to rescue his wife. Just as he arrives, she is on the roof where the Khan has sent her to welcome a Bird of Paradise, messenger from the gods. And they fly away.

CONNECTIONS. Animation. Artists. Bird of Paradise. Birds. Blacksmiths. Carvers. Cooperation. Cruelty. Escapes. Friendship. Healing. Khans. Love. Magical objects. Magicians. Princes. Rescues. Rings. Talents. Tibetan People, stories from. Travelers. Trees. Wife-stealing. Wooden birds.

86. The Piebald Calf

Carol Kendall and Yao-Wen Li, *Sweet and Sour*. China

When the Third Wife tells her scholar-official husband that she will greet his return from a temporary position with a baby in her arms, he is overjoyed and the First and Second Wives are intensely jealous. They take the boy born to Third Wife and feed it to Big Cow. They tell Third Wife that the baby was malformed. The cow gives birth to a beautiful piebald calf. The husband sends Third Wife to live in the drafty mill house, but he becomes quite attached to the little calf, who not only follows him around, but seems to understand what he is saying. The scholar-official tests the calf's understanding by asking him to bring dumplings to his mother. When the calf starts pushing the bowl to the mill house, First and Second Wives feign illness that they say only organs from the piebald calf will cure. The master cannot kill the piebald calf and switches calves with his neighbor Wang. According to custom, Wang's daughter will be throwing an embroidered ball from her window when it is time to choose a husband. It is the piebald calf who catches the ball on his horn and runs. She follows to retrieve the ball, and there stands a handsome young man with the ball in his hand. As he is also courageous and gentle, Wang's daughter is happy to marry him. Third Wife takes her rightful place in the scholar-official's home, and the other wives are banished to the mill.

CONNECTIONS. Calves. Cows. Cruelty. Deceit. Extraordinary children. Husbands and wives. Jealousy. Kiangsu, China, stories from. Love. Matches, marriage. Murder. Punishment. Scholars. Transformation.

HOW ELSE THIS STORY IS TOLD. The Pretty Little Calf — Wolfram Eberhard, *Folktales of China* (from Kiangsu).

87. The Flute

Grace James, *Green Willow*. Japan

O' Yoné's stepmother is jealous of her father's affection for her and treats O' Yoné cruelly. O' Yoné pleads with her father not to go away on a trip to Kyoto. She tells him he will not see her again and gives him a bamboo flute she made, so that he will think of her. In the third moon that he is away, O' Yoné's father comes across the flute and plays it. The flute wails and then cries for him to come back to Yedo. He leaves immediately for home. O'Yoné is not there, and his wife will not tell him her whereabouts. But when he plays the flute in the bamboo grove, it speaks, saying that the stepmother has killed her.

CONNECTIONS. Bamboo. Birds. Deceit. Fathers and daughters. Flute. Husbands and wives. Jealousy. Magical objects. Murder. Mysteries. Stepmothers and stepdaughters. Talking bamboo. Talking birds. Tibetan People, stories from. Truth.

HOW ELSE THIS STORY IS TOLD. *Chinese variation:* The Story of Three Hunters— A.L. Shelton, *Tibetan Folk Tales* (here, a bird sings the truth about a girl's murder by three wives). *Japanese variations:* The Flute — Lafcadio Hearn and Others, *Japanese Fairy Tales*. The Stepchild and the Flute — Fanny Hagin Mayer, *Ancient Tales in Modern Japan*.

88. Daka and Dalun
Folk Tales from China, Fourth Series. Zhuang People

Daka's stepmother becomes mean to her when the stepsister Dalun is born, and things get worse after her father dies. When Daka wants to go with them to a wedding feast, her stepmother mixes five piculs of sesame with soybeans and tells Daka that first she must separate them. The spirit of her mother in a crow sings instructions to Daka. Again, her mother's spirit sings to tell her how to fill three leaky jars with water and where to dig to find new clothes and shoes under the loquat tree. Dancing, Daka stumbles on her way to the feast, and one of her red shoes falls into the river. It is found by Hsiu Tsai, a teacher, who wonders if this belongs to the young woman he will marry. Dalun's mother says the shoe belongs to her pockmarked daughter Dalun. Daka says that it is hers. Hsiu Tsai declares that the shoe belongs to the young woman whose clothes stick to it. The wind blows Daka's coat onto the bramble. She marries Hsiu Tsai and gives birth to a boy. One day Dalun pushes her into the well and pretends to be Daka, making up lies about the change in her appearance. A cuckoo sings to Hsiu Tsai that the beautiful wife has changed. Hsiu Tsai wonders if his wife's spirit is in the bird and brings it home. When the cuckoo sings that Dalun is a murderer, Dalun cooks it. The soup tastes so bitter that Dalun spills it out, and a strange bamboo grove grows in that place. Once the bamboo catches Dalun's hair and lifts her. When Hsiu Tsai cuts the tree, he falls in pain. Dalun cuts down all the bamboo plants. An old woman requests a stalk of bamboo as a reel for her loom. She comes home one day to find a beautiful girl weaving there who says she is the spirit of a someone who was murdered, but that she will become real if the woman boils some new chopsticks and then drinks that water. The old woman invites Hsiu Tsai and his son to visit, and the boy recognizes Daka as his mother right away. Hsiu Tsai is so happy to have found Daka. When Dalun asks Daka how her skin became so white, Daka answers that her mother pounded her in a mortar. This is what Dalun requests that her mother do to her, and she is crushed. The spirits of Dalun and her mother become two chiu chio birds whose cry warns people not to harm others.

CONNECTIONS. Bamboo. Beauty. Birds. Chiu chio birds. Cinderella stories. Cows. Crows. Cruelty. Cuckoo birds. Devotion. Enchantment. Husbands and wives. Kindness from animals. Kwangtung, China, stories from. Life-giving. Lotus flowers. Love. Magical objects. Mothers and daughters. Mothers and sons. Murder. Origins. Physical difference. Pockmarks. Punishment. Rebirth. Shoes. Sparrows. Spirits. Stepmothers and stepsisters. Talking bamboo. Talking birds. Transformation. Teachers. Turtles. Ugliness. Weavers. Zhuang People, stories from.

HOW ELSE THIS STORY IS TOLD. *Chinese variations:* The Chao Ku Bird — M. A. Jagendorf and Virginina Weng, *The Magic Boat*. Cinderella — Wolfram Eberhard, *Folktales of China* (from Kwangtung). *Korean variations:* Kongji and Patji — Y.T. Pyun, *Tales from Korea* (here, the magic helpers include a cow, turtles, and sparrows, and a lotus flower from the pond where the stepsister drowns the heroine). *Kongjui and Patjui* — John Holstein. Kongjwi and Padjwi — Tae Hung Ha, *Folk Tales of Old Korea*. K'ongiwi and P'atjwi — James Huntley Grayson, *Myths and*

Legends from Korea. A Korean Cinderella — Frances Carpenter, *Tales of a Korean Grandmother. The Korean Cinderella* — Shirley Climo. The Tale of Kongjwi — Linda Soon Curry, *A Tiger by the Tail.*

89. Benizara and Kakezara

Keigo Seki, *Folktales of Japan.* Japan

Benizara, whose name means Crimson Dish, and Kakezara, whose name means Broken Dish, are stepsisters. The stepmother favors Kakezara, who is her child. She sends both girls out to gather chestnuts with the admonition not to return home until the bags are full, but Benizara's bag has a hole and is impossible to fill. It is growing dark, and Kakezara has long gone home. Benizara walks until she sees a light and finds an old woman spinning. The old woman tells Benizara that she cannot stay because her oni sons eat humans, but she gives Benizara chestnuts, a magic box, and a handful of rice for her to chew if she meets the onis. When she hears onis, Benizara chews the rice and lies down, and the oni sons think she is already dead. She makes it home that night, but another time, the stepmother takes Kakezara to see a play and leaves Benizara home with much work. Benizara's animal friends help her finish the tasks. Then she taps the little magic box three times and wishes for a beautiful kimono to replace her rags and goes to see the play. The next day a nobleman arrives in a palaquin. He wants to know which girl came to see the play. The stepmother insists it was Kakezara, but the nobleman does not think so. At last the stepmother takes Benizara from the bathtub where she has hidden her. The nobleman asks each girl to compose a poem using the salt on a plate with a pine needle in it as the subject. Kakezara sings about salt on a plate, but Benizara sings about mountains in snow where a lovely pine tree grows. The lord admires Benizara's poem, and she rides off to his palace. The stepmother drags Kakezara to the palace in a basket so roughly that Kakezara dies.

CONNECTIONS. Boxes. Chestnuts. Cinderella stories. Cruelty. Kimonos. Kindness from animals. Love. Magical objects. Mothers and daughters. Nobles and lords. Old woman, supernatural helper. Oni. Poetry. Rice. Salt. Stepmothers and stepsisters. Tests.

HOW ELSE THIS STORY IS TOLD. Benizara and Kakezara — Robert J. Adams, *Folktales of Japan.* Benizara and Kakezara — Margaret Read MacDonald, *Celebrate the World.* Benizara and Kakezara — Judy Sierra, *Cinderella.* Nukabuku, Komebuku — Fanny Hagin Mayer, *Ancient Tales in Modern Japan.* Sara-Sara Yama — Fanny Hagin Mayer, *Ancient Tales in Modern Japan.*

90. Sunshine and Moonshine

Eleanore Myers Jewett, *Wonder Tales from Tibet.* Tibetan People

When his wicked stepmother pretends to be ill and says that only Moonshine's heart's blood will save his brother Sunshine, Moonshine runs away with him. Struggling in the hot desert, Moonshine collapses, but Sunshine goes off to find water. He comes to a red door in a rock that is opened by an old man. The hermit saves Moonshine, and the two brothers stay with him until the Khan, who fears that a stranger will take his throne, arrives. Sunshine reveals himself so that the Khan, will not hurt the hermit, but he pretends that Moonshine is dead. As the Khan's men are taking Sunshine to the palace, the Khan's daughter sees him, and he sees her. They fall in love. The Khan cannot stand her pleading to marry Sunshine and has both his daughter and the young man placed in sacks in a cave close to the place where demon-bears come daily to drink. Sunshine and the Khan's daughter think only of how the other one must be suffering, and the demon-bears, moved by their unselfishness, set them free. Despite the prophecy, the Khan give his throne to Sunshine. Moonshine marries the Khan's other daughter.

CONNECTIONS. Bears. Brothers. Captivity. Demon bears. Demons. Devotion. Fate. Fathers and daughters. Fear. Foretellings. Hermits. Khans. Love. Old man, supernatural helper. Protection. Stepmothers and stepsons. Tibetan People, stories from. Unselfishness.

91. Looking-to-Mother Shoal

Wu Jingchao, translator, *Dragon Tales: A Collection of Chinese Stories*. China

Boy Nie sees a white shadow in a gully and gives chase, thinking it might be a rabbit. It disappears. He starts digging up some bamboo grass to transplant at home for the landlord's horse and the rabbit and finds a pearl in a pool of water beneath. Mom Nie tells him to hid it in the rice vat, and rice soon overflows. The pearl doubles whatever Boy Nie and Mom Nie place it on. They help their neighbors, but landlord Zhou Hong hears and wants that pearl. He and his steward invent a lie about Boy Nie's having stolen the pearl from his family. It is too late for Boy Nie to run away. He swallows the pearl while the landlord's men are beating him. Neighbors come to stop the beating, but he has an unquenchable thirst. After many bowls of water, he runs to the river in a storm. Now he has grown horns, tentacles, and red scales. Landlord Zhou Hong comes to cut open Boy Nie, but Boy Nie is a full red dragon and drowns the men with a giant wave. Boy Nie's mother is still holding his foot, reluctant to lose him, but he tells her he must go. Every time she calls to him, he turns, creating twenty-four shallow spots in the river.

CONNECTIONS. Bamboo. Children. Deceit. Devotion. Dragons. Greed. Landlords. Loss. Magical objects. Mothers and sons. Multiplication. Number. Pearls. Poverty. Rivers. Transformation.

92. The Listening Ear

Shirley Climo, *A Treasury of Mermaids*. Japan

Jiro, the second brother, returns a red fish to the water, and a maiden takes him to the underwater kingdom of Neriya to Rin Jin, the Dragon King. The maiden tells him to ask for the Listening Ear, a conch shell. Back on shore, Jiro puts the shell to his ear and can understand the language of the birds. They are saying that a nobleman's daughter is under the spell of a hungry snake trapped in the thatch of the roof of the house. Jiro goes to rescue her.

CONNECTIONS. Birds. Centipedes. Conch. Demons. Dragon King. Fish. Goblins. Kindness to animals. Language of animals. Magical objects. Maidens. Neriya, kingdom. Rescues. Rin Jin, Dragon King. Sea. Shells. Snakes. Spells. Talking birds. Underwater kingdom.

HOW ELSE THIS STORY IS TOLD. *Japanese variation:* The Magic Ear — Keigo Seki, *Folktales of Japan*. *Korean variation:* How Foolish Men Are! — O Sog-Gon in Zong In-Sob, *Folk Tales from Korea* (a boy overhears goblins and gets rid of the lurking centipede to save the girl, as well as solving some other problems for the village, but his greedy friend is tricked by the goblins when he tries to do the same thing).

93. The Magic Listening Cap

Yoshiko Uchida, *The Magic Listening Cap*. Japan

When a poor old man tells his guardian god that he has nothing left to offer but his life, the god rewards his goodness and honesty with a little red cap that will let him hear "as never before." The old man thanks the guardian god. Wearing his cap, he hears two crows talking. One tells the other that their friend the camphor tree is growing weaker because it was improperly cut down without the roots being dug up. The wealthy man who cut it is also ill. The old man wonders how he may be able to help in a way that the family will believe him about the link between the two. He pretends to be a fortune teller. The sick man's wife permits him to sleep in the guest house. The old man realizes the tree roots are underneath its floor. The next morning the old man tells the sick man that he must transplant the camphor tree where it can grow. The wealthy man gets well and rewards the man with the red cap with gold. The man with the listening cap brings gifts to his guardian god and, having enough now, packs the hat away.

CONNECTIONS. Birds. Camphor trees. Changes in fortune. Crows. Despair. Enchantment. Fortune tellers. Gods and goddesses. Hats. Healing. Illness. Iwate, Japan, stories from. Language of animals. Magical objects. Rewards. Trees.

WHERE ELSE THIS STORY APPEARS. The Magic Listening Cap — Yoshiko Uchida in I. K. Junne, *Floating Clouds, Floating Dreams.*

HOW ELSE THIS STORY IS TOLD. The Listening Cap — Pleasant DeSpain, *Thirty-Three Multicultural Tales to Tell.* The Listening Hood — Fanny Hagin Mayer, *Ancient Tales in Modern Japan* (from Iwate).

94. The Jewels of the Sea

Yoshiko Uchida, *The Dancing Kettle.* Japan

A young prince trades places with his brother for the day to try fishing, for he is tired of hunting. When he loses his brother's best fishhook, however, the older brother will not forgive him until that exact hook is found. As the young prince searches the seashore one day, an old man gives him a magic boat to take him underwater to the King of the Sea for help. The prince drops his royal stone, the maga-tama, into a cup for two Sea Princesses to take to their father. The King of the Sea listens to the young prince's story and summons all of the creatures who live in the sea to ask if they have seen the hook. One little fish says the red snapper has a sore throat and has, perhaps, swallowed it. Guards bring the red snapper and remove the fishhook from his throat. The brother stays with the King of the Sea for five years. As a token of friendship, the King gives him one jewel to call the waves and another to let waters recede. The prince thanks the King and rides a large alligator back to shore. While he was gone, the elder prince has seized power and wants to rule alone. The young prince hears his brother coming with his dagger drawn and holds one jewel overhead. The elder prince cries as the water crashes toward him. The young prince holds up the other jewel, and the waters flow back. The older prince thanks his brother for saving his life, and peacefully, they rule together.

CONNECTIONS. Alligators. Blame. Brothers. Conflict. Discontent. Fish. Fishhooks. Forgiveness. Jewels. King of the Sea. Loss. Magical objects. Old man, supernatural helper. Princes. Reconciliation. Red snapper. Rescues. Sea. Trades. Underwater kingdom.

HOW ELSE THIS STORY IS TOLD. The Happy Hunter and the Skilful Fisher — Yei Theodora Ozaki, *Japanese Fairy Book.* In the Palace of the Sea God — F. Hadland Davis, *Myths and Legends of Japan.* The Sea King and the Magic Jewels — Grace James, *Green Willow and Other Japanese Fairy Tales.* The Sea Palace — Yoshimatsu Suzuki, *Japanese Legends and Folk-Tales.* Tamanoi, the Jewel Spring — Iwaya Sazanami, *Iwaya's Fairy Tales of Old Japan.* Tamanoi, or the Jewel Spring — Alan Leslie Whitehorn, *Wonder Tales of Old Japan.* Umi-Sachi-Hiko and Yama-Sachi-Hiko — Keshi Nakajima, *Japanese Traditional Tales.*

95. The Story of the Fairy Boat

Lotta Carswell Hume, *Favorite Children's Stories from China and Tibet*. Central China

Ho Lai does not collect frogs for his cruel stepmother on the day he finds a bag of coins. He waits to see who may return for the lost money. The man who appears to claim the bag wants to give Ho Lai half the money, but Ho Lai replies that he was only doing what is right. His stepmother, however, is furious that he turned down money and turns him out of the house to beg. Ho Lai sees a tiny golden boat float down on a moonbeam. On the boat, tiny people are rowing and dancing and playing music. He holds out his basket, and the fairy people land there. They tell him they have come to help. They shrink the boat so small, and Ho Lai puts it in his pocket. The Emperor is enchanted by the tiny boat and offers to give his daughter in marriage in trade. Ho Lai agrees, for he likes the princess, but that night the Emperor shuts him in a house haunted by two creatures, one red and one green-faced, who eat people. They show Ho Lai where treasure lies hidden. The next day, finding Ho Lai alive and wealthy, the Emperor permits him to marry his daughter and turns over most of the governing, since he prefers to play with his boat.

CONNECTIONS. Boats. Captivity. Central China, stories from. Changes in fortune. Coins. Emperors. Fairies. Flesh-eaters. Golden boat. Honesty. Kindness. Princesses. Size. Stepmothers and stepsons. Supernatural creatures. Trades. Treasure.

96. The Magic Purse

Yoshiko Uchida. Japan

One April a poor young farmer decides to catch up with his friends to visit Iseh shrine and takes a shortcut down a strange road. A storm rages as he reaches Black Swamp, a place of quicksand and snakes. A sad woman in a silver-blue kimono with long, black hair comes toward him from the swamp, though she is not wet. She asks him to help her by taking a letter to her parents in the Red Swamp near Osaka. He tells her that no one ever leaves the Red Swamp alive. But when she begins to weep and tells him she is being held captive in the Black Swamp, he cannot refuse. Gratefully, she gives him the envelope and a small red purse with gold coins that will replenish as long as he leaves one coin inside. She thanks him and disappears. Everyone he asks for directions to the Red Swamp is horrified, but the young farmer cannot forget the young woman and presses on until he finds it. The Red Swamp is dark and frightening. He claps so her parents will know that he is there. The second time, an old man arrives in a creaky boat and asks if he has brought a message from his daughter. He invites the young farmer to get into the boat. The young man cannot keep his eyes open. When he wakes he is in a golden room with the old man and his wife. They thank him for his kindness in delivering the letter and give him gold coins before bringing him back to shore. When the young farmer arrives at the shrine, he gives thanks for the gold and for still being alive. He never forgets the young woman. Every year he returns to Black Swamp to float a tray with rice cakes and wine for her.

CONNECTIONS. Captivity. Changes in fortune. Coins. Devotion. Farmers. Fear. Gold. Golden room. Gratitude. Iseh, shrine. Letters. Longxi County. Love. Magical objects. Messengers. Parents and children. Rewards. Sadness. Supernatural beloveds. Swamps. Unselfishness.

WHERE ELSE THIS STORY APPEARS. The Magic Purse of the Swamp Maiden — Yoshiko Uchida, *The Sea of Gold*.

HOW ELSE THIS STORY IS TOLD. ***Chinese variation:*** Shepherd Girl — Dai Dongdong in Howard Giskin, *Chinese Folktales* (set in Longxi County in Gansu Province).

97. The Daughter and the Helper

Gioia Timpanelli, *Tales from the Roof of the World*. Tibetan People

One day a maid tricks the chief's daughter into throwing her golden bucket into the river to see if it will float. When it is carried away, the maid tricks her again by lying and saying that the chief will kill her, when, actually, the chief does not mind. The maid suggests that they exchange clothes and run away. At a neighboring chief's house, the chief's real daughter finds black and white stones that help her to round up cattle and wood pieces that turn branches into fine thread. This chief's son does not really believe she is the maid, but he does not say anything until the chief's false daughter grows angry when she cannot work the black and white stones or answer the chief's son's riddles. Then, he gets the false maiden to open her saddlebag too soon and partridges suddenly fly out, causing the horse to bolt and throw her. The chief's son and the chief's real daughter get married and become chiefs.

CONNECTIONS. Birds. Chieftains. Cleverness. Deceit. Golden bucket. Identity. Love. Magical objects. Partridges. Riddles. Servants. Stones. Tests. Tibetan People, stories from. Trades.

98. A Frog's Gift

Rafe Martin, *Mysterious Tales of Japan*. Japan

A snake bargains with a farmer. It will not eat the frog it has caught, if the farmer will take its place. The farmer offers the snake one of his daughters to marry instead. The snake agrees, and the frog hops off. The farmer's youngest daughter says she will go to the snake if her father will bring her one thousand gourds and one thousand iron needles. The snake arrives for her dressed as a warrior with one thousand men, who turn into hissing snakes once they reach the snake palace. The youngest daughter says she needs to test the snakes. They must sink one thousand gourds and float one thousand needles. The snakes think it will be easy, but the gourds float and the needles sink. The girl runs while they are concentrating on the task. In the marshes, a squat old woman with big eyes in a green robe gives her a new kimono and escorts her to the castle where the lord is looking for a bride. The old woman croaks good bye when the youngest daughter is chosen to come inside.

CONNECTIONS. Cleverness. Escapes. Fathers and daughters. Frogs. Gourds. Matches, marriage. Needles. Nobles and lords. Old woman, supernatural helper. Problem solvers. Shape-shifting. Snakes. Spirits. Supernatural bridegrooms. Tests. Tochigi, Japan, stories from. Trades.

HOW ELSE THIS STORY IS TOLD. The Snake Son-in-Law — Fanny Hagin Mayer, *Ancient Tales in Modern Japan* (from Tochigi).

99. The K'un-lun Slave

P'ei Hsing in Karl S. Y. Kao, *Classical Chinese Tales of the Supernatural and the Fantastic*. China

Requested by his father to inquire about His Excellency who has been ill, the young scholar Ts'ui is discomforted by the presence of three singing girls who pamper His Lordship. Then, the girl with red silk trousers who escorts him out points with three fingers and says, "Remember." Back at home, Ts'ui cannot concentrate or eat. The K'un-lun slave Mo-le asks Ts'ui to let him help. Mo-le interprets the girl's mysterious gestures to mean that she wants Ts'ui to come to her chambers on a certain night. He makes dark green gauze garments for Ts'ui to wear. Mo-le also slays the dog that guards the girls' quarters and carries Ts'ui on his back across ten walls. The girl is happy to see Ts'ui and bids Mo-le enter, too. She tells Ts'ui how she was forced to become an attendant to His Lordship. She says that she will serve Ts'ui as a servant if Mo-le can free her with his magic powers. Mo-le flies over the walls with Ts'ui and the girl, whom Ts'ui hides in his home for two years. His Lordship does not know where she has gone until one day she is spotted out for a carriage ride. Ts'ui tells everything to His Lordship, who decides that the girl should keep serving Ts'ui, but that Mo-le should be arrested for penetrating his dominion. Mo-le escapes over a wall.

CONNECTIONS. Captivity. Escapes. Mysteries. Nobles and lords. Problem solvers. Rescues. Scholars. Singing girls. Slaves. Supernatural skills.

100. Robe of Feathers

Florence Sakade, *Urashima Taro and Other Japanese Children's Stories*. Japan

A poor fisherman has just taken down a robe of colorful feathers he found hanging in a pine tree after a storm, when a beautiful woman runs after him. She tells him that she needs the robe. She says she is an angel, and the robe is her wings that she had hung there to dry. She will need the wings to return to heaven. Empathetic, the fisherman apologizes that he did not know the robe belonged to anyone. She gratefully offers to dance the angel's dance for him. Music fills the air as she dances in the robe. A rainbow fills the sky. Her dance takes her higher and higher until the fisherman can no longer see her. This lovely memory gives him pleasure for the rest of his life.

CONNECTIONS. Dancing. Feathers. Heavenly beings. Rising to the sky world. Robes. Wings.

WHERE ELSE THIS STORY APPEARS. Robe of Feathers— Florence Sakade, *Japanese Children's Favorite Stories, Book Two*.

HOW ELSE THIS STORY IS TOLD. The Celestial Robe of an Angel — Takeshi Nakajima, *Japanese Traditional Tales*. Feather-Robe Stone Mountain — Richard M. Dorson, *Folk Legends of Japan*. The Robe of Feathers— F. Hadland Davis, *Myths and Legends of Japan* and as The Feathery Robe in D. L. Ashliman, *Folktexts*, Online. Tanabata — Yoko Shibata at *Kids Web Japan*, Online.

101. Aniz the Shepherd

John Minford, *Favourite Folktales of China*. Uygur People

In Sinkiang Province there is a rich landlord who mistreats the young shepherd who works for him. He even breaks Aniz's flute one day and beats him. An old man makes a new bamboo flute for Aniz and teaches him to play so sweetly that animals come to listen. The landlord has ordered his three sons to fetch him the white rabbit with a black spot on top of its head that he has dreamed about. When they return emptyhanded, he challenges them to find the rabbit in return for all that he owns. The eldest son is directed to Aniz by the old man. Aniz says he will find the white rabbit if the son brings him 1000 strings of cash. Thinking about all he will inherit, the eldest son does. Aniz plays his flute, and the white rabbit comes to listen. Aniz tells the son to hold the rabbit firmly, but when he begins to play the flute again, the rabbit runs off. The same thing happens to the second and third sons. Finally, the landlord comes himself. As

Aniz plays the flute, the landlord is surrounded by forest beasts. He is terrified, but Aniz will only stop playing if the landlord promises to behave more generously to his workers and the poor.

CONNECTIONS. Animals. Bamboo. Cleverness. Coins. Cruelty. Dreams. Enchantment. Fathers and sons. Flutes. Herders. Landlords. Magical objects. Music. Old man, supernatural helper. Rabbits and hares. Sinkiang Province. Uygur People, stories from.

HOW ELSE THIS STORY IS TOLD. Anizu's Magic Wonder Flute — M.A. Jagendorf and Virginia Weng, *The Magic Boat and Other Chinese Folk Stories.*

102. Ma Lien and the Magic Brush

Hisako Kimishima. China

The peasant boy Ma Lien is too poor to own his own brush, so he draws scratching on stone or with his finger in sand. The animals he draws seem so real. Then a wizard gives him a magic brush with a warning to use it only to do good. Now the things Ma Lien paints really do come alive. He creates animals that help people with their work. Ma Lien's magic brush comes to the attention of the mandarin who demands that Ma Lien paint coins for him and throws Ma Lien in prison when he refuses. Ma Lien paints a door to free himself, but the mandarin finds him again and takes the brush away. However, the brush will not work for the court painter. The mandarin gives it back to Ma Lien if he will paint a mountain of gold. This time, Ma Lien agrees. He paints a mountain of gold, but in front of it, he paints a sea and a ship that the greedy mandarin steps into to sail him there. And then, Ma Lien paints a storm that sinks the ship the mandarin is on.

CONNECTIONS. Animation. Artists. Brushes. Captivity. Children. Cleverness. Empresses. Greed. Liaoning Province, China, stories from. Magical objects. Mandarins. Paintings and pictures. Peasants. Poverty. Problem solvers. Talents. Transformation.

HOW ELSE THIS STORY IS TOLD. The Boy with the Magic Brush — Zhang Dongdon in Howard Giskin, *Chinese Folktales* (Fushan, Liaoning Province). *Isabella and the Magic Brush* — B. Doumashkin, director, Film. *Liang and the Magic Paintbrush* — Demi. Ma Liang and His Magic Brush — Yin-lien C. Chin, Yetta S. Center, and Mildred Ross, *Traditional Chinese Folktales.* Ma Liang and His Magic Brush — A Han story in *Folk Tales from China,* First Series and *The Frog Rider.* Ma Liang and His Magic Brush — Robert Wyndham, *Tales the People Tell in China.* The Magic Brush — Catherine Edwards Sadler, *Treasure Mountain.* The Picture That Swallowed a Man — Lim Sian-tek, *More Folk Tales from China* (a demanding emperor vanishes into the magic cave painted in a scene by Wu Tao-tzu). Sausage Boy and His Magic Brush — Patrick Atangan, *Silk Tapestry* (the artist here is a simple young man, who angers the Dowager Empress, but gallops away on a stallion that he has painted, while she never gets to enter paradise).

103. The Magic Horse of Han Gan

Chen Jiang Hong. China

A young man who begins by sketching an innkeeper's horses in the sand continues to draw horses, even when he enters the Emperor's Academy. Han Gan always draws realistic horses tied up, so they will not gallop away if they ever do become truly alive. A great warrior asks Han Gan to paint an especially valiant horse. Han Gan tries, but is not happy with his work. When he throws it in the fire, however, a mighty horse leaps out. The warrior catches the horse and rides him hard. The horse seems to need no food or rest and takes the warrior through many victories. At last, weary of battle, the horse throws off the warrior and runs. When the warrior can find the horse nowhere else, he comes to Han Gan, who shows him how the horse has leaped back into a painting.

CONNECTIONS. Animation. Artists. Horses. Paintings and pictures. Talents. War. Warriors.

104. The One-Horned Ox

Louise and Yuan-Hsi Kuo, *Chinese Folk Tales.* Yao People

A young man who wishes he had an ox to help him plow draws a picture of a one-horned ox that he hangs in his room and talks to. One morning, the leaf he has drawn on is blank, and a real ox appears outside. The ox helps him till, and afterwards, he and the ox play. But the village chieftain seizes the ox for food. The young man buries the ox's bones and hangs its horn on his walls. Tall bamboo grows from the mound where the ox is buried, and the young man climbs to heaven where fairies are dancing. When they spy him, the bamboo shrinks and brings him back to the ground. In a dream, the ox tells the young man to draw one of the fairies on a banana leaf and to drill a hole in the ox horn and blow through it. The young man works on his drawing and the horn, and when he blows, the fairy he most remembers appears and becomes his wife. He draws another ox for them, too. They live happily until the chieftain takes the fairy to be his wife. The young man brings a winged tiger to life and rescues the fairy. The mountains where they live become known as Ox Horn Range.

CONNECTIONS. Animation. Bamboo. Bones. Enchantment. Fairies. Flying tiger. Horns. Husbands and wives. Jack and the Beanstalk stories. Killing. Loss. Love. Magical objects. Oxen. Paintings and pictures. Rescues. Supernatural wives. Wife-stealing. Yao People, stories from.

105. The Wooden Bowl

Lafcadio Hearn and Others, *Japanese Fairy Tales.* Japan

As she is dying, a mother warns her beautiful daughter not to remove a lacquered bowl from her head. She hopes that it will shadow her daughter's face and keep her safe. People laugh at the girl when she works in the fields with the bowl upside down on her head. Some try to pull it off, but the wooden bowl does not move. A rich farmer brings the young woman to wait on his sick wife, and their son falls in love with her gentle ways. None of his relatives want him to marry her; the bowl is just too strange. Then, considering his happiness, they relent, but the girl refuses, not wanting to cause tension. The girl's mother comes to her in a dream and tells her to marry this man. Even during the wedding ceremony, the bowl will not come off and seems to cry out. But as the daughter and her new husband complete the marriage ceremony with wine, the bowl breaks and precious gems fall on the floor.

CONNECTIONS. Bowls. Changes in fortune. Devotion. Dreams. Enchantment. Kindness. Magical objects. Matches, marriage. Mothers and daughters. Protection. Shyness. Spirits. Unselfishness.

WHERE ELSE THIS STORY APPEARS. The Wooden Bowl — Lafcadio Hearn, *The Boy Who Drew Cats and Other Japanese Fairy Tales.*

How Else This Story Is Told. The Black Bowl — Grace James, *Green Willow and Other Japanese Fairy Tales*. The Girl With the Wooden Helmet — Andrew Lang, *A World of Fairy Tales*. The Maiden with the Wooden Bowl — F. Hadland Davis, *Myths and Legends of Japan*. The Maiden with the Wooden Helmet — Pearl S. Buck, *Fairy Tales of the Orient*. The Princess of the Bowl — Yei Theodora Ozaki, *Warriors of Old Japan*. The Wooden Bowl — Eric Quayle, *The Shining Princess*.

106. The Cub's Triumph

T. H. James. Japan

Hunters have killed all of the animals in the forest except for a badger and a mother fox with one cub. They are hungry, afraid to come out of hiding. And then the badger comes up with a plan. He will pretend to be dead, and the fox can change into a man and sell him in town. When he escapes, the badger will run back and share the food. The following week the fox will pretend to be dead. The fox agrees and transforms herself into a woodcutter. She sells the badger and buys food which they share. The next week, the badger privately tells the man who buys the fox that the fox is only pretending to be dead. The man hits the fox with a big stick and kills her. The badger does not share any of the food he brings back. The crying cub is sure the badger is responsible for his mother's death. He hides his anger and suggests that the badger and he transform into men one at a time and make a contest out of trying to identify each other among other people. The fox cub announces that he will change first into someone grand. He actually remains a fox and hides. When the badger sees a procession with a daimyo being carried, he is sure this daimyo is the fox. When the badger runs up, one of the daimyo's retainers takes off his head.

Connections. Arrogance. Badgers. Calves. Children. Cleverness. Competition. Cubs. Deceit. Foxes. Hiroshima, Japan, stories from. Identity. Killing. Kitsune. Loss. Revenge. Shapeshifting. Tanuki. Tibetan People, stories from. Tigers. Transformation. Tricksters.

How Else This Story Is Told. *Chinese variation:* How the Fox Fell Victim to His Own Deceit — A. L. Shelton, *Tibetan Folk Tales* (a baby tiger cub and a calf who are friends together trick the fox who tries to separate them). *Japanese variations:* Comparing Disguises — Fanny Hagin Mayer, *Ancient Tales in Modern Japan* (from Hiroshima). How the Wicked Tanuki Was Punished — Andrew Lang, *The Crimson Fairy Book*. Kitsune no Tegara: The Cub's Triumph — T. H. James.

107. Green Dragon Pond

Yang Guangyong in He Liyi, *The Spring of Butterflies and Other Folktales of China's Minority Peoples*. Bai People

One rainstorm, a young man seeks shelter in the temple by the pond in a valley below Ma long Peak in Dali. He turns out to be a challenging chess opponent, to the old monk's surprise and delight. The young man, Li Aiqi, returns to play chess with the monk for many days. The monk wonders who he is. One day Aiqi tells the monk that he is a dragon who lives in Green Pond. He dives down and emerges with a beautiful robe for the monk. The monk begs to see Aiqi as a dragon, but Aiqi answers that not only would the monk be terrified, but if a mortal sees him, he will never be able to become human again. But the monk keeps begging. Aiqi has the monk put on his magic robe and then changes himself into a horned snake. Still, the monk imagines that Aiqi can be much bigger and begs to see him as grand a dragon as he can be. They plan for the monk to send his two novices away and lock the temple gate. Suspicious, though, the novices peer over the wall just as the Green Dragon has grown over twenty meters long. The dragon screams, the two monks die of fright, and a storm rages. The dragon's tail lashes the temple to rubble. Waters sweep the sorrowful dragon into Dali Lake. The monk wanders in the valley. It is said that people disappear in the icy waters of Green Pond.

CONNECTIONS. Bai People, stories from. Chess. Curiosity. Dragons. Floods. Friendship. Green Pond. Identity. Loss. Monks. Mysteries. Ponds. Robes. Shape-shifting. Size. Transformation.

WHERE ELSE THIS STORY APPEARS. The Dragon King of Langchong—*Folk Tales from China*, Fourth Series.

108. Sticks and Turnips! Sticks and Turnips!

Frances Carpenter, *Tales of a Korean Grandmother*. Korea

Discontent, Cho leaves his rice fields and his family to try to receive an appointment as a government official in Seoul. The Prime Minister keeps putting him off, though, and after four years, with no position and no more cash, Cho starts for home. He stays overnight with a country couple, but in the morning the man taps him with four little sticks, and Cho becomes an ox. The country man sells him in the market, but Cho escapes when the man who bought him stops in a wineshop. He stops to eat a turnip in a field, begins to itch, and turns human again. He returns to the country couple to get hold of those magic sticks for he wants to punish the Prime Minister. Cho returns to Seoul and taps the sleeping Prime Minister with two sticks. The Prime Minister grows horns and his hands become hooves. The next day there is a commotion in the capital. No one can cure the Prime Minister, who must certainly have been bewitched. Cho says that he can take away the hooves and horns if the Prime Minister agrees to make him an official. The Prime Minister agrees, and Cho grinds up turnips and administers them to the Prime Minister, who is cured. Cho receives the position at last and sends for his family.

CONNECTIONS. Changes in fortune. Discontent. Enchantment. Healing. Illness. Magical objects. Ministers. Officials. Onions. Oxen. Revenge. Sticks. Transformation. Travelers. Turnips. Work.

HOW ELSE THIS STORY IS TOLD. The Lazy Man—*Long Long Time Ago*. The Man Who Became an Ox—Suzanne Crowder Han, *Korean Folk and Fairy Tales*. Onions—Zong In-Sob, *Folk Tales from Korea* (onions are the transforming vegetable here).

109. How the Ox Star Fell from Heaven

Lily Toy Hong. China

In the beginning, life on earth is hard for people who must farm without oxen, for all oxen live at the Imperial Palace of the Emperor of All the Heavens. The imperial oxen never have to work. The Emperor of All the Heavens decrees that people must eat at least every three days. He chooses the Ox Star to be messenger, but the Ox Star messes up the message announcing that people must eat three times every day. The Emperor banishes the Ox Star from the sky. The ox now labors with people, who do appreciate their help, a little bit of heaven on earth.

CONNECTIONS. Jade Emperor. Mistakes. Origins. Oxen. Punishment. Stars. Transformation. Words. Work.

110. Heaven's Reward

Catherine Edwards Sandler, *Heaven's Reward*. China

When his good friend Shia fails the official examinations and dies, Yao pays for his funeral, but loses heart about continuing his own studies. He becomes a tradesman. One day, Yao pushes his own food over to a very tall man in an inn. The man tells Yao he will protect him and, indeed, carries Yao across the waves when their boat founders in a storm. Then the giant dives down to recover all of Yao's belongings, including one gold hairpin. Yao falls asleep wondering what thunder is and wakes in the sky, where stars are like seeds. He sneaks one star into his sleeve. As he sees other men up there do, Yao takes a bucket to sprinkle water onto the clouds, which sends rain to his parched village. The tall man tells Yao he became the Thunder God's assistant as a punishment when he did not give earth enough rain, but now his time is up. He gives Yao a rope to slide back down to earth with. When Yao's star begins to fade, it flies into his wife's mouth. That night Yao's friend Shia comes to him in a dream and says he is the star who will become Yao's son and grow up to be a scholar.

Connections. Clouds. Death. Friendship. Giants. Gods and goddesses. Heaven. Imperial examination. Journeys. Kindness. Punishment. Rain. Rebirth. Rescues. Rewards. Rising to the sky world. Scholars. Stars. Thunder. Tradesmen. Transformation. Work.

111. Theft of a Duck

Herbert A. Giles, *Chinese Fairy Tales*. China

The wastrel Lin steals one of farmer Chang's ducks and begins to itch agonizingly all over. Then his chest is covered with feathers. He dreams that a man tells him he must go back to farmer Chang and make him say, "You dirty thief." Instead, Lin tells Mr. Chang that old Wang stole the duck and will repay him if farmer Chang calls him a thief. Mr. Chang laughs and says he has no time to call people bad names. Lin's skin feels so itchy now that he confesses, but still Mr. Chang refuses to use bad language. Finally, the farmer sees Lin's feathers and takes pity. Mr. Chang, at last, calls Lin a thief. That ends Lin's duck-stealing career.

Connections. Changes in attitude. Ducks. Enchantment. Farmers. Feathers. Humorous stories. Laziness. Names. Thieves. Transformation. Tricksters. Words. Work.

112. Chang Feng

Li Fu-Yen in Karl S. Y. Kao, *Classical Chinese Tales of the Supernatural and the Fantastic*. Honan, China

Chang Feng stops at the Inn of the Waylaying Mountain toward the end of the Yüan-ho dynasty. It is close to evening when he goes for a stroll and rolls around naked in some lovely grass. He discovers that he has become a tiger. Powerfully, Chang Feng springs across mountains and ravines. Nearing a village, he remembers that he has come to Fu-t'ang County to capture Inspector Cheng. He hides and waits. When Inspector Cheng arrives, Feng carries him up the mountain and eats him. Feng then returns to the jade-green grass and rolls around again to become human. He puts his clothes back on and walks to the inn, where everyone has been worried about him because a tiger has eaten Inspector Cheng. A few years later, Feng is telling this story after dinner, when the scholar Cheng Hsia pulls out a knife to avenge his father. The other guests intervene, and Feng changes his name and is sent south across the Huai River. The opinion is that Feng murdered Cheng unintentionally, whereas Hsia's action, if he killed Fen in revenge, would be punishable.

CONNECTIONS. Enchantment. Fathers and sons. Flesh-eating. Honan, China, stories from. Huai River. Inspectors. Justice. Revenge. Shape-shifting. Storytelling. Tigers. Transformation. Travelers. Waylaying Mountain.

113. The Fairy Grotto

Wolfram Eberhard, *Folktales of China*. Central China

The young cousins Liu Ch'en and Yüan Chao go into the hills to fetch water. They leave their pails by the stream and follow a path up to a cave where two fairies are playing chess on a large stone. As a white hare jumps up and down nearby, flowers bloom and fade. The boys watch until the game ends a few hours later. They tell the fairies they must leave, and the fairies give them each a reed with instructions to point it at the cave, which will open if they find things changed at home and return to this place. The boys find only decayed earth where they had left their buckets. Their homes in the village are gone. Two old men say they are descendants of Liu Ch'en and Yüan Chao seven generations ahead, but no one believes the boys. Disheartened, Liu Ch'en and Yüan Chao return to the cave, but cannot get in because they have lost their reeds. They die from beating their heads against the rock that seals the cave. The ruler of heaven takes pity and makes them the gods of good fortune and bad.

CONNECTIONS. Age, suddenly old. Central China, stories from. Chess. Despair. Enchantment. Fairies. Fortune. Foxes. Go. Gods and goddesses. Kitsune. Magical objects. Paduk. Rabbits and hares. Rip Van Winkle stories. Spirits. T'ien-t'ai Mountains. Time. Visu. Xianqi.

HOW ELSE THIS STORY IS TOLD. *Chinese variations:* The Fairy Grotto—Leslie Bonnet, *Chinese Folk and Fairy Tales*. Liu Ch'en and Juan Chao—Karl S. Y. Kao, *Classical Chinese Tales of the Supernatural and the Fantastic* (they become lost in the T'ien-t'ai Mountains and marry two young women). Wang Chih and the Magic Chess Game—Lim Sian-tek, *Folk Tales from China*. *Japanese variations:* The Adventures of Visu and Visu's Return—F. Hadland Davis, *Myths and Legends of Japan*. Visu the Woodsman and the Old Priest—D. L. Ashliman, *Folktexts*, Online (here, the two women are kitsune, fox spirits, playing go. Visu is punished for always wanting to pray and neglecting his family). *Korean variations:* Kee-Wee, A Korean Rip Van Winkle—Eleanore M. Jewett, *Which Was Witch?* (the magical old men are playing changki). While the Axe Handle Rots—Suzanne Crowder Han, *Korean Folk and Fairy Tales* (the woodcutter watches old men playing paduk, a game like go). The Woodcutter and the Fairies—James Huntley Grayson, *Myths and Legends from Korea* (the fairies are also playing paduk). The Woodcutter and the Old Men—Frances Carpenter, *Tales of a Korean Grandmother*.

114. The Fountain of Youth

Lafcadio Hearn. Japan

One day a poor woodcutter ventures further in the mountains than he has ever walked before and drinks from a spring he finds there. Then he sees his reflection in the water. He is young! He has hair and feels new strength. He runs home. His wife is terribly frightened by his changed appearance. Finally, he convinces her to go to the spring and become young again, too. When she hasn't returned for a long while, the man runs to the spring. A baby is there. The old woman has drunk too much water. He tenderly carries the baby back home.

CONNECTIONS. Age, suddenly young. Babies. Childlessness. Enchantment. Greed. Humorous stories. Husbands and wives. Magical water. Water. Woodcutters.

WHERE ELSE THIS STORY APPEARS. The Woodcutter and His Wife — Lafcadio Hearn, *Japanese Fairy Tales.* The Fountain of Youth — Lafcadio Hearn, *The Boy Who Drew Cats and Other Japanese Fairy Tales.*

HOW ELSE THIS STORY IS TOLD. *Japanese variations:* Baby Wifie/Akanbo Baasan — Daiji Kawasaki on kamishibai story cards. The Water That Restores Youth — Fanny Hagin Mayer, *Ancient Tales in Modern Japan.* **Korean variations:** The Fountain of Youth — Lindy Soon Curry, *A Tiger by the Tail.* The Fountain of Youth — Suzanne Crowder Han, *Korean Folk and Fairy Tales.* The Fountain of Youth — *Long Long Time Ago.* The Magic Spring — Nami Rhee. Well of Youth — James Huntley Grayson, *Myths and Legends from Korea* (a childless couple who have been scorned by a couple with children end up adopting them when the parents become babies after drinking too deeply from the well).

115. My King Has Donkey Ears

Tae Hung Ha, *Folk Tales of Old Korea.* Korea

The king of Silla, Kyungmoon-wang, hides the two donkey ears on his head under a turban. His tailor is sworn to secrecy, but the burden of keeping this secret is too great. Visiting a temple in Kyungju, he yells the secret about the king's long ears aloud in a bamboo grove and falls down dead. Now, whenever wind blows through the bamboo, the tailor's words sound. The king orders that palm trees replace the bamboo, but they, too, sing the secret aloud.

CONNECTIONS. Bamboo. Ears. Enchantment. Khans. Kings. Long ears. Magical objects. Physical difference. Secrets. Silla, place. Tailor. Talking bamboo. Tibetan People, stories from. Words.

HOW ELSE THIS STORY IS TOLD. *Chinese variation:* The Secret of the Khan — Eleanor Myers Jewett, *Wonder Tales from Tibet.*

116. The Eyelash of the Tiger

Y. T. Pyun, *Tales from Korea.* Korea

A strange Buddhist monk gives a traveler an eyelash to hold in front of one eye. When the traveler does, he sees animals and one child in a field where there appeared to be all people before. The monk somersaults and becomes an enormous tiger. The animals flee, but the child brandishes a stick. The tiger somersaults and becomes human again. He says he has been ordered by the mountain genius to bring him a certain girl, who sounds exactly like the traveler's niece. The traveler begs the tiger not to take her, but the tiger does not want to disobey orders from the mountain genius. At last the tiger relents and tells the traveler that what tigers fear the most is fire. With this advice, the traveler surrounds his niece with candles. The tiger arrives as he has been commanded to do, but since he cannot get to the girl, he goes away.

CONNECTIONS. Fear. Fire. Knowledge. Magical objects. Protection. Outsmarting supernatural opponents. Rescues. Shape-shifting. Tigers. Transformation. Travelers.

117. Little Sima and the Giant Bowl

Zhi Qu. China

The dragon who used to weave clouds in the sky goes to live in a river instead and creates drought in the village for one hundred years. Little Sima's family offers hospitality to an old beggar one night, and in the morning, he gives them a blue *gang* with a warning not to let it break. The pot is decorated with nine dragons. That day nine dragons begin weaving clouds in the sky again and bring a much needed rain to the village. When one of Little Sima's friends falls in the water one day, Little Sima cracks the gang so he will not drown. Because he chooses to save his friend's life over keeping the pot intact, the dragons come back to the sky, and the cracks in the gang disappear.

CONNECTIONS. Animation. Beggars. Bowls. Choices. Dragons. Drought. Magical objects. Old man, supernatural helper. Pots. Problem solvers. Rescues. Warnings. Water.

HOW ELSE THIS STORY IS TOLD. The Boy Ssu-ma Kuang — Lim Siantek, *More Folk Tales from China* (there are no dragons in this story where a boy breaks an earthenware jar to keep his friend from drowning). The Golden Dragon — Gregory Crawford, *Animals in the Stars*. Sze-Ma Gwang, the Quick One — Frances Alexander, *Pebbles from a Broken Jar*.

118. The Magic Bird

John Minford, *Favourite Folktales of China*. Mongolian People

Yirtegel, Khan of the East, is sure he can capture the magical talking bird in the forests of the north where other emperors and lords have failed. He finds the bird in its pine tree and easily catches it, but as they leave, the magic bird tells him it will fly away if there are sighs or silences. The bird begins to tell the Khan a story about a man who asks a hunter and his dog to watch a broken-down ox-cart filled with precious things while he looks for someone to repair it. When the owner does not return, the hunter leaves the dog as sole guard. The owner rewards the dog with silver, but the hunter beats his dog, thinking the dog stole the silver from the cart. The Khan sighs, thinking about the hunter's blind temper in the story, and the magic bird flies away. This time, when the Khan catches the bird, the bird tells a story about a woman who leaves her cat to watch the baby and wrongfully punishes the cat when she finds the baby's ear has been bitten. The Khan sighs, and again the bird flies away. Again, the Khan captures it. The third story the bird tells is about a man who wrongfully kills a crow that is trying to protect him. The Khan cannot help sighing again. This time, however, he does not try to catch the clever bird again.

CONNECTIONS. Anger. Birds. Captivity. Cleverness. Justice. Khans. Mongolian People, stories from. Storytellers. Talking birds. Yirtegel, Khan of the East.

HOW ELSE THIS STORY IS TOLD. The Talking Bird — Herbert A. Giles, *Chinese Fairy Tales*. The Magic Bird — Stephen Hallett, translator, in *The Magic Bird*.

119. The Sun Sisters

Margaret Read MacDonald, *Three-Minute Tales*. China

Two maidens who live on the moon are shy about having people stare up and watch them embroider. They tell their brother they would like to live in the sun. He tells them that many more people will see them if they are out during the day. But he agrees to switch places. When people look up at the sun now, the sisters stick needles in their eyes.

CONNECTIONS. Discontent. Embroidery. Golden needles. Heavenly beings. Moon. Needles. Shyness. Sisters and brothers. Sun. Trades.

HOW ELSE THIS STORY IS TOLD. Golden Needles— Emily Cing and Ko-Shee Ching, *Golden Needles; Three Treasures.* The Sisters in the Sun — Frances Carpenter, *Tales of a Chinese Grandmother.*

120. Offering Sacrifice to the Fire Goddess

Liu Haiqi, *A Museum of Chinese Classic Stories*, Volume 3. Oroqen People

A mother in the Greater Hinanling Mountains stabs at the campfire when her young son's hand is burned. Afterwards, though, she can no longer make fires. She returns to the original campfire, where an old woman now sits beside the flames, bleeding. The old woman says that the mother hurt her. She realizes that the woman is the Fire Goddess and begs for forgiveness. The Goddess gives her a few embers, wrapped in bark, to light her fires at home.

CONNECTIONS. Anger. Blame. Consequences. Fire. Fire Goddess. Forgiveness. Gods and goddesses. Mothers and sons. Oroqen People, stories from.

121. The Phoenix and Her City

Kathleen Ragan, *Fearless Girls, Wise Women & Beloved Sisters*. Hui People, China

Seven Phoenix Sisters live on a mountain peak south of the Yangtze River, where people are happy and the land is healthy. To the north, though, in Ningxia Plain, people suffer because the Yellow River is too shallow to irrigate the dry fields. The wild goose brings the youngest Phoenix Sister to Ningxia, where she is warmly welcomed. The Phoenix works tirelessly to make Ningxia so green and lovely and decides to stay. Then a western tribe attacks and destroys everything. The Phoenix herself becomes a fortress city for three months. When the enemy withdraws and people can farm again, the Phoenix asks the wild goose to tell her sisters. However, tribal chiefs, warlords, emperors, and landlords move in and exploit people, conscript them into military service, and rob their belongings. Ningxia Plain goes dry again. One greedy official plans to steal the gold pony he has heard is sunk in Heiquan Lake. He cuts the Phoenix's throat so she will not know, but the Phoenix's heart remains alive and her blood flows into a new canal. An old ahong cries that the Phoenix told him she was being killed, and people mourn for nine days and nights. Then the Phoenix reappears in his dream to say that she will rise again and turn Ningxia beautiful after ninety-nine years, when a red cloud appears over the Liupan Mountains.

CONNECTIONS. Ahongs. Birds. Drought. Ecology. Foretellings. Geese. Greed. Heiquan Lake. Hui People, stories from. Irrigation. Liupan Mountains. Magical objects. Murder. Ningxia, China, stories from. Ningxia Plain. Phoenix. Promises. Rebirth. Transformation. War. Water.

WHERE ELSE THIS STORY APPEARS. The Phoenix and Her City — Shujian Li and Karl W. Luckert, *Mythology and Folklore of the Hui* (from Ningxia).

122. The First Storyteller

Louise and Yuan-Hsi Kuo, *Chinese Folk Tales*. China

This is the story of the first storyteller. When the king abandons his blind son in the mountains, animals care for him. The mountain and earth gods tell him stories, and the oriole teaches him to sing. When he is seven, a fairy teaches him to play the jade p'i-p'a that has fallen from heaven. Now the young boy says goodbye to his friends and goes off to make his living by singing and telling stories. Everything he learns and everyone he meets make his own stories deeper and richer. Then two hersdmen quarrel about which one he should go away with to tell stories to. When the horse owner takes him and runs, the cattle owner goes to see the king. The king listens to both sides; then he asks the boy to speak. As the youth tells how he was abandoned by his parents, the king and queen realize that he is their son. They want him to stay, but the storyteller keeps roaming. He teaches a limping beggar to tell stories in verse and keep time with specially-fashioned clappers. With one string from his p'i-p'a, he makes a measuring rod for Lu Pan, who goes on to construct great, strong things; another he gives to the scholar Chiang T'ai Kung for fishing in the River Wei. The three of them —carpenter, fisherman, and scholar share a wonderful friendship.

CONNECTIONS. Abandonment. Acknowledgment by father. Chiang T'ai Kung, scholar. Children. Conflict. Education. Fairies. Fathers and sons. Friendship. Identity. Kindness from animals. Kings. Lu Pan, builder. Music. P'i-p'a. Princes. Reconciliation. Wei River. Storytellers. Talents.

123. The Legend of Moody Mount Iwate

Samira Kirollos, *The Wind Children and Other Tales from Japan*. Japan

For hundred of years in Tōhoko and through all the seasons, strong, tall Mount Iwate has admired the gentle Mountain of the Divine Princess who stands near him. Finally, he asks her to marry him, and she consents. However, once she agrees, Mount Iwate grows bored. Now, he cannot stop looking at all the beautiful changes happening on elegant Mount Hayachine. He tries to break his engagement with the Mountain of the Divine Princess, but she flings a clump of her hair at him that becomes a forest on his side. Angry, Mount Iwate calls for Mount Heimt, the messenger mountain to move Mount Iwate far away. Mount Iwate begins to cry rivers, and the sympathetic messenger mountain only moves her to the Kitakami River, where Mount Iwate can still see her. Mount Iwate cuts off Mount Heimt's head, which lands at the top of Mount Kurakake. His anger continues to boil. For the next thirty-three years, Mount Iwate blows out smoke and ash, while the Mountain of the Divine Princess watches.

CONNECTIONS. Anger. Betrothal. Compassion. Conflict. Divine Princess, Mountain of the. Hayachine, Mount. Heimt, Mount. Iwate, Mount. Kitakami River. Kurakake, Mount. Love. Mountains. Selfishness. Tōhoko, place. Unfaithfulness.

~ IV ~

Supernatural Loves

124. Urashima Taro

Rafe Martin, *Mysterious Tales of Japan*. Japan

The fisherman Urashima Taro stops some boys from teasing a giant sea turtle. Later, out in his boat, he falls asleep and dreams that a woman rises from the sea. When he opens his eyes, the woman is there. She tells him she is the daughter of the Dragon King, who, because of Urashima's kindness to his messenger turtle, has sent her to see if the fisherman would like to marry her. Urashima Taro goes with the Dragon King's daughter to the Island Where Summer Never Dies. For three years, Urashima enjoys the wonders on that island, but then he wants to return home, for he never said goodbye to his parents and friends. His wife warns that he will never return if he does go. When Urashima Taro insists he will just be going to visit, she hands him a black lacquered box tied with a silken cord. She tells him not to open it. Back on the mainland, everything looks different, and Urashima Taro knows no one. An old man remembers a story about a fisherman with that name who disappeared three hundred years ago. Sad now, Urashima Taro opens the box, thinking perhaps it holds the secret to what has happened. A mist rises, and he suddenly grows old and turns to dust.

CONNECTIONS. Age, suddenly old. Death. Dragon Princess. Enchantment. Fishermen. Homesickness. Husbands and wives. Island Where Summer Never Dies. Journeys. Kindness to animals. Loss. Love. Mysteries. Rip Van Winkle stories. Sadness. Supernatural wives. Taiwan, stories from. Time. Transformation. Turtles. Urashima Taro. Warnings. Wonders.

WHERE ELSE THIS STORY APPEARS. Urashima Taro—Rafe Martin in David Holt and Bill Mooney, *Ready-to-Tell Tales*.

HOW ELSE THIS STORY IS TOLD. *Japanese variations:* The Adventures of a Fisher Lad—Eric Quayle, *The Shining Princess*. The Fisher Boy and the Turtle—Juliet Piggott, *Japanese Fairy Tales*. *The Fisherman Under the Sea*—Matsutani, Miyoko. *Seashore Story*—Taro Yashima. The Story of Urashima, the Fisher Boy—Alan Lesie Whitehorn, *Wonder Tales of Old Japan*. The Story of Urashima Taro, the Fisher Lad—Yei Theodora Ozaki, *Japanese Fairy Book*. The Story of Urashima Taro the Fisherman—Yasuda, Yuri, *Old Tales of Japan*, Vol. I. Uraschi-mataro and the Turtle—Andrew Lang, *Pink Fairy Book* and in Mike Ashley, *The Giant Book of Myths and Legends*. Urashima—Joanna Cole, *Best-Loved Folktales of the World*. Urashima—Japanese Fairy Tale Series, No. 2. Urashima—Lafcadio Hearn, *Japanese Fairy Tales*. Urashima—Grace James, *Green Willow*. Urashima—Teresa Pierce Williston, *Japanese Fairy Tales*. Urashima and the Tortoise—F. Hadland Davis, *Myths and Legends of Japan*. Urashima the Fisherman—Royall Tyler, *Japanese Tales* and in Jane Yolen, *Favorite Folktales from around the World*. Urashima Taro—Keshi Nakajima, *Japanese Traditional Tales*. Urashima Taro—Robert Nye, *Out of This World and Back Again*. Urashima Taro—Florence Sakade, *Urashima Taro* and *Japanese Children's Favorite Stories*, Book Two. Urashima Taro—Keigo Seki, *Folktales of Japan*. Urashima

Taro — Ichiro Wakabayashi, Kamishibai story cards. Urashima-Taro — Shoichi Shiomi at *Kids Web Japan*, Online. Urashima Taro and the Princess of the Sea — Yoshiko Uchida, *The Dancing Kettle and Other Japanese Tales*. Urashima Taro and the Turtle — Andrew Lang, *A World of Fairy Tales*. **Taiwanese variation:** Curious Taro — Cora Cheney, *Tales from a Taiwan Kitchen*.

125. The Pearl That Shone by Night

John Minford, *Favourite Folktales of China*. Han People

The Dragon King of the Eastern Sea does not want his beautiful and intelligent daughter to marry the orphan Ah Er, whom General Eel has found for her. He protests that the hunter may be honest and brave, but he does not come from the sea. A courtier proposes a test. In the night, Ah Er wakes and tells his brother Ah Da about the dream he has had that a maiden waits for him by the riverbank. Ah Da slips off to the riverbank himself, but Ah Er soon joins him. The maiden says that she will marry whichever one of them can get the luminous pearl that is kept by the Dragon King of the Eastern Sea. She hands them each a clasp that can open a path for them through the water. They do not know where the Eastern Sea is and separate to find it. On a borrowed horse, Ah Da arrives at a village that has been overwhelmed with floodwaters. Old villagers suggest Ah Da ask the Dragon King if they may borrow his Golden Dipper to bail their fields. They give Ah Da bread and a boat. Two days later, Eh Er, on foot, arrives. He works beside the villagers for a whole day and tells them he is going to the Dragon King and promises to ask for the Golden Dipper. Ah Er meets up with Ah Da on the shore of the Eastern Sea. Ah Da has been afraid to cross because the waves are high. Ah Er holds the clasp and dives, and the water parts. Ah Da follows, and they reach the palace. The Dragon King tells them they may each take one piece from his treasure house. Ah Da chooses a giant pearl whose light fills the room; Ah Er asks for the Golden Dipper. Ah Da gallops straight to the maiden with the luminous pearl; Ah Er first brings the Golden Dipper to the villagers and helps them bail. On the ground villagers find a black pearl inside an oyster which they give to him. Meanwhile, Ah Da's pearl loses its light. Ah Er arrives. He tells the maiden he does not have the luminous pearl, but when he takes out the black pearl, it begins to glow.

CONNECTIONS. Brothers. Clasps. Deceit. Dragon King. Dreams. Eastern Sea. Fathers and daughters. Floods. Golden Dipper. Han People, stories from. Helpfulness. Heroes, men. Hunters. Kindness. Love. Maidens. Matches, marriage. Pearls. Quests. Supernatural wives. Tests. Unselfishness.

HOW ELSE THIS STORY IS TOLD. *The Luminous Pearl* — Betty L. Torre.

126. The Daughter of the Dragon King

Frances Carpenter, *Tales of a Chinese Grandmother*. China

Liu Ye studies hard, but he does not pass the government examinations. Sadly walking home, he meets a young woman tending goats on a riverbank. She tells him that her husband, the son of the dragon in the River Ching is punishing her because of lies told by jealous servants. She gives him a letter to take to her father, the Dragon King in Lake Tung Ting. An armored man escorts Liu Ye to the Dragon King's crystal palace at the bottom of the lake. The Dragon King and his court all cry when they read the daughter's letter. His elder brother, a red gold dragon, flies in carrying the Dragon King's daughter. She wants to marry Liu Ye. He likes her, but he is afraid and leaves the sea. The first two women he marries die young. Then Liu Ye marries a young widow whom a matchmaker has found. After their first son is born, his wife tells him that she is the Dragon King's daughter. They move to a palace in Tung Ting Lake.

CONNECTIONS. Crystal Palace. Dragon King. Dragon Princess. Dragons. Fate. Fathers and daughters. Fear. Golden dragon. Han People, stories from. Herders. Imperial examination. Identity. Letters. Love. Maidens. Matches, marriage. Messengers. Rescues. Sadness. Scholars. Sea. Secrets. Shape-shifting. Supernatural wives. Tung-Ting Lake. Underwater kingdom.

HOW ELSE THIS STORY IS TOLD. The Dragon King's Daughter — *Dragon Tales: A Collection of Chinese Stories.* The Dragon-King's Daughter — Lim Sian-tek, *Folk Tales from China.* Dragon Princess — Haiwang Yuan, *The Magic Lotus Lantern and Other Tales from the Han Chinese.*

127. The Wife from the Dragon Palace

Fanny Hagin Mayer, *Ancient Tales in Modern Japan.* Kagoshima, Japan

When a young man cannot sell any of his flowers one day, he throws them into the sea for the Dragon God. A tortoise arrives to bring him to the Dragon Palace and advises him to ask for the Dragon God's daughter if he is offered anything. After three years, though it seems like three days, he does leave with the Dragon God's beautiful daughter. His mother has died of starvation. The Dragon God's daughter taps his mother back to life with three strokes of the Life Whip. She also creates a house, rice, and a storehouse for them with a magic mallet. The feudal lord wants her for his wife and demands an impossible amount of rice or the young man's wife. That night, the Dragon God's daughter beckons at the shore. Several hundred horses come out of the water loaded with rice. When the feudal lord demands one thousand fathoms of rope, she again obtains it from the sea. On New Year's Day, the feudal lord calls for rowdy entertainment, and she lets several hundred identical men out of one little box to dance. When he calls for quiet entertainment, she bring several hundred men with swords in their hands out of another little box. The swordsmen cut off everyone's heads. A river appears that washes the feudal lord and his men out to sea.

CONNECTIONS. Crystal Palace. Dragon King. Dragon Princess. Dragons. Enchantment. Faithfulness. Hui People, stories from. Kogoshima, Japan, stories from. Life-giving. Love. Mallets. New Year's. Ningxia, China, stories from. Nobles and lords. Revenge. Sea. Shaanxi, China, stories from. Snails. Spirits. Supernatural wives. Time. Tortoises. Ultimatums. Underwater kingdom. Warriors. Wife-stealing. Whips. Zithers.

HOW ELSE THIS STORY IS TOLD. **Chinese variation:** The Zither Master Hasang — Yang Zhouwen in Shujiang Li and Karl W. Luckert, *Mythology and Folklore of the Hui* (in this tale from Ningxia and Shaanxi, a dragon girl comes to the youngest of seven sons who plays the zither so well). **Korean variations:** The Snail Lady — *Long Long Time Ago.* The Snail Lady — Suzanne Crowder Han, *Korean Folk and Fairy Tales* (she gives a note to the Dragon King, who helps him win back his wife from the king). The Snail Woman — James Riordan, *Korean Folktales.*

128. Dragon Girl

Yan Fen in *Dragon Tales.* China

Tired of life in the underwater palace, Dragon Girl, the Daughter of White Dragon, wanders far from the Lancang River when she is sixteen. She tells a young farmer she has lost her way. Yan Maoyang invites her to his small bamboo cottage, but worries about sharing the house with her as night approaches. Dragon Girl tells him who she is and asks to become his wife. Dragon Girl helps the villagers in Mengyang Plain learn how to swim, how to build a bridge across the river, and how to summon rain. The headman hears about Dragon Girl. When ninety-nine trees walk away on the Jinghong Plain, Yan Maoyang is summoned to help. He worries about leaving Dragon Girl while she is pregnant, but the villagers promise to care for her. When Dragon Girl sends word, the Dragon King in the Lancang River sends fish and shrimp to help Yan Maoyang fish out the trees. The headman is now alarmed about Yan Maoyang's power and kills him. Furious, Dragon Girl sends word, and the Dragon King's forces block the Lancang River with boulders, which causes a huge flood and much hardship in Jinghong. The headman kneels before Dragon Girl and begs her forgiveness. Eventually, Dragon Girl asks her father to let the river flow again. She returns to the dragon palace and gives birth.

CONNECTIONS. Anger. Community. Devotion. Discontent. Dragon King. Dragon Princess. Dragons. Farmers. Fear. Floods. Forgiveness. Headmen. Jinghong Plain. Lancang River. Loss. Love. Maidens. Mengyang Plain. Mysteries. Murder. Pregnancy. Revenge. Supernatural wives. Trees. White Dragon.

129. The Dragon Prince: A Chinese Beauty and the Beast Tale

Laurence Yep. Southern China

A snake slid back into the water turns into a dragon, which now has captured a poor farmer. In return for his release, the farmer promises that he will give the dragon one of his seven daughters in marriage. Only the youngest, Seven, agrees to go. The dragon soars up with her and then down to his underwater kingdom. With her acceptance of him, the dragon transforms into a human prince. However, Seven becomes homesick and asks to go home for a visit. There, Seven's jealous third sister tries to drown her in order to take her place as princess. The prince, however, follows his heart to find his true wife.

CONNECTIONS. Beauty and the Beast stories. Deceit. Disguises. Dragon Prince. Dragons. Homesickness. Jealousy. Matches, marriage. Shape-shifting. Southern China, stories from. Supernatural husbands. Transformation. Underwater kingdom.

130. White Wave: A Chinese Tale

Diane Wolkstein. Southern China

One night, the shy farmer Kuo Ming stops to pick up a white stone that turns out to be a lovely moon snail. He prepares fresh leaves for the snail in a jar at home. When he returns for dinner, he finds food on the table. No one is there. After he peeks and sees a beautiful girl in an iridescent gown leap out of the jar one morning, he watches her every morning. Her presence makes him less lonely. One day he needs to touch her long black hair and rushes in. She says she must go, for she is the moon goddess. She will leave him her shell to call for White Wave if he ever needs her. She rises with the wind. Kuo Ming begins to work on a shrine for the moon goddess out of beautiful grey, white, and pink stones. There has been a bad harvest, and, weakened, the farmer accidentally knocks her shell out of the jar. He calls for White Wave and enough rice pours out to give him strength to go on.

CONNECTIONS. Farmers. Han People, stories from. Kindness to animals. Loss. Love. Maidens. Moon goddess. Mysteries. Rescues. Rice. Rising to the sky world. Shanghai, China, stories from. Shape-shifting. Shells. Shrines. Snails. Southern China, stories from. Supernatural wives. Transformation. Wind.

How Else This Story Is Told. *Chinese variations:* The Field-Snail Fairy — Haiwang Yuan, *The Magic Lotus Lantern and Other Tales from the Han Chinese.* Kertong — Carol Kendall and Yao-wen Li, *Sweet and Sour.* The Pure Maiden of the White Waters — Karl S. Y. Kao, *Classical Chinese Tales of the Supernatural and the Fantastic.* The River Snail Girl — Jia Jie in Howard Giskin, *Chinese Folktales* (from Shanghai). Two Dutiful Sons — Frances Carpenter, *Tales of a Chinese Grandmother* (the shell maiden story is included in this chapter). *The Shell Woman and the King* — Laurence Yep (here, the shell maiden, who can change form, comes from the sea and stays with her husband, after she uses magic to thwart the king who abducted her). *Korean variation:* The Mud-Snail Fairy — Zong In-Sob, *Folk Tales from Korea.*

131. The Princess and the Fisherman

Yoshiko Uchida, *The Dancing Kettle.* Japan

A fisherman pulls up only one clam this day, but his boat grows heavier and harder to row, and the clam grows larger and then opens. A beautiful, but sad, young woman is there, bewildered for she does not know where she belongs. The fisherman brings her home, and his mother welcomes her. Everyone in the village wants to meet this true princess, for that is what she seems. She begins to weave and tells the fisherman he must not enter the room for twenty-eight days. Then she presents him with wonderful cloth to sell for not less than 3,000 yen. No one can afford to buy the cloth, until a wealthy old man arrives who brings him to a palace, serves him dinner, and orders that the money be sent to the fisherman's home. The old man then summons a cloud and goes up to heaven. The palace vanishes, but the three bags of gold the fisherman finds at home are real. Now the princess says that she must leave him, as she was sent for just this while to bring him happiness.

Connections. Changes in fortune. Clams. Clouds. Fishermen. Happiness. Loss. Love. Maidens. Mysteries. Old man, supernatural helper. Palaces. Rising to the sky world. Shapeshifting. Spirits. Supernatural wives. Taiwan, stories from. Weavers.

How Else This Story Is Told. *Taiwanese variation:* The Clam Girl — Cora Cheney, *Tales from a Taiwan Kitchen.*

132. The Pagoda Tree

Linda Jennings, *Stories from Around the World.* China

Poor Tung Yung begins to regret his decision to work for a rich merchant for three years to pay for his father's funeral. He rests under a pagoda tree on his long walk over the mountains to the merchant's house. A young woman appears and suggests that they marry so she can come with him to help. The pagoda tree serves as their matchmaker. The merchant says that Tung Yung's wife can stay only if she weaves twenty-four pieces of linen in three days. She accomplishes this, seemingly effortlessly, and the merchant next demands fifty pieces of silk. Peeking, Tung Yung sees a white crane drop a shuttle into his wife's hand. When she throws it at the loom, it begins to weave all by itself. Now, the greedy merchants says he will release Tung Yung if his wife embroiders all the silk in ten days. On the ninth night Tung Yung sees six maidens and seven cranes assisting his wife. His wife tells him the cranes are her sisters. With the exquisite embroidery done, the merchant must let them go. On the way home Tung Yung thanks the pagoda tree for giving him his wonderful wife. Once they return home, however, the young woman tells him she is an immortal sent to help him and now must go. She leaves bales of silk with him, and seven cranes accompany her up into the air.

CONNECTIONS. Changes in fortune. Cranes. Embroidery. Gods and goddesses. Gratitude. Kindness. Loss. Love. Magical objects. Maidens. Matches, marriage. Merchants. Pagoda trees. Poverty. Rescues. Rising to the sky world. Sadness. Spirits. Supernatural wives. Ultimatums. Weavers.

HOW ELSE THIS STORY IS TOLD. The Legend of Tchi-Niu — Pearl S. Buck, *Fairy Tales of the Orient*. Three Hundred Yards of Silk That Saved the Devoted Son — Rena Krasno and Yeng-Fong Chiang, *Cloud Weavers*. Tung Yung, the Filial Son — Karl S. Y. Kao, *Classical Chinese Tales of the Supernatural and the Fantastic*.

133. The Peacock Maiden

Folk Tales from China, Third Series. Tai People

Chaushutun is born to the queen at the moment a man-child crawls out from the foot of a white elephant and vanishes. Armed with a magic bow, Chaushutun leaves Monbanja to find a maiden who will win his heart. The old hunter Gohagen brings Chaushutun to Lake Langsna where they see seven peacocks fly down and become maidens when they take off their peacock cloaks. Chaushutun falls in love with the seventh sister, Namarona, but then all of the sisters don their cloaks and fly away. To discover how to make the peacock maidens stay, Chaushutun follows an otter into the lake. Grateful to Gohagen for having released him from a net a while back, Bahna, the God of Waters lends Chaushutun his magic hook. The peacock maidens return, and Chaushutun hooks Namarona's cloak so she cannot fly off with the others. They begin talking, and Namarona is enchanted with his eloquence and intelligence. Chaushutun proposes to her. Wrapped in her cloak, they fly to his home. A plotting minister Mahashen tries to convince the king that Namarona is a witch, while also encouraging neighboring kings to abduct her. With Chaushutun away fighting, the king believes the minister's false bad news that they are losing the battle and blames Namarona. On the day of her execution, she begs to dance for the king and queen in her robe. Once it is on, she flies away. Chaushutun returns victorious, and the king is ashamed that he lost Namarona. Namarona has told a hermit to dissuade Chaushutun from following her, but, but seeing how determined the prince is, the hermit sends a monkey to guide him through dangers. Chaushutun encounters white-hot waters that melt his sword tip, crosses an enormous black python bridge, opens a passage through three mountains, travels through sandstorms and flying stones, loses his monkey to man-eating birds, and flies to Mongwudoon with one of their feathers. To test his love for her, Namarona's father makes Chaushutun use his bow to destroy a boulder that has been causing a river to flood and identify Namora's finger through a hole in the wall. All trials done, Chaushutun and Namarona ride off together on a flying horse and a flying elephant.

CONNECTIONS. Bahna, God of Waters. Birth, unusual. Clothes. Dancing. Devotion. Distrust. Elephants. Fairies. False accusations. Fathers and sons. Flying elephants. Flying horses. God of Waters. Gods and goddesses. Hooks. Horses. Kindness to animals. Kings. Love. Maidens. Ministers. Peacocks, supernatural. Plots. Supernatural wives. Tai People, stories from. Tests. Travelers. Underwater kingdom.

WHERE ELSE THIS STORY APPEARS. The Peacock Maiden — *The Peacock Maiden: Folk Tales from China* and at D.L. Ashliman, *Folktexts*, Online.

134. In the Moonlight Mist

Daniel San Souci. Korea

A woodcutter hides a deer from hunters one afternoon, and the grateful deer wants to fulfill the woodcutter's wish to have a loving wife and family. The deer tells him to climb to the top of the mountain on the next full moon and take the clothes of one of the heavenly maidens who will come to bathe in the lake. The woodcutter is uncertain about tricking someone into loving him, but the deer reassures him that his friend the Mountain Spirit will soften the maiden's heart. The deer warns that the woodcutter should not return the maiden's clothes until their second child is born. The woodcutter cuts his way through to the lake and sees five stars float down and become maidens. He takes the clothes belonging to one and hides. When the others leave, she cannot. He brings her home and treats her kindly. One baby girl is born. The wife misses heaven so much, that he shows the clothes to her to console her, but she slips into them and floats up to the sky holding their baby. The woodcutter is miserable. The deer tells him that when the heavenly maidens lower their silver bucket, he should climb in to go see his wife. The woodcutter does not want to leave his mother alone on earth and brings her to the bucket, too. However, the weight is too great. The mother says he should be the one to go, but he thinks she may have some joy in heaven and jumps out. Moved by the woodcutter's sacrifice, the heavenly king sends a dragon-horse to bring the woodcutter up to join his family.

CONNECTIONS. Clothes. Deer. Dragons. Fairies. Filial devotion. Gratitude. Heaven. Heavenly King. Homesickness. Husbands and wives. Journeys. Kindness to animals. Love. Maidens. Mountain spirit. Reunions. Rising to the sky world. Sacrifice. Spirits. Stars. Supernatural wives. Transformation. Warnings. Woodcutters.

HOW ELSE THIS STORY IS TOLD. The Heavenly Maiden and the Woodcutter — James Huntley Grayson, *Myths and Legends from Korea*. The Heavenly Maiden and the Woodcutter — *Long Long Time Ago*. The Heavenly Maiden and the Wood cutter — Zong Yong-Ha in Zong In-Sob, *Folk Tales from Korea*. The Legend of the Sang-Pal-Dam Pools — Y.T. Pyun, *Tales from Korea*. The Nymph and the Woodcutter — Chun Shin-Yong, *Korean Folk Tales*. The Sky Maiden — Yu Chai-Shin, Shiu L. Kong, and Ruth Y. Yu, *Korean Folk Tales*. Son-Nyo the Nymph and the Woodcutter — James Riordan, *Korean Folk-tales*. The Wife from Another World — Eleanore M. Jewett, *Which Was Witch?* The Woodcutter and the Heavenly Maiden — Suzanne Crowder Han, *Korean Folk and Fairy Tales*.

135. The Bride's Red Silk Handkerchief

Liu Haiqi, *Museum of Chinese Classic Stories*, Volume 5. Tujia People

The young hunter Pengshen lives in the mountain village of Xiopurang in western Hunan Province. For several days now the corn cakes he has hung from a tree for lunch have been replaced by hot rice and steaming salamander meat. Pengshen hides, and a beautiful girl emerges from a cave. As he approaches her, a wind picks up, and she turns into a white crane and flies back into the cave, which closes. Entranced by the White Crane Fairy Maiden, Pengshen brings one feather home. The feather changes into a poetry book. He reads that the White Crane Fairy Maiden is his wife, but that the village head's daughter is coming. Suddenly the village head's ugly, lazy daughter Kaliegu is there, and though, she falls instantly in love with him, Pengshen is repulsed. The book pages turn by themselves to foretell what will occur. A wind brings the suddenly ill Kaliegu home unconscious. Kaliegu's father wants to force Pengshen to marry her. Then, he demands that Pengshen bring the White Crane Fairy Maiden to be his concubine. Pengshen goes back to the cave, but it stays shut for three days. He is arrested, and the village head takes possession of the book. After the first poem, Kaliegu runs into the room well, saying she will marry the village head, but then she falls ill again and disappears. The book becomes a feather, which Pengshen chases to White Crane Cave. There he falls down unconscious. The White Crane Fairy Maiden transforms herself into an ugly girl to meet the village head, who no longer desires to marry her. Hiding her head beneath a red silk handkerchief to avoid recognition, she marries Pengshen. To this day, Tujia brides also cover their faces in red silk.

CONNECTIONS. Beauty. Books. Brides. Caves. Cranes. Disguises. Fathers and daughters. Feathers. Headmen. Hunan Province. Hunters. Illness. Love. Maidens. Physical difference. Red handkerchief. Shape-shifting. Supernatural wives. Traditions. Transformation. Tujia People, China, stories from. Ugliness. Ultimatums. Wind. Xiopurang, village.

136. The White Bird's Wife

Eleanor Myers Jewett, *Wonder Tales from Tibet*. Tibetan People

An old man who loves his goats more than his daughters beats them each day when one goat disappears. The third daughter, Ananda, follow hoofprints to a cave with a red door. Inside she finds a jeweled palace empty, except for a white bird in a cage. He says he will restore the lost goats if she will marry him. She decides it is better to live with the bird than with her father's anger and agrees. However, Ananda grows lonely. The white bird permits her to go to the village fair. There she falls in love with a mysterious man on a white horse. An old woman advises her that he is the white bird and tells Ananda to burn his cage and everything in it before he returns to keep him as a man. Ananda does, but when the rider returns, he sorrowfully tells her that she burned his soul with the feathers. For the next seven days and nights, good and evil spirits fight for him. She can win back his soul by pounding on the mother-of-pearl door for all of that time. Ananda beats continuously, but falls asleep exhausted in the last hour. Evil spirits carry off her husband, and she journeys to find him hauling water. She builds him a golden cage and sings with all her heart to woo his soul back into the bird.

CONNECTIONS. Beauty and the Beast stories. Birds. Cages. Devotion. Fathers and daughters. Feathers. Goats. Golden cage. Horseman, white. Loneliness. Love. Old woman, supernatural helper. Palaces. Rescues. Shape-shifting. Singing. Spirits. Supernatural husbands. Talking birds. Tests. Tibetan People, stories from. Transformation.

HOW ELSE THIS STORY IS TOLD. The White Rooster — Frederick and Audrey Hyde-Chambers, *Tibetan Folk Tales.*

137. The Fox Wife

Yoko Kawashima Watkins, *Tales from the Bamboo Grove*. Japan

Though he is so poor, Shinkichi, a kind young farmer, dreams of marrying a pretty young woman from the village. When a maiden faints by his rice field one hot summer day, he carries her to his home. She recovers and offers to work to repay him. She also tells him that her family was killed by wolves. She stays, and they marry and have a boy, Morime. One time Morime becomes so ill that Shinkichi stays to help nurse him and neglects his field. He is too tired to plant, but privately worries about how he will be able to pay the rice tax. He does not tell his wife, but he is afraid they will lose the rice field to the landowner. Walking to the field, Shinkichi sees that it has been planted, but that the seedlings are upside down. He tells his wife the news when he comes home. She leaps out, turning into a white fox as she runs. The white fox sings a song to the field that it should thrive to feed her son, but appear poor to the inspector. When the fox returns, she tells Shinkichi she must go. After that, Shinkichi's rice plants grow healthily for him, but fool the inspector's eyes.

CONNECTIONS. Changes in fortune. Children. Devotion. Farmers. Foxes. Illness. Kindness. Kitsune. Loss. Love. Maidens. Shape-shifting. Singing. Skin. Spirits. Supernatural wives. Taxes. Upside-down seedlings. Wishes.

HOW ELSE THIS STORY IS TOLD. *Chinese variation:* The Fox Wife Turns a Somersault — Lotta Carswell Hume, *Favorite Children's Stories from China and Tibet* (here the farmer takes the maiden's fox skin. They raise a family, and one day he returns her skin and she slips out the door). *Japanese variations:* The Fox Wife — Richard M. Dorson, *Folk Legends of Japan*. The Fox Wife — Fanny Hagin Mayer, *Ancient Tales in Modern Japan*.

138. The Blind Serpent-Wife

Richard M. Dorson, *Folk Legends of Japan*. Japan

The village headman of Fukae-mura invites in a girl who has taken shelter from the rain under his eaves. She says she is from Higo, and the headman thinks she may be a good wife for the young village doctor. The doctor and the girl do marry and have a son. One day, however, the doctor's mother sees a big serpent coiled around the child, snoring. The doctor wants a divorce. The woman sadly says she is a serpent from the pond on Mt. Fugen and has come to serve the doctor in gratitude for his having saved her a few years back. She tells him to come to the pond if he cannot find a wetnurse for their son and leaves. The doctor cannot find a nurse and brings their child to the pond. The wife emerges from the pond as a woman and gouges out one of her eyeballs. The baby begins to lick the eyeball and milk comes out. The doctor leaves with the eyeball, but patrolling samurai stop him. They take the bulging jewel ball they find in his shirt to their feudal lord, who gives it to the shogun in Edo. When the child cries because he has no milk, the doctor brings him back to Fugen Pond. The serpent-mother gouges out her other eyeball, even though now she is blind. Samurai rob the doctor of this eyeball, too. The serpent-wife is furious with the samurai. Perhaps that is the cause of a severe earthquake in the area around Fukae-mura.

CONNECTIONS. Babies. Blindness. Devotion. Doctors. Earthquakes. Eyeballs. Eyes. Fugen Pond. Fukae-mura, village. Loss. Love. Maidens. Milk. Revenge. Sacrifice. Samurai. Serpents. Shape-shifting. Supernatural wives. Thieves. Transformation.

HOW ELSE THIS STORY IS TOLD. The Blind Serpent — Yoshimatsu Suzuki, *Japanese Legends and Folk-Tales*. The Snake Wife — Fanny Hagin Mayer, *Ancient Tales in Modern Japan*.

139. The Noble Tiger

Yu Chai-Sin, Shiu L. Kong, and Ruth W. Yu, *Korean Folk Tales*. Korea

Legend says that if you pray nightly at the pagoda near Hyung Yun Temple, your wish will be granted. One night during the reign of King Wonsong in Silla, Kim Hyon senses a maiden behind him while he is praying. They stroll by the pagoda every night and fall in love. One night Kim Hyon walks her home to a thatched hut, where an old woman says they need to hide Kim Hyon from the woman's brothers. Suddenly three tigers roar that they smell a man. The old woman tells them that heaven is displeased that they have killed so many humans. The maiden tells the tigers that they have broken their promise to Buddha not to hurt living things. She tells them she will sacrifice her life for them. The tigers weep and leave. The young woman asks Kim Hyon if he will be the one to kill her. She says that she will run wild as a tiger in the marketplace, and he shall chase her into the forest, kill her, and claim the king's reward. Kim Hyon chases the tiger through the village and into the forest, but then he cannot kill her. His love changes back into a woman. As they embrace, she seizes Kim Hyon's sword and stabs herself. There, in the forest Kim Hyon is now holding a beautiful tiger. Remembering her fondly and with sadness, he uses the reward money to build "The Temple of Tiger's Wishes."

CONNECTIONS. Brothers and sisters. Buddhism. Choices. Killing. Loss. Love. Maidens. Old woman, supernatural helper. Prayer. Promises. Punishment. Respect for life. Rewards. Sacrifice. Shape-shifting. Suicide. Supernatural beloveds. Temples. Tigers. Transformation.

HOW ELSE THIS STORY IS TOLD. The Beautiful Tigress— Tae Hung Ha, *Folk Tales of Old Korea*. The Grateful Tiger — Kim So-un, *Korean Children's Favorite Stories*. The Tiger-Girl — Song Sog-Ha in Zong In-Sob, *Folk Tales from Korea*.

140. The Daughter of Hsü Hsüan-fang

Karl S.Y. Kao, *Classical Chinese Tales of the Supernatural and the Fantastic*. Canton, China

The magistrate's son sleeps in the stable and dreams that a young maiden tells him she has been unjustly killed by a demon four years before. She asks Pony to bring her back to life. Hair covers the floor by his bed. Bit by bit the rest of her appears. They have a delightful conversation. She teaches Pony how he will bring her back to life. On the appointed day, he spreads millet, wine, and a scarlet cock over her grave and digs up her coffin. He wraps her in felt. She begins to breathe. Four servant girls moisten her eyes and feed her and soon she can speak. In two hundred days, she can walk with a cane. After one year, her skin and strength are all back to normal. Word is sent to her father. Everyone comes to the wedding of Pony and the girl. They have two fine sons.

CONNECTIONS. Canton, China, stories from. Death. Devotion. Dreams. Ghosts. Healing. Life-giving. Love. Maidens. Marriage. Rebirth. Supernatural wives. Transformation.

141. Drolmakyid the Fairy

Folk Tales from China, Fifth Series. Tibetan People

When a prince makes amends for causing a hole in her bucket, an old woman wishes for the fairy Drolmakyid to become his wife. Following the old woman's instructions, the prince rides for ten days and fetches a special orange that he protects in his clothes. At home, the prince peels the orange. A golden ray shoots out and inside is a beautiful girl whom he marries. His parents have no idea that the handmaid they hire for her is a witch, who pushes Drolmakyid into the lake and takes her place. But now, the prince is drawn to a beautiful golden lotus flower on the lake. The witch burns the flower, but from its ashes a walnut tree grows, and she invites everyone in to gather the green walnuts and then burns the tree. However, a young boy finds one lone walnut, which he and his mother place on the windowsill in their house behind the palace. Someone begins to cook for them, and they see a young woman emerge from the shell. She tells them her story, and they keep her secret, but one day her hat blows off, and the witch recognizes her. Guards come to tie her up and burn her, but that night a nine-story palace appears in the glade where flowers appears as the prince walks. He enters the palace and finds his fairy inside. Drolmakyid tells him not to seek revenge on the witch, so they wait. The witch questions the groom, who has returned from riding alone, and tells her about the prince's disappearance into a palace that might be enchanted. The witch storms over and falls into a hole, and the prince's men burn her. He and Drolmakyid then live together until they are old.

CONNECTIONS. Cruelty. Devotion. Fairies. Fighting supernatural opponents. Golden ray. Lotus flowers. Love. Old woman, supernatural helper. Oranges. Palaces. Princes. Shape-shifting. Supernatural wives. Tibetan People, stories from. Transformation. Walnuts. Witches.

142. Lady White Snake

Aaron Shepard. China

Two snakes training for immortality on O Mei Mountain in western China take human form to look around in Jiang Lan, south of the Yangtze River. The white snake becomes the beautiful maiden, Bai Su-Tzin, and the green snake her servant girl, Shao Chin. Bai Su-Tzin causes a rain, so that the young pharmacy clerk Shu Shen, will offer her shelter under his umbrella. They fall in love. Bai Su-Tzin helps Shu Shen open his own pharmacy, where she also cures patients. Her beauty and talent start rumors flying. The abbot at Gold Mountain Monastery warns Shu Shen that his wife is not mortal. He says Shu Shen should offer her wine during the Dragon Boat Festival so that the evil spirit will show. At home Bai Su-Tzin drinks the wine Shu Shen offers her. He returns to see a white snake in his bed and collapses. Bai Su-Tzin rides a cloud to Kun Lun Mountain to steal some of the elixir of immortality for her husband. She gets caught but the Celestial Ruler is touched by her affection for her mortal husband and sends a package that helps Shu Shen recover. Shu Shen does not know whether to believe his wife or the monk, but at last the monk persuades him to stay at the monastery. Bai Su-Tzin calls for water spirits to raise the Yangtze River to bring her to Shu Shen, but, now pregnant, she faints, and the water spirits pull back. Bai Su-Tzin and Shao Chin go to live in Soochow. Shao Chin blocks Shu Shen from entering when he shows up. Bai Su-Tzin falls just then and gives birth to a son. The monk does not give up and goes to Lin Mountain to steal a special golden alms bowl to trap spirits. He turns into a turtle, waits, and then approaches the house as a peddler. Bai Su-Tzin tries on a crown from his wares, but it begins to squeeze her head tighter and tighter until she collapses. Bai Su-Tzin and Shao Chin turn back into two snakes. The monk gathers them into his golden bowl. And buries it under Thunder Hill Pagoda by West Lake. Shu Shen's son never learns the truth about his mother.

CONNECTIONS. Celestial Ruler. Children. Crowns. Death. Devotion. Distrust. Elixir of Immortality. Enchantment. Golden alms bowl. Gold Mountain Monastery. Han People, stories from. Healing. Identity. Jiang Lan, place. Kun Lun Mountain. Loss. Love. Maidens. Monks. Mysteries. O Mei Mountain. Pharmacists. Secrets. Shape-shifting. Soochow, place. Snakes. Spirits. Supernatural wives. Tests. Thunder Peak Pagoda. Transformation. Truth. Turtles. Warnings. West Lake. Yangtze River. Zhejiang Province, China, stories from.

HOW ELSE THIS STORY IS TOLD. The Legend of the White and Black Serpents — Lim Sian-tek, *Folk Tales from China* (In the happier ending here, their young son cries out at Thunder Peak Pagoda and releases the white snake from underneath). The Story of the White Snake — Shelley Fu, *Ho Yi the Archer* and in *Treasury of Chinese Folktales*. White Lady — Yu Fanquin, translator, in *The Lady in the Picture*. White Snake — Frances Carpenter, *Tales of a Chinese Grandmother*. The White Snake — Yin-lien C. Chin, Yetta S. Center, and Mildred Ross, *Traditional Chinese Folktales*. White Snake and Xuxian — Zhao Dinghua in Howard Giskin, *Chinese Folktales* (from Zhejiang Province). The White-Snake Lady — Leslie Bonnet, *Chinese Folk and Fairy*

Tales. Xu Xuan and His White-Snake Wife — Haiwang Yuan, *The Magic Lotus Lantern and Other Tales from the Han Chinese.*

143. The Centipede Girl

James Riordan, *Korean Folk-tales.* Korea

Feeling hopeless that he can no longer feed his family, a poor man throws himself off a cliff into the River Han in Seoul. He is rescued by a beautiful young woman and lives with her for weeks. He falls in love with her, but begins to think of his wife and children. The woman tells him that she cannot keep him against his will, but to ignore anyone who tries to keep him from returning to her. The man finds that his family is no longer poor. His wife has assumed that the money that arrives every day has come from him. He does not tell her about the mysterious woman. After a few months, though, he does leave his family to thank her. A voice claiming to be the spirit of his dead grandfather tells him that the woman is really an evil centipede and to spit strong tobacco juice in her face so he will not die. The man begins to doubt the woman and buys some tobacco. He does see a centipede's tail when he comes to the house, but then the woman herself is still beautiful and kind. He is about to spit tobacco juice at her, but she sobs, and he spits out the window instead. By doing that, he has broken a three-year spell. She was being punished by the Heavenly Ruler for kissing an evil serpent. They spend one last night together, and he awakes on the sandbank by the River Han.

CONNECTIONS. Centipedes. Choices. Despair. Enchantment. Han River. Homesickness. Husbands and wives. Jade Emperor. Love. Maidens. Poverty. Punishment. Rescues. Shape-shifting. Spells. Spirits. Suicide. Supernatural beloveds. Tests. Transformation. Tigers. Tobacco juice. Trust. Warnings.

HOW ELSE THIS STORY IS TOLD. The Centipede Girl — Yun Beg-Nam in Zong In-Sob, *Folk Tales from Korea.* The Rooster and the Centipede — Frances Carpenter, *Tales of a Korean Grandmother* (here, the Jade Emperor has set a rooster to pursue the centipede/wife through thousands of lives). Tiger Woman — Eleanore M. Jewett, *Which Was Witch?* (the mysterious woman is a tiger). Tiger Woman — Freya Littledale, *Strange Tales from Many Lands.*

144. A Dragon and Phoenix Match

Jin Deshun in *Dragon Tales.* China

A childless old couple give birth to a little snake. The third daughter next door is kind to the snake, and he asks his parents to propose a marriage to her. The girl's father sets two riddle tasks for the snake, which he accomplishes, and so the father must agree. On their wedding night, the snake changes into a young man when he and his bride are alone. He gives her his skin, telling her it must remain a secret and must not be burned. The bride's two sisters overhear. One time when he is away, they steal the skin and throw it into the brazier. The young man has just been named as the king's successor, when he feels a wrenching pain. He becomes a golden dragon and flies to his wife, who has taken her own life, and now becomes a red phoenix. They fly off together.

CONNECTIONS. Betrothal. Childlessness. Devotion. Dragons. Eavesdropping. Golden dragon. Kindness to animals. Love. Matches, marriage. Phoenix. Riddles. Secrets. Shape-shifting. Sisters. Skin. Snakes. Suicide. Supernatural husbands. Thieves. Transformation. Warnings.

HOW ELSE THIS STORY IS TOLD. The Fairy Serpent — Adele Marion Fielde, *Chinese Nights' Entertainment* (the youngest daughter sets the serpent/man free with her kindness).

145. The Son of the Turtle Spirit

Wolfram Eberhard, *Folktales of China*. China

A turtle living in the pond in a nobleman's garden falls in love with the nobleman's daughter. Every night he changes into a handsome youth and spends the night in her room, returning to the pond at dawn. After one year, the young woman becomes pregnant. The girl's mother makes the daughter promise to sew a red thread onto her mysterious visitor's coat. The next morning, the father traces the thread to the pond, drains the water out, and finds the turtle with a red thread folded into his skin. The father chops the turtle up into pieces. A while later, the young woman collects the bones. When her son is seven, a rich man offers a huge reward for someone to swim to a dragon-like formation in the Li Che River and lay his grandfather's bones in the dragon's mouth. The nobleman's daughter gives her son his father's bones to put there, too. He is a good swimmer and comes back with a huge reward and eventually becomes emperor.

CONNECTIONS. Bones. Children. Death. Devotion. Fathers and daughters. Killing. Li Che River. Loss. Love. Mothers and daughters. Nobles and lords. Pregnancy. Red thread. Secrets. Shape-shifting. Spirits. Supernatural beloveds. Swimmers. Talents. Turtles. Underwater caves.

HOW ELSE THIS STORY IS TOLD. The Son of the Turtle Spirit — Leslie Bonnet, *Chinese Folk and Fairy Tales*.

146. The Well at the World's End

Howard Giskin, *Chinese Folktales*. Henan Province, China

Lianhua's cruel stepmother sends her with a sieve to collect water from the Well at the World's End. Only a ragged old woman knows where the well is. A fat green frog tells the weeping Lianhua how to stop the holes in the sieve with moss and clay so it will hold water. In return, she promises to do everything the frog asks for one night. Back home, Lianhua is horrified when the frog actually shows up, but her stepmother smugly says she must keep her promise. The next morning, the frog asks Lianhua to chop off his head with an axe. A handsome prince replaces the frog and takes Lianhua away.

CONNECTIONS. Beauty and the Beast stories. Frogs. Henan Province, China, stories from. Kindness from animals. Old woman, supernatural helper. Sieves. Stepmothers and stepdaughters. Supernatural husbands. Tests. Transformation. Wells.

147. The Toad-Bridegroom

Zong Bog-Sun in Zong In-Sob, *Folk Tales from Korea*. Korea

A big toad — whom the fisherman refuses to bring home with him because he thinks the toad may have eaten up all the fish in the drying lake — shows up at his door anyway, saying he will bring good fortune. The fisherman's wife invites him in, and the toad stays with them for years. The toad asks his adoptive parents to ask the rich neighbor if he may marry one of his daughters. The rich man gets so angry, he beats the fisherman's wife. Pretending that a captured hawk is a messenger of the Heavenly King, the toad accuses the rich man of arrogance in refusing the marriage proposal. The rich man is frightened. His youngest daughter agrees to marry the toad. On their wedding night, the toad asks her to cut the skin on his back. A handsome young man steps out. In the morning, he puts the toad skin back on. When the toad goes hunting with the men, everyone comes back with nothing. The toad secretly requests that a white-haired man round up one hundred deer. The rich man is happily surprised to see all the deer. The frog steps out of his skin then and rises up to Heaven, holding his bride and his parents.

CONNECTIONS. Adoption. Beauty and the Beast stories. Bridegrooms. Changes in fortune. Fathers and daughters. Filial devotion. Fishermen. Love. Matches, marriage. Old man, supernatural helper. Rich man. Rising to the sky world. Secrets. Shape-shifting. Skin. Supernatural husbands. Toads. Transformation. Weddings.

WHERE ELSE THIS STORY APPEARS. The Toad-Bridegroom — Zong Bog-Sun in Jane Yolen, *Favorite Folktales from around the World* and at D. L. Ashliman, *Folktexts*, Online.

HOW ELSE THIS STORY IS TOLD. *Chinese variation:* The Frog Who Became an Emperor —*Folk Tales from China*, Third Series, in *The Peacock Maiden: Folk Tales from China*, and at D. L. Ashliman, *Folktexts*, Online (from the Zhuang People). How a Warty Toad Became Emperor — Judy Sierra, *Can You Guess My Name?* (from the Hmong People. The emperor sees a picture of the toad's sweetheart and purloins her, but toad and wife trick him into somersaulting into the toad's skin). *Korean variations:* A Fortune from a Frog — Frances Carpenter, *Tales of a Korean Grandmother*. A Frog for a Husband — William Elliot Griffis, *The Unmannerly Tiger and Other Korean Tales* and at D. L. Ashliman, *Folktexts*, Online. The Toad Bridegroom — Linda Soon Curry, *A Tiger by the Tail*. The Toad Bridegroom — Suzanne Crowder Han, *Korean Folk and Fairy Tales*.

148. The Frog Rider

Folk Tales from China, First Series. Tibetan People

A poor couple prays to the God of Mountains and Rivers for a child, and the woman gives birth to a frog. They are about to put him in a pool to live, when the Frog says that he will change the lives of the poor if they let him live with humans. Three years later he goes off to ask the Chungpon, the local district official, for one of his daughters to marry. The Chungpon is outraged by the Frog's request, but the Frog laughs so deeply that the earth shakes and the frightened Chungpon gives the Frog his eldest daughter. This daughter tries to kill the Frog with a millstone, and he brings her back. He also returns the second daughter. The kind-hearted youngest daughter finds the Frog rather clever and marries him. The frog stays home while she goes to the annual horse race. However, a mysterious man there, dressed all in green on a green horse, wins all the riding and hunting contests and disappears. This happens the next year, too. On the third year of the horse race, the wife comes back early and finds her husband's frog skin. She guesses that he is the mysterious green rider and flings the skin into the fire. He tells her he is the son of Mother Earth, but not yet strong enough to live without his skin. He wants her to tell officials in Peking that common people should be able to trade with their Han brothers. Her horrified father holds her horse so that she cannot go, and so her beloved dies.

CONNECTIONS. Beauty and the Beast stories. Childlessness. Community. Cruelty to animals. Death. Devotion. Distrust. Fathers and daughters. Fire. Frogs. God of Mountains and Rivers. Gods and goddesses. Horseman, green. Kindness to animals. Loss. Love. Officials. Peking. Poverty. Prayer. Promises. Shape-shifting. Skin. Social class. Supernatural wives. Tibetan People, stories from. Transformation. Unselfishness.

WHERE ELSE THIS STORY APPEARS. The Frog Rider — *The Frog Rider: Folk Tales from China.*

HOW ELSE THIS STORY IS TOLD. The Frog — Frederick and Audrey Hyde-Chambers, *Tibetan Folk Tales.*

149. Yuki-Onna

Lafcadio Hearn, *Kwaidan.* Japan

The woodcutter Old Mosaku and his young apprentice Minokichi take shelter in an abandoned ferryman's hut during a snowstorm in Musashi Province. Minokichi wakes in the night and sees a woman dressed in white blow a white breath out upon Mosaku. She tells Minokichi that she will spare him because he is young, but will kill him if he ever tells what he has seen. She leaves then and Minokichi discovers the old woodcutter frozen and dead. The terrified young woodcutter tells no one. One evening, Minokichi meets tall, slender O-Yuki, who says she is an orphan en route to find work in Yedo. Minokichi is charmed by her, and she comes home to live with Minokichi and his mother. They have ten children. One night as she is sewing, Minokichi tells her she looks like the beautiful white woman he saw when he was eighteen. Yuki cries that she is that woman and would kill him now for speaking, if it were not for their children. She says she will kill him if he does not take care of them and rises up through the smoke hole, a white mist.

CONNECTIONS. Breath of death. Fear. Husbands and wives. Killing. Loss. Love. Maidens. Musashi Province. Mysteries. Rising to the sky. Secrets. Shape-shifting. Snow. Spirits. Supernatural wives. Transformation. Ultimatums. Woodcutters.

WHERE ELSE THIS STORY APPEARS. Yuki-Onna — Lafacdio Hearn in Mike Ashley, *The Giant Book of Myths and Legends.*

HOW ELSE THIS STORY IS TOLD. The Cold Lady — Grace James, *Green Willow and Other Japanese Fairy Tales.* The Snow-Bride — F. Hadland Davis, *Myths and Legends of Japan* and at D. L. Ashliman, *Folktexts,* Online. *The Snow Wife*— Robert D. San Souci. The Snow Wife — Keigo Seki, *Folktales of Japan* (she does not have terrifying teeth and melts at the end). Snow Woman — Hiroko Fujita, *Folktales from the Japanese Countryside.* The Snow Woman — Rafe Martin, *Mysterious Tales of Japan.* Yuki-Onna — Pearl S. Buck, *Fairy Tales of the Orient.*

150. Green Willow

Lafcadio Hearn, *Japanese Fairy Tales.* Japan

The talented and kind young samurai Tomotada has been trusted with an important mission by the Lord of Noto. He must ride straight though at all costs, without stopping for any distractions, and return with an answer. On his third day out, though, a wild autumn storm blows up. Tomotada becomes lost, and his horse falters. Suddenly, the sky clears, and in a full moon, he sees a cottage with three green weeping willow trees before it. Tomotada lays his reins over one willow branch and knocks on the door. An old woman tells him he has left his horse in good hand with her daughter. A young girl with long black hair stands with the reins over her arm. The old woman and old man give him dry clothes and food. The young girl enters. He forgets his daimyo's warning and looks at her between the eyes and falls in love. Her name is Green Willow, and when he leaves the next morning, he can think of nothing else. That next night, she appears at the shrine where he is stopping, and he carries her off on his horse. They live in an unknown city for three years. As they watch the moon one night, she tells him she is dying. She says the willow tree was cut down and slides to the ground, where all that remains are her silken gown and her sandals. Tomotada becomes a monk, walking from shrine to shrine. One night, he comes across the cottage again. It is empty, and before it the stumps of three willow trees stand.

CONNECTIONS. Death. Devotion. Ecology. Husbands and wives. Loss. Love. Maidens. Mysteries. Samurai. Shape-shifting. Sadness. Spirits. Supernatural wives. Transformation. Travelers. Trees, destruction. Willow trees.

HOW ELSE THIS STORY IS TOLD. Green Willow — Grace James, *Green Willow and Other Japanese Fairy Tales*. Green Willow — Rafe Martin, *Mysterious Tales of Japan*. The Spirit of the Willow Tree — R. Gordon Smith, *Ancient Tales and Folk-lore of Japan*. The Story of Aoyagi — Pearl S. Buck, *Fairy Tales of the Orient*. The Story of Aoyagi — Lafcadio Hearn, *Kwaidan*. Willow Wife — F. Hadland Davis, *Myths and Legends of Japan* and at D. L. Ashliman, *Folktexts*, Online.

151. The Maid in the Mirror

Frances Carpenter, *Tales of a Chinese Grandmother*. China

Even though he has the best teachers, Lu is lazy about studying for the Emperor's examination. He meets the maiden Feng Hsieng out walking one day and wants to marry her, but she replies that she will return when he passes his examination. She hands him a mirror, saying that he will be able to see her there on times when he has studied well. When Lu looks in the mirror at home, Feng Hsiang's back is turned, and she appears to be walking away. At first Lu begins to study again, to his parents' delight, but then he drifts away from books and back into socializing with his friends. One time when Lu looks in the mirror, he sees Feng Hsiang with tears. It takes a few years, but at last Lu passes all three tests in the Emperor's examination, and Fen Hsiang in the mirror smiles. When notice of his success is posted, the wealthiest man in town wants Lu to marry his daughter. Lu really wants only to marry Feng Hsiang. From the mirror, she tells him to consent to the marriage, and he does, reluctantly. However, on the day of the wedding, it is Feng Hsiang who sits in the bridal chair, and she sticks by him for the rest of his life.

CONNECTIONS. Betrothal. Brides. Devotion. Encouragement. Faithfulness. Foxes. Imperial examination. Laziness. Love. Maidens. Matches, marriage. Mirrors. Motivation. Mysteries. Scholars. Spirits. Studiousness. Supernatural wives.

HOW ELSE THIS STORY IS TOLD. The Fox's Daughter — Alice Ritchie in I. K. Junne, *Floating Clouds, Floating Dreams* (here the young woman pushing him to study for his exams is a fox spirit, who stays mockingly far away, but then tells him to look for her in his books). The Magic Mirror — P'u Sung-ling, *Strange Stories from a Chinese Studio*, Online.

152. The Dark Maiden from the Ninth Heaven

Wolfram Eberhard, *Folktales of China*. Kwangtung, China

One New Year, a poor man spends almost all of his money on the picture of an enchanting girl. He bows to the picture and leaves an offering before every meal. One day he arrives home to find dinner cooked. He hides the next morning and sees the beautiful girl working. The picture is empty. When he walks in, she is back in the picture. That afternoon, he rolls up the paper and kneels at the girl's feet. She suggests they live together and one day tells him that she comes from the ninth heaven and has been condemned to earth for a few years. They have a daughter, but three years later, just when he thinks she may be staying forever, she asks to see the blank paper and steps back into the picture.

CONNECTIONS. Animation. Fairies. Husbands and wives. Kwangtung, China, stories from. Loss. Love. Maidens. Mysteries. New Year's. Ninth heaven. Paintings and pictures. Poverty. Supernatural wives. Transformation.

HOW ELSE THIS STORY IS TOLD. The Dark Maiden from the Ninth Heaven — Leslie Bonnet, *Chinese Folk and Fairy Tales*. The Mystery Maiden from Heaven — I. K. Junne, *Floating Clouds, Floating Dreams*.

153. A Beauty on a Painting Scroll

Haiwang Yuan, *The Magic Lotus Lantern and Other Tales from the Han Chinese*. Han People

A young stonecutter, Brother Zhuang, falls instantly in love with Sister Qiao after he saves her grandfather's life. However, the cruel emperor, continually on the hunt for beautiful women, sends soldiers to bring her to the palace. Sister Qiao throws herself from a cliff. A fairy catches her by unfurling a scroll. Sister Qiao becomes the image in the painting. The fairy gives Sister Qiao a needlework kit to work on while she waits until a safe time to leave the painting. At the New Year, the fairy in disguise sells Brother Zhuang the scroll. He recognizes Sister Qiao, but it is still safer for her to remain in the painting to avoid the emperor's soldiers. Each day, however, Brother Zhuang returns to find the household chores and cooking done. He pleads with Sister Qiao to stay out of the painting, and she hides in his house. After one year, she gives Brother Zhuang some of her exquisite needlework to sell, which catches the attention of the emperor's men who kill Brother Zhuang and seize Sister Qiao. At the emperor's palace, Sister Qiao jumps back into the painting. The fairy brings Brother Zhuang back to life. He storms the palace and throws a cauldron of hot charcoal at the emperor. That merely burns a hole in his robe. The emperor sentences Brother Zhuang to death. To save his life, Sister Qiao walks out of the scroll and offers to mend the emperor's robe. The emperor demands that she also embroider a red sun above waves before sunrise. Sister Qiao completes the task in time. The deceitful emperor says he will reward Sister Qiao with Brother Zhuang's heart. The fairy frees Brother Zhuang who snatches a knife from the executioner and slices the emperor's robe. The embroidered waves surge, becoming real ones that engulf the palace and drown the emperor. The fairy gives Brother Zhuang and Sister Qiao a boat to sail away in.

CONNECTIONS. Animation. Devotion. Embroidery. Emperors. Enchantment. Fairies. Han People, stories from. Life-giving. Paintings and pictures. Rebirth. Rescues. Stonecutters. Supernatural beloveds. Wife-stealing.

154. The Princess Peony

Richard Gordon Smith, *Ancient Tales and Folk-lore of Japan*. Japan

Princess Aya intends to love her betrothed, the second son of the Lord of Ako, though she has never seen him. But when she slips in the peony bed at Gamogun castle, she becomes enchanted with the mysterious young samurai who keeps her from falling in the pond and then vanishes. His clothes were embroidered with peonies. Princess Aya asks her maid to keep him a secret. After this encounter, however, she fades, and the wedding has to be postponed. When her father, Lord Naizen-no-jo, questions the maid if perhaps the princess does not like Lord Ako, the maid confesses that Princess Aya is in love with the samurai. The lord is sure that no shape-changers can slip past his guards and brings a biwa player to play music for his daughter. The samurai appears for a moment, and the princess revives. He appears again when her maids play music, though there are never footprints in the peony beds. Officer Maki Hiogo tries to seize the young samurai, but the officer faints and revives holding a peony. Lord Naizen-no-jo pronounces that the samurai is the spirit of a peony and that the princess should tend this flower with kindness. She does. Her health improves, and the peony blossoms until the day Princess Aya marries.

CONNECTIONS. Betrothal. Fathers and daughters. Healing. Illness. Loss. Love. Matches, marriage. Music. Mysteries. Nobles and lords. Peonies. Princesses. Rescues. Samurai. Spirits. Supernatural beloveds.

WHERE ELSE THIS STORY APPEARS. The Princess Peony — D.L. Ashliman, *Folktexts*, Online.

HOW ELSE THIS STORY IS TOLD. Flower of the Peony — Grace James, *Green Willow and Other Japanese Fairy Tales*. The Spirit of the Peony — F. Hadland Davis, *Myths and Legends of Japan*.

155. The Story of Ming-Y

Pearl S. Buck, *Fairy Tales of the Orient*. China

During the reign of the Ming dynasty, the serious Ming-Y is hired to be tutor for the children of Commissioner Tchang in Genii. He is traveling to visit his parents in Tching-tou when he meets a handsome young woman in the woods. On his return, a country house stands in that very same spot, and a servant beckons him to Sië, the young woman he had seen before. Sië says that she became a relative of Commissioner Tchang's through marriage, but that her husband has died. Her wine, conversation, and musical compositions beguile him. When Ming-Y is ready to leave, Sië gives him a yellow jade paperweight in the shape of a lion and bids him never to speak of their love. Ming-Y lies to Tchang that his mother would like to see him and now spends his evening with Sië. It happens, however, the Commissioner Tchang and Ming-Y's father meet, and they wonder where Ming-Y is spending his nights. Ming-Y vanishes, when they try to have him followed. In tears, Sië tells him they must part. Min-Y's father recognizes the lion and other gifts from Sië as the relics of a courtesan from an ancient city that no longer exists.

CONNECTIONS. Courtesans. Enchantment. Ghosts. Loss. Love. Mysteries. Scholars. Secrets. Supernatural beloveds. Teachers.

HOW ELSE THIS STORY IS TOLD. The Romantic Adventure of Ming-Yi — Lim Siantek, *More Folk Tales from China*.

~ V ~

Devotion

156. The Journey of Meng

Doreen Rappaport. China

A young woman travels north to find her husband who has been taken to build the Great Wall of China. It is an arduous journey. After she lies down in the snow exhausted, she is able to fly like a crow the rest of the way. But her husband is dead. Her anger brings down rain and washes men's bones out of the wall. She wraps her husband's bones. Soldiers drag her off to the Emperor. The Emperor is going to punish her for ruining a section of his wall until he sees how beautiful she is. He gives her a choice between being beheaded or becoming his mistress. She says she will give herself to him but asks first for her husband to be buried with honor. When the forty-nine days of mourning are over, she accuses Emperor Qin Shi Huangdi of killing thousands of people and leaps into the sea, where she is transformed into many tiny darting silver fish.

CONNECTIONS. Anger. Bones. Choices. Concubines. Death. Despair. Determination. Devotion. Emperors. Fish. Great Wall of China. Han People, stories from. Husbands and wives. Justice. Loss. Problem solvers. Shihuangdi, First Emperor of Qin Dynasty. Quests. Suicide. Separation. Transformation. Ultimatums.

HOW ELSE THIS STORY IS TOLD. The Faithful Lady Meng—Wolfram Eberhard, *Folktales of China* (this also appears as How the Faithful Wife became Eternal through the Cruel Emperor in earlier editions). The Faithful Wife—Leslie Bonnet, *Chinese Folk and Fairy Tales* (here, the young Meng Chiang is found in a pumpkin plant). Meng-Jiang Nyu—Yin-lien C. Chin, Yetta S. Center, and Mildred Ross, *Traditional Chinese Folktales*. Meng Jiang Wails at the Great Wall—Haiwang Yuan, *The Magic Lotus Lantern and Other Tales from the Han Chinese*. Seeking Her Husband at the Great Wall—*Folk Tales from China*, First Series and *The Frog Rider* (from the Han People). The Story of Men Jiang—Yu Fanquin, translator, in *The Lady in the Picture*.

157. Bride Island

James Riordan, *Korean Folk-tales*. Korea

So disheartened by her husband's mysterious wasting illness, a young woman prays at the shrine. She begs a fortune teller to tell her if there is anything she might do, and the fortune teller tells her that there is a yellow plant at the Seven Mountains on Devil's Island that has the power to bring a dead person back to life. The old fortune teller warns, however, that legend says a woman will become a monster if she goes there. The young woman is determined to save her husband and takes his fishing boat to Devil's Island. Finally, at twilight, she finds the yellow plant in a crevice. Suddenly, many snakes are hissing toward her. The young woman faints.

When she revives, the yellow plant is there, but she has become a long, green snake. Still desperate to return to her husband, she glides through the water holding the yellow plant in her mouth. Her husband, however, died when he heard that she had gone to Devil's Island. She returns to the sea. Devil's Island changes shape and becomes the young woman; villagers hear the grieving bride weep. Once a year a snake slides to the empty cottage bearing a yellow plant.

CONNECTIONS. Courage. Death. Despair. Determination. Devil's Island. Devotion. Fortune tellers. Heroes, women. Illness. Islands. Life-giving. Old man, supernatural helper. Plants. Prayer. Sacrifice. Seven Mountains. Snakes. Transformation.

HOW ELSE THIS STORY IS TOLD. The Bride's Island — Chun Shin-Yong, *Korean Folk Tales*.

158. The Red Spring

Folk Tales from China, Fourth Series. Han People

Hardworking Shih Tun runs away with his beloved wife Jade Flower when his stepmother makes her life miserable. On a steep mountain path, Jade Flower drinks red water from a spring. An old woman in a hamlet in the valley cries when she hears this. She tells them the spring is colored by maple tree roots, whose red leaves become a red-faced devil, who takes as a wife the most beautiful woman who has drunk water from his spring. That maple-tree wife becomes a tree when snow falls. Shih Tun and Jade Flower stay on with the kindly old woman, who grows more nervous as autumn approaches. One evening, a red leaf swirls down and the red-faced devil stands there with a bridal chair. He has red eyes that can see through walls and mountains, red beard, and red hair. A flick of his sleeve puts Jade Flower in the chair, and they disappear into the sky. Shih Tun accepts the old woman's dagger and rides his horse toward the highest mountain to get Jade Flower back. From two mountains away, the red-faced devil flicks his belt into a red-eyed tiger that springs at Shih Tun, who rides into its open mouth and slits the tiger's belly open. Now the red-faced devil flicks a landscape painting. Shih Tun finds himself struggling up a slippery mountain, but he persists and reaches the red mountain cave where Jade Flower is being held captive. The red-faced devil has turned two pillow cases into her likeness, so that Shih Tun must choose the real Jade Flower. She has tears in her eyes, but cannot move. She is sending him silent messages to leave her and go, but he picks her up. Suddenly a maple leaf flutters down, and the red-faced devil says he will never again separate a wife from her husband. The red-faced devil becomes a maple tree, and the dew it drops breaks the spell that has bound Jade Flower. She and Shih Tun ride back to the old woman in the valley.

CONNECTIONS. Autumn. Changes in attitude. Devils. Devotion. Fighting supernatural opponents. Han People, stories from. Identity. Leaves. Magical objects. Maple trees. Paintings and pictures. Separation. Shape-shifting. Tests. Transformation. Water. Wife-stealing.

HOW ELSE THIS STORY IS TOLD. The Red Stream — M. A. Jagendorf and Virginia Weng, *The Magic Boat and Other Chinese Folk Stories*.

159. A Woman's Love

Smae Yolerda in He Liyi, *The Spring of Butterflies and Other Folk Tales of China's Minority Peoples*. Uygur People

A young woman, marvelously talented at embroidery, turns down attention from the king and marries a hardworking, simple man. One day she gives her husband a bedspread with instructions to sell it for twenty silver coins, but not to go to 41st Street. Unable to sell the bed-spread for so much money, the man goes to 41st Street, home of the palace officials. The king buys the bedspread and says he will come to visit the next day. The woman hides herself, but the king finds her after giving her husband too much to drink. Before the king takes her away, she says she must follow the village custom of making cakes to leave by the wayside for the spir-its. She puts marks on the cakes to show her husband which direction she has gone. When he awakes, he follows her path to the palace, but cannot get in. With a coin from an old woman, he buys some things to sell by the palace gate. The wife slips her husband money to buy two horses. On the third day, a bald-headed scoundrel sees the woman drop down at midnight. Her husband is sleeping, and he secretly takes his place, which she only realizes once they have rid-den far away. She escapes from the scoundrel by pretending that boiling oil will get rid of his baldness; escapes from four hunters by shooting arrows in four directions and saying she will marry whichever one returns the arrow first; and escapes from four gamblers by challenging them to drink bowls of wine to win her. Alone, she disguises herself as a man and enters a city, where the Bird of Happiness is about to choose the next king. It lands on her head. She rules fairly and imprisons the hunters, gamblers, and king when they arrive. Her husband also shows up; he does not recognize her at first, but she has him dress as a woman, and they marry. One day, they reveal their secret, and by then, the scoundrels who have learned their lessons are released. The city is pleased with the way they govern.

CONNECTIONS. Cleverness. Deceit. Devotion. Embroidery. Escapes. Heroes, women. Husbands and wives. Identity. Kings. Leadership. Problem solvers. Separation. Uygur People, stories from. Wife-stealing.

WHERE ELSE THIS STORY APPEARS. A Woman's Love — Kathleen Ragan, *Fearless Girls, Wise Women & Beloved Sisters.*

HOW ELSE THIS STORY IS TOLD. The Clever Woman — *Folk Tales from China, Third Series* and *The Peacock Maiden: Folk Tales from China.*

160. How the Moon and Stars Were Created

Louise and Yuan-Hsi Kuo, *Chinese Folk Tales.* Yao People

Ya Lah plans to take his bow and arrow to shoot down a moon that is burning the crops. In a net made from his wife Ni Nigau's hair, they trap the tiger from the Southern Mountain and the deer from the Northern Mountain. He uses the tiger's tendon to make a bowstring, and the deer's horn to make an arrowhead. Ya Lah shoots the arrow one hundred times, and it chips off parts of the moon that become stars and bounces back. The moon is still too hot. Ni Nigau weaves a brocade that Ya Lah shoots up to cover the moon. This cools things off on earth, but Ni Nigau begins to float up to the sky to join her image in the brocade. Ya Lah cries to his wife. He wishes his image were also in the brocade so he could be with her. Ni Nigau stretches her braid so it reaches a mountaintop, and Ya Lah climbs up to the moon. You can see them herd-ing and weaving up there, together.

CONNECTIONS. Archers. Brocade. Devotion. Heat. Heaven. Helpfulness. Loss. Moon. Northern Mountain. Origins. Paintings and pictures. Rising to the sky world. Southern Moun-tain. Stars. Yao People, stories from.

HOW ELSE THIS STORY IS TOLD. How the Moon and Stars Were Created — Louise and Yuan-Hsi Kuo, *Chinese Folktales.* Shooting the Moon — Catherine Edwards Sadler, *Treasure Mountain.*

161. The Disembodied Soul

Karl S. Y. Kao, *Classical Chinese Tales of the Supernatural and the Fantastic.*
Hunan Province, China

The official's daughter Ch'ien-niang and the nephew Wang Chou, who came to work for him, always imagine that they will marry, but no one knows this. When the official gives his consent for someone else to marry Ch'ien-niang, Chou accepts a government post in the capital. He is on the boat, many li away, when he hears footsteps running along the riverbank. It is Ch'ien-niang with bare feet. He brings her aboard and they travel on to Shu, where they live for five years. Ch'ien-niang wants her parents to meet her two sons. She feels sorry for just having run off without saying anything. Chou agrees that they should pay their respects. He disembarks first and is startled when the official tells him that his daughter has been sick in her room all this time. Chou says Ch'ien-niang is in the boat. When the girl in the room hears that Ch-ieng-niang is in the boat, she rises from the bed and silently goes out to meet her. As soon as the two girls meet, their bodies fuse, clothes and all.

CONNECTIONS. Devotion. Fathers and daughters. Hunan Province, China, stories from. Husbands and wives. Identity. Love. Matches, marriage. Mysteries. Officials. Reunions. Shu, place. Souls. Transformation.

HOW ELSE THIS STORY IS TOLD. Chien-Nang — Ruth Manning-Sanders, *A Book of Charms and Changelings.* The Divided Daughter — Ch'en Hsüan-yu in Moss Roberts, *Chinese Fairy Tales and Fantasies.*

162. Oshidori

Lafcadio Hearn, *Kawidan.* Japan

In Tamura-no-Gō in the province of Mutsu, a hunter knows it is not good to kill mandarin ducks, but shoots at a pair of oshidori one day when he has found no other game. His arrow kills the male. That night, after he has eaten the duck, he dreams that a woman weeps by his bed. She sobs, asking why he killed her lover when they were so happy at Akanuma. The women says he will see what misery he wrought. The hunter wakes in the morning feeling uneasy and decides to travel to Akanuma. The female oshidori swims straight toward him. She rips her body open with her beak and dies. The hunter becomes a priest.

CONNECTIONS. Aichi, Japan, stories from. Akanuma, place. Changes in attitude. Despair. Devotion. Dreams. Ducks. Hunters. Husbands and wives. Killing. Loss. Love. Mutsu, province. Respect for life. Revenge. Suicide. Shape-shifting. Spirits. Tamura-no-Gō, place.

HOW ELSE THIS STORY IS TOLD. The Mandarin Ducks — Fanny Hagin Mayer, *Ancient Tales in Modern Japan* (from Aichi). The Origin of Enoo-Ji — Richard M. Dorson, *Folk Legends of Japan.* Oshidori — Pearl S. Buck, *Fairy Tales of the Orient.*

163. Husband and Wife in This Life and in the Life to Come

Wolfram Eberhard, *Folktales of China.* Central China

A lonely husband goes to seek his dead wife. A waiter tells him that, after a half-day's journey, he will see his wife drawing water at the well in the land of ghosts. The husband finds the well, but, though he can see his wife, she does not respond to him at all. The waiter tells him to throw a coin into her water pail. This time the husband and wife do speak. When she starts to leave and he follows, she tells him that she is now married to a cruel ghost official who will eat him. Still, her husband will not leave, so she pretends that he is her brother. After ten days, however, they flee together to the upper world. The woman takes half a coin with her to quench her thirst at a shop. When she does not reappear, the man asks if the owner has seen his wife. Just then, the owner's wife gives birth. For years, the child has her fist clenched tight, but when she is seventeen, she opens it and is holding half a coin. The husband marries his wife once more.

CONNECTIONS. Babies. Birth. Coins. Death. Devotion. Ghosts. Husbands. Identity. Loneliness. Loss. Love. Mysteries. Quests. Rebirth. Separation. Supernatural wives. Travelers. Underworld. Waiters.

164. The Man Who Lost His Wife

Basil Hall Chamberlain, *Aino Folktales*. Ainu People, Japan

The god of an oak tree, an old man, sympathizes with a husband who has been searching everywhere for his wife. The oak god gives him a golden horse to fly up to the sky. Up there, the world is beautiful, and the man sings as he rides in the streets like the old man instructed. However, the people in the sky do not like his smell, and the chief god sends him away. The man returns to the oak god, who tells him it was a demon who stole his wife, but that because of his singing, the demon is still looking up at the sky. The oak god sneaks around the demon to let the wife out of a box and returns her to the man. He also gives him the gold horse and tells him to stay on earth and breed it. The couple obey and become rich, raising horses for the Ainu people.

CONNECTIONS. Ainu People, stories from. Breeders. Demons. Devotion. Flying horses. Gods and goddesses. Husbands and wives. Loss. Oak god. Oak trees. Quests. Rescues. Rising to the sky world. Separation. Singing. Smells.

WHERE ELSE THIS STORY APPEARS. The Man Who Lost His Wife — Basil Hall Chamberlain at *Internet Sacred Text Archive*, Online.

HOW ELSE THIS STORY IS TOLD. *The Man Who Lost His Wife*— Basil Hall Chamberlain (a slightly different version, the man has a name, Penri. The demon has been changed to a goblin).

165. The Irises of the Sixth Day

Samira Kirollos, *The Wind Children and Other Tales from Japan*. Japan

When the hardworking farmer, Hōriō, marries beautiful Aoyagi, they are so much in love that he cannot separate from her to work. A painter paints a realistic portrait of her on a scarf that Hōriō can bring on a bamboo pole out to the field. However, one day a strong wind blows the scarf all the way from Ooe in Izumo to the Shōgun's palace in Edo. The Shōgun falls in love with Aoyagi from her portrait and sends men to find her and bring her to him. Though Hōriō fights, they take Aoyagi. At the palace, Aoyagi holds herself cold and distant from the Shōgun. Hōriō is distraught at their being separated. Aoyagi's parents tell Hōriō to go to the Shōgun's court, when he admits iris sellers on the fifth day of the fifth month. Hōriō arrives on the sixth day, but calls aloud as an iris vendor outside the walls. Aoyagi hears him. That night they sneak away. Concerned that the Shōgun's men will follow them, Hōriō does not stop as they flee. Aoyagi is not dressed for the cold and becomes ill and dies. Holding an iris in his hand, and unwilling to live without Aoyagi, Hōriō dies soon after. He never knows that the Shōgun, realizing that Aoyagi would never return his love, did not follow them.

CONNECTIONS. Captivity. Death. Devotion. Disguises. Edo. Escapes. Farmers. Heroes, men. Illness. Irises. Irony. Izumo. Loss. Love. Niigata, Japan, stories from. Paintings and pictures. Peddlers. Rescues. Separation. Shogun. Wife-stealing. Wind.

HOW ELSE THIS STORY IS TOLD. Peach Peddler — Hiroko Fujita, *Folktales from the Japanese Countryside.* Pine Trees for Sale! — Milbre Burch in David Holt and Bill Mooney, *More Ready-to-Tell Tales from Around the World.* The Wife's Picture — Fanny Hagin Mayer, *Ancient Tales in Modern Japan* (from Niigata). The Wife's Portrait — Keigo Seki, *Folktales of Japan* and in Joanna Cole, *Best-Loved Folktales of the World.*

166. The Red-Maned Horse

Leslie Bonnet, *Chinese Folk and Fairy Tales.* China

Deciding whom his daughter is to marry is fraught with politics for the Prime Minister, and so he decides to sidestep the problem and let Pao-ch'uan toss out a ball from a tower. That afternoon Pao-ch'uan wakes a young beggar asleep in the garden, and they get to talking. She likes Sieh and gives him gold to dress for the competition. The next day, Sieh catches the ball, but the Prime Minister will not let his daughter marry a beggar. She goes off to live in Sieh's cave. Sieh tames a wild horse with a red mane and soon acquires a position in the army. He begs Pao-ch'uan to return to her father while he away, but she refuses. In the army, Sieh is given dangerous, punishing assignments by the two generals who are married to Pao-ch'uan's sisters. When word comes that he has been slain, and her mother shows up at her poor cave, Pao-ch'uan will not leave. It turns out that Sieh has not been killed. Tied to his horse by one of the generals, he has been captured by a warrior princess who commands that he marry her. Reluctantly, Sieh does. Meanwhile, still in her cave, Pao-ch'uan has begun asking the birds if any have seen her husband on their travels. One day, after eighteen years, she writes a message in blood on a piece from her tattered gown for a bird to bring to Sieh. When he receives the message, Sieh gallops away from the warrior princess, who sorrowfully agrees that he should return to Pao-ch'uan.

CONNECTIONS. Beggars. Birds. Captivity. Caves. Choices. Death. Devotion. Fortune. Horses. Husbands and wives. Loss. Matches, marriage. Ministers. Misinformation. Princesses. Separation. Ultimatums. Unselfishness. War. Warriors.

167. Ondal the Fool

Cathy Spagnoli, *Asian Tales and Tellers.* Korea

Princess PyonKang's crying has annoyed her father since she was a baby. Always, the king has threatened that she will marry Ondal the Fool, who is an ugly beggar, if it does not stop. One day, she does stop crying and insists that now she must marry Ondal. She finds Ondal, who lives simply with his mother, and sees that he is a good man. They marry. Princess PyonKang trades her jewels in for a horse, sword, and books and gently encourages her husband to study, to learn to ride, and to become a warrior. Many months pass, and Princess PyonKang sends him to hunt with the king, who is amazed to learn that Ondal is so accomplished. He makes Ondal a general. Ondal fights fiercely to defend Koguryo, and the king sends him to reclaim land north of the Han river. Ondal is wounded at Achasong fortress. No one can lift his coffin until PyonKang arrives to mourn his loss.

CONNECTIONS. Beggars. Changes in attitude. Devotion. Education. Fathers and daughters. Han River. Heroes, women. Husbands and wives. Kings. Koguryo, place. Loss. Matches, marriage. Ondal. Separation. Social class. Tears. Ultimatums. Warriors. Words.

HOW ELSE THIS STORY IS TOLD. Princess Pynonggang and Ondal the Fool — Yu Chai-Shin, Shiu L. Kong, and Ruth W. Yu, *Korean Folk Tales.* The Weeping Princess — Linda Soon Curry, *A Tiger by the Tail.*

168. The Princess and the Herdboy

Florence Sakade, *Kintaro's Adventures.* Japan

The King of the Sky's daughter is the star Vega, also called Weaving Princess because she creates beautiful clouds, mists, and fog. He sends her to take a rest in the Milky Way. She sees a boy washing a cow in the water. He is the star Altair, who herds cows for the King of the Sky. She rides his cow to his home. The King of the Sky is worried when the Weaving Princess does not return. He sends a magpie to find her and then goes himself when she refuses to come. The King of the Sky pours more star water into the Milky Way to separate the Weaving Princess from Herdboy, for they have been neglecting their duties. She becomes too lonely to weave. The sky is empty of clouds. The King relents and says she may play with Herdboy once a year if she will weave again. On the seventh night of the seventh month, magpies fly to the Milky Way and make a bridge with their wings for the Weaving Princess to run across to Herdboy. The promise of this night is celebrated as the holiday Tanabata-sama, when children play.

CONNECTIONS. Altair. Devotion. Fathers and daughters. Festivals. Han People, stories from. Herders. Love. Magpies. Milky Way. Origins. Separation. Sky Princess. Stars. Tanabata. Vega. Weavers.

WHERE ELSE THIS STORY APPEARS. The Princess and the Herdboy — Florence Sakade — *Japanese Children's Favorite Stories,* Book Two.

HOW ELSE THIS STORY IS TOLD. **Chinese variations:** The Bank of the Celestial Stream — Wolfram Eberhard, *Folktales of China.* The Bridge of Magpies — Cheo-Kang Sié, *A Butterfly's Dream and Other Chinese Tales.* Cowherd and Girl Weaver — Liu Haiqui, *A Museum of Chinese Classic Tales,* Vol. 1. The Cowherd and the Spinning Girl — Mingmei Yip, *Chinese Children's Favorite Stories.* Cowherd and Weaving Girl — Haiwang Yuan, *The Magic Lotus Lantern and Other Tales from the Han Chinese.* Cowherd and Weaving Maid — Yin-lien C. Chin, Yetta S. Center, and Mildred Ross, *Traditional Chinese Folktales.* The Herd Boy and the Weaving Maiden — Richard Wilhelm, *The Chinese Fairy Book.* The Herdboy and the Spinning Maid — Lim Sian-tek, *More Folk Tales from China.* The Heavenly Spinning Maid — Leslie Bonnet, *Chinese Folk and Fairy Tales.* The Heavenly River — Shelley Fu, *Ho Yi the Archer* and *Treasury of Chinese Folktales. Legend of the Milky Way*— Jeanne M. Lee. The Marriage of the Cowherd — Yu Fanquin, translator, in *The Lady in the Picture. A Song of Stars*— Tom Birdseye. The Spinning Maid and the Cowherd — Frances Carpenter, *Tales of a Chinese Grandmother.* The Weaver and the Cowherd — Rena Krasno and Yeng-Fong Chiang, *Cloud Weavers.* **Japanese variations:** The Star Lovers — F. Hadland Davis, *Myths and Legends of Japan.* The Star Lovers — Grace James, *Green Willow and Other Japanese Fairy Tales. The Story of Tanabata/Tanabata Monogatari*— Shin Kitada, kamishibai story cards. The Wife from the Sky World — Takeda Akira in Fanny Hagin Mayer, *Ancient Tales in Modern Japan* (in a very different variation, this story of Tanabata tells of a peddler who steals the sky maiden's robe. She takes pity on him and pulls him up to the sky, but his immortal in-laws treat him terribly, which is why, the story says, the celebration of

Tanabata only occurs once a year). ***Korean variations:*** Across the Silvery Stream — Linda Soon Curry, *A Tiger by the Tail.* The Herdsman and the Weaver —*Long Long Time Ago.* The Herdsman and the Weaver — Gillian McClure, *The Land of the Dragon King and Other Korean Stories.* Kyon-u the Herder and Chik-nyo the Weaver — Suzanne Crowder Han, *Korean Folk and Fairy Tales.* *The Love of Two Stars*— Janie Jaehyun Park. *The Magpie Bridge*— John Holstein. The Skybridge of Birds— William Elliot Griffis, *The Unmannerly Tiger and Other Korean Tales.* Weaver and Herdsman Chik-Nyo and Kyun-Woo— James Riordan, *Korean Folk-tales.*

169. The Medicine Spring Assembly

Liu Haiqi, *A Museum of Chinese Classic Stories*, Volume 6. Daur People

Ameiqige rides up with her white horse to rescue her betrothed Kalasangbaiyin, who has been tied to a stake and whipped by a despotic sheep herd owner. Alerted by his dog, the herd owner's men chase them into the forest. A poison arrow hits Ameiqige's leg. The pursuers drop back, saying she will die from the poison anyway. Ameiqige's horse runs all the next day and finally collapses on the grassland. Kalasangbaiyin wakes early and sees a wounded fawn recover when it drinks from a puddle. He crawls over to the puddle and drinks, and his wounds also heal. Kalasangbaiyin carries the unconscious Ameiqige over to the puddle and pulls the poison arrow from her leg. They lie in the puddle all day, and Ameiqige also recovers. After that, Ameiqige and Kalasangbaiyin stay together and heal many other people.

CONNECTIONS. Arrows. Daur People, stories from. Devotion. Festivals. Healing. Herd owners. Heroes, men. Heroes, women. Love. Magical objects. Poison. Puddles. Rescues. Unselfishness. Water.

170. The Waiting Maid's Parrot

Hao Ko Tzu in Moss Roberts, *Chinese Fairy Tales and Fantasies*. China

The master's rare parrot has been conversing with an intelligent waiting maid, who is favored by the master, and she is tearful when the parrot flies away one day. The master does not blame her, knowing the other maids are jealous of her and may have let the parrot out. Some days later, the parrot flies in to the unmarried son in the Liang house and tells him to look at the waiting maid, who has come on an errand. Hsü falls in love with her, and she notices him. The parrot tells her he will let Hsü know her feelings, but she replies that her master will never let her go and that young Liang will never marry a waiting maid. The parrot recites a love poem the young man has written to her and delivers his love letter. Then Hsü receives word that the waiting maid has died. Not knowing how to write, she had sent the parrot with one of her earrings when he was felled by a stone. The other maids tell the master that the waiting maid converses with a man in her room. The master finds Liang Hsü's love letter to her and has the waiting maid beaten and buried alive. Hsü dreams that a woman dressed in feathers says that she is the parrot and that the waiting maid, her sister, is also a parrot who has been transformed. The parrot woman tells him where his love is buried. He digs the maid up, and she recovers at a Buddhist Convent. Hsü marries the waiting maid, and they set many parrots free.

CONNECTIONS. Buddhism. Cruelty. Deceit. Devotion. Escapes. Healing. Letters. Love. Masters. Messengers. Misunderstandings. Parrots. Rescues. Servants. Social class. Spirits. Talking birds.

WHERE ELSE THIS STORY APPEARS. The Serving Maid's Parrot — Hua Long, *The Moon Maiden.* The Waiting Maid's Parrot — Jane Yolen, *Favorite Folktales from Around the World.*

171. The Story of O-Tei

Lafcadio Hearn, *Kwaidan*. Japan

Long ago in Niigata, consumption turns Nagao Chosei's betrothed paler and more beautiful. On her fifteenth birthday before she dies, O-Tei tells Chosei that they are destined to meet again in this world in fifteen or sixteen years, once she has been reborn as a girl and grows up. He promises to wait for her, but does not know how he will recognize her. Meanwhile, as an only son, he must marry the wife his father chooses, but he never forgets O-Tei. Misfortune befalls Chosei. His wife and child die, and he wanders. In a mountain village, a young waitress seems to look like O-Tei. She says she is O-Tei and falls unconscious on the floor. When the young woman comes to, she cannot remember what she told him or anything about her previous existence, but they get to begin a good life together, anew.

CONNECTIONS. Death. Foretellings. Identity. Journeys. Loss. Love. Mysteries. Niigata, place. Rebirth. Reunions. Separation. Supernatural beloveds.

HOW ELSE THIS STORY IS TOLD. O-Tei — Lafacadio Hearn in *Kwaidan*, a video production by the Jim Henson Foundation. The Story of O-Tei — Pearl S. Buck, *Fairy Tales of the Orient*.

172. The White Butterfly

F. Hadland Davis, *Myths and Legends of Japan*. Japan

As old Takahama lies dying, a white butterfly returns to rest on his pillow three times. His nephew chases it to the nearby cemetery of Sozanji temple, where it hovers over a tomb, with the name Akiko, planted with flowers. The nephew asks his mother about the tomb, and she tells him that it belongs to Takahama's betrothed, who died right before their wedding. For the rest of his life, Takahama never married and tended her grave. They wonder if the white butterfly is the soul of Akiko that has come for him.

CONNECTIONS. Betrothal. Butterflies. Death. Devotion. Graves. Love. Mysteries. Separation. Souls.

WHERE ELSE THIS STORY APPEARS. The White Butterfly — D. L. Ashliman, *Folktexts*, Online.

HOW ELSE THIS STORY IS TOLD. Butterflies — Lafcadio Hearn, *Kwaidan*. **Korean variation:** Butterflies — Bag Sog-Ryong in Zong In-Sob, *Folk Tales from Korea* (a young woman grieves for her betrothed and tears her skirt; the pieces become live and flutter away).

173. The Spring of Butterflies

Yin Chang in He Liyi, *The Spring of Butterflies and Other Folk Tales of China's Minority Peoples*. Bai People

Every young man dreams of marrying farmer Lao Zhang's daughter, Wengu, but she loves only the orphan woodcutter Xiana. Wang, the local ruler of the Zansan Mountains and Dali Lake, sends men to beat the farmer and abduct Wengu. She refuses to become his eighth wife, and Wang ties her up. Xiana travels to Wang's palace with an axe. He frees Wengu, and they flee. When soldiers surround them, Wengu and Xiana leap into Bottomless Pond. Angry villagers march to Wang's palace and kill him. When they return, Bottomless Pond opens. First one pair of butterflies emerge, and then hundreds dance above the water that day and for every spring thereafter.

CONNECTIONS. Bai People, stories from. Bottomless Pond. Butterflies. Captivity. Dali Lake. Devotion. Governors. Kidnapping. Orphans. Revenge. Spirits. Springs. Suicide. Transformation. Woodcutters. Zansan Mountains.

174. Faithful Even in Death

Wolfram Eberhard, *Folktales of China*. Han People, Central China

Since his daughter has such a passion for reading and studying, Chu Yingt'ai's father dresses her as a boy and allows her to study at school along with Liang Hsienpo. They are together all the time, but Hsienpo never guesses that his companion is a girl. Yingt'ai loves Hsienpo, but, after her father dies, her sister-in-law arranges for her to marry Dr. Ma. Her sister-in-law forces Yingt'ai to come back from school. Yingt'ai answers none of Hsienpo's letters, and he arrives to visit. Hsienpo is startled to discover that his longtime friend is a girl and engaged. Suddenly all of the hints she left flood over him. Filled with regret, he falls ill and dies. On the way to her bridegroom's house, Yingt'ai asks that the carriage stop at Hsienpo's grave. She calls for the grave to open if she and Hsienpo were meant to be together. It does. Yingt'ai jumps in before anyone can stop her. When Dr. Ma has the grave reopened, two white stones are there that become a bamboo with two stems, that always grow back together. When the whole plant is cut down, Yingt'ai becomes the blue and Hsienpo the red in the rainbow.

CONNECTIONS. Bamboo. Butterflies. Central China, stories from. Death. Devotion. Disguises. Education. Fathers and daughters. Friendship. Graves. Han People, stories from. Identity. Knowledge. Love. Mandarin ducks. Matches, marriage. Misunderstandings. Mysteries. Rainbow. Remorse. Scholars. Sisters. Spirits. Stones. Suicide. Transformation. Zhejiang Province, China, stories from.

WHERE ELSE THIS STORY APPEARS. Faithful Even in Death — Joanna Cole, *Best-Loved Folktales of the World*.

HOW ELSE THIS STORY IS TOLD. The Butterfly Lovers — Haiwang Yuan, *The Magic Lotus Lantern* (from the Han People). Hsien-Po and Ying-Tai — Lim Sian-tek, *More Folk Tales from China*. Liang Shanbo and Ju Yingtai — Yin-lien C. Chin, Yetta S. Center, Mildred Ross, *Traditional Chinese Folktales*. Liang Shanbo and Zhu Yingtai — Chen Haiyan, translator, in *The Lady in the Picture* (the two lovers become mandarin ducks). *Liang Shan Bo and Zhu Ying Tai: The Butterfly Lovers* — He Xuejun. A Sad Love Story — Shen Beilun in Howard Giskin, *Chinese Folktales* (from Zhejiang Province). Tso Ying Tie — Cheo-Kang Sié, *A Butterfly's Dream and Other Chinese Tales*.

175. The Love of a Princess

Yu Chai-Sin, Shiu L. Kong, and Ruth W. Yu, *Korean Folk Tales*. Korea

A king in Southern Korea is pressing his beloved daughter to choose a husband. She loves the prince from the Northern Kingdom, but her father will not let her go so far away. Alone, she leaves the castle and is helped by an old woman who shows the way and a flock of birds that carry her across the sea in a net she has woven. She arrives at the palace of the North Kingdom and tells the king how much she loves his son. The king, like her father, cannot consider the match. She flings herself into the sea. Heartbroken, the prince follows suit. The King of the North and the King of the South regret their actions and resolve their differences. A white flower grows from the princess's grave that stretches south toward the crimson flower on the prince's.

CONNECTIONS. Birds. Changes in attitude. Despair. Devotion. Distance. Fathers and daughters. Fathers and sons. Flowers. Journeys. Kings. Love. Matches, marriage. Old woman, supernatural helper. Princes. Princesses. Romeo and Juliet stories. Separation. Suicide. Transformation.

HOW ELSE THIS STORY IS TOLD. Star-Crossed Lovers—Linda Soon Curry, *A Tiger by the Tail.*

176. The Mirror of Matsuyama: A Story of Old Japan

Yei Theodora Ozaki, *The Japanese Fairy Book*. Japan

In a loving family in the remote Province of Echigo, a father returns from a long journey to the capital with an engraved mirror for his wife. The wife has never seen a mirror before and marvels at her reflection and listens as her husband tells her the old tradition about the mirror representing a woman's soul and heart. She keeps the mirror carefully shut up in its wooden box. When the daughter grows to sixteen, the mother becomes very ill. She tells her daughter that she will be able to see her in the mirror and speak to her after the mother is gone. The daughter grieves for her mother, and then one day, looks into the mirror and is surprised to see her mother's face, young and healthy. In her innocence, she believes this to be her mother's soul. After a while, the father remarries, and the stepmother tries to come between the father and his daughter. Seeing the unhappy daughter speaking privately to something in her room, the stepmother goes to the father and accuses the daughter of making an image of her and cursing it. The father is torn; he asks his gentle daughter for the truth. As he walks into the room, she slips something up her sleeve. Her father demands to know what it is and voices her stepmother's accusation. The daughter shows her father the mirror then and tells how her mother promised to meet her in the glass. He realizes that she does not know it is her own face she has been seeing and weeps. The stepmother, too, recognizes the girl's filial devotion and asks for her forgiveness.

CONNECTIONS. Changes in attitude. Death. Echigo Province. Fathers and daughters. Filial devotion. Loneliness. Loss. Mirrors. Misunderstandings. Mothers and daughters. Realization. Reconciliation. Reflections. Stepmothers and stepdaughters.

WHERE ELSE THIS STORY APPEARS. The Mirror of Matsuyama: A Story of Old Japan — Kathleen Ragan, *Fearless Girls, Wise Women & Beloved Sisters.*

HOW ELSE THIS STORY IS TOLD. The Matsuyama Mirror—T. H. James in Lafcadio Hearn and Others, *Japanese Fairy Tales* and in a separate woodcut book in the Japanese Fairy Tale Series, #10. The Matsuyama Mirror—Eric Quayle, *The Shining Princess* (in this variation, the stepmother turns herself into a rat to spy on the daughter; the daughter sees the rat reflected in the mirror, and her father rushes in with a sword to kill it). The Mirror of Matsuyama—F. Hadland Davis, *Myths and Legends of Japan* and at D.L. Ashliman, *Folktexts*, Online. The Mirror of Matsuyama—Takeshi Nakajima, *Japanese Traditional Tales*. The Mirror of Matsuyama—Iwaya Sazanami, *Iwaya's Fairy Tales of Old Japan*. The Mirror of Matsuyama—Alan Leslie Whitehorn, *Wonder Tales of Old Japan*. The Mirror of Matsuyama—Teresa Pierce Williston, *Japanese Fairy Tales.*

177. Sim Chung, the Loving Daughter

Yu Chai-Sin, Shiu L. Kong, and Ruth W. Yu, *Korean Folk Tales*. Korea

For years now, Sim Chung has worked hard to care for herself and her blind father, who did everything he could for her when she was a baby. Wealthy Mrs. Chang offers to adopt her, but fifteen-year-old Sim Chung says that her father depends on her. That same day her father is pulled out of a ditch by a monk who tells him he will see again if he offers three hundred bags of rice to Buddha. Finding that much rice is on Sim Chung's mind when she offers herself to fisherman who will pay for a young woman to throw into the sea so the dragon king will calm the waters. She does not tell her father until that morning. He weeps and says he would rather keep living in darkness and have her present. The fishermen promise to take care of him. When they throw Sim Chung into the water a lotus flower opens. They present the flower to the prince, and Sim Chung rises from the flower. She marries the prince, and they hold banquets for blind men. At last, she finds her father, and suddenly, he can see.

CONNECTIONS. Blindness. Buddha. Devotion. Dragon King. Fathers and daughters. Fishermen. Lotus flowers. Poverty. Princes. Rebirth. Rice. Sacrifice. Trades. Transformation. Unselfishness.

HOW ELSE THIS STORY IS TOLD. The Blind Man's Daughter — Frances Carpenter, *Tales of a Korean Grandmother*. Blindman's Daughter Shim Chung — James Riordan, *Korean Folk-tales*. *A Father's Pride and Joy* — John Holstein. The Faithful Daughter Shim Ch'ong — Suzanne Crowder Han, *Korean Folk and Fairy Tales*. The Land of the Dragon King — Gillian McClure, *The Land of the Dragon King* (here, Shim Chong is returned to her father by the Dragon King). Sim Chung, the Dutiful Daughter — H. N. Allen, *Korean Tales*. Sim Chung, the Dutiful Daughter — Tae Hung Ha, *Folk Tales of Old Korea*.

178. Ko-Ai's Lost Shoe

Frances Carpenter, *Tales of a Chinese Grandmother*. China

Emperor Yung Lo has threatened to behead the bellmaker if his third bell for the new tower in Peking does not form correctly. Ko-Ai worries for her father. She hears from a fortune teller that a maiden's blood must be part of the molten metal for the bell to shape correctly and throws herself into the hot metal as her father is pouring it into the mold. Her old nurse reaches to stop Ko-Ai, but only catches one shoe. Some say the bell that bongs and then wails is Ko-Ai calling for her lost shoe.

CONNECTIONS. Babies. Bellmakers. Bells. Devotion. Emileh. Emperors. Fathers and daughters. Peking. Sacrifice. Shoes. Sounds. Ultimatums. Yung Lo, Emperor.

HOW ELSE THIS STORY IS TOLD. **Chinese variations:** The Bell Goddess— Jin Shoushen, *Beijing Legends*. The Great Bell — Pearl S. Buck, *Fairy Tales of the Orient*. The Legend of the Big Bell — Lim Sian-tek, *Folk Tales from China*. **Korean variations:** The Bell of Emileh — Tae Hung Ha, *Folk Tales of Old Korea*. The Voice of the Bell — William Elliot Griffis, *The Unmannerly Tiger and Other Korean Tales* (a baby boy is thrown into the molten metal to prevent the bell from cracking).

179. Village of the Bell

Cathy Spagnoli, *Asian Tales and Tellers*. Korea

Though her own health suffers, the grandmother in a loving, poor family continually gives most of her food to her little grandson. Her son and his wife sadly decide that they will need to take their son away so that the grandmother can live. As the man digs a grave for his son, he unearths a stone bell. His wife says that it is a sign from heaven to spare their child. They hang the bell in front of their house. The forty-second King of Silla hears its beautiful sound and sends men to investigate. Moved by their filial piety, he gives the family rich land to farm, so no one will be hungry.

CONNECTIONS. Bells. Changes in fortune. Family life. Filial devotion. Grandmothers and grandfathers. Hunger. Husbands and wives. Kings. Parents and children. Sacrifice. Silla, place. Sounds.

HOW ELSE THIS STORY IS TOLD. The Bell Village — Tae Hung Ha, *Folk Tales of Old Korea*. Heaven's Reward to a Filial Son — James Huntley Grayson, *Myths and Legends from Korea*. The Man Who Wanted to Bury His Son — Hong Og-Zong in Zong In-Sob, *Folk Tales from Korea*.

180. The Wise Old Woman Who Saved the Country in Great Crisis

Takeshi Nakajima, *Japanese Traditional Tales*. Japan

Long ago, a cruel lord in the province of Shinano rules that anyone over the age of seventy is useless and must be brought to an island where old people soon die for lack of food. One peasant decides to abandon his mother up on the mountain, rather than have her taken by the lord's men. He does not tell her what he has planned, but as he carries her, she breaks off sticks. Once there, she tells him she left the trail of twigs so he will be able to find his way back down. He finds himself unable to leave her and hides her, instead, under the floor back in his house. Now, there is new trouble. A nearby province has warned Shinano to produce a rope of ash or it will attack. The man asks his mother, and she makes the rope, which he brings to the lord. She also knows what to do to meet their other demands, how to run a single thread through a winding hole and how to make a drum that sounds without being beaten. This third time, the peasant lets the lord know that it was his clever mother who solved the all three tasks. The lord rescinds his order about banishing old people, and the neighboring warlike province backs down.

CONNECTIONS. Abandonment. Changes in attitude. Cruelty. Discrimination. Fathers and sons. Filial devotion. Mothers and sons. Nobles and lords. Old age. Peasants. Problem solvers. Respect. Shinano, province.

HOW ELSE THIS STORY IS TOLD. **Japanese variations:** The Mountain of Abandoned Old People — Richard M. Dorson, *Folk Legends of Japan*. The Mountain Where Old People Were Abandoned — Keigo Seki, *Folktales of Japan* and in Richard M. Dorson, *Folktales Told around the World*. The Mountain Where Old Women Were Abandoned — Fanny Hagin Mayer, *Ancient Tales in Modern Japan* (part 1 of the story above). A Thousand Bales of Rope — Fanny Hagin Mayer, *Ancient Tales in Modern Japan* (part 2 of the story above). *The Wise Old Woman—* Yoshiko Uchida (the cruel ruler is named Lord Higo here). The Wise Old Woman — Yoshiko Uchida, *The Sea of Gold and Other Tales*. **Korean variations:** The Aged Father — So Zu-Sig in Zong In-Sob, *Folk Tales from Korea* and at D.L. Ashliman, *Folktexts*, Online. The Son Who Abandoned His Father — James Huntley Grayson, *Myths and Legends from Korea*.

181. The Seven Chinese Brothers

Margaret Mahy. China

Emperor Ch'in Shih Huang is too hard on the workers who are building the great wall of China. The third of seven remarkable brothers repairs a hole in the wall, but then the emperor worries about the threat from someone who is strong enough to lift mountains and has him taken away to be executed. The fourth brother who has bones of iron takes his place. They cannot behead him. The first brother who can hear a fly sneeze hears the fourth brother's cry when they say they will now try to drown him, and fifth brother, who has legs that can grow extraordinarily long, takes his place. The sixth brother, who never gets too hot, goes when they say will burn him. The second brother sees what is coming next, and the seventh brother goes when they are going to shoot arrows into the sixth brother. He cries enough tears to free the sixth brother and himself and to wash the soldiers away.

CONNECTIONS. Brothers. Cooperation. Devotion. Emperors. Executions. Great Wall of China. Han People, stories from. Identity. Rescues. Shihuangdi, First Emperor of Qin Dynasty. Talents.

HOW ELSE THIS STORY IS TOLD. *Chinese variations: The Five Chinese Brothers—* Claire Bishop (a humorous retelling). Five Chinese Brothers—John Lone, narrator, on *Rabbit Ears Treasury of World Tales,* Volume One, Audio CD. Five Chinese Brothers—Jonathan Rodgers, author, *Rabbit Ears Storybook Collection,* DVD. The Five Queer Brothers—Adele Marion Fielde, *Chinese Nights' Entertainment.* The Five Queer Brothers—Lim Sian-tek, *More Folk Tales from China. Seven Magic Brothers—* Kuan-Tsai Hao. The Seven Brothers—*Folk Tales from China,* Second Series (in this story from the Han People, Enormous Mouth drains the sea and drowns the emperor when he spits it out). *Six Chinese Brothers: An Ancient Tale—* Cheng Hou-tien (a humorous retelling). *Korean variation:* The Six Brothers—Y.T. Pyun, *Tales from Korea.*

182. The Mynah Bird

Wolfram Eberhard, *Folktales of China.* China

A plasterer named Liu Shan is friends with a talking mynah bird, who keeps him company and warns him of danger. A magistrate wants to buy the bird. Liu refuses to sell it. But then he comes down with a fever and cannot work. He owes the magistrate money, and the magistrate has him thrown in jail. The mynah finds a way to reach Liu Shan in prison, but the magistrate sends soldiers to capture the bird. The mynah tells the magistrate that he has been eating human flesh, so the magistrate should eat him. The magistrate's cook plucks out his feathers. The mynah escapes into a pipe. He looks everywhere for Liu Shan who has also escaped. The mynah pretends to be a city deity and orders the magistrate to confess all of his sins and kowtow so many times that he loses consciousness.

CONNECTIONS. Captivity. Devotion. Disguises. Escapes. Kindness from animals. Magistrates. Mynah birds. Plasterers. Punishment. Rescues. Talking birds. Tricksters.

183. Jojofu

Michael P. Waite. Japan

Jojofu is Takumi's favorite hunting dog. One day, the young hunter follows her off the path into the forest. A landslide buries the path where they had just been walking. Now the forest grows thicker. Jojofu lies down and won't move when the other dogs go on. Takumi follows them and hears one of his dogs fall off a cliff. That night, Takumi sleeps in a tree, but wakes to hear Jojofu growling. The other dogs have vanished. Now Jojofu is rushing up the tree toward him, still angry. Takumi thinks perhaps she has gone mad and grabs his sword. But he does not want to kill her and leaps down from the tree just as Jojofu also jumps, holding a giant snake which has been above him. Takumi cuts open the snake, and his missing nine dogs jump out. Loyal Jojofu has truly been his "eyes and ears."

CONNECTIONS. Devotion. Dogs. Helpfulness. Hunters. Kindness from animals. Misunderstandings. Ravens. Realization. Snakes. Tibetan People, stories from. Warnings.

HOW ELSE THIS STORY IS TOLD. *Chinese variation:* How the Raven Saved the Hunter — A. L. Shelton, *Tibetan Folk Tales*. *Japanese variation:* Kuro, the Faithful Dog — Yashimatsu Suzuki, *Japanese Legends and Folk-Tales*.

184. The Snake and the Toad

Kim So-un, *Korean Children's Favorite Stories*. Korea

A poor girl feeds rice to the hungry toad who shows up in the kitchen one day. He stays for one year and grows enormous. A huge snake has been terrorizing the village, destroying crops and stealing animals and people to eat. After her mother dies, the girl thinks that maybe she can offer herself to the snake to save her village. She says goodbye to the toad and climbs the rocky hill to the snake's cave. The giant green snake that comes out at night so frightens her that she faints. Just then, white poison hits the snake from the enormous toad who has followed the girl up the hill. The snake shoots poison right back. After two hours, the toad's poison strengthens as the snake's weakens, and the snake dies. Grateful villagers heal the girl.

CONNECTIONS. Bullies. Children. Demons. Devotion. Fear. Fighting supernatural opponents. Helpfulness. Heroes, women. Kindness to animals. Poison. Rescues. Sacrifice. Snakes. Toads. Villagers.

HOW ELSE THIS STORY IS TOLD. A Fight between a Centipede and a Toad — James Huntley Grayson, *Myths and Legends from Korea*.

185. The Snow Monkey and the Boar: A Story of Old Japan

Shirley Climo, *Monkey Business*. Japan

Long ago in Shushin, a musician and his wife care for a snow monkey as if he were part of their family. The man rescued the monkey from the cold twelve years ago. They named the monkey Taro, a name which is usually given to a first son. Taro performs acrobatics as the man plays his samisen in one village and another. When the couple has a human baby, Taro becomes worn out from trying to entertain him. He becomes alarmed when he overhears the musician speak of replacing him with a younger monkey and runs off for advice. The fierce boar Taro meets might have attacked him, except that Taro looks so rundown. Instead, the boar hears his story and tells Taro to give chase the next time he sees him. The next morning Taro is watching the baby when the huge boar breaks down the gate and runs off holding the baby by his kimono sash. The baby wails. The mother and father see Taro dash after the boar. When the musician reaches Taro, the monkey is holding the baby in his arms. After his heroic rescue, Taro's position in the family is secure.

CONNECTIONS. Babies. Boars. Cleverness. Devotion. Monkeys and apes. Musicians. Performance. Problem solvers. Rescues. Respect. Shushin.

HOW ELSE THIS STORY IS TOLD. The Sagacious Monkey and the Boar — Yei Theodora Ozaki, *Japanese Fairy Book* and at D.L. Ashliman, *Folktexts*, Online.

186. The Silver Charm: A Folktale from Japan

Robert D. San Souci. Ainu People

A puppy and a fox follow young Satsu everywhere near his home on the island of Hokkaido. Around his neck, in a charm bag, the boy wears a silver ship that his fisherman father has warned him not to lose, for it has brought good fortune through the generations of men in his family. One day when the puppy and fox cub are playing in the waves, Satsu is lured from the seashore by the smell of berries. He walks into the forbidden woods and is caught by a giant ogre with hairy skin, red eyes, two white horns, and pointed teeth. Satsu trades his silver charm for his freedom just as the puppy and fox cub arrive and chase off the ogre. Satsu becomes very ill from eating the ogre's berries. The village shaman says he will die without his charm. Only the puppy and fox cub know where it might be. They trap a mouse who trades them magic words to transform things. They turn themselves into a boy and a girl and offer to dance for the ogre while the mouse secretly chews through the cord that hold the charm bag around the ogre's neck. As the boy suddenly lunges with his sword, the mouse runs off with the charm. The boy and girl run, too. The mouse transforms them back into a puppy and fox, and they lose the ogre who has come after them. With the silver charm back around his neck, Satsu recovers, and the family is ever grateful to the puppy, fox cub, and mouse.

CONNECTIONS. Ainu People, stories from. Charms. Children. Cooperation. Dancing. Devotion. Dogs. Fighting supernatural opponents. Foxes. Hokkaido. Illness. Magical objects. Mice. Ogres. Quests. Shape-shifting. Trades. Transformation.

HOW ELSE THIS STORY IS TOLD. The Stolen Charm — Basil Hall Chamberlain, *Aino Folktales* in print and online. The Stolen Charm — Teresa Pierce Williston, *Japanese Fairy Tales*.

187. How the Horse-Head Fiddle Was Created

Louise and Yan-Hsi Kuo, *Chinese Folk Tales*. Mongolian People

The orphan shepherd Suho returns with a helpless newborn foal one night. The white pony grows stronger under his care. Once it defends the sheep from a large wolf. Suho races his white horse in a competition to win the hand of the Khan's daughter and comes in first. The Khan, however, sees Suho as a simple herdsman, ignores the marriage reward, and offers three ingots of silver for his horse. Suho does not want to sell the pony. The Khan's men beat him and take the horse away. Shortly after, the horse appears at Suho's house with arrows sticking out of his body, having thrown the Khan when he tried to mount it. Suho mourns the death of his pony, and one night the horse appears, telling Suho to make a fiddle from his bones. Suho carves a bone to look like his horse's head. He uses the horse's tendons for strings, and its tail hairs for the bowstrings. Whenever Suho plays the fiddle, he remembers the pony he loved so well.

CONNECTIONS. Devotion. Dreams. Fiddle. Herders. Horses. Khans. Killing. Kindness to animals. Mongolian People, stories from. Music. Promises. Spirits. Thieves. Transformation.

HOW ELSE THIS STORY IS TOLD. How the Horse-Headed Fiddle Came to Be Made — *Folk Tales from China*, Second Series. The Fiddle with a Horse Head — Haiwang Yuan, *Princess Peacock*. The Legend of the Matouqin — Liu Haiqi, *A Museum of Chinese Classic Stories*, Vol. 1.

188. A Girl, a Horse

Cathy Spagnoli, *Asian Tales and Tellers*. Northern Tohoku, Japan

In the north of Japan, a girl who has grown up with her colt feels closer to him than she ever could to a man. Upset, her parents send her on an errand to a village that is far away. They lead the horse to a cliff and are about to push him off, when the horse whinnies and the thunder god rages. Lightning flashes, and the horse disappears. When she returns, they tell their daughter that the horse has run away, and the girl races off into the storm to find him. In a flash of lightning, the parents see their daughter on the cliff, and she disappears. They call for her all night, and the next morning find two worms on a rock below. Certain that the worms are the spirit of their daughter and the horse, the parents nurture them on mulberry leaves. And the silk threads which the worms produce represent the sensitivity and strength of their friendship.

CONNECTIONS. Deceit. Devotion. Han People, stories from. Heroes, women. Horses. Northern Tohoku, Japan, stories from. Origins. Parents and daughters. Suicide. Silkworms. Spirits. Transformation.

HOW ELSE THIS STORY IS TOLD. ***Chinese variations:*** The Betrothal — Carol Kendall and Yao-wen Li, *Sweet and Sour*. The Girl with the Horse's Head or the Silkworm Goddess — Richard Wilhelm, *The Chinese Fairy Book* (in this version, the father shoots the horse, and its hide wraps itself around the girl). The Horse and the Silkworm — Karl S. Y. Kao, *Classical Chinese Tales of the Supernatural and the Fantastic*. Lady with the Horse's Head — Frances Carpenter, *Tales of a Chinese Grandmother*. The Legend of the Silkworm — Lim Sian-tek, *Folk Tales from China*. The Silkworm — Louise and Yuan-Hsi Kuo, *Chinese Folk Tales* (from the Han People).

~ VI ~

Strange Events and Ghostly Encounters

189. The Boy Who Drew Cats

Lafcadio Hearn, *Japanese Fairy Tales*. Japan

A poor farmer and his wife bring their youngest boy to a temple to become a priest. The boy draws cats whenever he can and on whatever surface he finds. The priest tells him that in the future he may become a great artist, but he must leave the monastery now. The priest advises the boy to avoid large, open places at night. The boy arrives at the temple in the next village at dusk. He does not know that the temple there has been shut because of goblins. He enters the empty temple and, seeing a blank white screen, paints cats all over it. Then, as the priest advised, he tucks himself into a small cabinet to sleep. In the night he hears horrible noises, but stays hidden in his cabinet. In the morning, he emerges to find blood everywhere. A huge goblin-rat lies dead on the floor, and there is blood on all the cats' mouths he had drawn.

CONNECTIONS. Artists. Battles. Cats. Children. Compulsions. Death. Drought. Goblin rat. Goblins. Heroes, men. Paintings and pictures. Priests. Protection. Rats. Supernatural events. Talents. Temples. Warnings.

WHERE ELSE THIS STORY APPEARS. *The Boy Who Drew Cats*— Lafcadio Hearn, Japanese Fairy Tale Series. The Boy Who Drew Cats— Lafcadio Hearn and Others, *Japanese Fairy Tales.*

HOW ELSE THIS STORY IS TOLD. *The Boy Who Drew Cats*— Margaret Hodges. *The Boy Who Drew Cats*— William Hurt, narrator, *Rabbit Ears Storybook Collection*, Film. *The Boy Who Drew Cats*— Arthur A. Levine (the goblin rat has been responsible for a drought). The Boy Who Drew Cats— Rafe Martin, *Mysterious Tales of Japan*. The Boy Who Drew Cats— Aaron Shepard, *Aaron Shepard's World of Stories*, Online.

190. Shippeitarō

Samira Kirollo, *The Wind Children and Other Tales from Japan*. Japan

The brave warrior Chōshirō goes off to seek adventure, hoping to encounter a legendary supernatural creature. When it rains on the evening of the seventh day, he seeks shelter in an abandoned temple. That night, he hears shrieks and miaows. As he watches, hidden, nine old white cats come dancing on their tails. They ask whether Shippeitarō will come that night. In a circle in the temple, they miaow not to tell Shippeitarō and parade out. Chōshirō wonders who Shippeitarō is and why he scares the cats. In the morning, he follows a mysterious new path to a mansion from which he hears weeping. The family there says that they must sacrifice their daughter to the mountain spirit in the temple or a storm will destroy their fields. Chōshirō tells them he will return in seven days and goes looking for Shippeitarō. He finds him on the seventh day. Shippeitarō is the daimyō's black and white dog, whom Chōshirō asks to borrow. He places Shippeitarō in the temple box where the daughter is supposed to go. At midnight, a large black cat leads the nine white cats into the temple. Again, they chant not to tell Shippeitarō, but when the black cat lifts the lid of the box, Shippeitarō attacks him. Chōshirō cuts off the cat's head and slits his body so neither cat nor cat ghost will return. Together Chōshirō and Shippeitarō kill the nine white cats. His work here done, Chōshirō returns Shippeitarō to the daimyō.

CONNECTIONS. Cats. Dogs. Fighting supernatural opponents. Heroes, men. Mountain spirit. Mysteries. Parents and children. Sacrifice. Spirits. Supernatural events. Temples. Ultimatums. Warriors.

HOW ELSE THIS STORY IS TOLD. Destroying the Monkey Gods— Fanny Hagin Mayer, *Ancient Tales in Modern Japan* (here a cat chases off the old rats in a temple). *Schippettaro—* Japanese Fairy Tales Series, No. 17. Shippei Taro— Keigo Seki, *Folktales of Japan.* Shippeitaro— Teresa Pierce Williston, *Japanese Fairy Tales.* Shippeitaro and the Phantom Cats— F. Hadland Davis, *Myths and Legends of Japan.*

191. The Goblin-Spider

Lafcadio Hearn and Others, *Japanese Fairy Tales.* Japan

A samurai says that he will stay the night in a temple that is reputedly haunted by goblins. He crouches under the altar that holds a Buddha statue. A one-eyed goblin comes, announces that it smells a human, and goes away. A priest playing wonderful music arrives, who tells the samurai that his music keeps the goblins at bay. He holds the samisen out to the samurai. When the samurai reaches for it, his left hand becomes stuck in a spider web, as the priest becomes a goblin-spider. The samurai wounds the spider with his sword, but cannot free himself from the web. In the morning, villagers cut him free and follow a blood trail to the garden where they kill the goblin-spider.

CONNECTIONS. Fighting supernatural opponents. Goblins. Goblin spiders. Heroes, men. Music. Priests. Rescues. Samisens. Samurai. Shape-shifting. Spiders. Temples.

WHERE ELSE THIS STORY APPEARS. *The Goblin-Spider—* Lafcadio Hearn. The Goblin Spider — Lafcadio Hearn, *Japanese Fairy Tales.*

HOW ELSE THIS STORY IS TOLD. The Goblin Spider —F. Hadland Davis, *Myths and Legends of Japan.* The Goblin Spider — Yei Theodora Ozaki, *Warriors of Old Japan.* The Spider Web — Fanny Hagin Mayer, *Ancient Tales in Modern Japan.*

192. The Wrestler of Kyushu

Harold Courlander, *The Tiger's Whisker.* Japan

As a sumo wrestler stands on a river bank on the island of Kyushu, a snake appears in the water and nods as if to invite him into the river. The wrestler stands still. The snake disappears underwater, but then its tail lashes out and wraps around one of the wrestler's legs. The wrestler braces himself and does not move. The snake now wraps its tail around the other leg and pulls again. The wrestler calmly tells the snake that he wishes to stand on the shore and is not impressed with the snake's "raw force." Water churns as the snake pulls even harder, and then, it snaps in two. The wrestler goes home. Later the wrestler has a rope made in the same dimensions as the snake's tail. It takes one hundred and thirty men pulling to move his feet just a little.

CONNECTIONS. Demons. Fighting supernatural opponents. Kyushu Island. Rivers. Snakes. Strength. Wrestlers, sumo.

HOW ELSE THIS STORY IS TOLD. The Tug of War — Royall Tyler, *Japanese Tales.*

193. The One-Eyed Monster

Frances Carpenter, *People from the Sky.* Ainu People, Japan

In a time before there are insects in the world, a hairy spirit, with claws, big teeth, and one large eye in the center of its forehead, has been scaring the Ainu children. The hunters say their arrows bounce off its body. It seems to feed on all living things. The Old Man of the village convinces young Oto to go hunting for a deer. Deep in the woods, Oto sees the fiery eye of the monster. He aims a poisoned arrow at the eye, and the creature falls down dead. To make sure that the monster will not return to life, Oto burns the monster and scatters the ashes, but he does not know that each burning ash carried by the air becomes a little stinging mosquito, gnat, or fly.

CONNECTIONS. Ainu People, stories from. Fear. Fighting supernatural opponents. Flesh-eaters. Heroes, men. Hunters. Insects. Monsters. Origins. Spirits. Transformation.

194. The Boy Who Swallowed Snakes

Laurence Yep. China

In Southern China, when poor Little Chou sees a wealthy man drop a bamboo basket full of silver coins and run off, he chases him. The man angrily says he did not leave money and goes. Little Chou brings the basket home. That night his mother finds a snake coiled around Little Chou's leg, which they cannot remove. The wise old women tells them it is a ku snake that kills people and brings their treasure back to its master. Little Chou does not want to kill anyone and impulsively swallows the snake. That night two snakes emerge in a light from Little Chou's stomach, and he swallows those, too. The snakes keep multiplying, and Chou keeps eating them. A farmer offers to dig a hole to bury the snakes for one silver piece. Rich Mr. Owyang recognizes the silver as his own. He thinks that he could become even richer if he had 10,000 ku snakes to steal for him. At Chou's house, little snake lights now dart from the ground as they had from Chou's stomach. Mr. Owyang says that the snakes are his pets, and when Chou hands him the basket a snake coils around his arm and shortly kills the greedy man.

CONNECTIONS. Changes in fortune. Children. Coins. Courage. Greed. Honesty. Kindness. Ku snake. Mothers and sons. Multiplication. Old woman, supernatural helper. Outsmarting supernatural opponents. Punishment. Rich man. Silver. Snakes. Southern China.

195. The Fearless Captain

Im Bang and Yi Ryuk, *Korean Folk Tales.* Korea

The soldier Yee Man-ji of Yong-nam is not afraid of anything. He becomes Captain of the Right Guard and moves to North Ham-kyong Province, where goblins have killed all of his predecessors. When three dark objects back him up against his office wall, he demands to know what they want. When they tell him they are hungry, he says some magic words and snaps his fingers. He swats at the first devil, but then all three say they will go, if he treats guests this way.

CONNECTIONS. Courage. Goblins. Hospitality. Humorous stories. Outsmarting supernatural opponents. Soldiers. Ham-kyong Province.

WHERE ELSE THIS STORY APPEARS. The Fearless Captain — Im Bang in Kathleen Ragan, *Outfoxing Fear.*

196. Ah Shung Catches a Ghost

Pleasant DeSpain, *Thirty-Three Multicultural Tales to Tell.* China

One moonlit night, brave Ah Shung is startled when a cold-fingered ghost asks him the way to town. Thinking quickly, Ah Shung replies that he is also a ghost. The ghost says he is planning to scare the man Ah Shung. When the ghost hears that town is still three miles away, he suggests that they carry each other. Ah Sung cleverly answers that he is newly dead when the ghost complains about his weight and the amount of noise he makes. Now Ah Sung asks the ghost what it is that ghosts fear. The ghost replies if a human spits on them, ghosts cannot escape. When they reach Ah Shung's house, the ghost changes into a talking horse to frighten the man he thinks is inside. But Ah Shung spits on him and gains a horse for a few years.

CONNECTIONS. Cleverness. Courage. Fear. Ghosts. Horses. Humorous stories. Identity. Knowledge. Outsmarting supernatural opponents. Transformation. Tricksters.

HOW ELSE THIS STORY IS TOLD. The Man Who Sold a Ghost — Robert Wyndham, *Tales the People Tell in China.* Sung Ting-po and the Ghost — Karl S. Y. Kao, *Classical Chinese Tales of the Supernatural and the Fantastic.* Sung Ting-Po Catches a Ghost —*Stories About Not Being Afraid of Ghosts.* Sung Ting-po Catches a Ghost — Kan Pao in Moss Roberts, *Chinese Fairy Tales and Fantasies.*

197. The Magic Pancakes at the Footbridge Tavern

Lotta Carswell Hume, *Favorite Children's Stories from China and Tibet.* West China

The mysterious Mrs. Number Three runs the Footbridge Tavern, with stalls for her many donkeys at the back of the inn. One night, Mr. Chao hears strange noises coming from Mrs. Number Three's room and peeks in. He sees her remove small wooden figures from a wooden box and blow on them to bring them to life. One little man scatters dirt on the rug, and tiny oxen draw a plow through it. The little man sows buckwheat seeds and grinds the grain into flour when the sprouts mature. He hands the little sack of grain to Mrs. Number Three, who blows on him, and he becomes wooden again. The next morning, Mr. Chao declines the buckwheat pancakes that Mrs. Number Three has made. He watches as one by one the other guests who eat them start braying like donkeys and go down on all fours. Mrs. Number Three leads them to her stalls. Weeks later, Mr. Chao returns to the inn and switches three buckwheat pancakes of his own with the magic buckwheat pancakes, which he places on Mrs. Number Three's plate. When she turns into a donkey, he rides off on her back. One day a priest recognizes that the donkey is really Mrs. Number Three and transforms her back. No one ever sees her again.

CONNECTIONS. Animation. Breath of life. Buckwheat. Donkeys. Enchantment. Heroes, men. Horses. Innkeepers. Outsmarting supernatural opponents. Pancakes. Transformation. West China, stories from. Witches.

HOW ELSE THIS STORY IS TOLD. ***Chinese variation:*** The Magic at "Grasshopper Inn" — Lim Sian-tek, *Folk Tales from China.* Third Lady of the Wooden Bridge Inn — Karl S. Y. Kao,

Classical Chinese Tales of the Supernatural and the Fantastic. **Japanese variation:** Travelers Turned into Horses— Fanny Hagin Mayer, *Ancient Tales in Modern Japan.*

198. The School-Boy and the Fox

Y. T. Pyun, *Tales from Korea.* Korea

Everyone falls asleep at a village school one day, except for one boy who watches a girl come in and kiss the ninety-nine other boys. One by one they stop breathing. He climbs in among the boys to hide. She begins to count the shoes and says with one more kiss she will become a celestial being. However, she never does find him and when she leaves at dawn, he follows her until she vanishes in front of a large rock. Then she lifts him to her lap and kisses him, and a ball like a pearl passes back and forth between their mouths until he loses consciousness. Somehow, though, he swallows the ball and wakes to find the girl dead. The village parents blame him for the deaths of their sons. They do not believe his story until at the rock they find a bushy, yellow fox tail under clothes and hair copied from a young girl who had recently died.

CONNECTIONS. Children. Foxes. Identity. Killing. Kiss of death. Kitsune. Maidens. Misunderstandings. Pearls. Possession. Spirits. Transformation.

199. The Merchant's Son

Brian Brown, *Chinese Nights Entertainments: Stories of Old China.* China

A wife in Hunan, whose husband is trading abroad, awakes one night and thinks she sees a fox slip out of her room. The next night the fox returns, the wife mutters, and the cook calls out, but the wife is not herself after that. Her ten-year-old son runs to his mother in the nights, but she yells at him. The son blocks up all the windows and sits waiting with a knife and manages to cut two inches off a fox's tail as it dashes out. His father, too, is distressed by his wife's eccentricities, the way she changes rooms in the night and curses them. The boy hides in the neighbor's garden and overhears two men with fox tails say that they like wine. He prepares a poisoned bottle for them and delivers it to their servant by pretending to be a fox-person himself. In that conversation the servant mentions that one master has bewitched the wife of a trader and is beginning to put her under spells again. That night his mother does not mutter, and the next day he and his father find two dead foxes in the neighbor's garden.

CONNECTIONS. Children. Cleverness. Courage. Disguises. Enchantment. Foxes. Heroes, men. Husbands and wives. Illness. Mothers and sons. Outsmarting supernatural opponents. Possession. Shape-shifting. Spirits. Wine.

HOW ELSE THIS STORY IS TOLD. **Japanese variation:** Tamamo, the Fox Maiden — Grace James, *Green Willow and Other Japanese Fairy Tales* (when the fox woman leaves, a man's health improves).

200. The Fox Girl

Suzanne Crowder Han, *Korean Folk and Fairy Tales.* Korea

A daughter returns late to her family's stables one spring evening, and the next morning and the one after that a horse is found dead. The family posts a guard, and he dies. The son is sent to guard. He sees his sister rub her hands and arms with sesame oil and reach into a horse's anus and pull out its liver and eat it. The boy tells his parents what he has seen, but they think he must have been dreaming. The next night an old monk tells him that his sister must have been replaced by a fox that ate her. He gives the boy three bottles, a white horse, and instructions. The fox girl greets him and tells him their parents have died. He asks her to prepare food, and before she goes into the kitchen she ties one end of a string to his ankle, which he moves to the leg of a chest, and gallops away on the horse. The fox girl calls after him. She grabs the horse's tail and he throws the red bottle, which bursts into flame. She keeps coming after him, and he throw the yellow bottle which creates brambles that she manages to work through. He throws the blue bottle, which makes a lake, and she sinks.

CONNECTIONS. Bottles. Brothers and sisters. Escapes. Fighting supernatural opponents. Foxes. Heroes, men. Horses. Killing. Mysteries. Parents and children. Possession. Rope. Shape-shifting.

HOW ELSE THIS STORY IS TOLD. *Japanese variation:* The Younger Sister a Demon — Fanny Hagin Mayer, *Ancient Tales in Modern Japan.* **Korean variations:** The Fox Girl — James Riordan, *Korean Folk-tales.* The Fox Girl and Her Brother — Zo Gyong-Gu in Zong In-Sob, *Folk Tales from Korea.* The Fox-Sister and Her Three Brothers— James Huntley Grayson, *Myths and Legends from Korea.*

201. Destroying the Fox

Fanny Hagin Mayer, *Ancient Tales in Modern Japan.* Japan

A fox tricks women by appearing as a man to women passing through the pine grove in Shirasu and as a woman to men. Ichibei is sure that the woman who now approaches him is a fox, but he does not let on. She asks if she may walk with him, as she is going to Kyōraishi and is afraid to walk alone. He says she may and asks where she is going in Kyōraishi. She tells him where her mother lives. Ichibei secretly spits three times and wipes some on his eyebrows. He tells her that he saw a large dog before he entered the pine grove who held two young foxes in its mouth. He supposes that the mother fox will be upset. At that, the fox-woman turns pale and vanishes. Ichibei laughs to have fooled a fox.

CONNECTIONS. Cleverness. Filial devotion. Foxes. Humorous stories. Kitsune. Kyōraishi, place. Outsmarting supernatural opponents. Shape-shifting. Shirasu, place. Spit.

202. The Painted Skin

Herbert A. Giles, *Chinese Fairy Tales.* China

Mr. Wang stops a pretty girl trying awkwardly to walk quickly on her bound feet. She tells him she is running away from a cruel master and mistress. Sympathetic, he takes her home and hides her in his library. A priest in the street looks hard at him and tells him that he is in the power of a witch. When Mr. Wang shrugs off the comment, the priest mutters that he will die. Mr. Wang is frightened and locks the library door. Through the library window, he sees a green-faced witch with jagged teeth paint a girl's skin and then put it on to become the lovely maiden he brought home. He rushes out to find the priest and begs him for help. The priest gives him a fly-brush to hang at his bedroom door. Angrily, the girl comes out of the library, tears up the fly-brush, and then rips out Mr. Wang's heart. Distraught, Mrs. Wang sends Mr. Wang's brother for the priest, who says that the witch is still in the house. She is, on the brother's side, disguised as an old woman. The priest hits her with a wooden sword. The old woman's skin drops off, and the priest swings again and takes off the witch's head. She turns into a column of smoke.

The priest catches the smoke in a gourd. He sends Mrs. Wang to a madman in the mud, with instructions to accept whatever he does to her. The madman beats Mrs. Wang and reviles her, but she does not get angry. Then he disappears. She runs home sobbing, and the lump in her throat falls into Mr. Wang's wound. It becomes his heart, which begins beating again.

CONNECTIONS. Devotion. Enchantment. Fighting supernatural opponents. Fly-brush. Hearts. Heroes, men. Husbands and wives. Killing. Life-giving. Madmen. Maidens. Priests. Skin. Tears. Tests. Transformation. Witches.

203. The Vampire Cat

D. L. Ashliman, *Folktexts.* Japan

No one notices when a large white cat follows the Prince of Hizen's favorite concubine into her room and strangles her and takes her form. The prince suspects nothing and caresses the false O Toyoko, but his strength begins to wane. Every night, one hundred retainers keep watch, but they fall asleep mysteriously, and the false O Toyoko enters the palace. The priest invites a young soldier he has observed praying to Buddha for the prince's recovery to stand guard. Ito Soda is surprised to be asked, as his rank is not so high, but he tells the priest that he believes the prince has been bewitched. That night, Ito Soda thrusts his dirk into his own thigh to try to fight the mysterious sleepiness that has overcome the other soldiers; still, it is difficult to stay awake. Then he sees a beautiful woman enter the prince's room. She senses Ito Soda's presence and leaves. The same thing happens the next night. As Ito Soda keeps watch, the prince gradually recovers his strength. Ito Soda goes to O Toyoko's room and draws his dirk. The woman fights back with a halberd and then suddenly turns into a cat and springs to the roof. The white cat eludes capture for a while, but at last, it is killed and the loyal Ito Soda is rewarded.

CONNECTIONS. Buddhism. Cats. Concubines. Determination. Fighting supernatural opponents. Heroes, men. Killing. Maidens. Mysteries. Possession. Prayer. Princes. Shapeshifting. Soldiers. Spirits. Transformation.

WHERE ELSE THIS STORY APPEARS. The Vampire Cat of Nabéshima — Baron Algernon Bertram Freeman-Mitford Redesdale, *Tales of Old Japan.*

HOW ELSE THIS STORY IS TOLD. The Vampire Cat — O Toyo — F. Hadland Davis, *Myths and Legends of Japan.*

204. The Witch's Daughter

Wolfram Eberhard, *Folktales of China.* Kiangsu, China

In the wild mountains, an old man plays chess with a old widow, who tells him that he must send his three sons to be husbands for her daughters if he loses. He loses every game and sends his sons to the valley one at a time. The first son is eaten by a lion, and the second by a tiger. A hermit tells the third son that the old widow is a witch and gives him an iron pearl to throw to the lion and an iron rod for the tiger. He would have been crushed by an iron block if he had not used a stick from the cherry tree to open the third door to her house. First the witch makes him sow linseed in a weed-covered field, which a swine helps him to do, and then makes him pick up every seed, which ants help him accomplish. Then she tells him he must find her when she hides. A lovely maiden on the roof calls down that her mother has become a half-green, half-red peach in the garden and that he should bite into the red part. He does, and there is the witch with blood running down her cheek. The witch tells him he can marry her daughter if he brings a bed of white jade from the palace of the dragon king. Her daughter give him magic objects to finish that task and then others, to bring back a big drum from the western mountain of the monkey king, to cut down two bamboo sticks from a garden where the hairy gardener eats men's fingers, and to bring snakes out of his mouth to counter the poisoned noodles the witch has fed him. At last, the third son marries the witch's daughter, but even then, the witch sends a flying knife that seeks blood against them. The witch's daughter says she will sacrifice herself to the knife, because she can be reborn if the third son puts her in a lotus pail for forty-nine days. He does this, but when he hears groans on the forty-eighth day, he lifts the lid, and he loses her forever.

CONNECTIONS. Ants. Chess. Dragon King. Fate. Kiangsu, China, stories from. Fighting supernatural opponents. Flying knife. Kindness from animals. Loss. Lotus pail. Love. Maidens. Matches, marriage. Monkey King. Mothers and daughters. Old man, supernatural helper. Pearls. Pigs. Poles. Rebirth. Sacrifice. Snakes. Supernatural wives. Tests. Witches.

205. Black Hair

Rafe Martin, *Mysterious Tales of Japan*. Japan

When he loses his position, a samurai in Kyoto becomes a ronin, masterless and without honor. His good and beautiful wife sells cloth she has woven, but he leaves, though she begs him to stay. In another city, he marries a lord's vain daughter just to secure a new position. After a while, he regrets this marriage and travels back to see his first wife. He arrives at midnight. The house appears abandoned, but he finds his wife weaving at her loom. He begs her forgiveness, and she welcomes his return. In the morning, he finds he has been holding a skeleton. His wife has died heartbroken long before.

CONNECTIONS. Ghosts. Husbands and wives. Illusions. Loss. Love. Reunions. Revenge. Sadness. Samurai. Selfishness. Skeletons. Supernatural wives. Unfaithfulness. Weavers.

HOW ELSE THIS STORY IS TOLD. Black Hair — Brenda Wong Aoki in *Best-Loved Stories Told at the National Storytelling Festival*. She Died Long Ago — Royall Tyler, *Japanese Tales*.

206. One Hundred Recited Tales

Richard M. Dorson, *Folk Legends of Japan*. Japan

A young novice has invited his friends to the temple to tell stories. When someone finishes a story, he is to walk into the hall and blow out one of the one hundred candles that are lit. The bravest people go last as the hall is quite dark; most have already gone home or been carried away. Finally, only the village headman's son remains. He fears that his turn to disappear is next, but then the rooster crows. Every day after that the headman's son passes the same girl on his way back from the shrine. They marry. One evening the man sees his wife blowing the fire in the kitchen with a hollow bamboo. She looks just like the ghost in the temple a year ago. He cries out. His wife runs over and blows into his face, and he dies.

CONNECTIONS. Breath of death. Candles. Fear. Ghosts. Headmen. Killing. Love. Maidens. Priests. Shape-shifting. Storytellers. Supernatural wives. Temples.

207. The Goblin of Adachigahara

Yei Theodora Ozaki, *Japanese Fairy Book*. Japan

A priest who does not know the legend of the cannibal goblin that haunts the plain of Adachigahara in the shape of an old woman comes to a little cottage. The old woman there agrees to let him in and feeds him rice. She tells him that he must not look in the back room, while she goes out for more wood. When she does not return for so long that the fire goes out, he decides to look. Human bones are on the floor, and the walls are splashed with blood. The man races from the house. The old woman changes into her demon form and chases him with a large knife angry that he looked in the back room. As he runs, he utters the holy invocation to Buddha over and over and escapes.

CONNECTIONS. Adachigahara Plain. Bones. Buddha. Escapes. Fighting supernatural opponents. Flesh-eaters. Goblins. Horror. Prayer. Priests. Shape-shifting.

208. On Cat Mountain

Françoise Richard. Japan

Good-hearted Sho makes a perilous journey in search of the black cat, Secret, which her cruel mistress has discovered and thrown out of the house. When Sho finds Secret, the cat has become a cat-faced girl, who saves her from the unwanted village cats who eat people who stray onto Cat Mountain. Secret also rewards her friendship with gold enough to buy her freedom. Then Sho's nasty mistress sets off to acquire her own fortune on Cat Mountain, with grisly results.

CONNECTIONS. Cats. Changes in fortune. Cruelty to animals. Flesh-eaters. Freedom. Gold. Journeys. Kindness from animals. Kindness to animals. Mistresses. Mountains. Punishment. Servants. Transformation.

HOW ELSE THIS STORY IS TOLD. Cat Mountain — Fanny Hagin Mayer, *Ancient Tales in Modern Japan.*

209. Mujina

Lafcadio Hearn, *Kwaidan.* Japan

An old merchant sees a woman crying bitterly by a moat on the Akasaka Road in Tōkyō. She appears to be well-dressed and keeps moaning into her sleeve. He stops to offer her assistance. She turns to face him, and he sees with horror that she has no eyes or nose or mouth. He screams and runs away until he comes to the light of a traveling soba-seller. The merchant flings himself down. The soba-seller asks if he is hurt, and the terrified merchant tries to tell the soba-seller what he saw, but he cannot. At that, the soba-seller asks if what he saw was anything like this — and shows the merchant his own featureless face.

CONNECTIONS. Akasaka Road. Demons. Faces. Fear. Horror. Merchants. Mujina. Tears. Tōkyō.

HOW ELSE THIS STORY IS TOLD. Surprised Twice — Fanny Hagin Mayer, *Ancient Tales in Modern Japan.*

210. Jikininki

Lafcadio Hearn, *Kwaidan.* Japan

Lost in the mountain district of Mino, the Zen priest Musō Kokushi stops at a rundown hermitage to ask if he may stay the night. It is unusual, but the old priest there refuses him lodging and directs him to the valley. Musō Kokushi finds a crowd gathered at the headman's house there, but he is kindly given a little room. Before midnight, he hears sobbing. A young man tells him that his father has died and that it is the custom that no one remain in the hamlet the night after a death. The young man urges Musō to join them and leave, but the priest says he is not afraid of demons or ghosts and will stay with the father's body until morning. Musō prays and enters a meditative state. Then Musō becomes aware of a large, indistinct shape that lifts the corpse and eats it all, from the head down. The young man returns in the morning, relieved that the priest has not been harmed. Musō tells him about the shape. He asks if the villagers ever ask the priest on the hill to perform the funeral service, and the young man replies that there is no hermitage on the hill. Musō Kokushi walks back up the mountain to see for himself. He finds the hermit priest, who tells him that he was reborn as a jikininki, an eater of human flesh, because for years he performed all of the priestly rites only thinking of himself. He begs Musō Kokushi to perform the Buddhist service for hungry spirits that will let him escape this existence. Musō does, and suddenly a priest's tomb appears beside him on the mountain.

CONNECTIONS. Buddhism. Courage. Death. Flesh-eaters. Funerals. Ghosts. Headmen. Illusions. Jikininki. Mino, district. Mysteries. Outsmarting supernatural opponents. Prayer. Priests. Rebirth. Traditions.

HOW ELSE THIS STORY IS TOLD. Jikininki — Lafacadio Hearn in *Kwaidan*, a video production by the Jim Henson Foundation.

211. Rokuro-Kubi

Lafcadio Hearn, *Kwaidan*. Japan

Five hundred years ago, a samurai who cut off his hair and became the traveling priest Kwairyō is preparing to sleep in the mountains when a woodcutter warns him about haunted things in the woods and invites him to his cottage. Four others are there when they arrive. The woodcutter tells the priest that he once served a daimyō, which accounts for his civilized manner in such an isolated spot. The priest reads sûtras until late, but then he sees their five bodies without heads. Kwairyō recognizes that he has been lured to the home of a Rokuro-Kubi. He pushes the body of the woodcutter out the window, so that the head will never be able to find it, and it will die. In the garden he sees the five heads eating insects and worms. The heads are beginning to speak about going in to dine on the priest. One head reports back that not only is the priest gone, but so is the woodcutter's body. The woodcutter's head comes at Kwairyō, but the priest uproots a young tree and whacks the heads away as fast as they come. The other heads go off to reunite with their bodies, but the woodcutter's head clings to the priest's sleeve. Kwairyō travels to Suwa in Shinano with the head hanging from his sleeve. People flee screaming, and the police arrest him, thinking the man he had been trying to murder grabbed hold of him. They do not believe that the head belongs to a goblin until they examine it and find no marks that show it has been severed. Later a robber buys the head from Kwairyō by switching robes with him. Then, growing uneasy, the robber never can find the body to bury with the head.

CONNECTIONS. Arrests. Fighting supernatural opponents. Flesh-eaters. Goblins. Headless bodies. Heads. Misunderstandings. Nukekubi. Priests. Shinano, province. Suwa. Woodcutters. *Note:* Lafcadio Hearn mis-labeled the vicious supernatural creatures in this tale. The cannibalistic *rokurokubi* are actually *nukekubi* (see Appendix B).

212. The Fortuneteller and the Demons

Suzanne Crowder Han, *Korean Folk and Fairy Tales*. Korea

When a blind fortune teller from Han Yang senses that evil spirits follow several errand boys into a house and the master's daughter dies, he tells the nobleman that he can revive his daughter. The fortune teller covers the doors and windows with paper and chants. The demons begin to groan loudly to get out, and they do find a chance to escape when a curious servant girl pokes a hole in the paper to see what is happening. The dead girl revives, but the fortune teller knows that the demons will come after him. Meanwhile, the king wants to test the blind fortune teller's ability to "see." He places one rat in front of the fortune teller and when the blind man says that three rats are there, the king denounces him as a fraud and orders his execution. Later the king discovers that there were really two fetuses inside the rat. He tries to cancel the fortune teller's execution, but a strong wind keeps the signal flag from communicating his intent. Demon laughter is heard.

CONNECTIONS. Blindness. Curiosity. Death. Demons. Executions. Fetuses. Fighting supernatural opponents. Fortune tellers. Healing. Identity. Kings. Misunderstandings. Paper, covering openings. Prayer. Rats. Rebirth. Remorse. Revenge. Servants. Spirits. Tests. Wind.

HOW ELSE THIS STORY IS TOLD. Blindman and the Demons— James Riordan, *Korean Folk-tales*. The Blind Man and the Devils— Zong Teg-Ha in Zong In-Sob, *Folk Tales from Korea*.

213. Ho-ichi the Earless

Rafe Martin, *Mysterious Tales of Japan*. Japan

Traveling from village to village, the blind storyteller Ho-ichi strums on his biwa and tells the tragic story of the Heiki royal family who were destroyed by the Genji and of the nursemaid who leapt into the sea holding the baby emperor. A priest at the temple built to remember the Heiki nobles invites him to stay. One summer night, a samurai approaches and tells Ho-ichi that he has come to bring the storyteller to his lord who would like to hear the story of the Heiki clan. The samurai guides him to a gathering of nobles. Ho-ichi begins. He can hear them weeping. The nobles tell him he must come again to continue the story, but that he must tell no one where he has been. The samurai comes for Ho-ichi again. The priest is worried; he does not know where Ho-ichi is going, but the strain of his nights is beginning to show. At last, Ho-ichi confides in the priest. The priest tells him that the people he has been singing to are ghosts of the royal Heiki family who will destroy him once the story is finished. On the fourth night, the priest has servants write sacred words all over Ho-ichi's body to make him invisible to the ghosts. He tells Ho-ichi not to respond to the samurai's summons in any way. That night, the samurai cannot see Ho-ichi, except for his two ears, which the servants forgot to paint. Even when the samurai rips his ears off, Ho-ichi sits silently. After this, the ghosts never come for him again, but he adds them into his story.

CONNECTIONS. Biwa. Blindness. Calligraphy. Ears. Fukushima, Japan, stories from. Ghosts. Hoichi. Invisibility. Music. Mysteries. Nobles and lords. Outsmarting supernatural opponents. Prayer. Protection. Priests. Rescues. Sadness. Samurai. Silence. Storytellers. Temples. Tragedies.

HOW ELSE THIS STORY IS TOLD. Dan'ichi Whose Ears Were Cut Off— Fanny Hagin Mayer, *Ancient Tales in Modern Japan* (from Fukushima). *Earless Ho-ichi: A Classic Japanese Tale of Mystery*— Lafcadio Hearn. The Earless Jizo of Sendatsuno— Richard M. Dorson, *Folk*

Legends of Japan. Hoichi — Naomi Baltuck, *Apples from Heaven*. Hoichi — Lafcadio Hearn in *Kwaidan*, a video production by the Jim Henson Foundation. Hoichi-the-Earless — F. Hadland Davis, *Myths and Legends of Japan*. Mimi-Nashi Hoichi — Lafcadio Hearn, *Kwaidan*.

214. The Disowned Student

Kim So-un, *Korean Children's Favorite Stories*. Korea

A young student returns after three years of study and meditation in a mountain temple to find an identical young man in his house. His parents think their son is the imposter. He wanders sadly until he meets a priest who guesses what has gone wrong and knows how to fix it. The priest tells the student to bring a cat back to his parents' house. The cat flies at the false son's neck and bites, exposing a field rat inside. That rat had stolen his identity when the student had left clippings when he trimmed his nails.

CONNECTIONS. Cats. Identity. Mysteries. Nail clippings. Nails. Parents and children. Priests. Problem solvers. Rats. Shape-shifting. Students.

HOW ELSE THIS STORY IS TOLD. Nails — Zong Zin-Il in Zong In-Sob, *Folk Tales from Korea*.

215. Chin Chin Kobakama

Lafcadio Hearn and Others, *Japanese Fairy Tales*. Japan

Every night, little men only one-inch high, dance around a lazy woman's pillow. They mock her and make faces. Her warrior husband returns and stays up to watch for them. When the little warriors come, they seem more comical than frightening to him. However, he pulls out his sword to chase them away, and they all turn into toothpicks ... the toothpicks the woman had kept sliding under her mat, rather than pick up.

CONNECTIONS. Fear. Humorous stories. Husbands and wives. Laziness. Mysteries. Size. Toothpicks. Transformation. Warriors, supernatural.

WHERE ELSE THIS STORY APPEARS. *Chin Chin Kobakama*-Lafcadio Hearn, Japanese Fairy Tale Series.

HOW ELSE THIS STORY IS TOLD. Hiroko — Diane Wolkstein, *Lazy Stories*. The Toothpick Warriors — Florence Sakade, *Japanese Children's Favorite Stories* and *Peach Boy*.

216. Adventures of the Three Sons

James Riordan, *Korean Folk-tales*. Korea

With their dying father's good wishes, the eldest son inherits his father's millstone; the middle son inherits his bamboo walking stick and gourd bowl; and the youngest son inherits his drum. The three brothers separate. The eldest son frightens two robbers when he urinates on them and grinds his millstone from his perch in a tall tree. They run away, and he collects their jewels and marries a beautiful girl. The middle son falls asleep on a burial mound and tricks a tokkaebi who feels the stick and bowl and thinks that the boy has died. Together, tokkaebi and the second son travel to a rich man's house where the tokkaebi steals the daughter's spirit and puts it in the son's purse. The son returns to the girl's house, papers over all the windows and cracks and opens the purse under her nose, and the spirit reenters her. This is the girl he marries. The youngest son is walking along and beating his father's drum when a tiger jumps out and starts to dance. He keeps playing and walking backwards until he reaches the village, where the villagers shower him with money, thinking he has trained a tiger. He walks backwards all the way to the capital city where the emperor's youngest daughter falls in love with him. So, he becomes a royal prince, with the tiger as their pet. Ten years later the brothers meet and visit their father's grave to thank him for his gifts.

CONNECTIONS. Bowls. Brothers. Changes in fortune. Cleverness. Dancing. Drums. Gifts. Gratitude. Inheritance. Life-giving. Millstones. Outsmarting supernatural opponents. Paper, covering openings. Princesses. Problem solvers. Rebirth. Rescues. Rich man. Spirits. Tigers. Tokkaebi. Tricksters.

HOW ELSE THIS STORY IS TOLD. The Three Sons— Zong In-Mog in Zong In-Sob, *Folk Tales from Korea*. The Three Brothers' Inheritance — Suzanne Crowder Han, *Korean Folk and Fairy Tales*. Three Who Found Their Hearts' Desires— Eleanore M. Jewett, *Which Was Witch?*

217. Li O Sent Back from the Dead

Karl S. Y. Kao, *Classical Chinese Tales of the Supernatural and the Fantastic.*
Hunan Province, China

Wealthy Li O has been buried for fourteen days in Ch'ung County in Wu-ling, when her neighbor Ts'ai Chung tries to loot the grave with an axe. He hears Li O cry out to watch out for her head and flees. The Grand Administrator of Wu-ling asks Li O how she came to be buried. The sixty-year-old woman tells him that she had been brought to the Arbiter of Life by mistake and was heading out of the western gates when she saw her cousin and told him she was feeling weak and did not know how she would get out of the grave. Her cousin sent someone to ask the Chancellor of the Bureau of Households, who said that another man who was also being sent back to Wu-ling would escort her. The chancellor told the escort to have the neighbor free her. The Grand Administrator decides that since ghosts and spirits made Ts'ai Chung break into the grave, he should not be punished. However the administrator is puzzled by the letter that Li O's cousin sent back for his son. At last a necromancer deciphers the letter. It tells the cousin's son to be in Wu-ling on the eighth day of the eighth month for his father will be there inspecting the watercourse with the Lord of the Underworld. The son T'o waits and hears his deceased father's voice. T'o tells his father about the sickness that has been in Wu-ling, and his father tells him to smear the gates and door with medicine that he gives him. There is an epidemic, but T'o's family is spared.

CONNECTIONS. Changes in fortune. Ch'ung County. Death. Fathers and sons. Ghosts. Graves. Hunan Province, China, stories from. Justice. Letters. Mistakes. Mysteries. Officials. Protection. Rebirth. Thieves. Underworld.

218. Football on a Lake

Herbert A. Giles, *Chinese Fairy Tales*. China

One night, Young Chai anchors his boat in the lake where his father drowned. Five men come up out of the lake and lay a huge mat on top of the water. They bring up food and wine. An older man and a boy seem to be servants for the other three. The older servant resembles Chai's father. After they picnic, the servant boy comes up with a monster, glittering ball, and all five begin a football game. At one point the ball lands in Chai's boat. A good football player, like his father, Chai kicks it hard. His foot goes through the surprisingly light material. The ball arcs high, and colored lights stream from the hole his foot has made. The players are angry when the ball comes down and fizzes out in the water. Three players, now armed with swords, tell the servants to bring Chai over. Chai pulls out his own sword. He calls out to his father that he is his son. As the other players jump on the boat with their black faces and huge, rolling eyes, young Chai cuts off one man's arm and another's head. Chai and his father are fleeing in the boat, when a mouth opens up in the lake, blowing giant winds that create waves that threaten to capsize them. Chai hurls one anchor stone and then another in the great mouth, and the waters calm. As they leave together, Chai's father tells him that the men he was with are fish goblins who serve the Dragon King. He himself was spared from being eaten because he was a good football player. The ball was made of fish fin.

CONNECTIONS. Dragon King. Fathers and sons. Fighting supernatural opponents. Fish goblins. Football. Goblins. Lakes. Rescues.

219. The Story of the Man Who Did Not Wish to Die

Yei Theodroa Ozaki, *Japanese Fairy Book*. Japan

Wealthy Sentaro worries about death and climbs peaks seeking legendary Horaizan to find the monks who may know about the Elixir of Life, but he never finds them. He is praying at the shrine of the Emperor's courtier Jofuku who is said to have gone to Horaizan, when Jofuku himself appears and tells Sentaro that he is selfish, but that he will send him to the country of Perpetual Life. Sentaro flies on a little paper crane that becomes real to an island where the people long for death so they can reach Paradise. After 300 years there with nothing happening, Sentaro prays for Jofuku to bring him back home where he will be mortal again. A storm drops the paper crane into the sea, and when a shark is about to swallow Sentaro, he screams for help. A messenger comes from Jofuku saying that Sentaro's scream means he does not really want to die, but now what he must do is go back home and live a good life, provide for his children's futures, and stop worrying about death.

CONNECTIONS. Acceptance of life's changes. Animation. Changes in attitude. Cranes. Death. Generations. Immortality. Jofuku. Journeys. Paper birds. Perspective. Prayer. Rip Van Winkle stories. Sentaro. Sharks. Tests.

HOW ELSE THIS STORY IS TOLD. *Japanese variation:* The Old Rip Van Winkle of Old Japan — F. Hadland Davis, *Myths and Legends of Japan* (Sentaro returns from the Land of Perpetual Youth after three hundred years). *Korean variation:* The Man Who Lived a Thousand Years— Frances Carpenter, *Tales of a Korean Grandmother* (a man tricks the heavenly Messenger and gets to live much longer until one day, he gives up immortality to save his son).

220. Janghwa and Hongnyun

Tae Jung Ha, *Folk Tales of Old Korea*. Korea

Jang Si, the wife of a country gentleman during the Yi Dynasty, dreams of a fairy dancing on a rainbow who holds out a red flower that becomes another fairy that enters her bosom. She gives birth to one daughter Janghwa, Rose, and later to Hongnyun, Red Lotus. The daughters are beloved by both parents, but after Jang Si dies, their father marries a wicked woman who bears three sons. Their jealous stepmother puts a dead rat in Janghwa's bed and pretends it is a miscarried baby. She tells her husband that Janghwa must go. He sends the half-brother out with instructions to force Janghwa into the water, but a tiger attacks him. Hongnyun calls out to her sister in a trance, and Janghwa answers that she is in the Dragon Palace in another world. Janghwa urges Hongnyun not to follow her, but Hongnyun sinks in the lotus pond. People walking near the pond hear two girls crying; magistrates who see ghosts in the shape of a red and white lotus flower there later die. The king sends the young nobleman Jung Dong Ho to the county of Chulsan which is suffering from a drought. The two ghostly girls tell him about their wicked stepmother. They also let him know that the famine will end when Janghwa's honor is avenged. Janghwa and Hongnyun tells him to cut the dead rat open so he will know it was not a baby. He learns the truth, punishes the wicked stepmother and her son, drains the lotus pond, and gives Janghwa and Hongnyun an honorable burial.

CONNECTIONS. Birth, unusual. Consequences. Deceit. Devotion. Dreams. Drought. Fathers and daughters. Ghosts. Magistrates. Murder. Mysteries. Problem solvers. Punishment. Rats. Sisters. Stepmothers and stepbrothers. Stillbirth. Suicide. Truth.

HOW ELSE THIS STORY IS TOLD. These tales were all adapted from the novel *Gaze Zib. All for the Family Name*— John Holstein. The Two Sisters, Rose and Lotus— Gim Dong-Hul in Zong In-Sob, *Folk Tales from Korea.*

221. The Tiger in Court

Lotta Carswell Hume, *Favorite Children's Stories from China and Tibet.* Southwest China

Despairing when her only son is eaten by a tiger, an old woman pressures the magistrate to try the tiger in court. At last he agrees, but no one can catch the tiger. The magistrate's attendant Li Neng is praying at Cheng-huang temple one month later, when a tiger lies in the doorway and allows himself to be bound. The magistrate tells the tiger that he will be pardoned if he agrees to be the old woman's son. Every day after that the tiger brings her food. She was expecting a different kind of justice, but takes comfort in the tiger's presence. When the old woman dies, the tiger roars and disappears.

CONNECTIONS. Cheng-huang Temple. Death. Justice. Magistrates. Mothers and sons. Remorse. Retribution. Southwest China, stories from. Tigers.

HOW ELSE THIS STORY IS TOLD. The Tiger of Cho-cheng — P'u Sun-ling, *Strange Stories from a Chinese Studio* and in Michael Bedard, *The Painted Wall.* Tiger Sorrowful — Lim Sian-tek, *More Folk Tales from China.*

222. A Taoist Priest

Joanna Cole, *Best-Loved Folktales of the World.* China

Wealthy Mr. Han and Mr. Hsü often drink together. One day a shabby Taoist priest approaches, and Mr. Hsü offers him hospitality that day and many more. Finally, Mr. Hsü asks why the priest never hosts them. The priest invites them to come to his place, which the two friends are surprised to find sumptuous and well-staffed. They are entertained and keep drinking. When Mr. Hsü accuses the priest of previous rudeness, the priest runs out. Mr. Hsü and Mr. Han fall asleep. They wake in the road; nothing is there but a couple of huts.

CONNECTIONS. Hospitality. Illusions. Manners. Mysteries. Poverty. Precepts. Priests. Rich man. Rudeness. Taoism. Wealth.

223. The Origin of the Room

Fanny Hagin Mayer, *Ancient Tales in Modern Japan*. Niigata, Japan

After four or five days, a new wife grows pale. She tells her mother-in-law that she has been trying not to break wind. Old Granny tells her that she may break wind at any time. The new wife warns Granny to hold onto the hearth. However, when the wife's wind blasts Granny up to the ceiling, the old woman and her son decide she is too dangerous and should go home. At the edge of the village, children are trying to get persimmons down from a tall tree. She breaks wind to blow them down. When she reaches the river, her wind unsticks a boat loaded with rice so that it is free to sail. The boatmen give her all the rice. She hauls the rice back to the old woman's house. Granny and the son decide she has a valuable talent. They build her a special little house, a *heya*, just for breaking wind.

CONNECTIONS. Acceptance. Breaking wind. Changes in attitude. Exile. General Pumpkin. Helpfulness. Humorous stories. Mothers-in-law and daughters-in-law. Niigata, Japan, stories from. Origins. Rewards. Rice. Rooms. Talents. Thieves.

HOW ELSE THIS STORY IS TOLD. *Japanese variation:* The Bride with an Unusual Talent/Hekkoki Yome — Shozo Mizutani on kamishibai story cards. *Korean variations:* The Daughter-in-Law Who Broke Wind Frequently — James Huntley Grayson, *Myths and Legends from Korea*. In the next two variants, a large, strong man who eats only pumpkins routs a robber gang at a Buddhist temple by breaking wind. General Pumpkin — *Long Long Time Ago*. General Pumpkin — Zong In-Sob, *Folk Tales from Korea* and in D.L. Ashliman, *Folktexts*, Online.

224. The Rescue

Laurence Yep, *Tree of Dreams*. China

Min-Chung's mother instructs Li Min-Chung to be polite if he meets a crooked man on his travels to a distant village, where the village head has commissioned him to paint his portrait. Min-Chung rushes off without asking the spirits to protect him on his journey. On his way home he snaps at a crooked man who asks for some food, but the crooked man follows him. The road is getting dark. The crooked man scolds Min-Chung for not sharing and trips him, so that Min-Chung falls down the mountain without his paints or his food. At home, neither Min-Chung's mother or wife know that he is there. A little old man appears who says that one of Min-Chung's souls knocked loose when he fell. The old man drags Min-Chung through a wall and back up the mountain to his body. The crooked man kicks Min-Chung's body. The little old man holds out Min-Chung's food, and Min-Chung inhabits his body again. When he returns home again, Li Min-Chung thanks the spirit of their home, and after that, he always carries food for the crooked man, spirit of the mountain road.

CONNECTIONS. Artists. Changes in attitude. Disembodied. Food. Invisibility. Manners. Old man, supernatural helper. Physical difference. Protection. Punishment. Realization. Rudeness. Selfishness. Souls. Spirit of the Mountain Road. Spirits.

225. The Story of Umétsu Chūbei

Lafcadio Hearn, *A Japanese Miscellany*. Japan

As a young samurai heads for night-duty at the castle of Lord Tomura Jūdayū in the province of Dewa, a young woman with a young child in her arms stops him. He worries that she may be a goblin in human form, but he is kind. When she addresses him by name and asks him to hold her baby until she returns, he takes the child. The baby appears to be newborn, but grows heavier and heavier. Umétsu knows he has been tricked, but wants to keep his promise. Now, the baby weighs 600 pounds and Umétsu's muscles are shaking. He calls on Buddha three times, and on the third time, the child vanishes. The woman reappears, telling him that he has done a great service. She is the Ujigami for this night and needed his strength and courage to help her after the Gates of Birth have closed for a mother who had prayed to the deity. When Umétsu prayed, Lord Buddha opened the Gates, and the child he had been holding was able to be born to her. In thanks, Umétsu's children and grandchildren are also rewarded with strength.

CONNECTIONS. Babies. Birth, unusual. Buddha. Deities. Dewa Province. Generations. Kindness. Mysteries. Prayer. Promises. Rewards. Samurai. Spirits. Strength. Tests. Ujigami. Weight.

226. Three Strong Women

Claus Stamm. Japan

Forever-Mountain, the strongest sumo wrestler in Japan and proud of his strength, is on his way to the wrestling competition in the capital, when he decides to tickle a girl carrying a water bucket. Maru-me clamps her arm down on his hand and drags him up the mountain. She tells him that her family can turn him into a really strong wrestler, as strong as her mother who carries the cow or as strong as her grandmother who pulls a tree up by the roots. At first Forever-Mountain is mortified, but he decides to stay and learn from them. When at last, he can actually pin the grandmother, they decide Forever-Mountain is ready to compete. They have prepared him so well, there is no competition at the meet that year. When Forever-Mountain stamps his foot, his opponent bounces in the air and out of the wrestling circle. None of the other wrestlers want to try to go against him, and the emperor makes him promise to retire from competition. Forever-Mountain wins the prize money and goes back up the mountain to ask Maru-me to marry him.

CONNECTIONS. Arrogance. Competition. Education. Emperors. Generations. Heroes, women. Humorous stories. Love. Strength. Wrestlers, female. Wrestlers, sumo. Wrestling.

WHERE ELSE THIS STORY APPEARS. Three Strong Women — Claus Stamm in Ethel Johnston Phelps, *Tatterhood*.

HOW ELSE THIS STORY IS TOLD. The Strongest Wrestler in Japan — Richard M. Dorson, *Folk Legends of Japan*.

227. The Wrestling Match of the Two Buddhas

Yoshiko Uchida, *The Magic Listening Cap*. Japan

A poor servant carves a piece of wood in the image of Buddha, since his master keeps his own golden image of Buddha locked away except for festival days. The servant prays to this wooden Buddha before meals on a little altar in his room. The master and other servants mock him. One day the master calls for a public wrestling match between the two Buddhas. If the servant's wooden Buddha loses, then the servant will have to work for the master for the rest of his life. If the master's golden Buddha loses, then the master will give the servant all of his belongings. The wooden Buddha tells the servant not to worry. When the two Buddhas are placed in sand, they begin to rock and then to shove each other. The golden Buddha tires and falls over. The wooden Buddha goes to the master's house and stands upon the altar, where the servant is now master. The former master wanders, remorseful for the love he had not shown to his Buddha or his servant.

CONNECTIONS. Animation. Buddha, statues. Changes in attitude. Changes in fortune. Competition. Faith. Golden Buddha. Masters. Remorse. Servants. Statues. Wrestling.

228. The Tiny God

Yoshiko Uchida, *The Magic Listening Cap.* Japan

When Prince Okuninushi sees a little man hop off a boat made from a sweet potato leaf that has been floating in the Japan Sea, he pinches the little man's nose. When the little man bites the Prince's cheek, the Prince apologizes. A scarecrow tells the Prince that the little man is a god, and the Prince apologizes again. The little god suggests they have an endurance contest. The Prince thinks it will be harder to carry a heavy pack than to walk one-legged up a mountain. The little god, who is carrying the heavy pack while the Prince hops, wins. They become friends. What the little god teaches the Prince about planting and governing, the Prince teaches his people. At last, the little god says it is time to go and leaps from a stalk of grain into the sky. Missing his friend, the Prince looks for the little god each day, until a boat arrives with a message from the little god for the Prince to work for his people, instead of waiting by the shore.

CONNECTIONS. Acceptance of life's changes. Changes in attitude. Competition. Friendship. Gods and goddesses. Japan Sea. Knowledge. Leadership. Leaves. Loss. Princes. Rising to the sky world. Rudeness. Size. Teachers.

~ VII ~

The Power of Dreams

229. Cricket Boy

Feenie Ziner. China

The scholar Hu's main passion is collecting crickets and cricket fighting. Word spreads about his champion fighter, Black Dragon. One day a courier arrives from the Emperor to summon Hu to bring Black Dragon to fight the Emperor's champion. The magistrate of Yung Ping, where Hu lives, frets that the Emperor may punish the whole village if Hu's cricket wins. Hu's son Hu Sing worries that the magistrate may harm Black Dragon and lifts the lid of the jar where Hu keeps his special cricket. But, Black Dragon jumps out, and as Hu Sing reaches to catch him, the jar falls and kills the cricket. Distraught, the boy throws himself in the river. He is rescued, but unconscious. The scholar sits by his bed. Now the magistrate fears that the Emperor will be angry if Hu does not show up for the competition. The scholar dreams that his dead wife points to a rock in the garden. He walks to the garden and lifts that rock, and a tiny cricket springs into his hand. The little cricket wins over all other crickets in his fighting bowl. With his mother keeping the vigil over Hu Sing, the scholar brings the tiny cricket to the Emperor's fight, and it defeats the Emperor's big champion. When the Emperor asks what he might wish to have as a reward, Hu answers that he wants only for his son to live. Back in Yung Ping, Hu Sing opens his eyes and tells his father that he dreamed he had wrestled and won against the Emperor's champion.

CONNECTIONS. Competition. Cricket fighting. Crickets. Despair. Dreams. Emperors. Fathers and sons. Fear. Guilt. Han People, stories from. Healing. Magistrates. Mysteries. Remorse. Size. Suicide.

HOW ELSE THIS STORY IS TOLD. Cheng's Fighting Cricket — Frances Carpenter, *Tales of a Chinese Grandmother*. The Cricket — P'u Sung-ling in Moss Roberts, *Chinese Fairy Tales and Fantasies*. A Cricket Boy — Haiwang Yuan, *The Magic Lotus Lantern* (from the Han People). The Fighting Cricket — P'u Sung-ling, *Strange Stories from a Chinese Studio*, Online. The Fighting Cricket — Laurence Yep, *Tree of Dreams*.

230. The Dream of the Butterfly

Mingmei Yip, *Chinese Children's Favorite Stories*. China

The scholar Zhuang Zi dreams that he is a butterfly. When he wakes, he wonders whether he is a butterfly dreaming of being a man or vice versa. No matter which one is true, what is real is his appreciation for the natural world.

CONNECTIONS. Butterflies. Dreams. Ecology. Harmony. Perspective. Reality. Scholars. Truth.

HOW ELSE THIS STORY IS TOLD. The Butterfly — Chuang Tzu in Moss Roberts, *Chinese Fairy Tales and Fantasies*. A Butterfly's Dream — Cheo-Kang Sié, *A Butterfly's Dream and Other Chinese Tales* (in this adult variant, only the thought that perhaps he is a butterfly dreaming consoles the man who has enjoyed feeling free of human worries, fears, and jealousy and wakes as he is making love to a beautiful butterfly).

231. Night Visitors

Ed Young. China

When ants invade his family's rice storehouse in southern China, the young scholar Ho Kuan persuades his father to give him a month to seal the walls to keep the ants out, rather than to drown them. Ho Kuan is contemplating how to accomplish this when soldiers arrive and summon him to His Majesty's palace. He gets into their black carriage and days later arrives at a beautiful mountain city. The king gives Ho his daughter in marriage. Red warriors attack, however, and kill Ho's wife. Ho drives these invaders from the country, but he returns to the king, sorrowful about the loss of his wife. The king thanks him for his devotion and tells him to look under the cassia tree at his parent's home. Ho Kuan awakes at his desk. He thinks this has all been a dream until he follows a line of ants to what looks like a palace, where one large black ant sits on an earthen jar as if it were a throne at the foot of the cassia tree. Spilling from the jar are silver coins, which Ho Kuan spends to seal his father's storehouse and reinforce his belief in a respect for all life.

CONNECTIONS. Ants. Coins. Dreams. Fathers and sons. Harmony. Kindness to animals. Mysteries. Problem solvers. Reality. Respect for life. Scholars. Treasure.

HOW ELSE THIS STORY IS TOLD. *Chinese variation:* South Branch — Li Kung-tso in Laurence Yep, *Tree of Dreams* (a one thousand-year-old story). *Japanese variation:* Dream of Akinosuké — Lafcadio Hearn, *Kwaidan.*

232. The Cypress Pillow

Karl S. Y. Kao, *Classical Chinese Tales of the Supernatural and the Fantastic.*
Anhwei Province, China

The curate of the temple at Lake Chiao invites an unmarried merchant to sleep beside the crack in a cypress pillow he has had for thirty years. The merchant enters the crack. Inside he sees exotic jeweled palaces and finds good fortune. The Grand Marshal Chao arranges a marriage for him. He raises six children and is appointed Assistant Director of the Imperial Library and then promoted. When he runs into trouble in his career, he hears the curate calling for him to come back out. The merchant has only been inside the pillow for a moment.

CONNECTIONS. Anhwei Province, China, stories from. Changes in fortune. Curates. Cypress wood. Dreams. Merchants. Mysteries. Pillows. Porcelain. Reality. Temples. Taoism.

HOW ELSE THIS STORY IS TOLD. Contentment in Humbleness — Brian Brown, *Chinese Nights Entertainments: Stories of Old China* (a young man who experiences the power and fall of his career inside the porcelain pillow is grateful now for the life he has). The Magic Pillow — Herbert A. Giles, *Chinese Fairy Tales*. The Pillow of Contentment — Lim Sian-tek, *Folk Tales from China.*

233. The Firefly

D.L. Ashliman, *Folktexts*. Japan

A young man of Matsue is surprised to see a firefly in the winter. He pushes it away with his stick as it flies toward him. The next day, his betrothed tells him that she dreamed she was a firefly and that he pushed her away. The young man feels it wiser not to tell his story.

CONNECTIONS. Betrothal. Dreams. Fireflies. Matsue. Mysteries. Peace. Spirits.

HOW ELSE THIS STORY IS TOLD. A Strange Dream — F. Hadland Davis, *Myths and Legends of Japan.*

234. Choon Hyang — Spring Fragrance

Yu Chai-Shin, Shiu L. Kong, and Ruth W. Yu, *Korean Folk Tales*. Korea

One spring morning, Yi Doryung, son of the magistrate of Nam Won is enchanted by a kisueng, the dancing girl he sees swinging in the summer pavilion at Gwanghalloo. He goes to Choon Hyang's house and declares his everlasting love, but she tells him that a nobleman's son cannot marry a kisueng. Still, he persists, and they marry secretly. But now, Yi Doryung's father is going to take Yi Doryung with him to Seoul where he has been promoted to Minister of Finance. Yi Doryung gives Choon Hyang his jade ring to keep until he returns. Shortly after he leaves, the new magistrate of Nam Won throws Choon Hyang in prison for spurning his attentions. Meanwhile in Seoul, Yi Doryung's intelligence and poetry are admired by the king, who offers him a position as His Majesty's Royal Envoy. Yi Doryung travels in disguise, observing how districts are governed. He hears about the corrupt new magistrate in Nam Won. Villagers tell him that Choon Hyang has stayed faithful to the husband who abandoned her. She is fading in prison and dreams of withered flowers, a shattered mirror, and empty shoes. Yi Doryung learns that Choon Hyang is to be executed in two days. He goes to the prison and tells her that he loves her. Yi Doryung goes to the magistrate's palace dressed as a beggar and recites poetry. Everyone realizes that he is no beggar. He punishes the magistrate and sends for Choon Hyang. The king praises her virtue and makes Choon Hyang a duchess. After that, Choon Hyang and Yi Doryung no longer have to hide.

CONNECTIONS. Captivity. Changes in attitude. Changes in fortune. Dancing girls. Devotion. Disguises. Dreams. Envoys. Gwanghalloo, place. Husbands and wives. Illness. Jade ring. Justice. Kisueng. Love. Magistrates. Matches, marriage. Nam Won, place. Rescues. Seoul, capital city. Social class. Unfaithfulness.

HOW ELSE THIS STORY IS TOLD. Charan — Im Bang and Yi Ryuk, *Korean Folk Tales.* Chun Yang, the Faithful Dancing-Girl Wife — H. N. Allen, *Korean Tales.* Spring Fragrance — Tae Hung Ha, *Folk Tales of Old Korea.* Hwang Jini, The Dancing Girl — Tae Hung Ha, *Folk Tales of Old Korea.*

235. The Sandman: The Dream Hunters

Neil Gaiman and Yoshitaka Amano. Japan

In competition with each other, a badger and a fox conspire to get a solitary monk to vacate his temple. The badger takes fearsome forms. The fox appears as a beautiful, green-eyed woman collapsed outside his door. The monk recognizes them for what they are and resists both the badger's bullying and the fox's allure. Now the fox has truly fallen in love with the monk and wants to protect him from the plot she overhears where three female creatures want to cause the monk's death through three dream events so the Master of Yin-Yang can acquire the monk's peacefulness. The little fox brings a carving of a dragon she has kept to the sea, where she hopes to be crafty enough to catch one of the Dream Eaters, the Baku, so she can keep the monk from dying. In the first dream event the monk is given a box; in the second his grandfather gives him a key. The little fox wants to stop the third dream when the monk will open the box with the key and die. The monk finds the fox limp upon his threshold. He carries her into the temple and warms her and speaks to her, but she does not improve. He heads for the village, but an old man along the way tells him that the right thing is to bring the fox back to the temple and sleep with a token of the King of All Night's Dreaming beneath his head, for the fox is trapped in his dreams. The monk sleeps with the fox wrapped in his robe. In his dream, he pleads with the King of Dreams to spare the fox, but the king tells him that the fox opened the box with the key and took his death upon herself. It is what she wants. The King of Dreams brings the fox back as a woman to tell the monk how she got the Baku to let her enter his dreams. The monk tells the fox that he cares for her. He tells the King of Dreams that he wants his dream returned to him. He walks into the heart of a mirror and dies. The little fox despairs that all she did was for nothing. Despite the monk's advice that she seek Buddha rather than revenge, she tempts the Master of Yin-Yang as a woman and leaves him naked and bitter, with nothing of his own.

CONNECTIONS. Badgers. Baku. Buddhism. Competition. Death. Despair. Devotion. Dream Eaters. Dreams. Fighting supernatural opponents. Foxes. Helpfulness. Heroes, women. King of All Night's Dreaming. Mirrors. Monks. Rebirth. Revenge. Sacrifice. Shape-shifting. Spirits. Supernatural beloveds. Temptation. Transformation. Unselfishness.

236. The Hunter in Hades

Basil Hall Chamberlain, *Aino Folktales*. Ainu People, Japan

A skilled hunter, who has been chasing a bear without being able to shoot it with a poisoned arrow, ends up following the bear down into a hole. There is a whole world even more beautiful than the world above down there. He is still looking for the bear and walks along, eating grapes and mulberries. Then he sees he has become a hateful serpent. He glides back toward the cavern where he first entered and falls asleep under a giant pine tree. He dreams the goddess of the pine tree tells him that because he has eaten food in the Underworld, he must climb the tree and throw himself off the top to become human again. He awakes, climbs the tree, and flings himself down. He is a man. He thanks the pine tree and exits to the mountaintop. At home he dreams again of the goddess of the pine tree. This time she says he may not remain in the world of men because he has eaten the food of the Underworld. She tells him that a goddess down there wishes to marry him, and that she had taken the form of the bear to lure him underground. Several days later, the man returns to the Underworld cavern and is seen no more.

CONNECTIONS. Ainu People, stories from. Bears. Curiosity. Gods and goddesses. Hunters. Journeys. Pine trees. Rebirth. Serpents. Shape-shifting. Supernatural wives. Transformation. Underworld.

WHERE ELSE THIS STORY APPEARS. The Hunter in Hades—Basil Hall Chamberlain, *Aino Folk-Tales* in *Internet Sacred Text Archive*, Online. The Hunter in FairyLand—Basil H. Chamberlain. The Fairy-Tale Hunter—B. H. Chamberlain in Lafcadio Hearn, *Japanese Fairy Tales*, 1888.

237. Miss Lin, the Sea Goddess

Frances Carpenter, *Tales of a Chinese Grandmother*. China

Hundreds of years ago, the daughter in a fisherman family by the Eastern Sea dreams that the five dragon brothers who live under the ocean are angry and cause a mighty ocean storm while her father and two brothers are out in their little boats. In her dream, the daughter wades through rough waves, catches the ropes on their boats, and pulls them toward shore with her hands and teeth. Her mother hears the daughter cry out in her sleep and tries to awaken her. As the daughter opens her mouth to answer, the rope holding her father's boat in the dream slips away from her, and he drowns. That night, her brothers return alone, saying their father's boat is lost. Filled with self-reproach, the daughter runs into the sea to find her father. She never returns, but sailors often say they see her lantern right before a storm to show them the way to safety.

CONNECTIONS. Despair. Dragon Prince. Dreams. Eastern Sea. Failure. Family life. Fathers and daughters. Fishermen. Foretellings. Loss. Reality. Remorse. Rescues. Sea. Storms.

HOW ELSE THIS STORY IS TOLD. The Empress of Heaven — Wolfram Eberhard, *Folktales of China*.

238. Misokai Bridge

Fanny Hagin Mayer, *Ancient Tales in Old Japan*. Japan

A poor charcoal maker Chō Kichi, who lives in Sawakami village in Niukawa-mura, dreams that a hermit has told him to stand by Misokai Bridge in Takayama to hear good news. Chō Kichi sells charcoal along the way to Takayama. Then he stands on the bridge for three days, but does not hear anything special. On the fifth day, the owner of a tofu shop near Misokai Bridge asks Chō Kichi why he stands there every day. Chō Kichi tells him about his dream. The man scoffs at the thought of believing dreams. He says he has dreamed about a man named Chō who lives in a village called Sawakami and has a treasure buried at the foot of a cryptomeria tree beside his house. Chō rushes home to dig at the foot of the cryptomeria tree and finds gold and silver buried there.

CONNECTIONS. Bridges. Changes in fortune. Charcoal makers. Cryptomeria trees. Dreams. Foretellings. Gojo Bridge. Irony. Journeys. Kyoto. Misokai Bridge. Mysteries. Niukawamura, province. Sawakami, village. Takayama, place. Treasure.

HOW ELSE THIS STORY IS TOLD. Gojo Bridge in Kyoto — Lafcadio Hearn, *Kwaidan*.

239. The Bee and the Dream: A Japanese Tale

Jan Freeman Long. Japan

One day, as Tasuke naps while he and his friend are gathering cedar branches for firewood, Shin sees a bee fly from Tasuke's nose. When he awakes, Tasuke tells Shin that he dreamt of gold buried in the garden of the richest man in Naniwa. Shin offers to buy Tasuke's dream and find that gold. He promises to give Tasuke a portion of whatever he finds, and Tasuke agrees. Promising to repay his relatives, Shin borrows money for his long journey and at last recognizes the garden in Naniwa with a pine tree and a white camellia from Tasuke's dream. The rich man who owns the garden agrees to let Shin dig the next day, but has his servants sneak out in the night and dig beneath the camellia bush. All they find is a pot full of bees. They rebury the pot.

The next day, Shin digs up the empty pot. He heads home, feeling foolish and unhappy, because he will not be able to repay his relatives. His wife greets him with excitement. She left the house when a swarm of bees flew in, but when she returned, gold coins, silks, and gems were scattered on the floor.

CONNECTIONS. Bees. Changes in fortune. Deceit. Dreams. Foretellings. Friendship. Husbands and wives. Mysteries. Noses. Rich man. Treasure.

HOW ELSE THIS STORY IS TOLD. The Bee and the Dream — Fanny Hagin Mayer, *Ancient Tales in Modern Japan*. The Man Who Bought a Dream — Timmy Abell in David Holt and Bill Mooney, *More Ready-to-Tell Tales from Around the World*. The Man Who Bought a Dream — Richard M. Dorson, *Folktales Told Around the World*. The Man Who Bought a Dream — Keigo Seki, *Folktales of Japan*. The Man Who Bought a Dream — Yoshiko Uchida, *The Magic Listening Cap*. Sanya Choja — Richard M. Dorson, *Folk Legends of Japan*.

240. Luck from Heaven and Luck from the Earth

Keigo Seki, *Folktales of Japan*. Japan

An honest old man suggests to his evil old neighbor that they each try to have a dream that will predict their new year. Three days later, the honest man says that he dreamed that luck had come to him from heaven. The evil man says that he dreamed that luck had come from the earth. When the honest man hoes the ground for beans, he digs up a jar filled with oban and koban coins. He honorably leaves the jar there, for the honest man is sure that this is the lucky thing from the earth his neighbor dreamed about, so it belongs to him. When the evil man reaches the field, the jar is full of snakes. He thinks his neighbor must have played a mean trick on him and goes to tip the jar of snakes into the snake hole on top of his neighbor's roof. However, coins, not snakes, fall down in the honest man's house — the luck that his dream told him would come from heaven.

CONNECTIONS. Anger. Changes in fortune. Coins. Dreams. Earth. Foretellings. Fortune. Greedy neighbor. Heaven. Honesty. Snakes. Supernatural events. Yamanashi, Japan, stories from.

HOW ELSE THIS STORY IS TOLD. *Chinese variations:* The Buried Treasure — Laurence Yep, *Tree of Dreams* (here, the youngest brother who has helped to arrange for his father's funeral digs up two jars of gold, but when the disrespectful older brother goes to retrieve his, he finds a jar of snakes). A Jar Full of Ants — Wolfram Eberhard, *Folktales of China* (this appears in the 1937 edition as A Bottle full of Ants, from Chêkiang). *Japanese variations:* Heavenly Treasure, Earthly Treasure — Elizabeth Scofield, *Hold Tight, Stick Tight*. Heaven's Blessings and Earth's Blessings — Fanny Hagin Mayer, *Ancient Tales in Modern Japan* (from Yamanashi). Kitchomu Fools His Neighbor — Richard M. Dorson, *Folk Legends of Japan*. The Snake and the Treasure of Gold — Fanny Hagin Mayer, *Ancient Tales in Modern Japan*.

241. The Grateful Ghost

Im Bang and Yi Ryuk, *Korean Folk Tales*. Korea

A scholar is journeying over the mountains to the imperial examination in Seoul, when he hears sneezing. No one is there, but he hears the sneezing again and stops to investigate. His servant digs up a dead man's skull, with vines wending through its nostrils. The scholar feels sorry for the skull and cleans it, wraps it in paper, and reburies it with an offering of food. That night an old scholar come to the man in a dream, thanks him for his kindness in caring for his skull, and tells him what will be on the examination. The next day the scholar is amazed that the examination is exactly in the same form and subject as what the ghost told him it would be. He uses the poem the ghost composed and passes with honors.

CONNECTIONS. Dreams. Ghosts. Gratitude. Imperial examination. Kindness. Old man, supernatural helper. Scholars. Skulls. Sneezing. Travelers.

WHERE ELSE THIS STORY APPEARS. The Grateful Ghost — Im Bang at D. L. Ashliman, *Folktexts*, Online.

242. The Helpful Badger

Laurence Yep, *Tree of Dreams*. Japan

Kitabayashi and his wife are too tired to clean up after their son's wedding feast. That night, Kitabayashi sees twelve badgers gather around the rice and red beans. As he watches the badger parents teaching the young ones how to eat properly, he decides that they, too, should share in his good fortune. The next day, he blocks a hole in the wall, but worried about the little ones, he leaves leftovers for them outside. The following night, he and his wife sit up to watch the badgers. They continue to leave food for them. One night robbers enter their house. One holds a sword to the man and demands money. The bedroom door crashes down, and two wrestlers stand there. They catch the swordsman's wrist as he slashes and stamp to scare the thieves away. Then the wrestlers, too, disappear. That night in his dream the badgers thank Kitabayashi and his wife for the food.

CONNECTIONS. Badgers. Dreams. Education. Food. Gratitude. Helpfulness. Husbands and wives. Kindness from animals. Kindness to animals. Parents and children. Protection. Shape-shifting. Thieves.

243. The Ghost Catcher

Mingmei Yip, *Chinese Children's Favorite Stories*. China

One time when the Emperor Xuan Zong returns from travel with a fever, he sleeps for a month. In one of his dreams, a ghost in rags arrogantly snatches the emperor's jade flute, jeweled crown, and money with its sharp nails. The ghost laughs that he is Empty Waste and likes to take people's money and waste it. When Emperor Xuan Zong shouts angrily for his guards, an even larger ghost comes and eats Empty Waste. Big Ghost bows to the emperor and tells the story of his bandaged head and heavy boots; he was a student from South Mountain who killed himself when he failed the imperial examination. However, grateful for the proper burial Xuan Zong's father gave him. Big Ghost now devours all the wicked ghosts who terrorize the kingdom. Big Ghost hands Xuan Zong his possessions, and as the emperor reaches for them, he wakes from his long sleep. The emperor asks the court painter to paint his vivid dream. This ghost-catcher painting and others help Big Ghost continue his work.

CONNECTIONS. Arrogance. Burial. Coins. Dreams. Emperors. Failure. Ghosts. Gratitude. Illness. Imperial examination. Paintings and pictures. Protection. Respect. Selfishness. South Mountain. Students. Suicide. Thieves. Xuan Zong, Emperor.

~ VIII ~

Supernatural Creatures: Tangling with Tengu, Tokkaebi, Yamaubas, Kappa, Ogres

244. The Badger and the Magic Fan

Florence Sakade, *Japanese Children's Favorite Stories*. Japan

Three tengu children are fanning their noses with one side of a magic fan to make them longer and with the other side of the fan to shrink them. Badger wants that magic fan. He takes the shape of a little girl and, carrying a plate with four bean-jam buns, asks to play. The tengu children argue about which one will get the last bun. Badger suggests they close their eyes and hold their breath to see who can do it the longest. The minute their eyes are closed, Badger snatches the magic fan and runs. At a temple in the city he sees the daughter of a wealthy man and stealthily fans her nose. It grows three feet long. Her father calls doctors, but none can help. Finally the father offers half of his wealth and his daughter's hand in marriage to the one who can cure her. Badger just happens to have the cure. He fans the daughter's nose to make it shorter. At their wedding feast, however, badger overeats and sleepily starts fanning himself with the magic fan. He does not notice that he is making his nose so long it grows through to the clouds. Some heavenly workers think his nose is a useful pole, and, ouch!, they pull Badger clear up to the sky.

CONNECTIONS. Badgers. Drums. Fans. Fathers and daughters. Healing. Humorous stories. Long nose. Magical objects. Matches, marriage. Nagasaki, Japan, stories from. Noses. Poles. Rising to the sky world. Tengu. Thunder God. Tricksters.

WHERE ELSE THIS STORY APPEARS. The Badger and the Magic Fan — Florence Sakade, *Little One-Inch*.

HOW ELSE THIS STORY IS TOLD. *The Badger and the Magic Fan* — Tony Johnston. The Bird Fan — Fanny Hagin Mayer, *Ancient Tales in Modern Japan* (in this story from Nagasaki, it is a clever boy who cures the girl). *Gengoroh and the Thunder God* — Miyoko Matsutani (Gengoroh has a magic drum that plays these same tricks on a girl; he is pulled up to the heavens and learns how to make storms). The Tengu's Magic Nose Fan — Yoshiko Uchida, *The Sea of Gold* (here, too, the fan wielder is a boy).

245. Long-Nosed Goblins

Florence Sakade, *Japanese Children's Favorite Stories*. Japan

A blue long-nosed goblin and a red long-nosed goblin always compete about which has the finest nose. The blue goblin sends his nose across seven mountains to the enticing smells at a princess's party. The princess and her guests think the nose is a lovely blue pole and hang their dress cloths upon it. The cloth tickles, and when the blue goblin retracts his nose, it comes back with all the wonderful cloth. Jealous, the red goblin sends his nose down to the same mansion, but the lord's son and his friends swing on the red pole they see. Then one guest tries to carve his initials in it with a knife. The red goblin has a hard time shaking everyone off so he can pull his hurt nose back.

CONNECTIONS. Ainu People, stories from. Competition. Goblins. Humorous stories. Identity. Long nose. Nobles and lords. Penises. Princesses. Tengu. Vanity.

WHERE ELSE THIS STORY APPEARS. The Long-Nosed Goblins— Florence Sakade, *Peach Boy*.

HOW ELSE THIS STORY IS TOLD. Panaumbe, Penaumbe, and the Lord of Matomai— Basil Hall Chamberlain, *Aino Folk-Tales* (two characters each stretch their penises across to another town). *A Tale of Two Tengu*— Karen Kawamoto McCoy.

246. The Exchange at Tengu Rock

Samira Kirollos, *The Wind Children and Other Tales from Japan*. Japan

Baka-San is idly playing with a stick he found, when a Tengu flies by wearing a straw hat and coat. Baka-San would like to own that hat and coat. He pretends his bamboo stick is a magic telescope and trades the stick for the straw hat and coat that the Tengu says will make him invisible. Back in town and now invisible, Baka-San starts playing tricks on people, some funny and some mean. He teases women by pulling their sashes, eats cakes, trips a boy and then his father, and mixes up everyone's fish orders. Then he goes home to take a nap. Baku-San's wife burns the straw hat and coat because they smell. There is enough magic left in the ashes that Baka-San rubs then all over him and returns to playing eating tricks. This time, however, he drinks too much sake and sweats the ash off, so everyone can see him. As Baka-San walks home disgraced, he sees the Tengu fly by wearing a new straw hat and coat and holding a real telescope.

CONNECTIONS. Coats. Goblins. Hats. Humorous stories. Husbands and wives. Invisibility. Magical objects. Nagano, Japan, stories from. Sticks. Straw clothing. Tengu. Tokkaebi. Trades. Tricksters. Wang Liang.

HOW ELSE THIS STORY IS TOLD. **Chinese variation:** A San and the Wang Liang— Leslie Bonnet, *Chinese Folk and Fairy Tales* (A San demands a straw cap of invisibility from a Wang Liang, a large hairy mountain creature). **Japanese variations:** Exchanging Treasures— Fanny Hagin Mayer, *Ancient Tales in Modern Japan* (from Nagano). The Straw Cape— Juliet Piggott, *Japanese Fairy Tales*. *Tengo no KaKuremino*— Tomoji Noda at *Kids Web Japan*, Online. The Vanishing Rice-straw Coat— Helen and William McAlpine, *Oxford Tales from Japan*. **Korean variations:** Hats to Disappear With— I. K. Junne, *Floating Clouds, Floating Dreams* and in Joanna Cole, *Best-Loved Folktales of the World* (here, a bandit snatches a hat from one or more goblins that makes him invisible and free to play pranks for a while). The Magic Cap— Zo Song-Gab in Zon In-Sob, *Folk Tales from Korea*. The Magic Clothes— James Huntley Grayson, *Myths and Legends from Korea* (a man who thinks he is invisible gets caught while wearing a jacket he stole from the tokkaebi.)

247. The Promise of Massang

Eleanor Myers Jewett, *Wonder Tales from Tibet*. Tibetan People

A poor, bitter man with one cow wishes for a calf. Instead, a ragged boy appears in his shed soon after. The boy, Massang, promises to bring him wealth, even though the man chases him off. Massang meets a Green man, a Black man, and a White man, but he worries that they may not be trustworthy companions, as each night the dinner has disappeared. When it is Massang's turn to cook, a little old woman asks to taste the stew. Massang is sure she is a witch and sends her off with a perforated pail to fetch water so he can examine her bundle. He finds iron scissors, an iron hammer, and catgut, all of which grow larger as he takes them out. He breaks the catgut as she tries to bind him and hammers on her head. His companions follow her blood trail to the cave where she dies. As they hold the catgut, Massang climbs down to the bottom of the cave and sends up bags of jewels, but the three men abandon him down there. Massang buries three cherry pits. They grow into trees overnight, and he climbs the tallest tree up out of the cave. Massang's wicked companions now live in fancy houses and think he is a ghost when he appears. He orders them to take half of their riches to the poor man by the river with one cow.

CONNECTIONS. Catgut. Caves. Cherry trees. Deceit. Fighting supernatural opponents. Iron hammer. Iron scissors. Jewels. Magical objects. Promises. Tibetan People, stories from. Trust. Witches.

248. Yamanba of the Mountain

Cathy Spagnoli, *Asian Tales and Tellers*. Japan

Behind a quiet village there is a high mountain no villagers ever climb because they fear the yamanba, a witch, who lives on top. One day, a voice thunders that it is the yamanba's new son speaking. He threatens to devour all the villagers if they do not bring him mochi. The villagers pound and boil and shape the rice balls. Only a very old woman volunteers to bring them up the mountain. She perseveres in the face of a great wind, even after the two young men with her turn back. At last, the old woman reaches the top, where she finds a hollering baby and a yamanba, who accidentally knocks her down and then welcomes her with unexpected friendliness. The lonely yamanba apologizes if the baby wasn't being polite and asks if the woman will stay and help her for two weeks. In thanks for her kindness, the yamanba gives the woman a magic swatch of gold brocade. When the old woman returns to the village, she cuts the brocade into pieces for each family. After that, the villagers visit with the yamanba, and she looks out for them.

CONNECTIONS. Babies. Changes in attitude. Courage. Fear. Friendship. Heroes, women. Identity. Kindness. Mochi. Mountains. Peace. Ultimatums. Villagers. Witches. Yamauba.

HOW ELSE THIS STORY IS TOLD. *The Witch's Magic Cloth*—Miyoko Matsutani.

249. The Mountain Witch and the Peddler

Yoshiko Uchida, *The Magic Listening Cap*. Japan

A peddler crossing the mountains runs from a witch with wild hair, a huge mouth, and fiery eyes who demands all of his salted mackerel or she will eat him and his horses. He is so tired, he enters a little house in the woods where no one is home and lies down upstairs. The witch enters in the middle of the night and starts fixing food for herself, asking questions aloud. From upstairs, the peddler whispers answers, and she follows his advice. He whispers that she should sleep in the kettle. And she does. He creeps down, lights a fire underneath the kettle, and races back to his village, where no one is bothered by the witch anymore.

CONNECTIONS. Chases. Cleverness. Humorous stories. Mountains. Outsmarting supernatural opponents. Questions. Peddlers. Travelers. Ultimatums. Witches. Words. Yamauba.

250. Three Charms

Cathy Spagnoli, *Asian Tales and Tellers.* Japan

A kind monk does not want the boy to go pick chestnuts because there is a shape-changing, boy-eating yamanba in the woods. When the boy insists, the monk gives him three slips of paper with special writing for protection. The boy becomes lost in the woods and knocks at a cottage door. He is fed dinner and given a place to sleep by a friendly-looking old woman. Waking in the night, he discovers that the old woman is now a scary yamanba with glowing eyes and a red tongue who roars that she will eat him. When he tells her he needs to go to the outhouse, she ties her obi around his waist. Once outside, he reties the obi to a post with one of the monk's papers and tells the post to answer the yamanba in his voice. He flees. Eventually, the yamanba angrily yanks on the obi and pulls the whole outhouse down. Then she gives chase. The boy throws another charm, telling it to make a river, and his last charm, telling it to make a mountain. He reaches the temple before the yamanba does, and the monk hides him. The monk asks the mountain witch if she can truly become gigantic. She fills the room to show him. He asks how small she can make herself. When she is as tiny as a soybean, he eats her.

CONNECTIONS. Akita, Japan, stories from. Charms. Chases. Children. Cleverness. Flesh-eaters. Magical objects. Monks. Oni. Ōnyūdō. Outsmarting supernatural opponents. Protection. Shape-shifting. Witches. Woods. Yamauba.

HOW ELSE THIS STORY IS TOLD. Eating a Demon in One Bite — Fanny Hagin Mayer, *Ancient Tales in Modern Japan* (here, the priest tricks an ōnyūdō). The Three Charms — Fanny Hagin Mayer, *Ancient Tales in Modern Japan* (from Akita). The Three Lucky Charms — Keigo Seki, *Folktales of Japan* (in this tale, the yamauba is a female oni). *The Three Magic Charms/ Taberareta Yamanba* — Miyoko Matsutani on kamishibai story cards. The Privy at the Demon's House — Fanny Hagin Mayer, *Ancient Tales in Modern Japan* (in this telling there are three boys, and the witch drowns trying to chase them).

251. Lon Po Po: A Red-Riding Hood Story from China

Ed Young. China

When a mother needs to leave her three girls in the house alone, she warns them to lock the door because of wolves in the woods. A wolf does come to the door pretending to be the children's mother. At last, they do open the door, thinking it is their grandmother. The wolf blows out the candle and is thinking about eating the plump children. In bed, they question her hairy tail and claws, but the wolf seems have explanations ready. And then the eldest girl lights the candle long enough to catch a glimpse of the wolf's tail. She leads her sisters outside, saying they will pick special ginko nuts for their grandmother. Once they are all safely up in the tree, they invite the wolf to pick the nuts herself. Twice they drop the basket, while trying to haul the wolf up, and the third time, the wolf breaks into pieces.

CONNECTIONS. Children. Cleverness. Deceit. Fear. Ghosts. Gingko nuts. Han People, stories from. Heroes, women. Identity. Liaoning Province, China, stories from. Moon. Origins. Outsmarting supernatural opponents. Problem solvers. Red Riding Hood stories. Rising to the sky world. Sun. Supernatural creatures. Taiwan, stories from. Tigers. Witches. Wolves. Woods. Yamauba.

HOW ELSE THIS STORY IS TOLD. **Chinese variations:** A Family and a Ghost — Yao Li in Howard Giskin, *Chinese Folktales. Auntie Tiger* — Laurence Yep. Auntie Tigress — Gia-Zhen Wang, *Auntie Tigress* (this story combines elements present in several other stories: a child's unlocking the door to a dangerous imposter, being allowed to go to the outhouse tied by a rope, and being given three magic charms, the last of which is golden hair that becomes hundreds of mice who terrify the tigress and enable the girl to escape). Grandmother Wolf—*Folk Tales from China*, Second Series (from the Han People). The Panther — Richard Wilhelm, *The Chinese Fairy Book*. Small Sweep and the Wolf — Yao Ming in Howard Giskin, *Chinese Folktales* (from Liaoning Province). *Wolf-"Mother"*— Haiwang Yuan, *The Magic Lotus Lantern and Other Tales from the Han Chinese*. **Japanese variations:** The Golden Chain from Heaven — Keigo Seki, *Folktales of Japan*. Mr. Sun's Chain — Hiroko Fujita, *Folktales from the Japanese Countryside* (it is a yamauba who tries to trick the children). O, Sun, the Chain — Fanny Hagin Mayer, *Ancient Tales in Modern Japan*. **Korean variations:** (in many of these variations, the tiger demands that the mother give him various body parts before eating her totally and moving on to trick the children. The children escape by being hauled up to heaven on a golden chain where they become celestial bodies). Mister Moon and Miss Sun —*Long Long Time Ago*. The Origin of the Sun and the Moon — Y.T. Pyun, *Tales from Korea*. Sun and Moon — Linda Soon Curry, *A Tiger by the Tail*. Sun and Moon — Suzanne Crowder Han, *Korean Folk and Fairy Tales*. The Sun and the Moon — O Hwa-Su in Zong In-Sob, *Folk Tales from Korea*. The Sun Girl and the Moon Boy— Yangsook Choi. The Sun, the Moon, and the Stars— James Riordan, *Korean Folk-tales*. Sun, Moon and Stars— Chun Shin-Yong, *Korean Folk Tales*. The Three Little Girls— Kim So-un, *Korean Children's Favorite Stories*. **Taiwanese variation:** The Tiger Witch — Cora Cheney, *Tales from a Taiwan Kitchen*.

252. Which Was Witch?

Eleanore M. Jewett, *Which Was Witch?* Korea

The scholar Kim Su-ik grows hungry one midnight while he is studying in his house just outside of Seoul. His wife appears with a bowl of hot roasted chestnuts for him. Then the door opens and another woman identical to his wife also stands holding a bowl of roasted chestnuts. Which is his true wife? Kim Su-ik knows one woman must be a witch. He seizes each by the arm, one in each hand. Neither reacts strongly, even when he shakes them. Kim Su-ik holds on until dawn, when the woman in his left hand begins to struggle and snarl to get away. She becomes a wildcat and springs out the window. Kim Su-ik's true wife murmurs that he has been studying too hard, but she has no memory of what transpired this past night.

CONNECTIONS. Chestnuts. Husbands and wives. Identity. Outsmarting supernatural opponents. Scholars. Transformation. Witches.

253. The Old Man with a Wen

Florence Sakade, *Urashima Taro and Other Japanese Children's Stories*. Japan

An old woodcutter with a lump on his right cheek hides in a hollow tree when it begins to rain. He falls asleep, and when he wakes, it is night. Red and green elves are dancing. One elf drags him over and makes him dance for them. He dances a jig the best he can. The elves are so entertained that they take his wen, saying they will only return his lump when he comes back to dance for them again. The old man is delighted not to have his wen. His next door neighbor goes to the mountain hoping to get rid of his wen, too. The elves, however, are not happy with his dancing and give him the other man's lump to keep him from returning.

CONNECTIONS. Dancing. Dwarfs. Elves. Goblins. Humorous stories. Physical difference. Rewards. Talents. Tibetan People, stories from. Wens. Woodcutters.

WHERE ELSE THIS STORY APPEARS. The Old Man with a Wen — Florence Sakade, *Japanese Children's Favorite Stories*, Book Two.

HOW ELSE THIS STORY IS TOLD. *Chinese variations:* Hok Lee and the Dwarfs — Pearl S. Buck, *Fairy Tales of the Orient*. The Story of the Man with the Goitre — A. L. Shelton, *Tibetan Folk Tales* and at D. L. Ashliman, *Folktexts*, Online. The Story of Hok Lee and the Dwarfs — Andrew Lang, *The Green Fairy Book* and at D. L. Ashliman, *Folktexts*, Online. *Japanese variations:* The Elves and the Envious Neighbor — Baron Algernon Bertram Freeman-Mitford Redesdale, *Tales of Old Japan* and at D. L. Ashliman, *Folktexts*, Online. How an Old Man Lost His Wen — Yei Theodora Ozaki, *Japanese Fairy Book*. How an Old Man Lost His Wen — F. Hadland Davis, *Myths and Legends of Japan* and at D. L. Ashliman, *Folktexts*, Online. *Kobutori: The Old Man and the Devils* — Japanese Fairy Tales Series, No. 7. Lump Off, Lump On — Helen and William McAlpine, *Oxford Tales from Japan*. The Man with the Wen — Indries Shah, *World Tales*. The Old Man and the Devils — Lafcadio Hearn and Others, *Japanese Fairy Tales*. The Old Man Who Got a Tumor — Fanny Hagin Mayer, *Ancient Tales in Modern Japan* (from Yamagata). The Old Man Who Had Wens — Keigo Seki, *Folktales of Japan*. The Old Man with the Bump — Yoshiko Uchida, *The Dancing Kettle*. The Old Man with the Wen — Iwaya Sazanami, *Iwaya's Fairy Tales of Old Japan*. The Old Man with the Wen — Alan Leslie Whitehorn, *Wonder Tales of Old Japan*. The Story of the Old Man Who Had His Wen Taken Off by a Goblin — Takeshi Nakajima, *Japanese Traditional Tales*. *Korean variation:* The Singing Lump — Suzanne Crowder Han, *Korean Folk and Fairy Tales*.

254. The Outsize Candy Figure

Folk Tales from China, Second Series. Han People

Lao Erh, the younger brother, works odd jobs and never complains that his older brother, Lao Ta, grabs all of the family property when their father dies. One day Lao Erh slides in the mud, carrying two buckets of syrup through the rain. Goblins think he is a giant candy man and rush him to their cave. They bring out a little drum that produces food when they beat it. Lao Erh does not move until they carry their festivities outside. Then, he snatches the magic drum and runs home. He now has plenty to eat. Lao Ta hears about the drum and pours syrup all over himself. Goblins carry him to their cave, but a long-horned goblin says that since he got away the last time, they should boil him first. Lao Ta too jumps out of the pot, but he cannot run very fast and the goblins catch him. To punish him, they each pull his nose until it is seven feet long. Lao Erh hides in the cave to see if he can find a cure for his brother. He overhears the goblin's laughing that all Lao Ta has to do is rap on the drum and say "shrink" to cure his nose. Back at home, Lao Ta's wife grabs the drum and pounds it so furiously that Lao Ta's nose disappears into his head.

CONNECTIONS. Brothers. Caves. Clubs. Drums. Fairies. Goblins. Hammers. Han People, stories from. Humorous stories. Husbands and wives. Identity. Jealousy. Long nose. Magical objects. Mallets. Tokkaebi.

WHERE ELSE THIS STORY APPEARS. The Outsize Candy Figure — At D.L. Ashliman, *Folktexts*, Online.

HOW ELSE THIS STORY IS TOLD. *Chinese variations:* The Candy Man — Catherine Edwards Sadler, *Treasure Mountain*. The Long Nose — Leslie Bonnet, *Chinese Folk and Fairy Tales* (here and in the story below, the youngest brother takes a food-producing stick from the Immortals). The Long Nose — Wolfram Eberhard, *Folktales of China* (from Central China). The Wishing Cup—Lotta Carswell Hume—*Favorite Children's Stories from China and Tibet* (the cave contains eight fairies). **Korean variations:** The Ghost's Treasure-Mallet—Chun Shin-Yong, *Korean Folk Tales.* The Goblins' Magic Stick—Gillian McClure, *The Land of the Dragon King and Other Korean Stories.* The Magic Club—James Riordan, *Korean Folk-tales.* The Magic Hammer—I. K. Junne, *Floating Clouds, Floating Dreams.* The Mallet of Wealth—Zon Bog-Sul in Zon In-Sob, *Folk Tales from Korea.* The Ogres' Magic Clubs—*Long Long Time Ago.* The Tokkaebi's Club—Suzanne Crowder Han, *Korean Folk and Fairy Tales.* The Two Brothers—Y.T. Pyun, *Tales from Korea.*

255. A Kappa and a Fish Peddler

Hiroko Fujita, *Folktales from the Japanese Countryside.* Japan

One day a fish peddler buys a kappa to stop several village boys from tormenting the stretchy water monster. He warns the kappa not to play tricks on human children who think that he is drowning them. The next morning and every morning for three months, the peddler finds a heap of fish outside his door, which he sells for a lot of money. He decides that he will get lazy and goes to the river. He calls for the kappa not to bring him any more fish. A voice from the river answers that kappas give rewards for a whole year, so he will have to accept the fish for nine months more. The peddler does get lazy, and when all of his money is gone, he goes to the river to fish and catches a very tiny kappa. This little kappa says that he is the god of kappas and will bring the man a lifetime's supply of rice if he releases him. The peddler releases the kappa and receives one bag of rice the next morning. He is surprised, for he expected more, the lifetime supply the kappa promised. Kappas always keep their promises, and the supply of rice is dwindling. He is just wondering when more rice will arrive when a thunderbolt strikes him dead.

CONNECTIONS. Death. Fish. Humorous stories. Kappa. Kindness. Laziness. Misunderstandings. Peddlers. Promises. Rewards. Rice.

256. The Funny Little Woman

Arlene Mosel. Japan

One day a little old woman who likes to laugh and likes to make rice dumplings chases one of her dumplings down into a hole that opens in her floor. She runs past two Jizo statues, who warn her not to continue to follow the dumpling because wicked oni live down the way. She laughs and keeps running. She hides behind the third Jizo when the oni comes, but her laughter gives her away, and he rows her to a strange house across the lake where he teaches her how to make rice dumplings with a magic paddle that quickly multiplies the rice. After a while, the woman tucks the magic paddle into her sash and jumps in a boat to cross the water and go home. The onis drink all of the water from the lake to stop her, but the sight of the little woman floundering in the mud makes them laugh. Water spills from their mouths back into the lake. The little woman jumps back in the boat and escapes with the magic rice paddle.

CONNECTIONS. Captivity. Chases. Escapes. Goblins. Humorous stories. Jizo. Laughter. Magical objects. Oni. Paddles. Rice dumplings. Underground.

HOW ELSE THIS STORY IS TOLD. The Funny Little Woman—Kate D. Wiggin, *Tales of Laughter. The Magic Rice Paddle*—Etsu Sasaki on kamishibai story cards. The Old Woman and the Rice Cakes— Ethel Johnston Phelps, *The Maid of the North*. The Old Woman Who Lost Her Dumplings— Lafcadio Hearn and Others, *Japanese Fairy Tales*; in *The Boy Who Drew Cats and Other Japanese Fairy Tales*; in Joanna Cole, *Best-Loved Folktales of the World*, and as a crepepaper book *The Old Woman Who Lost Her Dumpling*. The Rice Cake That Rolled Away — Yoshiko Uchida, *The Magic Listening Cap* and in *I.K. Junne, Floating Clouds, Floating Dreams* (here, a kindly old man following his runaway rice cake is protected by jizo from goblins and ends up with gold. His greedy neighbor does not fare so well).

257. The Three Brothers Who Grew Up in a Year

Samira Kirollos, *The Wind Children*. Japan

A father tells his three teenage sons to go away for a year and each learn something that will be useful when they are grown. Tarō, the eldest son agrees to collect wood for an Oni Baba with long fingernails and fangs at the top of the mountain. At the end of the year, however, she wants him to stay and tells him that he cannot leave until his jimbé is worn out. It will not wear out. A little voice tells him to hit the jimbé with a white stone near his foot and that tatters the jimbé. At last, he is free to go. Oni Baba gives him a mud doll that she says will both help him and provide amusement. The doll surprises Tarō by helping to get food as he travels to meet his brothers. Saburō and Jirō have both become Samurai warriors and excel at shooting arrows and working with swords. The doll tells Tarō to say that he has become a famous thief. Reluctantly, Tarō does. His uncle sets up tests, and with the doll's help, Tarō gets hold of Chinese lions and creates enough confusion to steal his uncle's well-guarded box of gold coins. The uncle is so pleased with Tarō's resourcefulness that Tarō inherits his father's house.

CONNECTIONS. Aomori, Japan, stories from. Bowls. Brothers. Dolls. Fathers and sons. Identity. Magical objects. Oni. Tests. Thieves. Travelers. Tricksters. Uncles.

HOW ELSE THIS STORY IS TOLD. Goro's Broken Bowl — Fanny Hagin Mayer, *Ancient Tales in Modern Japan* (from Aomori). The Thief Who Took the Money Box — Richard M. Dorson, *Folk Legends of Japan*. The Thief's Gambling — Fanny Hagin Mayer, *Ancient Tales in Modern Japan*. The Wonderful Talking Bowl — Yoshiko Uchida, *The Sea of Gold*.

258. The Oni and the Three Children

Keigo Seki, *Folktales of Japan*. Japan

A poor mother abandons her three boys in the mountains because she can no longer provide for them. They come to a rundown hut where an old woman hides them underground as an oni arrives. The oni smells humans and begins to search for them. When the old woman tells him that the children ran away, he pulls on his Thousand Ri in One Step boots and tears off after them. When he does not find them, he thinks he may have gone too far and lies down to rest. The old woman sends the boys out the back door. They hear thunder and find the oni sleeping. The oldest two are scared, but the youngest softly pulls off the oni's boots. The oldest boy puts on the boots and strapping his brothers to his back zips through the air back home, where they help their mother.

CONNECTIONS. Abandonment. Boots. Children. Courage. Magical objects. Mothers and sons. Mountains. Old woman, supernatural helper. Oni. Outsmarting supernatural opponents. Poverty.

259. Oniroku

Judy Sierra, *Can You Guess My Name?* Japan

A master builder stands thinking that no bridge he can build will be able to withstand the raging river below that has claimed so many lives, when a horned oni with yellow tusks and fiery eyes rises from the water. The oni roars that the builder will fail without his help. The builder agrees to pay the oni's price without knowing what that will be. The oni builds a magnificent wooden bridge across the river. Now, he demands the man's eyes. When the builder begs, the oni gives him a chance to guess the oni's name by sunset. The man runs into the woods in despair. He happens upon young oni children drumming and chanting about how happy they will be when Oniroku brings the eyes. The master builder races back to the river with the oni's name, which the oni commands he must never let anyone else know.

CONNECTIONS. Bridges. Builders. Eyes. Heroes, men. Identity. Mysteries. Names. Oni. Questions. Rivers. Secrets. Ultimatums.

HOW ELSE THIS STORY IS TOLD. The Ogre Who Built a Bridge — Yoshiko Uchida, *The Sea of Gold.*

260. The Festival of Pouring Water

Wolfram Eberhard, *Folktales of China.* Yunnan Province, China

An indestructible and cruel goblin king has just kidnapped a seventh girl to be his wife. She asks him if he can live forever and flatters him until he reveals his one vulnerability — he fears that someone will strangle him with one of his own hairs. The seventh wife decides to try. While he sleeps, she pulls a hair from his head and wraps it around his neck. His head does fall off, but then it starts rolling by itself. Flames with ghosts spring from the ground. Her screams bring the other wives. One wife lifts the head up off the earth, and the ghosts disappear. So, all of the wives take turns carrying the goblin's head for a year. When one young woman passes it over to another, they pour water over the head to wash away blood and keep the head from starting fires. When each has a turn, it dies.

CONNECTIONS. Captivity. Cleverness. Coins. Cooperation. Dai People, stories from. Fear. Festivals. Fire. Goblins. Hair. Heads. Husbands and wives. Identity. Kidnapping. Kings. Knowledge. Okinoshima, Japan, stories from. Problem solvers. Questions. Snakes. Tengu. Tokkaebi. Water. Witches. Yi People, stories from. Yunnan Province, China, stories from.

WHERE ELSE THIS STORY APPEARS. The Festival of Pouring Water — Wolfram Eberhard in Kathleen Ragan, *Fearless Girls, Wise Women and Beloved Sisters.*

HOW ELSE THIS STORY IS TOLD. ***Chinese variations:*** Sprinkling Water Festival — Liu Haiqi, *Museum of Chinese Classic Stories,* Volume 4 (from the Dai People). The Vulnerable Spot — John Minford, *Favourite Folktales of China* (in this tale from the Yi People, a witch gets chopped by asking the man to avoid her black mark). ***Japanese variations:*** The Terrible Black Snake's Revenge — Yoshiko Uchida, *The Sea of Gold and Other Tales from Japan* (here it is a man named Badger who tricks the vicious snake monster, once inadvertently when the snake thinks he is a badger spirit pretending to be human and then by cleverly revealing his "fear" of gold coins). What Are You the Most Scared Of? — Franny Hagin Mayer, *Ancient Tales in Modern Japan* (in this tale from Okinoshima, an old woman tricks a tengu as they swap fears. He tells her what he is really afraid of, dense brush, and she pretends to fear botamochi cakes and gold coins, which he sends down into her house with great satisfaction). ***Korean variation:*** You Can't Trust a Woman — Suzanne Crowder Han, *Korean Folk and Fairy Tales* (she befriends a tokkaebi to get hold of its mallet and then asks him what he is afraid of).

261. My Lord Bag-o'-Rice

B. H. Chamberlain in Lafcadio Hearn and Others, *Japanese Fairy Tales*. Japan

It is impossible for a Warrior to cross the bridge over a lake without stepping on a huge snake, so he does. The snake turns into a Dwarf who begs him to fight on his behalf against a Centipede who lives on the mountain. The Dwarf brings the Warrior underwater to a coral summer house, but then they hear the Centipede clumping down the mountain on his 2000 poisonous feet. The Centipede is longer than one mile, and the Warrior's arrows bounce off the Centipede's head. The Warrior spits on his last arrow, and this one hits its mark. The Centipede dies, causing the ground to shudder as if there were an earthquake. The grateful Dwarf rewards the Warrior with his own castle, special armor, and both a roll of silk and bag of rice that never run out.

CONNECTIONS. Arrows. Centipedes. Dwarfs. Fighting supernatural opponents. Heroes, men. Magical objects. Rewards. Shape-shifting. Snakes. Spit. Underwater kingdom. Warriors.

WHERE ELSE THIS STORY APPEARS. *My Lord Bag-o'-Rice* — B. H. Chamberlain. Japanese Fairy Tale Series, No. 15. My Lord Bag-o'-Rice — Lafcadio Hearn and Others, *The Boy Who Drew Cats and Other Japanese Fairy Tales.*

HOW ELSE THIS STORY IS TOLD. Hidesato of the Rice Bale — Alan Leslie Whitehorn, *Wonder Tales of Old Japan.* My Lord Bag-o'-Rice — Eric Quayle, *The Shining Princess.* My Lord Bag of Rice — F. Hadland Davis, *Myths and Legends of Japan.* My Lord Bag of Rice — Yei Theodora Ozaki, *Japanese Fairy Book* and in Mike Ashley, *The Giant Book of Myths and Legends.* Tawara Toda — Takeshi Nakajima, *Japanese Traditional Tales.* Tawara Toda Hidesoto: Hidesoto o, the Rice Bale — Iwaya Sazanami, *Iwaya's Fairy Tales of Old Japan.*

262. The Ogre and the Cock

Florence Sakade, *Japanese Children's Favorite Stories*. Japan

When the farmers find all of their vegetables yanked from the ground and trampled, they yell at the blue ogre with a single horn who lives at the top of the steep mountain. The ogre brags that he can do anything he wants. The farmers challenge him to build a stone stairway with one hundred steps in one night. If he can do it, they will send him the one human a day he requests for dinner. If he cannot, he will go. The ogre sneaks into a farmyard and covers the chickens with straw hoods so they will not crow at dawn, and he will have more time to work. A good fairy sees his trick and pulls the hood off of one rooster. It crows at daybreak. The stairway is one step short. The ogre goes away.

CONNECTIONS. Arrogance. Fairies. Farmers. Flesh-eaters. Ogres. Outsmarting supernatural opponents. Roosters. Stone stairway. Tests. Ultimatums.

WHERE ELSE THIS STORY APPEARS. The Ogre and the Rooster — Florence Sakade, *Japanese Children's Favorite Stories* (later editions).

HOW ELSE THIS STORY IS TOLD. The Demons' Cave — Richard M. Dorson, *Folk Legends of Japan.*

263. The Three Families

Liu Haiqi, *A Museum of Chinese Classic Stories*, Volume 2. Bonan People

Three families that live in Dahejia near the Yellow River always work together. The head of the eastern family has Distant Ears that can hear from far away. The head of the western family has Farsighted Eyes that can see through mountains. The head of the northern family has Omnipotent Hands. Jealous, the Devil in South Mountain calls for the God of the Yellow River to flood Dahejia. Distant Ears warns the two heads. Distant Eyes buys two cows that are being slaughtered under the mountain and from their hides Omnipotent Hands makes two rafts on which the families survive the flood. Then Distant Ears overhears the Devil call the plague gods. Again, the heads of the other two families find and prepare mugwort to keep everyone safe from illness. The Devil sends the mountain bird Chijiaozi to create dissension among the families. This time the families quarrel and separate. Now the Devil can kill them. The heads of the three families warn their descendants to work together again.

CONNECTIONS. Bonan People, stories from. Chijiaozi, supernatural bird. Community. Conflict. Cooperation. Dahejia. Devils. Ears. Eyes. Fables. Fighting supernatural opponents. Hands. Jealousy. Parables. South Mountain. Talents. Yellow River.

264. The Four Sworn Brothers

Y. T. Pyun, *Tales from Korea*. Korea

A man of great strength who walks from one mountain peak to another in Stone Shoes sees a man in Iron Shoes. They decide to join up and wrestle to see which one will become the elder brother. Then they see a tall tree in the valley that has been set swaying by the snores of a giant and ask him to become their brother, too. When the Snorer blows his nose and knocks them over, he becomes the elder brother. A giant who spits so hard that he creates a new stream joins their teams as the fourth and eldest brother. An old woman invites them in, but they become prisoners of her and her human-eating sons. One of the old woman's sons proposes a contest. First the four sworn brothers pull up trees and toss them over, while the four real brothers stack them high. So many trees come flying that the four real sons give up for the first time in their lives. The next day the four sworn brothers stack the trees three times as high as the real brothers did the day before. They are caught inside, and the old woman and her sons set fire to the stack. The Spitter puts out the fire with so much water that the old woman and her sons swim for their lives until the Snorer blows and freezes their bodies in ice, at which point Stone Shoes and Iron Shoes knock off their heads.

CONNECTIONS. Brothers. Competition. Cooperation. Extraordinary children. Fire. Flesh-eaters. Iron shoes. Magical objects. Outsmarting supernatural opponents. Shoes. Snoring. Spit. Stone shoes. Strength. Supernatural creatures. Talents. Tests. Tigers. Trees.

HOW ELSE THIS STORY IS TOLD. The Four Mighty Brothers— James Riordan, *Korean Folk-tales* (extraordinarily strong baby boy Iron Back sets off and meets other extraordinary companions and outwits four tiger brothers and their mother who try to harm him). Four Sworn Brothers— Zo Ze-Ho in Zong In-Sob, *Folk Tales from Korea*.

265. The Twins of Paikala Mountain

M. A. Jagendorf and Virginia Weng, *The Magic Boat and Other Chinese Folk Stories*. Oroqen People

After their parents are caught by the ferocious, hairy mani on Paikala Mountain, a boy twin and a girl twin look after each other. One day, however, Altanay and the mani both die in a fight. Katuyen cannot bring her brother back to life. The Spirit of the Pine tree she leans against tells her to spread its oil over her brother's body and to send a skilled archer to Chief Salgutai who lives by the ocean with three daughters. Katuyen puts on her brother's clothes and practices shooting with his bow and arrow until she is skillful. With a branch from The Spirit of the Pine that becomes a magic horse she gallops to the ocean, where the horse grows wings to fly her over to Salgutai's island. Chief Salgutai does not want his daughters to return with Katuyen and tries to poison her, but Katuyen, suspicious, is careful. Then she surprises the soldiers Salguti sends by shooting an arrow through ninety-nine of their torches. At last Salgutai sends his daughters home with Katuyen with a silver hairpin to use at the right moment. Magic goose feathers help them fly back to Paikala Mountain. The first and second daughters draw a circle around Altanay, mistaking him for Katunya dead. When he does not move, they fly home. The third daughter sticks the hairpin into the earth near Altanay, and he begins to breathe. The third daughter and Altanay get married and Katuyen lives with them.

CONNECTIONS. Archers. Brothers and sisters. Chieftains. Devotion. Feathers. Fighting supernatural opponents. Flesh-eaters. Flying horses. Hairpins. Heroes, women. Horses. Identity. Kidnapping. Love. Magical objects. Mani. Oroqen People, stories from. Paikala Mountain. Pine oil. Pine tree spirit. Rebirth. Rescues. Spirits. Supernatural wives. Tests. Trees. Twins. Wooden horses.

266. Bowl Mountain

Zhao Ye in Howard Giskin, *Chinese Folktales*. Liaoning Province, China

One year, a man and his three sons are visited by an ugly river spirit that demands their harvest. One by one, each son goes to the wise man in the East for help. The wise man wants the sons to pull two of their own teeth to replace the missing teeth in the stone horse's mouth. The horse will eat grass and become real, and they will be able to ride it after going through a mountain of fire and a cold sea to retrieve a magic bowl. The wise man gives each young man a choice between taking this journey or taking a box of gold. The first two sons take the gold and disappear. The third son accomplishes the tasks and finds the magic bowl. When the river spirit demands vegetables and pigs, the third son throws the magic bowl at him. The ugly river spirit is trapped underneath and can no longer bother them. The two elder sons spend all the gold and become beggars.

CONNECTIONS. Animation. Bowls. Brothers. Choices. Courage. Determination. East. Fathers and sons. Fire. Gold. Heroes, men. Liaoning Province, China, stories from. Magical objects. Old man, supernatural helper. Outsmarting supernatural opponents. Quests. Rivers. River spirit. Sacrifice. Sea. Spirits. Stone horse. Trials. Ultimatums. Wise man.

267. The Lushung Festival

Liu Haiqi, *A Museum of Chinese Classic Stories*, Volume 1. Miao People

The greedy Pheasant Demon on the other side of the mountain is determined to have beautiful, accomplished Awang as his wife. Disguised as a rich stranger, he brings many gifts, but Awang's father sees the evil within him and refuses his suit. One day while Awang is sewing with some girls, a sandy wind flings them to the ground. When the dust clears, Awang is gone. The young men organize a Fighting Pheasant Demon Group to rescue her. They fight valiantly, but the Pheasant Demon's wings beat them back. The wandering hunter Moosha arrives and fights relentlessly. He succeeds in shooting an arrow into the demon's neck. Moosha brings Awang home and disappears. She grows weaker, missing him. To rally her spirits, Awang's father makes a bamboo pipe instrument he teaches all the young men to play. Moosha returns during one festival and falls in love with Awang.

CONNECTIONS. Bamboo. Cooperation. Demons. Disguises. Festivals. Fighting supernatural opponents. Heroes, men. Hunters. Kidnapping. Loss. Love. Miao People, stories from. Music. Pheasant demon. Pipes, bamboo. Rescues. Shape-shifting. Talents. Wind.

HOW ELSE THIS STORY IS TOLD. How Panpipes Came to Be Played — *The Seven Sisters: Folk Tales from China.*

268. The Mountain Witch and the Dragon King

Gim Han-Yong in Zong In-Sob, *Folk Tales from Korea.* Korea

A turtle promises to help a warrior who rescues it from being tormented by boys. Later, a beautiful woman, who is really a thousand-year-old fox, threatens to kill the warrior with swords of flame that materialize from the air if he will not marry her. The warrior goes to the shore and calls for the Dragon-King to help him. The Dragon-King sends his three brothers back with him. The fox woman severs them with pillars of flame. The warrior requests another month to decide about marriage. The Dragon-King tells him that they must ask the Heavenly King to punish her. Three warriors go to the mountain. A thunderbolt falls on the woman's house and kills her. They find a dead fox inside.

CONNECTIONS. Dragon King. Fighting supernatural opponents. Fire. Foxes. Heavenly King. Kindness to animals. Matches, marriage. Shape-shifting. Supernatural creatures. Turtles. Ultimatums. Warriors.

269. The Son of the Mountain

Folk Tales from China, Second Series. Mongolian People

A ruthless queen has sent ten men to kill a fifty-foot monster in a lake in the northwest so she can make a magic garment from its skin that will keep the king comfortable in all temperatures. Son of the Mountain, a young hunter with an iron bow, helps them on the condition that they not tell the king who actually kills the monster. However, the king finds out and forces Son of the Mountain to make the coat from the monster's hide. Now the queen sends Son of the Mountain to get the demon's magic hat to go with it. At a purple yurt, Son of the Mountain kills the snake that has been picking off the daughters of the phoenix each day. The grateful mother phoenix takes him on her back to the demon's home. She tells Son of the Mountain to shout for the demon, while she snatches the hat. However, the hat is held on with a chinstrap, so the demon rises in the air with them, until Son of the Mountain hits him with his bow. Next, the queen prompts the king to demand that Son of the Mountain obtain a heavenly handmaid for him. The phoenix flies him first to some kind people in the sky and then on to the South Gate of Heaven and tells him how to make his request of the immortal's mother. Son of the Mountain is able to leave with an immortal and stops back at the houses in the sky, where he picks up one daughter from each house plus a silver needle, yellow satin, and a little mirror. The queen plans to kill Son of the Mountain, as she thinks he is too dangerous. The king and queen tell him that overnight he must raise a yellow satin yurt with silver pillars and a glass city on top of the mountain or die. With the help of the magic objects from the sky, it is done. The immortal tells Son of the Mountain to shoot his arrows at the royal warriors. He does, the glass city cracks, and water pours down the mountain and drowns the king and queen. Son of the Mountain becomes king with the immortal as his wife.

CONNECTIONS. Cooperation. Deceit. Demons. Fighting supernatural opponents. Floods. Glass city. Hats. Heaven. Heroes, men. Hunters. Immortals. Kings. Magical objects. Mongolian People, stories from. Monsters. Phoenix. Queens. Skin. Snakes. Supernatural wives. Tests. Ultimatums.

WHERE ELSE THIS STORY APPEARS. The Son of the Mountain — *The Peacock Maiden: Folk Tales from China.*

270. The Heavenly Song of the Green-Spotted Dove

M.A. Jagendorf and Virginia Weng, *The Magic Boat.* Lisu People, China

The son of a rich mountain lord and the son of a poor farmer are floating down the river on a raft of banana logs when the rich son throws his sword at a carp and accidentally cuts the boat in two. The young farmer drifts to a deserted village where he finds two young women hiding in a cupboard. They tell him that a python and an eagle have killed many people while they were out collecting herbs. The python and eagle attack the farmer, but he bravely kills them. The two young women come with him to look for his lost friend, whom they do find in the woods at last. The young lord marries the vain elder girl, and the young farmer marries the younger daughter who has done all of the cooking along the way. The young lord sees the farmer's wife all washed one day and wants her for himself. Faking a hunting expedition, he tricks his friend, who falls into a magic cave. The young farmer finds himself surrounded by little ant people. He helps them plant crops. The King of the Ants is grateful, but concerned that the farmer will eat too much, as he is a giant and keeps him captive. Some of the ant people sneak him food. He makes a bamboo flute. Enchanted, animals offer to help him escape in exchange for the flute. Plans keep failing, though, until the Green-Spotted Dove gets her friends to bend bamboo branches down so that when they spring back they fling him home, where the farmer rescues his wife. Ever after, the Green-Spotted Dove sings the flute song with her heart.

CONNECTIONS. Ants. Bamboo. Captivity. Deceit. Doves. Eagles. Farmers. Fighting supernatural opponents. Flutes. Husbands and wives. Kindness from animals. Lisu People, China, stories from. Maidens. Music. Nobles and lords. Origins. Pythons. Rescues. Rivers. Snakes. Trades. Wife-stealing.

271. The Great Flood

Wolfram Eberhard, *Folktales of China.* Shantung, China

One day a poor old woman shares rice with a beggar monk, who tells her to ask her son Chou to make a boat from paper and flour, for when she sees the eyes of two lions in front of the temple turn red, there will be a flood that covers the town. The monk tells her that she and Chou may rescue sparrows, ants, and snakes, but to bring no men or wolves into the boat. Two rascals in town secretly paint the lions' eyes red, but Chou and his mother take that as a sign and get into their boat. Suddenly water surrounds them. They do save a sparrow, ants, and a snake, as well as a wolf and a man his mother feels sorry for. They land on an island and build themselves a little house. Then Chou and Wu, the rescued man who calls himself Chou's brother, go to sell firewood in town. Thinking a certain black cloud may be an evil spirit, Chou throws his axe in the air. It falls down bloody. He chases the cloud. When Chou lifts the stone under which the cloud has disappeared, he sees a hole. Back at home, the wolf has eaten his mother. In town there is a notice offering gold and His Excellency's daughter in marriage to the man who rescues her from the evil spirit who carried her off in a cloud. Chou asks Excellency Wang for a basket and a long chain. Wu lowers Chou down into the hole he had found before. Underground, Chou sees a sleeping ogre with a gray-blue face and two tusks. He also finds the maiden washing a wound on its black foot. Chou struggles with cutting off the ogre's seven heads that appear one by one, and the ogre dies. The grateful maiden gives him one-half of her golden hair clasp. Chou sends her up in the basket, but, before Chou can exit, Wu closes the hole, telling everyone the evil spirit is coming up. Abandoned below, Chou frees a little white dragon. They both lick a stone which takes away their hunger and thirst. Days pass. The dragon flies Chou up to earth. Chou arrives so tattered, however, that Excellency Wang thinks he is an imposter. Excellency Wang sets Chou the impossible task of separating rice from corn. The ants Chou helped in the flood divide it for him. The snakes help with the second task of carrying gold to the east room. Then Chou shows his half of the gold hair clasp, and the daughter tells her father that he is her true rescuer.

CONNECTIONS. Abandonment. Ants. Beggars. Buddha. Captivity. Clouds. Deceit. Dragons. Eyes. Fathers and daughters. Fighting supernatural opponents. Floods. Foretellings. Generosity. Golden clasp. Heads. Identity. Ingratitude. Kidnapping. Lions. Love. Magical objects. Monks. Mothers and sons. Needles. Ogres. Old man, supernatural helper. Princesses. Red eyes. Rescues. Rewards. Shantung, China, stories from. Snakes. Sparrows. Spirits. Tests. Tsunamis. Underground. Warnings. Wolves.

HOW ELSE THIS STORY IS TOLD. The Bird with Nine Heads—Richard Wilhelm, *The Chinese Fairy Book* (there is no flood here, but the male hero does rescue the princess from a cave and prove himself against an imposter by showing that he possesses the second half of a long hair needle). The Great Flood—Richard Wilhelm, *The Chinese Fairy Book* (this tale does include the red eyes and subsequent flood, along with the rescue of animals and one deceitful man with black hair). A Warning from the Gods—Robert Wyndham, *Tales the People Tell in China*. **Korean variations:** When the Buddha Wept Blood—Suzanne Crowder Han, *Korean Folk and Fairy Tales* (here, it is the statue of a Buddha whose eyes turn red. The story ends with a tsunami flooding the village when no one believes her). The Three Princesses—Kim So-un, *Korean Children's Favorite Stories* and *The Story Bag* (this story begins with the rescue of the three princess who were carried off by an eagle and are being held by an ogre underground). *See also*, The Great Flood, story #38.

272. The Shawl with Seven Stars

Liu Haiqi, *A Museum of Chinese Classic Stories*, Volume 6. Naxi People

When the cruel Drought Demon throws eight hot suns into the sky and scorches the fields and dries up Lijiang Lake, people are suffering. Yinggu makes a shawl from the feathers of birds who have died of thirst and, under its protection, crosses ninety-nine mountains to the East Sea to beg the Dragon King for help. At the shores of the East Sea she sings. The Dragon King's third Prince hears her and promises to help. Holding his arm, Yinggu flies with the Prince back to Lijiang, where he transforms into a dragon and sends a thunderstorm down from the sky. When the Drought Demon tries to burn him, the Prince changes into a stream. The Drought Demon challenges the Prince to come to his cave, where the Prince falls into a pit guarded by an elephant and a lion. The Drought Demon burns Yinggu to ashes when she tries to catch him. This violence shocks the God of Kindness, Bei Shi San Dong, who sends a Snow Dragon to swallow the eight suns. The Snow Dragon spits out one frozen sun, which becomes the moon. He presses the Drought Demon to death. The Prince's tears surround Yinggu's body. The Naxi God of Kindness turns the seven suns into shining stars for her shawl.

CONNECTIONS. Bei Shi San Dong, God of Kindness. Conflict. Cruelty. Death. Demons. Determination. Dragon Prince. Dragons. Drought. East Sea. Elephants. Feathers. Fighting supernatural opponents. Gods and goddesses. Heroes, women. Killing. Kindness. Lijiang Lake. Lions. Magical objects. Moon. Music. Naxi People, stories from. Origins. Quests. Sacrifice. Shawls. Suns. Unselfishness.

273. The Princess' Veil

Louise and Yan-Hsi Kuo, *Chinese Folk Tales*. Zhuang People

The princess Gurtashi says that she will only marry a young man who understands the meaning of the head veil she started weaving when she was eight. The chieftain hangs the veil on the palace door. A young man takes the veil at midnight, but brings it back. He says that the veil tells of a demon that guards a cave and that inside the cave is a five-colored phoenix, who will bring its rescuer great fortune. Princess Gurtashi says he is correct, but the chieftain is displeased with the young man's brashness. He orders him to get the phoenix. The princess gives the young man the red ruby from her headdress. Dazzling light from the ruby blinds the demon guard at the mountain cave. The young man returns with the five-colored phoenix, but the chieftain will not yet let him take the princess home. He tells the young man that he must first clarify the water in all fifty scummy palace ponds by morning. The young man accomplishes this task with the green emerald from the princess's headdress. The chieftain comes up with additional unreasonable tasks that the young man must accomplish or be beheaded. The princess suggests that they leave. She takes her veil and the phoenix, and they flee on horseback. When the chieftain catches up, Gurtashi chastises her father for failing to keep his word and for being so harsh. She and the young man fly into the sky on the back of the phoenix. Her spread veil renders them invisible and protects them from the her father's arrows.

CONNECTIONS. Chases. Chieftains. Demons. Embroidery. Fathers and daughters. Fighting supernatural opponents. Jewels. Love. Magical objects. Matches, marriage. Mysteries. Phoenix. Princesses. Promises. Quests. Tests. Ultimatums. Uygur People, stories from. Veils. Zhuang People, stories from.

HOW ELSE THIS STORY IS TOLD. The Gauze Engagement Scarf—Liu Haiqi, *A Museum of Classic Chinese Stories*, Vol. 1 (from the Uygur People). The Princess's Veil—Wunamarji in He Liyi, *The Spring of Butterflies and Other Folk Tales of China's Minority Peoples* (from the Uygur People).

274. The Story Bag

Kim So-Un, *The Story Bag*. Korea

There is a boy who stows all the stories he hears in a small bag he wears at his belt. By the time he is a young man, the bag is crammed full and tied tight. As the household prepares for the young man's wedding, an old servant hears whispering coming from the bag as it hangs on the wall. Voices from the stories complain about being packed up and plan revenge on the young man's wedding day. Alarmed, the faithful servant decides to leads the bridegroom's horse himself the next day to protect his young master. The servant ignores the young man's command to stop for the red berries and water he knows are poisonous, and he knocks the bridegroom over so the traditional bag of chaff he plans to step on will not have a chance to burn his feet. The bridegroom is angry at his servant, but he cannot berate him in public. After the wedding, the servant bursts into the bridal chamber with a sword and kills the hundreds of string snakes that await under the mattress. Then the servant tells the young man what he overheard from the story bag about the need for stories to be passed on.

CONNECTIONS. Bags. Berries. Chaff. Changes in attitude. Cleverness. Consequences. Devotion. Poison. Rescues. Selfishness. Servants. Silence. Snakes. Spirits. Storytelling. Weddings.

WHERE ELSE THIS STORY APPEARS. The Story Bag — Kim So-un, *Korean Children's Favorite Stories.* The Story Bag — Kim So-un at *Learning to Give*, Online.

HOW ELSE THIS STORY IS TOLD. The Pouch of Stories — Lindy Soon Curry, *A Tiger by the Tail.* The Story Spirits — Naomi Baltuck, *Apples from Heaven.* The Story Spirits — Amabel Williams-Ellis, *Round the World Fairy Tales.* The Story Spirits — Mun Czang-zun in In-Sob Zong, *Folk Tales from Korea.*

~ IX ~

The Heroes: There Is No Danger Which These Women and Men Will Not Brave for the Good of All

275. The Long-Haired Girl

John Minford, *Favourite Folktales of China*. Dong People

There is a village near a high mountain where people have to haul water from two miles away. When a girl goes up the mountain one day to gather greens for the pigs, she pulls a green turnip out of the cliff and spring water spurts up. Immediately, the turnip jumps from her hands to plug the hole back up. A gust of wind blows the girl to a cave where a hairy man tells her that he is the god of the mountain and will kill her if she tells anyone about his spring. Her long hair turns white trying to keep the spring a secret. After she sees an old man stumble while hauling a heavy water bucket, she tells the whole village to follow her to cut up the turnip plug and release the water they need. However, the girl herself vanishes. The angry god tells the girl she will have to lie on the cliff and let the spring water fall on her body. She asks to be able to return home first to arrange for someone to care for her mother. The god threatens to kill everyone if she does not come back. The girl sadly says goodbye to a banyan tree on her way back up the mountain. An old man with green hair and beard steps out. He says he has carved a stone girl who can take her place on the mountain if she pulls out her white hair for the stone girl's head and lays the statue down in her place. Her hair takes root in the stone, and the mountain god is fooled. She returns to the village above which there is now a waterfall that resembles a young girl with long, flowing, white hair.

CONNECTIONS. Bai People, stories from. Banyan trees. Community. Dali, ancient capital. Deities. Dong People, stories from. Fighting supernatural opponents. Hair. Heroes, men. Heroes, women. Old man, supernatural helper. Outsmarting supernatural opponents. Sacrifice. Spirits. Springs. Statues. Stone girl. Tree spirits. Unselfishness. Water. Waterfalls.

WHERE ELSE THIS STORY APPEARS. The Long-Haired Girl — John Minford in Kathleen Ragan, *Outfoxing Fear*.

HOW ELSE THIS STORY IS TOLD. The Long-haired Girl — Stephen Hallett, translator, in *The Magic Bird*. *The Long-Haired Girl* — Doreen Rappaport. The Story of Washing Horse Pond — A Bai tale arranged by Yang Cheng in *The Spring of Butterflies* (here it is a young man in Dali who is turned to stone by the God of the mountain peak in order to free water for his village). The White-Hair Waterfall — M. A. Jagendorf and Virginia Weng, *The Magic Boat and Other Chinese Folk Stories*.

276. Golden Chisel and the Stone Ram

John Minford, *Favourite Folktales of China*. Han People

There is only salty water in the upper Zuli River. People have heard a prophecy about spring water coming from the mouth of a Stone Ram, but no one knows what it is or where it may be. One night, the talented young stone mason, Golden Chisel digs up a ram-like looking stone from the center of a dried pond south of the village. He carves that stone into a ram over nine days and nights. The ram comes to life and wants to repay Golden Chisel for creating him. Golden Chisel says the village needs pure water most of all. The Stone Ram tells Golden Chisel that he must keep his existence secret. Every night for ninety-nine nights, the ram runs thirty miles to the Yellow River to drink up water which he empties into the village's dry pond. When he does not return on the hundredth day, Golden Chisel searches and finds the Stone Ram injured. The god of the Yellow River has cut off one of his front hooves. Golden Chisel carries the ram home and nurses him, but the village pond dries up. Golden Chisel carves a golden hoof for the little ram and rides him to the god of the Yellow River. The god is angry that his water has been stolen. He will turn Golden Chisel into a block of ice, but Golden Chisel blocks the god's icy wind with his ancestral Sun-and-Moon talisman. The god calls up water spirits and turtle demons who rush at Golden Chisel, but fire streams from the swinging talisman to stop them. Golden Chisel threatens to burn the god of the Yellow River unless he allows them to take water, and the god gives in. He takes a pearl from his mouth and tells Golden Chisel that when the ram holds this pearl in his mouth, spring water will flow. Golden Chisel and the ram race back to the village at daybreak, but they are seen. The Stone Ram becomes a pile of rocks from which sweet water flows.

CONNECTIONS. Animation. Demons. Devotion. Fighting supernatural opponents. Goats. Gods and goddesses. Golden hoof. Han People, stories from. Heroes, men. Magical objects. Sculptors. Secrets. Spirits. Statues. Stone. Stone ram. Stonecutters. Turtle demons. Warnings. Water. Water spirits. Yellow River. Zuli River.

HOW ELSE THIS STORY IS TOLD. Golden Chisel and the Stone Ram — Hua Long, *The Moon Maiden*.

277. A Stone Sheep

Liu Guirong in *The Spring of Butterflies*. Yi People, China

The Dragon King of Dali Lake in western Yunnan falls in love with the daughter of the Dragon King of Donting Lake and seizes her while she has come to watch fishermen singing. When she refuses to marry him, he sends her to look after sheep in a valley far away. That year there is a drought, and the Yi people are suffering. Two hundred of her sheep die, so she climbs over ninety-nine hilltops and ninety-nine rocky peaks to find water. Camellias bloom where drops of blood fall from the thorns that pierce her feet; grass grows where her sweat falls. She reaches the Dragon King's spring, and her tears crack the stone seal so that water flows. She then leaves to find salt for the Yi villagers. She walks over ninety-nine hilltops and ninety-nine rocky peaks until her clothes are tattered and her food gone. When the last sheep pushes at the ground, the Dragon King's brave daughter digs with her bare hands. That is how the young men find her, with her hands buried in the ground at a vein of salt and a stone sheep beside her.

CONNECTIONS. Camellias. Dali Lake. Donting Lake. Dragon King. Dragon Princess. Drought. Herders. Heroes, women. Kidnapping. Quests. Sacrifice. Salt. Sheep. Springs. Stone sheep. Tears. Unselfishness. Yi People, stories from. Yunnan Province.

278. The Hunter: A Chinese Folktale

Mary Casanova. China

In a time of drought, Hai Li Bu searches deeper into the forest to hunt for food. One day, he sees a crane snatch up a little white snake that cries for help. Hai Li Bu shoots an arrow so close, that the crane drops the snake. The next day the little snake tells him that she is the Dragon King's daughter and invites him to come with her to the crystal palace, where the Dragon King would like to thank him. Instead of precious jewels, Hai Li Bu tells the Dragon King that he wishes to help his village by understanding the language of animals. The Dragon King gives him a stone from his own mouth, but tells Hai Li Bu that he will turn to stone if he ever reveals this secret. With the stone, Hai Li Bu becomes a better hunter, and the villagers recover. But one day, Hai Li Bu overhears the animals say that the village will be flooded. No one back in the village will listen to his warning. He will die if he tells them how he knows. As rain falls, Hai Li Bu begins to speak, and he begins to turn to stone. Now, the villagers believe him and flee to higher ground. When they return, they place his stone statue on the mountaintop where it reminds them to listen to each other.

CONNECTIONS. Courage. Cranes. Crystal Palace. Dragon King. Dragon Princess. Drought. Floods. Halibu. Heroes, men. Hui People, stories from. Hunters. Knowledge. Language of animals. Magical objects. Mongolian People, stories from. Naxigaer. Sacrifice. Secrets. Snakes. Stone. Transformation. Underwater kingdom. Unselfishness. Warnings.

HOW ELSE THIS STORY IS TOLD. *Hui Chinese variation:* Naxigaer — Shuijiang Li and Karl W. Luckert, *Mythology and Folklore of the Hui* (when the small golden turtle's eyes turn red, there will be a disastrous earthquake, but Naxigaer will turn to rock if he warns people). *Mongolian Chinese variations:* Hailibu the Hunter — Stephen Hallett, translator, in *The Magic Bird*. Halibu the Hunter — John Minford, *Favourite Folktales of China*. Hunter Halibu's Great Sacrifice — M.A. Jagendorf and Virginia Weng, *The Magic Boat and Other Chinese Folk Stories*.

279. Chang-E Flies to the Moon

Mingmei Yip, *Chinese Children's Favorite Stories*. China

In ancient China ten suns, all sons of the Heaven King, are drying up everything on earth. The Heaven King sends the warrior Hou Yi down to help save earth. His wife Chang-E comes, too. She suggests that Hou Yi shoot down the suns. Nine fall into the ocean, and the tenth begs to be allowed to stay. Things are better on earth, but the Heaven King is angry about losing his sons and forbids Hou Yi to return to Heaven, which makes Chang-E sad, especially because Hou Yi is away fighting monsters much of the time. Chang-E fights with Hou Yi, who goes to Kunlun Mountain to seek advice from the Queen Mother of the West. The Queen Mother is sleeping, and he steals her immortality pills. Chang-E finds them and swallows them all. As she rises high into the sky, Hou Yi weeps. However, the guardians of heaven will not let Chang-E enter because she has left Hou Yi. She cannot return to Earth and goes to the Moon, where her only companion is a jade rabbit, forever pounding a mortar to make immortality pills. Heartbroken, Hou Yi tries to send love letters on his arrows, but his bow no longer has the power to allow them to reach her.

CONNECTIONS. Archers. Chang'e. Cruelty. Drought. Elixir of Immortality. Gods and goddesses. Han People, stories from. Heaven. Heavenly King. Heroes, men. Hou Yi. Husbands and wives. Jade rabbit. King of Heaven. Kun Lun Mountain. Loneliness. Moon. Mortars. Queen Mother of the West. Rising to the sky world. Sichuan Province, China, stories from. Suns.

HOW ELSE THIS STORY IS TOLD. The Beautiful Lady in the Moon — Lim Sian-tek, *Folk Tales from China*. Heng O, the Moon Lady — Frances Carpenter, *Tales of a Chinese Grandmother*. Ho Yi the Archer — Shelley Fu, *Ho Yi the Archer* and *Treasury of Chinese Folktales*. The Lady of the Moon — Richard Wilhelm, *The Chinese Fairy Book*. The Moon Goddess— Kathleen Ragan, *Outfoxing Fear* (here, the queen swallows the elixir of immortality to keep her cruel husband from forever making life miserable for the people of the land). The Moon Maiden — Hua Long, *The Moon Maiden*. The Origin of the Mid-Autumn Festival — Haiwang Yuan, *The Magic Lotus Lantern and Other Tales from the Han Chinese* (Hou Yi takes solace from Chang'e's presence as a shadow on the moon and spreads her favorite fruits and cakes out on a table for her to see, a practice that has become an annual tradition among some Han People). The Rabbit in the Moon — Gregory Crawford, *Animals in the Stars*. Yee and the Nine Suns— Li Yuan in Howard Giskin, *Chinese Folktales* (from Sichuan Province).

280. The Bridge of Ch'uan-chou

Wolfram Eberhard, *Folktales of China*. Fukien, China

The ruler of heaven splits open his own body and throws his entrails into the Loyang River in Fukien where sea and mountain rivers meet. They turn into an evil tortoise spirit and snake spirit who drown men with cruel winds and waves. A voice from the sky predicts that Ts'ai Hsiang will be the one to build a bridge over the Loyang. Ts'ai Hsiang, now governor of Ch'uan-chou, wonders how he is going to lay the foundations for the bridge in the rough water on the twenty-first day at the hour of yu, a time set by the dragon king. Then eight strangers appear who say they will work without pay. They play chess until yu, and the river dries up. A sand-storm obscures Ts'ai Hsiang's vision, but when it clears, the pillars have been set, and the men, perhaps the Eight Immortals, are gone. The monk I-po helps strengthen the construction and when the wood runs out, sticks his foot into the stone to cook food. He, too, becomes immortal. Ts'ai Hsiang invests his entire personal fortune in building the bridge, but he needs still more funds to complete construction. To help him, the goddess Guanyin turns herself into a beautiful woman and sails up the river. Men throw money at her, hoping to become her husband. The only piece that touches her is the fruit-seller's money helped by Lü Tung-pin's magic as he flies by on a cloud, but Guanyin vanishes. The fruit-seller drowns in the river, and Guanyin turns his body into thousands of little white fishes to feed the workmen. Construction continues, but at the end of Ts'ai Hsiang's life, the bridge is still underwater at high tide. Seven hundred years later, Li Wu digs up buried money by the temple of the earth deity and is arrested for banditry. After getting soaked crossing the river, Li Wu vows that he will build a bridge over the Loyang if he ever escapes. His guilt cannot be proven. Guanyin gives him a snail with a golden shell to present to the empress, who presses for Li Wu's release. In the end, it is Li Wu who does complete the bridge.

CONNECTIONS. Bridges. Builders. Chaochou Bridge. Ch'uan-chou, Bridge. Dragon King. Eight Immortals. Fighting supernatural opponents. Foretellings. Fukien, China, stories from. Fukien Province. Gods and goddesses. Golden snail. Governors. Guanyin, Goddess of Mercy. Han People, stories from. Heroes, men. Li Wu. Monks. Promises. Temples. Transformation. Ts'ai Hsiang. Water.

WHERE ELSE THIS STORY APPEARS. The Bridge of Ch'uan-chou — Wolfram Eberhard in Richard M. Dorson, *Folktales Told Around the World*.

HOW ELSE THIS STORY IS TOLD. Chaochou Bridge — *Folk Tales from China*, Fifth Series (from the Han People).

281. Carp Jumping Over the Dragon Gate

Mingmei Yip, *Chinese Children's Favorite Stories*, Volume 1. China

The River God is drowning many people in the angry Yellow River. The village chief tries containing the river with boulders to no avail. The struggle passes to his son. Now, for thirteen years, Yu, has been trying to channel the water. The Jade Emperor takes pity and sends his daughter Tushan Nu to help, along with a holy plow and a ghostly axe as wedding gifts. Assisted by the villagers, Yu and Tushan Nu succeed in digging a deep gorge that directs water away from the village. To honor them, the villagers build a gate over the Yellow River. However, the carp complain that with the water level so low, they can no longer swim upstream in the spring. They threaten to make giant waves. Yu challenges the carp to jump through the new Yu Gate. Tushan Nu asks her father what can be done to keep the fish from getting battered on the rocks Yu's father placed there. The Jade Emperor sends back a message that the carp that do jump high enough over the tall Yu Gate will become dragons, and the rest will remain ordinary fish. So, it is for people, too. The same golden future lies ahead for those who study hard.

CONNECTIONS. Carp. Dragons. Gates. Gods and goddesses. Gun, supernatural character. Han People, stories from. Heroes, men. Jade Emperor. Motivation. Princesses. Problem solvers. River God. Taiwan, stories from. Tests. Transformation. Tushan Nu, supernatural character. Water. Xirang. Yellow River. Yu, supernatural character. Yu Gate.

HOW ELSE THIS STORY IS TOLD. The Great Deeds of King Yu — A Han tale in M. A. Jagendorf and Virginia Weng, *The Magic Boat. Yu the Great Conquering the Flood: A Chinese Legend*— Paul D. Storrie (this graphic novel contains the legend of Yu who emerges from his father Gun as a golden dragon and becomes a man. Yu's great-grandfather, the Emperor of Heaven, Huang Di, helps him with a tortoise who dives down to fill the waters with xirang, a magical earth, against GongGong who is causing the floods. Yu's wife, here — Nu Jiao— is the daughter of a Tushun lord). Gun and Yu Conquer the Deluge — Haiwang Yuan, *The Magic Lotus Lantern and Other Tales from the Han Chinese*. **Taiwanese variation:** How to Become a Dragon — Cora Cheney, *Tales from a Taiwan Kitchen*.

282. Xueda and Yinlin

Kathleen Ragan, *Outfoxing Fear*. Hui People

In a poor community at the foot of Mount Gancialin, a widow and her daughter, Yin lin, take special care of the orphan boy, Xueda. One day, in the mountains, an old man gives Xueda three golden arrows. After that, he never misses. An old woman gives Yinlin a flute that makes people forget their troubles. When one year some villagers are afflicted with an illness that distends their bellies, Yinlin and Xueda resolve to help them. Xueda crosses steep mountains to Rock Cliff, where he has to wait for the one hot day a year when the leopard spirit comes out. His first two arrows hit their mark, and he takes the leopard's gallbladder back to the village. Yinlin arrives at the frightening Birds Cave, The four girls who have come with her turn back, but Yinlin puts the guard birds to sleep with her flute. She travels through the cave and out across a valley for three days. On Flower Mountain, a girl with a basket of irises asks Yinlin to play her flute. Surrounded by children, she sings of the suffering of the villagers. The boys and girls gather a big basket of irises for her to bring to them. A magic wind carries her swiftly home. With irises and the leopard's gallbladder, Yinlin and Xueda cure the sick villagers and live happily together.

CONNECTIONS. Arrows. Children. Community. Flower Mountain. Flutes. Gallbladder. Gancialin, Mount. Golden arrows. Healing. Heroes, men. Heroes, women. Hui People, stories from. Illness. Irises. Leopards. Love. Magical objects. Malianxian, medicinal herb. Ningxia, China, stories from. Old man, supernatural helper. Old woman, supernatural helper. Orphans. Ten Thousand Birds Cave. Ten Thousand Flowers Mountain. Ten Thousand Rock Chasm. Tinder Ridge Mountain. Wind.

WHERE ELSE THIS STORY APPEARS. Xueda and Yinlin — Wang Juenqing in Shuijiang Li and Karl W. Luckert, *Mythology and Folklore of the Hui* (from Ningxia).

HOW ELSE THIS STORY IS TOLD. Big Xue and Silver Bell — Tania Wickham, translator, in *The Magic Bird* (when the villagers at the foot of Tinder Ridge become ill, the two male heroes separate and trek to Ten Thousand Rock Chasm and through Ten Thousand Birds Cave to Ten Thousand Flowers Mountain for the leopard's gallbladder and medicinal herb that will save them).

283. The Tale of the Magic Green Water-Pearl

M.A. Jagendorf and Virginia Weng, *The Magic Boat*. Nung People, China

Villagers on the southern border of Yunnan Province flee to the mountains when a meteor flames Black Bottom Village and burns for two years. Nothing can grow in the scorched valley, and now a drought threatens to destroy the four couples who have fled to the mountain. Yen-Kang's uncle tells him that an old shaman once said life would be good if they could get the Green Water-Pearl from the pond in a cave on Spring Mountain in the east. It is guarded by a golden spider, and the only way to get past him is to kill him with the golden stinger from the stomach of Old King Bee who lives, surrounded by bees, on Flower Mountain in the west. Yen-Kang says he will try. He travels to Flower Mountain where he throws his golden shoulder pole to keep an eagle from stealing a crow child from its nest. The grateful mother crow calls for hundreds of crows to pile leaves and twigs on Flower Mountain. Yen-Kang sets the mountain on fire and flushes out Old King Bee. Mother crow brings the bee to Yen-Kang, who fights his way through a heavy web on Spring Mountain with the bee's golden stinger and then stabs the golden spider before it swallows him. The pearl he finds in the pond is too icy to hold. Yen-Kang pops it into his mouth and loses consciousness. When he awakens, he is a giant. Water pours down from his mouth to the valley below and extinguishes the meteor fires. As the shaman predicted, life is good in the village again.

CONNECTIONS. Bee monster. Bees. Crows. Drought. Eagles. Fighting supernatural opponents. Flower Mountain. Golden stinger. Gratitude. Heroes, men. Meteorites. Monsters. Nung People, stories from. Pearls. Ponds. Quests. Rivers. Sacrifice. Spider monster. Spiders. Spring Mountain. Transformation. Yenkang River. Yunnan Province.

HOW ELSE THIS STORY IS TOLD. The Water Pearl — *Folk Tales from China*, Fourth Series.

284. The Eight-Headed Dragon

Yoshiko Uchida, *The Dancing Kettle*. Japan

To trick his sister, goddess of the sun, mischievous Prince Susano destroys her handmaiden's loom one day. This time she cannot forgive him. The goddess shuts herself in a cave, leaving the earth all dark. The gods send Prince Susano away. In Izumo, he follows a stream that a pair of red chopsticks float down to a cottage where an old man, an old woman, and a young girl are weeping. An eight-headed dragon as long as eight valleys has eaten all of their other daughters and is coming for this last one. Prince Susano places jugs of wine at the foot of a boulder and tells the daughter to sit so still on top that her face reflects in each jug. The terrifying dragon arrives and, thinking he sees eight separate maidens, drinks all of the poisoned wine at once. Prince Susano chops off all eight heads. In the dragon's tail he finds a silver sword with a jeweled hilt that he presents to the emperor. For this good deed, the gods and goddesses forgive him, but Prince Susano chooses to stay in Izumo and marries the lovely daughter.

CONNECTIONS. Cleverness. Dragons. Eight-headed dragon. Exile. Fighting supernatural opponents. Forgiveness. Gods and goddesses. Heroes, men. Izumo. Poison. Problem solvers. Rescues. Self-control. Sun Goddess. Supernatural husbands. Susano. Swords. Weavers. Wine.

HOW ELSE THIS STORY IS TOLD. Ama-terasu and Susa-no-o plus Susa-no-o and the Serpent—F. Hadland Davis, *Myths and Legends of Japan*. The Dragon with the Sword in Its Tail—Juliet Piggott, *Japanese Fairy Tales*. The Eight-Headed Serpent—Teresa Pierce Williston, *Japanese Fairy Tales*. The Eight-Tailed Dragon—Takeshi Nakajima, *Japanese Traditional Tales*. *The Serpent with Eight Heads: Yamata no Orochi*—B.H. Chamberlain. Fairy Tales Series, No. 9. The Story of Susa, the Impetuous—Grace James, *Green Willow*.

285. The Wave

Margaret Hodges. Japan

The wise old man, Ojisan, lives with his grandson Toda high on a mountainside above a village by the sea. Ojisen watches an earthquake come from the sea one hot day and shake the land. He knows what it means when the waters grow dark and draw far back from the beach. There is no time to warn the four hundred villagers. Frightened, Toda does not understand when Ojisan sets fire to his own rice fields so close to harvest time. Down below, priests see the fire and ring the temple bell. Villagers rush up the mountain, but Ojisan will let no one fight the fire until everyone has arrived. The villagers, and even Toda, think he has gone mad, but then the sea returns, a tidal wave that shakes the mountain and sweeps all of the village houses away.

CONNECTIONS. Changes in attitude. Community. Earthquakes. Farmers. Fire. Grandfathers and grandsons. Heroes, men. Misunderstandings. Mountains. Problem solvers. Rescues. Sea. Tsunamis. Unselfishness. Villagers.

HOW ELSE THIS STORY IS TOLD. *Tsunami*—Kimiko Kajikawa.

286. The Tale of the Oki Islands

Eric Protter and Nancy Protter in Kathleen Ragan, *Fearless Girls, Wise Women, & Beloved Sisters*. Japan

Emperor Hojo Takatoki banishes a samurai to the feared Oki Islands around the year 1320. When people are too afraid to take her to see her father, the samurai's daughter Tokoyo, an excellent pearl diver, sails there herself. Even once she lands, a fisherman warns her not to ask about her father, but she continues to search. One night, sleeping by a shrine, she hears a girl crying. The priest is about to push the white-robed girl off the cliffs. Tokoyo stops him. He says that once a year the evil god Yofune-Nushi demands that they sacrifice one girl under fifteen years old or he will send storms that kill fishermen. Tokoyo takes the girl's place, diving down with a dagger between her teeth. She finds a wooden statue of the emperor in an underwater cave. She ties it on and battles with the giant, snakelike Yofune-Nushi. Triumphant, she brings both the statue and the creature to the surface. She is hailed as a hero by the emperor, and he releases her father.

CONNECTIONS. Courage. Devotion. Emperors. Exile. Fathers and daughters. Fighting supernatural opponents. Gods and goddesses. Heroes, women. Hojo Takatoki, Emperor. Oki Islands. Rescues. Sacrifice. Samurai. Serpents. Supernatural serpents. Tokoyo. Ultimatums. Underwater battles. Underwater caves. Yofune-Nushi.

WHERE ELSE THIS STORY APPEARS. The Tale of the Oki Islands—Eric Protter and Nancy Protter, *Folk and Fairy Tales of Far-Off Lands*. The Tale of the Oki Islands—Eric Protter and Nancy Protter in Joanna Cole, *Best-Loved Folktales of the World*. The Tale of the Oki Islands—Eric Protter and Nancy Protter in Kathleen Ragan, *Fearless Girls, Wise Women & Beloved Sisters*.

HOW ELSE THIS STORY IS TOLD. *The Samurai's Daughter*—Robert D. San Souci. The Samurai Maiden—Jane Yolen, *Not One Damsel in Distress*. A Story of Oki Islands—Richard Gordon Smith, *Ancient Tales and Folk-lore of Japan*. Tokoyo—Samira Kirollos, *The Wind Children and Other Tales from Japan*.

287. Li Chi Slays the Serpent

Kan Pao in Moss Roberts, *Chinese Fairy Tales and Fantasies*. China

For nine years, a giant serpent, almost eighty feet long, has terrorized people in Fukien in the Yung Mountain range in Yüeh. It kills officers and demands a young girl to eat in the eighth month every year. Li Chi, sixth daughter of Li Tan, volunteers to go to the serpent this time, thinking it is the best way to help her family. She sneaks off from her loving parents and asks the officials to arm her with a sharp sword and a snake-hunting dog. Li Chi places a large number of rice balls at the mouth of the serpent's cave. When the serpent emerges, she sets the dog loose to bite the giant snake. Then Li Chi creeps up behind and slashes the serpent. The serpent springs fully out of its cave and dies. Li Chi returns to Fukien with the nine skulls of the serpent's female victims, bringing honor to her family. The King of Yüeh marries her.

CONNECTIONS. Caves. Cleverness. Courage. Fighting supernatural opponents. Fukien Province. Heroes, women. Kings. Li Chi. Problem solvers. Rice balls. Sacrifice. Supernatural serpents. Ultimatums. Unselfishness. Yueh. Yung Mountains.

WHERE ELSE THIS STORY IS FOUND. Li Chi Slays the Serpent—Kan Pao in Jane Yolen, *Not One Damsel in Distress* and *Favorite Folktales from around the World*.

HOW ELSE THIS STORY IS TOLD. **Chinese variations:** Li Chi, the Serpent Slayer—Karl S. Y. Kao, *Classical Chinese Tales of the Supernatural and the Fantastic*. Li Chi Slays the Serpent—Hua Long, *The Moon Maiden*. The Serpent Slayer—Carol Kendall and Yao-wen Li, *Sweet and Sour*. The Serpent Slayer—Katrin Tchana, *The Serpent Slayer*.

288. The Bird of Happiness

John Minford, *Favourite Folktales of China*. Tibetan People

In a poor region of Tibet, where people suffer from hunger and cold, they imagine happiness as a beautiful bird that lives far away in the east on a snow-covered mountain. They say that three old monsters guard the Bird of Happiness by blowing through their beards. The villagers send people out to find the bird, but none return. Now they spread barley on the boy

Wangjia's head for luck and send him off to find the bird. When Wanjia refuses to kill some-one's mother, the monster with the black beard blows and fills the mountain road with rocks as sharp as knives. Wanjia struggles for three hundred miles until his feet and hands are cut up. When he refuses to poison another stranger, the monster with the brown beard blows his bread-bag to the sky. Wangjia struggles through three hundred miles of desert, hungry and thirsty. He comes to the monster with a white beard who tells him he must bring pretty Baima's eye-balls or have his own taken. When Wangjia refuses to blind her, the white-bearded monster blows and blinds him. Wangjia feels his way for nine hundred miles. At last, he hears the voice of the Bird of Happiness at the top of a snowy mountain. He asks her to return to the village with him. As the Bird of Happiness caresses Wangjia, his wounds heal. She flies him home and fulfills his wish for happiness with warmth, forests, flowers, fields and rivers.

CONNECTIONS. Bird of Happiness. Blindness. Choices. Courage. Determination. Fighting supernatural opponents. Healing. Heroes, men. Killing. Monsters. Mountains. Poverty. Quests. Snow. Tibetan People, stories from. Transformation. Unselfishness.

289. T'ien the Brave, Hero of the Hsia River

M. A. Jagendorf and Virginia Weng, *The Magic Boat and Other Chinese Folk Stories.* T'uchia, China

One night as the giant T'ien and his friends are floating logs down the Hsia River, the innkeeper from the Black Inn and his men attack, intending to rob and murder them. T'ien throws them all into the sky, and it takes them a long time to come down. T'ien strengthens the wharf, but the innkeeper still wants to kill T'ien. T'ien climbs a mast and, pretending not to be himself, calls for T'ien to appear. Then he twists heavy logs. The men fear that if this man is so strong, T'ien will be even stronger. The innkeeper offers a kungfu fighter gold to get rid of T'ien. Again pretending to be someone else, T'ien invites him in for tea and twists brass rods into the powder that he says T'ien smokes. This fighter also runs. The innkeeper manages to wound T'ien, who instructs his wife to take his body to Hsia River and shout his name three times, bite the mattress three times, throw him in the river, and run to the top of the hill. She does, and the river waters rise until they cover the inn. And, so, T'ien brings justice to Hunan Province.

CONNECTIONS. Competition. Floods. Heroes, men. Hsia River. Hunan Province. Innkeepers. Justice. Murder. Revenge. Strength. Supernatural events. T'uchia, China, stories from. Thieves. T'ien the Brave.

290. The Legend of Hong Kil Dong, the Robin Hood of Korea

Anne Sibley O'Brien. Korea

Kil Dong's birthmark foretells a great destiny, but because his mother is a maidservant, Kil Dong cannot be treated as a full son by his father, Minister Hong, a wealthy and powerful advisor to the king. Minister Hong, favors Kil Dong, but will not go against the law which will never permit Kil Dong to rise in position. Kil Dong goes off to study with the monks and learns secrets of martial arts, divination, and magic from an ancient sage. These skills protect him from the assassin a jealous concubine sends, but he leaves his home then for good. Bandits set Kil Dong the impossible task of lifting an enormous rock, which he does with magic and help from Heaven. He becomes leader of these men, who all became bandits under desperate circumstances. Kil Dong sends seven men all looking like him to reclaim wealth stolen unjustly and to challenge greedy monks and corrupt officials everywhere in the country. King Se Jong arrests eight Kil Dongs and calls for Minister Hong to identify his son. Minister Hong faints. All eight sons rush over to help revive him. They tell the King about corruption in his land and fall on the floor, becoming straw men. After this escape, Hong Kil Dong sends word that the king should appoint him Minister of War as he cannot be captured. After one more attempt, the king decides that Kil Dong's power is positive and gives him the minister's position. Later, Hong Kil Dong rules an island of his own.

CONNECTIONS. Acknowledgment by father. Changes in attitude. Changes in fortune. Cleverness. Fathers and sons. Foretellings. Heroes, men. Hong Kil Dong. Identity. Justice. Kings. Leadership. Respect. Robin Hood stories. Shape-shifting. Social class. Thieves.

HOW ELSE THIS STORY IS TOLD. *The Legend of Hong Kil Dong* above is a graphic novel rendition of the first novel written in Korean language from the Chosun dynasty. Here are shorter retellings: Hong Kil Tong; Or, the Adventures of an Abused Boy — H. N. Allen, *Korean Tales*. The People's Fight — John Holstein. The Story of Hong Gil-Dong — Ho Gyun in Zong In-Sob, *Folk Tales of Korea*.

291. The Ogre of Rashomon

Yei Theodora Ozaki, *Japanese Fairy Book*. Japan

Long ago, people in Kyoto say that an ogre caused folk to disappear at dusk by the Gate of Rashomon. The knight Watanabe scoffs that such an ogre is still around. The others challenge him to ride to the gate in a storm and post a list of their names. Watanabe has just posted the list when a voice tells him to wait, and a hairy, thick arm grabs his helmet from behind. Watanabe immediately slices at the arm. It is as wide as a tree trunk and falls on the ground. An ogre as tall as the gate itself, with flashing eyes, moves in front of him, and they fight. Watanbe is tenacious, and the ogre runs off. Watanabe rides off with the ogre's arm and locks it away in a box. One night, an old woman comes to the door, his old nursemaid. Watanabe politely invites her in. She wants to see the arm and, softened by his childhood affection for her, Watanabe opens the box. At that moment, the nursemaid turns back into a ferocious ogre. They fight again. The ogre takes his arm and leaves Kyoto for good.

CONNECTIONS. Arms. Courage. Deceit. Fighting supernatural opponents. Heroes, men. Iwate, Japan, stories from. Knights. Kyoto. Ogres. Rashomon Gate. Shape-shifting. Tests. Transformation.

HOW ELSE THIS STORY IS TOLD. The Ogre of Rashomon — Eric Quayle, *The Shining Princess*. The Origin of Fleas and Mosquitoes — Fanny Hagin Mayer, *Ancient Tales in Modern Japan* (from Iwate). Rashomon — Takeshi Nakajima, *Japanese Traditional Tales*.

292. Driving Out the Monster with Ice Lanterns

Liu Haiqi, *A Museum of Chinese Classic Stories*, Volume 5. Manchu People

An enormous Nine-Headed Bird Monster stirs up storms that darken skies and kill people and livestock in a village near the Songhua River. Batulu leads the young men with their bows and arrows to fight the monster. An evil wind blows the others into a cave, but he clings to a vine and is swept up to the sky. When the wind subsides, Batulu is holding a green python, which becomes a beautiful girl, who says that the Nine-Headed Bird Monster has killed her parents. She tells him the powerful middle head of the Bird Monster has eyes that are sensitive to light and that Batulu should get two meteorites from Star Mountain and warm them with the bodies of one hundred people until they become bright. She transforms into a green vine once again and, wrapping aground Batulu, carries him far to the foot of Star Mountain. Following her instructions, Batulu picks up a white eagle's feather, which he is able to ride to the top of the mountain. He picks up two meteorites and opens the blocked door of the Bird Monster's cave with the green vine. Inside Batulu brings the captive young men back to consciousness. He has them hold the meteorites until they begin to shine so brightly that the Nine-Headed Bird Monster is blinded by their light. Batulu swings his sword and cuts off the monster's heads one by one. At the very end, the Bird Monster shoots out poisonous black blood that kills Batulu and flies away.

CONNECTIONS. Bird monster. Community. Courage. Death. Determination. Feathers. Fighting supernatural opponents. Heroes, men. Maidens. Manchu People, stories from. Meteorites. Monsters. Nine-headed Bird Monster. Pythons. Rescues. Rising to the sky world. Shapeshifting. Songhua River. Star Mountain. Transformation. Unselfishness. Wind.

293. Singing Hali

Liu Haiqi, *A Museum of Chinese Classic Stories, Volume 6*. Donxiang People who call themselves Saerta

A fierce Boa Demon on Kangterhy Mountain has forced the villages to flee, but the brave hunter Lu Tui goes hunting on an opposite mountain, reassuring his wife that he will bring her shoes from the Boa Demon's hide. However, the Boa Demon comes to Lu Tui's campfire and sucks him up. Lu Tui's wife determines to avenge his death. She gathers red cloth, white cloth, and a jar of wine and goes to the Boa Demon's cave with twenty hunters. She instructs the hunters to come forward when she waves the red cloth and sings "Hali Ah-Hong-na" and to retreat when she waves the white cloth. The hunters hide. Lu Tui's wife calmly greets the Boa Demon, whom she charms into closing his eyes. She waves the red cloth. Then she follows the demon into his cave, pretending to agree to their marriage, and entices him to drink wine, singing all the while and waving the hunters slowly forward. The drunk Boa Demon falls asleep, and the hunters chop him up. Lu Tui's wife becomes their new chief.

CONNECTIONS. Boa demon. Cleverness. Demons. Donxiang People, stories from. Fighting supernatural opponents. Heroes, women. Husbands and wives. Kangterhy Mountain. Leadership. Loss. Mountains. Revenge. Saerta People, stories from. Singing. Snakes.

294. Fa Mulan: The Story of a Woman Warrior

Robert D. San Souci. China

As her father is elderly when he is called to fight Tartar invaders in the Khan's army, the girl Mulan puts on his armor and takes his place. She rides and fights alongside the men under harsh conditions. Her bravery, and ability win her the command of a small company of men that makes surprise attacks. Her strategic strength is in having the troops appear weaker than they are, so the enemy lets down its defenses. She becomes a general, leading three armies. It is not until the end, that she reveals herself to be a woman.

CONNECTIONS. Cleverness. Courage. Disguises. Filial devotion. Generals. Han People, stories from. Heroes, women. Leadership. Mulan. Warriors.

HOW ELSE THIS STORY IS TOLD. *The Ballad of Mulan*—Song Nan Zhang. *Disney's*

Mulan— Katherine Poindexter. *Mulan*— Tony Bancroft and Barry Cook, directors, Film. Mulan Fights in the Guise of a Male Soldier — Haiwang Yuan, *The Magic Lotus Lantern and Other Tales from the Han Chinese*. Mulan Goes to War — Rena Krasno and Yen-Fong Chiang, *Cloud Weavers*. *Mulan Saves the Day*— Nancy E. Krulik. The Story of Hua Mulan — Yu Fanquin, translator, in *The Lady in the Picture*.

~ X ~

Propitious Births and Extraordinary Children

295. Momotaro, the Peach Boy

Lafcadio Hearn and Others, *Japanese Fairy Tales*. Japan

An old woman brings the ripe peach she has pulled from a stream home for her husband. It bursts open, and a baby boy is inside. The baby eats both halves of the peach and grows strong. The old man and the old woman take good care of their "eldest son of the peach." One day Momotaro requests that his mother make millet dumplings for him to take on a journey to Ogres' Island to acquire treasure. En route, he gives a dumpling each to the monkey, pheasant, and dog he meets, and they join him on his venture. Momotaro's plan is for the pheasant to fly over the castle wall to spy, for the monkey to climb over the wall and pinch the ogres, and for the dog and he to break into the castle. They fight successfully with claws and teeth and Momotaro's sword. In the end, they share the treasure of magic jewels and clothing.

CONNECTIONS. Births, unusual. Cooperation. Dogs. Extraordinary children. Fighting supernatural opponents. Heroes, men. Heroes, women. Iwate, Japan, stories from. Leadership. Monkeys and apes. Parents and children. Peaches. Pheasants. Strength. Treasure. Unselfishness.

WHERE ELSE THIS STORY APPEARS. Momotaro or The Peach Boy — Lafcadio Hearn in Joanna Cole, *Best-Loved Folktales of the World*.

HOW ELSE THIS STORY IS TOLD. *The Adventure of Momotaro, the Peach Boy* — Ralph F. McCarthy. The Adventures of Little Peachling — Pearl S. Buck, *Fairy Tales of the Orient* and in I. K. Junne, *Floating Clouds, Floating Dreams*. The Adventures of Little Peachling — Takeshi Nakajima, *Japanese Traditional Tales*. The Adventures of Little Peachling — Baron Algernon Bertram Freeman-Mitford Redesdale, *Tales of Old Japan*. The Adventures of Momotaro plus The Triumph of Momotaro — F. Hadland Davis, *Myths and Legends of Japan*. Little Peachling — A. B. Mitford, *Tales of Old Japan* and at D.L. Ashliman, *Folktexts*, Online. Momotaro — Yamada Chitose at *Kids Web Japan*, Online. Momotarō — Fanny Hagin Mayer, *Ancient Tales in Modern Japan* (from Iwate). Momotaro — Iwaya Sazanami, *Iwaya's Fairy Tales of Old Japan*. Momotaro: Boy-of-the-Peach — Yoshiko Uchida, *The Dancing Kettle*. Momotaro, or the Little Peach Child — Alan Leslie Whitehorn, *Wonder Tales of Old Japan*. Momotaro or The Peach Boy — Joanna Cole, *Best-Loved Folktales of the World*. Momotaro or The Story of the Son of a Peach — Virginia Haviland, *Favorite Fairy Tales Told in Japan*. Momotaro, or the Story of the Son of a Peach — Yei Theodora Ozaki, *Japanese Fairy Book*. Momotaro, the Peach Boy — Miyoko Matsutani, kamishibai story cards. *Momotaro, the Peach Boy* — Linda Shute. Momotaro — The Peach Warrior — Eric Quayle, *The Shining Princess*. The Peach Boy — Helen and William McAlpine, *Oxford Tales from Japan*. Peach Boy — Florence Sakade, *Peach Boy* and as Momotaro or The Story of the Son of a Peach in *Japanese Children's Favorite Stories*. Prince Yuriwaka — Fanny Hagin Mayer, *Ancient*

Tales in Modern Japan. The Story of Momotarō; The Peach Boy—Yuri Yasuda, *Old Tales of Japan*, Volume II. *Tasty Baby Belly Buttons*—Judy Sierra (told with a female hero who comes out of a melon). The Triumph of Momotaro—F. Hadland Davis, *Myths and Legends of Japan*.

296. The Lion Tamer

Folk Tales from China, Fifth Series. Tibetan People

A young exiled queen gives birth to a son with a scarlet head and scarlet breast who speaks immediately and grows to full height in three days. The boy becomes skilled with a bow and arrow. One day he brings home a tiger and says he would like to present the skin to his father. His mother tells him then that his father is the king, and the boy leaves for the palace. The king is suspicious about the boy's motive in showing up and tells him that if he kills a lion, the king will claim him as his son. The boy cannot find a lion until he lets a temple lama beat him, after which the lama gives him instructions on how to get it to obey. The king is frightened when the boy shows up with the lion. First he agrees to bring the boy and his mother back to the palace, but then changes his mind and says the boy must first bring Satan's daughter to be his wife. A woman gulping half the sea takes him to the Devil King's palace. They pick up a giant and a girl with a golden bow along the way. The chattering of crows tells them that they will recognize Satan's daughter when she comes with her maidens for water because she has "Om" on her forehead and "Hum" on her breast. The boy grabs the daughter, but her screams bring Satan, at which point the girl with the golden bow hits him, the burly woman swallows down every devil in the palace, and the giant scoops them all up and brings them to the king. When the king continues to stall, the giant tramples the palace and the girl archer shoots him. The lad becomes king, marries Satan's daughter, and brings his mother back to live with them.

CONNECTIONS. Acknowledgment by father. Age, growing up quickly. Births, unusual. Cooperation. Devils. Exile. Extraordinary children. Fathers and sons. Fighting supernatural opponents. Filial devotion. Giants. Heroes, men. Hunters. Kings. Language of animals. Lions. Monks. Mothers and sons. Physical difference. Princes. Queens. Supernatural wives. Tests. Tibetan People, stories from.

297. Kintaro's Adventures

Genichi Kume in Florence Sakade, *Kintaro's Adventures*. Japan

One day a bear runs into a woodcutter's cabin and carries off the baby boy Kintaro, who has a piece of red coral hung around his neck. The bear leaps off a cliff and crosses a river where the woodcutter cannot follow. The bear brings Kintaro to his wife who has lost a cub. All of the animals teach him their special skills. When Kintaro is eight, his bear father dies, and Kintaro becomes King of the Forest. Meanwhile, the woodcutter and his wife have another child, a girl, Misuzu, who wears a white coral piece around her neck. Her parents tell her about Kintaro and ask her to keep watch for him. One day Misuzu sees Kintaro by a waterfall, but at that moment a wolf runs off with her. Kintaro gives chase, but stops to help a drowning monkey and loses Misuzu's trail. The girl is locked in the wolves' castle. Kintaro helps to put out the forest fire that breaks out around the castle. Woodcutters also arrive to cut a path. Wolves, too, are wetting their bodies and rolling on the grass to put out the fire. Misuzu runs out and identifies Kintaro to her father. They bring Kintaro home and teach him human language and skills to go along with all that he has learned from the animals.

CONNECTIONS. Bears. Brothers and sisters. Extraordinary children. Fire. Helpfulness. Heroes, men. Identity. Kidnapping. Raised by animals. Reunions. Wolves. Woodcutters.

WHERE ELSE THIS STORY APPEARS. Kintaro's Adventures—Florence Sakade, *Japanese Children's Favorite Stories*, Book Two.

HOW ELSE THIS STORY IS TOLD. The Adventures of Kintaro, the Golden Boy—Yei Theodora Ozaki, *Japanese Fairy Book*. Kintaro—Juliet Piggott, *Japanese Fairy Tales*. Kintaro—Shoichi Shiomi at *Kids Web Japan*, Online. Sakata-No-Kintoki—Takeshi Nakajima, *Japanese Traditional Tales*. Kintaro, the Golden Boy in chapter The Transformation of Issunboshi and Kintaro, the Golden Boy—F. Hadland Davis, *Myths and Legends of Japan*. The Story of Kintaro, the Strong Boy—Alan Leslie Whitehorn, *Wonder Tales of Old Japan*.

298. The Tiger and the Dwarf

Zong Bog-Sul in Zong In-Sob, *Folk Tales from Korea*. Korea

A famous hunter disappears on the dangerous Diamond Mountain in the Province of Gangwon. He never sees his son, who is born a dwarf and gets teased by the other boys. The son asks his mother for a gun when he is eight. He practices shooting for six years to be able to avenge his father's death, until, like his father, he can shoot the eye off a needle from a quarter mile away. He comes to the house of an old woman on the mountain who tells him his father could shoot an ant off a rock. He stays with her for three more years to practice. Then he sets off, looking for the tiger that killed his father. He shoots a priest with tiger's fangs, an old woman with tiger's claws, a girl with a tiger's back, and a young man with a tiger's tail. He shoots at a crowd of tigers in the valley until he runs out of ammunition, and they take him captive. The tigers suggest that their leader eat the dwarf, and the enormous tiger swallows him in one gulp. Inside the tiger's stomach, the son finds a gun with his father's initials and his father's bones. He helps a girl recover consciousness and then cuts a hole in the king tiger, which goes into a frenzy of pain and kills the other tigers and then dies. The son and the girl skin the tiger. The old woman is delighted to see him, as are the girl's parents and his mother. He buries his father's bones, and he and the girl are wed.

CONNECTIONS. Bones. Diamond Mountain. Fighting supernatural opponents. Gangwon Province. Heroes, men. Hunters. Old woman, supernatural helper. Physical difference. Quests. Revenge. Size. Supernatural events. Talents. Teasing. Tiger King. Tigers.

HOW ELSE THIS STORY IS TOLD. The Revenge of the Huntsman's Son—James Huntley Grayson, *Myths and Legends from Korea*.

299. The Golden Reed Pipe

John Minford, *Favourite Folktales of China*. Yao People

As a little girl all dressed in red is snatched by a dragon one day, she calls out that her brother will come to rescue her. The little girl does not have a brother, until her mother eats a red bayberry and gives birth to a boy with a round head and red cheeks. Little Bayberry grows fourteen years in just a few days. One day a crow tells him that Evil Dragon is making his sister dig rocks with her bare hands. Learning that he has a sister, Bayberry sets off to rescue Little Red. He lifts a large rock that blocks his path, and, when he blows the golden reed pipe he finds in the hole, it sets all the little creatures in the woods to dancing. He sees the fierce-looking dragon coiled at the entrance to a cave, whipping Little Red with its tail because she will not marry him. Bayberry starts blowing his pipe, and the dragon cannot keep from dancing. Bayberry does not stop even to speak to his sister. He keeps blowing; the dragon is steaming and begs the boy to stop, promising to release Little Red. Bayberry edges toward a pond and the Evil Dragon falls in. He promises to stay at the bottom of the pond and not bother people, but as Bayberry and Little Red walk off, the dragon comes after them. So, Bayberry plays for another seven days and nights until the dragon dies in the pond.

CONNECTIONS. Age, growing up quickly. Bayberry Boy. Births, unusual. Brothers and sisters. Captivity. Dancing. Dragons. Extraordinary children. Foretellings. Helpfulness. Henan Province, China, stories from. Heroes, men. Kidnapping. Knowledge. Little Red. Magical objects. Miao People, stories from. Mulberry Boy. Music. Outsmarting supernatural opponents. Pipe, reed. Rescues. Secrets. Yao People, stories from.

HOW ELSE THIS STORY IS TOLD. The Golden Sheng — Louise and Yuan-Hsi Kuo, *Chinese Folk Tales* (from the Miao People). Red String — Shang Lijuan in Howard Giskin, *Chinese Folktales* (from Henan Province).

300. The Tiger King's Skin Cloak

Folk Tales from China, Fifth Series. Mongolian People

The wife of a poor herdsman whose first three sons died gives birth to a boy who grows from the moment he is born. On his first day Ku-nan eats a whole goat. His parents worry about how they will feed him, but on his third day Ku-nan goes to find work. He eats the wolf who attacks him on the way to the Khan's yurt. When he gets there, the Khan keeps him as a personal bodyguard. After Ku-nan grabs a tiger by the legs and swings it against a tree, the Khan demands that he bring him the pelt of the Tiger King, which seems impossible. Ku-nan is helped with a pony that speeds yurts to a blur and given a magic sheep-bone when he saves a young girl from a wolf. A turtle who asks him to remove his aching eye flies off, as a dragon. The eye becomes a pearl that parts the wide river. Ku-nan promises a shepherd he will rescue his daughter who has been stolen by the Tiger King. The sheep-bone distracts the Tiger'King's guards, so that Ku-nan finds the shepherd's daughter. Then the Tiger King flies down, an ogre with the head of a tiger and the body of a man all covered with golden hair. Ku-nan shoots an arrow into the ogre's eye, and the ogre swats him waist-deep into the ground. They continue to fight until Ku-nan kills the Tiger King. He marries the shepherd's daughter, fights off eleven more tigers that sweep in on a wind, and returns with the tiger skin. Now the Khan demands that Ku-nan's wife make it into a cloak with not one hair missing. When the Khan puts the cloak on in front of assembled guests, he becomes a tiger that Ku-nan smites with his bare hands. After that Ku-nan shares his kill with poor herdsmen and cures blindness by placing the pearl in blind people's eye sockets.

CONNECTIONS. Age, growing up quickly. Blindness. Extraordinary children. Eyeballs. Fighting supernatural opponents. Healing. Herders. Heroes, men. Khans. Kindness. Mongolian People, stories from. Ogres. Magical objects. Pearls. Punishment. Rescues. Skin. Tiger King. Tigers. Transformation. Ultimatums.

301. The Tale of the Bamboo Cutter

Yaunari Kawabata. Japan

Life gets better for an old bamboo cutter after he finds a three-inch high girl in a glowing stalk of bamboo. Not only do he and his wife now have a beautiful daughter that they cherish, but he often finds gold in other bamboo stalks. When the girl becomes a young woman, they call her Nayotake no Kaguya-hime, Shining Princess of the Young Bamboo. Kaguya-hime is not interested in her many suitors, and her father worries for her future as he is old. She tells him she is not of this world. At last, she gives each man a different task to prove that he is noble and deserving. The tasks include finding a begging-bowl of Buddha, a branch with fruit from the golden tree with silver roots at the Mountain of Paradise, and a robe made from the magic fur of Chinese fire-rats that cannot be burned. Though, they seem impossible, four men try and fail. The emperor has heard of the Shining Princess and would like to meet her, but she becomes invisible when he tries to bring her by force. After a while, he steps back, and they become friends. The Princess grows sad, however. She was sent to earth from the Palace of the Moon as a punishment, but now needs to return. The Emperor surrounds the bamboo cutter's house with two thousand soldiers on the day of the full moon, but all of their strength drains when the moon men ride in on white clouds. Kaguya-hime writes a letter to her parents and the Emperor of her feelings for them and apologizes if she causes unhappiness now. She tastes the elixir of immortality and puts on the celestial robe of feathers that will erase all of her earthly emotions and ascends in a chariot. She has sent some of the elixir to the Emperor, but he has it burned high on the mountain that becomes Mount Fuji, not wanting to live forever if she is not here.

CONNECTIONS. Bamboo cutters. Bamboo Princess. Changes in fortune. Elixir of Immortality. Emperors. Extraordinary children. Fighting supernatural opponents. Filial devotion. Fuji, Mount. Kaguya-hime. Loss. Love. Magical objects. Matches, marriage. Moon. Princesses. Rising to the sky world. Robes. Sadness. Size. Suitors. Supernatural beloveds. Tests. Transformation.

HOW ELSE THIS STORY IS TOLD. All of the following are modern retellings of the *Taketori Monogatari*, the oldest surviving work of Japanese fiction: The Bamboo-Cutter and the Moon-Child — Yei Theodora Ozaki, *Japanese Fairy Book*. The Bamboo-Cutter and the Moon-Maiden plus The Celestial Robe of Feathers — F. Hadland Davis, *Myths and Legends of Japan*. *The Bamboo Princess/Kaguya-Hime* — Kyoko Iwasaki on kamishibai story cards. The Bamboo Princess — Juliet Piggott, *Japanese Fairy Tales. The Child in the Bamboo Grove* — Rosemary Harris. Kaguya Hime-Tomoji Noda at *Kids Web Japan*, Online. Kaguya Himé — Yoshimatsu Suzuki, *Japanese Legends and Folk-Tales*. The Maiden from the Sky — Royall Tyler, *Japanese Tales*. The Moon Maiden — Grace James, *Green Willow and Other Japanese Fairy Tales*. The Princess of Light — Yoshiko Uchida, *The Dancing Kettle. Princess Splendor, The Woodcutter's Daughter* — Japanese Fairy Tale Series Extra. The Shining Princess — Eric Quayle, *The Shining Princess. The Tale of the Shining Princess* — Sally Fisher.

302. Little One-Inch

Florence Sakade, *Japanese Children's Favorite Stories*. Japan

A childless couple find a tiny baby boy in the grass. They call him Little One-Inch and bring him home to be their son. When Little One-Inch decides it is time to seek his fortune in the world, his parents supply him with a wooden rice bowl for a boat and a needle as a sword. After a collision with a frog throws Little One-Inch into the river, he makes his way to a lord's house and offers to serve in the guard. The lord is amused and assigns him the task of being the princess's companion. Little One-Inch and the princess become friends. At the temple one day Little One-Inch tries to stop a green devil from seizing the princess by running up the devil's body and leaping into its mouth, slashing with his sword. The devil spits Little One-Inch out and flees, dropping its magic hammer. The princess holds the hammer and wishes for Little One-Inch to be taller. Each time she shakes the hammer he grows one inch, until he is just the right height. A few years later they marry and live happily.

CONNECTIONS. Courage. Devils. Extraordinary children. Fighting supernatural opponents. Friendship. Hammers. Height. Heroes, men. Issun Boshi. Little people. Love. Magical objects. Niigata, Japan, stories from. Nobles and lords. Oni. Physical difference. Princesses. Size. Supernatural husbands.

WHERE ELSE THIS STORY APPEARS. Little One-Inch — Florence Sakade, *Japanese Children's Favorite Stories.*

HOW ELSE THIS STORY IS TOLD. *The Inch Boy*— Junko Morimoto. Issun Bōshi — Fanny Hagin Mayer, *Ancient Tales in Modern Japan* (from Niigata). Issun Boshi — Takeshi Nakajima, *Japanese Traditional Tales.* Issun-boshi — Kyoko Yamada at *Kids Web Japan*, Online. *Issunbōshi*— George Suyeoka. Isun Boshi, the One-Inch Lad — Yoshiko Uchida, *The Dancing Kettle. Little Fingerling*— Monica Hughes. *Little Inchkin*— Fiona French. Little One Inch — Keigo Seki, *Folktales of Japan. The One-Inch Boy Issun-boshi*— Joji Isubota, kamishibai story cards. One-Inch Fellow — Virginia Haviland, *Favorite Fairy Tales Told in Japan* (here, the devil that One-Inch fights is an Oni). One-Inch Priest in chapter The Transformation of Issunboshi and Kintaro, the Golden Boy — F. Hadland Davis, *Myths and Legends of Japan.*

303. Tsubu the Little Snail

Carol Ann Williams. Japan

A rice farmer's wife who prays to the Water God for any baby at all is blessed with a snail they call Tsubu. For twenty years they love him and care for him in a bowl of water in front of their household shrine. When Tsubu's father says he is too tired to deliver the yearly rice tax, Tsubu calls that he will bring it to the choja. And he does, riding on the top bale and singing driver's songs, though it looks like the horses have no driver. The choja marvels over Tsubu's competence and manners and wants him to become a son-in-law. Only his youngest daughter agrees to marry the snail. She becomes part of the rice farmer's family. When Tsubu's wife wants to go to the shrine for the Festival of Healing, Tsubu rides in her sash. It seems to passersby that she is talking to no one. Reluctantly, carefully, she puts Tsubu down by the side of the road while she enters to pray. When she comes out, she cannot find him and frantically plunges into a nearby rice paddy, picking up every snail. She hears a crack and thinks she has killed him, but there stands a handsome young man. Because she loves him without caring what other people think, the Water God allows Tsubu to become human.

CONNECTIONS. Acceptance. Aomori, Japan, stories from. Chojas. Devotion. Extraordinary children. Farmers. Festivals. Gods and goddesses. Husbands and wives. Kindness. Loss. Love. Matches, marriage. Parents and children. Shape-shifting. Size. Snails. Supernatural husbands. Transformation. Water God.

HOW ELSE THIS STORY IS TOLD. **Chinese variation:** The Man in a Shell — Adele Marion Fielde, *Chinese Nights' Entertainment.* **Japanese variations:** The Mud Snail Son — Betty Jean Lifton. Mudsnail Chōja — Fanny Hagin Mayer, *Ancient Tales in Modern Japan* (from Aomori). The Snail Choja — Keigo Seki, *Folktales of Japan.*

304. Gazelle Horn

Indries Shah, *World Tales.* Tibetan People

One day a gazelle doe gives birth to a boy, but leaves him because he is too different from her. The holy man, a Rishi, finds the boy and raises him in his hermitage. As the boy grows, gazelle horns appear on his head. The Rishi tells his son to welcome other Rishis who come to the hermitage. When the Rishi dies, the boy finds that he has now attained the Five Kinds of Insight and has himself become a Rishi. There comes a day when so much rain falls that the Rishi drops his pitcher of water and yells at the deity to not send any more rain for twelve years. The deity sends no rain, and the people are starving. The King's seers tell him that the famine has been caused by a Rishi's anger, and no rain will fall as long as he is holy. The King's daughter prepares to undo him by studying to be a Rishi herself. Then she dresses in bark and grass and goes to the Rishi with the gazelle horns. The Princess seduces him with wine and then women, and his magical powers vanish. The deity sends rain. The King gives the Princess to the Rishi as his wife, but the Rishi begins to love other women. Filled with jealousy one day, the Princess hits the Rishi. The Rishi thinks that he, who could once control the weather, is now too bound by earthly concerns. He once again becomes a hermit and possesses the Five Kinds of Insight.

CONNECTIONS. Abandonment. Anger. Arrogance. Asceticism. Births, unusual. Deities. Determination. Drought. Extraordinary children. Famine. Gazelles. Gods and goddesses. Holiness. Horns. Hunger. Husbands and wives. Monks. Physical difference. Princesses. Rain. Sages. Selfishness. Supernatural skills. Tibetan People, stories from. Unfaithfulness.

305. Little Boy from the Dragon Palace

Fanny Hagin Mayer, *Ancient Tales in Modern Japan*. Kumamoto, Japan

When a poor old man has not sold any wood one day, he prays to the Ryūjin and drops the wood he has gathered into the river. Suddenly a maiden stands on the water then holding a little child. She tells him that Little Runny-Nose Boy is a gift from the Dragon Spirit for his hard work. She hands Little Running-Nose Boy to the wood gatherer and tells him that the boy will grant his wishes, but he must feed him raw shrimp relish every day. The old man happily carries the boy home. Whenever he wishes for something, Little Runny-Nose Boy makes a sound like blowing his nose, and the thing appears. The old man acquires a larger house and storehouses. His only work now is to fix raw shrimp relish. When that becomes a chore, he tells Little Runny-Nose Boy to go back to the Dragon Spirit. Little Runny-Nose Boy goes outside. The old man can hear him snuffling. Suddenly everything new and fancy disappears.

CONNECTIONS. Abandonment. Consequences. Dragon Spirit. Extraordinary children. Kumamoto, Japan, stories from. Laziness. Noses. Prayer. Punishment. Rewards. Selfishness. Snuffling. Spirits. Supernatural events. Unfaithfulness. Wishes. Woodcutters. Work.

HOW ELSE THIS STORY IS TOLD. Boy with a Runny Nose — Hiroko Fujita, *Folktales from the Japanese Countryside*. Little Snot Nose Boy — Margaret Read MacDonald, *Celebrate the World*.

306. Nezha Fights Sea Dragons

Haiwang Yuan, *The Magic Lotus Lantern and Other Tales from the Han Chinese*. Han People

Sliced by his father, Gewneral Li, from a ball of flesh his mother gives birth to after a pregnancy that lasts three and one-half years, Nezha grows immediately to the age of six. The Taoist master, Taiyi Zhenren, flies in on the back of a crane with magic weapons for Nezha to use only for the good of people. The Chentown region has been suffering from drought, because the cruel Dragon King of the East Sea has been withholding rain. When people refuse to give into his demand that one boy and one girl be sacrificed to him as food, the Dragon King sends a man-eating monster, a yecha, to grab them. The first time Nezha uses his magic ring is to keep the yecha from trying to snatch two children. His ring breaks the yecha's head into pieces with one touch. Outraged, the Dragon King sends his third son to capture Nezha. When the dragon prince comes at Nezha with his sword drawn, Nezha flings his magic silk tie again and again until the ribbon immobilizes the prince. The dragon prince breaks his neck as he falls to the sand. Now the Dragon King calls in all of his brothers, who flood Chentown with torrential rains. The only way he will stop is if General Li kills his son. Nezha grabs his father's sword and kills himself to save his parents torment. The Taoist master sends for his spirit, which is brought to Golden Light Cave on Qianyuan Mountain. There, Tauyi Zhenren reconstructs Nezha from lotus leaves and blossoms and arms him with a new magical spear and fenghuolun, a pair of wind-and-fire wheeled shoes for transportation. Nezha is also now able to transform into a giant with three heads and six arms. Armed with this new power, Nezha vanquishes the Dragon King.

CONNECTIONS. Age, growing up quickly. Chentown Pass. Birth, unusual. Cranes. Dragon King. Dragon Prince. Dragons. Drought. East Sea. Fighting supernatural opponents. Floods. Giants. Golden Light Cave. Han People, stories from. Helpfulness. Heroes, men. Lotus flowers. Magical objects. Mazes. Monsters. Qianyuan Mountain. Rebirth. Sacrifice. Sages. Spirits. Taiyi Zhenren, sage. Taoism. Transformation. Ultimatums. Yecha.

307. Bawshou Rescues the Sun

Chun-Chan Yeh and Allan Baillie. Han People

Thousands of years ago, by West Lake in Eastern China, Liu Chun and his wife Hui Niang are awaiting the birth of their first child, when the sky grows dark. Rice plants begin to wither. The Old Man of the Village is sure the sun has been stolen by the King of the Devils. Liu Chun says he will go to find it. His wife makes him a special pair of slippers from her own long hair. Just as he is to leave, a golden phoenix lands on his shoulder. It seems like a good omen, but Liu Chun does not return for months. The earth is still dark. Hui Niang gives birth to a son, Bawshou. The phoenix returns alone, and a new star appears in the sky. When a breeze touches the infant Bawshou, he stands and speaks. A second breeze brings him to his feet, walking. With the third breeze, he is a giant. When the phoenix flies to his shoulder, Bawshou promises his mother that he will find the sun. He follows the new star many li, until his shoes have worn through. One hundred families in one village make him a sheepskin coat to keep him warm and help him float across an icy river. Bawshou is weak when he reaches the other side, but villagers there share warmth and their last food and give him a special package of earth, a shirang. An old woman by the road tells him to go home, that the sun is dead, but Bawshou wants to see for himself. He comes to an oddly happy village and is offered a cup of dark wine. Just at that moment, the phoenix drops the hair shoe his mother had made, and he realizes that his father died in this place, that the wine is poison, and that the old woman is a plant. The village vanishes. He walks until he comes to the East Ocean, but does not know how he will cross it. Then he remembers the parcel of earth. He throws in one pinch, and it forms an island. Another pinch forms another island, and he walks across thousands of islands to a black crag where he can hear evil laughter. He fills his chest with storm wind and roars into a cleft in the crag. Frightened Devils jump into the sea. He wanders through their fortress and finds the imprisoned sun, now dimly flickering, in a cave. The phoenix helps him bring it out. The Devils shriek, but they can do nothing. The sun gains strength as it climbs from the sea towards the bright new star. Its light burns the King of the Devils and restores light and warmth to the earth.

CONNECTIONS. Age, growing up quickly. Community. Darkness. Death. Devils. Earth. East Ocean. Extraordinary children. Fighting supernatural opponents. Han People, stories from. Helpfulness. Heroes, men. King of the Devils. Magical objects. Mothers and sons. Mysteries. Phoenix. Poison. Promises. Quests. Shoes. Sun. Wind. West Lake. Xirang.

308. Posting the Dragon Tablet

Folk Tales from China, Fifth Series. Hui People

An old woman and an old man who have had no child for thirty years pray to Allah, and then she is pregnant for three years before giving birth during a drought to a boy Kan-han, "In time for drought." He can walk by two months, speak by three, and by six months follow his mother on her chores. At two years old, when Kan-han learns that his parents do not plant because there has been no rain, he says he will go to the Dragon King. First, though, he must learn the ways of water. He cannot find the Dragon King until the Dragon King's daughter tells him about the underwater cave in a dream while he is lying in a lake. Kan-han struggles past knife-sharp rocks to find that he needs also to have the Dragon Tablet to unlock the gates. His mother brings him to the mosque where the Ahun and the whole congregation accompany him to the Lake of the Black Dragon. Kan-han dives into the water with the tablet and bangs on the gates. They open. The Dragon King is sleeping with a ruby in his mouth. Kan-han swallows the ruby. The Dragon King awakes roaring for the ruby, and Kan-han yells at him for bringing famine to so many people. He strikes the Dragon King with the tablet three times and takes off his head. Kan-han becomes a dragon and flies out of the cave to bring rain.

CONNECTIONS. Age, growing up quickly. Birth, unusual. Ahongs. Dragon King. Dragon Princess. Dragons. Drought. Extraordinary children. Fighting supernatural opponents. Helpfulness. Heroes, men. Hui People, stories from. Hunger. Lake of the Black Dragon. Mosques. Parents and children. Prayer. Rubies. Stone tablet. Transformation. Underwater caves. Unselfishness. Water. Yunnan Province, China, stories from.

HOW ELSE THIS STORY IS TOLD. The Dragon Tablet — Wang Dong in Shuijiang Li and Karl W. Luckert, *Mythology and Folklore of the Hui* (from Yunnan).

309. The Small Yellow Dragon

Margaret Read MacDonald, *Celebrate the World*. Pai People

In Yunnan Province on the shore of Lake Erh, a poor young woman pulls something from the water that turns out to be a dragon's egg. Sometime later she has a baby boy, who is protected by a Phoenix and a snake. At three years old the boy helps her work; at five, he can read and write. The boy tells his mother he wants to keep the Black Dragon from flooding the land. He gives the magistrate a list of things he needs: three large straw dragons, three hundred flour dumplings, three hundred iron dumplings, a little bronze dragon mask and bronze dragon claws, six sharp swords, and a yellow silk shirt. The Black Dragon attacks the straw dragons and then eats the iron dumplings and sinks down. Dressed in the yellow silk shirt with a bronze claw on every finger and wearing the bronze mask, the boy presents himself as a small Yellow Dragon. When he calls that he is hungry, they feed him the flour dumplings and then give more of the iron ones to the Black Dragon. The Yellow Dragon leaps into the Black Dragon's mouth, slashing with swords all the way to his stomach. Finally the Black Dragon lets the Yellow Dragon out through his eye. The Yellow Dragon remains in the water to guard Lake Erh.

CONNECTIONS. Age, growing up quickly. Birth, unusual. Black Dragon. Disguises. Dragons. Dumplings. Eggs. Erh Lake. Extraordinary children. Fighting supernatural opponents. Floods. Helpfulness. Heroes, men. Masks. Mothers and sons. Pai People, stories from. Straw dragons. Yunnan Province.

HOW ELSE THIS STORY IS TOLD. Small Yellow Dragon and the Big Black Dragon — *Folk Tales from China*, Fourth Series.

~ XI ~

Animal Fables

310. The Tiger's Tale

Demi, *The Dragon's Tale*. China

To escape from a tiger's clutches, a fox tells him that the Heavenly Dragon has made him, the fox, king of all the animals. The tiger does not believe him. The fox tells the tiger to follow him and see how the other animals all fear him. Sure enough, the animals all run as the fox and tiger approach. Only the tiger does not know that it is his presence, not the fox's, that they run from.

CONNECTIONS. Cleverness. Dragons. Escapes. Fear. Foxes. Frogs. Han People, stories from. Heavenly Dragon. Hierarchy. Humorous stories. Kings. Tibetan People, stories from. Tigers. Tricksters.

HOW ELSE THIS STORY IS TOLD. *Chinese variations:* The Fox and the Tiger — Richard Wilhelm, *The Chinese Fairy Book*. A Fox and a Tiger — Who Is the Real King of the Jungle — Haiwang Yuan, *The Magic Lotus Lantern and Other Tales from the Han Chinese*. The Fox Outwits the Tiger — Lotta Carswell Hume, *Favorite Children's Stories from China and Tibet*. The Fox That Flaunted the Tiger's Treasure —*Selected Chinese Fables*. How the Fox Tricked the Tiger — Mingmei Yip, *Chinese Children's Favorite Stories*. The Officer of Heaven — Pleasant DeSpain, *Thirty-Three Multicultural Tales to Tell*. The Tiger and the Frog — A. L. Shelton, *Tibetan Folk Tales* and at D.L. Ashliman, *Folktexts*, Online. The Tiger Behind the Fox — Chan Kuo Ts'e in Moss Roberts, *Chinese Fairy Tales and Fantasies*. The Wicked Empress— Brian Brown, *Chinese Nights Entertainments: Stories of Old China*. **Korean variation:** A Fox Deceives a Tiger — James Huntley Grayson, *Myths and Legends from Korea*.

311. The Greatest of All

Eric A. Kimmel. Japan

Father Mouse is not ready to accept an ordinary field mouse as the husband for his daughter. He wants her husband to be the greatest of all, like the emperor. However, the emperor points to the sun as greater than he is. The sun says it may be covered by the cloud, which may be scattered by the wind, which may be stopped by a rock wall. The rock wall says that the humble field mouse is greatest for it can tunnel inside. So, Father Mouse give permission for his daughter to marry the field mouse, after all.

CONNECTIONS. Animal fables. Changes in attitude. Clouds. Fathers and daughters. Fathers-in-law and sons-in-law. Hierarchy. Matches, marriage. Mice. Moles. Perspective. Power. Rats. Stone. Sun.

HOW ELSE THIS STORY IS TOLD. *Chinese variations:* The Mouse Bride: A Chinese Folk-

tale — Monica Chang. The Mouse Bride — Minmei Yip, *Chinese Children's Favorite Stories. Mouse Match* — Ed Young. **Japanese variations:** The Espousal of the Rat's Daughter — Grace James, *Green Willow. The Mouse's Wedding*— Seishi Horio on kamishibai story cards. The Mole's Bridegroom — Keigo Seki, *Folktales of Japan.* The Mouse's Marriage —*Kids Web Japan*, Online. *The Mouse's Wedding/Nezumi no Yomeiri*— Seishi Horio on Kamishibai story cards. The Rats and Their Daughter — D. L. Ashliman, *Folktexts*, Online. *The Rats' Daughter*— Joel Cook. The Rat's Tale — Demi, *The Dragon's Tale.* The Rat's Wedding — Takeshi Nakajima, *Japanese Traditional Tales.* The Story of Nezumi No Yomeiri: The Marriage of a Mouse — Yuri Yasuda, *Old Tales of Japan.* The Wedding of the Mice — Juliet Piggott, *Japanese Fairy Tales.* The Wedding of the Mouse — Yoshiko Uchida, *The Dancing Kettle.* **Korean variations:** A Bridegroom for Miss Mole — William Elliot Griffis, *The Unmannerly Tiger and Other Korean Tales.* The Mole and the Miryek — Frances Carpenter, *Tales of a Korean Grandmother.* The Rat's Bridegroom — Zong Mi-Og in Zong In-Sob, *Folk Tales from Korea.* The Vanity of the Rat —*Long Long Time Ago.* The Vanity of the Rat — Suzanne Crowder Han, *Korean Folk and Fairy Tales.* The Vanity of the Rat — Y.T. Pyun, *Tales from Korea.* See also *The Stonecutter*, Story #429.

312. The Biggest in the World

Florence Sakade, *Urashima Taro and Other Japanese Children's Stories.* Japan

A huge bird on an island continually brags about his strength. A seagull lets him know that there is a larger creature in the Southern Sea. The bird goes to see and rests on one of two red columns that are sticking up. The red column belongs to a giant lobster, who laughs at frightening the bird. The seagull then lets the lobster know there is something bigger than he is. The lobster crawls into a cave in a huge mountain that turns out to be a whale's nostril.

CONNECTIONS. Animal fables. Birds. Boastfulness. Competition. Hierarchy. Knowledge. Lobsters. Perspective. Realization. Seagulls. Shrimp. Size. Southern Sea. Strength. Whales.

WHERE ELSE THIS STORY APPEARS. The Biggest in the World — Florence Sakade, *Japanese Children's Favorite Stories*, Book Two.

HOW ELSE THIS STORY IS TOLD. The Idol and the Whale — William Elliot Griffis, *The Fire-Fly's Lovers.* The Idol and the Whale — Alan Leslie Whitehorn, *Wonder Tales of Old Japan.* The Shrimp and the Big Bird — Fanny Hagin Mayer, *Ancient Tales in Modern Japan.*

313. A Frog in a Well

Haiwang Yuan, *The Magic Lotus Lantern and Other Tales from the Han Chinese.* Han People

Frog has lived in a well all his life. It is the whole world to him and seems to contain everything he needs. When the frog brags to a sea turtle who wanders by the top of the well, the sea turtle offers to take him to the sea, which he describes as a much vaster body of water than what is in the well. The frog is overwhelmed. He never brags again, and his descendants move to where they can see more than a little round circle of sky.

CONNECTIONS. Animal fables. Boastfulness. Changes in attitude. Han People, stories from. Frogs. Knowledge. Perspective. Sea. Turtles. Wells.

HOW ELSE THIS STORY IS TOLD. The Frog in the Well — Zhuang Zi in *Ancient Chinese Tales.* The Frog in the Well —*Selected Chinese Fables.* The Goat's Tale — Demi, *The Dragon's Tale.*

314. The Dragon's Tale

Demi, *The Dragon's Tale*. China

When a flood causes many rivers to run together, the fish think they must be in the largest body of water in the world. From the large river they swim into the huge ocean where they meet the Dragon King. The Dragon King tells them that even this large ocean is only a small part of an even bigger world.

CONNECTIONS. Animal fables. Dragon King. Fish. Floods. Harmony. Knowledge. Perspective. Rivers. Sea. Size.

315. Holding Up the Sky

Margaret Read MacDonald, *Peace Tales*. China

An elephant asks a hummingbird why the hummingbird is lying on his back, feet in the air. The hummingbird answers that he is holding up the sky. The elephant laughs at him because he is too small to keep the sky from falling. The hummingbird agrees; he says he is doing his small part.

CONNECTIONS. Animal fables. Birds. Community. Elephants. Hummingbirds. Perspective. Size.

WHERE ELSE THIS STORY APPEARS. Holding Up the Sky — Margaret Read MacDonald, *Three-Minute Tales*.

316. Three Samurai Cats: A Story from Japan

Eric A. Kimmel. Japan

A daimyo asks the senior monk to send a samurai cat to rid his castle of a troublesome rat. The rat quickly bests the first cat the dōchō sends, as well as the second larger and more experienced cat. The dōchō next sends Neko Roshi, a martial arts master who seems too old for the job. Neko Roshi keeps putting off fighting. Flaunting his ability to run free in the castle, the rat rolls a giant rice ball that uses every bit of the daimyo's rice. When he accidentally gets pinned beneath it, however, the wise master finally gets up and offers to free the rat if he promises to leave the castle for good.

CONNECTIONS. Animal fables. Bullies. Cats. Cleverness. Conflict. Daimyos. Monks. Patience. Problem solvers. Rats. Samurai. Warriors.

317. The First to Be Served

Suzanne Crowder Han, *Korean Folk and Fairy Tales*. Korea

Deer, Hare and Toad are arguing about which one of them is oldest, for the oldest will eat first at a celebration. Deer says he helped to nail stars to the sky. Hare says he planted the tree that gave the wood to build the ladder used to nail stars to the sky. Toad begins to cry, remembering his three sons who were all involved in the star-making but died. Toad's story puts him as honored eldest, and he gets to eat first.

CONNECTIONS. Competition. Deer. Hierarchy. Honor. Humorous stories. Old age. Rabbits and hares. Storytelling. Toads.

HOW ELSE THIS STORY IS TOLD. *Chinese variation:* The Fox, the Hare, and the Toad Have an Argument — Lotta Carswell Hume, *Favorite Children's Stories from China and Tibet.* *Korean variations:* The Deer, the Hare, and the Toad — Zong Zin-Il in Zong In-Sob, *Folk Tales from Korea.* The First to Be Served — Linda Soon Curry, *A Tiger by the Tail.* Me First — Gillian McClure, *The Land of the Dragon King.*

318. The Rabbit's Revenge

Folk Tales from China, Second Series. Tibetan People

The rabbit has had enough of the lion's always looking down upon her. She tells the lion that she has met someone who looks like the lion, but brags that he is stronger. The lion wants to see this arrogant creature. The rabbit leads the lion to a well. The lion roars down the well, and the other creature roars back. Then the lion throws himself down the well to get at his enemy.

CONNECTIONS. Animal fables. Arrogance. Cleverness. Competition. Hierarchy. Hui People, stories from. Humorous stories. Lions. Ningxia, China, stories from. Pride. Rabbits and hares. Reflections. Revenge. Social class. Tibetan People, stories from. Tigers. Tricksters.

WHERE ELSE THIS STORY APPEARS. The Rabbit's Revenge — D.L. Ashliman, *Folktexts,* Online.

HOW ELSE THIS STORY IS TOLD. *Chinese variations:* How the Rabbit Killed the Lion — A. L. Shelton, *Tibetan Folk Tales.* The Little Hare's Clever Trick — Lotta Carswell Hume, *Favorite Children's Stories from China and Tibet* (from the Tibetan People). The Tiger and the Hare- Bao Xuecheng in Shujiang Li and Karl W. Luckert, *Mythology and Folklore of the Hui* (from Ningxia).

319. Cat and Rat

Ed Young. China

All of the creatures desire to be first when the Jade Emperor announces a race that will determine the cycle of twelve years named after them. Cat and Rat are friends as the story begins, but since neither can swim, they ask the water buffalo to carry them across the river. Then Rat pushes Cat into the water. He later plays another trick on the water buffalo and so wins the honor of first place. Cat struggles to catch up, but she ends up finishing after tiger, rabbit, dragon, snake, horse, goat, monkey, rooster, dog, and pig and is angry to not be included in the twelve-year cycle at all.

CONNECTIONS. Cats. Competition. Deceit. Enemies. Han People, stories from. Hierarchy. Jade Emperor. Origins. Rats. Water buffalo. Years. Zodiac.

HOW ELSE THIS STORY IS TOLD. From the Year of the Rat to the Year of the Pig — Yin-lien C. Chin, Yetta S. Center, and Mildred Ross, *Traditional Chinese Folktales. How the Years Were Named/Rainen wa Nanidoshi—* Chizuko Kamichi on kamishibai story cards. *The Rat, the Ox, and the Zodiac—* Dorothy Van Woerkom (this tale specifically concerns the rivalry between the wise Rat and the strong Ox over which should become Beast of the First Year). The Origins of the Twelve Zodiac Animals— Haiwang Yuan, *The Magic Lotus Lantern and Other Tales from the Han Chinese.* The Snake, the Deer, and the Old Man — Gregory Crawford, *Animals in the Stars. Story of the Chinese Zodiac—* Monica Chang.

320. Soo Tan the Tiger and the Little Green Frog

Lotta Carswell Hume, *Favorite Children's Stories from China and Tibet*. Southwest China

When a tiger catches a frog, the little frog proposes a jumping competition, and then a spitting competition, bragging to the tiger that he has killed and eaten a tiger before. The tiger leaves and tells this to a fox, who laughs at him for worrying about a frog. When the fox returns with the tiger, the frog asks him if he brought this little dog for his evening meal. And the tiger takes off then, running away very very fast.

CONNECTIONS. Bears. Cleverness. Competition. Deer. Escapes. Foxes. Frogs. Goats. Hierarchy. Humorous stories. Jackals. Perspective. Rabbits and hares. Sheep. Southwest China, stories from. Talents. Tibetan People, stories from. Tigers. Tricksters. Wolves.

HOW ELSE THIS STORY IS TOLD. **Chinese variations:** The Black Bear and the Fox — Hua Long, *The Moon Maiden* (here a goat pretends to be a bear-eater). The Jackals and the Tiger — Lotta Carswell Hume, *Favorite Children's Stories from China and Tibet* (in this story from the Tibetan People, Father Jackal and his family pretend to be fearsome creatures when they take over the tiger's den and then thank the baboon for bringing them a tiger to eat). One Hairball — Carol Kendall and Yao-wen Li, *Sweet and Sour*. The Sheep, the Lamb, the Wolf, and the Hare — W. F. O'Connor, *Folk Tales from Tibet* (a clever hare saves the sheep and her lamb by pretending that she has been deputized by the Emperor of China to collect wolf-pelts for the King of India). The Tiger and the Frog — A. L. Shelton, *Tibetan Folk Tales*. The Tiger, the Deer and the Fox — Lim Siantek, *More Folk Tales from China*.

321. The Chachatatutu and the Phoenix

Folk Tales from China, Second Series. Tibetan People

The small, ugly chachatatutu asks the beautiful, grand phoenix to take action against a pika that has eaten two eggs from her nest. The phoenix does not want to be bothered. The chachatatutu stabs the pika with a blade of grass the next time it comes by. The pika runs around blindly startling a lion who startles a dragon, who accidentally tips over the phoenix's nest and breaks her only egg. When the phoenix tries to blame the chachatatutu for starting the chain of events, the indignant chachatatutu points out that the phoenix considered her too insignificant to be counted before.

CONNECTIONS. Animal fables. Beauty. Chachatatutus. Conflict. Dragons. Eggs. Hierarchy. Lions. Phoenix. Pikas. Recognition. Responsibility. Revenge. Size. Social class. Tibetan People, stories from. Unkindness. Vanity.

322. The Boastful Tortoise

Folk Tales from China, Second Series. Tibetan People

A tortoise weeps that he will not be able to leave a dried-up lake because he cannot fly. Two egrets suggest that he hold tightly to the middle of a stick while they fly with him, one at each end, carrying the stick in their beaks. The egrets keep flying when people call out how clever the tortoise is to let the egrets carry him. But when some children exclaim how clever the egrets are, the tortoise open his mouth to add that it was his plan. And he falls.

CONNECTIONS. Animal fables. Egrets. Falls. Helpfulness. Mongolian People, stories from. Rescues. Tibetan People, stories from. Tortoises. Vanity.

WHERE ELSE THIS STORY APPEARS. The Boastful Tortoise—At D.L. Ashliman, *Folktexts*, Online.

HOW ELSE THIS STORY IS TOLD. *Chinese variation:* The Flying Frog—Carolyn Han, *Why Snails Have Shells* (from the Mongol People).

323. The Silly Jelly Fish

B.H. Chamberlain in Lafcadio Hearn and Others, *Japanese Fairy Tales*. Japan

The wife of the Sea Dragon king says only Monkey's liver will cure her illness. The Dragon King asks his Jelly-Fish servant to bring Monkey into the sea. The Jelly-Fish coaxes Monkey onto his back, but when they are halfway across the water Monkey discovers why Jelly-Fish has come for him. He feigns dismay, saying that he left his liver in a tree back on the land. Jelly-Fish floats Monkey back to get his liver, but the minute Monkey touches land, he zips up high in the tree and says he cannot find it. Jelly-Fish reports to the Dragon King, who has his officers beat the Jelly-Fish until there are no bones in his body.

CONNECTIONS. Cleverness. Dragon King. East Sea. Escapes. Hearts. Hui People, stories from. Humorous stories. Illness. Jellyfish. Livers. Messengers. Monkeys and apes. Problem solvers. Rabbits and hares. Tibetan People, stories from. Tortoises. Tricksters. Turtles.

WHERE ELSE THIS STORY APPEARS. *The Silly Jelly Fish*—B.H. Chamberlain. Japanese Fairy Tale Series, No. 13. The Silly Jelly-Fish—B.H. Chamberlain in Lafcadio Hearn, *The Boy Who Drew Cats and Other Japanese Fairy Tales*.

HOW ELSE THIS STORY IS TOLD. *Chinese variations:* The Dragon and the Monkey—Lim Sian-tek, *More Folk Tales from China*. The Foolish Dragon—E.T. C. Werner, *Myths and Legends of China* and at D.L. Ashliman, *Folktexts*, Online (in the ending, Buddha tells his followers he is the monkey when the monkey tricks the dragon by scampering up the tree to get his heart). The Monkey and the Turtle—Wang Weiguo in Shujiang Li and Karl W. Luckert, *Mythology and Folklore of the Hui* (from Ningxia). The Story of the Tortoise and the Monkey—Lotta Carswell Hume, *Favorite Children's Stories from China and Tibet* (from the Tibetan People). The Story of the Tortoise and the Monkey—W. F. O'Connor, *Folk Tales from Tibet*. *Japanese variations:* The Jelly-Fish and the Monkey—F. Hadland Davis, *Myths and Legends of Japan*. How the Jelly-Fish Lost His Shell—William Elliot Griffis, *The Fire-Fly's Lovers*. The Jelly-Fish Takes a Journey—Grace James, *Green Willow*. The Jellyfish and the Monkey—Yei Theodora Ozaki, *Japanese Fairy Book*. The Jellyfish and the Monkey—F. Hadland Davis, *Myths and Legends of Japan*. The Jellyfish Messenger—Takeshi Nakajima, *Japanese Traditional Tales*. The Monkey and the Jellyfish—Andrew Lang, *The Violet Fairy Book* and at D. L. Ashliman, *Folktexts*, Online. The Monkey's Liver—Keigo Seki, *Folktales of Japan*. Why the Jellyfish Has No Bones—Florence Sakade, *Japanese Children's Favorite Stories* and *Little One-Inch*. Why the Jellyfish Has No Shell—Alan Leslie Whitehorn, *Wonder Tales of Old Japan*. *Korean variations:* The Hare Liver—Tae Hung Ha, *Folk Tales of Old Korea*. Harelip—John Holstein. The Hare's Liver—Suzanne Crowder Han, *Korean Folk and Fairy Tales*. The Hare's Liver—James Riordan, *Korean Folk-tales*. *The King of the Fish*—Marian Parry. *The Rabbit and the Dragon King*—Daniel San Souci (a turtle is the messenger sent to bring the rabbit for his heart). The Rabbit and Other Legends—H. N. Allen, *Korean Tales*. The Rabbit That Rode on a Tortoise—Frances Carpenter, *Tales of a Korean Grandmother*. Rabbit Visits the Palace of the Dragon King—James Huntley Grayson, *Myths and Legends from Korea* (the Dragon King lives in the East Sea). *The Rabbit's Escape*—Suzanne Crowder Han. The Rabbit's Eyes—William Elliot Griffis, *The Unmannerly Tiger and Other Korean*

Tales. The Tortoise and the Hare —*Long Long Time Ago*. The Turtle and the Rabbit — Yu Chai-Shin, Shiu L. Kong, and Ruth Y. Yu, *Korean Folk Tales*.

324. The Tiger Finds a Teacher

Folk Tales from China, Second Series. Han People

A clumsy tiger asks a cat if she will teach him to be as graceful as she. He promises that he will not use what he learns against her. The cat teaches the tiger and finally tells him that she has shared everything she knows. The tiger breaks his word and pounces on the plump cat, who quickly runs up a tree. He cannot follow her, for this is one last trick the cat never trusted the tiger enough to share.

CONNECTIONS. Animal fables. Cats. Cleverness. Education. Escapes. Han People, stories from. Humorous stories. Knowledge. Problem solvers. Promises. Teachers. Tigers. Trust.

WHERE ELSE THIS STORY APPEARS. The Tiger Finds a Teacher — At D. L. Ashliman, *Folktexts*, Online.

HOW ELSE THIS STORY IS TOLD. Tiger Finds a Teacher — Hua Long, *The Moon Maiden*.

325. The Tiger and the Hare

Y.T. Pyun, *Tales from Korea*. Korea

A clever hare convinces a hungry tiger not to eat her, but to bake some rocks like cake while she goes for sauce. Of course, she does not return, and he burns his mouth on the hot rocks. A while later, she tricks the tiger by saying that she will drive sparrows into his open mouth if he keeps it open wide. The third time, the hare tells the tiger that the only way he will be able to catch fish is by sticking his tail into the river. The tiger's tail freezes there overnight, which makes it easy for the villagers to catch him in the morning.

CONNECTIONS. Cleverness. Escapes. Humorous stories. Foxes. Otters. Problem solvers. Rabbits and hares. Tails. Tigers. Tricksters.

HOW ELSE THIS STORY IS TOLD. *Japanese variation:* The Sky-Watcher — Hiroko Fujita, *Folktales from the Japanese Countryside* (in the second half of this story, an otter gets revenge against a trickster fox). *Korean variations:* The Rabbit and the Tiger —*Long Long Time Ago*. The Rabbit and the Old Tiger — Suzanne Crowder Han, *Korean Folk and Fairy Tales*. The Old Tiger and the Hare — Bag Mal-Bong in Zong In-Sob, *Folk Tales from Korea*. The Tiger and the Hare — I. K. Junne, *Floating Clouds, Floating Dreams*. The Tiger and the Rabbit — Kim So-un, *Korean Children's Favorite Stories*. The Tiger Catching Fish — Chun Shin-Yong, *Korean Folk Tales*.

326. How Two Water Snakes Moved House

Margaret Read MacDonald, *Three-Minute Tales*. China

Two snakes need to cross the road as their marsh is drying up. They want to do it without getting killed. The larger one says that he will lead, but the smaller one says that will give away their plans. The smaller snake suggests that he ride on the larger snake. If they each hold the other's tail in his mouth, no one will know what they are or where they are going.

CONNECTIONS. Cooperation. Disguises. Perspective. Problem solvers. Secrets. Snakes.

HOW ELSE THIS STORY IS TOLD. How Two Water Snakes Moved House — Han Fei Zi in *Ancient Chinese Tales.*

327. The Crab and the Monkey

Florence Sakade, *Japanese Children's Favorite Stories.* Japan

Monkey finds a persimmon one day while he is out walking with Crab, and Crab finds a rice ball. Monkeys persuades Crab to trade. Monkey eats the rice ball, and Crab plants the persimmon seed, which does grow into a fine tree. When the persimmons are ready to pick, Crab asks Monkey to climb the tree for him. Monkey does, but once up there, he eats up all the ripe persimmons and pelts Crab with the green ones. Crab gathers his friends to help punish Monkey. He invites Monkey to his house, where mortar, hornet, and chestnut are hiding. They surprise Monkey, stinging, burning, and hitting him one after the other as Monkey tries to run out. After that, Monkey begs Crab to forgive him and never cheats again.

CONNECTIONS. Animal fables. Changes in attitude. Chestnuts. Cooperation. Crabs. Deceit. Hornets. Monkeys and apes. Mortars. Persimmons. Reconciliation. Revenge. Rice balls. Trades.

WHERE ELSE THIS STORY APPEARS. The Crab and the Monkey — Florence Sakade, *Little One-Inch.*

HOW ELSE THIS STORY IS TOLD. The Ape and the Crab — William Elliot Griffis, *The Fire-Fly's Lovers* and *Other Fairy Tales of Old Japan.* The Battle Between the Monkey and the Crab — Fanny Hagin Mayer, *Ancient Tales in Modern Japan.* The Battle of the Ape and the Crab — Takeshi Nakajima, *Japanese Traditional Tales.* The Battle of the Ape and the Crab — Baron Algernon Bertram Freeman-Mitford Redesdale, *Tales of Old Japan.* The Cancerian-Simian War, The Revenge of the Crab upon the Monkey — Iwaya Sazanami, *Iwaya's Fairy Tales of Old Japan.* The Crab and the Monkey — Andrew Lang, *The Crimson Fairy Book.* The Fight Between the Crab and the Monkey — Juliet Piggott, *Japanese Fairy Tales.* Monkey and Crab — Yoko Kawashima Watkins, *Tales from the Bamboo Grove.* The Monkey and the Crab — Keigo Seki, *Folktales of Japan. The Monkey and the Crab/Saru to Kani—* Miyoko Matsutani on kamishibai story cards. The Quarrel of the Monkey and the Crab — Yei Theodora Ozaki, *Japanese Fairy Book. Saru Kani Kanen/ The Battle of the Monkey and the Crab—* Japanese Fairy Tale Series, No. 3. The Story of the Monkey and the Crab — Alan Leslie Whitehorn, *Wonder Tales of Old Japan.*

328. The Fox and the Bear

Yoshiko Uchida, *The Magic Listening Cap.* Japan

Times are bad, and the fox suggests that Mr. Bear and he work together to plant seeds. Somehow, at each step, the fox manages to get the bear to do all of the work. At the beginning, the fox wants them to decide which one will take the crop that will come in above ground and which will take the crop growing below. The fox quickly chooses the crop below the ground and, since it turns out to be carrots, he gets it all. The next time the bear chooses bottom, but the crop is strawberries. There are other tricks, and the bear has had enough. He tells the fox he can get some delicious meat like what the bear is eating by tying his tail to the tail of the biggest horse and then biting its hind leg. The fox runs to try this, and the horse drags him all around the meadow.

CONNECTIONS. Animal fables. Bears. Deceit. Farmers. Foxes. Han People, stories from. Horses. Humorous stories. Landlords. Monkeys and apes. Rats. Revenge. Shirkers. Strawberries. Weasels. Work. Yunnan Province, China, stories from.

HOW ELSE THIS STORY IS TOLD. *Chinese variations:* The Fox, the Monkey, the Hare, and the Horse —*Folk Tales from China*, Second Series and at D.L. Ashliman, *Folktexts*, Online (from the Han People). Living King of Hell Dies of Anger — William Eberhard, *Folktales of China* (this post-communist variation from Yunnan Province features an evil landlord and exploited farmer. It first appears in the 1965 edition of Eberhard's book). *Japanese variation:* The Rice Field the Rat and the Weasel Cultivated — Fanny Hagin Mayer, *Ancient Tales in Modern Japan*.

329. The Cat and the Mice

John Yeoman and Quentin Blake, *The Singing Tortoise*. Tibetan People

When the old cat tells the mice she will give up hunting them if they file past and bow to her twice a day, the mice agree. The cat, however, pounces on the last mouse in line each time. Two mice suspect something is up and position themselves one in the front and one in the back of the line. They keep calling. The cat cannot pounce undetected that day or the next and, frustrated, eventually leaves the barn.

CONNECTIONS. Cats. Cooperation. Deceit. Hierarchy. Humorous stories. Mice. Problem solvers. Promises. Tibetan People, stories from.

HOW ELSE THIS STORY IS TOLD. The Story of the Cat and the Mice — W. F. O'Connor, *Folk Tales from Tibet* and at D. L. Ashliman, *Folktexts*, Online.

330. The Frog from Osaka and the Frog from Kyoto

Margaret Read MacDonald, *Three-Minute Tales*. Japan

A frog from Osaka meets a frog coming the opposite direction from Kyoto on top of a mountain. To see what the new city is like where each is going, the frogs stand up on their hind legs and hold onto each other. Osaka looks like Kyoto to the Kyoto frog and vice versa. So, the frogs each decide to go back home. Because frogs' eyes are in the back of their heads, they never realize that the cities they think they see lying ahead are the same ones they have left behind.

CONNECTIONS. Cooperation. Frogs. Humorous stories. Journeys. Knowledge. Kyoto. Misunderstandings. Osaka. Perspective.

HOW ELSE THIS STORY IS TOLD. *Japanese variations:* Sea Frog, City Frog— Dorothy O. Van Woerkom. The Two Frogs— Andrew Lang, *The Violet Fairy Book*, also in Marie L. Shedlock, *The Art of the Story-Teller* and at D.L. Ashliman, *Folktexts*, Online. The Travels of the Two Frogs— William Elliot Griffis, *The Fire-Fly's Lovers and Other Fairy Tales of Old Japan*. The Travels of Two Frogs— Alan Leslie Whitehorn, *Wonder Tales of Old Japan*. *Korean variation:* Two Frogs— Suzanne Crowder Han, *Korean Folk and Fairy Tales*.

331. Plop!

Folk Tales from China, Second Series. Tibetan People

Six rabbits flee in terror when a large piece of fruit falls in the lake. They yell that Plop is coming. Word spreads to fox, monkey, deer, pig, buffalo, rhinoceros, elephant, black bear, brown bear, leopard, tiger, and lion, who are also afraid. Another lion wants to know why they are all running, and they take him to see. Just then, everyone watches another big piece of fruit fall down.

CONNECTIONS. Bears. Buffalo. Deer. Elephants. Fear. Foxes. Fruit. Humorous stories. Identity. Leopards. Lions. Misunderstandings. Monkeys and apes. Pigs. Rabbits and hares. Rhinoceros. Tibetan People, stories from. Tigers.

WHERE ELSE THIS STORY APPEARS. Plop!— At D.L. Ashliman, *Folktexts*, Online. Plop — In Carl Withers, *I Saw a Rocket Walk a Mile*.

HOW ELSE THIS STORY IS TOLD. *Chinese variations:* Plop!— Hua Long, *The Moon Maiden*. The Rabbit's Tale — Demi, *The Dragon's Tale*.

332. The Two Foolish Cats
Yoshiko Uchida. Japan

A big cat and a small cat are friends until they find two rice cakes and start to fight over which one gets to eat the bigger rice cake. An old badger tells them to find the old monkey of the mountain who will ensure that they get equal shares. The old monkey keeps evening up the two sides, nibbling one rice cake and then the other, until the rice cakes are gone.

CONNECTIONS. Badgers. Cats. Conflict. Humorous stories. Monkeys and apes. Problem solvers. Rice cakes. Sharing. Size. Tibetan People, stories from.

WHERE ELSE THIS STORY APPEARS. Two Foolish Cats— Yoshiko Uchida, *The Sea of Gold*.

HOW ELSE THIS STORY IS TOLD. *Tibetan variation:* Two Quarrelsome Cats— Carolyn Han, *Why Snails Have Shells*.

333. The Monkey's Tale
Demi, *The Dragon's Tale*. China

The King of Monkeys summons his subjects to fish the moon he sees up from the bottom of a well. They make a chain down to the water, each one hanging from the other's arms and tails. The smallest monkey keeps trying unsuccessfully to pick the moon up out of the water. The other monkeys grow tired. Then they stop trying, for they see a new moon in the sky.

CONNECTIONS. Animal fables. Fools. Han People, stories from. Humorous stories. Kings. Leadership. Misunderstandings. Monkeys and apes. Moon. Quests. Reflections. Tibetan People, stories from. Water. Wells.

HOW ELSE THIS STORY IS TOLD. *Chinese variations:* (the emphasis in the Tibetan tales is to be wary about following an unwise ruler). *Monkeys Fish the Moon*— Zhou Kequin, director, Film. *The Monkeys Fish Out the Moon*— Hou Guanbin. The Monkeys and the Moon — Frederick and Audrey Hyde-Chambers, *Tibetan Folk Tales*. Monkeys Fishing the Moon — Haiwang Yuan, *The Magic Lotus Lantern and Other Tales from the Han Chinese*. Reaching for the Moon — Margaret Read MacDonald, *Peace Tales* (from the Tibetan People).

334. Why White Rabbits Have Long Ears and Pink Eyes
Folk Tales from China, Second Series. Zhuang People

An old mother rabbit, with the short ears and blue eyes rabbits used to have, tells her lazy son that he should go out to look for his own food. He has a few mishaps, but does manage to find some ripe berries and comes back with attitude. The next day, he does not get any food because a farmer swings a pole at him. The rabbit does not tell his mother, but returns to the same field for melons the next day. Getting cocky with a scarecrow that he thinks is a man, the rabbit sticks to its pasty rice. His eyes become bloodshot as he tries to yank away. Just then the farmer comes and pulls and pulls the rabbit free by the only unstuck part, his ears.

CONNECTIONS. Animal fables. Arrogance. Ears. Education. Eyes. Farmers. Laziness. Mothers and sons. Origins. Rabbits and hares. Scarecrows. Zhuang People, stories from.

HOW ELSE THIS STORY IS TOLD. How Rabbits Got Pink Eyes and Long Ears—Louise and Yuan-Hsi Kuo, *Chinese Folk Tales.*

335. How the Cock Got His Red Crown

Lotta Carswell Hume, *Favorite Children's Stories from China and Tibet.* Miao People

Six suns blaze in the sky during the time of Emperor Yao and scorch all the crops. The ten elders think someone should shoot down the suns. The best archers cannot reach the suns, but Prince Howee from a neighboring kingdom has the idea to shoot the reflections of the suns in a pool. He shoots five, but the sixth runs to hide in a cave. Now the land is too dark. The ten elders try to find someone to call forth the sixth sun. The sun does not like the call of either the tiger or the cow, but when he hears the cock's crow he appears.

CONNECTIONS. Archers. Bulang People, stories from. Darkness. Emperors. Han People, stories from. Miao People, stories from. Moon. Origins. Princes. Reflections. Roosters. Sounds. Sun.

HOW ELSE THIS STORY IS TOLD. Gumiya —*The Seventh Sister: Folk Tales from China* (from the Bulang People). How the Cock Got His Red Crown — Ruth Q. Sun, *The Asian Animal Zodiac. How the Rooster Got His Crown*— Amy Lowry Poole. Why Rooster Crows— Gregory Crawford, *Animals in the Stars.* Why the Sun Rises When the Rooster Crows— M. A. Jagendorf and Virginia Weng, *The Magic Boat and Other Chinese Folk Stories* (from the Han People).

336. Peacock with the Fiery Tale

Hua Long, *The Moon Maiden.* China

The beautiful Peacock Fairy, with human arms and head and with a peacock's tail and body, brings together all of the peacocks and announces that she can only choose one to be her apprentice. She challenges them to return at midnight looking individually different. Little Peacock decides that he does not stand out enough and will not worry about the competition. He gives some of his tail feathers to an old man who looks so hot and more feathers away through to day to other people in need. When the peacocks assemble that night, they look dazzling, all decorated with fireflies and flowers. But it is Little Peacock the Peacock Fairy notices. And when she hears what has happened to his feathers, she waves her hand. One feather flies from each peacock's tail to form a fan that comes down to cover his bare tail. Then she teaches Little Peacock the magic words to make his tail burst into flashing colors that light up the night sky and bring the joy of fireworks all around the land.

CONNECTIONS. Compassion. Education. Fairies. Feathers. Generosity. Helpfulness. Humility. Kindness from animals. Origins. Peacocks. Physical difference. Recognition. Rewards. Tails.

HOW ELSE THIS STORY IS TOLD. *Japanese variation: The Little Peacock's Gift*— Cherry Denman. *Chinese variation:* The Peacock's Tail — M.A. Jagendorf and Virginia Weng, *The Magic Boat and Other Chinese Folk Stories* (in this tale from the Miao People, an ugly peacock is the only animal humble enough to think that the Immortal can improve him).

337. The Wisdom of the Ants

Margaret Read MacDonald, *Three-Minute Tales*. China

Fire spreads on a mountain below where one thousand ants live. How will they get down? They form a large ball and roll through the fire, saving most of the ants inside.

CONNECTIONS. Animal fables. Ants. Community. Cooperation. Death. Fire. Problem solvers.

338. The Ant That Laughed Too Much

Frances Carpenter, *Tales of a Korean Grandmother*. Korea

An earthworm asks a wise old ant to act as matchmaker and find him a wife. The ant speaks to a centipede she thinks may be the right one. The centipede complains that an earthworm would be too long to make coats for and has no feet. The ant laughs. The earthworm is insulted. He says it would take too much straw to make shoes for all of the centipede's feet anyway. The ant laughs so hard that the straw rope around her middle squeezes in her waist.

CONNECTIONS. Animal fables. Ants. Centipedes. Earthworms. Feet. Humorous stories. Insults. Laughter. Matches, marriage. Matchmakers. Physical difference. Quantity. Origins. Size.

HOW ELSE THIS STORY IS TOLD. Sir One Long Body and Madame Thousand Feet — William Elliot Griffis, *The Unmannerly Tiger and Other Korean Tales.*

339. The Kindhearted Crab and the Cunning Mouse

Richard M. Dorson, *Folktales Told Around the World*. Korea

A crab feeds his mouse friend well when he invites him over. However, when the crab is invited to the mouse's house, the mouse is looking up at the sky and does not acknowledge the crab at all. The following day the mouse excuses himself, saying he must have been deep into his meditation. The crab entertains the mouse and again feeds him well. However, the second time the mouse invites the crab over, the mouse stares at the ground the whole time. The third time the mouse ignores the crab, the crab goes from doubting his own religious spirit to just being angry. The next time the mouse shows up, the crab pinches him hard with his claw. After that, they go their separate ways.

CONNECTIONS. Animal fables. Conflict. Crabs. Foxes. Friendship. Hospitality. Mice. Otters. Spirituality. Unkindness.

HOW ELSE THIS STORY IS TOLD. *Japanese variation:* The Sky Watcher — Hiroko Fujita,

Folktales from the Japanese Countryside (the two protagonists here are a gracious otter and an ungenerous fox).

340. The Birds' Party

Basil Hall Chamberlain. Ainu People, Japan

Mr. and Mrs. Pigeon invite five different kinds of birds to their party, but not the Crow. The Crow flies over the feast and drops a large stone that breaks dishes and scatters guests. The birds all blame Mr. and Mrs. Pigeon for faulty preparations. The Jay and the Woodpecker, who were also not invited, say that it is not their business to patch up relations between the Pigeons and the party-goers. When planning a party, it is better to invite all of your friends.

CONNECTIONS. Animal fables. Birds. Community. Conflict. Crows. Harmony. Hospitality. Jays. Pigeons. Woodpeckers.

WHERE ELSE THIS STORY APPEARS. *The Birds' Party*—B.H. Chamberlain, Online.

341. An Endless Story

Keigo Seki, *Folktales of Japan.* Japan

When there is no food left in Nagasaki, the rats sail to Satsuma. They meet the rats from Satsuma who are sailing to Nagasaki for food. Without hope now, all of the rats jump into the water one by one — the first rat cries and jumps, the second rat cries and jumps....

CONNECTIONS. Famine. Humorous stories. Journeys. Nagasaki. Rats. Repetition. Satsuma. Storytelling.

WHERE ELSE THIS STORY APPEARS. An Endless Story — Jane Yolen, *Favorite Folktales from Around the World.*

HOW ELSE THIS STORY IS TOLD. Endless Story — Yei Theodora Ozaki, *Japanese Fairy Book* (here the rats crawl out from a storehouse). An Endless Story — Keigo Seki, *Folktales of Japan.* Endless Story — Cathy Spagnoli, *Asian Tales and Tellers.* The Mice Make a Pilgrimmage — Hiroko Fujita, *Folktales from the Japanese Countryside* (in this playful variation, mice who have no money for a ferry cooperate by holding onto each other after they dive into the river one by one). The Rats of Nagasaki — Margaret Read MacDonald, *Three-Minute Tales.* The Rats of Nagasaki — Carl Withers, *I Saw a Rocket Walk at Mile.*

~ XII ~

Tricksters and Fools

342. The Magical Monkey King: Mischief in Heaven

Ji-li Jiang. China

Born from a black stone egg that was breathed on by a dragon wind, a small stone monkey comes alive on the peak of the Mountain of Flowers and Fruits. When he laughs, a beam of light shoots up to Heaven, but the Jade Emperor of Heaven and Earth thinks a little golden monkey is nothing to worry about. The little monkey challenges a bunch of monkeys who are afraid to go through a waterfall to the other side. He says he will do it if they make him their king. They agree, and he leaps through. Behind the waterfall, the little monkey finds a room with marble beds, that seems like a palace. He somersaults back through the waterfall to tell the other monkeys all about it, and they name him Magnificent Monkey King. During one birthday celebration, however, Monkey bursts into tears for he does not want ever to die. He wants to learn how to live forever like the Immortals. The Magnificent Monkey King travels for nine years to find a sage. At last he comes to Master Subhodi's cave. Master Subhodi strikes Monkey, but then Monkey convinces the master to take him on as a student, even though he does not want to waste time reading and breathing. He learns magic spells that let him transform himself, see things that are far away, and stay young for a long time. However, Monkey gets bored and begins to misbehave. He lies to the master, saying he has been practicing cloud soaring, but then falls off a cloud because he hasn't been. Monkey really does want to become immortal and promises once again to obey the rules. This works for five years, but when Monkey brags that he is smarter than another student Master Subhodi sends him away. Monkey's clan is in hiding, having been attacked by the Demon of Havoc. Monkey rides a cloud to the Demon and outwits him in a fight with all his newly-learned magic. He brings the captured monkeys home and teaches his clan to defend itself. Monkey is rude to the Dragon King, when he goes to the bottom of the sea to acquire a special weapon. He ends up seizing the pillar that anchors the Sacred Island, which he shrinks to be a staff. Monkey then spins so fast that the 42,000 crabs the Dragon King sends after Monkey can't catch him. The Dragon King goes to complain about Monkey to the Jade Emperor, who sends Thousand-League Eye to invite him up to Heaven.

Monkey impulsively somersaults onto a cloud and reaches Heaven without waiting for the Emperor's escort. He tries to browbeat the guards into letting him in, but at last Thousand-League Eye appears, and Monkey is dazzled by the magnificence of Heaven. When the Jade Emperor suggests Monkey work there, Monkey cockily exclaims that he is the Magnificent Monkey King, so why should he work. The Jade Emperor offers Monkey the important post of Heavenly Horse Deity, in charge of transportation. Monkey accepts, but then he finds out that his is a low-ranking position. He tromps off to talk to the Jade Emperor, who offers him the position of protector in the Heavenly Peach Garden. It turns out that one kind of peach in the garden ripens every 9,000 years and will let the being who eats it live forever. This is just what Monkey has been looking for. Every day, he sneaks in and eats peaches from the purple-leafed tree. However, one day fairies preparing for a banquet discover that the peaches are missing. Monkey goes on the offensive, accusing them of stealing the peaches and he puts a freezing spell on the fairies. Monkey decides to go to the banquet. He transforms himself to look like the goddess Lotus-Feet Immortal, but en route tastes some liquid that is bubbling in the kitchen and cannot stop laughing inappropriately. The Jade Emperor sees Monkey's tail, and Monkey quickly somersaults back to earth. The Jade Emperor sends one hundred thousand soldiers to arrest Monkey. Monkey's clan is ready to fight, and Monkey uses all the magic he knows to humiliate the general and kings. The goddess Guan-yin suggests that the Emperor send Magician Lang, who transforms herself as swiftly as Monkey can, but the fight is stalled when Gyuan-yin throws down a vase that traps Monkey inside. Monkey is bound and brought to Heaven, but he just laughs at all the punishments they throw at him because, having eaten the peaches, he is now immortal. Then a deep voice tells everyone to stop fighting. It is Great Buddha. Monkey says he would like to replace the Jade Emperor. Great Buddha says that if Monkey can somersault out of the palm of his hand in one push, he will get to rule Heaven. Otherwise, he will be punished. Monkey is sure this will be easy, and he leaps. When he lands, he does not recognize where he is and is sure it must be far, far away. He pisses against a pillar to mark that he has been there and cloud-soars back. But jumping off the cloud, Monkey discovers he has been in the Great Buddha's hand the whole time; the pillar was one of Buddha's great fingers. Buddha tells Monkey he must stay under a mountain for five hundred years, and Monkey laughs.

CONNECTIONS. Arrogance. Buddha. Changes in attitude. Curiosity. Deceit. Demon of Havoc. Demons. Disobedience. Education. Flowers and Fruits, Mountain of. Forgiveness. Han People, stories from. Gods and goddesses. Guanyin, Goddess of Mercy. Heaven. Humorous stories. Immortality. Impulsiveness. Jade Emperor. Laughter. Leadership. Monkeys and apes. Monks. Peaches. Performance. Sages. Self-esteem. Stone monkey. Talents. Tests. Tricksters.

HOW ELSE THIS STORY IS TOLD. Picture books and story collections capture pieces of the whole tale about the irrepressible Monkey King, taken from Wu Cheng-en's Chinese epic *Journey to the West*, also translated as *The Pilgrimmage to the West*. The Adventures of the Stone Monkey — Lim Sian-tek, *Folk Tales from China*. Journey to the West — Shelley Fu, *Ho Yi the Archer* and *Treasury of Chinese Folktales* (also continues the Monkey King story after the 500-year punishment). The King of the Monkeys — Frances Carpenter, *Tales of a Chinese Grandmother. The Making of Monkey King* — Robert Kraus and Debby Chen. The Mighty Monkey King — Rena Krasno and Yen-Fong Chiang, *Cloud Weavers*. Monkey — David Kherdian, *Feathers and Tails. Monkey and the Water Dragon* — Troughton, Joanna (this episode involves Monkey, Tripitaka, and Pigsy). *Monkey and the White Bone Demon* — Jill Morris. Monkey King and the Iron Fan Princess — Haiwang Yuan, *The Magic Lotus Lantern* (from the Han People). Monkey King Strikes the White-Bone Demon Three Times — Haiwang Yuan, *The Magic Lotus Lantern*. The Monkey King Turns the Heavenly Palace Upside Down — Mingmei Yip, *Chinese Children's Favorite Stories. Monkey King Wreaks Havoc in Heaven* — Debby Chen. Monkey That Became King — Brian Brown, *Chinese Nights Entertainments: Stories of Old China*. The Monkey Who Would Be King — Anthony Horowitz, *Myths and Legends*. The Monkey Wu Kong Learns His Lesson — Mingmei Yip, *Chinese Children's Favorite Stories*. The Stone Monkey — Herbert A. Giles, *Chinese Fairy Tales. Tang Monk Disciples Monkey King* — Debby Chen.

343. The Boy of the Three-Year Nap
Diane Snyder. Japan

On the banks of the Nagara River there lives a boy who sleeps so much that he is called "The Boy of the Three-Year Nap." His mother is hopeful that her son Taro will change. One day, when Taro is already a young man, he watches a rich merchant build a large house next door. Taro comes up with a plan. He puts on a priest's black kimono and hat and draws charcoal lines on his face. That night when the merchant walks past the shrine of the ujigami, the patron god of the town, a black-clad figure startles the merchant, saying that he must marry his daughter to Taro or she will turn into a clay pot. The merchant is aghast, but the next day, he goes to see Taro's mother. When she hears the story of the ujigami, she suspects what Taro has been up to, but only suggests that if the merchant's daughter is to marry her son, the merchant will want to provide them with a bigger house. The merchant expands their house. Then, the mother, who has plans of her own, says that Taro will need a job. Taro does marry the merchant's daughter, goes to work for the merchant, raises a family, and lives happily in his new life.

CONNECTIONS. Changes in attitude. Changes in fortune. Disguises. Gods and goddesses. Humorous stories. Laziness. Matches, marriage. Merchants. Nagara River. Priests. Secrets. Sleep. Tricksters. Ujigami. Words. Work.

HOW ELSE THIS STORY IS TOLD. Do-Nothing Taro—Iwaya Sazanami, *Iwaya's Fairy Tales of Old Japan.* Netarō, the Lazy Man Next Door — Fanny Hagin Mayer, *Ancient Tales in Modern Japan.* Sannen Netaro: The Young Man Who Slept for Three Years—Chitose Yamada at *Kids Web Japan,* Online. The Story of Lazy Taro—Yei Theodora Ozaki, *Warriors of Old Japan.* The Story of Lazy Taro—Alan Leslie Whitehorn, *Wonder Tales of Old Japan* (grateful for the kindness of a governor who asks nothing in return, this Taro is eventually motivated to work and surpasses all expectations). The Three-Year Sleeping Boy—Keigo Seki, *Folktales of Japan.*

344. Chu the Rogue

Wolfram Eberhard, *Folktales of China.* Kiangsu, China

Chu loves playing pranks. He scolds the sun for entering his room uninvited, and the sun leaves a pot of silver for him outside. He scolds the moon for the same thing, and the moon leaves him gold. Always, he says he is going to complain to Yü huang-ti. When he threatens the plague deities, however, they complain to Yen-lo-wang, the king of hell, who sends a bee spirit up to fetch Chu. Chu, however, has pasted paper over every opening in his house, except one, which he covers with a pig's bladder. The bee spirit gets trapped there. When the bee spirit doesn't return, Yen-lo-wang sends the one-legged spirit, but Chu surrounds himself with thorns. The one-legged spirit gets stuck and becomes Chu's prisoner. The king of hell himself mounts his thousand-league horse and appears at Chu's house with Oxhead and Horseface. Chu sends his wife to invite Yen-lo-wang to dinner. Afterwards, she hangs two hot arrows on Chu's old water buffalo's back, so it runs like a thousand-league buffalo. Yen-lo-wang begs to ride it. They exchange clothes, so the buffalo will think Yen-lo-wang is its master. Now seated on the thousand-league horse in Yen-lo-wang's clothes, Chu tells the rakshasas and small servant ghosts in hell to beat Chu the Rogue on the water buffalo when he arrives. They beat Yen-lo-wang until Oxhead and Horseface arrive and tell about the switch. Yen-lo-wang tries to boil Chu in oil, but Chu has convinced the little spirits to sell most of the oil, and he is able to hold himself above its level in the cauldron. Yen-lo-wang then orders the spirits to drag Chu to the Yin-Yang River and leave him there to freeze to death. A sympathetic carp offers him a ride to the upper world. Chu is thinking he could sell this carp once he gets aboveground ... which he exactly what he does.

CONNECTIONS. Bee spirit. Bees. Carp. Chu the Rogue. Deities. Disguises. Ghosts. Gods and goddesses. Horses. Humorous stories. Husbands and wives. Kiangsu, China, stories from. King of Hell. One-legged spirit. Plague deities. Punishment. Spirits. Tricksters. Underworld. Water buffalo. Yen-lo, Lord of the Underworld. Yin-Yang River.

WHERE ELSE THIS STORY APPEARS. Chu and the King of the Underworld — Leslie Bonnet, *Chinese Folk and Fairy Tales*. Chu the Rogue — *Chinese Traditional Tales*, The Tent Archive, Online. Chu the Rogue — Richard Dorson, *Folktales Told Around the World*. Chu the Rogue — Lim Sian-tek, *More Folk Tales from China*. The Trickster in the Underworld China, Chu the Rogue — Josepha Sherman, *Trickster Tales*.

345. A Rare Bargain

Carol Kendall and Yao-wen Li, *Sweet and Sour*. China

The sign at the wine shop reads: "1 calty of sweet wine — 1 copper; 1 calty of aged vinegar — 2 coppers." Two friends order wine, but it tastes like vinegar. The second friend is afraid that if he complains they will be charged more.

CONNECTIONS. Coins. Fools. Frugality. Humorous stories. Wine.

346. The Wine Bibber

Carol Kendall and Yao-wen Li, *Sweet and Sour*. China

A gentleman has let a servant go for sampling his fine wines. Now he questions potential replacements about their knowledge of wine. If they know too much, he turns them down, figuring that they will be much too interested in his collection. The third applicant, however, does not recognize a certain bottle of wine as even being wine, and so, the gentleman takes him on. One day, the gentleman is going out and tells his new servant to guard the chickens and the ham and to make sure not to touch the two bottles that he tells him contain poison. As soon as he has left, the servant eats the ham and the chickens. Then he drinks the two bottles of wine called poison. The gentleman returns to find his servant lying on the floor. When he rouses him, the young man tells him that as a cat was making off with the ham, a dog gave chase and let the chickens out. The servant says that he was so upset at messing everything up, he drank first one bottle of poison, and then the other.

CONNECTIONS. Consequences. Deceit. Fools. Honey. Humorous stories. Identity. Knowledge. Persimmons. Poison. Remorse. Servants. Storytelling. Suicide. Tricksters. Truth. Warnings. Wine.

HOW ELSE THIS STORY IS TOLD. In some variations, the servant or student truly thinks the "poison" is poison and takes some after he messes up. *Chinese variation:* The Unsuccessful Suicide — Wolfram Eberhard, *Folktales of China* (from Central China). *Japanese variation:* Syrup — Royall Tyler, *Japanese Tales*. *Korean variations:* For the Love of Honey — Suzanne Crowder Han, *Korean Folk and Fairy Tales*. The Honey Pot — Lindy Soon Curry, *A Tiger by the Tail*. Poisonous Persimmons — O Wi-Yong in In-Sob Zong, *Folktales from Korea* and at D.L. Ashliman, *Folktexts*, Online.

347. Ten Jugs of Wine

Carol Kendall and Yao-wen Li, *Sweet and Sour*. China

Ten old friends decide that they will welcome the New Year together with hot wine. They agree that each person will bring one jug of wine. The first old man privately decides that he could bring water instead and no one would know. The second old man thinks that his wine is too sour. He brings water so as not to spoil the mix. A third man decides that he should bring water because his wine is so pale it looks like water. A fourth man decides his wine is too weak. A fifth man thinks his wine is too strong. And so it goes. On the eve of the New Year, each old man solemnly empties his jug into the big bowl. When the liquid is ladled out, no one will admit that they are all drinking water.

CONNECTIONS. Community. Deceit. New Year's. Selfishness. Tricksters. Truth. Water. Wine.

348. Stories About Nasrdin Avanti

Folk Tales of China, First Series. Uygur People, China

Here is a medley of thirteen stories about Nasrdin Avanti, also known as Effendi Nasreddin. Avanti tricks some suspicious horsemen by climbing into a grave and pretending that he is a dead man who has come up for air. He hides in a chest as his house is being robbed and tells the thief he is ashamed that there is so little to steal. He follows thieves making off with furniture from his house and thanks them for helping him move. Avanti manages not to pay when he confuses a shopkeeper into thinking he is just exchanging trousers for a shirt. Avanti buys back his own cow, when the dealer who is supposed to sell it gives an irresistible pitch. Avanti declares that the moon is better than the sun because it shines when there is no sun to make things bright. He pours tea into the pocket of a wedding guest he sees hiding away sweetmeats so the pocket will not get thirsty. Out on a hunt with the king, Avanti pretends to know the language of the birds and tells the king that an owl is saying that the kingdom will fall apart just like its nest if the king keeps treating people so badly. On another occasion, the king asks Avanti some absurd questions, so unanswerable that he cannot fault the responses Avanti offers. When a businessman tries to trick Avanti into giving him his ring, saying it will remind him of Avanti, Avanti replies that he needs to have the ring to always remember his friend when he thinks how his friend asked for the ring and did not get it. Avanti borrows a big iron pot and returns it to a stingy man with a smaller iron pot, saying the pot gave birth. The stingy man gives him the pot to hold in case it should have more sons, but Avanti returns emptyhanded to tell him that the big pot has now died. When an innkeeper wants to charge someone who ate chicken the price of the future eggs that were lost, Avanti asks the Imam to hold a public trial and arrives late, saying that he had to roast seeds before he could plant them. Then, as defense lawyer, he claims that the hen cannot lay eggs after it has been eaten. Avanti's wife sends him with a bowl for oil and when the shopkeeper fills the bowl, and asks Avanti where he should put the rest, Avanti turns the bowl over to an indentation on the underside. Avanti's wife thinks he is a fool, but secretly is happy to know that his neighbors hold Avanti in esteem.

CONNECTIONS. Avanti. Birth. Chickens. Cows. Effendi. Graves. Humorous stories. Husbands and wives. Imagination. Kings. Language of animals. Nasrdin Avanti. Perspective. Purchases, unusual. Thieves. Tricksters. Uygur People, stories from. Words.

WHERE ELSE THIS STORY APPEARS. The following are two stories included in the medley: Effendi and the Riddles—Josepha Sherman, *Trickster Tales*. The Pot Bears a Son—D.L. Ashliman, *Folktexts*, Online.

349. The Story of the Three Thieves

W. F. O'Connor, *Folk Tales from Tibet*. Tibetan People

Three thieves each have a special talent — one can pull eggs out from under a hen without her noticing, one can cut the soles off a man's boots while he is walking without his noticing, and one can eat the food from another man's plate without anyone's noticing. They decide to join together and play their tricks at the court of the Emperor of China to catch his attention. Then they call for an audience with the Emperor himself and return all of the purloined items. The Emperor puts the three men to a test to steal three pearls from his well-guarded Treasury. If they fail, they will be put to death. The thieves request that the emperor inventory the pearls first, so he will absolutely know that the three they bring are indeed Treasury pearls. During the inventory, the three thieves intermingle with the counters and each hide one pearl. The Emperor is astonished and rewards the three thieves with lands and money.

CONNECTIONS. Changes in fortune. Emperors. Pearls. Talents. Tests. Thieves. Tibetan People, stories from. Tricksters. Ultimatums.

350. The Gold Colt of the Fire Dragon

John Minford, *Favourite Folktales of China*. Han People

To get even with Skinflint, their stingy landlord, the peasants pool all of their silver and buy a rundown little colt. They stuff all of the leftover ingots up his behind. They send the talkative peasant Bigmouth to Skinflint with the horse. Bigmouth tells Skinflint that he had a dream that a white-bearded man told him to catch the colt that used to carry ingots for the God of Wealth. Bigmouth says this must be the colt. He lights incense and unobtrusively pulls the plug from the colt's behind. Silver ingots fall out. Skinflint buys the horse from him for thirty bushels of grain. However, when Skinflint lights incense and tries, the horse only splatters him. In a rage, Skinflint kills the horse. He does not find Bigmouth until the winter, but when he does, Skinflint shuts him in his mill without a coat. To keep from freezing, Bigmouth carries the millstone back and forth all night until he is sweating. He tells Skinflint that it is his magic shirt of Fire Dragon's pelt made by the Queen of the Western Heaven that gives off heat. Skinflint has to have this shirt and trades Bigmouth his fox-fur gown and fifty taels of silver for it. Skinflint goes to see his father-in-law dressed only in the Fire Dragon shirt and freezes to death. His family finds him in a burned-out tree, which confirms Bigmouth's opinion that Skinflint got so hot he burned up.

CONNECTIONS. Coins. Death. Greed. Han People, stories from. Horses. Hui People, stories from. Landlords. Millstones. Misers. Ningxia, China, stories from. Peasants. Punishment. Purchases, unusual. Revenge. Shirts. Tricksters.

HOW ELSE THIS STORY IS TOLD. Suoli's Story — Shujiang Li and Karl W. Luckert, *Mythology and Folklore of the Hui* (from Ningxia). The Wise Ma Tsai — *Folk Tales from China*, Third Series and *The Peacock Maiden: Folk Tales from China*.

351. Of Course

John Minford, *Favourite Folktales of China*. Han People

A cruel, rich man, named Pepper-peel, drives off Zhao, a loyal farmhand, when he falls ill. Zhao's neighbors pool money to get Zhao medical care, and they buy him a parrot, which they train to say, "Of course." They aim to teach Pepper-peel a lesson. One year later, Zhao dresses well and brings his parrot to visit Pepper-peel. Zhao says that a god has appeared to him in a dream, directing him to this parrot who knows where gold and silver lie buried. Pepper-peel wants to see the parrot in action. Zhao brings the parrot to two sites where he has already buried silver and asks the parrot if treasure is there. The parrot squawks, "Of course." Pepper-peel is amazed and publicly offers to trade all of his property for the parrot. The deal is made. But when Pepper-peel brings the parrot to this place and that and asks if gold or silver is buried there, the parrot always answers, "Of course," though nothing is there.

CONNECTIONS. Birds. Cooperation. Deceit. Farmers. Han People, stories from. Landlords. Parrots. Purchases, unusual. Revenge. Rich man. Trades. Tricksters.

352. The Golden Vase and the Monkeys

Folk Tales from China, Third Series. Tibetan People

Two good friends cannot agree about what to do with the golden vase they find. The first friend wants to keep it for himself; the second friend wants to sell it and share the wealth with the poor. The first friend suggests leaving the vase with him so he can have it tested to see if it is real gold. When the second friend returns, the first man sadly says the vase melted in the fire, so it must have only been tin. The second man invites the first man to send his two children to visit for a while. The second man catches two monkeys on the way over to his house, and the children are delighted to teach them tricks. They call the monkeys by their own names. Three months later, the second man sends the children off to pick fruit. When the first man arrives, the second man sadly reports that the children have somehow turned into monkeys. He calls the children's names, and the monkeys respond. The first friend understands and confesses about playing a trick with the vase. His children return, and he shares the vase.

CONNECTIONS. Children. Conflict. Deceit. Fathers and children. Golden vase. Greed. Identity. Monkeys and apes. Names. Reconciliation. Selfishness. Tibetan People, stories from. Tricksters. Vases.

WHERE ELSE THIS STORY APPEARS. The Golden Vase and the Monkeys—*The Peacock Maiden: Folk Tales from China*.

HOW ELSE THIS STORY IS TOLD. The Missing Treasure — Frederick and Audrey Hyde-Chambers, *Tibetan Folk Tales*. The Pewter Vase — A. L. Shelton, *Tibetan Folk Tales*. The Story of the Two Neighbours—W.F. O'Connor, *Folk Tales From Tibet*. The Tale of the Golden Vase and the Bright Monkeys—M.A. Jagendorf and Virginia Weng, *The Magic Boat and Other Chinese Folk Stories*.

353. Kim Sondal and the River

Cathy Spagnoli, *Asian Tales and Tellers*. Korea

Kim Sondal watches tired men carrying water from the Daedong River to rich men's houses. The unfairness bothers him. Kim Sondal suggests a plan. He gives the water-carriers coins to pay him with the next day as they walk to the river. The rich men ask Kim Sondal what he is doing. He tells them that he is collecting a tax on his river water. The fact that the men are paying him proves that they know the water is his. The rich men offer to buy the river from Kim Sondal. However, the following day the water-carriers walk to the river without paying. The rich men have been tricked.

CONNECTIONS. Daedong River. Greed. Purchases, unusual. Rich man. Social class. Taxes. Tricksters. Water. Water-carriers.

HOW ELSE THIS STORY IS TOLD. Practical Jokes of Bong-i Gim-sun-dal — Y.T. Pyun, *Tales from Korea*. The Story of Kim Son-dal— Mark C.K. Setton.

354. Working the Field

George Shannon, *Stories to Solve*. Japan

Yasohachi rests a lot, and his land is bumpy with clumps of earth and stones. Now the rich landlord has ordered him to make it smooth. Yasohachi puts up a notice in the village, inviting people to see him climb to heaven on a bamboo pole that Sunday. The landlord is angry with Yasohachi. However, on Sunday villagers flock to Yasohachi's field to see him try. Each time, Yasohachi climbs to the top of the pole, he falls. At last, everyone leaves, but the landlord sees that all those feet tromping over the land have indeed smoothed it out.

CONNECTIONS. Earth. Farmers. Landlords. Laziness. Performance. Poles. Rising to the sky world. Tricksters. Work.

HOW ELSE THIS STORY IS TOLD. Kichigo Ascends to the Sky — Richard M. Dorson, *Folk Legends of Japan.*

355. Under the Shade of the Mulberry Tree

Folk Tales of China, First Series. Uygur People

A rich man wants to chase a poor man away from resting under his mulberry tree, even though the man is sitting in the road where the tree hangs over outside the wall of his house. The poor man offers to buy the shade. Middlemen negotiate a price, and the rich man is happy to make extra money. But there is nothing the rich man can do when the poor man enters the rich man's courtyard as the shade moves around. The rich man is so exasperated and humiliated that he moves away. The poor man moves into the house and turns no one away from resting in the shade in the road.

CONNECTIONS. Consequences. Greed. Humorous stories. Mulberry trees. Purchases, unusual. Rich man. Shade. Social class. Trees. Tricksters. Uygur People, stories from. Zelkova tree.

HOW ELSE THIS STORY IS TOLD. *Korean variations:* A Bit of Shade — Gillian McClure, *The Land of the Dragon King and Other Korean Stories* (here the tree is a zelkova). The Good Neighbor — Lindy Soon Curry, *A Tiger by the Tail.* Shade Selling — Suzanne Crowder Han, *Korean Folk and Fairy Tales.*

356. Big Brother-Man; Little Brother-Rabbit

M.A. Jagendorf and Virginia Weng, *The Magic Boat*. Ch'iang People

By smearing a rock with sticky pine pitch, a poor mother and son in Szechun Province catch a rabbit that has been stealing yams and peas from their garden. Rabbit begs to become their son. He helps Big Brother get food. He leads a wedding party and then an official on a chase that enable Big Brother to bring home their food and fancy clothes. Now that Big Brother is well-dressed, Rabbit brings him to a village where the chieftain is delighted to offer his daughter in marriage. Big Brother worries what will happen when they arrive back at his poor house, but Rabbit has a plan. He tricks a cruel chieftain from another village into thinking Heaven wants him to leave his home because of his evil deeds. Rabbit tells Big Brother to bring his new bride to the chieftain's large, now vacant, house. With his work all done, Rabbit returns to the woods.

CONNECTIONS. Adoption. Changes in fortune. Ch'iang People, stories from. Chieftains. Foxes. Gratitude. Matches, marriage. Mongolian People, stories from. Mothers and sons. Rabbits and hares. Social class. Tricksters. Uygur People, stories from.

HOW ELSE THIS STORY IS TOLD. (In these tales, a fox comes up with the tricks that enable a poor man to appear wealthier than he is in order to marry the lord's daughter/princess). The Clever Red Fox — Stephen Hallet, translator, in *The Magic Bird* (from the Mongolian People). The King of the Pomegranate Tree — *Folk Tales from China*, Third Series and in *The Peacock Maiden* (from the Uygur People).

357. The Ugly Son

Jane Yolen, *Favorite Folktales from Around the World*. Japan

A gambler and his wife want to trick a rich man who seeks a handsome bridegroom for his daughter into marrying their ugly son. They tell him that their son, whose eyes and nose appear smooshed together, is the "fairest youth in all the land." A marriage with covered faces is arranged. Eventually, though, the young woman will see what her husband looks like. His parents come up with a plan. On the wedding night, a gambler friend hides above the ceiling and three times calls out for the "fairest youth." The voice accuses him of taking the demon's bride. The groom begs the demon not to hurt him. The voice asks if the young man cherishes his life or his looks the most. The groom asks his in-laws what he should answer, and they advise him to choose looks. There is a horrible noise. The groom seems to collapse. Everyone can see that he is ugly, but the rich family is glad that he is alive.

CONNECTIONS. Choices. Deceit. Demons. Disguises. Identity. In-laws and husbands. Matches, marriage. Perspective. Physical difference. Secrets. Tricksters. Ugliness.

WHERE ELSE THIS STORY APPEARS. The Ugly Son — Royall Tyler, *Japanese Tales*.

358. The Prayer That Was Answered

Jane Yolen, Favorite *Fairy Tales from Around the World*. Tibetan People

Though she has no dowry to offer, a poor woman prays that her daughter will make a good marriage match, one that will make her wealthy, as well as happy. A poor man from another village comes up with a plan to wed the girl. Concealing himself in the shrine room, he tells the woman that a rich man will appear on a white horse and ask to marry her daughter. The woman is sure a god has spoken to her. When the man appears on a white horse in borrowed clothes, she agrees to the marriage. The man is afraid, though, that the girl will leave when she arrives at his poor home. So, on the journey home, he locks her in a trunk. He tells her that he wants her to be surprised when she arrives, but he leaves the trunk in the forest. He continues home alone and warns the villagers that his new bride is nervous and may scream. Then he returns for her. But, meanwhile, a wealthy chieftain has opened the trunk and fallen in love with the beautiful girl inside. He takes her away and leaves a bear in her place. The young man is mauled when he opens the trunk at home, but the neighbors, forewarned, pay no attention to his screams. The mother's prayers have been answered — her daughter lives happily as the chieftain's wife.

CONNECTIONS. Bears. Changes in fortune. Deceit. Disguises. Matches, marriage. Prayer. Punishment. Tibetan People, stories from. Tricksters.

WHERE ELSE THIS STORY APPEARS. The Prayer That Was Answered — Frederick and Audrey Hyde-Chambers, *Tibetan Folktales.*

HOW ELSE THIS STORY IS TOLD. *Korean variation:* A Monk Gets a Surprise — Suzanne Crowder Han, *Korean Folk and Fairy Tales.*

359. Goldhair Becomes Minister

Wolfram Eberhard, *Folktales of China.* Central China

Blonde Liu Ta, called Goldenhair, never studies. So when he announces that this time he will study, his uncle gives him two hundred ounces of silver. Liu Ta actually wanders until the silver is gone. Then he returns to his uncle and announces that he is a midwife. His uncle thinks Goldenhair should go to help the emperor's wife, who has been in labor for three days. Liu Ta faces the empress with two dolls. Over and over he calls for the little emperor to come out. The empress laughs, and her child is born. However, the officials do not want to reward Liu Ta with an official position. They suggest he first go up against the barbarians in battle. Liu Ta is shaking so much that his horse throws him against a tree, which he pulls up by its roots. Then, he falls into a manure bucket. Terrified barbarians retreat when they see a lone warrior coming armed with a many-pointed lance and a steaming cauldron. The emperor asks Liu Ta to guess what he has pulled from a sack. In frustration, sure he cannot guess, Liu Ta repeats his own name, "Goldenhair, Goldenhair." The emperor is amazed, as he is indeed holding a gold cat. Liu Ta wins a position.

CONNECTIONS. Birth. Central China, stories from. Changes in fortune. Cleverness. Deceit. Dolls. Laughter. Luck. Midwives. Ministers. Misunderstandings. Mysteries. Queens. Tests. Tricksters. War. Work.

360. A Wife for a Grain of Millet

Suzanne Crowder Han, *Korean Folk and Fairy Tales.* Korea

A young man who is traveling to Hanyang to take the national examination asks an innkeeper to keep a grain of millet safe for him overnight. The next day the innkeeper tells him a rat has eaten the millet, and the young man demands to be given the rat. At the next inn, he acquires the cat who has eaten the rat in the night and after that, a horse and a bull. When this last innkeeper says that he has sold the bull to the Minister, the Minister first offers to house the young man and then, impressed with his enterprise, offers his daughter in marriage.

CONNECTIONS. Bulls. Cats. Changes in fortune. Flax. Han People, stories from. Hanyang. Horses. Humorous stories. Imperial examination. Innkeepers. Luck. Matches, marriage. Millet. Rats. Scholars. Seeds. Trades.

HOW ELSE THIS STORY IS TOLD. *Chinese variation:* The Story of a Pint of Flax Seeds — John Minford, *Favourite Folktales of China* (from the Han People). *Korean variations:* A Grain of Millet — *Long Long Time Ago.* A Grain of Millet — Gim Yang-Ha in Zong In-Sob, *Folk Tales from Korea.*

361. The Noodle

Carol Kendall and Yao-wen Li, *Sweet and Sour.* China

A future father-in-law, an important man, is regretting the match he arranged for his daughter long ago now that it seems like the young man has turned out to be a simpleton. Meanwhile, the Noodle's father sends him off with one hundred pieces of silver to make his way. The Noodle offers twenty pieces of silver to a gardener to teach him a rhyme about regretting that a pond has no fish. He offers another twenty pieces to a farmer to learn a rhyme about one board not being enough to move a lot of rice across a stream. He offers twenty coins each to two hunters to learn their rhyme about which one of them will shoot the red bird. And he pays his last twenty coins to a man who teaches him a rhyme where one departing man tells another he'll see him in court. Preparations for a wedding are happening when he arrives at his future bride's house. He does not know that it is not for him. They invite him in for a meal, thinking to make sport. At points during the meal, the Noodle speaks the rhymes he has learned. They fit in such a way as philosophical and witty comments and threats that the father-in-law believes that the Noodle is brilliant. He decides that Noodle is the fitting bridegroom for the daughter of a prominent family after all.

CONNECTIONS. Changes in fortune. Consequences. Fathers-in-law and husbands. Fools. Humorous stories. Identity. Misunderstandings. Reconciliation. Poetry. Purchases, unusual. Taiwan, stories from. Tibetan People, stories from. Words.

HOW ELSE THIS STORY IS TOLD. *Chinese variation:* A Wise Idiot — A.L. Shelton, *Tibetan Folk Tales*. *Taiwanese variation:* A Thoroughly Goofy Son-in-Law — Gary Marvin Davison, *Tales from the Taiwanese*.

362. Medical Techniques

P'u Sung-ling in Moss Roberts, *Chinese Fairy Tales and Fantasies*. China

A Taoist priest tells poor Chang, who lives in the mountains of Yi county in Shantung, to become a doctor even though he cannot read. So, Chang sets up shop in town with some natural ingredients he finds. One day the governor of Ch'ingchou has a bad cough, and the magistrate is instructed to bring Chang, a local, to treat him. Chang is worried. His own cough is not going away. En route, a woman in a hamlet nearby gives him some water that has been left over from preparing her vegetables. His cough improves, and this is what he fixes for the governor, who also gets better. After that many people come to see Chang. Sometimes his mistakes actually work.

CONNECTIONS. Advice. Ch'ingchou, place. Doctors. Illiteracy. Illness. Luck. Mistakes. Priests. Taoism. Work. Yi County.

WHERE ELSE THIS STORY APPEARS. The Doctor — P'u Sung-ling, *Strange Stories from a Chinese Studio*, Online.

363. Kotgam

Yu Chai-Shin, Shiu L. Kong, and Ruth W. Yi, *Korean Folk Tales*. Korea

Proud of his fierceness, a tiger creeps down to a village looking for dinner. He hears a mother trying to comfort a crying baby and feels affronted when even the threat of a tiger eating it does not stop the baby's tears. Then, the mother offers the baby kotgam, and the baby stops crying. The tiger thinks that kotgam must be far more powerful than he is. He does not know that it is only dried persimmon. Still hungry, he goes to the barn to dine on a cow, but a thief is there, who mistakes the tiger for the cow in the dark and jumps on its back. The tiger is sure that only the creature kotgam would not fear him and shoots out of the barn, trying to shake his rider. The thief clings on until dawn and flees when he sees that he is on a tiger. Now free of kotgam, the tiger flees, too.

CONNECTIONS. Arrogance. Babies. Chases. Consequences. Deer. Fear. Fools. Han People, stories from. Hui People, stories from. Humorous stories. Husbands and wives. Identity. Kagawa, Japan, stories from. Leaks. Misunderstandings. Monkeys and apes. Mothers and children. Ningxia, China, stories from. Origins. Persimmons. Rain. Thieves. Tigers. Wolves.

HOW ELSE THIS STORY IS TOLD. *Chinese variations:* How the Deer Lost His Tail—Lotta Carswell Hume, *Favorite Children's Stories from China and Tibet*. The Leaking Pot—Yang Shengjun in Shujiang Li and Karl W. Luckert, *Mythology and Folklore of the Hui* (from Ningxia). A Monkey and a Tiger—Haiwang Yuan, *The Magic Lotus Lantern* (the monkey and the tiger in this story from the Han People both wonder why the old couple fear "Leak" more than them). *Japanese variations:* (a wolf and a thief end up scaring each other after a man says that what he fears most is a leaky roof). The Leak in an Old House—Fanny Hagin Mayer, *Ancient Tales in Modern Japan* (from Kagawa). Rain Leak in an Old House—Keigo Seki, *Folktales of Japan*. The Terrible Eeek—Patricia A. Compton. The Terrible Leak—Yoshiko Uchida, *The Magic Listening Cap*. *Korean variations:* The Fierce Old Dried Persimmon—Gillian McClure, *The Land of the Dragon King and Other Korean Stories*. The Rabbit's Tail: A Story from Korea—Suzanne Crowder Han. The Tiger and the Dried Persimmon—*Long Long Time Ago*. The Tiger and the Persimmon—Ma He-Song in Zong In-Sob, *Folk Tales from Korea*. The Tiger, the Persimmon and the Rabbit's Tale—Suzanne Crowder Han, *Korean Folk and Fairy Tales*.

364. A Foolish Old Man Tries to Remove Two Mountains

Haiwang Yuan, *The Magic Lotus Lantern and Other Tales from the Han Chinese*. Han People

It takes ninety-year-old Mr. Foolish and his family a long time to go around Taihang and Wangwu Mountains to work their farm. He suggests they dig up the mountains. His wife has doubts. She asks where they will put all the dirt. The son announces that they will dump the dirt in the Bohai Sea, hundreds of miles away. The next day, they start digging. One trip to the sea with the dirt and rocks takes a whole year. Mr. Smart comes to see what they are doing. Mr. Foolish assures him that even though leveling the mountains may take generations, mountains do not grow and eventually the work will be done. The Jade Emperor hears about their perseverance and sends two giants to pick up the mountains and move them.

CONNECTIONS. Angels. Bohai Sea. Determination. Distance. Emperor of Heaven. Fools. Giants. Han People, stories from. Humorous stories. Jade Emperor. Mountains. Taihang Mountain. Wangwu Mountain. Work.

HOW ELSE THIS STORY IS TOLD. How the Fool Moved Mountains—Lie Zi in *Ancient Chinese Fables*. Moving a Mountain—Lim Sian-tek, *Folk Tales from China*. Old Man Stupidity—Cheo-Kang Sié, *A Butterfly's Dream and Other Chinese Tales* (here, the Emperor of Heaven sends angels to help with the task). The Old Man Who Moved Mountains—Margaret Read MacDonald, *Three-Minute Tales*.

365. Fishing for a Sword Dropped into a River from a Moving Boat

Haiwang Yuan, *The Magic Lotus Lantern and Other Tales from the Han Chinese*. Han People

While traveling on a ferry, a man from the state of Chu drops his sword into the river. At once, he borrows a knife and carves a mark on the side of the boat where his sword slipped into the water. The boatman and his fellow passengers cannot understand why he is doing this. As the boat nears the riverbank, the man, to everyone's laughter, begins to search the water exactly under where the mark is on the boat.

CONNECTIONS. Boats. Fools. Han People, stories from. Humorous stories. Loss. Swords. Water.

HOW ELSE THIS STORY IS TOLD. The Lost Sword—Wu Huiyuan, *Selected Chinese Fables*. Marking the Boat to Locate the Sword —*Ancient Chinese Fables*. Marking the Boat to Locate the Sword — Robert Wyndham, *Tales the People Tell in China*.

366. The Chinese Mirror

Mirra Ginsberg. Korea

A Korean man travels from his small village to China. In a store, he sees a man in a mirror who smiles back at him. When he makes faces, the man in the mirror does, too. He brings this object back home, but fearing that it may lose its magic, he keeps it in a trunk and only takes it out at night. His wife wonders what he is laughing at in the night. The next day, she takes the mirror out of the trunk and is upset to see a beautiful young woman there. She brings the mirror to her mother-in-law who sees a wrinkled old woman. The old man is called over, and he sees the neighbor's grandfather. While they are arguing about who is in the mirror, the son takes it outside. He sees a boy and thinks the boy has stolen the pebble he is holding in his hand. The boy tells a man who comes by, and that man sees a bully in the mirror. He draws his hand back into a fist to punish the bully. And that is the end of the mirror.

CONNECTIONS. Chêkiang, China, stories from. Family life. Gansu, China, stories from. Hui People, stories from. Humorous stories. Identity. Knowledge. Mirrors. Misunderstandings. Reflections. Tokushima, Japan, stories from. Villagers.

HOW ELSE THIS STORY IS TOLD. *Chinese variations:* Clod's Comb—Carol Kendall and Yao-wen Li, *Sweet and Sour*. The Mirror—Wolfram Eberhard, *Folktales of China* (from Chêkiang). Simple Wang—Leslie Bonnet, *Chinese Folk and Fairy Tales* and Joanna Cole, *Best-Loved Folktales of the World*. Treasure Mirror—Fen Jun in Shujiang Li and Karl W. Luckert, *Mythology and Folklore of the Hui* (from Gansu). *Japanese variations:* The Mirror at Matsuyama—Fanny Hagin Mayer, *Ancient Tales in Modern Japan* (from Tokushima). Reflections—Lafcadio Hearn, *Japanese Fairy Tales*. Reflections—Grace James, *Green Willow*. The Visit to the Dragon Palace—Fanny Hagin Mayer, *Ancient Tales in Modern Japan* (reflections in a jar of sea water given to the husband by Ryūjin cause jealousy at home). *Korean variations:* The Bridegroom's Shopping—Kim So-un, *Korean Children's Favorite Stories*. The Face in the Mirror—Suzanne Crowder Han, *Korean Folk and Fairy Tales*. The Mirror—Pleasant DeSpain, *Thirty-Three Multicultural Tales to Tell*. The Mirror — Chai-Sin Yu, Shiu L. Kong, and Ruth W. Yu, *Korean Folk Tales*. Reflections—Lindy Soon Curry, *A Tiger by the Tail*. The Tiger Hunter and the Mirror—Frances Carpenter, *Tales of a Korean Grandmother*.

367. The Lazy Farmer

Yong-Sheng Xuan, *The Dragon Lover*. China

A farmer is chasing a rabbit, when the rabbit runs into a tree-stump and breaks its neck. The lazy farmer thinks that if it is so easy to catch a rabbit, perhaps he can give up farming and just wait by the stump. He sits by the stump every day, letting his crops go to ruin, but no more rabbits come.

CONNECTIONS. Farmers. Fools. Han People, stories from. Humorous stories. Laziness. Rabbits and hares. Taiwan, stories from. Trees. Work.

HOW ELSE THIS STORY IS TOLD. *Chinese variation:* At the Wrong Post — Han Fei Tzu in Moss Roberts, *Chinese Fairy Tales and Fantasies.* The Wait for the Hare — *Selected Chinese Fables.* Waiting for a Hare to Turn Up — Han Fei Zi in *Ancient Chinese Fables.* Waiting for a Rabbit to Bump into a Tree — Haiwang Yuan, *The Magic Lotus Lantern and Other Tales from the Han Chinese. Taiwanese variation:* Waiting for Rabbits — Coa Cheney, *Tales from a Taiwan Kitchen.*

368. Saburo the Eel-Catcher

Florence Sakade, *Kintaro's Adventures.* Japan

One day, as Saburo pulls an eel from the water, it springs from the water and lands in the field behind him. He hears a grunt. There is a wild boar with the eel on top of it. Saburo is afraid of boars, but this one is dead. Saburo decides to bring both the eel and the boar home to eat. However, the vines he pulls to tie the boar to his back are attached to wild yams, which Saburo would like to bring home, too. The yams lead him to a pheasant's tail attached to a pheasant, which is also dead, beside a nest with thirteen eggs. Finding a way to wear everything, Saburo looks silly, but he is happy to be so good at catching eels.

CONNECTIONS. Boars. Consequences. Eggs. Eels. Luck. Pheasants. Saburo. Self-esteem. Yams.

WHERE ELSE THIS STORY APPEARS. Saburo the Eel-Catcher — *Florence Sakade, Japanese Children's Favorite Stories*, Book Two.

369. Silly Saburo

Florence Sakade, *Japanese Children's Favorite Stories.* Japan

A boy can keep only one instruction in his head at a time. When his father tells him to let the potatoes on their farm dry in the sun, he does the same with a pot of gold coins he finds and, of course, it disappears. His father tells him that the next time he should wrap what he finds carefully and bring it home. That is what he does with a dead cat. His father says next time, he should throw it in the river. That is what he does with a tree stump, which is valuable for firewood. The neighbor says next time he should break it up into pieces. That is just what he does to a teacup from his father's lunch ... so why do his parents leave him home the next day?

CONNECTIONS. Coins. Consequences. Fathers and sons. Fools. Humorous stories. Memory. Misunderstandings. Saburo.

WHERE ELSE THIS STORY APPEARS. Silly Saburo — Florence Sakade, *Peach Boy and Other Japanese Children's Favorite Stories.*

370. Whew!

Richard M. Dorson, *Folk Legends of Japan.* Japan

Shuju loves the delicious dinner at his uncle's house and asks what the food is called. His uncle tells him it is "dumpling." Shuju repeats the word over and over as he walks home. But, huffing up a steep slope, he replaces "dumpling" with "whew" and repeats that word over and over. When Shuju arrives home, he asks his wife to prepare some whew. She has no idea what whew is. Shuju gets angry and hits her with a tool. His wife cries out that he has given her a lump as big as a dumpling, and he remembers the word.

CONNECTIONS. Dumplings. Fools. Humorous stories. Husbands and wives. Memory. Words.

371. Foolish Greetings

Hiroko Fujita, *Folktales from the Japanese Countryside.* Japan

A father tries to instruct his foolish son on what to say in various situations. To greet a man he is to comment on what a beautiful day it is, but the son offends those at a funeral with the same words. The next time, he offends those at a wedding by offering his sympathies. He offers congratulations to people whose house is on fire and pours water on a blacksmith's fire to put it out. He joins in and strikes a woman in a fight with her husband and is injured trying to separate two bulls who have locked horns.

CONNECTIONS. Fathers and sons. Fools. Humorous stories. Manners. Misunderstandings. Taiwan, stories from. Words.

HOW ELSE THIS STORY IS TOLD. ***Chinese variation:*** The Fool meets his End — Wolfram Eberhard, *Folktales of China.* ***Taiwanese variation:*** The Goofiness of Chen Ah Ai — Gary Marvin Davison, *Tales from the Taiwanese.*

372. Memory Trouble

Lo Cho in Moss Roberts, *Chinese Fairy Tales and Fantasies.* China

A man in Ch'i forgets everything. His wife thinks he should go to Ai Tzu, who might be able to cure him. On his way there, the man gets off his horse to relieve himself and lays his arrows on the ground. Afterwards, he thinks the arrows indicate that someone has been trying to shoot at him. He is so distracted he steps in his own dung. Then, he thinks someone has left a horse there for him and he rides back to Ch'i. When he arrives, he does not recognize his own house, and he wonders why a strange woman (his wife) is scolding him.

CONNECTIONS. Ch'i. Fools. Humorous stories. Husbands and wives. Identity. Journeys. Memory. Misunderstandings. Travelers.

373. The Two Fools

Leslie Bonnet, *Chinese Folk and Fairy Tales.* China

Lin comes into possession of ten pieces of silver. This is more money than he has ever owned before, and he hides the silver in the wall of his hut. Still, he is ill at ease, for he thinks that if someone were to come to the bare hut, they would know that the treasure has to be in the wall because there is nowhere else to hide it. So, he writes on the wall that no money is hidden there. The villager Wan comes to Lin's hut when Lin is not there and sees the writing on the wall, which makes him think that maybe something is hidden there. He digs the silver out of the wall with his hands, but is worried that he will be suspected and punished for the robbery. Then, Wan has an idea. On the pillar of his own house, he brushes a sign that says he did not take Lin's money.

CONNECTIONS. Calligraphy. Coins. Deceit. Fools. Humorous stories. Poverty. Thieves. Truth. Words.

HOW ELSE THIS STORY IS TOLD. Fool robs Fool — Wolfram Eberhard, *Folktales of China.*

374. Silent Debate

Cathy Spagnoli, *Asian Tales and Tellers*. Korea

A Chinese scholar wants to see if there are great thinkers in Korea. He decides to begin with the Korean boatman who is taking him there. The scholar does not speak Korean and holds up his fingers to form a circle. He intends this circle to symbolize the universe and wants to know what the boatman knows about heaven. The boatman thinks that the scholar is asking about round rice cakes. He, himself, prefers square ones, so he hold up his fingers to form a square. The scholar is startled. He thinks the boatman is giving the square character for secrets of heaven and earth. After two more exchanges like this, the scholar decides that if even the boatmen of Korea are so brilliant about Confucian relationships, there is no point in continuing on.

CONNECTIONS. Boatmen. Competition. Fools. Humorous stories. Knowledge. Misunderstandings. Peddlers. Priests. Scholars. Social class. Silence. Tests.

HOW ELSE THIS STORY IS TOLD. *Japanese variation:* A Debate in Sign Language — Hiroko Fujita, *Folktales from the Japanese Countryside* (the debate is between a priest and a konnyaku-ya, who sells tofu).

375. A Selfish Husband

Son Zin-Tĕ in In-Sob Zong, *Folk Tales from Korea*. Korea

An old married couple argue over which one should eat the one cake they have received. They decide that the one who speaks first forfeits the cake. A thief enters their house, and they continue to sit in silence. Even when the thief collects all their belongings and then beats the old woman, the husband does not speak. When his wife cries out that he is heartless to do nothing, the husband claims the cake.

CONNECTIONS. Competition. Hiroshima, Japan, stories from. Humorous stories. Husbands and wives. Selfishness. Stubbornness. Thieves.

WHERE ELSE THIS STORY APPEARS. A Selfish Husband — Son Zin-Tĕ at D.L. Ashliman, *Folktexts*, Online.

HOW ELSE THIS STORY IS TOLD. *Japanese variation:* The Silence Match — Fanny Hagin Mayer, *Ancient Tales in Modern Japan* (from Hiroshima). *Korean variation:* The Stubborn Couple — Suzanne Crowder Han, *Korean Folk and Fairy Tales.*

376. The Unanswerable

Carol Kendall and Yao-wen Li, *Sweet and Sour*. China

A man who makes and sells armor is flamboyantly displaying his weapons to a crowd. He announces that one spear is so sharp because of the way it was cast that nothing can stop its blade. He shows the crowd a bronze shield that he says cannot not be pierced by anything. A heckler asks what happens if he sends his special spear against his special shield.

CONNECTIONS. Armor. Arrogance. Ch'u. Han People, stories from. Markets. Performance. Tradesmen. Truth. Words.

HOW ELSE THIS STORY IS TOLD. The Armor-Maker of Ch'u — Lim Sian-tek, *More Folk Tales from China*. The Invincible Spear Versus the Impenetrable Shield — Haiwang Yuan, *The Magic Lotus Lantern and Other Tales from the Han Chinese*. The Man Who Sold Spears and Shields — Han Fei Zi in *Ancient Chinese Fables*. The Shield or the Spear — Wu Huiyuan, *Selected Chinese Fables*.

377. The Magic Fox

Margaret Read MacDonald, *Twenty Tellable Tales*. Japan

Zuiten, a boy whose job it is to sweep the temple, to dust the altar where the golden statue of Lord Buddha sits, and to cook rice, thinks he hears someone call his name. It is a magic fox, brushing against the shoji doors and knocking against the rice paper panes, that sounds like he is saying Zuiten's name. When Zuiten slides the shoji open, the magic fox tumbles into the temple and vanishes. Now Zuiten sees two gold Buddhas on the altar, but he does not know which one is the fox. He bows and speaks aloud, saying that the real Buddha always sticks out its tongue when he prays. The fox thinks he should stick out his tongue and does. The Zuiten says that Buddha always follows him to the kitchen and bathes in the rice pot. The fox does that, too. Zuiten starts a fire under the fox, and it takes off into the forest.

CONNECTIONS. Buddha, statues. Children. Cleverness. Foxes. Identity. Kitsune. Mysteries. Prayer. Problem solvers. Statues. Temples.

378. A Story for Sale

Frances Carpenter, *Tales of a Korean Grandmother*. Korea

Rich Yi is looking for entertainment and sends his gatekeeper with a chest of cash to buy a good story. The gatekeeper meets a farmer and asks him if he has a story to sell. The farmer is not a storyteller, but he does want the money. He is trying to figure out what to say when he sees a stork. He begins to narrate every movement of the stork, about how the stork comes and stops and listens and steps again and looks. The gatekeeper hands the strings of cash over to the farmer and passes the story on to his master. Yi is puzzling over the story one night, when he starts speaking it aloud. This happens just as a thief is creeping around outside. It seems to the thief that old Yi is narrating his every action of stepping and stopping and listening. He flees.

CONNECTIONS. Farmers. Fools. Gatekeepers. Humorous stories. Kwantung, China, stories from. Misunderstandings. Mysteries. Purchases, unusual. Storks. Storytelling. Thieves. Words.

HOW ELSE THIS STORY IS TOLD. **Chinese variation:** The Deluded Thief — Wolfram Eberhard, *Folktales of China* (from Kuantung). **Japanese variation:** Sutra of the Mouse — Hiroko Fujita, *Folktales from the Japanese Countryside*. **Korean variation:** A Tale for Sale — Lindy Soon Curry, *A Tiger by the Tail*.

379. Backing Up a Story

Naomi Baltuck, *Apples from Heaven*. China

A wife warns her husband that stretching the truth to tell a good story may get him into trouble, and one day it does. His relatives are on their way to see three treasures he made up: a bullock that can run 1,000 li a day, a rooster that crows to begin day and night, and a dog that can read and write. His wife tells him to hide. When the relatives arrive, she tells them that her husband has gone to Peking and will not return for eight days or so. They marvel that he can travel so quickly. She says that he is riding the special bullock. When their ordinary rooster crows, she tells them that it is announcing visitors. As for the literate dog, she tells them he is in Peking where he runs a school. The relatives leave, believing everything.

CONNECTIONS. Bulls. Cooperation. Dogs. Humorous stories. Husbands and wives. Literacy. Peking. Roosters. Storytellers. Truth.

HOW ELSE THIS STORY IS TOLD. The Remarkable Ox, Rooster, and Dog — Carl Withers, *A World of Nonsense*.

380. The Story of the Man Who Loved Stories

Samira Kirollos, *The Wind Children and Other Tales from Japan*. Japan

The fat man wants Kitchamu-San to tell him a story, and Kitchamu-San makes a deal. If the fat man says "But that's impossible," the way he usually does, then he will have to give Kitchamu-San a bag of rice. Kitchamu-San begins. In his story a Daimyō is traveling to pay respects to the Shogun when a bird keeps circling and calling. When the Daimyō gets out of his palanquin to see, a bird dropping lands on his black hakama. The Daimyō does not let his retainers shoot the bird and calmly calls for a clean hakama. Again the bird returns, circling and crying. When the Daimyō leans out, a bigger bird dropping lands on the hilt of his family sword. The Daimyō calmly asks his retainers to bring another sword. The next time, the bird leaves a dropping on the Daimyō's head. He cuts off his dirty head and replaces it with a clean one. The fat man has stopped himself from calling out before, but finally he says, "But that's impossible." He owes Kitchamu-San a sack of rice, but says the story is worth it.

CONNECTIONS. Birds. Competition. Daimyos. Humorous stories. Ōita, Japan, stories from. Rice. Self-control. Storytellers.

HOW ELSE THIS STORY IS TOLD. Wagering on Stopping Bad Habits— Fanny Hagin Mayer, *Ancient Tales in Modern Japan* (from Ōita).

381. The Dragon King's Feast

Naomi Baltuck, *Apples from Heaven*. China

Two brothers love to compete when telling tall tales. The older brother dives into the water with a piece of meat hidden in his hand. He emerges from the water eating the meat and tells his brother he got it at the Dragon King's underwater picnic. He describes fairies and the wonders there. The younger brother dives into the water. He hits his head on a rock. It bleeds, but as his older brother comes over to help him, the younger one says that things were just as the older brother described — except that the Dragon King was angry that he arrived late and hit him with a stick.

CONNECTIONS. Brothers. Competition. Humorous stories. Imagination. Storytellers. Tricksters.

HOW ELSE THIS STORY IS TOLD. *Chinese variation:* The Dragon King's Feast — Jon Kowllis, *Wit and Humor of Old Cathay*. *Japanese variation:* A Tall Tale Contest — Keigo Seki, *Folktales of Japan*.

382. Two Lies

An Zŏng-og in Zong In-Sob, *Folk Tales from Korea*. Korea

A minister offers that the person who tells him two interesting lies shall marry his daughter. No one measures up until a young man arrives who says that the minister will find treasure when he digs under a certain street in Seoul in the hot weather. His second claim is that the minister's late father signed a bond of debt for 100,000 yang, which the young man has come now to collect. What choice does the minister have?

CONNECTIONS. Cleverness. Deceit. Matches, marriage. Ministers. Storytellers. Tricksters. Underworld.

HOW ELSE THIS STORY IS TOLD. *Chinese variation:* "Never Heard of This Before"— San Bao in He Liyi, *The Spring of Butterflies and Other Folktales of China's Minority Peoples*. *Korean variations:* Lies Rewarded with a Bride — Y.T. Pyun, *Tales from Korea*. In the next two variants, a petty government official dismisses a man's debt so he will not be embarrassed by the man's claim that he has just returned from the underworld where he lent the official's father a coin and drank wine at a tavern run by the official's mother, who is now married to his father. A Pilgrimmage to the Hell — Chun Shin-Yong, *Korean Folk Tales*. A Trip to Hell and Back — Suzanne Crowder Han, *Korean Folk and Fairy Tales*.

~ XIII ~

The Way Things Are

383. Red Thread

Ed Young. China

The orphan Wei Gu hears that a matchmaker in Songcheng is looking for a husband for General Pan's daughter and goes there. An old man studying a large book in a language from the spirit world tells Wei Gu that the wife he is destined to marry in fourteen years is still a child. He shows Wei Gu the red thread that links couples by the feet when they are born. When Wei Gu presses for details about his future wife, the old man tells him that she lives near the inn where he is staying and that she will live long and happily and receive a title because of her son. Near his inn, Wei Gu sees a half-blind woman selling vegetables with an ugly baby on her back. He pays his servant to kill the baby. The servant stabs the girl and runs. Over the next fourteen years, Wei Gu travels. He becomes a judge in Xiangzhou, where he marries the governor's daughter. They are happy, but one day Wei Gu asks his wife why she always wears a flower seed between her eyebrows. She tells him that when her father died, she was taken in by the poor, half-blind woman who had been her wet nurse. One day a crazy man stabbed her, leaving an ugly scar. She was then found by her uncle, the governor, and raised in his house. Wei confesses his story to her. He and his wife love each other, and, as the old man foretold, their son becomes governor of Yanmen province.

CONNECTIONS. Betrothal. Changes in attitude. Fate. Foretellings. Forgiveness. Husbands and wives. Identity. Love. Matches, marriage. Murder. Mysteries. Old man, supernatural helper. Orphans. Physical difference. Red thread. Secrets. Songcheng, place. Spirits. Truth. Yanmen Province. Xiangzhou, place.

HOW ELSE THIS STORY IS TOLD. The Bride with One Eyebrow — Lim Sian-tek, *Folk Tales from China* (here, the protagonist throws a stone and unintentionally wounds his future wife). The Inn of the Betrothal — Karl S. Y. Kao, *Classical Chinese Tales of the Supernatural and the Fantastic*.

384. Music to Soothe the Savage Breast

Margaret Read MacDonald, *Peace Tales*. Japan

When his ship is attacked by pirates in the harbor at Aki, Mochimitsu shuts himself in his cabin. He calls to the pirates to listen as he plays his hichiriki. Mochimitsu pours everything he has into playing music, sure it will be his final act. The pirates do listen and, no longer wishing to harm him, row away.

CONNECTIONS. Aki, city. Chang Liang, General. Changes in attitude. Conflict. Flutes. Harmony. Hichirikis. Music. Musicians. Peace. Pirates. Tigers. Woodcutters.

HOW ELSE THIS STORY IS TOLD. *Chinese variation:* The Homesick Flute — Lim Sian-tek, *More Folk Tales from China* (the enemy leaves for home in the dead of night, when they hear strains of General Chang Liang's sorrowful flute). *Japanese variation:* To Soothe the Savage Beast — Royall Tyler, *Japanese Tales*. *Korean variations:* (in the stories below, a musician saves his life by getting tigers to dance, which collapses the tower they have been building to reach him). The Charming Flute — Linda Soon Curry, *A Tiger by the Tail*. The Wonderful Flute — Yu Chai-Shin, Shiu L. Kong, and Ruth W. Yu, *Korean Folk Tales*. The Woodcutter and the Dancing Tiger — Suzanne Crowder Han, *Korean Folk and Fairy Tales*.

385. The Zither-Met Friends

Cathy Spagnoli, *Asian Tales and Tellers*. China

The official Yu Boya is heading back to the State of Jin from the State of Chu when a storm forces him to set anchor at the Han Yang River. The storm clears, and in the light of a full moon, he calls for his zither and begins to play. The woodcutter Zhong Ziqi has been walking along the riverbank with a load of firewood and is moved by the melody. When a zither string snaps, Yu Boya thinks there must be someone listening. Zhong Ziqi steps forward. Yu Boya scoffs, saying that a woodcutter cannot appreciate the music of the zither, an instrument of scholars. Zhong Ziqi responds that the zither has "six taboos, eight excellences, and seven never-plays." He tells Yu Boya that he should not have been playing if no one was listening. Surprised by this knowledge, Yu Boya shoots many more questions about the zither at Zhong Ziqi, who answers them all, as he has once been an official, himself, but is now helping his elderly parents. Zhong Ziqi tells Yu Boya that he has brought the beautiful mid-autumn night into his piece.

CONNECTIONS. Autumn. Changes in attitude. Flutes. Han Yang River. Harmony. Knowledge. Misunderstandings. Music. Musicians. Nature, appreciation for. Officials. Questions. Social class. Storms. Tests. Travelers. Woodcutters. Zithers.

HOW ELSE THIS STORY IS TOLD. The Broken Harp — Lim Sian-tek, *Folk Tales from China*. Kung Peng Tah and the Woodcutter — Tung Chou Kion in Brian Brown, *Chinese Nights Entertainments: Stories of Old China*.

386. The Musician and the Water Buffalo

Demi, *The Dragon Lover*. China

A renowned musician is playing one of his best pieces on the zither, when a water buffalo starts munching grass nearby. The zither player tries to get the water buffalo's attention with his music, but the buffalo keeps eating. Now the musician angrily bangs on the zither strings. This time, the buffalo raises his head. The music sounds like something he knows, a cricket. After that, the player always tries to give audiences music they will appreciate.

CONNECTIONS. Changes in attitude. Harmony. Musicians. Performance. Perspective. Qin. Self-esteem. Water buffalo. Zithers.

HOW ELSE THIS STORY IS TOLD. Playing the Harp to an Ox — Mou Zi in *Ancient Chinese Fables*. Playing Qin for the Water Buffalo — Mingmei Yip, *Chinese Children's Favorite Stories* (in this variation, the water buffalo is indifferent to the qin player's music).

387. Number Is Security

Haiwang Yuan, *The Magic Lotus Lantern and Other Tales from the Han Chinese*. Han People

Mr. Nanguo, hears that the emperor of Qi, who loves to hear the yu played in chorus, is hiring musicians. Now, Mr. Nanguo cannot play the bamboo pipes of the yu, but he wants to get into the emperor's band. He bribes the audition interviewer. At last, three hundred yu players assemble to play for the emperor. When Mr. Nanguo pretends that he is playing, no one notices. However, when the emperor dies, the new emperor likes solo music and asks the yu players to play individually. Mr. Nanguo must flee.

CONNECTIONS. Community. Deceit. Emperors. Han People, stories from. Musicians. Pipes. Qi, feudal state. Silence. Yu.

HOW ELSE THIS STORY IS TOLD. The Man Who Faked His Music — Wu Huiyuan, *Selected Chinese Fables*. The Man Who Pretended He Could Play Reed Pipes — Han Dei Zi in *Ancient Chinese Fables*. The Yu Player from the South — Margaret Read MacDonald, *Three-Minute Tales*.

388. Painting Ghosts

Han Fei Zi in *Ancient Chinese Fables*. China

The hardest things to draw are animals. There are too familiar. Everyone can criticize. Everyone knows what they look like. The easiest things to paint are ghosts and monsters, for no one can argue with the artist's creation.

CONNECTIONS. Artists. Criticism. Ghosts. Ogres. Paintings and pictures. Reality. Supernatural creatures. Truth.

HOW ELSE THIS STORY IS TOLD. Ghosts Are Easiest to Draw — Wu Huiyuan, *Selected Chinese Fables*. Painting Ghosts — Margaret Read MacDonald, *Three-Minute Tales*.

389. A Lover of Dragons

Margaret Read MacDonald, *Three-Minute Tales*. China

Zighao, the Lord of Yeh, says that he loves dragons. There are carved and painted images of them all over his house. However, when the dragon in heaven hears about this and comes to see, Zighao flees. He much prefers the idea of dragons to the real thing.

CONNECTIONS. Dragons. Fear. Han People, stories from. Images. Nobles and lords. Reality. Truth. Yeh, place.

HOW ELSE THIS STORY IS TOLD. The Dragon Lover — Demi, *The Dragon Lover*. The Lord Who Loved Dragons — Shen Zi in *Ancient Chinese Fables*. A Professed Dragon Lover — Haiwang Yuan, *The Magic Lotus Lantern and Other Tales from the Han Chinese*.

390. The Blind Men and an Elephant

Louise and Yuan-Hsi Kuo, *Chinese Folk Tales*. Han People

One day three blind men have a chance to find out what an elephant is like. A merchant leads them, one by one, to touch the elephant. The first blind man touches the forelegs, top to bottom. The second man touches the swishing tail. The third touches the elephant's curling trunk. They thank the merchant and begin to argue. A elephant is like a fan, two tree trunks, a snake — each blind man is sure he knows about elephants from the one part he has touched.

CONNECTIONS. Blindness. Conflict. Curiosity. Elephants. Han People, stories from. Knowledge. Perspective. Truth.

391. Crying Wolf

Wang Min in Howard Giskin, *Chinese Folktales*. Jiangshu Province, China

While watching the sheep one day, the bored shepherd A'shan cries that there is a wolf, and villagers climb the grassy hill to help him dispatch the wolf with their tools. He laughs at them. The same thing happens the next day. On the third day, when a real wolf attacks A'shan and the sheep, no one arrives.

CONNECTIONS. Consequences. Deceit. Herders. Jiangshu Province, China, stories from. Punishment. Sheep. Tigers. Wolves. Words.

HOW ELSE THIS STORY IS TOLD. *Korean variation:* The Boy Who Cried Tiger Too Often — James Huntley Grayson, *Myths and Legends from Korea*.

392. Quarreling Leads to Losses

Margaret Read MacDonald, *Three-Minute Tales*. China

A heron swoops down to eat an oyster. The oyster snaps his shell tight, trapping the heron's beak and will not let him go. As the heron and the oyster threaten each other, a fisherman comes by and bags them both.

CONNECTIONS. Animal fables. Birds. Clams. Conflict. Consequences. Cranes. Dai People, stories from. Fables. Fishermen. Geese. Heron. Mussels. Oxen. Oyster. Phoenix. Snipes. Storks. Tigers. Vulnerability.

HOW ELSE THIS STORY IS TOLD. *Chinese variations:* The Bird with Two Heads— Ding Yazuo in Howard Giskin, *Chinese Folktales*. The Clam and the Snipe —*Selected Chinese Fables*. The Crane and the Clam — Yong-Sheng Xuan, *The Dragon Lover*. The Double-Headed Phoenix — John Minford, *Favourite Folktales of China* (from the Dai People). Mussels and Snipe — Margaret Read MacDonald, *Peace Tales* (here it is a snipe who has caught a mussel). The Fate of the Troublemaker — Louise and Yuan-Hsi Kuo, *Chinese Folktales* (in a twist, a little buffalo and a little tiger work together to trick the fox who tries to disrupt their friendship). The Ox's Tale — Demi, *The Dragon's Tale* (a herd becomes vulnerable to tigers when they allow themselves to be separated by gossip). The Snipe and the Mussel — Peng Tong in *Ancient Chinese Fables*. Stewed, Roasted or Live?— Carol Kendall and Yao-wen Li, *Sweet and Sour* (as two hunters argue about the best way to cook geese, their prey fly away). The Two-Headed Phoenix — Wolfram Eberhard, *Folktales of China* (once the two heads quarrel, the emperor is able to separate one from the other). Two Ways of Cooking the Goose — Xian Yi Pian in *Ancient Chinese Fables*. **Korean variations:** The Clam, the Stork, and the Fisherman — Tae Hung Ha, *Folk Tales of Old Korea*. Two Foolish Friends— I.K. Junne, *Floating Clouds, Floating Dreams* (two men argue over dividing the reward for catching a tiger before they have caught it).

393. Temper

Paul Rep, *Zen Flesh, Zen Bones*. Japan

A Zen student would like to control his temper. But when the student cannot take out his temper to produce it, Bankei, the master, tells him that it must not then really be part of his nature.

CONNECTIONS. Anger. Bankei, sage. Buddhism. Self-control. Students. Reality. Sages. Truth.

HOW ELSE THIS STORY IS TOLD. Temper — Margaret Read MacDonald, *Peace Tales.*

394. Tikki Tikki Tembo

Arlene Mosel. China

Many years ago in China, first sons were honored with long names and second sons received short ones. One day, Chang, the second son, falls into the well. His brother, the first son Tikki Tikki Tembo No Sa Rembo Chari Bari Ruchi Pip Peri Pembo, runs to his mother, who sighs and sends Tikki Tikki Tembo to fetch the old man with the ladder to bring Chang out of the well. Chang recovers. One day as the boys are once again playing around the well, Tikki Tikki Tembo No Sa Rembo Chari Bari Ruchi Pip Peri Pembo falls in. Chang runs to his mother and then to the old man with the ladder, but it is so difficult to say his brother's long name over and over that Tikki Tikki Tembo takes a while to recover. Ever since then, first sons, too, are given short names.

CONNECTIONS. Brothers. Ladders. Mothers and sons. Names. Niigata, Japan, stories from. Origins. Rescues. Wells.

WHERE ELSE THIS STORY APPEARS. Tikki Tikki Tembo — Arlene Mosel on *Stories from Near and Far*, DVD. Also issued with different illustrations by Weston Woods on *Stories from the Asian Tradition*, VHS, 2003.

HOW ELSE THIS STORY IS TOLD. **Chinese variation:** Tikki Tikki Tembo — D.L. Ashliman, online at *Folktexts.* **Japanese variations:** The Child with a Long Name — Fanny Hagin Mayer, *Ancient Tales in Modern Japan* (from Nigata. Here the first son's name is Itchō giri-nichō giri-chōnai-chōsaburō-gorgoro-heiji-atchiyama-kotchiyama-tori-no-tokkasa-tate-ebōshi-tongarabyō).

395. A Polite Idiosyncrasy

Kathleen Ragan, *Fearless Girls, Wise Women and Beloved Sisters.* China

An old woman goes to visit her married daughter, who lives in the house with her husband's mother. The lamp blows out. Thinking she is alone with her daughter, the woman says that the largest portions of meat should be turned towards her at dinner. When the lamp comes on, the woman is embarrassed to see that she has been speaking to her son-in-law's mother. To cover for her remark, she says that whenever the light goes out, she prattles nonsense. The mother-in-law responds that whenever the light goes out, she cannot hear anything.

CONNECTIONS. Cleverness. Family life. Forgiveness. Harmony. Humorous stories. Manners. Mistakes. Mothers-in-law. Peace. Problem solvers. Words.

WHERE ELSE THIS STORY APPEARS. A Polite Idiosyncrasy — Adele Marion Fielde, *Chinese Nights' Entertainment.*

HOW ELSE THIS STORY IS TOLD. A Wit to Outwit — Tehyi Hsieh, *Chinese Village Folk Tales.*

396. The Wild Pigeon

Cathy Spagnoli, *Asian Tales and Tellers*. Japan

There is a boy who always does the opposite of whatever his mother asks. So, she learns to say the opposite of what she actually wants him to do. When she is dying, she requests that he bury her on the beach, when what she really wants is to be buried on the hillside. The son regrets all the times he did not listen to his mother. With great love this time, he buries her by the ocean near the city of Kanazawa. He worries so much that her grave lies unprotected from the elements, that he turns into a wild pigeon, sadly crying the mournful call of pigeons by the seashore.

CONNECTIONS. Birds. Children. Death. Disobedience. Family life. Filial devotion. Frogs. Graves. Irony. Language of animals. Misunderstandings. Mothers and sons. Pigeons. Stone.

HOW ELSE THIS STORY IS TOLD. *Japanese variations:* The Girl Who Turned Into a Stone — Richard M. Dorson, *Folk Legends of Japan*. The Unfilial Pigeon — Fanny Hagin Mayer, *Ancient Tales in Modern Japan*. The Unfilial Tree Frog — Fanny Hagin Mayer, *Ancient Tales in Modern Japan*. *Korean variations:* The Contrary Frog — Yu Chai-Shin, Shiu L. Kong, and Ruth W. Yu, *Korean Folk Tales*. The Disobedient Frog — Suzanne Crowder Han, *Korean Folk and Fairy Tales*. The Green Frog —*Long Long Time Ago* (the remorseful frog croaks when the weather is wet). The Green Frog — Zong Yong-Og in Zong In-Sob, *Folk Tales from Korea*. Why the Green Frog Croaks— James Huntley Grayson, *Myths and Legends from Korea*.

397. The Lost Horse

Ed Young. China

When Sai's swift horse bolts during a thunderstorm, Sai says it may not be such a bad thing. Sure enough, the horse returns with a healthy mare. Sai says this might not be such a good thing. Sure enough, the mare throws Sai's son, who breaks his leg. It could be that this is not such a bad thing. When enemies invade the northern border, Sai's son is spared from fighting and from becoming injured or dying. Such are the changing fortunes of life.

CONNECTIONS. Acceptance of life's changes. Changes in fortune. Fathers and sons. Han People, stories from. Horses. Perspective. Tibetan People, stories from.

HOW ELSE THIS STORY IS TOLD. Bad Luck or Good Luck — Margaret Read MacDonald, *Three-Minute Tales*. From Bad to Good to Bad to Good — Carol Kendall and Yao-wen Li, *Sweet and Sour*. The Lost Horse — Heather Forest, *Wisdom Tales from Around the World*. The Lost Horse — Lui An in Moss Roberts, *Chinese Fairy Tales and Fantasies*. The Lost Horse — Jane Yolen, *Favorite Folktales from Around the World* (this exact retelling appears in Moss Robert's book). The Old Man Who Lost His Horse — Wu Huiyan, *Selected Chinese Fables*. A Steed Lost Is More Horses Gained — Haiwang Yuan, *The Magic Lotus Lantern and Other Tales from the Han Chinese*. Yeshi's Luck — Naomi C. Rose, *Tibetan Tales for Little Buddhas*.

398. The Missing Axe

Lieh Tzu in Moss Roberts, *Chinese Fairy Tales and Fantasies*. China

When a man's axe is missing, his neighbor's son suspiciously appears to be a thief. When the man finds his axe, his neighbor's son appears the same as any other boy.

CONNECTIONS. Axes. Changes in attitude. Harmony. Identity. Misunderstandings. Perspective. Snakes. Trust.

WHERE ELSE THIS STORY APPEARS. The Missing Axe — Lieh Tzu in Jane Yolen, *Favorite Folktales from Around the World*.

HOW ELSE THIS STORY IS TOLD. The Missing Axe — Lie Zi in *Ancient Chinese Fables*. The Neighbor's Shifty Son — Margaret Read MacDonald, *Peace Tales*. The Snake's Tale — Demi, *The Dragon's Tale* (here it is a spotted snake that cannot find his egg and suspects a striped snake).

399. The King's Favorite

Han Fei Tzu in Moss Roberts, *Chinese Fairy tales and Fantasies*. China

The beautiful, favored Mi Tzu-hsia can get away with anything. When she borrows the lord of Wei's carriage without permission to visit her ill mother, he commends her filial devotion. When she tastes a peach before handing it to him, the lord appreciates her love for him. Once she is no longer beautiful, however, he complains that she takes his carriage without permission and hands him a peach she has already bitten.

CONNECTIONS. Changes in attitude. Concubines. Harmony. Identity. Love. Manners. Nobles and lords. Perspective.

WHERE ELSE THIS STORY APPEARS. The King's Favorite — Han Fei Tzu in Joanna Cole, *Best-Loved Folktales of the World*. The King's Favorite — Han Fei Tzu in Jane Yolen, *Favorite Folktales from Around the World*.

400. The Plucky Maiden

Im Bang in Im Bang and Yi Ryuk, *Korean Folk Tales*. Korea

When Han Myong-hoi, Governor of Pyong-an Province, tells the Deputy Prefect of Son-chon that he would like to take his daughter as a concubine, sight unseen, the Deputy is greatly distressed. His daughter, however, reassures him that it would be better for him to obey the order than to lose his life. The daughter asks her father to prepare as if the wedding will be for a real marriage, not a concubine's. When the Governor arrives, he finds the daughter holding a sword. She tells him that if he forces her, a gentleman's daughter, to become his concubine, she will kill herself, but if he marries her, she will serve him. The Governor, impressed with her beauty and determination, signs a certificate making her his wife. The Governor already has a first wife, though, and back in his home, the others do not treat her with respect. When King Se-jo comes to visit, the young woman prostrates herself and says she does not want to live in disgrace. She states that her papers prove that she is a real wife, but that the law only recognizes first wives. The king immediately writes a document legitimizing the young woman and her children.

CONNECTIONS. Concubines. Courage. Family life. Fathers and daughters. Governors. Hierarchy. Husbands and wives. Kings. Ministers. Pyong-an Province. Respect. Social class. Son-chon, county.

WHERE ELSE THIS STORY APPEARS. The Plucky Maiden — Im Bang in *Fearless Girls, Wise Women & Beloved Sisters*.

401. The Advice That Cost a Thousand Ryo

Keigo Seki, *Folktales of Japan*. Japan

A poor man heads home to his wife with thirty yen he has made working in the capital so that they will be able to pay the imperial taxes. He stops overnight with an old man who says he can stay if he likes to hear advice. The old man then charges him for three pieces of advice: not to take shelter under a rock cliff in the rain, not to travel too fast, and not to be too quick to anger. The man is annoyed at having to pay, but he does follow each piece of advice, and they all come in handy. He is not underneath a rock cliff when it crumbles; he gets off a fast boat that ends up capsizing; and he does not lose his temper when his sees his wife drinking miso with a man, who turns out to be the temple priest who has come to thank her for a good deed.

CONNECTIONS. Advice. Fate. Foretellings. Perspective. Anger. Luck. Old man, supernatural being.

402. The Piece of Straw

Yoshiko Uchida, *The Dancing Kettle*. Japan

As a poor man kneels at the shrine of the Goddess of Mercy, waiting for her advice, he dreams that an old man tells him to hold onto the first thing that touches his hand. The young man trips as he is leaving the temple. He stands and finds himself holding a piece of straw. When a horsefly annoys him, he ties the straw to the fly and attaches it to his stick. A boy riding with his mother wants the fly on a stick, and the young man gives it to him. In return, the boy's mother hands him three oranges. One thing leads to another. Each time, the poor man kindly gives away the new item he has acquired, he unexpectedly receives something of greater value in return. When he prays, the goddess Guanyin even revives a horse that has died. At last, with the harvest money from a rice field, he marries a lovely maiden, and they live happily ever after in Toba.

CONNECTIONS. Bodhisattvas. Changes in fortune. Despair. Dreams. Gods and goddesses. Guanyin, Goddess of Mercy. Hiroshima, Japan, stories from. Luck. Old man, supernatural helper. Poverty. Straw. Toba. Trades. Travelers.

HOW ELSE THIS STORY IS TOLD. The Bundles of Straw and the King's Son — Keigo Seki, *Folktales of Japan* (it's more than one piece of straw, but a young man follows his mother's advice to trade them at the miso shop after her death, after which he keeps trading up). Choja from a Straw — Fanny Hagin Mayer, *Ancient Tales in Modern Japan* (from Hiroshima). A Fortune from a Wisp of Straw — Royall Tyler, *Japanese Tales*. Mr. Lucky Straw — Florence Sakade — *Japanese Children's Favorite Stories* and *Peach Boy*. Warashibe Choja — *Kids Web Japan*, Online.

403. Continually Promoted

Hu Fangren in Howard Giskin, *Chinese Folktales*. Hunan Province, China

When a monk flatters ordinary Zhang Haogu by telling him he will pass the imperial. examination, Zhang Haogu heads for the capital city, Ch'ang an. He arrives at night and tells the soldiers outside the examination hall that he must hurry, for he is going to place second in the exam. The official Wei Zhonxian thinks he must be special and gives him a card to enter. Zhang Haogu is late, but with the admissions card signed by Wei Zhonxian, the examiners let him take the test. Despite the fact that he cannot read or write well, they give Zhang Haogu second place, which lands him a position in the emperor's palace. When Zhang. Haogu asks his secretary to brush birthday respects for Wei Zhonxian on silk, the secretary, tricking Zhang Haogu writes an insult, instead. Wei Zhonxian knows that Zhang Haogu is ignorant, but favored. by the emperor. He hides the silk, which is discovered by some of the emperor's servants. They use the cloth to prove that Wei Zhonxian is plotting against the emperor, and Zhang Haogu becomes advisor to the emperor.

CONNECTIONS. Ch'ang-an, imperial capital. Changes in fortune. Deceit. Emperors. Foretellings. Hunan Province, China, stories from. Illiteracy. Imperial examination. Luck. Officials. Self-esteem.

404. The Treasure of Li-Po

Alice Ritchie. China

A merchant looks forward to visiting Li-Po the basket maker, in his simple hut on the Yangtze River twice a year. Li-Po has been saving the coins he gets from the merchant. Now he asks the merchant to buy a jewel to give to the most virtuous and accomplished woman the merchant knows. Reluctantly, for he thinks Li-Po, should keep his money, the merchant does present a virtuous young woman with a jade necklace. She sends a gift back to thank her admirer. Li-Po asks the merchant to bring that gift to the most generous and noble young man he knows. This young lord sends packages in return, which Li-Po begs the merchant to present to the young woman. The anonymous exchange ends with a meeting between the young man and the young woman, who fall in love. Li-Po has revealed his identity only to the young lord, who asks the basket maker to adopt him and leaves him gold. Li-Po uses his new wealth to help the poor and happily returns to his simple life, welcoming the merchant's visit every six months.

CONNECTIONS. Adoption. Basket makers. Changes in fortune. Fathers and daughters. Friendship. Gifts. Humility. Kindness. Love. Matches, marriage. Merchants. Messengers. Nobles and lords. Yangtze River.

WHERE ELSE THIS STORY APPEARS. The Treasure of Li-Po— Alice Ritchie in I. K. Junne, *Floating Clouds, Floating Dreams*.

405. Money Makes Cares

Wolfram Eberhard, *Folktales of China*. Fukien, China

Worrying about and managing money occupies so much of rich Ch'en Po-shih's time that his wife regrets he has no time to be happy. They can hear their poor neighbor Li the Fourth singing happily at night. Ch'en says that if Li had money, he would stop singing. Ch'en's wife thinks Li would be even happier. The next day Ch'en presents Li with a gift of five hundred pieces of silver to start a business. Li thanks Ch'en, but then, all day, he thinks about what he will do with the money. He does not sing for two nights. On the third day, the deity of luck appears and tells Li to forget the money. Li hurries over to Ch'en's house to return the silver. And the next evening, he sings again.

CONNECTIONS. Changes in fortune. Coins. Deities. Family life. Fukien, China, stories from. Gifts. Happiness. Harmony. Husbands and wives. Luck. Music. Poverty. Rich man. Tests.

WHERE ELSE THIS STORY APPEARS. Money Makes Cares— Joanna Cole, *Best-Loved Folktales of the World*. Money Makes Cares— Richard M. Dorson, *Folktales Told Around the World*.

406. The Most Frugal of Men

Joanna Cole, *Best-Loved Folktales of the World.* China

The most frugal man in the kingdom wants to learn how to save even better from a man that he has heard is more frugal than he is. On one-half of one sheet of cheap paper, the frugal man draws a pig's head and tucks it into a covered basket, as if it were a real pig he was bringing as a gift. The son of the most frugal man in the kingdom takes the basket to the most frugal man in the world, who happens to be out. The son of the most frugal man in the world pantomimes putting four oranges in the basket as a thank you. When the most frugal man in the world comes home and hears what his son gave in return for the drawing, he cuffs the boy for measuring out such large oranges with his hands, when smaller ones would do.

CONNECTIONS. Curiosity. Fathers and sons. Frugality. Gifts. Humorous stories. Manners. Oranges.

HOW ELSE THIS STORY IS TOLD. The Most Frugal of Men — Adele Marion Fielde, *Chinese Nights' Entertainment.*

407. A True Money Tree

M.A. Jagendorf and Virginia Weng, *The Magic Boat and Other Chinese Folk Stories.*
Han People

When Long Life's father dies, his stepmother keeps the house and the best fields for herself and her son, Good Life. Long Life works his rocky land and fares well. Without him, though, Good Life and his mother get poorer. They wonder if Long Life has something he is not sharing. Long Life says their father gave him a money tree with two trunks and five branches on each. Good Life sneaks a tree that resembles what Long Life has described back to his own land, but no money falls. Then Long Life tells him the gift from their father was his own two arms and ten fingers. Good Life realizes that he also has everything he needs.

CONNECTIONS. Brothers. Changes in attitude. Changes in fortune. Fables. Han People, stories from. Jealousy. Laziness. Money tree. Mothers and sons. Naxi People, stories from. Realization. Stepmothers and stepsons. Storytelling. Work.

HOW ELSE THIS STORY IS TOLD. The Two Brothers — Yang Zai in He Liyi, *The Spring of Butterflies and Other Folk Tales of China's Minority Peoples* (this story from the Naxi People also includes elements contained in How the Brothers Divided Their Property, story # 44).

408. The Discovery of Salt

Wolfram Eberhard, *Folktales of China.* Chêkiang, China

Because all treasures must be reported, a peasant brings the emperor some of the earth he saw a phoenix pushing. He is sure that earth must contain treasure. Unamused, the emperor thinks the peasant is playing him for a fool and beheads him. Servants lay the earth overhead. Shortly after, rainwater drips through that earth. Some gets into the emperor's food, and the emperor loves the taste. Pieces are dug from the earth and dried to become white salt crystals. The emperor grants the peasant's son a high position to honor his father's memory.

CONNECTIONS. Chêkiang, China, stories from. Death. Earth. Emperors. Misunderstandings. Peasants. Phoenix. Punishment. Reconciliation. Remorse. Salt. Tragedies.

HOW ELSE THIS STORY IS TOLD. Discovery of Salt — Robert Wyndham, *Tales the People Tell in China.*

409. The Refugee Empress

Emily Ching, Ko-Shee Ching, and Theresa Austin, *The Refugee Empress; Chi Juang Cookies.* China

The formidable Empress Dowager Tzu Hsi, also called "Old Buddha," declares war on the whole world after she is tricked into believing that her people in Shandong Province have magical powers to protect them from foreign guns. Eight foreign countries invade; the people in Shandong flee; and the Empress Dowager herself runs from the capital with her servants. She is hiding at a farmhouse when she gets hungry. Her guardian eunuch tells the farmers to prepare food for the empress. With food in short supply and because they have always eaten simply, the farm people prepare bean curd stir-fried with spinach. The Empress Dowager loves the food and wants to know its name. Her eunuch invents an elaborate name to suit what she is accustomed to. After the empress has signed a peace treaty, she asks the palace chef to prepare "Golden rim of white jade platter with the red-beaked green parrot," but he is totally baffled.

CONNECTIONS. Cleverness. Empresses. Eunuchs. Farmers. Food. Harmony. Names. Pride. Shandong Province. Tzu Hsi, Dowager Empress. War.

410. The Palace Plot

Yin-lien C.Chin, Yetta S. Center, and Mildred Ross, *Traditional Chinese Folktales.* China

The Emperor Jin Dzung has never had time to take a wife, and now he worries about not leaving an heir. He tells two concubines he cares for that the first to give him a male child will become queen. They have never been rivals before. Lady Li gives birth to a son first. Lady Liu tells the eunuch Guao Hai to exchange Lady Li's baby for a skinned cat. Then she orders her maid Pearl to drown the baby. Instead, Pearl gives the baby to a sympathetic eunuch, Chen Lin, who brings the boy to the emperor's cousin's house hidden in a bowl of fruit. Lady Liu becomes queen, even though her son dies shortly after he is born; Lady Li is in disfavor for having produced a monstrosity. The emperor is taken with his cousin's boy and asks to adopt him. When Queen Liu sees the resemblance between the boy and Lady Li, she has Guo Huai demand that the eunuch Chen Lin beat Pearl to death. Chen Lin tells Lady Li to flee. Ten years later, the emperor dies, without ever knowing the real identity of his adopted son who succeeds him as emperor. One day a ragged woman throws herself before a judge's sedan chair, screaming that she is the emperor's true mother. She shows the judge a gold phoenix brooch from the emperor. Guo Huai is imprisoned, but denies everything until a fake phantom voice of Pearl frightens him into confessing. Lady Li is made the rightful queen mother.

CONNECTIONS. Competition. Concubines. Confessions. Cruelty. Deceit. Emperors. Eunuchs. Family life. Fathers and sons. Golden brooch. Identity. Injury. Jealousy. Jin Dzung, Emperor. Justice. Mothers and sons. Queens.

How Else This Story Is Told. The Baby Prince Who Was Replaced by a Cat — Rena Krasno and Yeng-Fong Chiang, *Cloud Weavers.*

411. The Golden Eggplant

Fanny Hagin Mayer, *Ancient Tales from Modern Japan.* Ōshima-gun, Japan

The king's consort breaks wind one day when they are walking. He angrily sets her adrift in a boat with their young son. The boat lands on an island where they are terribly poor, and other boys make fun of him as an illegitimate child. The boy asks his mother about his father, and she tells him the story. When he is thirteen, he wants to go to request that his father restore his mother's place in the palace. Uncertainly, she lets him go. Every day, the youth calls in front of the palace gate asking if anyone wants a seed that grows golden eggplant. The king asks if the golden eggplant will really grow. The boy tells the king that the seed must be planted by someone who does not break wind. The king exclaims that everyone breaks wind. The boy tells the king about his mother, then, and, impressed with his son's wisdom, the king takes her back immediately.

CONNECTIONS. Acknowledgment by father. Arrogance. Breaking wind. Changes in attitude. Compassion. Eggplant. Exile. Fathers and sons. Filial devotion. Helpfulness. Husbands and wives. Kings. Manners. Mothers and sons. Ōshima-gun, Japan, stories from. Problem solvers. Queens. Realization. Reconciliation. Seeds. Tests. Tolerance.

How Else This Story Is Told. The Golden Eggplant — Keigo Seki, *Folktales of Japan.* The Jewel That Grew Golden Flowers — Richard M. Dorson, *Folk Legends of Japan.*

412. The Blue Rose

Maurice Baring. China

The Emperor's accomplished daughter has one hundred fifty suitors, but will only marry the man who can bring her a Blue Rose. Some are determined to succeed. One merchant threatens a shopkeeper, whose wife comes up with a plan to dip a white rose stem in blue dye. The Lord Chief Justice hires a skillful artist to make an exquisite china cup with a painted blue rose. All fail in their quest to find an acceptable blue rose. One night the Princess overhears a strolling minstrel singing in another part of the garden. They meet and talk and enjoy each other's company. The next day, the minstrel brings the Princess a white rose. She tells the Emperor that this minstrel has found exactly the Blue Rose she has been looking for.

CONNECTIONS. Blue rose. Competition. Emperors. Fathers and daughters. Love. Minstrels. Music. Perspective. Princesses. Roses. Suitors. Tests.

How Else This Story Is Told. The Blue Rose — Marie L. Shedlock, *The Art of the Story-Teller.* The Blue Rose — Anita Stern, *World Folktales.*

413. The Greatest Treasure

Gia-Zhen Wang, *Auntie Tigress and Other Favorite Chinese Folktales.* China

Frustrated when she will not choose a rich man to marry, Yomei's father, Master Liu, opens the door and sends her off with the poor snail peddler, Tian Lee. Yomei admires that Tian Lee is hardworking and kind. One day Tian Lee discovers shining black rocks in a cave. The God of the Earth tells him he may take one, but that the rest are for D.K. Lee. The rock is black gold. Years later, when their son is born, Yomei and Tian Lee bring the baby to visit Master Liu, who calls him D.K. for short, since the boy is entranced by all the door knockers in the house. Yomei and Tian Lee realize that this means that it is their son owns all the black gold in the cave. They surprise Master Liu with a basket of black gold covered with snails for New Year's celebration. They buy a big piece of land, which Master Liu gives to the poor in his village.

CONNECTIONS. Black gold. Changes in attitude. Changes in fortune. Charity. Coal. Exile. Fathers and daughters. Foretellings. Gods and goddesses. Grandfathers and grandsons. Husbands and wives. Love. Marriage. Matches, marriage. Mysteries. Names. New Year's. Peddlers. Reconciliation. Respect. Snails. Social class. Taiwan, stories from.

HOW ELSE THIS STORY IS TOLD. *Taiwanese variation:* The Much-Deserved Good Fortune of Li Menhuan — Gary Marvin Davison, *Tales from the Taiwanese.*

414. The Girl Who Ate a Baby

Richard M. Dorson, *Folk Legends of Japan.* Japan

Three young men all apply to marry the choja's daughter. The choja cannot decide which is the most able and has them each cultivate a different rice field — one in the east, one in the west, and one to the front. Work that should take ten days, they all finish in one. The choja still cannot decide. One night, two of them see the choja's daughter take a coffin out from underneath the floorboard, remove a baby from the coffin, cut off its head, and start to eat it. She turns and offers the two young men a bloody arm. They run from the house. The third young man decides to look for himself. Watching carefully, he realizes that the she-demon is a girl wearing a mask and that the baby is a doll made of mochi that has been covered with rouge. He asks to eat one of the legs. It is this courageous brother that the choja's daughter marries.

CONNECTIONS. Babies. Chojas. Competition. Disguises. Farmers. Misunderstandings. Mochi. Perspective. Problem solvers. Reality. Rice. Suitors. Tests. Truth.

HOW ELSE THIS STORY IS TOLD. *Japanese variations:* Of Ghosts and Goblins, VI — Lafcadio Hearn, *The Writings of Lafcadio Hearn.* A Test of Love — F. Hadland Davis, *Myths and Legends of Japan.* **Korean variation:** The Final Test — James Huntley Grayson, *Myths and Legends from Korea.*

415. The Choosy Maid of Yen-pien

M. A. Jagendorf and Virginia Weng, *The Magic Boat and Other Chinese Folk Stories.* Korean Chinese People

Many young men try to accomplish their planting extra fast to impress the Korean maiden in Yen-pien, who is renown for the speed at which she works. However, she turns them all down. One rejected suitor pushes the maid off a narrow mountain path. A young blacksmith in the village below sees her falling. He quickly cuts twigs, weaves them into a basket, and catches the maiden in time. Now, this is the man for her.

CONNECTIONS. Anger. Blacksmiths. Competition. Farmers. Humorous stories. Korean Chinese People, stories from. Problem solvers. Rescues. Speed. Suitors. Yen-pien, place.

416. Three Dead Wives

James Riordan, *Korean Folk Tales*. Korea

An emperor questions three of his ministers about why they are not married. He thinks something may be lacking that will affect their ability to lead. The Prime Minister tells the king that he is faithful to the memory of his wife, who sacrificed herself to save a ship in a storm. The Minister for Home Affairs says that his wife died from shock when she saw him, after trying to balance one egg on top of another for five years to bring him back from exile. The Minister of Education tells the king that he was too shy on his wedding night and ran out to study on a mountain top. However, when he passed his examinations and was traveling to Nam Yang, he stopped in a village where his deserted bride lay in her wedding dress. She looked young and alive, but when he kissed her forehead, wanting to beg her forgiveness, she turned to dust. The emperor decides that tragic love has given these three men the remorse and kindness they need to be good ministers.

CONNECTIONS. Devotion. Emperors. Husbands and wives. Kindness. Leadership. Love. Marriage. Ministers. Questions. Realization. Remorse. Storytelling. Tragedies.

HOW ELSE THIS STORY IS TOLD. The Three Unmarried Ministers—Song Ssi in Zong In-Sob, *Folk Tales from Korea*.

417. Baling with a Sieve

Kathleen Ragan, *Outfoxing Fear*. Kwantung, China

A young woman instructs her foolish husband to sell the linen she has woven for a certain price, saying "Among all whose nostrils open downward, not one is honest." At the market, he is confused, for it seems to him that everyone's nostrils open downward. Then he sees a man whose head is tilted back to read a proclamation. He approaches the man, who sees he is dealing with a fool. The man tells the husband to tell his wife that the cloth was bought by Mr. Seven-Eight and to send for payment the next day to "the house beside the wasps' nest behind a grove of jointless bamboo." The wife solves this riddle and sends her husband to the boy's school where Mr. Seven-Eight teaches fifteen-year-olds. Mr. Seven-Eight hands over the payment plus a basket that has a pomegranate blossom stuck in a lump of dirt. The wife starts crying, as she interprets this to mean she is a flower married to a clod. Her husband, though, thinks she is crying because he accepted too little money for the linen. Wanting to make the young wife feel better, Mr. Seven-Eight goes to a pond near her house and tries to bail it out with a sieve. When she sees him, he tells her that he is trying to find his wife's needle. His intent is to let her think that if his wife has survived being married to a fool, she can too.

CONNECTIONS. Cleverness. Fools. Harmony. Helpfulness. Husbands and wives. Kwantung, China, stories from. Mysteries. Perspective. Riddles. Sieves. Tolerance. Weaving.

WHERE ELSE THIS STORY APPEARS. Bailing with a Sieve—Adele Marion Fielde, *Chinese Nights' Entertainment*.

418. The Fish Seller and the "One-Eyed Yak"

Folk Tales from China, Second Series. Tibetan People

A king offers a reward to anyone who will bring him fish during a drought. A peasant brings some salted fish to the palace, but the guard, One-Eyed Yak, will not let him enter unless the peasant promises to give him half of the reward. The peasant agrees, but asks the guard his name. When the king asks the peasant what he wants as his reward, the peasant says to be flogged one thousand strokes. After five hundred very light strokes, the peasant says that by rights the other five hundred strokes belong to the guard One-Eyed Yak and lets the king know what happened. One-Eyed Yak does not get off as lightly.

CONNECTIONS. Bullies. Drought. Fish. Gifts. Guards. Kings. Names. Peasants. Punishment. Revenge. Rewards. Taiwan, stories from. Tibetan People, stories from. Tricksters.

HOW ELSE THIS STORY IS TOLD. *Taiwanese variation:* The Reward — Cora Cheney, *Tales from a Taiwan Kitchen.*

419. The Empty Pot
Demi. China

When he needs to choose a successor, an emperor who loves plants, decides to let the flowers choose. He distributes seeds to children, planning to judge their plants in one year. Nothing grows in Ping's pot, though he has faithfully tended the seed. Ping wonders whether he should substitute another plant, but at the end of the year, he brings his empty pot to the emperor's courtyard, which is filled with many children and their beautiful blooms. The emperor, however, praises Ping for being honest. It turns out all of the seeds have first been cooked.

CONNECTIONS. Children. Competition. Emperors. Flowers. Honesty. Seeds. Succession. Tests.

420. Golden Life
Carol Kendall and Yao-wen Li, *Sweet and Sour.* China

There is an emperor who has riches, but now wants to live forever. A Taoist arrives who says he is carrying a golden grain of immortality. In the throne room, a guard suddenly grabs the golden grain and swallows it. The emperor, angry, at first condemns the guard to death and then rescinds his order. If the grain really works then he will not be able to behead the guard. If the grain does not work, the emperor will lose face for beheading a lowly man over nothing.

CONNECTIONS. Choices. Consequences. Emperors. Golden grain. Guards. Harmony. Immortality. Leadership. Priests. Punishment. Social class. Taoism.

HOW ELSE THIS STORY IS TOLD. The Elixir of Long Life — Lim Sian-tek, *More Folk Tales from China.* Living Forever — Herbert A. Giles, *Chinese Fairy Tales.*

421. The King and the Poor Man
John Minford, *Favourite Folktales of China.* Kazak People

An old man advises his son never to make friends with someone he does not trust, never to borrow money from someone newly rich, and never to reveal his secrets. Curious to see if this advice works, the son does the opposite. The son's wife goes right to the king with the secret that her husband killed a man, when he has actually killed a goat. However, the son's best friend will not testify on his behalf. The son confesses to the king that he was just testing his father's advice. The king has both father and son buried alive, thinking they must be smarter than he is. Then the king gets a bone caught in his throat. The father and son offer to save him, but tell him that his son must die. The king reluctantly agrees. Everything is ready, but when the king hears a cry, he is so upset that he wails, too, and the bone flies out of his throat. It turns out, the cry was from a goat, not his son, but the king hands all of his possessions over to the wise old man.

CONNECTIONS. Advice. Bones. Changes in fortune. Cleverness. Deceit. Compassion. Fathers and sons. Friendship. Healing. Husbands and wives. Jealousy. Kazak People, stories from. Kings. Poverty. Problem solvers. Realization. Secrets. Tests.

HOW ELSE THIS STORY IS TOLD. The King and a Poor Man — He Liyi, *The Spring of Butterflies.*

422. The Headman and the Magician

Folk Tales from China, Third Series. Tibetan People

A powerful headman in the Bol area of Tibet asks a poor magician to make him happy. The magician tells the headman that his magic does not last, but the headman promises he will not punish the magician when his happiness ends. Just then a large yurt with gold and silver thrones and hundreds of soldiers and servants set up in his pasture. Sa-i-nibu, the God of Fate, and his son have arrived from the underworld to stop the heavenly gods from plucking all the figs from their tree. The headman suggests that the son stay, thinking he might be able to arrange a marriage with his daughter. One stormy day body parts fall from the sky, and one of the heads looks like Sa-i-nibu. The son throws himself onto the funeral pyre, but it turns out Sa-i-nibu was not killed and is now furious with the headman for his son's death. The God of Fate tells the headman to look around. Everything is gone, except for the poor magician who has created the illusion.

CONNECTIONS. Acceptance of life's changes. Bol, place. Conflict. Death. Despair. Fate. Fathers and sons. Gods and goddesses. Happiness. Headmen. Heads. Illusions. Magicians. Sa-i-nibu. Tibetan People, stories from.

WHERE ELSE THIS STORY APPEARS. The Headman and the Magician — *The Peacock Maiden: Folk Tales from China.*

HOW ELSE THIS STORY IS TOLD. Dreams — Yu Hsiung in Brian Brown, *Chinese Nights Entertainments: Stories of Old China.*

423. Wagging My Tale in the Mud

Chuang Tzu in Moss Roberts, *Chinese Fairy tales and Fantasies.* China

The poet Chuang Tzu is fishing in the River Pu. The King of Ch'u sends two noblemen to invite him to work in an official position. The poet replies that he has heard about the sacred, ancient tortoise that the king keeps enshrined in a box. He questions whether that tortoise is happier being an honored shell, than it would be being a turtle in the mud.

CONNECTIONS. Choices. Ch'u. Freedom. Kings. Life, appreciation of. Officials. Parables. Poets. Pu River.

WHERE ELSE THIS STORY APPEARS. Wagging My Tale in the Mud — Jane Yolen, *Favorite Folktales from Around the World.*

424. Keeping a Promise

Margaret Read MacDonald, *Three-Minute Tales*. China

Zeng Shen's son begs to go to the market with his mother. She tells him that he must stay home, but that they will kill a pig for him when she returns. That night, Zeng Shen gets ready to kill the pig, and she stops him. She says she was just saying that so their son would go home. He answers that they must set a good example for their son and always follow through on their words.

CONNECTIONS. Consequences. Family life. Parables. Parents and children. Pigs. Promises. Words.

HOW ELSE THIS STORY IS TOLD. Keeping One's Word — Wu Huiyuan, *Selected Chinese Fables*. Why Zeng Shen Killed the Pig — Han Fei Zi in *Ancient Chinese Fables*.

425. Lao Lai-Tse, the Tactful

Frances Alexander, *Pebbles from a Broken Jar*. China

Seventy-year-old Lao Lai-Tse knows how to make his older parents forget their aches and pains when they come to visit him. He prepares soft food, eliminates steps, and pretends to be a young child.

CONNECTIONS. Compassion. Family life. Filial devotion. Lao-tsu, sage. Manners. Old age. Parents and children. Sages. Taoism.

426. A Final Lesson

Cathy Spagnoli, *Asian Tales and Tellers*. China

Lao-tsu begs his old teacher for some final advice. The teacher tells him to step on the ground when he returns to his birthplace so he will never forget it. Then, the teacher opens his mouth to show Lao-tsu that his teeth are gone. He tells Lao-tsu that the tongue was more flexible and survived.

CONNECTIONS. Advice. Flexibility. Lao-tsu, sage. Perspective. Sages. Taoism. Teeth.

427. Logic

Carol Kendall and Yao-wen Li, *Sweet and Sour*. China

An old man asks a boy whether the capital city, Ch'ang an, or the sun is closer to them. The boy answers that the sun must be closer because he can see it from where he is. The man thinks the boy is very clever and shows him off in the busy marketplace. This time when he asks which is closer, the boy answers Ch'ang an. He has now seen people from the capital at the market, and he has never seen anyone from the sun.

CONNECTIONS. Ch'ang-an, imperial capital. Children. Cleverness. Distance. Dogs. Humorous stories. Questions. Sun.

HOW ELSE THIS STORY IS TOLD. The Dog's Tale — Demi, *The Dragon's Tale* (conversation is between dog and smart pup). The Little Prince Ponders — Lim Sian-tek, *More Folk Tales from China*.

428. The Official and the Hermit

Louise and Yuan-Hsi Kuo, *Chinese Folk Tales.* Han People, China

Fung Ch'ung and T'ang Yi are scholars and friends from Hunan Province with differing approaches to life. When gentle Fung casually aims a pebble at a willow branch and hits it, he says this will predict his future success. Muscular, bold T'ang aims his arrow, and when it misses, he breaks his bow. Fung tries to console his friend that it is just a game, but that year, Fung passes his examinations and T'ang does not. Fung becomes Tsin-tzee, with an official post in Fukien Province. T'ang ignores Fung's invitation to join him and wanders. For ten years Fung does not hear from T'ang. One night, the houseboy who fiercely routs robbers at Fung's house mysteriously vanishes. Years later, Fung sees the houseboy on a sandbar after his boat has drifted on its own up the Yangtze River. The young man says that his master has been waiting, and Fung follows him to the summit of a mountain, where T'ang and his people live in simple huts. Fung and T'ang embrace and then part. The two friends embody the differences between Taoism and Confucianism, between living in harmony with natural order and with social order.

CONNECTIONS. Acceptance of life's changes. Confucianism. Fate. Friendship. Fukien Province. Han People, stories from. Harmony. Imperial examination. Mysteries. Natural order. Officials. Parables. Professions. Protection. Social class. Taoism. Travelers. Yangtze River.

429. The Stonecutter: A Japanese Folk Tale

Gerald McDermott. Japan

Each day, Tasaku chips away at a mountain, cutting blocks of stone that are used to build great structures. He is content with his life. However, watching a princely procession pass by, Tasaku suddenly longs for more power. The spirit in the mountain transforms him into a prince. He feels grand until he sees the sun burning flowers in the garden. Then, Tasaku longs to be the sun. He becomes the sun. When a cloud covers him, he wants to be a cloud. He enjoys sending storms down on the land. Despite all the fury he rains down on earth, though, the mountains remain, so Tasaku asks the spirit to change him into a mountain. He is happy as a mountain — greater than prince or sun or clouds — until one day, he feels a stonecutter chiseling his feet.

CONNECTIONS. Discontent. Happiness. Harmony. Mountains. Parables. Realization. Spirits. Stonecutter. Transformation. Wishes.

WHERE ELSE THIS STORY APPEARS. The Stonecutter — Gerald McDermott on *Asian Folk Tales*, DVD.

HOW ELSE THIS STORY IS TOLD. **Chinese variations:** A Stonecarver's Dream — Emily Ching and Ko-Shee Ching, *Sun Valley; A Stone Carver's Dream.* The Stone Mason — Louise and Yuan-Hsi Kuo, *Chinese Folk Tales* (T'ung People). The Stone Mason — Catherine Edwards Sadler, *Treasure Mountain* (T'ung People). The Stone-Mason Who Was Never Satisfied — *Folk Tales from China,* Second Series and at D. L. Ashliman, *Folktexts,* Online. *The Stonecutter*—Demi. **Japanese variations:** The Stone-Cutter — Andrew Lang, *The Crimson Fairy Book* and as The Stonecutter, online in D.L. Ashliman, *Folktexts.* The Stonecutter — Joanna Cole, *Best-Loved Folktales of the World.* The Two Stonecutters — Eve Titus. *See also,* The Mouse's Wedding, story # 311, where a mouse father thinks no mouse is great enough to marry his daughter.

430. What's a Life Span?

Emily Ching and Ko-Shee Ching, *Lugging Mountains; What's a Life Span?* China

The mountain gets 10,000 years to live. The river in a canyon receives 1,000 years to live. Man is asleep and does not hear God's call for the 100-year life span. So, man gets five years, after the horse, cow, and dog receive their allocations. However, rooster says 100 years is too long for him; all of his feathers fall out. They switch; rooster takes the five years, but man always rises when rooster crows.

CONNECTIONS. Discontent. God. Life span. Man. Mountains. Origins. Rivers. Roosters. Time. Trades.

431. All the Way to Lhasa

Barbara Berger. Tibetan People

A man on horseback stops to ask an old woman how far it is to Lhasa, and she tells him it is too far away. A boy leading his yak asks the old woman the same question. She tells the boy he can make it by nightfall. Step by step by step up a steep and windy slope, across a narrow bridge, and through snow, he does.

CONNECTIONS. Children. Determination. Distance. Irony. Lhasa, place. Old woman, supernatural helper. Parables. Questions. Tibetan People, stories from. Travelers. Yaks.

432. Muddy Road

Paul Rep, *Zen Flesh, Zen Bones.* Japan

Two monks meet a beautiful young woman in a silk kimono during a heavy rainstorm. One monk carries her across a muddy intersection. Much later, the second monk broods that monks should not touch females. The first monk answers that he set the young woman down way back and asks if the second monk is still carrying her.

CONNECTIONS. Beauty. Buddhism. Maidens. Manners. Monks. Mud. Parables. Precepts. Temptation.

433. A Parable

Paul Rep, *Zen Flesh, Zen Bones.* Japan

A man, fleeing from a tiger, now hangs from a vine over the edge of a cliff. Mice start gnawing on the vine. The man reaches for a ripe strawberry that grows right there. It tastes so sweet.

CONNECTIONS. Buddhism. Death. Life, appreciation of. Mice. Parables. Perspective. Strawberries. Tigers.

434. Real Prosperity

Paul Rep, *Zen Flesh, Zen Bones.* Japan

A rich man asks Sengai to write something that will continue his family's good fortune. The master writes "Father dies, son dies, grandson dies." This sounds like a curse to the rich man until Sengai explains that preserving the natural order will insure his family's happiness.

CONNECTIONS. Buddha. Buddhism. Death. Generations. Happiness. Harmony. Luck. Natural order. Parables. Perspective. Realization.

435. The Value of Salt

Linda Soon Curry, *A Tiger by the Tail*. Korea

The aristocratic parents of a man oppose his marriage to a salt peddler's daughter and make her life miserable after the wedding with verbal abuse. Her own parents wish that they could do something to help her. They invite the in-laws to dinner, where they serve food so bland the parents-in-law cannot eat. The salt peddler speaks up then saying that surely now they see how indispensable salt is. The parents-in-law agree, and everyone lives with respect and harmony after that.

CONNECTIONS. Changes in attitude. Family life. Food. Harmony. In-laws and wives. Peddlers. Reconciliation. Respect. Salt. Social class. Tolerance.

HOW ELSE THIS STORY IS TOLD. The Value of Salt — Suzanne Crowder Han, *Korean Folk and Fairy Tales*.

436. What Do They Respect?

Shujiang Li and Karl W. Luckert, *Mythology and Folklore of the Hui*. Ningxia, China

An ahong who gives away as much as he acquires is invited to a rich man's house as a teacher. However, when he arrives in shabby clothes, he is seated as a commoner far away from his host. Another dinner invitation arrives, which the ahong would like to decline, but he is told to come well-dressed. This time, when the ahong arrives, he is given a place of honor. He takes his clothes off and puts them on the table, telling his host that it is really only the clothes he truly respects.

CONNECTIONS. Ahongs. Charity. Clothes. Manners. Ningxia, China, stories from. Parables. Realization. Respect. Rich man. Social class.

437. The Subjugation of a Ghost

Paul Rep, *Zen Flesh, Zen Bones*. Japan

A dying young wife tells her husband that if he remarries she will return as a ghost to trouble him. After three months, he becomes engaged, and the ghost of his wife appears every night to describe in detail all of his doings with his betrothed. The man goes to a Zen master for help. The master tells him first to admire the tenacity and intelligence of his first wife, and then to bargain with her and promise to break his engagement if she can tell him how many beans he holds in his hand. She cannot do this, for she has sprung from his imagination.

CONNECTIONS. Advice. Betrothal. Buddhism. Death. Ghosts. Haunting. Husbands and wives. Jealousy. Peace. Reality. Revenge. Sages. Tests. Truth.

438. The Ahong Who Saved a Snake

Bei Keyu in Shujiang Li and Karl W. Luckert, *Mythology and Folklore of the Hui*. Guangxi, China

A Muslim man asks an ahong to accompany him to his ancestral grave, where they see a large spotted snake. The ahong keeps him from killing the snake for, as Muhammad has said, one should not kill without reason. The following year, the ahong goes to that same graveyard on his own and meets the same snake. The snake reaches out to bite him. The ahong protests that he saved the snake's life in the past. The snake answers that biting is in its nature.

CONNECTIONS. Ahongs. Graves. Guangxi, China, stories from. Hui People, stories from. Ingratitude. Kindness to animals. Muslims. Natural order. Parables. Perspective. Snakes.

439. An Ox for a Persimmon

Suzanne Crowder Han, *Korean Folk and Fairy Tales*. Korea

Every day kind Mr. Kim waters the stump of a persimmon tree until it flowers and bears large fruit. He shares fruit with his neighbors, but wraps the largest persimmon to bring as a present for the king in Hanyang. The king is pleased and thanks Mr. Kim with a gold nugget the same size as the persimmon from his store of recent gifts. Mr. Kim's neighbor, Mr. Pak, is jealous. He sells his property and buys an ox to present to the king, thinking he will receive an even bigger gold nugget. But when he gives the king the ox, the king has his servants search the storeroom for something large and sends Mr. Pak home with Mr. Kim's watermelon-sized persimmon as his reward.

CONNECTIONS. Gifts. Greed. Hanyang. Humorous stories. Irony. Jealousy. Kindness. Kings. Oxen. Persimmons. Rewards.

~ XIV ~

The Problem Solvers

440. The Young Head of the Family

Kathleen Ragan, *Fearless Girls, Wise Women and Beloved Sisters*. Kwantung, China

A father-in-law gives permission for his two daughters to visit their own village if they bring back fire and wind both wrapped in paper. The girls are baffled, but a young girl they meet solves the riddle with a lantern and a fan. The father-in-law is impressed and brings her into his household as his youngest son's wife. The clever young woman watches out for their welfare. She tells the sons always to carry something both to and from the fields and correctly suspects there may be more to their rock pile than ordinary rocks when a stranger offers a money for it. The father-in-law is so pleased, he inscribes "No Sorrow" where everyone can see. A magistrate accuses him of bragging and demands that the young head of the family weave cloth as long as the road. She says she will as soon as he tells her how long the road is. He also wants her to guess whether or not he will squeeze the quail in his hand to death. In response to how many gallons of oil equal water in the sea, she asks the magistrate a question he cannot answer, and so he leaves.

CONNECTIONS. Cleverness. Emperors. Family life. Fathers-in-law and daughters-in-law. Harmony. Helpfulness. Heroes, women. Hui People, stories from. Husbands and wives. Kwantung, China, stories from. Magistrates. Ningxia, China, stories from. Pride. Problem solvers. Riddles. Scholars. Tests. Wife-stealing. Wisdom.

WHERE ELSE THIS STORY APPEARS. The Young Head of the Family—Wolfram Eberhard, *Folktales of China*. The Young Head of the Family—Joanna Cole, *Best-Loved Folktales of the World*. The YoungHead of the Family—Ethel Johnston Phelps, *Tatterhood*.

HOW ELSE THIS STORY IS TOLD. ***Chinese variations:*** The Beautiful Young Woman as the Head of the Family—Tehyi Hsieh, *Chinese Village Folk Tales*. The Clever Daughter-in-Law—Yin-lien C. Chin, Yetta S. Center, and Mildred Ross, *Traditional Chinese Folktales*. The Clever Daughter-in-Law—Margaret Read MacDonald, *Celebrate the World*. The Clever Wife—Louise and Yuan-Hsi Kuo, *Chinese Folktales*. The Clever Wife—Carol Kendall and Yao-wen Li, *Sweet and Sour* and at *Learning to Give*, Online. Sailimai Goes to an Examination—Wang Yanyi in Shujiang Li and Karl W. Luckert, *Mythology and Folklore of the Hui* (in this tale from Ningxia, the emperor proclaims Sailimai as Female Number One Scholar). The Shrewd Daughter-in-law—Lim Sian-tek, *Folk Tales from China*. The Young Head of the Cheng Family—Robert Wyndham, *Tales the People Tell in China*. The Young Head of the Family—Adele Marion Fielde, *Chinese Nights' Entertainment*. The Young Head of the Family—Kate Douglas Wiggin, The Fairy Ring. ***Korean variation:*** The Three Riddles—Yu Chai-Shin, Shiu L. Kong, and Ruth Y. Yu, *Korean Folk Tales* (here, the government official wants to take the clever wife away from her husband).

441. Sailimai's Four Precious Things

Wang Yanyi in Shujiang Li and Karl W. Luckert, *Mythology and Folklore of the Hui*. Hui People

Ali accidentally breaks a precious vase while he is doing some work for the emperor. The emperor says that he will spare Ali's life if Ali pays with something blacker than the bottom of a pan, something as clear as a mirror, something as hard as steel, and something as large as the sea. As the deadline draws near, Sailimai tells her father-in-law to let the emperor know she has the four things. With her answers to the emperor's riddles, Sailimai becomes known for wisdom throughout the land.

CONNECTIONS. Cleverness. Emperors. Family life. Helpfulness. Heroes, women. Hui People, stories from. Ningxia, China, stories from. Problem solvers. Riddles. Ultimatums. Wisdom.

WHERE ELSE THIS STORY APPEARS. Sailimai's Four Precious Things—Wang Yanyi in Kathleen Ragan, *Fearless Girls, Wise Women and Beloved Sisters* (from Ningxia).

442. The Tibetan Envoy

Shao Chong Su in He Liyi, *The Spring of Butterflies and Other Folk Tales of China's Minority Peoples*. Tibetan People

Seven envoys arrive to woo Princess Wencheng, beloved daughter of the emperor of the Tang dynasty. The emperor, however, considers Tibet too far away and would like to discourage the Tibetan prince's suit. He sets up a test whereby all of the envoys must match five hundred mares with their foals. None succeed, except for the Tibetan envoy who calls for the mares to be fed, after which they each call their own foal. The Tibetan envoy uses an ant to bring a thread through an intricate, tiny passageway to hang a piece of jade. For the third test, the emperor asks that each envoy tell him which is the top and which is the bottom of a log. Although the Tibetan envoy passes this test, too, the emperor still does not want to send his daughter to Tibet. For a final test, he asks that the envoys pick the princess from among three hundred girls. From an old laundress, the Tibetan discovers that the princess likes to oil her hair, around which bees buzz. At last, impressed with the cleverness of the Tibetan envoy, the emperor agrees that his daughter may marry the Tibetan prince. The Tibetan envoy requests that she ask her father to give them seeds for the land as a wedding gift, instead of jewels, and the emperor complies.

CONNECTIONS. Cleverness. Distance. Emperors. Envoys. Fathers and daughters. Knowledge. Matches, marriage. Princesses. Problem solvers. Reconciliation. Seeds. Suitors. Tests. Tibetan People, stories from. Wisdom.

HOW ELSE THIS STORY IS TOLD. Princess Wencheng—Haiwang Yuan, *Princess Peacock*. The Tibetan Envoy's Mission—M.A. Jagendorf and Virginia Weng, *The Magic Boat and Other Chinese Folk Stories*. The Tibetan Envoy and the T'ang Dynasty Princess—Louise and Yuan-Hsi Kuo, *Chinese Folk Tales*.

443. The Right Site

Cathy Spagnoli, *Asian Tales and Tellers*. Korea

A young woman from a rich home loses both her father and her father-in-law at the same time. She worries that her husband's poorer family will not be able to afford to hire a geomancer to find the right place to bury his father. She overhears her family's geomancer say that if the site that he found for her father stays dry after the rain, it will bring blessings to future generations. She pours water on that site, so the geomancer will reject it. Then the young woman gives this site to her husband for his father. The poor family's fortunes increase.

CONNECTIONS. Changes in fortune. Cleverness. Geomancers. Graves. Harmony. Helpfulness. Heroes, women. Husbands and wives. Problem solvers. Social class.

444. Finding a Wife for the River God

Yin-lien C. Chin, Yetta S. Center, Mildred Ross, *Traditional Chinese Folktales*. China

The new prefect Syimen Bau notices the disparity between rich officials and the poverty of the villagers when he arrives in Ye. The elders tell him that heavy taxes are levied against the people to pay for expenses associated with finding a wife for the River God each year. It is the Village Sorceress who arranges the marriages. She chooses a beautiful young girl and prepares her in her large house with many disciples. In a grand ceremony, the bridal bed is pushed into the river. It sinks downstream. The Sorceress says they must do this to protect their land from flooding. At the next wedding, Syimen Bau calls out that he wants to judge if the girl is pretty enough. He then says that she will not do and has his servants toss the Sorceress into the river to report to the River God. When she does not return, they toss in a disciple and then the Officer in Charge of Ceremonies. The Magistrate and officials save themselves by saying there are enough messengers, and Syimen Bau agrees. To further take away all belief in the old superstition, the Magistrate has canals dug to irrigate the fields and redirect flood waters, and the town prospers.

CONNECTIONS. Bullies. Changes in attitude. Cleverness. Deceit. Floods. Heroes, men. Justice. Magicians. Magistrates. Peace. Problem solvers. River God. Sacrifice. Social class. Taxes. Ultimatums. Villagers. Weddings.

HOW ELSE THIS STORY IS TOLD. Based on the book *Shr Ji* by Sz-Ma Chyan. The Black General — Kuo Yüan-chen in Moss Roberts, *Chinese Fairy Tales and Fantasies*. A Bride for the River God — Louise and Yuan-Hsi Kuo, *Chinese Folktales*. How the River God's Wedding Was Broken Off — Lim Sian-tek, *More Folk Tales from China*. How the River-God's Wedding Was Broken Off — Richard Wilhelm, *The Chinese Fairy Book*. The Wedding of the Dragon God — S. Y. LuMar, *Chinese Tales of Folklore*.

445. The Story of the Three Genjias

John Minford, *Favourite Folktales of China*. Tibetan People in Sichuan Province

A tribal chief, a carpenter, and the chief's steward all have the same name. The steward covets the carpenter's wife, but she will have nothing to do with him. When the chief's father dies, the steward plots to kill the carpenter. He brushes a document in old-fashioned calligraphy that says that the chief's father needs a carpenter to construct a mansion for him in heaven. The chief orders Genjia the carpenter to go to heaven at once. The carpenter sees through the steward's plot. He requests seven days to prepare for a Twig Burning Ceremony that will send him up to heaven. The carpenter confides in his wife, and they secretly dig a tunnel from the hemp field to their house. When faggots of wood are lit for the ceremony, the carpenter secretly escapes. His wife brings him whatever he needs for living underground, and he practices calligraphy. She avoids the steward. Exactly one year later, the carpenter reappears with his tools and a document that tells the chief that his father is very happy but now needs a steward for his mansion. The conniving steward never makes it back from his trip to heaven.

CONNECTIONS. Calligraphy. Carpenters. Ceremonies. Chieftains. Cleverness. Death. Deceit. Escapes. Fathers and sons. Filial devotion. Heaven. Husbands and wives. Justice. Mongolian People, stories from. Names. Plots. Problem solvers. Revenge. Rising to the sky world. Sichuan Province, China, stories from. Stewards. Talents. Tibetan People, stories from. Twig Burning Ceremony. Wife-stealing.

HOW ELSE THIS STORY IS TOLD. The Jealous Artist and the Architect — Louise and Yuan-Hsi Kuo, *Chinese Folktales* (from the Mongolian People). The Wise Carpenter — A. L. Shelton, *Tibetan Folk Tales.*

446. Chan's Strategy

S. Y. LuMar, *Chinese Tales of Folklore.* China

Morale is low as Hwei-Yang city is about to be surrounded by the enemy. General Chang Shuen of the Tan Dunasty announces that fresh supplies of food and arrows will be arriving. The skeptical mayor does not know how this can happen, but General Chang tells him to buy straw and hay from the people of the city and to build 1,500 figures in human form. At midnight, General Chang gives the signal for attack. Drums and gongs sound from the lookout tower, and soldiers raise and lower the straw dummies over the city wall for four nights. The enemy camp lets their arrows fly. They hit the straw dummies. General Chang collects all of the arrows before sending the dummies back over the wall. On the fifth night, he sends one thousand young men over the wall to attack. The enemy has not wanted to fall for the trick again, and they are routed sleeping.

CONNECTIONS. Arrows. Chang Shuen, General. Chu-Ko Liang, General. Cleverness. Dummies. Generals. Helpfulness. Hwei-Yang City. Mayors. Problem solvers. Strategy. Straw. Tricksters. War. Yangtze River.

WHERE ELSE THIS STORY APPEARS. One Hundred Thousand Arrows— Frances Alexander, *Pebbles from a Broken Jar.*

HOW ELSE THIS STORY IS TOLD. Borrowing the Enemy's Arrows— Lim Siantek, *More Folk Tales from China.* The Borrowing of 100,000 Arrows— Robert Wyndham, *Tales the People Tell in China.*

447. An Old Horse

Yong-Shen Xuan, *The Dragon Lover.* China

The Lord of Qi and his troops are lost in the deep snows of a mountain range. An advisor suggests that he release one horse. As it finds its way home, they follow.

CONNECTIONS. Advice. Direction. Horses. Nobles and lords. Problem solvers. Warriors. Wisdom.

HOW ELSE THIS STORY IS TOLD. The Horse Who Knew the Way — Gregory Crawford, *Animals in the Stars.*

448. A Lesson Well Learned

George Shannon, *Still More Stories to Solve.* China

Students go to a cave to learn from their wise teacher. He tells them that the lesson is to find a way to make him leave the cave. The first student says that there is a dragon nearby. The second student claims that the emperor will arrest them. The teacher does not leave the cave until the third student says that he is certain that if the teacher were sitting outside, they could get him to go in.

CONNECTIONS. Caves. Cleverness. Humorous stories. Problem solvers. Sages. Students. Tests. Words.

HOW ELSE THIS STORY IS TOLD. *Chinese variations:* The Master and the Disciples—Lim Sian-tek, *Folk Tales from China*. A Merry Prank of Pa-Leng-Ts'ang—M. A. Jagendorf and Virginia Weng, *The Magic Boat*. The Sage in the Cave—Frances Alexander, *Pebbles from a Broken Jar*. **Korean variation:** The Story of Admiral Yi—Zong He-Ryong in Zong In-Sob, *Folk Tales from Korea*.

449. Bokuden and the Bully

Stephen Krensky. Japan

The nobleman Tsukahara often travels disguised as a commoner. He remains silent when a warrior demands that peasants give up their spots to him in a ferry line. He closes his eyes when the warrior flashes his skills with a sword. When the warrior directly confronts Bokuden, the nobleman replies that he sword fights without swords. The warrior challenges him. They row to a nearby island, where Bokuden leaves him and rows away.

CONNECTIONS. Arrogance. Bullies. Cleverness. Disguises. Harmony. Hierarchy. Justice. Nobles and lords. Patience. Peace. Social class. Strategy. Swords. Tricksters. Warriors. Wisdom.

450. O-sung and Han-um

Cathy Spagnoli, *Asian Tales and Tellers*. Korea

O-sung's father is not please to find the new ondal floor pocked with holes. O-sung tells him that it was not his fault as he was chasing a bothersome flea with a drill, and his father says nevertheless the boy will need to be punished. The next day O-sung's father asks him to figure out how many rice grains are in a wooden chest or face punishment. O-sung's friend Han-um comes over, and O-sung forgets all about counting the rice till late. Han-um suggests they fill one cup with rice, count that, and then multiply by how many cups would fit in the chest. This they can accomplish in time. O-sung tells his father the exact number of thousands of grains that are in the chest, and his father rewards the boys' clever thinking.

CONNECTIONS. Boats. Children. Cleverness. Elephants. Fathers and sons. Harmony. Problem solvers. Punishment. Quantity. Ultimatums. Weight.

HOW ELSE THIS STORY IS TOLD. *Chinese variations:* In all three of these, a young boy figures out how to weigh an elephant by placing the elephant on a boat, marking the water line, removing the elephant, and then filling the boat with stones to the same line. *The Emperor's Big Gift*—Dell Britt. How to Weigh an Elephant—Frances Alexander, *Pebbles from a Broken Jar*. Weighing an Elephant—Lim Siantek, *More Folk Tales from China*.

451. The Monkey Keeper

Lieh Tzu in Moss Roberts, *Chinese Fairy Tales and Fantasies*. China

A monkey keeper looks after the welfare of the ten monkeys in his care as if he were their father. One year he cannot give them each the usual eight chestnuts each day. They chitter unhappily when he tells them he will give them each three chestnuts in the morning and four in the afternoon. However, things look much better to the monkeys the next day when he tells them he will give them the usual four chestnuts in the morning PLUS three more in the afternoon.

CONNECTIONS. Acceptance of life's changes. Animal keepers. Changes in attitude. Chestnuts. Cleverness. Food. Harmony. Monkeys and apes. Nuts. Perspective. Problem solvers. Strategy. Quantity. Words.

HOW ELSE THIS STORY IS TOLD. The Monkey and the Chestnuts—Gregory Crawford, *Animals in the Stars*. The Monkey Keeper—Shirley Climo, *Monkey Business*. The Monkey's Ration—*Selected Chinese Fables*. Three Chestnuts or Four—Lie Zi in *Ancient Chinese Tales*.

452. The Tiger's Whisker

Harold Courlander, *The Tiger's Whisker*. Korea

Yun Ok wishes her husband were as loving as before he went to war. She asks the mountain hermit for a special potion. The hermit tells her that he will need the whisker from a tiger. Yun Ok thinks about how she will obtain this. For several days, she approaches close to the tiger's cave with rice and meat sauce. Each day the tiger comes a little closer to the bowl, becoming accustomed to her presence. She speaks softly and, at last, the tiger eats food from her bowl. At the end of six months, the tiger lets Yun Ok pull one of his whiskers. She brings the whisker to the hermit, who horrifies her by dropping it in the fire. Then he suggests she reach her husband with the same patience and understanding.

CONNECTIONS. Advice. Changes in attitude. Harmony. Hermits. Heroes, women. Husbands and wives. Patience. Problem solvers. Strategy. Tibetan People, stories from. Tigers. Trust. Wisdom. Wise man.

WHERE ELSE THIS STORY APPEARS. The Tiger's Whisker—Harold Courlander in Joanna Cole, *Best-Loved Folktales of the World*.

HOW ELSE THIS STORY IS TOLD. **Chinese variation:** Jomo and the Dakini Queen—Naomi C. Rose, *Tibetan Tales for Little Buddhas*. **Korean variations:** The Tiger's Whisker—Anita Stern, *World Folktales*. Yun Ok's Potion—Linda Soon Curry, *A Tiger by the Tail*.

453. The King of the Mountain

Lotta Carswell Hume, *Favorite Children's Stories from China and Tibet*. North China

What can be done when a ferocious tiger, they call King of the Mountain, carries off livestock and children in the valley? Their teacher Lao-tzu tells them that they must understand the tiger. He chooses Wang to go up with him to the tiger's cave with a kid goat, which they leave for the tiger, amid the bones of other animals the King of the Mountain has eaten. Hiding, they see the tiger return and, not finding the kid to be a threat, lick the kid and play with it. Lao-tzu says the village will be safe. Three months later, Wang goes up to the cave and sees that the tiger now has a tiger's head, but the bottom half of him has become a man. The villagers tell him that a half-man, half-snake creature rescued a child from a snake while he was gone. Love has transformed the King of the Mountain. Three months later, Lao-tzu rides down from the sky in a chariot and brings a mysterious young man up with him to the Western Heaven.

CONNECTIONS. Buddhism. Bullies. Changes in attitude. Fear. Goats. Harmony. Hierarchy. Lao-tsu, sage. Love. North China, stories from. Parables. Problem solvers. Rising to the sky world. Sages. Strategy. Taoism. Tigers. Transformation. Western Heaven. Wisdom.

454. The Tiger and the Coal Peddler's Wife

Suzanne Crowder Han, *Korean Folk and Fairy Tales*. Korea

A coal peddler needs to leave his pregnant wife to sell coal many ri away, but a rainstorm delays sales, and he cannot return home. His wife gives birth, and, that same night, their dog has three puppies. Hearing a noise, the woman opens the door, thinking it is her husband, but a large tiger stares at her. She is frightened, but calmly thinks what to do. She grabs one of the new puppies and throws it out the door. The tiger gulps down the puppy and stares at her hungrily. She tosses the tiger another puppy. The tiger still stares hungrily, but she looks around, not wanting to sacrifice the last puppy, and tosses the tiger a hot coal wrapped in cotton instead. The tiger swallows the coal, staggers, and falls over. The next morning, the coal peddler is greatly relieved to find that his wife and new baby are fine.

CONNECTIONS. Babies. Coal. Compassion. Dogs. Fear. Heroes, women. Husbands and wives. Peddlers. Problem solvers. Sacrifice. Strategy. Tigers.

WHERE ELSE THIS STORY APPEARS. The Tiger and the Coal Peddler's Wife — Suzanne Crowder Han in Kathleen Ragan, *Fearless Girls, Wise Women and Beloved Sisters*.

455. The Bad Tiger

Kim So-un, *Korean Children's Favorite Stories*. Korea

A poor old woman invites the tiger who has been eating her radishes to come for red bean gruel and prepares for his arrival. She lights the charcoal brazier, floats hot cayenne pepper in her jug of water, sticks needles in the kitchen towel, scatters cow dung around the kitchen door, spreads a straw mat in the yard, and props a frame upside down against the fence. When the tiger arrives, she asks him to bring in the hot brazier, and he blows ashes into his eyes. This begins a calamitous chain of events for the tiger, from the stinging pepper water he puts on his eyes to the slippery dung. In the end, the mat wraps itself around the tiger, and the clever old woman throws him into the sea.

CONNECTIONS. Ashes. Beetles. Bullies. Consequences. Cooperation. Crabs. Determination. Dung. Eggs. Handre. Heroes, women. Needles. Nung gwama. Pepper. Problem solvers. Revenge. Strategy. Tibetan People, stories from. Tigers. Tricksters.

WHERE ELSE THIS STORY APPEARS. The Bad Tiger — Kim So-un, *The Story Bag*.

HOW ELSE THIS STORY IS TOLD. *Chinese variations:* A Dreadful Boar — Adele Marion Fielde, *Chinese Nights' Entertainment*. The Nung-guama — Leslie Bonnet, *Chinese Folk and Fairy Tales*. The Old Woman and the Tiger —*Folk Tales from China*, Second Series. The Tale of the Nungguama — Wolfram Eberhard, *Folktales of China* and as The Tale of Nung-kua-ma in Kathleen Ragan, *Outfoxing Fear* (here, in this story from Kuangtung, a woman plays tricks on the Nung-kua-ma, a man-eating monster with a body like a bull, a head like a measure of rice, sharp teeth and claws, a hairy coat, and glowing eyes). *The Terrible Nung Gwama*— Ed Young. The Two Little Cats— A. L. Shelton, *Tibetan Folk Tales* (the cats meet a Handre who is going to eat them up in this Tibetan variation, and the other animals help them set a trap). *Korean variations:* The Old Woman and the Tiger — Suzanne Crowder Han, *Korean Folk and Fairy Tales.* The Old Woman and the Tiger — Y.T. Pyun, *Tales from Korea.* The Young Gentleman and the Tiger — GimDu-Ri in Zong In-Sob, *Folk Tales from Korea* (here, a may-beetle, an egg, and a crab help a young man who has been kind to them protect a girl's house from the tiger).

456. The Monkey Bridegroom

Keigo Seki, *Folktales of Japan.* Japan

A monkey helps an old man pull gobo roots with the promise that the old man will give him one of his daughters as a bride. The youngest daughter agrees to go with the monkey if her father will give her a heavy mortar, a heavy maul, and one *to* of rice. The monkey bears this heavy load on his back at his bride's request. At a place where cherry trees bloom at the edge of a canyon, she also asks the monkey to pluck her a branch of blossoms from the very top of the tree. He climbs to please her, but the branch breaks under all his weight, and he is swept away by the river below. The youngest daughter happily returns home.

CONNECTIONS. Cleverness. Fathers and daughters. Heroes, women. Matches, marriage. Mauls. Monkeys and apes. Mortar. Problem solvers. Promises. Rice. Strategy. Supernatural bridegrooms. Supernatural husbands. Weight. Yamagata, Japan, stories from.

WHERE ELSE THIS STORY APPEARS. The Monkey Bridegroom — Keigo Seki in Kathleen Ragan, *Fearless Girls, Wise Women & Beloved Sisters.*

HOW ELSE THIS STORY IS TOLD. The Monkey Son-in-Law — Fanny Hagin Mayer, *Ancient Tales in Modern Japan* (from Yamagata).

457. The Trial of the Stone

S. Y. LuMar, *Chinese Tales of Folklore.* China

Twelve-year-old Wong Lin sells all of his fritters for the day and tucks the money into the greasy cloth in his basket. He sets the basket on a stone to hear a storyteller in a crowd, but when he is ready to leave, his two hundred coins are gone. Wong Lin runs to Magistrate Bao Lung Tu, the renowned judge of Kai Feng in Hunan Province. Wong Lin bows and presents his case. The magistrate pronounces that the stone is the culprit and has it carried to court. The magistrate has the stone flogged with a board for not answering. When the flogging board breaks and the crowd laughs, the magistrate threatens to arrest everyone unless they pay ten coins each. One by one, each person drops coins into a jug full of water. As the last man drops in his coins, a film of oil forms on the surface of the water. The magistrate has this man searched, and the rest of Wong Lin's coins are found.

CONNECTIONS. Children. Coins. Donkeys. Garlic. Guilt. Hunan Province. Hui People, stories from. Humorous stories. Justice. Liaoning Province, China, stories from. Magistrates. Ningxia, China, stories from. Problem solvers. Punishment. Stone. Thieves. Tibetan People, stories from. Zhuang People, stories from.

HOW ELSE THIS STORY IS TOLD. **Chinese variations:** In variations from the Tibetan People, the donkey is also arrested for kicking over some oil that is perched on the accused rock. Bao Gong Tries the Stone — Zhang Ying in Howard Giskin, *Chinese Folktales* (from Liaoning Province). *Donkey and the Rock* — Demi. The Guilty Stone — George Shannon, *Stories to Solve.* Stolen Garlic — Adele Marion Fielde, *Chinese Nights' Entertainment* (the magistrate has the garlic hutch beaten after the garlic is stolen). The Story of the Donkey and the Rock — A. L. Shelton, *Tibetan Folk Tales*. The Trial of the Stone — Lim Sian-tek, *Folk Tales from China*. The Wise Judge — Frances Alexander, *Pebbles from a Broken Jar*. Yimamu Questions a Stone — Ma Chenshan in Shujiang Li and Karl W. Luckert, *Mythology and Folklore of the Hui* (from Ningxia). **Japanese variation:** The Wise Judge — Susan Klein in David Holt and Bill Mooney, *Ready-to-Tell Tales*. **Korean variation:** Trial of the Stone Statue — Suzanne Crowder Han, *Korean Folk and Fairy Tales*.

458. The Thief Who Kept His Hands Clean

Carol Kendall and Yao-wen Li, *Sweet and Sour*. China

In Southern China, Magistrate Chen is famous for his wisdom. One time a constable turns to Chen to help him sort out the suspects' stories in a robbery case. Before he confronts the suspects, Magistrate Chen has firepots set around the bronze bell in the Temple of the Great Buddha. He then swathes the bell in cloth. Minister Chen informs everyone that the bell will ring when a guilty person rubs it. He orders them to reach under the cloth and rub the bell one by one. The bell does not sound at all for any of them, but in the end, only one suspect, scared to touch the bell at all, has no soot at all on his hands.

CONNECTIONS. Bells. Guilt. Humorous stories. Justice. Magistrates. Mysteries. Problem solvers. Soot. Thieves.

HOW ELSE THIS STORY IS TOLD. A Clever Judge — Chang Shih-nan in Moss Roberts, *Chinese Fairy Tales and Fantasies* and in Joanna Cole, *Best-Loved Folktales of the World*. The Magic Bell — S. Y. LuMar, *Chinese Tales of Folklore*. Self-Convicted — Adele Marion Fielde, *Chinese Nights' Entertainment*. Self-Convicted — Tehyi Hsieh, *Chinese Village Folk Tales* (here the guilty man rubs against soot from the walls so that a "god" in the dark cell cannot put his stamp on the back of the criminal).

459. Two Brothers and the Magistrate

Zong In-Mog in Zong In-Sob, *Folk Tales from Korea*. Korea

Two brothers who can read signs in nature and understand the language of birds find a murdered man and are accused of murdering him. The magistrate is unimpressed when they tell him that the crane told them that the murdered man stole eggs from her nest. He is a little more interested when they will not eat or drink, and it turns out to be true that the butcher fed the calf with his wife's milk and the wheat was grown beside a cemetery. Then, the two brothers tell the magistrate that his father was a wandering monk. The magistrate asks his mother, for he thought his father held an official position. She admits that this is true; she dallied with a Buddhist monk when her husband went to Seoul to take the examinations.

CONNECTIONS. Brothers. Cleverness. Language of animals. Magistrates. Mothers and sons. Problem solvers. Truth. Words.

460. One Word Solves a Mystery

George Shannon, *Stories to Solve*. China

A boatman drowns a local merchant who waits for his servant before boarding the vessel. The boatman steals the merchant's goods and then goes to the merchant's house to ask the merchant's wife where her husband might be. The magistrate asks the wife to repeat the sequence of events. She says her husband left, and then the boatman came asking for her. The magistrate now knows that the boatman is guilty. Someone who did not know that the boatman was dead would have come asking to see him.

CONNECTIONS. Boatmen. Deceit. Guilt. Justice. Magistrates. Merchants. Murder. Mysteries. Problem solvers. Words.

HOW ELSE THIS STORY IS TOLD. One Word Solves a Mystery — Chu Yün-ming in Moss Roberts, *Chinese Fairy Tales and Fantasies.*

461. A Wise Judge

Yang Yü in Moss Roberts, *Chinese Fairy Tales and Fantasies.* China

A poor grocer finds fifteen notes of money on his way to the market to buy vegetables. His mother tells him that he must take the money back and see if the owner returns looking for it. The owner of the money does come back, and the grocer hands it over without asking him how much he lost. The owner, a miser, claims that one-half of the money is missing. The case is brought before the country magistrate, who hears everyone's story. The magistrate concludes that because the money the grocer found is a different amount than what the miser claims he lost, it must not then be his money. And the magistrate hands the money back to the poor mother and son.

CONNECTIONS. Grocers. Han People, stories from. Magistrates. Misers. Money. Mothers and sons. Mysteries. Problem solvers. Tibetan People, stories from. Words.

HOW ELSE THIS STORY IS TOLD. The Decision of the Official as to Who Owned the One Hundred Ounces of Silver — A. L. Shelton, *Tibetan Folk Tales.* Fifteen Honest Coins — Louise and Yuan-Hsi Kuo, *Chinese Folk Tales* (from the Han People).

462. Two Mothers

George Shannon, *Stories to Solve.* Tibetan People

To protect her son from the older wife's jealousy, a younger wife gives him to her. However, when their husband dies, the two wives argue over whose child he is. The king decides that they should each hold onto one arm and whoever pulls the strongest will own him. When the boy cries out, the younger wife immediately lets go. The king pronounces her the boy's true mother.

CONNECTIONS. Children. Devotion. Identity. Jealousy. Justice. Kings. Love. Mothers and sons. Problem solvers. Tibetan People, stories from. Truth. Wisdom.

HOW ELSE THIS STORY IS TOLD. **Chinese variations:** The Judge Decides — Lim Sian-tek, *Folk Tales from China.* Like unto Solomon — A. L. Shelton, *Tibetan Folk Tales.* Ooka and the Wasted Widsom — Sharon Creeden, *Fair Is Fair.* **Korean variation:** The True Mother — James Huntley Grayson, *Myths and Legends from Korea.*

463. Umbrellas and Straw Shoes

Suzanne Crowder Han, *Korean Folk and Fairy Tales.* Korea

A woman is worried all of the time. One of her sons sells umbrellas for rain, and the other son sells straw shoes for sunny days. She wants them both earn a good living. A neighbor shows her how to think positively, being happy for one son at a time.

CONNECTIONS. Advice. Changes in attitude. Happiness. Harmony. Mothers and sons. Perspective. Weather. Worry.

464. Making Choices

Selected Chinese Fables. China

Confucius tells the wise teacher Zi Songhu that his friends abandoned him in the states of Lu, Son, and Wei, where he was expelled without achieving his goals. Zi Songhu tells Confucius the story of Lin Hui from Jia who left his jade behind and fled carrying his baby on his back. The teacher says that in challenging times, ties of love bind people together and business ties tend to fall apart.

CONNECTIONS. Abandonment. Confucius, sage. Friendship. Jia, place. Love. Loyalty. Lu, state. Parables. Sages. Son, state. Wei, state. Wisdom. Zi Songhu, sage.

465. The Pear Seed

Sharon Creeden, *Fair Is Fair.* China

A hungry, poor man is caught stealing a pear and brought before the emperor. He offers the emperor a plain brown pear seed, telling him it will grow into a tree that bears golden pears. The emperor orders the man to plant the seed. The man digs a hole, but then stops. He says the magic will only work if the seed is planted by someone who has never stolen, never cheated, or never told a lie. He hands the seed to the emperor who passes it on. No court official feels like he can take responsibility for planting the seed. Seeing this, the emperor lets the prisoner go free.

CONNECTIONS. Emperors. Honesty. Hunger. Justice. Officials. Pears. Poverty. Problem solvers. Seeds. Social class. Tests. Thieves. Tolerance. Wisdom.

HOW ELSE THIS STORY IS TOLD. *Chinese variation:* The Marvelous Pear Seed — Robert Wyndham, *Tales the People Tell in China.* *Korean variation:* The Clever Thief — Joanna Cole, *Best-Loved Folktales of the World.*

466. The Groom's Crimes

Yen Tzu Ch'un Ch'iu in Moss Roberts, *Chinese Fairy Tales and Fantasies.* China

When Lord Ching's favorite horse dies suddenly, he blames the horse's groom and wants to cut off his limbs. Yen Tzu stops him, saying that the wise kings Yao and Shun ruled by their own example. Lord Ching cancels the order. Still, though he condemns the groom to death. Yen Tzu asks Lord Ching if he may inform the groom of his crime before he is killed. He tells the groom that he is guilty of being assigned to care for the horse, caring for a horse that is the king's favorite, and causing the lordship to put a man to death because of a horse, which will weaken him in everyone's eyes. Hearing these "crimes," Lord Ching lets the groom go free.

CONNECTIONS. Changes in attitude. Groom. Guilt. Harmony. Horses. Justice. Kings. Leadership. Nobles and lords. Punishment. Sages. Tolerance. Wisdom. Yen Tzu, sage.

WHERE ELSE THIS STORY APPEARS. The Groom's Crimes— Yen Tzu Ch'un Ch'iu in Joanna Cole, *Best-Loved Folktales of the World.*

467. The Chain

Liu Hsiang in Moss Roberts, *Chinese Fairy Tales and Fantasies.* China

The king of Wu will not allow anyone to criticize his plan to attack the state of Ching. One young man walks in the gardens with his slingshot for three mornings, but does not kill anything. The king questions him. The boy answers that he goes to the tree where the cicada does not know that a praying mantis waits to catch it, and the mantis does not know that an oriole is ready to eat it and the oriole does not know that he stands there with his slingshot. The king of Wu cancels the attack.

CONNECTIONS. Advice. Changes in attitude. Ching, state. Choices. Ch'u, place. Cicadas. Hunters. Kings. Leadership. Peace. Perspective. Praying mantises. Problem solvers. Sparrows. War. Wisdom. Wu, place.

HOW ELSE THIS STORY IS TOLD. *Chinese variations:* The Cicada, the Praying Mantis and the Sparrow — Liu Xiang in *Ancient Chinese Tales.* Plan of Attack — Margaret Read MacDonald, *Three-Minute Tales.* A Prince Went Hunting — Carl Withers, I Saw a Rocket Walk a Mile. The Words and Weapons of Mo Ti — Lim Siantek, *More Folk Tales from China* (Mo Ti and Kung-shu Pan use magical simulation to show the king of Ch'u that the upcoming battle he wants to wage may not go as he plans). *Japanese variation:* You Are Watched — Hiroko Fujita, *Folktales from the Japanese Countryside* (a hunter decides not to shoot).

468. The Gates of Paradise

Paul Rep, *Zen Flesh, Zen Bones.* Japan

A warrior asks Hakuin if paradise and hell really exist. Hakuin shows the warrior hell by first insulting him. The warrior draws his sword. When the warrior understands and sheaths his sword, Hakuin shows him that that is where paradise lies.

CONNECTIONS. Anger. Conflict. Hakuin, sage. Harmony. Heaven. Hell. Parables. Peace. Sages. Self-control. Swords. Warriors. Wisdom.

HOW ELSE THIS STORY IS TOLD. The Gates of Paradise — Margaret Read MacDonald, *Peace Tales.*

Appendix A: Chinese, Japanese, Korean, and Taiwanese Stories Listed by Country

For detailed places and peoples see Subject Index.

Chinese Stories

A San and the Wang Liang
The Adventures of the Stone Monkey
Ah Shung Catches a Ghost
The Ahong Who Saved a Snake
The Alchemist
All the Way to Lhasa
Aniz the Shepherd
Anizu's Magic Wonder Flute
Ants
The Armor-Maker of Ch'u
At the Wrong Post
Auntie Tiger
Auntie Tigress
The Baby Prince Who Was Replaced by a Cat
Backing Up a Story
Bad Luck or Good Luck
Bagged Wolf
Baling with a Sieve
The Ballad of Mulan
The Bank of the Celestial Stream
Bao Gong Tries the Stone
Bawshou Rescues the Sun
The Beautiful Lady in the Moon
The Beautiful Young Woman as the Head of the Family
A Beauty on a Painting Scroll
The Beggar Scholar
The Beggar's Magic: A Chinese Tale
The Bell Goddess
The Betrothal
Big Brother-Man, Little Brother-Rabbit
Big Xue and Silver Bell
The Bird of Happiness
The Bird with Nine Heads
The Bird with Two Heads
The Black Bear and the Fox
The Black General
The Blind Men and an Elephant
The Blue Rose

The Boastful Tortoise
The Borrowing of 100,000 Arrows
Borrowing the Enemy's Arrows
Bowl Mountain
The Boy, His Sisters, and the Magic Horse
The Boy Ssu-ma Kuang
The Boy Who Swallowed Snakes
The Boy with the Magic Brush
A Bride for the River God
The Bride with One Eyebrow
The Bride's Red Silk Handkerchief
The Bridge of Ch'uan-chou
The Bridge of Magpies
The Broken Harp
The Buried Treasure
The Butterfly
The Butterfly Lovers
The Butterfly Robe
A Butterfly's Dream
The Candy Man
Carp Jumping Over the Dragon Gate
Cat and Rat
The Cat and the Mice
The Chachatatutu and the Phoenix
The Chain
Chan's Strategy
Chang Feng
Chang-E Flies to the Moon
The Chao Ku Bird
Chaochou Bridge
Chen Ping and His Magic Axe
Cheng's Fighting Cricket
Chien-Nang
A Chinese Cinderella
The Choosy Maid of Yen-pien
Chu and the King of the Underworld
Chu the Rogue
The Chuang Brocade
The Cicada, the Praying Mantis and the Sparrow
Cinderella

The Clam and the Snipe
The Clever Daughter-in-Law
A Clever Judge
The Clever Red Fox
The Clever Wife
The Clever Woman
Clod's Comb
A Compassionate Scholar and an Ungrateful Wolf
Contentment in Humbleness
Continually Promoted
Cowherd and Girl Weaver
The Cowherd and the Spinning Girl
Cowherd and Weaving Girl
Cowherd and Weaving Maid
The Crane and the Clam
A Crane and Two Brothers
The Cricket
Cricket Boy
Crying Wolf
The Cypress Pillow
Daka and Dalun
A Dancing Crane
The Dancing Yellow Crane
The Dark Maiden from the Ninth Heaven
The Daughter and the Helper
The Daughter of Hsü Hsüan-fang
The Daughter of the Dragon King
The Decision of the Official as to Who Owned the One Hundred Ounces of Silver
The Deluded Thief
The Discovery of Salt
The Disembodied Soul
Disney's Mulan
The Dissatisfied Benefactor
The Dissatisfied Good Man
The Divided Daughter
The Doctor
The Dog's Tale
Donkey and the Rock
The Double-Headed Phoenix

I Want Your Finger
The Inn of the Betrothal
The Invincible Spear Versus the Impenetrable Shield
Iron Crutch and Gold Finger Wang
Isabella and the Magic Brush
The Jackals and the Tiger
A Jar Full of Ants
The Jealous Artist and the Architect
Jomo and the Dakini Queen
The Journey of Meng
Journey to the West
The Judge Decides
The K'un-lun Slave
Keeping a Promise
Keeping One's Word
Kertong
The King and the Poor Man
The King of the Monkey
The King of the Mountain
The King of the Pomegranate Tree
The King's Favorite
Ko-Ai's Lost Shoe
Kuan-yin, Gentle Mother of Mercy
Kung Peng Tah and the Woodcutter
The Lady of the Moon
Lady White Snake
Lady with the Horse's Head
Lao Lai-Tse, the Tactful
The Lazy Farmer
The Leaking Pot
The Legend of Tchi-Niu
The Legend of the Big Bell
The Legend of the Matouqin
The Legend of the Silkworm
The Legend of the White and Black Serpents
The Legend of Wang Xiao
A Lesson Well Learned
Li Chi Slays the Serpent
Li Chi, the Serpent Slayer
Li Jing
Li O Sent Back from the Dead
Liang and the Magic Paintbrush
Liang Shanbo and Ju Yingtai
Liang Shanbo and Zhu Yingtai
Like unto Solomon
Ling-Li and the Phoenix Fairy: A Chinese Folktale
The Lion Tamer
The Little Goddess
The Little Hare's Clever Trick
The Little Prince Ponders
Little Sima and the Giant Bowl
Liu Ch'en and Juan Chao
Living Forever
Living King of Hell Dies of Anger

The Living Kuan-yin
The Lost Sword
A Lover of Dragons
Logic
Lon Po Po: A Red-Riding Hood Story from China
The Long Nose
The Long-Haired Girl
Looking-to-Mother Shoal
Lord of the Cranes
The Lord Who Loved Dragons
The Lost Horse
The Lost Star Princess
The Luminous Pearl
The Lushung Festival
The Man in the Moon
Ma Liang and His Magic Brush
Ma Lien and the Magic Brush
The Magic Pole
The Magic Boat
The Magic at "Grasshopper Inn"
The Magic Bell
The Magic Bird
The Magic Brocade
The Magic Brocade: A Tale of China
The Magic Brush
The Magic Carrying Pole
The Magic Horse of Han Gan
The Magic Kettle
The Magic Melons
The Magic Mirror
The Magic Moneybag
The Magic Pancakes at the Footbridge Tavern
The Magic Pear Tree
The Magic Pillow
The Magic Pot
The Magic Tapestry
The Magical Monkey King: Mischief in Heaven
The Maid in the Mirror
The Maiden in Green
Making Choices
The Making of Monkey King
The Man in a Shell
The Man Who Faked His Music
The Man Who Pretended He Could Play Reed Pipes
The Man Who Sold a Ghost
The Man Who Sold Spears and Shields
Marking the Boat to Locate the Sword
The Marriage of the Cowherd
The Marvelous Pear Seed
The Master and the Disciples 448
Medical Techniques
The Medicine Spring Assembly
Memory Trouble
Meng Jiang Wails at the Great Wall
Meng-Jiang Nyu

The Merchant's Son
A Merry Prank of Pa-Leng-Ts'ang
The Mighty Monkey King
The Mirror
The Miserly Farmer
Miss Lin, the Sea Goddess
The Missing Axe
The Missing Treasure
Money Makes Cares
Monkey
A Monkey and a Tiger
The Monkey and the Turtle
Monkey and the Water Dragon
Monkey and the White Bone Demon
The Monkey Keeper
Monkey King and the Iron Fan Princess
Monkey King Strikes the White-Bone Demon Three Times
The Monkey King Turns the Heavenly Palace Upside Down
Monkey King Wreaks Havoc in Heaven
Monkey That Became King
The Monkey Who Would Be King
The Monkey Wu Kong Learns His Lesson
The Monkey's Ration
The Monkey's Tale
The Monkeys and the Moon
The Monkeys Fish Out the Moon
Monkeys Fish the Moon
Monkeys Fishing the Moon
The Moon Goddess
The Most Frugal of Men
The Mother of Heaven
The Mouse Bride
The Mouse Bride: A Chinese Folktale
Mouse Match
Mulan
Mulan Fights in the Guise of a Male Soldier
Mulan Goes to War
Mulan Saves the Day
Musa
The Musician and the Water Buffalo
Mussels and Snipe
The Mynah Bird
The Mystery Maiden from Heaven
Naxigaer
The Neighbor's Shifty Son
"Never Heard of This Before"
Nezha Fights Sea Dragons
Night Visitors
The Noodle
The North Country Wolf
Number Is Security

The Tale of the Golden Vase and the Bright Monkeys
The Tale of the Magic Green Water-Pearl
The Tale of the Nungguama
The Talking Bird
Tang Monk Disciples Monkey King
A Taoist Priest
Ten Jugs of Wine
Ten Thousand Treasure Mountain
The Terrible Nung Gwama
Theft of a Duck
The Thief Who Kept His Hands Clean
Third Lady of the Wooden Bridge Inn
The Third Son and the Magistrate
The Three Aged Worthies and the Wolf
Three Chestnuts or Four
The Three Families
Three Hundred Yards of Silk That Saved the Devoted Son
Three Magic Charms
Three Treasures
The Tibetan Envoy and the T'ang Dynasty Princess
The Tibetan Envoy
The Tibetan Envoy's Mission
The Tiger and the Frog
The Tiger and the Hare
The Tiger Behind the Fox
The Tiger Finds a Teacher
The Tiger General
The Tiger in Court
The Tiger King's Skin Cloak
The Tiger of Cho-cheng
Tiger Sorrowful
The Tiger, the Deer and the Fox
The Tiger's Tale
Tikki Tikki Tembo
Treasure Mirror
Treasure Mountain
The Treasure of Li-Po
The Trial of the Stone
The Trickster in the Underworld China, Chu the Rogue
A True Money Tree
Tso Ying Tie
Tung Caho-chih and the King of the Ants
Tung Yung, the Filial Son
The Twins of Paikala Mountain
The Two Brothers
Two Dutiful Sons
The Two Fools
The Two Little Cats
The Two Melons
Two Mothers
Two of Everything

The Two Travellers
Two Ways of Cooking the Goose
The Two-Headed Phoenix
The Umbrella Tree
The Unanswerable
Under the Shade of the Mulberry Tree
The Ungrateful Ones
The Unsuccessful Suicide
The Vulnerable Spot
Wagging My Tale in the Mud
The Wait for the Hare
Waiting for a Hare to Turn Up
Waiting for a Rabbit to Bump into a Tree
The Waiting Maid's Parrot
Wang Chih and the Magic Chess Game
A Warning from the Gods
The Water Pearl
The Weaver and the Cowherd
The Weaving of a Dream
The Wedding of the Dragon God
Weighing an Elephant
The Well at the World's End
What Do They Respect?
What's a Life Span?
When Rocks Rolled Crackling Wisdom
Whence Came the Ox?
The White Bird's Wife
White Lady
The White Rooster
White Snake
White Snake and Xuxian
White Wave: A Chinese Tale
The White-Hair Waterfall
The White-Snake Lady
Why the Sun Rises When the Rooster Crows
Why We Have the Ox
Why White Rabbits Have Long Ears and Pink Eyes
Why Zeng Shen Killed the Pig
The Wicked Empress
The Wild Goose Lake
The Wine Bibber
The Wine Well
The Wisdom of the Ants
The Wise Carpenter
A Wise Idiot
A Wise Judge
The Wise Judge
The Wise Ma Tsai
The Wishing Cup
A Wit to Outwit
The Witch's Daughter
The Wolf and the Scholar
The Wolf of Zhongshan Mountain
Wolf-"Mother"

A Woman's Love
Women's Words Part Flesh and Blood
The Wonderful Brocade
The Wonderful Pear Tree
The Wooden Horse
The Words and Weapons of Mo Ti
Xu Xuan and His White-Snake Wife
Xueda and Yinlin
Yee and the Nine Suns
Yeh-hsien
Yeh-Shen: A Cinderella Story from China
Yeshi's Luck
Yimamu Questions a Stone
Yinbolaxi
The Young Head of the Cheng Family
The Young Head of the Family
The Young Man Who Refused to Kill
The Yu Player from the South
Yu the Great Conquering the Flood: A Chinese Legend
Zhuang Brocade
The Zither Master Hasang
The Zither-Met Friends

Japanese Stories

The Accomplished and Lucky Teakettle
The Accomplished and Strange Teakettle
The Adventure of Momotaro, the Peach Boy
The Adventures of a Fisher Lad
The Adventures of Kintaro, the Golden Boy
The Adventures of Little Peachling
The Adventures of Visu
The Advice That Cost a Thousand Ryo
Ama-terasu and Susa-no-o
The Ape and the Crab
Baby Wifie/Akanbo Baasan
The Badger and the Magic Fan
Bamboo Hats and a Rice Cake
The Bamboo Princess
The Bamboo Princess/Kaguya-Hime
The Bamboo-Cutter and the Moon-Child
The Bamboo-Cutter and the Moon-Maiden
The Battle Between the Monkey and the Crab
The Battle of the Ape and the Crab

Sakata-No-Kintoki
The Salt-Grinding Millstones
The Samurai Maiden
The Samurai's Daughter
The Sandal-Seller
The Sandman: The Dream
    Hunters
Sannen Netaro: The Young Man
    Who Slept for Three Years
Sanya Choja
Sara-Sara Yama
Saru Kani Kanen/ The Battle of
    the Monkey and the Crab
Schippettaro
Screen of Frogs
Sea Frog, City Frog
The Sea King and the Magic Jew-
    els
The Sea of Gold
The Sea Palace
Seashore Story
Sedge Hats for Jizo
The Serpent with Eight Heads:
    Yamata no Oroch
She Died Long Ago
The Shining Princess
Shippei Taro
Shippeitarō
Shippeitaro and the Phantom Cats
Shitakiri Suzume : Tongue-Cut
    Sparrow
Sh-Ko and His Eight Wicked
    Brothers
The Shrimp and the Big Bird
The Silence Match
The Silly Jelly Fish
Silly Saburo
The Silver Charm: A Folktale
    from Japan
The Singing Turtle
The Skeleton's Dance
The Skeleton's Song
The Sky Watcher
The Sky-Watcher
The Slaying of the Tanuki
The Slit-Tongue Sparrow
The Snail Choja
The Snake and the Treasure of
    Gold
The Snake Son-in-Law
The Snake Wife
The Snow Monkey and the Boar:
    A Story of Old Japan
The Snow Wife
Snow Woman
The Snow-Bride
The Sparrow with a Broken Back
The Sparrow with the Slit
    Tongue
The Spider Weaver
The Spider Web
The Spirit of the Peony
The Spirit of the Willow Tree

The Star Lovers
The Stepchild and the Flute
The Sticky-Sticky Pine
The Stolen Charm
The Stonecutter: A Japanese Folk
    Tale
The Stone-Cutter
The Stork Wife
The Story of Nezumi No Yomeiri:
    The Marriage of a Mouse
The Story of Bunbuku Chagama,
    the Lucky Cauldron
The Story of Hanasaka Jijii, The
    Flower Blossomer
The Story of Kintaro, the Strong
    Boy
The Story of Kōgi the Priest
The Story of Lazy Taro
The Story of Momotarō, The
    Peach Boy
A Story of Oki Islands
The Story of O-Tei
The Story of Princess Hotoru
The Story of Shitakiri Suzume,
    The Tongue-Cut Sparrow
The Story of Susa, the Impetuous
The Story of Tanabata/Tanabata
    Monogatari
The Story of the Man Who Did
    Not Wish to Die
The Story of the Man Who
    Loved Stories
The Story of the Monkey and the
    Crab
The Story of the Old Man Who
    Had his Wen Taken Off by a
    Goblin
The Story of the Old Man Who
    Made Withered Trees Blossom
The Story of the Old Man Who
    Made Withered Trees to Flower
The Story of Umétsu Chūbei
The Story of Urashima Taro, the
    Fisher Lad
The Story of Urashima Taro the
    Fisherman
The Story of Urashima, the
    Fisher Boy
A Strange Dream
The Straw Cape
The Strongest Wrestler in Japan
The Subjugation of a Ghost
Surprised Twice
Susa-no-o and the Serpent
Sutra of the Mouse
Syrup
The Tale of the Mandarin Ducks
The Tale of the Bamboo Cutter
The Tale of the Oki Islands
The Tale of the Shining Princess
A Tale of Two Tengu
A Tall Tale Contest
Tamamo, the Fox Maiden

Tamanoi, the Jewel Spring
Tanabata
Tasty Baby Belly Buttons
Tawara Toda
Tawara Toda Hidesoto: Hidesoto
    o, the Rice Bale
The Tea-Kettle
The Tea-Kettle of Good-Luck
    Temper
Tengo no KaKuremino
The Tengu's Magic Nose Fan
The Terrible Eeek
The Terrible Black Snake's Re-
    venge
The Terrible Leak
A Test of Love
The Thief Who Took the Money
    Box
The Thief's Gambling
A Thousand Bales of Rope
The Three Brothers Who Grew
    Up in a Year
Three Charms
The Three Lucky Charms
The Three Magic Charms/Taber-
    areta Yamanba
Three Samurai Cats: A Story
    from Japan
Three Strong Women
The Three-Year Sleeping Boy
The Tiny God
To Soothe the Savage Beast
Tokoyo
The Tongue-Cut Sparrow
The Tongue-Cut Sparrow/Shi-
    takiri Suzume
The Toothpick Warriors
Travelers Turned into Horses
The Travels of the Two Frogs
The Triumph of Momotaro
Tsubu the Little Snail
Tsunami
Tsuru no Ongaeshi
The Tug of War
The Two Foolish Cats
The Two Frogs
The Two Stonecutters
The Ugly Son
Umi-Sachi-Hiko and Yama-
    Sachi-Hiko
The Uneatable Pears
The Unfilial Pigeon
The Unfilial Tree Frog
Uraschimataro and the Turtle
Urashima
Urashima and the Tortoise
Urashima Taro
Urashima Taro and the Princess
    of the Sea
Urashima Taro and the Turtle
Urashima the Fisherman
The Vampire Cat
The Vampire Cat — O Toyo

The Vampire Cat of Nabéshima
The Vanishing Rice-straw Coat
The Visit to the Dragon Palace
Visu the Woodsman and the Old Priest
Visu's Return
Wagering on Stopping Bad Habits
Warashibe Choja
The Water That Restores Youth
The Wave
The Wedding of the Mice
The Wedding of the Mouse
What Are You the Most Scared Of?
Whew!
The White Butterfly
The White Hare
The White Hare and the Crocodiles
The White Hare of Inaba
The White Hare of Oki
The White Rabbit and the Crocodiles
Why Is Seawater Salty?
Why the Jellyfish Has No Bones
Why the Jellyfish Has No Shell
The Wife from the Dragon Palace
The Wife from the Sky World
The Wife's Picture
The Wife's Portrait
The Wild Pigeon
Willow Wife
The Wise Judge
The Wise Old Woman
The Wise Old Woman Who Saved the Country in Great Crisis
The Witch's Magic Cloth
The Woman Who Loved a Tree-Spirit
The Wonderful Talking Bowl
The Wonderful Tea-Kettle
The Woodcutter and His Wife
The Wood-Cutter's Sake
The Wooden Bowl
Working the Field
The Wrestler of Kyushu
The Wrestling Match of the Two Buddhas
Yamanba of the Mountain
Yayoi and the Spirit Tree
You Are Watched
The Younger Sister a Demon
Yuki-Onna

Korean Stories

Across the Silvery Stream
Adventures of the Three Sons
The Aged Father
All for the Family Name

Another Tiger by the Tail
The Ant That Laughed Too Much
The Bad Tiger
The Beautiful Tigress
The Bell of Emileh
The Bell Village
A Bit of Shade
The Blind Man and the Devils
The Blind Man's Daughter
Blindman and the Demons
Blindman's Daughter Shim Chung
The Boy Who Cried Tiger Too Often
Bride Island
The Bride's Island
A Bridegroom for Miss Mole
The Bridegroom's Shopping
Butterflies
The Cat and the Dog
The Centipede Girl
Charan
The Charming Flute
The Chinese Mirror
Choon Hyang — Spring Fragrance
Chun Yang, the Faithful Dancing-Girl Wife
The Clam, the Stork, and the Fisherman
Clever Rabbit
The Clever Thief
The Contrary Frog
The Daughter-in-Law Who Broke Wind Frequently
The Deer, the Hare, and the Toad
The Disobedient Frog
The Disowned Student
The Distant Journey
The Dog and the Cat
The Enchanted Wine Jug
The Enchanted Wine-Jug, Or, Why the Cat and Dog Are Enemies
The Eyelash of the Tiger
The Face in the Mirror
The Faithful Daughter Shim Ch'ong
Fate and the Faggot Gatherer
A Father's Pride and Joy
The Fearless Captain
The Fierce Old Dried Persimmon
A Fight between a Centipede and a Toad
The Final Test
The First To Be Served
The Flying Beauty
For the Love of Honey
A Fortune from a Frog
The Fortuneteller and the Demons

The Fountain of Youth
The Four Mighty Brothers
The Four Sworn Brothers
A Fox Deceives a Tiger
The Fox Girl and Her Brother
The Fox Girl
The Fox-Sister and Her Three Brothers
A Frog for a Husband
General Pumpkin
The Ghost's Treasure-Mallet
The Goblins' Magic Stick
The Good Brother's Reward
The Good Neighbor
The Gourd Seeds
A Grain of Millet
The Grateful Ants
The Grateful Ghost
The Grateful Magpies
The Grateful Tiger
The Grave of the Golden Ruler
The Great Flood
The Greedy Princess
The Green Frog
The Green Leaf
The Hare Liver
The Hare's Judgement
The Hare's Liver
Harelip
Hats to Disappear With
Heaven's Reward to a Filial Son
The Heavenly Maiden and the Woodcutter
The Herdsman and the Weaver
The Honey Pot
Hong Kil Tong, Or, the Adventures of an Abused Boy
How Cat Saved the Magic Amber
How Foolish Men Are!
Hwang Jini, The Dancing Girl
In the Moonlight Mist
Janghwa and Hongnyun
K'ongiwi and P'atjwi
Kee-Wee, A Korean Rip Van Winkle
Kim Sondal and the River
The Kindhearted Crab and the Cunning Mouse
The King of the Fish
Kongji and Patji
Kongjui and Patjui
Kongjwi and Padjwi
A Korean Cinderella
Kotgam
Kyŏn-u the Herder and Chik-nyŏ the Weaver
The Land of the Dragon King
The Lazy Man
The Legend of Hong Kil Dong, The Robin Hood of Korea
The Legend of the Sang-Pal-Dam Pools
Lies Rewarded with a Bride

The Long-Nosed Princess
The Love of a Princess
The Love of Two Stars
The Magic Amber
The Magic Cap
The Magic Clothes
The Magic Club
The Magic Gem: A Korean Folk-
  tale About Why Cats and Dogs
  Don't Get Along
The Magic Hammer
The Magic Pot
The Magic Spring
The Magic Vase
The Magpie Bridge
The Mallet of Wealth
The Man Who Became an Ox
The Man Who Lived a Thousand
  Years
The Man Who Saved Four Lives
The Man Who Wanted to Bury
  His Son
Me First
The Mirror
Mister Moon and Miss Sun
The Mole and the Miryek
A Monk Gets a Surprise
The Mountain Witch and the
  Dragon King
The Mourner Who Sang and the
  Nun Who Danced
The Mud-Snail Fairy
My King Has Donkey Ears
Nails
The Noble Tiger
Nolbo and Heungbo
The Nymph and the Woodcutter
The Ogres' Magic Clubs
The Old Tiger and the Hare
The Old Woman and the Tiger
Ondal the Fool
Onions
The Origin of the Sun and the
  Moon
O-sung and Han-um
An Ox for a Persimmon
The Peasant and the Pheasants
The People's Fight
The Pheasants and the Bell
A Pilgrimmage to the Hell
The Plucky Maiden
Poisonous Persimmons
The Pouch of Stories
Practical Jokes of Bong-i Gim-
  sun-dal
Princess Pynonggang and Ondal
  the Fool
The Pumpkin Seeds
The Pumpkin Sparrow
The Queen Swallow's Gift
The Rabbit and Other Legends
The Rabbit and the Dragon King
The Rabbit and the Old Tiger

The Rabbit and the Tiger
The Rabbit That Rode on a Tor-
  toise
Rabbit Visits the Palace of the
  Dragon King
The Rabbit's Eye
The Rabbit's Judgment
The Rabbit's Tail: A Story from
  Korea
The Rabbit's Escape
The Rat's Bridegroom
Reflections
The Revenge of the Huntsman's
  Son
The Revenge of the Serpent
The Right Site
The Rooster and the Centipede
The School-Boy and the Fox
A Selfish Husband
Shade Selling
Silent Debate
Sim Chung, the Dutiful Daughter
Sim Chung, the Loving Daughter
The Singing Lump
Sir One Long Body and Madame
  Thousand Feet
The Six Brothers
The Sky Maiden
The Skybridge of Birds
The Snail Lady
The Snail Woman
The Snake and the Toad
The Son of the Cinnamon Tree
The Son Who Abandoned His
  Father
Son-Nyo the Nymph and the
  Woodcutter
The Sparrow and the Flies
The Sparrow and the Snake
Spring Fragrance
Star-Crossed Lovers
Sticks and Turnips! Sticks and
  Turnips!
The Story Bag
A Story for Sale
The Story of Admiral Yi
The Story of Hong Gil-Dong
The Story of Kim Son-dal
The Story Spirits
The Stubborn Couple
Sun and Moon
The Sun Girl and the Moon Boy
The Sun, the Moon, and the
  Stars
The Swallow Queen's Gift
A Tale for Sale
The Tale of Kongjwi
The Talking Turtle
The Three Brothers' Inheritance
Three Dead Wives
The Three Little Girls
The Three Princesses
The Three Riddles

The Three Sons
The Three Unmarried Ministers
Three Who Found Their Hearts'
  Desires
The Tiger and the Persimmon
The Tiger and the Coal Peddler's
  Wife
The Tiger and the Dried Persim-
  mon
The Tiger and the Dwarf
The Tiger and the Hare
The Tiger and the Rabbit
A Tiger by the Tail
The Tiger Catching Fish
The Tiger Hunter and the Mirror
The Tiger, the Persimmon and
  the Rabbit's Tale
Tiger Woman
The Tiger's Grave
The Tiger's Tail
The Tiger's Whisker
The Tiger-Girl
The Toad Bridegroom
The Toad-Bridegroom
The Tokkaebi's Club
The Tortoise and the Hare
The Traveller and the Tiger
Trial of the Stone Statue
A Trip to Hell and Back
The True Mother
The Turtle and the Rabbit
Two Brothers
Two Brothers and the Magistrate
The Two Brothers
Two Foolish Friends
Two Frogs
Two Kins' Pumpkins
Two Lies
The Two Sisters, Rose and Lotus
Umbrellas and Straw Shoes
The Ungrateful Tiger
The Unmannerly Tiger
The Value of Salt
The Vanity of the Rat
Village of the Bell
The Voice of the Bell
Weaver and Herdsman Chik-
  Nyo and Kyun-Woo
The Weeping Princess
Well of Youth
When the Buddha Wept Blood
Which Was Witch?
While the Axe Handle Rots
Why the Dog and the Cat Are
  Not Friends
Why the Green Frog Croaks
Why the Sea Is Salty
A Wife for a Grain of Millet
The Wife from Another World
The Wonderful Flute
The Woodcutter and the Bird
The Woodcutter and the Dancing
  Tiger

The Woodcutter and the Fairies
The Woodcutter and the Heavenly Maiden
The Woodcutter and the Old Men
You Can't Trust a Woman
The Young Gentleman and the Tiger
Yun Ok's Potion

Taiwanese Stories

The Clam Girl
Curious Taro
The Goofiness of Chen Ah Ai
How Saltwater Came to Fill the Seas
How to Become a Dragon
The Man Who Loved Tiny Creatures

The Much-Deserved Good Fortune of Li Menhuan
The Reward
A Thoroughly Goofy Son-in-Law
The Tiger Witch
Waiting for Rabbits
A Wealthy Landowner, a River Spirit, a City God

Appendix B: Glossary

A selective list of terms not defined by context in the story entries.

Ahong— Name for a Chinese Muslim spiritual leader, especially among the Hui People. Ahongs are responsible for leading religious services and performing religious ceremonies.

Baku— Supernatural dream-eaters of Japanese folklore. Baku spirits have the power to destroy nightmares. They were characteristically portrayed as having an elephant's head, trunk, and tusks, and sometimes, tiger's claws. Modern anime tends to picture them as resembling a tapir.

Biwa— Japanese lute, fretted and with a short neck, a descendant of the Chinese pipa.

Chang'e— Chinese goddess of the Moon.

Choja— Japanese name for a self-made, rich man.

Jikininki— In Japanese Buddhism, this is the ghostly spirit of a person who has been selfish or impious and is now condemned to eat human corpses after he dies. Jikininki are filled with self-loathing at having to do this. By day, they may appear as normal people, but at night they take on the fearsome appearance of a rotting cadaver, sometimes with glowing eyes or animal claws.

Kappa— Supernatural Japanese water imps that swim very well, but may also live on land. Kappa are yellow-green, short, with a beak-like snout, fins on their hands and feet, a shell or fish scales on their backs, and a weakness for cucumbers. The tops of their heads are scooped like a bowl. Kappa retain their supernatural powers only as long as that bowl is full of water. In the folkloric past, kappa had a reputation for both helping people by setting their bones and harming them by dragging them into the water and pulling their livers out through their anuses. Lately, because of their cute images, more lovable kappas are featured in cartoons.

Kitsune— Japanese fox-maidens, who are often seductive shape-shifters.

Koban— Valuable, large, oval gold coins used in the Edo period of feudal Japan

Kun Lun Mountain— Mystical mountain said to be the home of the Taoist gods and site of the palace where the Queen Mother of the West and the Yellow Emperor abide; also known as *Eastern Mountain* and *Mount Tai.*

Mochi— A Japanese cake made of glutinous rice that has been pounded and then molded into an oval shape. Mochi are traditionally eaten for New Year's. *Botamochi* have been only half-pounded and then completely covered with sweet brown azuki/redbean jam. Chinese rice cakes for the lunar New Year are called *niangao.*

Mujina— This shape-shifting raccoon dog (and in some regions, badger) in Japanese tales takes the form of a faceless ghost in Lafcadio Hearn's story.

Nung gwama— A frightening Chinese monster who devours human beings, described by Leslie Bonnet as having "a bull's body, a head as big as a wine jar, and its teeth gritted and its claws twitched."

Oni— Large Japanese ogres or demons with blue, black, or red bodies and horns. They often carry a large iron club and are known for being mean, but not particularly smart.

Ōnyūdō— A legendary Japanese giant with a long, sinuous neck, often depicted with enormous eyeballs, which can bring harm to people merely by looking at them. The onyudo is an elusive, shape-shifter and rarely seen.

Nukekubi— These terrifying Japanese monsters take human form by day. By night, however, nukekubi heads and necks release from their bodies and rise up to fly about biting and eating people. Nukekubi often deceptively live in groups that resemble normal families. According to legend, a nukekubi head must rejoin its body by daybreak.

P'i-p'a— Chinese stringed, pear-shaped wooden lute with a short neck; also spelled *pipa.*

Paduk— Korean name for the Chinese game of Go, a strategic board game played with black and white stones; also spelled *baduk.*

Qin— Former name for the *guqin*; a seven-stringed Chinese musical instrument related to the zither.

Rokurokubi— Japanese name for a female monster with a long, flexible neck that can appear normal by day, but then change at night to spy and frighten humans. To keep their existence secret, Rokurokubi often ply their tricks on drunks, who will not be sure of what they have seen.

Ryō— Japanese coin used during the thirteenth century, based on units of weight from China. At one point the amount of gold in a *koban* was equal to one *ryō*, but this changed as less gold was placed into successive *ryō* mintings.

Tanabata— The Japanese star festival that is also celebrated in China at night on the seventh day of the seventh lunar month, when, according to legend, the Weaver Princess and the Cowherd lovers, cross the Milky Way to meet.

Tanuki— Name for the malevolent shape-changing canine, often described as a badger in the English versions of Japanese and Korean stories. As Fran Stallings writes, "tanuki is tanuki;" it is not a badger or a raccoon dog.

Tengu— There are two kinds of prankish tengu in the mountains of Japan. One is part bird and part human with feathers, wings, and a long beak. The other is red and also has a long nose, which it can fan to make longer or shorter.

Tokkaebi— Mischievous Korean spirits who transform from the ordinary objects people abandon. Tokkaebi often carry clubs or mallets that reward good people and punish the bad. They are also known as *Dokkaebi* and sometimes are one-legged.

Xianqi— A strategic Chinese stone game, similar to Go; also spelled *Changki*.

Xirang— Magical earth given by the Chinese Emperor of Heaven. Pinches are used to build the earth up again where land has been flooded or to create a path through the sea; also spelled *shirang*.

Yamauba— The hag-like, white-haired woman who lives in the mountains in Japanese folklore. She possesses some demon characteristics, like a female oni who devours humans, but may also sometimes be nurturing. By the end of the seventeenth century she became known as the mother of Kintaro, the legendary strong boy and her image was gentled to that of an outsider. She is also known as a mountain-witch-like *yamanba*.

Zither— A stringed musical instrument based on the ancient Chinese guqin, an elongated wooden box strung with seven strings, to produce subtle sound.

Yecha— This Buddhist supernatural creature may be both a man-eating ogre that preys on travelers in the mountains and a nature fairy, looking after the mountains and the forests. It is also known as a yaksha.

Yu— A reed-pipe instrument played in the court orchestras of ancient China

Bibliography

Alexander, Frances, retold by. *Pebbles from a Broken Jar: Fables and Hero Stories from Old China*. Indianapolis/New York: The Bobbs-Merrill Company, Inc., 1967, c1963.

Allen, H. N. *Korean Tales*. New York: G. P. Putnam's Sons, 1889.

Ancient Chinese Fables. Trans. Yang Xianyi and Gladys Yang & others, Illust. Feng Zikai. Beijing: Foreign Languages Press, 1981.

Ashley, Mike, ed. *The Giant Book of Myths and Legends*. New York: MetroBooks, 1995.

Ashliman, D. L. *Folktexts, a Library of Folktales, Folklore, Fairytales, and Mythology*, 2002–8. Online <http://pitt.edu/~dash/folktexts.html>.

Asian Folk Tales. DVD. Weston, Connecticut: Weston Woods/Scholastic, 2008.

Atangan, Patrick. *Silk Tapestry and Other Chinese Folktales*. Graphic novel. New York: NBM Publishers, 2004.

Baltuck, Naomi. *Apples from Heaven: Multicultural Folktales About Stories and Storytellers*. North Haven, Connecticut: Linnet Books, 1995.

Bang, Molly. *Dawn*. New York: William Morrow & Co., 1983.

_____. *The Paper Crane*. New York: HarperCollins, 1985.

Baring, Maurice. *The Blue Rose*. Illust. Anne Dalton. Kingswood: Kaye & Ward, 1982.

Batt, Tanya Robyn. *The Fabrics of Fairytale: Stories Spun from Far and Wide*. Illust. Rachel Griffin. New York: Barefoot Books, 2000.

Bedard, Michael. *The Painted Wall and Other Strange Tales*. Toronto: Tundra Books, 2003.

Berger, Barbara. *All the Way to Lhasa*. New York: Philomel Books, 2002.

Best-Loved Stories Told at the National Storytelling Festival. Introd. by Jane Yolen. Jonesborough, Tennesee: National Storytelling Press, distributed by August House Publishers, Inc., Little Rock Arkansas, 1991.

Birdseye, Tom. *A Song of Stars*. Illust. Ju-Hong Chen. New York: Holiday House, 1990.

Bodkin, Odds. *The Crane Wife*. Illust. Gennady Spirin. New York: Gulliver Books/Harcourt Brace & Company, 1998.

Bonnet, Leslie. *Chinese Folk and Fairy Tales*. Previously published by Curtis Brown, Ltd., London, 1958. Illust. Maurice Brevannes. New York: G. P. Putnam's Sons, 1st Amer. ed., 1963, c1958.

Brown, Brian, ed. & selecter. *Chinese Nights Entertainments: Stories of Old China*. Introd. by Sao-Ke Alfred Sze. New York: Brentano's Publishers, 1922.

Bryan, Ashley, reteller. *Sh-Ko and His Eight Wicked Brothers*. Illust. Fumio Yoshimura. New York: Atheneum, 1988.

Buck, Pearl S., selector. *Fairy Tales of the Orient*. Illust. Jeenyee Wong. New York: Simon and Schuster, 1965.

Carpenter, Frances. *People from the Sky: Ainu Tales from Northern Japan*. Illust. Betty Fraser. Garden City, New York: Doubleday & Company, Inc., 1972.

_____. *Tales of a Chinese Grandmother*. Illust. Malthe Hasselriis. Mattituck, New York: Rivercity Press, 1937.

_____. *Tales of a Korean Grandmother*. Garden City, New York: Doubleday & Company, Inc., 1954.

Casanova, Mary. *The Hunter: A Chinese Folktale*. Illust. Ed Young. New York: Atheneum Books for Young Readers, 2000.

Chamberlain, Basil Hall. *Aino Folk-Tales*. Reprinted by Nendeln/Liechtenstein, Germany: Kraus Reprints Limited, 1967. Introd. by Edward B. Taylor. London: The Folk-Lore Society, 1888.

_____. *Aino Folk-Tales*. Introd. by Christopher M. Weimer, 1888. Internet Sacred Text Archive, 2002. Online <http://www.sacred-texts.com/shi/aft.htm>.

_____. *The Birds' Party*. No. 2 Aino Fairy Tales. Tokyo: T. Hasegawa, 1887.

_____. *The Birds' Party*. Aino Fairy Tales, No. 2, 1887. George C. Baxley, 1999–2008 scan of book published by Hasegawa with original illustrations. Online <http://www.baxleystamp.com/litho/hasegawa/aino_ft_3.shtml>.

_____. *The Hunter in FairyLand*. Aino Fairy Tales, No.1. Tokyo: The Kobunsha/T. Hasegawa, 1887.

_____. *The Hunter in FairyLand*. Aino Fairy Tales, No.1. Online <http://www.baxleystamps.com/litho/hasegawa/aino_ft_1.shtml>: George C. Baxley, 1999–2008 scan of book published by Hasegawa, with original illustrations, 1887.

_____. *The Man Who Lost His Wife*. No. 3 Aino Fairy Tales, 1889. George C. Baxley, 1999–2008 scan of book published by Hasegawa with original illustrations. Online <http://www.baxleystamp.com/litho/hasegawa/aino_ft_3.shtml>.

_____. *The Man Who Lost His Wife*. No. 3 Aino Fairy Tales. Tokyo: The Kobunsha/T. Hasegawa, 1889.

_____. *My Lord Bag-O'-Rice*. Japanese Fairy Tale Series, No. 15. Tokyo: The Kobunsha/T. Hasegawa, 1887.

_____. *The Serpent with Eight Heads: Yamata no*

Orochi. Japanese Fairy Tale Series, No. 9. Tokyo: The Kobunsha/T. Hasegawa, 1886.

_____. *The Silly Jelly-Fish*. Japanese Fairy Tale Series, No. 13. Tokyo: The Kobunsha/T. Hasegawa, 1887.

Chang, Isabelle C. *Tales from Old China*. New York: Random House, 1969.

Chang, Margaret S. and Raymond Chang. *The Beggar's Magic: A Chinese Tale*. David A. Johnson. New York: Simon & Schuster, 1997.

Chang, Monica, reteller. *The Mouse Bride: A Chinese Folktale*. Bilingual. Illust. Lesley Liu. Taipei, Taiwan: Pan Asian Publications, 1994.

_____, reteller. *Story of the Chinese Zodiac*. Bilingual. Illust. Arthur Lee, trans. Rick Charette. Taipei, Taiwan: Yuan-Liou Publishing Co., Ltd., 1994.

Chen, Debby, reteller. *Monkey King Wreaks Havoc in Heaven*. Bilingual. Illust. Wenhai Ma. Adventures of Monkey King 2. Union City, California: Pan Asian Publications, 2001.

_____, reteller. *Tang Monk Disciples Monkey King*. Bilingual. Illust. Wenhai Ma. Adventures of Monkey King 3. Union City, California: Pan Asian Publications, 2005.

Chen, Jiang Hong. *The Magic Horse of Han Gan*. Trans. Claudia Zoe Bedrick. New York: Enchanted Lion Books, 2006.

Chen, Kerstin. *Lord of the Cranes*. Trans. J. Alison James, Illust. Jian Jiang Cheng. New York: North-South Books, Inc., 2000.

Cheney, Cora. *Tales from a Taiwan Kitchen*. New York: Dodd, Mead, 1976.

Cheng, Hou-tien. *Six Chinese Brothers: An Ancient Tale*. New York: Holt Rinehart & Winston, 1979.

Chin, Yin-lien C., Yetta S. Center, and Mildred Ross. *Chinese Folktales: An Anthology*. Illust. Lu Wang. Armonk, New York: North Castle Books, 1989.

_____. *Traditional Chinese Folktales*. Illust. Lu Wang. Armonk, New York/London: M.E. Sharpe, Inc., 1989.

Chinese Traditional Tales. Online <http://enargea.org/tales/Chinese/sinolist.html>: The Tent Archive: Texts and Explorations of Narrative Tradition, 1998–2008.

Ching, Emily and Ko-Shee Ching. *Golden Needles; Three Treasures*. Bilingual. Cerritos, California: Wonder Kids Publications, English ed., 1991; Chinese ed., 1988.

_____. *Lugging Mountains; What's a Life Span?* Bilingual. Cerritos, California: Wonder Kids Publications, English ed., 1991; Chinese ed., 1988.

_____. *Sun Mountain; A Stone Carver's Dream*. Bilingual. Cerritos, California: Wonder Kids Publications, English ed., 1991; Chinese ed., 1988.

_____. *Sun Valley; A Stone Carver's Dream*. Bilingual. Cerritos, California: Wonder Kids Publications, English ed., 1991; Chinese ed., 1988.

Ching, Emily, Ko-Shee Ching, and Theresa Austin, eds. *The Refugee Empress; Chi Jiguang Cookies*. Bilingual. Cerritos, California: Wonder Kids Publications, English ed., 1991; Chinese ed., 1988.

Choi, Yangsook. *The Sun Girl and the Moon Boy: A Korean Folk Tale*. New York: Knopf Books for Young Readers, 1997.

Chun, Shin-Yong, general ed., Kim Yol-Gyu, ed. *Korean Folk Tales*. Bilingual. Trans. Tae-Dong Lee and Dolores Geier. Seoul: International Cultural Foundation, 1979.

Climo, Shirley. *The Korean Cinderella*. Illust. Ruth Heller. New York: HarperCollins Publishers, 1993.

_____. *Monkey Business: Stories from Around the World*. Illust. Erik Brooks. New York: Henry Holt & Company, 2005.

_____. *Someone Saw a Spider*. Illust. Dirk Zimmer. New York: Crowell/HarperCollins Publishers, 1985.

_____, reteller. *A Treasury of Mermaids: Mermaid Tales from Around the World*. Illust. Jean and Mou-sien Tseng. New York: HarperCollins Publishers, 1997.

Cole, Joanna, selector. *Best-Loved Folktales of the World*. Illust. Karla Schwarz. New York: Doubleday, 1982.

Compton, Patricia A. *The Terrible Eeek*. Illust. Sheila Hamanaka. New York: Harcourt Brace & Company, 1991.

Cook, Joel. *The Rats' Daughter*. Honesdale, Pennsylvania: Caroline House/Boyds Mills Press, Inc., 1993.

Courlander, Harold. *The Tiger's Whisker and Other Tales from Asia and the Pacific*. Illust. Enrico Arno. New York: Henry Holt and Company ; 1959 ed. published by Harcourt Brace & World, 1995, c. 1987.

Crawford, Gregory. *Animals in the Stars: Chinese Astrology for Children*. Rochester, Vermont: Bear Cub Books, 2002.

Creeden, Sharon. *Fair Is Fair: World Folktales of Justice*. Little Rock, Arkansas: August House Publishers, Inc., 1994.

Curry, Lindy Soon. *A Tiger by the Tail and Other Stories from the Heart of Korea*. World Folklore Series. Ed. Chan-eung Park. Englewood, Colorado: Libraries Unlimited, 1999.

Davis, F. Hadland. *Myths and Legends of Japan*. Illust. Evelyn Paul. New York: Thomas Y. Crowell Company, Publishers; republished by Dover in 1992, 1912.

Davison, Gary Marvin, reteller. *Tales from the Taiwanese*. World Folklore Series. Westport, Connecticut: Libraries Unlimited, 2004.

Demi. *Chen Ping and His Magic Axe*. New York: Dodd, Mead & Company, 1987.

_____. *Donkey and the Rock*. New York: Henry Holt & Company, 1999.

_____. *The Dragon's Tale and Other Animal Fables of the Chinese Zodiac*. New York: Henry Holt & Company, Inc., 1996.

_____. *The Empty Pot*. New York: Henry Holt & Company, 1990.

_____. *The Greatest Treasure*. New York: Scholastic Press, 1998.

_____. *Liang and the Magic Paintbrush*. New York: Holt, 1980.

_____. *The Magic Boat*. New York: Henry Holt & Company, 1990.

_____. *The Magic Tapestry*. New York: Henry Holt & Company, 1994.

_____. *The Stonecutter*. New York: Crown, 1995.

_____. *Under the Mulberry Tree*. Englewood Cliffs, New Jersey: Prentice-Hall, Inc., 1979.

Denman, Cherry. *The Little Peacock's Gift.* New York: Bedrick/Blackie, 1987.

DeSpain, Pleasant. *Thirty-Three Multicultural Tales to Tell.* Illust. Joe Shlichta. Little Rock, Arkansas: August House, 1993.

Dorson, Richard M. *Folk Legends of Japan.* Illus Yoshie Noguchi. Rutland, Vermont: Charles E. Tuttle Company, Inc., 1962.

_____. *Folktales Told Around the World.* Chicago: University of Chicago Press, 1975.

Dragon Tales: A Collection of Chinese Stories. Beijing: Panda Books/Chinese Literature Press, 1990.

Eberhard, Wolfram. *Folktales of China.* Folktales of the World. London: Routledge and Kegan Paul, LTD, 1965, rev. ed.

Eleven Nature Tales: A Multicultural Journey. Little Rock, Arkansas: August House, Inc., 1996.

Faye, Fernandez, adapter. *The Man Who Did Not Wish to Die.* Adapted from folktale by Yei Theodora Ozaki, Downloadable audio (New York Public Library). Prod. Kerplunk Studios, Read by Richard Joson. Hong Kong: Wualou Ltd., 2005.

Fielde, Adele Marion. *Chinese Nights' Entertainment: Forty Stories Told by Almond-Eyed Folk Actors in the Romance of the Strayed Arrow.* New York: G. P. Putnam's Sons, 1893.

Fisher, Sally. *The Tale of the Shining Princess.* Trans. Donald Keene. New York: The Metropolitan Museum of Art and a Studio Book/The Viking Press, 1980.

Folk Tales from China, First Series. Peking: Foreign Languages Press, 1957.

Folk Tales from China, Second Series. Reissued as The Water-Buffalo and the Tiger: Folk Tales from China. Illust. Mi Ku, trans. Gladys Yang. Peking: Foreign Language Press, 1958.

Folk Tales from China, Third Series. Illust. Cheng Shih-fa. Peking: Foreign Language Press, 1958.

Folk Tales from China, Fourth Series. Peking: Foreign Languages Press, 1960.

Folk Tales from China, Fifth Series. Peking: Foreign Languages Press, 1960.

Forest, Heather. *Wisdom Tales from Around the World.* Little Rock, Arkansas: August House, 1996.

Fregos, Claudia. *The Pumpkin Sparrow.* New York: Greenwillow Books, 1977.

French, Fiona. *Little Inchkin.* New York: Dial Books for Young Readers, 1994.

The Frog Rider; Folk Tales from China. Beijing: Foreign Languages Press, 3rd ed.1980.

Fu, Shelley. *Ho Yi the Archer and Other Classic Chinese Tales.* Reprinted as Treasury of Chinese Folktales, Tuttle Publishing, 2008. Joseph F. Abboreno and Chinese calligraphy by Sherwin Fu. North Haven, Connecticut: Linnet Books, 2001.

_____. *Treasury of Chinese Folk Tales: Beloved Myths and Legends from the Middle Kingdom.* A reprint of Ho Yi the Archer, with new illustrations. Illust. Patrick Yee. Rutland, Vermont: Tuttle Publishing, 2008.

Fujika, Hiroko. *Folktales from the Japanese Countryside.* World Folklore Series. Ed. Fran Stallings. With Harold Wright and Miki Sakurai. Westport, Connecticut: Libraries Unlimited, 2008.

Gaiman, Neil, and Yoshitaka Amano. *The Sandman: The Dream Hunters.* New York: DC Comics, 1999.

Giles, Herbert A. *Chinese Fairy Tales, Told in English.* London: Gowand & Gray, LTD, 1911.

Ginsburg, Mirra. *The Chinese Mirror.* Illust. Margot Zemach. Orlando, Florida: Gulliver Books/Harcourt Brace Jovanovich, 1988.

Giskin, Howard. *Chinese Folktales.* Lincolnwood, Illinois: NTC Publishing Group, 1997.

Grayson, James Huntley. *Myths and Legends from Korea: An Annotated Compendium of Ancient and Modern Materials.* Richmond, Surrey: Curzon, 2001.

Greene, Ellin. *Ling-Li and the Phoenix Fairy: A Chinese Folktale.* Illust. Zong-Zhou Wang. New York: Clarion Books, 1996.

Griffis, William Elliot. *The Fire-Fly's Lovers and Other Fairy Tales of Old Japan.* New York: T.Y. Crowell & Co. Publishers, 1908.

_____. *The Unmannerly Tiger and Other Korean Tales.* New York: Thomas Y. Crowell Company, 1911.

Ha, Tae Hung. *Folk Tales of Old Korea.* Seoul: Yonsei University Press, 1958.

Hamanaka, Sheila. *Screen of Frogs.* New York: Orchard Books, 1993.

Han, Carolyn. *Why Snails Have Shells: Minority and Han Folktales of China.* Illust. Li Ji, trans. Jay Han. Honolulu: University of Hawaii Press, 1993.

Han, Suzanne Crowder. *Korean Folk and Fairy Tales.* Elizabeth, New Jersey & Seoul, Korea: Hollym Corporation, 1991.

_____. *The Rabbit's Escape.* Bilingual. Illust. Yumi Heo. New York: Henry Holt & Company, 1995.

_____. *The Rabbit's Judgment.* Bilingual. Illust. Yumi Heo. New York: Henry Holt & Company, 1994.

_____. *The Rabbit's Tail: A Story from Korea.* Bilingual. Illust. Richard Wehrman. New York: Henry Holt & Company, 1999.

Hana Saki Jiji / The Old Man Who Made Trees Blossom. Trans. David Thompson, Illust. Eitaku. Japanese Fairy Tale Series. Tokyo: Kobunsha, 1885.

Hao, Kuang-Tsai, reteller. *Seven Magic Brothers.* Illust. Eva Wang, trans. Rick Charette. Taipei, Taiwan: Yuan-Liou Publishing, Ltd., 1994.

The Hare of Inaba. Japanese Fairy Tale Series, #11. Tokyo: T. Hasegawa Publisher & Art-Printer, 1898.

Harris, Rosemary. *The Child in the Bamboo Grove.* Illust. Errol Le Cain. New York: S. G. Phillips, 1971.

Haviland, Virginia. *Favorite Fairy Tales Told in Japan.* Illust. George Suyeoka. Boston:: Little Brown and Company, 1967.

He, Liyi, trans. *The Spring of Butterflies and Other Folk Tales of China's Minority Peoples.* First published 1985 William Collins Sons & Co. Ltd, Great Britain. Ed. Neil Philip. Illust. Pan Aiqing and Li Zhao. New York: Lothrop, Lee & Shepard Books, 1986.

He, Xuejun. *Liang Shan Bo and Zhu Ying Tai : The Butterfly Lovers.* Bilingual. Illust. Yan Baozhen. Taipei: Sharp Point Publishing Co. Ltd., 1995.

Hearn, Lafcadio. *The Boy Who Drew Cats.* Japanese Fairy Tale Series, No. 23. Tokyo: T. Hasegawa Publisher & Art-Printer, 1898.

_____. *The Boy Who Drew Cats.* Japanese Fairy Tale

Series, No. 23, 1898. George C. Baxley, 1999–2008 scan of book published by Hasegawa, with original illustrations. Online <http://www.baxleystamps.com/litho/hasegawa/cats.shtml>.

_____. *The Boy Who Drew Cats and Other Japanese Fairy Tales*. Illust. Yuko Green. Mineola, New York: Dover, 1998.

_____. *Chin Chin Kobakama*. Japanese Fairy Tale Series No. 25, 1903. George C. Baxley, 1999–2008 scan of book published by Hasegawa, with original illustrations. Online <http://www.baxleystamps.com/litho/hasegawa/ft_25.shtml>.

_____. *Chin Chin Kobakama*. Japanese Fairy Tale Series No. 25. Tokyo: T. Hasegawa Publisher & Art-Printer, 1903.

_____. *Earless Ho-Ichi: A Classic Japanese Tale of Mystery*. Illust. Masakuzu Kuwata, Introd. by Donald Keene. Tokyo: Kodansha International, 1966.

_____. *Fountain of Youth*. Japanese Fairy Tale Series. Tokyo: T. Hasegawa Publisher & Art-Printer, 1922.

_____. *Fountain of Youth*. Japanese Fairy Tale Series, 1925 ed. George C. Baxley, 1999–2008 scan of book published by Hasegawa, with original illustrations. Online <http://www.baxleystamps.com/litho/hasegawa/hearn_fountain_1925.shtml>.

_____. *The Goblin-Spider*. Japanese Fairy Tales, Second Series No. 1, 1898. George C. Baxley, 1999–2008 scan of book published by Hasegawa, with original illustrations. Online <http://www.baxleystamps.com/litho/hasegawa/spider.shtml>.

_____. *The Goblin-Spider*. Japanese Fairy Tales, Second Series No. 1. Tokyo: T. Hasegawa Publisher & Art-Printer, 1898.

_____. *Japanese Fairy Tales*. Illust. Valenti Angelo, prologue by Edward Laroque Tinker. Mount Vernon, New York: The Peter Pauper Press, 1936.

_____. *A Japanese Miscellany: Strange Stories, Folklore Gleanings, Studies Here and There*. New York: ICG Muse, Inc., 2001.

_____. *Kwaidan: Stories and Studies of Strange Things*. Boston: Houghton Mifflin Company, 1904.

_____. *Kwaidan: Three Japanese Ghost Stories*. Videorecording. Prod. executive producer Cheryl Henson, Leslee Asch, Dir. presented by The Center for Puppetry Arts and Ping Chong & Company and Ping Chong, based on the book by Lafcadio Hearn. International Festival of Puppet Theater. New York: Character Generators, Inc., 1998.

_____. *The Old Woman Who Lost Her Dumpling*. Japanese Fairy Tale Series. Tokyo: T. Hasegawa Publisher & Art-Printer, 1902, c.1898.

_____. *The Old Woman Who Lost Her Dumpling*. Japanese Fairy Tale Series, 1902, c.1898. George C. Baxley, 1999–2008 scan of book published by Hasegawa, with original illustrations. Online <http://www.baxleystamps.com/litho/hasegawa/ft_24a_dumpling.shtml>.

_____. *The Writings of Lafcadio Hearn*. Boston: Houghton Mifflin Company, 1922.

Hearn, Lafcadio and Others. *Japanese Fairy Tales*. Illust. Kay. New York: Liveright Publishing Corporation, 1953.

Heyer, Marilee. *The Weaving of a Dream*. New York: Viking Kestrel, 1986.

Hodges, Margaret. *The Boy Who Drew Cats*. Illust. Aki Sogabe. New York: Holiday House, 2002.

_____. *The Wave*. Illust. Blair Lent. Boston: Houghton Mifflin Company, 1964.

Holstein, John. *All for the Family Name*. Bilingual. Illust. Kim Kwang-bae. Korean Folk Tales. 6. Seoul: Si-sa-young-o-sa, Inc., 1985.

_____. *A Father's Pride and Joy*. Bilingual. Illust. Kim Hee-joon. Korean Folk Tales. 2. Seoul: Si-sa-young-o-sa, Inc., 1985.

_____. *Harelip*. Bilingual. Illust. Kim Chun-jong. Korean Folk Tales. 4. Seoul: Si-sa-young-o-sa, Inc., 1985.

_____. *Konjui and Patjui*. Bilingual. Illust. In-Choon Kang. Korean Folk Tales. Seoul: Si-sa-young-o-sa, Inc., 1985.

_____. *The Magpie Bridge*. Bilingual. Illust. Joo Young-bok. Korean Folktales. 5. Seoul: Si-sa-young-o-sa, Inc., 1985.

_____. *The People's Fight*. Bilingual. Illust. Choi Choong-hoon. Korean Folk Tales. 7. Seoul: Si-sa-young-o-sa, Inc., 1985.

_____. *Two Kins' Pumpkins*. Bilingual. Illust. Lee Woo-bum. Korean Folk Tales. 1. Seoul: Si-sa-young-o-sa, Inc., 1985.

Holt, David, and Bill Mooney, editors. *More Ready-to-Tell Tales: Sure-Fire Stories from America's Favorite Storytellers*. Little Rock, Arkansas: August House Publishers, Inc., 1995.

_____. *Ready-to-Tell Tales: Sure-Fire Stories from America's Favorite Storytellers*. Little Rock, Arkansas: August House Publishers, Inc., 1994.

Hong, Lily Toy. *How the Ox Star Fell from Heaven*. Morton Grove, Illinois: Albert Whitman, 1991.

_____. *Two of Everything: A Chinese Folktale*. Morton Grove, Illinois: Albert Whitman, 1993.

Horio, Seishi. *The Mouse's Wedding/Nezumi no Yomeiri*. Bilingual story cards. Illust. Masao Kubo. New York: Kamishibai for Kids, Accessed 2008.

Horowitz, Anthony. *Myths and Legends*. New York: Kingfisher Books, 1994.

Hou, Guanbin. *The Monkeys Fish Out the Moon: Xiao Hou Zi Lao Yue Liang*. Bilingual. Beijing: Dolphin Books/China International Publishing Group, 2006.

Hua Long, adaptators and illustrators. *The Moon Maiden and Other Asian Folktales*. Members of the Hua Long collective. San Francisco: China Books and Periodicals, 1993.

Hughes, Monica. *Little Fingerling: A Japanese Folk Tale*. Brenda Clark. Toronto: Kids Can Press Ltd., 1989.

Hume, Lotta Carswell. *Favorite Children's Stories from China and Tibet*. Illust. Lo Koon-chiu. Rutland, Vermont: Charles E. Tuttle Company, 1962.

Hurt, William, narrator. *The Boy Who Drew Cats*. DVD. Illust. David Johnson, music by Mark Isham. Rabbit Ears Storybook Collection. Chicago, Illinois: Clearvue & SVE, 1991.

Hyde-Chambers, Frederick, and Audrey Hyde-Chambers. *Tibetan Folk Tales*. Boulder, Colorado: Shambhala Publications, 1981.

Im Bang and Yi Ryuk. *Korean Folk Tales: Imps, Ghosts*

and Fairies. Trans. James S. Gale. New York: J.M. Dent & Sons, 1913.

Inaba no Shiro-Usagi / The Hare of Inaba. Trans. David Thompson, Illust. Eitaku. Japanese Fairy Tale Series. Tokyo: Kobunsha, 1886.

Isabella and the Magic Brush. 16 mm film. Dir. B. Doumashkin. Studio City, California: FilmFair.

Ishii, Momoko, reteller. *The Tongue-Cut Sparrow*. Illust. Suekichi Akaba. New York: Lodestar Books/ E.P. Dutton, 1982.

Isubota, Joji. *The One-Inch Boy/Issun-Boshi*. Bilingual story cards. Illust. Hisao Suzuki. New York: Kamishibai for Kids, Accessed 2008.

Iwasaki, Kyoko. *The Bamboo Princess/Kagua-Hime*. Bilingual story cards. Illust. Teruyo Endo. New York: Kamishibai for Kids, Accessed 2008.

Jagendorf, M.A., and Virginia Weng. *The Magic Boat and Other Chinese Folk Stories*. Illust. Wan-go Weng. New York: The Vanguard Press, 1980.

James, Grace. *Green Willow and Other Japanese Fairy Tales*. Illust. Warwick Goble. London: Macmillan & Co, Limited, 1926.

James, T. H. *The Cub's Triumph*. Japanese Fairy Tale Series No. 12. Tokyo: T. Hasegawa Publisher & Art-Printer, 1898.

_____. *The Matsuyama Mirror*. Japanese Fairy Tale Series No. 10. Tokyo: T. Hasegawa Publisher & Art-Printer, 1898.

_____. *Three Reflections*. Japanese Fairy Tale Series No. 21. Tokyo: T. Hasegawa Publisher & Art-Printer, 1898.

_____. *The Wooden Bowl*. Japanese Fairy Tale Series No. 16. Tokyo: T. Hasegawa Publisher & Art-Printer, 1898.

Jennings, Linda, selector. *Stories from Around the World*. Boston: Kingfisher, 1993.

Jewett, Eleanore Myers. *Which Was Witch? Tales of Ghosts and Magic from Korea*. Illust. Taro Yashima. New York: The Viking Press, 1959.

_____. *Wonder Tales from Tibet*. Illust. Maurice Day. Boston: Little, Brown, and Company, 1922.

Jiang, Ji-li. *The Magical Monkey King: Mischief in Heaven*. Illust. Hui Hui Su-Kennedy. New York: HarperCollins Publishers, 2002.

Jin Shoushen. *Beijing Legends*. Beijing: Panda Books, 1982.

Johnston, Tony. *The Badger and the Magic Fan*. Illust. Tomie DePaola. New York: G. P. Putnam's Sons, 1990.

Journey to the Sun: Folk Tales from China. Beijing: Foreign Languages Press, 1984.

Junne, I.K., ed. *Floating Clouds, Floating Dreams: Favorite Asian Folktales*. Garden City, New York: Doubleday & Company, Inc., 1974.

Kachi-Kachi-Yama / Kachi-Kachi Mountain. Trans. David Thompson, Illust. Eitaku. Japanese Fairy Tale Series. Tokyo: Kobunsha, 1886.

Kamichi, Chizuko. *How the Years Were Named/ Rainen Wa Nanidoshi*. Bilingual story cards. Illust. Yuko Kanazawa. New York: Kamishibai for Kids.

Kao, Karl S. Y., editor. *Classical Chinese Tales of the Supernatural and the Fantastic: Selections from the Third to the Tenth Century*. Bloomington, Indiana: Indiana University Press, 1985.

Kawabata, Yasunari. *The Tale of the Bamboo Cutter*. Bilingual. Trans. Donald Keene, Illust. Masayuki Miyata. New York: Kodansha International, 1998.

Kawasaki, Daiji. *Baby Wifie/Akanbo Baasan*. Bilingual story cards. Illust. Yuko Kanazawa. New York: Kamishibai for Kids.

_____. *The Old Man and the Mice/Nezumi Choja*. Bilingual story cards. Illust. Masao Kubo. New York: Kamishibai for Kids.

Kendall, Carol and Yao-wen Li. *Sweet and Sour: Tales from China*. Illust. Shirley Felts. New York: Houghton Mifflin/Clarion Books, 1978.

Kherdian, David. *Feathers and Tails*. Illust. Nonny Hogrogian. New York: Philomel Books, 1992.

Kids Web Japan. Japanese Ministry of Foreign Affairs, Illust. Yamada Chitose. Japan Echo Inc. Online <http://web-Japan.org/kidsweb/folk> Accessed 2008.

Kim, So-un. *Korean Children's Favorite Stories*. Previously published as The Story Bag, Tuttle, 1955. Illus Kyoung-Sim Jeong. Rutland, Vermont: Tuttle Publishing, 2004.

_____. *The Magic Gem: A Korean Folktale About Why Cats and Dogs Don't Get Along*. Illus Kyoung-Sim Jeong. Rutland, Vermont: Tuttle Publishing, 2006.

_____. *The Story Bag: A Collection of Korean Folk Tales*. Reprinted as Korean Children's Favorite Stories. Illus Kyoung-Sim Jeong. Rutland, Vermont: Charles E. Tuttle Co., 1955.

Kajikawa, Kimiko. *Tsunami*. Illust. Ed Young. New York: Philomel, 2009.

Kimishima, Hisako. *Ma Lien and the Magic Brush*. English trans Alvin Tresselt. New York: Parents' Magazine Press, 1968.

Kimmel, Eric A., retold by. *The Greatest of All: A Japanese Folktale*. Illust. Giora Carmi. New York: Holiday House, 1991.

_____, retold by. *Three Samurai Cats: A Story from Japan*. Illust. Mordicai Gerstein. New York: Holiday House, 2003.

Kirollos, Samira, reteller. *The Wind Children and Other Tales from Japan*. London: Andre Deutsch Limited, 1989.

Kobutori/The Old Man and the Devils. Trans. David Thompson, Illust. Eitaku. Japanese Fairy Tale Series. Tokyo: Kobunsha, 1886.

Kowallis, Jon. *Wit and Humor of Old Cathay*. San Francisco: Chinese Literature Press, 1984.

Krasno, Rena, and Yeng-Fong Chiang. *Cloud Weavers: Ancient Chinese Legends*. Berkeley, California: Pacific View Press, 2003.

Kraus, Robert, and Debby Chen, retellers. *The Making of Monkey King*. Bilingual. Illust. Wenhai Ma. Adventures of Monkey King 1. Union City, California: Pan Asian Publications, 1998.

Krensky, Stephen. *Bokuden and the Bully*. On My Own Folklore. Illust. Cheryl Kirk Noll. Millbrook Press, In press, 2008.

Krulik, Nancy E. *Mulan Saves the Day*. Illust. Atelier Philippe Harchy. New York: Disney Press, 1998.

Kuo, Louise and Yuan-Hsi. *Chinese Folk Tales*. Millbrae, California: Celestial Arts, 1976.

Kwan, Michael David. *The Chinese Storyteller's Book: Supernatural Tales*. Rutland, Vermont: Tuttle Publishing, 2002.

The Lady in the Picture: Chinese Folklore. Beijing: Chinese Literature Press, 1993.

Lang, Andrew. *The Green Fairy Book*. Ed. Brian Alderson. Illust. Antony Maitland. New York: Kestrel Books/Viking Press; originally published by Longmans, Green with different illustrations in 1906, 1978.

_____. *The Pink Fairy Book*. Ed. Brian Alderson. New York: The Viking Press, 1982.

_____. *The Rainbow Fairy Book*. Illust. Michael Hague. New York: William Morrow & Company; also published by Schocken Books with illustrations by Margery Gill in 1977, c.1967., 1993.

_____. *Violet Fairy Tales*. Ed. Brian Alderson. New York: Longmans, Green, 1901.

_____. *A World of Fairy Tales*. Selected and introduced by Neil Philip and Illustrated by Henry Justice Ford. New York: Dial Books, 1994.

_____, editor. *The Crimson Fairy Book*. Illus H.J. Ford. New York: Dover, Publications; reprinted from Longmans, Green & Co., London, 1903, 1967.

Learning to Give. Http://www.learningtogive.org/materials/folktales: The LEAGUE, Inc., Accessed 2008.

Lee, Jeanne M., reteller. *Legend of the Milky Way*. New York: Holt, Rinehart & Winston, 1982.

_____. *The Song of Mulan*. Written in free verse. Arden, North Carolina: Front Street, 1995.

Levine, Arthur A. *The Boy Who Drew Cats: A Japanese Folktale*. Illust. Frederic Clement. New York: Dial, 1993.

Li, Shujiang, and Karl W. Luckert. *Mythology and Folklore of the Hui: A Muslim Chinese People*. Translators Feng lan Yu, Zhilin Hoo, and Ganhui Wang. Albany, New York: State University of New York Press, 1994.

Lifton, Betty Jean. *The Mud Snail Son*. Illust. Fuku Akino. New York: Atheneum, 1971.

Litteldale, Freya. *Strange Tales from Many Lands*. Illust. Mila Lazarevich. Garden City, New York: Doubleday, 1975.

Liu, Haiqi, ed. *A Museum of Chinese Classic Stories =Da Zhonghua Jing Dian Gu Shi Bo Wu Guan*. Bilingual. Trans. Fu Dawei. Volume 1. Shandong Sheng, Jinan: Ming tian chu ban she, 2001.

_____, ed. *A Museum of Chinese Classic Stories=Da Zhonghua Jing Dian Gu Shi Bo Wu Guan*. Bilingual. Trans. Zhang Weixing. Volume 2. Shandong Sheng, Jinan : Ming tian chu ban she, 2001.

_____, ed. *A Museum of Chinese Classic Stories=Da Zhonghua Jing Dian Gu Shi Bo Wu Guan*. Trans. Fu Dawei and Zhang Weixing. Volume 3. Shandong Sheng, Jinan: Ming tian chu ban she, 2001.

_____, ed. *A Museum of Chinese Classic Stories=Da Zhonghua Jing Dian Gu Shi Bo Wu Guan*. Bilingual. Trans. Fu Dawei and Zhang Weixing. Volume 4. Shandong Sheng, Jinan : Ming tian chu ban she: Ming tian chu ban she, 2001.

_____, ed. *A Museum of Chinese Classic Stories=Da Zhonghua Jing Dian Gu Shi Bo Wu Guan*. Bilingual. Trans. Fu Dawei. Volume 5. Shandong Sheng, Jinan: Ming tian chu ban she, 2001.

_____, ed. *A Museum of Chinese Classic Stories=Da Zhonghua Jing Dian Gu Shi Bo Wu Guan*. Trans. Zhang Weixing. Volume 6. Shandong Sheng, Jinan: Ming tian chu ban she, 2001.

Long, Jan Freeman. *The Bee and the Dream: A Japanese Tale*. Illust. Kaoru Ono. New York: Dutton Children's Books, 1996.

Long Long Time Ago: Korean Folk Tales. Illust. Dongsung Kim. Elizabeth, New Jersey/Seoul: Hollym Corporation; Publishers, 1997.

Louie, Ai-Ling, reteller. *Yeh-Shen: A Cinderella Story*. Illust. Ed Young. New York: Philomel Books, 1982.

LuMar, S. Y. *Chinese Tales of Folklore*. Illust. Howard Simon. New York: Criterion Books, 1964.

MacDonald, Margaret Read. *Celebrate the World; Twenty Tellable Folktales for Multicultural Festivals*. Illust. Roxanne Murphy Smith. New York: The H. W. Wilson Company, 1994.

_____. *Earth Care: World Folktales to Care About*. New Haven, Connecticut: Linnet Books, 1999.

_____. *Peace Tales: World Folktales to Talk About*. Little Rock, Arkansas: August House Publishers, 1992.

_____. *Three-Minute Tales: Stories from Around the World*. Little Rock, Arkansas: August House Publishers, Inc., 2004.

_____. *Twenty Tellable Tales: Audience Participation Folktales for the Beginning Storyteller*. Illust. Roxanne Murphy. New York: The H. W. Wilson Company, 1986.

The Magic Bird: Folk Tales from China. Seventh Series. Ed. Ellen Hertz. Peking: Foreign Languages Press, 1985.

The Magic Knife: Folk Tales from China. Beijing: Foreign Languages Press, 3rd ed. 1982.

Mahy, Margaret. *The Seven Chinese Brothers*. Jean and Mou-sien Tseng. New York: Scholastic, 1990.

Manning-Sanders, Ruth. *A Book of Charms and Changelings*. Illust. Robin Jacques. New York: E.P. Dutton & Co., Inc., 1971.

Martin, Rafe. *The Fisherman Under the Sea*. Trans. Alvin Tresselt, Illust. Chihiro Iwasaki. New York: Parents Magazine Press, 1969.

_____. *The Hungry Tigress: Buddhist Legends and Jataka Tales*. Illust. Tatsuro Kiuchi. Berkeley, California: Parallax Press, 1990.

_____. *Mysterious Tales of Japan*. Illust. Tatsuro Kiuchi. New York: G. P. Putnam's Sons, 1996.

Matsutani, Miyoko. *The Crane Maiden*. Trans. Alvin Tresselt, illus Yasuo Segawa. New York: Parents' Magazine Press, 1968.

_____. *Gengoroh and the Thunder God*. Trans. Alvin Tresselt, illus Yasuo Segawa. New York: Parents' Magazine Press, 1970.

_____. *Hats for the Jizos/Kasa Jizo*. Bilingual story cards. Illust. Fumio Matsuyama. New York: Kamishibai for Kids.

_____. *Momotaro, the Peach Boy*. Bilingual story cards. Illust. Eigoro Futamata. New York: Kamishibai for Kids.

_____. *The Monkey and the Crab/Saru to Kani*. Bilingual story cards. Illust. Kayako Nishimaki. New York: Kamishibai for Kids.

_____. *The Three Magic Charms/Taberareta Yamanba*.

Bilingual story cards. Illust. Eigoro Futumata. New York: Kamishibai for Kids.

_____. *The Tongue-Cut Sparrow/Shitakiri Suzume.* Bilingual story cards. Illust. Seichi Horiuchi. New York: Kamishibai for Kids.

_____. *The Witch's Magic Cloth.* Trans. Alvin Tresselt, illus Yasuo Segawa. New York: Parents' Magazine Press, 1969.

Matthews, John, reteller. *The Barefoot Book of Giants, Ghosts & Goblins: Traditional Tales from Around the World.* Giovanni Manna. Cambridge, Massachusetts: Barefoot Books, 1999.

Mayer, Fanny Hagin, selector and translator. *Ancient Tales in Modern Japan: An Anthology of Japanese Folk Tales.* Bloomington, Indiana: Indiana University Press, 1984.

McAlpine, Helen and William. *Tales from Japan.* Oxford, England;New York: Oxford University Press, 2002, c. 1958.

McCarthy, Ralph F. *The Adventure of Momotaro, the Peach Boy.* Bilingual. Illust. Ioe Saito. Tokyo/New York: Kodansha International, 1993.

McCaughrean, Geraldine. *The Crystal Pool: Myths and Legends of the World.* Illust. Bee Willey. New York: Margaret McElderry Books, 1998.

McClure, Gillian. *The Land of the Dragon King and Other Korean Stories.* London: Frances Lincoln Children's Books, 2008.

McCoy, Karen Kawamoto. *A Tale of Two Tengu.* Illust. Koen Fossey. Morton Grove, Illinois: Albert Whitman & Company, 1993.

McDermott, Gerald. *The Stonecutter: A Japanese Folk Tale.* New York: Viking Penguin, 1975.

Minford, John, translator. *Favourite Folktales of China.* Illustrators He Youzhi and others. Singapore: Graham Brasch LTD. First published by New World Press, Beijing., 1983.

Mizutani, Shozo. *The Bride with an Unusual Talent/ Hekkoki Yome.* Bilingual story cards. Illust. Katsuji Fujita. New York: Kamishibai for Kids.

Momotaro (Little Peachling). Trans. David Thompson, Illust. Eitaku. Japanese Fairy Tale Series. Tokyo: KobunshaT./ Hasegawa Publisher & Art-Printer, 1885.

Morris, Jill. *Monkey and the White Bone Demon.* Illust. Lin Zheng, trans. Ye Pingkuei, Adapt. Zhang Xiu Shi. New York: Kestrel Books/Viking Press, 1984.

Mosel, Arlene. *The Funny Little Woman.* Illust. Blair Lent. New York: Dutton, 1972.

_____. *Tikki Tikki Tembo.* Illust. Blair Lent. New York: Holt, Rinehart, and Winston, 1968.

Mulan. Animated film. Dir. Barry Cook, et al. Burbank, California: Walt Disney Home Entertainment, 1998.

Mulan. DVD. First released as a motion picture in 1998. Dir. Tony Bancroft, et al. Burbank, California: Walt Disney Home Entertainment, 2004.

Nakajima, Takeshi, translator. *Japanese Traditional Tales: Myths, Legends and Nursery Tales.* Osaka: The Izumiya Company, Inc., 1996.

Newton, Patricia Montgomery. *The Five Sparrows.* New York: Atheneum, 1982.

Nye, Robert. *Out of This World and Back Again.* Illust. Bill Tinker. New York: The Bobbs-Merrill Company, Inc., 1978.

O'Brien, Anne Sibley. *The Legend of Hong Kil Dong, The Robin Hood of Korea.* A graphic novel. Watertown, Massachusetts: Charlesbridge Publishing, Inc., 2006.

O'Connor, W. F. *Folk Tales From Tibet with Illustrations by a Tibetan Artist and Some Verses From Tibetan Love Songs.* London: Hurst and Blackett, Ltd./ reprint by Kessinger Publishing, 1906.

Ozaki, Yei Theodora. *Japanese Fairy Book.* Republished by Tuttle Publishing, 2007. Originally published by Archibald Constable & Co., Ltd., 1903. Illust. Kazuko Fujiyama. New York: E.P. Dutton Co., English ed., 1922.

_____. *Warriors of Old Japan.* Illust. Shusui Okakura and others. Boston: Houghton Mifflin Company, 1909.

P'u Sun-ling. *Strange Stories from a Chinese Studio.* Trans. Herbert Allen Giles. Shanghai, Hong Kong, Singapore, Yokohama: Kelly & Walsh, Limited, 3rd ed. 1916.

Pan Cai Ying. *Monkey Creates Havoc in Heaven.* Adapted from the novel The Pilgrimage to the West by Wu Cheng En. Illust. Xin Kuan Liang, et al. New York: Viking Kestrel, 1987.

Park, Janie Jaehyun. *The Love of Two Stars.* Toronto: Groundwood Books/House of Anasi Press, 2005.

Parry, Marian. *King of the Fish.* New York: Macmillan Publishing Company, Inc., 1977.

Partridge, Elizabeth. *Kogi's Mysterious Journey.* Illust. Aki Sogabe. New York: Dutton, 2003.

Paterson, Katherine. *The Tale of the Mandarin Ducks.* Illustrators Leo and Diane Dillon. New York: Lodestar Books/ Dutton, 1990.

The Peacock Maiden: Folk Tales from China. Illust. Cheng Shih-fa. Beijing: Foreign Languages Press, 3rd ed. 1981.

Phelps, Ethel Johnston, ed. *The Maid of the North: Feminist Folk Tales from Around the World.* Illust. Lloyd Bloom. New York: Holt, Rinehart & Winston, 1981.

_____. *Tatterhood and Other Tales.* Illust. Pamela Baldwin Fox. Old Westbury, New York: Feminist Press, 1978.

Piggott, Juliet. *Japanese Fairy Tales.* Chicago: Follett Publishing Company, 1967.

Poindexter, Katherine. *Disney's Mulan.* Illust. José Cardona and Don Williams. New York: Random House, 2005.

Poole, Amy Lowry. *How the Rooster Got His Crown.* New York: Holiday House, 1999.

Princess Splendor, The Woodcutter's Daughter. Japanese Fairy Tale Series Extra No. 1. Trans. E. Rothesay Miller. Tokyo: Kobunsha, 1889.

Protter, Eric, and Nancy Protter. *Folk and Fairy Tales from Far-Off Lands.* Trans. Robert Egan. New York: Duell, Sloan and Pearce, 1965.

Pyun, Y.T. *Tales from Korea.* Introd. by Horace H. Underwood. Seoul: Il-Cho-Kak, 1947.

Quayle, Eric, reteller. *The Shining Princess and Other Japanese Legends.* Illust. Michael Forman. New York: Arcade Publishing, 1989.

Rabbit Ears Treasury of World Tales, Volume One.

Audio CD. South Norwalk, Connecticut: Rabbit Ears Entertainment, 2006.

Ragan, Kathleen, editor. *Fearless Girls, Wise Women & Beloved Sisters: Heroines in Folktales from Around the World.* Pref. by Jack Zipes. New York: W. W. Norton & Cpmpany, Inc., 1998.

_____. *Outfoxing Fear : Folktales from Around the World.* Pref. by Jack Zipes. New York: W. W. Norton & Cpmpany, Inc., 2006.

Rappaport, Doreen. *The Journey of Meng.* Illust. Yang Ming-Yi. New York: Dial Books for Young Readers, 1991.

_____. *The Long-Haired Girl.* Illust. Yang Ming-Yi. New York: Dial Books for Young Readers, 1995.

Redesdale, Algernon Bertram Freeman-Mitford, Baron. *Tales of Old Japan.* London: Macmillan and Company, Limited, 1908.

Reps, Paul, comp. *Zen Flesh, Zen Bones: A Collection of Zen and Pre-Zen Writings.* Rutland, Vermont: Charles E. Tuttle Company, 1975.

Rhee, Nami. *The Magic Spring, A Korean Folktale.* New York: Putnam, 1993.

Richard, Francoise. *On Cat Mountain.* Adapt. Arthur A. Levine, Illust. Anne Buguet. New York: Putnam, 1994.

Riordan, James. *Korean Folk-Tales.* Oxford: Oxford University Press, 1994.

Ritchie, Alice. *The Treasure of Li-Po.* New York: Harcourt, Brace and Company, 1949.

Roberts, Moss, translator and editor. *Chinese Fairy Tales and Fantasies.* New York: Pantheon Books, 1979.

Rodgers, Jonathan. *Five Chinese Brothers.* DVD. First issued as a video cassette in 1997. Illust. Kurt Vargo, Prod. Ken Hoin, Dir. John McCally, music by Bill Douglass, et al. Rabbit Ears Storybook Collection. Chicago, Illinois: Clearvue & SVE, 2005.

Rose, Naomi C. *Tibetan Tales for Little Buddhas.* Santa Fe, New Mexico: Clear Light Publishing, 2004.

Sadler, Catherine Edwards, reteller. *Heaven's Reward: Fairy Tales from China.* Cheng Mun Yun. New York: Atheneum, 1985.

_____. *Treasure Mountain: Folktales from Southern China.* Cheng Mun Yun. New York: Atheneum, 1982.

Sakade, Florence, editor. *Japanese Children's Favorite Stories.* Includes Peach Boy and Other Japanese Children's Favorite Stories plus Little One-Inch and Other Japanese Children's Stories. Trans. Meredith Weatherby, illus Yoshisuke Kurosaki. Rutland, Vermont: Charles E. Tutttle Company, 2003.

_____. *Japanese Children's Favorite Stories, Book Two.* First published in 1958 as Urashima Taro and Other Japanese Children's Favorite Stories. Trans. Meredith Weatherby, illus Yoshisuke Kurosaki. Rutland, Vermont: Charles E. Tutttle Company, 1964.

_____. *Kintaro's Adventures and Other Japanese Stories.* Included in Japanese Children's Favorite Stories, Book Two. Illus Yoshio Hayashi. Rutland, Vermont: Charles E. Tutttle Company, 2008.

_____. *Little One-Inch and Other Japanese Children's Favorite Stories.* Included in Japanese Children's Favorite Stories, 2003, 2005. Trans. Meredith Weatherby, illus Yoshisuke Kurosaki. Rutland, Vermont: Charles E. Tutttle Company, 2008.

_____. *Peach Boy and Other Japanese Children's Favorite Stories.* Included in Japanese Children's Favorite Stories, 2003, 2005. Trans. Meredith Weatherby, illus Yoshisuke Kurosaki. Rutland, Vermont: Charles E. Tutttle Company, 2008.

_____. *Urashima Taro and Other Japanese Children's Stories.* Included in Japanese Children's Favorite Stories, Book Two, 2005. Trans. Meredith Weatherby, illus Yoshio Hayashi. Rutland, Vermont: Charles E. Tutttle Company, 2008.

San Souci, Daniel. *In the Moonlight Mist.* Illust. Eujn Kim Neilan. Honesdale, Pennsylvania: Boyds Mills Press, 1999.

_____. *The Rabbit and the Dragon King.* Illust. Eujn Kim Neilan. Honesdale, Pennsylvania: Boyds Mills Press, 2002.

San Souci, Robert D. *The Enchanted Tapestry.* Illust. Lazlo Gal. New York: Dial Books for Young Readers, 1987.

_____. *Fa Mulan: The Story of a Woman Warrior.* Illust. Jean and Mou-Sien Tseng. New York: Hyperion Books for Children, 1998.

_____. *The Samurai's Daughter: A Japanese Legend.* Illust. Stephen T. Johnson. New York: Dial Books for Young Readers, 1992.

_____. *The Silver Charm: A Folktale from Japan.* Illust. Yoriko Ito. New York: Doubleday Books for Young Readers, 2002.

_____. *The Snow Wife.* Illust. Stephen T. Johnson. New York: Dial Books for Young Readers, 1993.

Saru Kani Kanen / Battle of the Monkey and the Crab. Trans. David Thompson, Illust. Eitaku. Japanese Fairy Tale Series. Tokyo: Kobunsha, 1885.

Sasaki, Etsu. *The Magic Rice Paddle/Fushigina Shamoji.* Bilingual story cards. Illust. Hiroshi Suzuki. New York: Kamishibai for Kids.

Say, Allen. *Once Under the Cherry Blossom Tree.* New York: Harper & Row, 1974.

Sazanami, Iwaya. *Iwaya's Fairy Tales of Old Japan.* Other editions published in 1938, 1942, and 1955. Comp. and ed. Tomita Yoshiji. Tokyo: Hokuseido Press, 1919.

Schippettaro. Japanese Fairy Tale Series, #17. Trans. T. H. James, Illust. Suzuki Kason. Tokyo: T. Hasegawa Publisher & Art-Printer, 1902.

Scofield, Elizabeth. *Hold Tight, Stick Tight : Collection of Japanese Folk Tales.* Illust. K. Wakana. Palo Alto, California: Kodansha International Ltd., 1966.

Seki, Keigo, editor. *Folktales of Japan.* Trans. Robert J. Adams. Chicago: University of Chicago Press, 1953.

Setton, Mark C. K. *The Story of Kim Son-Dal.* Bilingual. Illust. Kim Young-je. Seoul/New York: Si-sa-yong-o-sa, Inc., 1985.

Shah, Indries. *World Tales: The Extraordinary Coincidence of Stories Told in All Times, in All Places.* New York: Harcourt Brace Jovanovich, 1979.

Shannon, Goerge. *Still More Stories to Solve: Fourteen Folktales from Around the World.* Illust. Peter Sis. New York: Greenwillow Books, 1994.

_____. *Stories to Solve: Folktales from Around the*

World. Illust. Peter Sis. New York: Greenwillow/ HaperCollins Publishers, 1985.

Shedlock, Marie L. *The Art of the Story-Teller*. New York: D. Appelton & Company, 1917. 1915.

Shelton, A.L. *Tibetan Folk Tales*. Ed. Flora Beal Shelton. Illust. Mildred Bryan. New York: George H. Doran Company, 1925.

Shepard, Aaron. *Aaron Shepard's World of Stories*. http://www.aaronshep.com/stories, Accessed 2008.

_____, reteller. *Lady White Snake; A Tale from Chinese Opera*. Bilingual. Illust. Song Nan Zhang. Union City, California: Pan Asian Publications, 2001.

_____. *The Magic Brocade: A Tale of China*. New York: Pan Asian Publications, 2000.

Sherman, Josepha. *Trickster Tales: Forty Folk Stories from Around the World*. Illust. David Boston. Little Rock, Arkansas: August House, 1996.

Shitakiri Suzume / Tongue-Cut Sparrow. Trans. David Thompson, Illust. Eitaku. Japanese Fairy Tale Series. Tokyo: Kobunsha, Meiji, 1886.

Shute, Linda. *Momotaro, The Peach Boy*. New York: Lothrop, Lee and Shepard, 1986.

Sian-tek, Lim. *Folk Tales from China*. Illust. William Arthur Smith. New York: The John Day Company, 1944.

_____. *More Folk Tales from China*. Illust. William Arthur Smith. New York: The John Day Company, 1948.

Sié, Cheo-Kang. *A Butterfly's Dream and Other Chinese Tales*. Illust. Chi Kang. Rutland, Vermont and Tokyo, Japan: Chalres E. Tuttle Company, 1970.

Sierra, Judy. *Can You Guess My Name?* Illust. Stefano Vitale. New York: Clarion Books, 2002.

_____. *Cinderella*. Illust. Joanne Caroselli. Phoenix, Arizona: Oryx Press, 1992.

_____. *Tasty Baby Belly Buttons*. Illust. Meilo So. New York: Knopf, 1999.

The Seven Sisters: Folk Tales from China. Beijing: Foreign Languages Press, 1982.

Smith, Richard Gordon. *Ancient Tales and Folk-Lore of Japan*. London: A. amd C. Black, 1908.

Snyder, Diane. *The Boy of the Three-Year Nap*. Illust. Allen Say. Boston: Houghton Mifflin Company, 1988.

Song Nan Zhang. *The Ballad of Mulan*. Bilingual. Union City, California: Pan Asian Publications, 1998.

Spagnoli, Cathy. *Asian Tales and Tellers*. Little Rock, Arkansas: August House Publishers, Inc., 1998.

Stamm, Claus. *Three Strong Women: A Tall Tale from Japan*. Illust. Kazue Kizamura, et al. New York: Viking Press, 1990.

Stern, Anita. *World Folktales: An Anthology of Multicultural Folk Literature*. New York: McGraw-Hill ESL/ELT, 2001.

Stories About Not Being Afraid of Ghosts. Trans. Yang Hsien-yi, et al. Peking: Foreign Languages Press, 1961.

Stories from Near and Far. DVD. Weston, Connecticut: Weston Woods/Scholastic, 2007.

Storrie, Paul D. *Yu the Great Conquering the Flood: A Chinese Legend*. Sandy Carruthers. Minneapolis: Graphic Universe/Lerner Publications Company, 2007.

Sun, Ruth Q. *The Asian Animal Zodiac*. Rutland, Vermont: Charles E. Tutttle Company, 1974.

Suyeoka, George. *Issunbōshi*. Ed. Robert B. Goodman and Robert A. Spicer. Waipahu, Hawaii: Island Heritage Publishing, 2003.

Suzuki, Yoshimatsu. *Japanese Legends and Folk-Tales*. Tokyo: The Sakurai Shoten, 1949.

Tchana, Katrin. *The Serpent Slayer and Other Stories of Strong Women*. Illust. Trina Schart Hyman. New York: Little, Brown and Company, 2000.

Tehyi, Hsieh, ed. and trans. *Chinese Village Folk Tales*. Boston: Bruce Humphries, Inc., 1948.

Tibetan Traditional Tales. http://enargea.org/tales/Tibetan/tibetlist.html: The Tent Archive: Texts and Explorations of Narrative Tradition, 1998–2008.

Timpanelli, Gioia. *Tales from the Roof of the World: Folktales of Tibet*. Illust. Elizabeth Kelly Lockwood. New York: The Viking Press, 1984.

Titus, Eve. *The Two Stonecutters*. Garden City, New York: Doubleday and Co., 1967.

Tompert, Ann. *Bamboo Hats and a Rice Cake*. Illus Demi. New York: Crown Publishers, Inc., 1993.

Torre, Betty L. *The Luminous Pearl: A Chinese Folktale*. Illust. Carol Inouye. London: Orchard Books, 1990.

Troughton, Joanna, reteller and illustrator. *Monkey and the Water Dragon*. Also published by Penguin Books Ltd., London, 1997. New York: Dutton, 1995.

Tyler, Royall, selector. *Japanese Tales*. New York: Pantheon Books, 1987.

Uchida, Yoshiko, adapter. *The Sea of Gold and Other Tales from Japan*. Illus Marianne Yamaguchi. New York: Charles Scribner's Sons, 1965.

Uchida, Yoshiko, reteller. *The Dancing Kettle and Other Japanese Tales*. Originally published by Harcourt, Brace & World. Berkeley, California: Celestial Arts Book Company, 1949.

_____. *The Magic Listening Cap: More Folktales from Japan*. Berkeley, California: Creative Arts Book Company, 1987.

_____. *The Magic Purse*. Illus Keiko Narahashi. New York: McElderry Books, 1993.

_____. *Two Foolish Cats*. Illus Margot Zemach. New York: Margaret McElderry Books, 1987.

_____. *The Wise Old Woman*. Illus Martin Springett. New York: Margaret McElderry Books, 1994.

Urashima. Trans. B.H. Chamberlain, Illust. Eitaku. Japanese Fairy Tale Series. Tokyo: Kobunsha, 1886.

Van Woerkom, Dorothy. *The Rat, the Ox, and the Zodiac*. Illust. Errol LeCain. New York: Crown Publishers, Inc., 1976.

_____. *Sea Frog, City Frog*. Illust. Jose Aruego and Ariane Dewey. New York: Macmillan Publishing Company, Inc., 1975.

Waite, Michael P. *Jojofu*. Illust. Yoriko Ito. New York: Lothrop, Lee & Shepard Books, 1996.

Wakabayashi, Ichiro. *Urashima Taro*. Story cards. Illust. Saburo Nishiyama. New York: Kamishibai for Kids.

Wang, Gia-Zhen. *Auntie Tigress and Other Favorite Chinese Folktales*. Illust. Eva Wong, trans. Annie Kung. New York: Purple Bear Books, 2006.

Wang, Rosalind C. *The Fourth Question: A Chinese Tale*. New York: Holiday House, 1991.

The Water-Buffalo and the Tiger: Folk Tales from China. Published in 1958 as Folk Tales from China, Second Series. Illust. Mi Ku, trans. Gladys Yang. Beijing: Foreign Languages Press, 3rd ed. 1980.

Watkins, Yoko Kawashima. *Tales from the Bamboo Grove*. Jean and Mou-sien Tseng. New York: Bradbury Press, 1992.

Weng, Wango, dir. *The Magic Pear Tree*. 16 mm film. New York: Pictura, 1972.

Whitehorn, Alan Leslie. *Wonder Tales of Old Japan*. Illus Shozan Obata. London: T. C. and E. C. Jack, 1911.

Wiggin, Kate Douglas and Nora Archibald Smith, eds. *The Fairy Ring*. Originally published in 1906 with different illustrations. Illust. Ethna Sheehan. Garden City, New York: Doubleday & Co., 1967.

_____, eds. *Tales of Laughter*. Garden City, New York: McClure & Doubleday & Co., 1908.

Wilhelm, Richard, ed. *The Chinese Fairy Book*. Originally published by J.B. Lippincott Company, Ltd., Philadelphia in 1921, Last story omitted in 2008 edition. Mineola, New York: Dover, 2008.

Williams, Carol Ann. *Tsubu the Little Snail*. Illust. Tatsuro Kiuchi. New York: Simon and Schuster Books for Young Readers, 1995.

Williams-Ellis, Amabel. *Round the World Fairy Tales*. New York: Frederick Warne & Co., 1963.

Williston, Teresa Pierce. *Japanese Fairy Tales*. Illus Sanchi O. Gawa. Chicago: Rand McNally & Company, 1904.

Withers, Carl. *I Saw a Rocket Walk a Mile: Nonsense Tales, Chants & Songs from Many Lands*. Illust. John E. Johnson. New York: Holt, Rinehart & Winston, 1965.

_____. *A World of Nonsense*. Illust. John E. Johnson. New York: Holt, Rinehart & Winston, 1968.

Wolkstein, Diane, reteller. *Lazy Stories*. Illust. James Marshall.

_____. *White Wave: A Chinese Tale*. Illust. Ed Young. New York: Gulliver Books/ Harcourt Brace & Company, 1996.

The Wonderful Tea-Kettle. Japanese Fairy Tale Series, #16. Tokyo: T. Hasegawa Publisher & Art-Printer, 1898.

Wu, Huiyuan. *Selected Chinese Fables*. Bilingual. Hong Kong: Sun Ya Publications (HK) Ltd., 1995.

Wyndham, Robert. *Tales the People Tell in China*. Illust. Jay Yang. New York: Julian Messner, 1971.

Xuan, Yong-Sheng. *The Dragon Lover and Other Chinese Proverbs*. Auburn, California: Shen's Books, 1999.

Yagawa, Sumiko. *The Crane Wife*. Trans. Katherine Paterson, Illust. Suekichi Akaba. New York: William Morrow & Co., 1981.

Yashima, Taro. *Seashore Story*. New York: The Viking Press, 1967.

Yasuda, Yuri. *Old Tales of Japan*. Illust. Yoshinobu Sakakura. Japan: Dai-Nippon Printing Co., 1947.

_____. *Old Tales of Japan*. Illust. Yoshinobu Sakakura. Japan: Dai-Nippon Printing Co., 1947.

Yeh, Cun-Chan and Allan Baillie. *Bawshou Rescues the Sun*. Illust. Michelle Powell. New York: Scholastic Inc., 1991.

Yeoman, John and Quentin Blake. *The Singing Tortoise and Other Animal Folktales*. New York: Tambourine Books, 1993.

Yep, Laurence. *Auntie Tiger*. Illust. Insu Lee. New York: HarperCollins, 2008.

_____. *The Boy Who Swallowed Snakes*. Illust. Jean and Mou-sien Tseng. New York: Scholastic Inc., 1994.

_____. *The Dragon Prince: A Chinese Beauty and the Beast Tale*. Illust. Kam Mak. New York: HarperCollins, 1997.

_____. *The Shell Woman and the King*. Illust. Yang Ming-Yi. New York: Dial Books for Young Readers, 1993.

_____. *Tree of Dreams: Ten Tales from the Garden of Night*. Illust. Isadore Seltzer. Bridgewater Books/ Troll, 1995.

Yip, Mingmei. *Chinese Children's Favorite Stories*. Rutland, Vermont: Tuttle Publishing, 2004.

Yoda, Junichi. *The Rolling Rice Ball*. Illust. Saburo Watanabe, trans. Alvin Tresselt. New York: Parents MagazinPress, 1969.

Yolen, Jane, collector and reteller. *Mightier Than the Sword: World Folktales for Strong Boys*. Illust. Raul Colon. New York: Silver Whistle/Harcourt, Inc., 2003.

_____. *Not One Damsel in Distress: World Folktales for Strong Girls*. Illust. Susan Guevara. New York: Silver Whistle/Harcourt, Inc., 2000.

_____, editor. *Favorite Folktales from Around the World*. New York: Pantheon Books, 1986.

Young, Ed. *Cat and Rat*. New York: Henry Holt & Company, 1998.

_____. *Lon Po Po: A Red-Riding Hood Story from China*. New York: Philomel Books, 1989.

_____. *The Lost Horse*. Published with puppets. San Diego: Silver Whistle, 1998.

_____. *Monkey King*. New York: HarperCollins Publishers, 2001.

_____. *Mouse Match*. New York: Silver Whistle/Harcourt Brace & Company, 1997.

_____. *Night Visitors*. New York: Philomel Books, 1995.

_____. *Red Thread*. New York: Philomel Books, 1993.

_____. *The Terrible Nung Gwama: A Chinese Folktale*. Adapted from a retelling by Leslie Bonnett. New York: William Collins + World Publishing Company, 1978.

Yu, Chai-Shin, Shiu L. Kong, and and Ruth W. Yu. *Korean Folk Tales*. Illus Hai-ja Bang. Toronto: Kensington Educational, 1986.

Yuan, Haiwang. *The Magic Lotus Lantern and Other Tales from the Han Chinese*. World Folklore Series. Foreword by Michael Ann Williams. Westport, Connecticut: Libraries Unlimited, 2006.

_____. *Princess Peacock: Tales from the Other Peoples of China*. World Folklore Series. Foreword by Zhang Chunde. Westport, Connecticut: Libraries Unlimited, In press, 2008.

Zhi Qu. *Little Sima and the Giant Bowl*. On My Own Folklore. Illust. Lin Wang. Millbrook Press, In press, 2008.

Zhou Kequin, dir. *Monkeys Fish the Moon*. 16 mm film. Prod. Shanghai Animation Studio. New York: Italtoons, Distribution 16, 1982.

Ziner, Feenie. *Cricket Boy*. Illust. Ed Young. Garden City, New York: Doubleday & Company, Inc., 1977.

Zong, In-Sob, collector and translator. *Folk Tales from Korea*. London: Routledge & Kegan Paul Ltd., 1952.

Story Title Index

References are to story numbers.

Subject Index

References are to story numbers.

www.ingramcontent.com/pod-product-compliance
Lightning Source LLC
Chambersburg PA
CBHW081402090726
47908CB00012B/2761